MW01346026

As far as Szentkuthy is concerned, the question may be posed as to whether a country, or a culture, can be rendered a more significant 'service' than to have a masterpiece written in that country's language, raising said culture to hitherto unseen heights? *Prae* is one of the most important experimental novels because virtually all of the problems of the old and the 20th-century experimental novel can be found in it, and there are some elements (e.g, the theory of the novel, the theory of architectural wordplay) that are to be found solely in Szentkuthy's novel... The role of language grows tremendously: *language is the home of being.*

— Pál Nagy

There is no other Hungarian book as intelligent as *Prae*. It skips lightly, playfully, ironically and in consummately individual fashion around the highest intellectual peaks of the European mind. It will become one of the great documents of Hungarian culture that this book was written in Hungarian.

— Antal Szerb

If *Prae* were no more than a loosely linked series of reflections, it would still impress us with its sheer flood of ideas and the delicate veining of its concepts, which reminds us at times of the representations provided by medieval idea-miniatures, those masterworks of subtle distinctions. But like in the Baroque novel, one of its inspirations, the modern recreation of which he consciously attempts, extreme intellectualism is united to luxuriant vegetation, with hosts of sumptuous similes, orgies of words, visionary imagination and, above all, matchlessly vivid sensory impressions.

— Gábor Halász

PRAE

VOL. 1

MIKLÓS SZENTKUTHY

TRANSLATED BY

TIM WILKINSON

Contra Mundum Press New York · London · Melbourne

Selected Other Works by
Miklós Szentkuthy

Narcissus's Mirror

A Chapter on Love

St. Orpheus Breviary

Divertimento: Variations on the Life of W. A. Mozart

Europe is Closed

Frivolities & Confessions

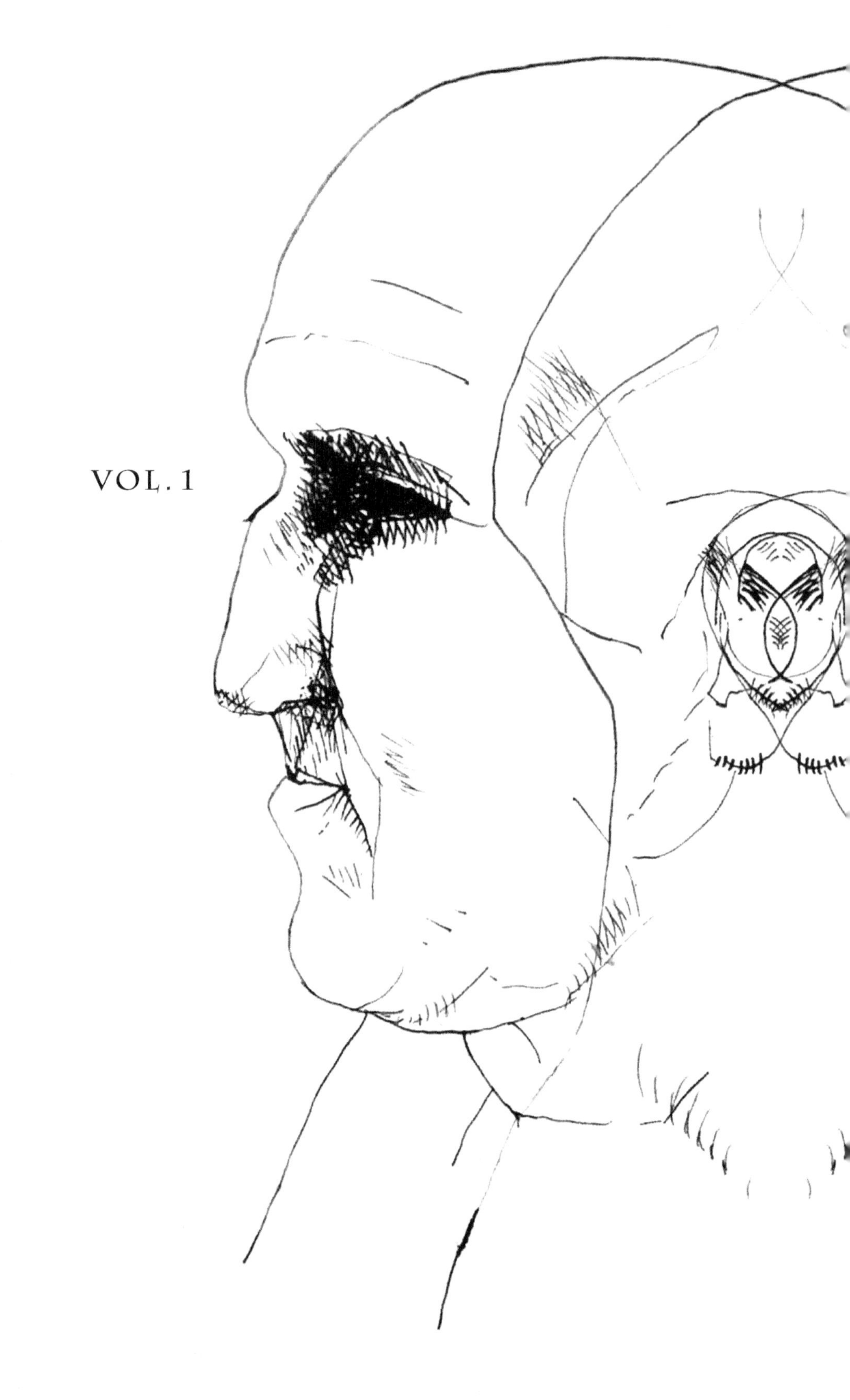
VOL. 1

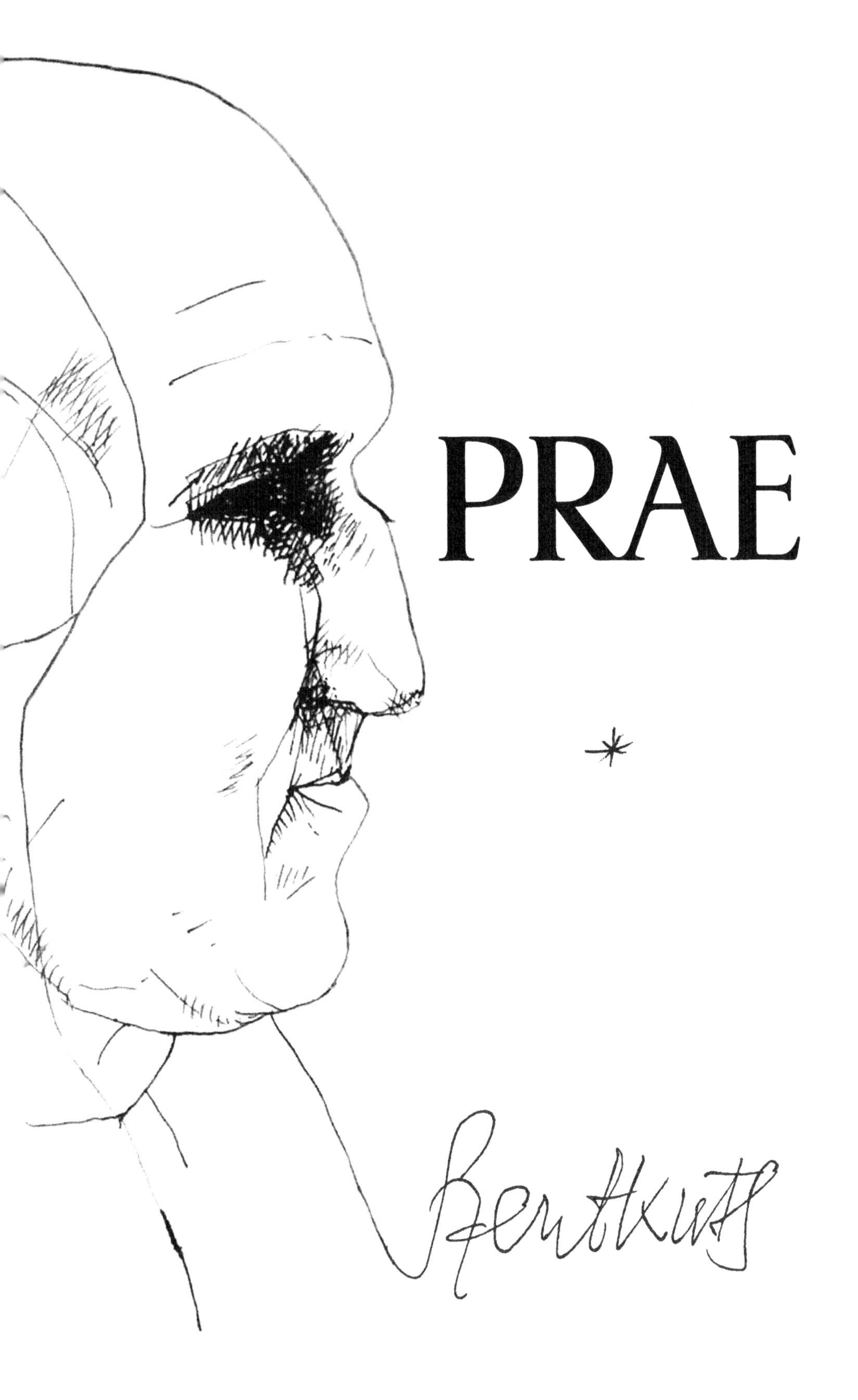
PRAE

Published by arrangement with Mariella Legnani-Pfisterer & Maria Tompa of the Szentkuthy Estate.

First Contra Mundum Press Edition 2014. This edition of *Prae* is based on the version published by Magvető in 1980.

Library of Congress Cataloguing-in-Publication Data

Szentkuthy, Miklós, 1908–1988

[Prae. English.]

Prae / Miklós Szentkuthy; translated from the original Hungarian by Tim Wilkinson

—1st Contra Mundum Press Edition
788 pp., 6x9 in.

ISBN 9781940625089

I. Szentkuthy, Miklós.
II. Title.
III. Wilkinson, Tim.
IV. Translator.

2014958637

Contra Mundum Press would like to extend its gratitude to the Hungarian Books & Translations Office at the Petőfi Literary Museum for rewarding us with a subvention to aid this publication.

Table of Contents

I.

II.

III.

IV.

V.

VI.

VII.

VIII.

PRAE

I.

From experiencing to expression: a cataloguing of the most ordinary possibilities. Leville-Touqué sees the hat: bringing women's fashion & philosophy to a first playful common denominator

the roots & problems of expression:

A) *three unconnected starting-points*

1. *the sunflower-fragment in the brain arising from biological involuntariness*
2. *the unelaboratability of any "theme"* (absolute *theme*) *all* thematic *themes devised with rational high-handedness*
3. *the* big *picture expressing absolute "evocativeness": a Venetian ship under construction at night*

relationship of tautology & oscillator

B) *the way in which it is possible to utilize and connect the above three elements: the necessary relativity of the concepts of connected and unconnected: wordplay*

1. *wordplay with words*
2. *wordplay with spatial elements: modern architecture*
3. *'wordplay' of elements listed under A) new-substance gastronome*

C) *the annihilation (over-realization?) of 'person' or 'romantic' hero in the dehumanizing novel technique. To be absorbed partly into a supra-ontological stratum, partly into a supra-fictional stratum separation of 'object'-novel and 'hyperaction'-novel*

Leville-Touqué wrote an article on the subject of "Outline of a Starting Point, or New Composition," for his periodical *Antipsyche*. In this he had advanced the case of an imaginary novelist, or maybe a philosopher who assumes the role of a novelist purely in order to gather arguments for his new logic from another field, and he gets that character to observe the point before which there was not yet a logical or artistic inspiration to write a new system or a new novel, but at which point the first germs of inspiration were already present; and with the help of the very first germ & its immediate continuations, he attempts to investigate the nature of the new compositional fashion, the special relationship of analysis and unity, fortuitousness and regularity. After the "Outline of a Starting Point" he had provisionally summarized his conclusions in a second article entitled "Toward a New Culture of Wordplay, or Concerning the Rules of Dogmatic Accidentalism."

The content of the first article was as follows: for months I had been in love with a girl (the article, it should be noted, was written in the first person) with whom one sunny forenoon I was looking at Paris shop windows, the colorful shelves of flower shops, jewelers and drug stores, when we arrived in front of a milliner's shop. Just one hat was on display behind the window, and even that barely resembled a hat: it was a small hemisphere in shape, one part of which was composed of shining, thin nickel tubules, with the gaps between being left empty, grid-like, the other part consisting of some thin, greenish-grey membrane about which I could not determine whether it was metal, paper, glass, or some textile. The sight of the superb structure of this marvel made my senses reel, but the girl remained rather cool. My feeling was that one could not construct a more splendid symbol of spring than that half-logical, half radio-technological hat: even in springtime I always took pleasure in some naïve ribbed regularity, the rational inspiration of babbling order (that was superbly represented by the clove-like arrangement of the nickel straws) and, at the same time, paradoxical brightness, glittering gloom, the certainty and conscious uncertainty of clumsy instincts (that was symbolized by the other part of the hat, folded & puffed out of an indefinable material).

It is undoubtedly conspicuous that my brain accomplishes that symbolism with such a raw mechanism, but here I want to hint at something of the taste of my obsession, with the usual brutality of didacticism: the tight and instinctive coherence & desire to cohere, the cohering voracious technique of the most universal, & thus most obscure, feelings (like, for instance, the complex feeling that we feel in relation to spring and which could be called the infinitely private definition of spring along with some randomly different thing, such as, for instance, those nickel tubules and glass bags here in the milliner's shop window).

What was the hat intended to declare? The glittering rigidity of the tubules, as rib-like they embraced the small globe of an to it as yet unknown female head, has always been considered the incarnation of the rule, the system, logical distinctions, chapters and ground-plans: tubules are the eternal symbol-lackeys of order. When those metal filaments and nickel runners cling to a black or blonde skull, they create strict Tropics of Cancer and Capricorn, pedantic equators and Greenwich-meridians:[1] the brain and short-cropped hair will become imprisoned between the scorpion fingers of the rule. But the rule that the aforementioned tubules represented nonetheless did not mean an old-fashioned cage of rules: partly in the degree of curvature there was a tendency to the grotesque, partly in their luster there was some exaggerated, cynical glitter, blind-white sparking: the original order, the puritanical scheme that such rigid and uniform runners always represent, inclined, in part, toward the world of burlesque, humor, game, and, in part, toward the world of luxury, self-serving elegance, & ascetic pose.

The two kinds of inclination do not count to the detriment (or richness) of order: it was then that I suspected with a discoverer's naïve self-satisfied nose that new possibilities of editing styles are opening up for me; a bit of humorous distortion on the one hand and a bit of frivolous decorativeness on the other will express the forever desired and indispensable artistic or logical order much more energetically than the parallel wires of the old cage of order. I shall express the essence of the beauty of a splendid lily much more precisely with two artificial inaccuracies: a grotesque cactus somewhat resembling it (that is the game) and a hat ornament made of a glittering manufactured material (that is worldliness): caricature & practical ornament together would make artistic and jurisprudential order.

Yet I learned something else from that window there on the street, for by that time I had read quite a number of books in which philosophy was making its own hypochondria law with a certain grandeur: the concept of a concept, the foundation of foundations, the possibilities of possibilities, the infra-principle preceding the precondition supposing all preconditions, the sense of conjunctions (*"reine Und-heit," "absolutes So-tum"*),[2] the most elementary cognitive fundamentals; in short, in puritanical agitation, those books analyzed the whole 'hyperlogical prelogic.'

Because they were indisputably puritanical: they looked behind the notions of conventional regularity, sense, orderliness, and consequentiality for an elemental order, which hardly resembled our ideas of order; this was an utter failure or triumph (or maybe failed triumph) of puritanism when absolute order was composed of obscure filaments, cell torsos, & plasma secessions. Because after reading German phenomenologies and systematologies it was my impression that these logical infras, the orders and absurd points of origin prior to order, were completely lacking certain geometrical or 'compositional' features of the notion of order and were rather a hypothetical gallery of opalescent frames, hesitant variations, and Proteus portraits. That is what the bigoted search for order, truly puritanical puritanicalness, led to.

At this point my pedagogical tactlessness interrupts, and it will symbolize this concept of order with the other half of the girl's hat seen in the shop window, with that strange, uncertain, but massive material of which I did not know whether it was glass or felt. In front of the window, therefore, I had three ideas, which all related more or less to the 'order,' the 'rule': burlesque, wordliness, & infralogic.

I asked the girl, who, until now, had all along behaved rather indifferently, whether she would like a hat like that. In dry tones she said that she would not willingly put it on because she had the feeling there was no hat on her head, but — as I had told her just before — a radio apparatus or a fancy outfit of arteries that had been surgically removed & nickel-plated. Anyway she did not like to spend money on absurdities like that.

When she called that springtime fetish from which I had begun to extract the Boileau-esque rules of the style of the new novel an absurdity, I felt I had been hit in the head by a bullet. In a flash, I ran my eyes over the girl's clothes like a bloodthirsty bailiff over the items in a suspect stock-list: flat-footed lace-up shoes on her feet, above them thick brown lisle stockings; a grey English two-piece suit with two buttons, a belt & grey buckle, a narrow-brimmed, grey felt hat with a single hatband around it. All at once my whole love for her became nonsensical: there was no point in my sniffing round so-called 'discrete' skirts. I knew that the girl had loads of money, and she was lacking in taste. I took speedy and cold leave of the girl, irately, dispiritedly animated by loathing for her.

So far, then, two important motifs have played a part in my story: an incipient theory and after it immense anger, desolation, & hatred. This was the ideal state for my imagination: the rudiments of a contrived theory coupled with strong revulsion.

The two components, the skeleton theory and the mass of emotions, suddenly combined in an odd resultant, to wit, an unexpected, strange, seemingly completely nonsensical pictorial fragment, or, to be more accurate, an enlarged metaphor. I saw two or three giant sunflowers with large, black carpals and short, golden-yellow ray-florets which were placed, crumpled and almost smoking, over a small, pale-blue lakelet like long plumes and crowns above and around the crest in a heraldic device. Although I saw no need for this picture for the time being, I sensed that it had taken the place of my trial theory and emotional repletion, stifling them and switching them out of reality.

This was both pleasant and unpleasant at the same time: I enjoyed the numbing gift of the sunflower image, its curative surprise, but I painfully missed the gymnastics of consistent thought and desire that had been styled by my body. Whereas before I had felt in every step I took the aggressive cruelty of a wild animal stalking after its prey, now every step was as empty as the empty splinters of shrapnel used as decorations in the homes of soldiers; all that was floating above my head with flirtatious tenacity was the uninvited guest metaphor. The reason for my referring to the intrusive and nameless friend as a metaphor, rather than as an image, is because I sensed that it had to relate to something, be a part of something: maybe more, maybe less than a symbol.

I have already indicated that I liked to research the organic connections of something universal and something completely random; I supposed that I was now standing before a task like that: my experimenting with theories & elementary hatred of the girl had no relation to this sunflower still life, whereas the latter rose into my consciousness with such sudden determination that I nevertheless strongly suspected a tight relationship between the two. When I looked more closely at the sunflower gift that could not be shaken off, I was able to convince myself that there was nothing pictorial about it: although it was wholly made up of pictorial elements, this was a characteristically metaphorical symptom, just a few contrasts and a few lines in it were emphasized, close-up it could be seen that the black receptacle base was a detail of a detail, almost just a black emphasis; the petals were just little flutterings, trembling yellow motors, and all around they could not be seen. It was all like when one looks too closely at a flower and sees in part enlarged details, yet also in part very poorly & dimly. Perhaps the plant's collecting cluster microscopic vision would correspond to the inceptions of theory and its dim vision to the spreading of sentiment? I felt that the unexpected picture had a logic, but I also suspected that it was not as vulgar as had been conceivable at the first moment.

As I was unable to find satisfaction with the free sunflowers, I reverted to my previous state: to the compositional theory and the anger, and I endeavored to find a story with which to express my disgust for discrete clothing and the girl acquaintance who represented it. In that way I switched to a new state, for the next step into the "Outline of an Opening."

I invented the following story against the stingy girl: a Spanish duke had at one time been in love with a girl who didn't love him. They separate and meet no more. The girl becomes a nun, and before long acquires a reputation for saintliness: her chief virtues are thriftiness and forgiveness; she neglects the nunnery's art treasures, sells them off, and calmly tolerates attacks on her and her convent. The convent's belongings thus gradually fall into the hands of Venetian Semitic traders: the girl, who by then is famous as a saint, had stemmed from the Christianized Sicilian branch of a likewise Venetian merchant family, but that is not suspected by the fellow nuns of her sisterhood. The 'saintly' mother superior (for she soon became that) suddenly dies, and proceedings to canonize her commence. That is where the story began, in fact.

Among the pre-eminent priests and prelates who gather for the canonization is the Spanish duke, the former lover of the girl who is to be canonized, who had similarly become a priest and there soon stood out for his dialectical adroitness and feverish, erotic rationalism, which he sought to exploit now as an antagonist & assailant of sainthood. He is clear that he does not wish to oppose the girl's sanctification because she had not reciprocated his love back then, but because he holds her type of asceticism to be characteristically unchristian, indeed anti-Catholic: he wants to prove from her extant writings and sayings that her modesty was rooted in mercantile money-grubbing, her forgiving was none other than indifference to the truth, whilst her puritanicalness was ignorant laziness, and, as far as the practical side of things was concerned: those of the convent's goods that she had deprived herself of with such exemplary self-denial had become the property of Semitic merchants, which they had devoted to women, wine, and, above all, the manufacture of weapons that the Ottoman sultan purchased as he was preparing for a devastating campaign against Christian Europe.

He discourses at length on the difference between exotic (i.e., truly Catholic) self-denial and naïve-mercantile secular puritanicalness: in the latter he does not see a disdain for the material but an almost calculated cult, which does not annihilate material but collects it, so that the luxury which spends the winnings on artistic entertainments or even frivolous reveling is still a more moral way of handling money than hoarding it. He manages to demonstrate that the reason the mother superior had cultivated a style of such extreme poverty was because she did not find in the world anything which was of so great a value as the magnitude that money signified for her. In his speech for the prosecution (which is what it was) he characterizes the whole convent as a dark symbol of "materialist self-denial."

Meanwhile, he learns by chance that the mother superior stemmed from the Sicilian branch of a famous Venetian merchant family, one of whose members had rescued the duke's family financially. The duke travels to Venice in order to observe merchants: there he meets the new pope and learns that he has Lutheran sympathies. This new pope had found a stash of manuscripts by the deceased mother superior in which she had expounded Catholic dogmas with the purest possible orthodoxy. For that reason, the Lutheranizing pope wishes to hinder sanctification, and is very glad to encounter in Venice the celebrated scholarly opponent of sanctification. The duke, naturally, is unwilling to come to terms with the pope, who is attacking the mother superior's virtues from the viewpoint of Protestant-flavored puritanism. The duke loathes simplicity of mercantile origin just as much as Protestant simplicity, and he leaves off his backbiting, not wanting to be in one and the same party as the pope.

The duke vanishes in Venice (Semite merchants, diplomatic Lutherans, & a vanished Catholic apologist: *ça, c'est pittoresque!*).

The conclave discussing sanctification is still together as a body in Sicily where two guests arrive from two sides at the same time: from the north the pope, & from the south, by ship, a Turkish army. The pope is none other than a machiavellianistically thinking Lutheran, who, making use of his oratorical and literary brilliance, had attained the papal throne in a hypocritical manner and from there now seeks to terrorize Catholics. At the head of the Ottoman army is the girl of Semitic descent whom, as it happened, the Sicilian conclave was seeking to sanctify. In other words, the girl is still alive; her entire nunnish career had been superficial (not hypocritical!), she escaped on the first Turkish ship onto which she had been lured. In her place a stranger's smuggled corpse was buried. The Turks scatter the conclave, but the girl disappears just as did the duke in Venice.

If I take the trial of a theory and my loathing for the girl as preparations, and the spontaneous sunflower fragment as the first phase of the "Outline of an Opening," then this worked-out story is the second big step of my development into a novel.

This second step is characterized by a deliberate weaving of the abstract lines of the plot: a heap of tendentiously sketched dilemmas, nodes of tragedy, and mechanically condensed moral crises — it was in these that my hatred for the girl was lived out. That hatred was perhaps directed less against the 'discretely clad' rich girl than against those broad swathes of humanity which believe that the girl's discretion is a virtuous and upper class matter, not noticing that is vulgar shopkeeper mediocrity, obstinate stinginess. When I had the Ottoman army lay waste to the Catholic conclave in Sicily, I had the sense that I was hitting with my own hands at the naïve masses who had hallucinated moral modesty into the taste-impotence of my female acquaintance. However consciously I had mapped out the above story, that consciousness nevertheless did not operate on the level of mundane life, because the sunflower stump stood before it and transformed consciousness's rhythm: the sunflower was the initial that performed the hygienic work of rendering things improbable, transposed consciousness onto a more frivolous and disquieting plane.

That would have left the 'elaboration' of the story. Where to start? The story as I wrote it down here did not arise in my brain as the sketch of a novel that was to be worked out later but was a stand-alone ready entity like the sunflower sign which preceded it, with the difference that I had deliberately forced the issue. But the aim of the whole thing was that I pour out my anger against the girl into a structure, a linear formula: if I had found the formula, the matter was no longer of interest, and it would have been an absurd idea to 'elaborate' the plot formula. An algebraic equation expressing a law of physics cannot be expanded into a narrative: & the essential feature of the above plot subject was that by its very nature it was not a narrative; it had no novelistic aims, it was a closed, finished formula. With me theme and development never depended on each other: I had subjects that were perennial themes and it was just as impossible to 'elaborate' them as it is impossible to construct or 'elaborate' the Great Wall of China from a ball of mercury completely contracted onto itself: an outline can never be related to a later elaboration; every outline is self-contained and uncontinuable.

A 'theme' & a 'novel' are separate genres, and the two have nothing in common: one cannot discover even the remotest relationship between novelists & thematicists. A theme, which has no novelistic aim, means pure composition, and in my 'elaborations' (which of course are not based on any 'theme') there have occurred 'themes' as compositional plans; those compositions, however, did not signify the structure of the work, the whole work, but 'structural' chapters inserted as interludes, or in other words, if I had written two chapters (without a 'theme') and afterwards some compositional trick or compositional possibility came into my mind, I did not set the two already written scenes into a structural unity but used the 'structure' as, so to speak, a third scene after the already finished two scenes. The so-called artistic structure was not the skeleton, a coherent system of girders, of the novel, but an independent character, as if one of the active roles of *Romeo and Juliet* were to turn into the plot line of the same tragedy. The composition thereby becomes unending, it proliferates forever, constantly changing shape, incorporating everything, but at any moment it might also lose everything, but this structure elevated into a separate character will float as a cork ornament above the eternal foam of this continuum of elaborations: as if I were suddenly to deprive a white lily (which previously, with the aid of a cactus & white hatpins, I had been able to express more precisely than with itself) of its contours and thus end up with only an endlessly crumbling and contracting, stray white stream, a white stream onto which I toss the lace-like sample of a now self-reliant contour (painting has been using that technique for fair time).

What am I to do, then? I had two things at hand: the automatically presenting stump of a sunflower, the poverty and visual limitations of which were compensated for by the fact that it popped into my mind with biological self-evidentness and therefore allowed me to observe nature's secret style. The other was this 'theme,' an arithmetic creation of deliberate abstraction that could lead no further. I could not have started with a description of Venice or one of the duke's pleadings, because Venice was just an algebraic node, the duke's speech just a sign in the operation, nothing more: the plot meant nothing, the words which played a part in it, like Venice, duke, Semite, Lutheran, or pope, had no conceptual scope: they just touched on the notions and immediately dropped them, otherwise they could not have become part of the structure: structure excludes 'meaning.'

There is nothing for it but to look for a third step, i.e., this time an image (a genuine 'scene,' not the root of a metaphor like the sunflower rudiments) in which I can move freely: where the pictorial elements are unstable, between them hover the mobile waves of time and space in the manner of unregulated water, or an intoxicating wind, and thus washes down or blows away the rough corners of the target & meaning that are sometimes revealed. Into this free sketch the 'theme' which floats about has to be sucked across, completely transformed, broken down to its atoms, or in the form of larger fragments, in the new and strange picture, like the fallen yellow leaves of chestnut trees on the surface of a distant lake. And in any case a more fortunate situation cannot befall a 'theme' than this leaf-like oscillation in parallel to an inorganic movement of the image.

The sunflower sample and the lines of the theme were characterized by a stifling staticness; this third picture (which I shall introduce right away) by a redeeming openness. Openness, not movement in the way that even a tranquil but tiny lake signifies infinite openness: a black mirror of sincerity. The sincerity of lakes is not a moral gesture but the optical chic of infinity: the further I look, the closer I am carried to a dormant stratum, which ever-more precisely expresses the substratal stratum; it's like a speeding lead ball that always keeps sinking deeper and deeper: it may be that physically this is called movement, but spiritually the great bounds of lasciviousness of a lake mean the perpetually strippable, ever-further strippable nakedness of spatial life: every openness can be a smidgen more open: that is the sadistic suggestion of quiet garden lakes.

The first property that I sense from the picture that occurs in the third degree of the "Outline of an Opening" is ever-continuable openness: if I draw a circle then after the 360th degree I reach the starting-point, and if I carry on turning the compass, at most I can thicken the line of the already drawn line — the openness of quiet lakes and of the picture employed in the third phase consisted precisely of, if I had already opened it up 'completely' (that is, its sincerity is on a par with a glove turned inside-out: the openness of a picture is not measured in degrees but in units of a glove turned completely inside-out), & I open it up further, then I shall not be proceeding on the same spot, or rather opening on the spot, after 360° comes 361° of openness, 420°, and the actual number of degrees becomes infinite: the essence of openness is that the properties of a circle and a spiral of infinitely narrow thread are unified in it as spirals of 361° or 420° circles and so on to infinity are conceivable. *Apertura sempiterna additiva*: that can only be perceived and explained with movements, but in reality that is in no case a movement. I am facing closedness and openness, not staticness & movement.[3]

Two calibrations of opposite direction take place at three places in the "Outline of an Opening," as far as the material of the novel is concerned, that is ever-narrower, but as far as the sidereal field of the novel is concerned, that is ever-expanding. Materially, the sunflower sketch came first, then the theme, and finally a picture; e.g., in the present case (as will immediately be clear), a Venetian ship under construction. At first sight one has the impression that it is not a matter of gradual narrowing, but on looking closer one perceives these three stages of 'material,' like English traders of porcelain in China looking at what the glaze was, what the enamel was, what the inlay was, what was burned in, was the red an added glaze or was it maybe fired out of the material, etc., and classing their pails of clay accordingly; so we, too, can experience that the most materialistic was the involuntary sunflower flip, compared to which the theme was of a lot more diluted, not to say more fake, material, while the picture of the ship under construction was unable to offer anything material: it was all a big reflex. In contrast (and as a result) the sunflower, despite its being a fragmentary grimace of deficiency, inhaled the whole space into itself, like a small fish which puffs itself up to death by swallowing its entire water orchard; the theme, which from the viewpoint of material, was poorer and more limited than even the scrap of sunflower, left more space around itself, the way a part of sugar is left undissolved in tea, and in the end the ship under construction was like a door that has been smashed into smithereens by the continuation of absolute openness and the curtailment of the spatial nude figure (*perpetuum nudile*). Which, then, was the picture that represented the concluding, third stage in the initial scheme of my novel, leveled against the stingy, 'discretely clothed' girl as it was?

In a Venetian winter's night, the sheer bulk of a giant ship under construction in a tight lagoon dock (more than likely ships were never constructed in places like that): the black iron bridge is taller than the surrounding houses. On one side of the ship is a big, grass-green blotch, the Moon. In this part the shadows are so sharp that their parasitic roots have grown deep into the body of the ship, and every dangling cord, ratlin, ladder, left-behind girder, improvised bridge or strut occurs twice over like synonymous entries in two languages in a dictionary: in shadow & in moonlight.

The air is warm, yet snow is falling sporadically in large flakes: the water around the ship, petrified into a blade of pitch, strains so quietly that the snowflakes remain in exactly the place on which they happened to fall: for some time they are still visible on the surface of the water while, as sparks, they become momentarily even whiter then dissolve, dissolution being preceded by a sweet geometrical rearing — when they seesawed in the air like miniature green perukes, they were only small knots of oakum, but when they touched the water with their bristly star branches, they suddenly clarified into regular stars, icy asterisk sparks, like ballerinas balleting on a glass stage, leaving only a black navel at the place on the water's indolent body where the glass-hungry night swallowed them.

On the façades of the houses, with their spinster wrinkles, the snowflakes traced as precisely as one sees (marked with a penciled circle) on plaster statues & which are needed, so I believe, in carving into marble or in casting (I have no idea which). The houses loll besides the green, concave saucer of the firmament like the remains of foam spilled onto a tabletop besides an overturned green tankard; it is not a full moon but a full sky, the whole night bursting with spring light that could only be followed for a couple of degrees counted from sea level; afterwards it was already green wind, spring water burgeoning, the moon's ostensive counterfeit coin, and the snow's big Danaë centenary.

The clouds rise vertically in snow-white spores, while the light-green cone of the firmament drills its nose into a distant unknown goal: the whole glittering atlas is a fugue of a racing propeller or corkscrew. The harlequin architecture of the clouds counterbalances the shiny and transparent leap of the firmament like a vertical mast, the horizontal graze of foam arising in the wake of a propeller.

Around the ship there is dead silence. The huge blade of the rudder, the stained divinity of direction, is lifted entirely out of the water. When one sees 'direction' embodied separately in this fashion, one thinks involuntarily of a bad direction: as if all morality were based on us feeling, willy-nilly, that a thing placed outside functioning is bad. Nothing good could be supposed about that huge rudder, only evil: it was like one of the wings of a window that has been left open and was made of shade rather than glass, and behind it resides the most malicious intention. Anyway, this palsied backdrop of direction here above the water was so gigantic and helpless that it was inconceivable that this big Luciferian fin could be placed parallel to the fastidious and affected slight directional lisp of a compass needle: the compass indicated too *précieuse* a direction, the blade of the rudder — too Calibanesque: *how* was it possible for that giant shark donjon to move all the same? The blade of the rudder, besides seeming to denote a wrong direction, was also a direction-heretic: things raised out of their function not only bode a bad function but always a precept according to which that particular function is only a sophism, it does not exist, in its place there is something else: in place of the goal's artificial sophistication the self-centeredness of the raised device. Besides its immorality, the rudder blade also suggested some kind of muddy ataraxia that could not be bothered with anything beyond itself: in its skewedness there was a dose of provocative lack of direction, zodiac-defiance (the way the wings of the window ripped out by the wind also do not point in any sort of direction unless toward self-interested dimensions of insanity) coupled with a certain elfish old-geezer composure. The bottom had been overgrown by moss and some kind of waterweed, the way mournful ivy is in the habit of overrunning Biedermeier gravestones: silt, muddy streaks, top-class aqueous plush and root tweezers gave a grey light to the lower, sparser, and cheaper layer of the moon. The giant rudder was, for all practical purposes, only attached to the ship's stern at one point, the way the colossal earflaps of beagles dangle from their skull on just a single thread.

The whole ship was an ungainly climatic Janus: its side proclaimed every marvel of a snow-covered & moonlit clear spring, its stern (probably due to the sharp maneuvering of its monumental control vane) strove to maintain the anachronistic world of fog, rancid oil, moldy shadows and rusty catarrh among the rags of lifeboats.

The picture, incidentally, derived great pleasure in every kind of anachronistic feature: vernal warmth and pelting snow, nocturnal darkness & diurnal brightness, medieval sailors & a modern steamship: as if with the aid of those features it would have managed to make the area still more spacious and airier.

At the end of the lagoon, where it debouches into a broad canal, a diminutive yellow bridge was visible: a skewed, crooked, tottering bridge that had slipped sideways, at which it did not enter one's head that it would serve any practical purpose but could be just some sort of appendix or partner of the hulking ship, like another form of hovering over the water: both boat and bridge were made of cumbersome, clumsy, and slack material, the one from iron plates buttoned together at one side like a soutane, the other from stones that had been forced together &, like a fan, possessed only restricted local value, but still, that black salmon mausoleum and lemon-yellow parabola-Guignol represented hovering much more completely than a featherweight gondola or a gull scudding low as it rubbed the sea.

The dilapidated yellow bridge was the brightest spot of the night, brighter than the side of the ship through which the moon is shining: behind it the stone-deaf setting of black houses, under it the water's black ground-plan secretion, which Venice's solitary body yields with gliding abundance. Which triumphs over the water more elegantly: the big repaired fish or this constrained barely-a-bridge, suffocated by reliefs: the one gets immersed, in accordance with Archimedean decorum, with the black '*secretio venetica*' and thus ends up above it, the other accomplishes impossible gymnastic exercises, air acrobatics, and tightrope walking over a teensy-weensy gap in liturgical vestments of stone.

No doubt that heavy little bridge had been built by raising a thick wall, an embankment across the lagoon, and when that compact castle wall was completed the waters pushed through a small hole as if they were extracting a jammed cork with a blockbusting so-called battering ram: this is actually the other end of the bridge-building. (For, in point of fact, other bridges are constructed by shooting a long road over the river in the air, and from this a thinned row of subsequent pillars drops down in long drips.) Of course, the main attraction of the little yellow bridge (*pontifex minimus fecit*)[4] is that nowhere is there a scrap of curvature, spring, jump, or hovering: every column, statuette, and ornamentation proclaims the unconcerned statics of the driest of dry-land art and nevertheless manages to get stuck in the air, and the undulating, completely slack unbound water under it does not even suspect what kind of accident it has to thank that it is able to reach the central canal of its desires.

That, then, was the third stage in "Outline of an Opening": the open landscape (Pandora Canaletti, Linnæus). Two things are conspicuous in this three-step course: one is that the first, biological metaphor-refuse, and the last, broad tableau, represent two regular extremes; the other is the radical disconnectedness, the foreignness of content, of the three stages that I nevertheless feel to be a logical kinship, indeed, I feel the relationship to be rational, because their pictorial parts are so disconnected.

Let us look first of all at the extreme features of the first and last visual stages: The first automatically sprang from my brain, the last I deliberately hunted for. The automatism of the first indicates that an incident in my life, in the present case the beginnings of a theory of the novel, coupled with my fury against a girl and the stingy pseudo-gentility of her dress, my soul or my body suddenly switches over an event like that into an inner concern: just as an exterior vibration of air evokes a pure C# minor or F in my soul, so an external event evokes that scrap of sunflower in my soul, signaling that the event, external history, has suddenly become an anatomical part of me: of course with the sonic example I immediately experience the C# minor or F, while in perceiving the event as the 'stimulus' is much more ramifying, processing of it occurs in installments — that sunflower is nothing more than a temporary signal that the story stimulus has been transposed to an esthetic inner plane: it has transformed into anatomy, & it is being handled as an esthetic symptom.

The sunflower snippet, therefore, exactly and with absolute taciturnity, merely signifies the event becoming my body or turning into my body: that tiny but significant + that a consciousness, a biologically reacting area, has been connected to an external story, as a matter of fact only a spark-like discharge between the story and the lowest, unconscious stratum of the estheticizing soul. Here my will had no role as of yet: here the lowest reflexes of my instinct perform the first subjective modification on the story as if a sand sculpture was suddenly surrounded by a wave of water, or a mimosa thin as a wisp of hair were suddenly caught by a gust of wind: the first alteration of the sand sculpture, the first change of form, becomes a reflex-like transformation that is determined in every inch, powerless & fated, what is called a 'blind force,' working on its own. The way the scudding wind snatches at the defenseless mimosa, so the lowest biological stratum of my personality captures the external event & immediately yields that first sunflower metamorphosis.

All that means is that the novel or thought which had been set in train by the external event on this level is in a suffocating relationship with the biological arrangement of my personality: on me the novel is like wet tissue paper pressed on a bronze figure, its material may be self-contained but it totally displays the unalterable structure of my being: a slave novel, captive logic.

Touqué was clear about the fact that he had expressed his emphasis of the biological character of the sunflower in a highly tautologous fashion, but he found that the antidote to tautology was not abbreviation, greater concentration, and omission, but setting a special 'oscillator,' an identity-oscillator, which in the present study consisted of sunflowers from a special issue of *The Studio* devoted to gardens,[5] indeed he had also enclosed pictures of poppies & hortensias, and had printed a dialogue diagonally, the daybreak chatter of two Englishwomen about their gardens. The two extremes, namely, the 'infinite-definition' & 'infinite-whatever,' had to appear once beside each other: the truth always seeks to loop more positive rings around itself, but it falls into the fatal absent-mindedness that ultra-definition does not lay concentric circles around a theme (in the present case the biological nature of the sunflower) but draws a helix, which can be continued forever, so that from the everyday point of view it does not seem to be a narrowing of precision as by virtue of its eternally valid nature its course is everywhere equally open, loose, and impotent. But Touqué wished fully to try out a schoolboyish delirium of verbosity, he wanted to wind out the phenomenologist's open helical spool of self-repetition a good bit further because he sensed that even if on the rational plane of the first degree that was just unproductive idling on the spot, on the rational plane of the second or nth degree even tautology is a useful logical dough.

For the 'truth' is always composed of two elements — one an eternal spiraling around the theme, a million thick shackles, but each one running over into the next, so that the theme to be defined lives behind it in only humbug-captivity (this is chiefly the Heideggerian automatism of German technology: the "opened identity"); the second is the oscillator, which indiscriminately shreds, intersects, diverts, refutes and betrays this eternal spiral (one might, with a touch of unscrupulous rashness, more just for the sake of neatness, call this English technology on the basis of the Baconian essay: the automatism of "playful role-flashing"). Truth therefore has two elements, which are directions, & irreconcilable directions at that; it is never possible to "lock up" the truth, at most to harry both the "definition" and the "oscillator" to the limit in their opposing directions: on the one hand into mythically stifling-tautology, & on the other, into sweating, anarchic flashing-apart. One can find no better oscillator than aimless conversation.

"... Yesterday evening I heard a great thud or scraping noise, I don't know what it was, you don't mean you hit the fence with your car at night?" "I did, good and proper too: you know that they are mending the fence at our place: they have dismantled everything, including the gate, so we organized a special patrol around the garden. I now drive in at the back of the garden because a little wooden gate was left still intact there..." "Are you so attached to the gate? Is the gate more important than the driveway to the garage?" "Laugh if you want; everyone does when I tell them, but believe me, I literally suffer from vertigo and get seasick whenever I enter the garage of a place that

has no fence." "Well anyway, what happened last night?" "Our old gardener had stacked all the buckets of sunflowers that used to stand beside the dismantled fence over the small gate at the back, because he had no idea that when the entire park fence was taken down, I would drive around the whole lot so as to drive in precisely through that little wooden contraption to get to the garage." "So you hit it, of course!" "And how! And there were those unusual sunflowers with huge seeds and huge florets." "I don't understand. I bought the same seeds and nothing came of them." "Maybe your gardener just hasn't got the knack. Why don't you ask mine?..." "Ask him? I can't imagine an unfriendlier chap. It's incredible how a person who works with so many marvelous flowers can be so curmudgeonly and obnoxious. Are you annoyed?" "No, I'm not annoyed at all. But he's only like that on the outside. If you get into a more prolonged conversation with him, he's a sweet teddy bear. I dote on him." "I can't stand people like that who you have to test out for half-an-hour like a piece in a jigsaw puzzle and then they pompously turn all amiable. Was your car scratched at all? Judging from your appearance, nothing..." "Thanks. The fender was a little crumpled like the peeled-down tinfoil on a champagne bottle, on the other hand, I was hugely amused this morning from the bedroom window." "At what?" "All of a sudden I heard my husband's voice arguing with somebody in the garden. So I got up and went to the window and I saw that with his foreman he was inspecting all sorts of stone debris between the overturned pots of sunflowers. I shouted down to ask what was it, perhaps last night I had tipped over a stone amphora, or even a freshly built and still weak wall, trying to be like a Biblical vehicle and pass solely & exclusively through the eye of a needle into the garage? My hubby shouted back in a weepy voice that far from smashing any of the vases, it was a good deal worse: I had knocked down an artificial ruin which had been just in the process of construction." "Good Lord! That's amusing: ruining a ruin." "Fortunately, the bits of the ruin had been marked with big daubed numbers so that they were able to restore them into the disorder that they had spent weeks calculating, but I still had a big laugh." "Tell me, do sunflowers always keep their heads pointing toward the sun? I always thought they had nothing to do with the sun." "It shows how frank you are to think of something like that! It would never have entered my head to ask something like that. Anyway, come over for tea and we'll watch from the terrace whether they turn with the setting sun." "I can't spare the time today because I have an appointment for trying on a housecoat. Just fancy, my girl will make an evening gown for two fittings but has difficulty with even as few as six for a housecoat." "Tell you what! Then I'll go across to your place to look at your things. My husband detests housecoats, so I never have one made: he says he can't abide coming back home to have breakfast after he's been out riding or playing tennis, full of fresh air and the joys of exercising, in his white shirt and trousers, to be greeted by a sleepy fake geisha in a swathe of silk." "That's interesting. My own husband said something to the effect that a housecoat makes a person spastic: knee-length sleeves and skirt pinned to the shoulder blades, so that the pattern of the textile is intact, but the girl is a Japanese hunch-backed monstrosity." "That's it, exactly that. In fact, my trousseau included, among other things, a housecoat that was cut every which way in such a manner that the whole thing looked like a clumsy bandage on a wound that extended the whole length of my body; on the other hand, embroidered on the endless flaps of the right arm and on the quite narrow waist area, there was a single giant sunflower..." "Apropos! Apropos!" "Yes, yes. In order for the sunflower to be easily and clearly visible I had to perform all sorts of grotesque movements, and my husband just hated that." "I'm very fond of big patterns; indeed, on one of them the pattern is larger than the housecoat." "How's that?" "On the back the pattern printed into the material is cut in half, the thing has been tailored to the shoulders, with the missing half fastened in the shape of a stiffened plate like an angel's wing or Stuart fin."

"Is your girl still the same as the one you took on that time we holidayed together?" "That's her." "But I seem to remember you moaning from dawn to dusk about how inaccurate she was." "I still moan now, but she's highly skilled. Recently I've developed a particular loathing for models. Nowadays she comes here so often I'm not bothered if she comes three times in a week, don't get into a flap if she doesn't show up on days she has promised. I don't go out, I'm always at home," et cetera, et cetera.

That is how an oscillator functions after a tautology.

The other visual state (the third phase) is the exact opposite of the sunflower: there freedom, an everlasting game, and unlimited artifice, rule. Everything fits into that picture, indeed, has to fit; only then is it perfect: all the elements, all the flowers, conceivable fifth, sixth, and seventh seasons, man and girl, supplemented with a couple of independent, untraced human genuses, all the stars, and all the fashionable, important dimensions: freedom and artifice operated with such impetus that something of which there were seven, like, for instance, stars in the Big Dipper, the seven days of the week, or the number of Wordsworth siblings & children, here starts straight away with the eighth, taking no notice of the preceding seven, which are just a kind of *comme il faut* prelude before the truth, starting at the eighth.

So in its first phase the incipient novel is essentially indistinguishable from my own anatomy: in point of fact only the retouching of a wave in the well of blood that softly sprinkles my brain; the last picture, however, leaves my thoughts, my life, my special theme, my theory of the novel, & the girl's annoying and immoral miserliness, a long way behind and pushes it into a foreign and infinite delta of almost lexical and alphabetical pantheism of freedom.

If, then, I truly wish to draw a lifelike portrait of the sweetheart I had come to loathe, then, first of all, I must draw a quite insignificant thing, a poor sketch of a sunflower, i.e., the 'absolute detail'; secondly, every imaginable thing in the world: ships, bridges, historical eras, and statistics about the distribution by occupation of those who will rise again at the last judgment: or in other words, 'absolutely everything.' These two are bound together by the second degree with colorless-odorless-insubstantial & transparent threads: the 'theme' produced. The third degree is linked together by no more than my intellectual will: I want all of this to stand in the service of my incipient, novelistic revenge against the miserly girl. At the beginning there are just two symbols, one a minus sign, the other the recumbent eight of the infinity sign: I am unable to get anywhere with the actual 'theme' between them.

As I mentioned, the first point of interest is that the first minus metaphor and the third infinite image are in an entirely contrasting relationship, while the second consists of, or rather arises, if I utilize all the three phases in the actual description of the novel or theory, and I relate all three to each other and separately to the central idea, namely, the tight-fisted girl. What will happen then? That is what was related by Leville-Touqué's study in *Antipsyche* entitled "Toward a New Culture of Wordplay, or Concerning the Rules of Dogmatic Accidentalism."

He started off from architecture, as so many times, and called attention to the following trick occurring at every turn: the engineer draws a square, and after that another, but in such a way that the latter square falls partially onto the area of the first square, and thus a shared area arises: that overlapping area will be the central and essential form of the whole construction; if the two squares occurred on the ground plan, then the self-contained box of the stairwell would rise above the overlapping area;

although it was perceptible that the form was not self-contained but a by-product, shadow, or reflex relationship of two almost accidentally superimposed foreign forms, out of it one of the most important parts of the whole building would nevertheless come. If the two squares did not occur on the ground-plan but, say, on a sketch of the façade, then double-thick balcony rails would be set up just as on the maps, where the statistical grid of colored lines on mutually intersecting but identically ruled areas would also be double thick.

No end of variations on that method are possible, but everywhere the principle is the same, with a bunch of forms being given that are pulled together so that a common area always arises, but the essential pillars of the whole construction will always be these 'fortuitously' doubled or tripled areas. Imagine a tree on which the leaves do not grow the way books of natural history describe, but on every branch the only formations to be seen are those arising such that two, three, or more leaves cover each other, and now only the common areas exist: in the place where a single leaf surface was left nothing at all figures at present. The style of the above-mentioned buildings is comparable to a tree like that. But that is nothing other than an architectural cult of wordplay.

Take a linguistic play on words, for example, the nickname of *Hippopochondra Stylopotama* given to a girl writer by a friend, where he drew on the scientific name for a hippopotamus to hint at the girl's widely known hypochondria and literary inclinations. With that wordplay exactly the same thing happened as in the 'chance' dropping of the two figures, one above the other, in architecture: the 'hippopotamus' designates one of the squares, 'hypochondriac' the other, and now with an engineering trick I push the two over each other in such a way that there will be a double arc: the linguistic blob where the hippopotamus life and hypochondriac life concur and they become shared, with two simple areas to the right and left where the notions of hippopotamus alone and hypochondriac alone lie. One can find no meaningful, logical connection between hippopotamus and hypochondriac; both have a vitally foreign essence, and we nevertheless force these two foreign entities and two substances onto one another in order to make their shared area a single, true substance: just as an architect does not make the foci of an ellipse the structural centers of a building, the diagonals of a square the internal bridges of ratios, but tosses onto the ellipse a non-pertaining, foreign, inorganic and risky form (let's say a row of four small, contiguous circles), and the covered area which arises in that fashion is made a carrier of the gist, something which shows people a completely new state of their sensitivity to substance: it can only enjoy accidents as dogma. The old substance was always an intellectual product of internal proportionality & arithmetical regularity — a kind of rational focal point; the new substance is rather the result of a biological operation: for it to appear or be effected it needs external fertilization, an alien form which sprinkles its own capricious form-pollen, & that is when the new substance is born.

What can easily be solved in the body of language and accomplished architecturally must also be realizable in novels: from the three initial phases — from the sunflower discharge, the T-squared network of plots, and the picture of the endless Venetian ship — what will likewise be essential is what arises if I push those three states slightly on top of each other, like three playing cards on a green baize card table, on each an independent digit still showing, but the bodies of the figures, the hearts, clubs, queens & kings, are bettered into a common game of forms & game-substance. Thus, wordplay does not mean cheap humor, quite the opposite: a modification of the essence-sensualism, the essence instinct, extending to the whole culture.

Let us take as an example the following wordplay, where grammatical pushing together is replaced by the pushing together of human lips: what becomes of a kiss if I treat the inflexible collision of lips as wordplay? The lips will have a shared area, and on both sides there will be residues of the original two non-united (non-conformist) pairs of lips. The essence of a kiss does not consist of two people meeting in it, but only in what would clearly be visible if both sets of lips were caked in lipstick and a thin plate of glass were to be placed between them: the red imprints that would be visible falling onto one another on the two sides of the glass plate would be the play substance of the kiss, the new, accidental anatomy of the lips, with the help of which one might also one day be able to cure mouth diseases more easily than by the old-fashioned way.

To put it another way, a true positive is always the relationship of two things, and specifically not an intellectual relationship but a quite accidental connection: in playing cards, when after a deal one is holding cards that one has been dealt by chance and immediately strives to treat that unconnected haphazard fan of numbers and court cards that one sees before one's eyes as fundamental truths on which one must build the entire hand: it is precisely the capricious incoherence of the cards through which one must calculate the essential course of the entire hand; if the cards lie systematically in the hand, one could deduce very little about the future and the neighboring hands, but if, on the other hand, there is considerable disarray, the broader the perspective the greater the order one sees around and in front of one. If an engineer builds a house, the blueprint of which is an infinitely narrow area that has arisen from two barely touching ellipses — precisely that hair's breadth fortuity allows one to infer the horizons to the left and the right of two large ellipses, whereas an elliptically shaped house does not allow one to infer any dynamic supplementation or spatial prediction.

The whole century is progressing toward wordplay —, Leville-Touqué wrote in his essay. Wordplay is an expression of the instinct that we consider relations ordained by chance as being much more eternal realities and much more typical beings than the individual things which are the characters of the relationship. One can imagine a new arrangement of the world whereby trees vanish from an alley of trees & only the smudges of touching boughs are left; the constitutive elements disappear from chemical compounds, and lines of bonding force are all that remain as sole material reality; the cells of living tissues have all been annihilated to give way to the relation between cells: in the places where hitherto there had been nothing, where only purely intellectual bonds of relation had run, in other words, in practice, an emptiness yawned, that is precisely where realities live nowadays. Every right bank and every left bank fades away, but the world is filled up with an endless multiplicity of hard bridges. If previously one had been interested in rose gardens because of the roses in it, one is now interested in the area between roses; in other words, for us a rose garden will not mean the aggregate of roses but something like a house painter's template, being a single large sheet of linoleum, out of which, however, the roses are cut off: that sheet of templates can be perceived as a separate space of the relationships of the roses, a materialized mass of relationships which is so dense that the roses are negligible abstractions in comparison.

I said previously that the essence of a rose is what another rose or a parrot's beak that falls over it happens to be covering: if I sense that concealment too strongly, however, even if I pull the covering rose away from the first rose and take it a long way away, I still feel that it is hiding it, and that second kind of concealment or coincidence, when the covering and covered are far from each other, but even so the instinct for wordplay senses, at least in shadow-like form, the mutual falling on each other:

that is precisely what is called a relation. The relationship is nothing more than an opened-up falling upon each other: the furthermost things in the world cast some kind of shadow on each other, and in many cases the paradoxical case comes about that the shadow cuts nothing from the other thing but only a black communicating path between the two things, say, the two roses.

It is matter of two states of one and the same wordplay situation: the first, more primitive and more naïve state when two roses do actually partially cover each other, and the shared part is the *'flos substantialis'*; the other state is when the two roses end up far from each other, but in such a way as if in falling onto each other they had been stitched together, & now, when I pull them apart, the second pulls with it the cotton threads which had bound it to the other: that is when what we call a relation actually arises. (In days gone by they used to manufacture a substance with similar industrial tricks as the above rose positionings, but in a significantly different direction: to start with, it was not just two roses placed one above the other in a possibly meaningless situation, but ten or thirty or two hundred roses placed one above the other in a possibly meaningful situation, exactly fallen onto each other, completely covering one another, and thus [the second crucial difference] the picture-like essence pressed out at the end of the old technological procedure was the innermost kernel of a single object, an end in itself and unique, whereas the picture-like essence manufactured by the wordplay technique is never the most intimate nucleus of an object but, quite the contrary, a surface & superficial torso, not for its own sake but rather expansive, something pointing to another thing.)

Two characteristic features of the new notion of essence are, first of all, that it is always composed of a capricious detail, which is raised to the strength of dogma (the second characteristic feature), that it receives that torso from another object and thus it relates to another object: this social streak, let us call it, counterbalances the torso nature. This is where the essay connected to the program of *Antipsyche*, the mind being the means of individualization in man; the mind, for one thing, is the center of intelligence and moral center of gravity, and for a second thing, its strength is closed in on itself. On the other hand, the new essence, for one thing, is a torso, for a second, it is something which leads out of itself and into something else so that it cannot be concerned with the human mind in the sense it has hitherto had. Obviously, in the new novel, there will hardly be any role for humans & their minds: just as we shall soon forget that there was a 'hippopotamus' and 'hypochondriac' in the world and instead concern ourselves with 'Hippopochondra,' which is a new substance made of the two: a torso & not self-directing (the 'torso' is not to be taken in the sense of sculptor-Romantic but, for example, that of an open conic section).

Wordplay has an extraordinary poetic value alongside its rational, not to say philosophical, use: by forcing two foreign things together it excites the fantasy most advantageously, for instance by adding to the picture of a hippopotamus the mental world of a pale, thin, and pretentiously decadent poet, while in the word 'Stylopotama' the academic-flavored scientific notion of the style is, all at once, crowded substantially with the green waves of tropical waters. Along with that we also have within us the instinct for involuntarily imagining two unconnected things as extremes, as if they denoted two ends of an extraordinarily rich series, boundary stones of arithmetical precision: beyond the hippopotamus there is nothing, absolutely nothing in the one direction, and similarly after hypochondria only space ensues in the other direction — thus, with the assistance of wordplay, which fuses these two endpoints of the phenomena of the world, we are always in possession of a huge arc, a reliable amplitude with which, as it were, we sum up the affairs of the world:

through holding the two boundary values (because those are what we sense these two unconnected things to be) we almost symbolically possess the sum of intervening values, the million other values falling between the hippopotamus and the hypochondriac.

After the analysis and propagation of wordplay culture it was necessary to examine the role of the thus nullified humans in the novel (which of course real society will follow somewhat later) or rather to imagine that non-featuring more precisely. That was the idea that was expressed in a newer paper entitled 'Style-Person and *Sache*-Person.'[6]

Touqué set off from his memory of a love and strove to keep it in a novelistic vein, in contrast to the spoon-feeding manner of his notes on substance. One summer he had had a rendezvous at five in the morning on a pier in Cannes, but he had spent the preceding evening in Nice & had not slept a wink. The whole night he had walked between trees, his soul drifting in winds, in stars, in leaves, in times, and in paths among all the raw & vast categories of lyric and logic. He then noticed that in fact he was a 'man of sentiments,' as the old phrase went. That surprised him since on the basis of the substance experiments, in the pedagogical elastic-sided boots of roses sewed with thread, he had begun to feel very much like a village schoolmaster who felt like he was dissolving in the superfluous effort of making comprehensible things clear. He realized later that his massive sentimentality lay at the bottom of the intellectual sterility of spoon-feeding (or already on the surface): massive because it was not a mental nuance but an edifice in space that was independent of him.

Tautology is always a lamentable effort toward where we nepotize a thought from our soul into a component part of a strange, inhuman space — a truly intelligent thought is like an elegant girl in a druggist's shop weighing out quinine in a transparent pharmacy shaped like a lamp bulb: she tosses a weight onto one pan of the balance, a knife-tip of powder onto the other pan, selects a new weight, takes off the first weight, replaces it with a glass bottle, flicks, stirs, withdraws, tips the scale, checks the balance pan; one might think that the quinine and the weights, multiplication and therapy, were going to fly out of the druggist's shop into the world, like pollen from an autumnal flower, yet everything remains between the glass lamellae and tungsten table wires. The second possibility, however, is to load everything onto one of the pans, weight on weight, quinine on quinine, so that it all overturns, the sense of the balance ceases the handlebar-mustachioed selfishness of balance, and to install an asymmetrical block in its place. People sometimes believe that a person discussing tautology enjoys the milieu of his thinking like a dog's nose the axillæ of its own thighs, when on falling asleep it sticks its nose there, though actually wanting to be free of it, distance itself, become estranged from & forget it, but not by turning back but seeking to cut across its own jungle of thoughts and forestall itself.

Now at nighttime, when he was observing his feelings, he had no need of the tipping of the balance because it had already tipped over long ago of its own accord; a single pan was all there was on the world's big sentimental balance, so it was not sentimentalism but trees, stars, times and paths. Every ontology is without fail a tautology, only the freshly tasted ontology of sensitivity, amorous hypochondria, & fermentation of memory is not exposed to the danger of prolixity in a grammatical sense; if the long longed-for & again longed-for longing is made a longing, the repetition falls smoothly in a single clean wave from the brim of the mind's well in order that it be absorbed in the big '*ens*' basin of nature, space, & God.[7] Humans did not yet truly feel, he thought with chaste daring. If they had truly had feeling, there would not have been any lyrical poetry, which means that the feeling was not so strong as to throw the mind's internal balance pan over toward the glass window and thereby scatter its blonde quinine for primrose powder onto English and Greek fields at the same time. That is how the '*Sache*'-person had come to mind, who is nothing other than a pure-sentiment-person, but as he was an extremely pure-sentiment-person, not even a psyche-owner, indeed not even human, just an ontological dough, a pain-tree, pleasure-rain, desire, kiss-time & dream-space. Tree, rain, and time, of course, are not pantheistic case endings, only naïve & temporary signposts of an as-yet unknown ontological language.

When Touqué thought meanwhile of the girl and their morning rendezvous, he thought it was pointless; both the girl and he himself were ridiculous little grubs in the independent space of the sensation of love. When he turned against the wind, he did not expose his feelings to the star-acidy breath of the night like hair that girls uncover in order to dry it, but he displayed his little birth-certificate personality to the flow of emotions pouring from the distance, which was not him and which wanted nothing, just the sentiment qua sentiment, detached from the person. Women cannot be reached because they are much closer to us than our own conscience is to ourselves: love, consummation, everything has long been ready. He would be meeting the girl tomorrow morning? They were already past everything; at least that was how the oncoming feeling spoke to him on the school stage of "onto-mania."

The morning, the girl, the thought of the meeting, were a frightful nuisance to him; he saw the whole thing as ill-timed adolescent canoodling. Love in him was so grand, sentimentalism so infinitely sniveling, that he hated the petty social dramaturgy of love, or simply love itself, the existence of sexes. All that he liked was this cold Nice night that united the girl's body and his own lyricism in a single dark gesture. But if one is pursuing narrative, then the technique for expressing this sentimental "Sachlichkeit" has to be found: the feelings that are not to be found either in the soul or in the trees but are new mythological realities in which decadent nervous disorders are so self-consistent that only the most savage realist branch of scholasticism is capable of expressing them: they became stronger and more positive than one did oneself. On the other hand, in the morning, he still had to meet the girl, as per arrangement, though when the first daylight clung like a lemon-green parasite to the breakers on the shore, he mourned for the girl as for a dead person (the fact that we imagine the girl as often as possible to be dead & decline her into the grave is merely an artificial trick for the purpose of smuggling her into the ontology).

The girl was not there. He waited half an hour for her then went up to her room in the hotel. The room was empty, the bathroom locked; only the gurgle of water in the wall plumbing being run out of the bathtub. He did not knock, just peeked through the keyhole. The girl was sitting before the mirror, or rather in the mirror, because in this hotel the fashion was for semicircular strip mirrors that could be rotated (rather like the wheel of a water-mill), so that a springed chair rose up if the mirror went deep down, possibly under the chair: thereby women could inspect themselves from quite wild & crazy perspectives, from which it was only natural that they immediately absorbed a quite new demeanor. The chair comprised two horizontal semicircles parallel to each other, armrest cocainism without a seat. Between the interstellar mousetrap of the armrest armature & the inverted light trough of the mirror on a glass board lay some diminutive boxes with which the girl was working at such short intervals, it was as if she were piano-playing back in a high-speed shot the coins that she had lost. Right then, as it happened, she was fiddling with her eyebrows, holding what looked like a small toothbrush, black mascara on a small plate in front of her, beside that a grimy rag with black smudges on it. One of her eyes was as yet unprepared, on the other were huge black needles like those at the ends of escalators in the London underground where giant steel combs are set against the gamut of the deep creases of the steps as they melt away.

He looked at the boxes: a long column of lipstick, a dinky Venetian coffin of face powder, nail varnish flat as a British silver coin ironed out on a railway line by the Orient Express; the face cream in a white porcelain jar like a fattener for sick infants; the perfume bottle as a scroll — the sole glass flourish, twisted shepherd's crook, or a moving-coil Kelvin galvanometer; the rouge — a small princely crown with a crimson brain inset already visible on her cheeks in the form of a first rough daubing. What shone through the keyhole was not desire, not love, not the stare of an inquisitive male like beams of light in a physics laboratory, but the lump of ontological dough rested on the bridge of cosmetic articles.

Touqué was unashamed, he left the antithesis as an antithesis: ontology and frippery, analogy *entis* and empty cosmetics — there you have it: a love story. Now, for a second time he ceased to be intelligent and human: at first he had been so much what he is that that identity became the cause of the greatest asymmetry, swaying & drawing away, while now the girl had so much vanished and been reduced to nothing behind the fiction-mathematics of cosmetics that this again rendered impossible regular love, as described in books. The girl was, in point of fact, in those boxes: cream, powder, oil, varnish and mascara, & in the implements: brush, sponge, rag, tweezers, scissors, perfume atomizer. His lover that night was the world itself, trees, roads, times and stars all together, in God's Jacobius Maritanus *Ens*-salon, his sentiments the virtually unbearable positivity of being — now an artificially assembled figure of deceptive anatomy, a game, algebra, fiction.

Love, therefore, fluctuates between two non-human poles: between ontological *Sachlichkeit* and cosmetic, radical artificiality. That made him optimistic. What, he wondered, could be the most faithful epic expression of this ersatz person who had fled into cosmetics? Perhaps that the protagonist of the novel (having already transformed into a material pain-constellation for the sake of ontology) transforms into the style, structure, grammar of the novel concerning him, becomes a 'style-person.'

The novel is thus not a closed affair but two counterposed infinite cones with rounded ends; the two mirrors absorb different things about the 'hero' arranged around them. One sucks out his soul, his sentimental kernel, the nest of sentimentalism, and projects it beyond the most universal, absolute world of existence, beyond even categories; the other cone-mirror, by contrast, absorbs the surface of the surface, the outermost of outer boundaries, slips it through into the world of fiction, abstraction & cosmetics, where (unlike the other cone's world of pure raison) only grammar, only word, empty & self-serving grammar rules.

Touqué tried to write something like that under the title "Kiss." The first part was scene-setting (the setting is always the first, ready-to-hand device for ontologically-intended dehumanization): night sky, crepuscular pink, with golden veils, analysis of the pink, idyll, sorrow, fire, flesh-color, time, flower, girl, weariness, virtue, irony, daybreak, dream convention; in it pale-green acacia leaves: ash, line, something, a fault, commutator brushes; a spherical early arc light in the pink sky: total light, total absence of rays, light, isolated color, no color, no light. The impressing upon one of the scenery's impossible totality, the nature of the absolute godly nude and infinitely compensated repleteness with paradox, signifies the kiss's emotional content, which naturally is beyond and foreign to the kiss. The second part is a fragment of a strange story, describing the curriculum vitae of an electric current flowing through the shunt of an ammeter and the repeated wing-beats of tamed seagulls: everywhere mouth, teeth, redness, collision, parallel, double & quadruple numbers, polarity, choice. Of course it is hard not to describe a cosmetic fiction but to give a sense of the humbug through linguistic formulæ. The kiss novella also had a subtitle: "An attempt at a permanent definition of 'onto-fict.'" 'Onto-fict' seems a fairly toothpaste logo, but what Touqué wished to signal with this witticism was the inseparable (but at the same time also infusible!) parallelism of extreme truth and extreme falsehood in the new intellectual & ordinary life.

Touqué experienced this duality not just in his own life but also in other areas. One and the same university published, in one and the same month, two books, one with the laconic title of *Ens Ens*, the other that of *Berkeley*. The ens-ens one had a single basic idea, which was to demonstrate that there is no such thing as an individual mental life, zero psychology, but on the other hand all those moods that shiver on the surface of our mind are great surges of ontological essence, the incandescing of the wires of existence in man, the way that the incandescent filaments of light bulbs give light not through any lyricism of their own but through a massive extrinsic electric current. A new mythology is under development, and people are taking out ever more of the hitherto neglected, despised quantity and raising it to a mythically positive plane of reality; just as in the past dogmas migrated into the world of hallucinations, now the most fleeting nerve-shadows get into the ontological divine hall of dogmas, with name, body, infinite concreteness.

The *Berkeley*-book likewise had a fundamental idea: a new, ferocious idealism was under development, because people had realized that they were unable to recognize the essence of things, the ultimate points of life & matter, in their immediate nakedness, the pudency-tension of existence being so fantastic that it is impossible to bend the ring of virginity apart and therefore the true basic structure can only be substituted by symbolic signs, mathematical façades. The Berkeleian finite idealism of old had a melodramatic flavor — "we must renounce knowledge of reality" — which is completely lacking from neo-Berkeleianism: the ontological need is in fact a primitive and barbarian need, and the grand fiction-systems that act in place of "reality" completely satisfy man's more sensible need for a "probable reality."

When Touqué read the two books in quick succession he knew that he did not have to "choose" here: he accepted both, because he found equally sharp guarantees of both in his most intimate experiences, in his amorous adventures. If he read a new book on physics, the sort of things that he noted down for himself from the chapters on optics were that light simultaneously manifested in the most medieval of material particles and in the most Berkeleian-tinged clouds of probability, perhaps-mists & uncertainty-fields — on the one hand, naïve material, on the other, de Broglie-fiction.[8]

Every phenomenon is composed of a great heterogeneity of existence and equivocation: briefly, being is a dark ontological night, then blinding lightness of symbolism, only then creasing back into the selfish blue womb of reality, of course not so as to stay there. Neither the darkness nor the light delirium permits vision, yet one can hardly count on temporary gentle lighting in the present style.

Could there be any sense to his love? The desire, the feeling, got nowhere, it was always rambling in an endless sea of existence without wanting anything ('vitalism' is the conceptual, vacantly joyless plaything of weekenders' 'ontologism', the dark underworld drink of tragedians), it is never possible to make buds blossom in a higher world if they had opened there, never possible to accomplish plans hatched there, because that is the underwater, bereaved Nereid world of eternal premises that forever turns toward itself on the indigo-blue serpentines of an endless umbilical vortex. When embracing pairs settle on a plan for tomorrow, that is seemingly usually realized since Touqué, too, had in the end met the Cannes girl at 5:30 in the morning, but there was no connection between the plans and what transpired afterwards, the meeting was just a mathematical de Broglie equation of action for the approximating & more hypothetical expression of the ontologically complete encounter conceived in the plan.

Every love is, first of all, 'something' that a person senses with mythologizing rapture and physical determination, but then the acting (theatrical marking rather than expression) of that closed 'something,' that unapproachable identity, which runs with eternal conditionality above or beside the 'something,' with the mendacious taste of symbolism — a tiring series of games or arbitrary formulas which hang in the air. Perhaps the twentieth century will feel and formulate 'theologizing sentimentalism,' the absurd forces of feelings, the blue waves, alien to life and self-serving (ontology is not 'life'), that Touqué lived through in great solitude, where pleasure, weeping, desire and questioning turned into '*Sache*,' which is a bigger record than Werther's. In vain does tomorrow come round for the lovers in the calendar, in their souls the tomorrow feeling does not transform into a today feeling but carries on as a tomorrow wave, which pushes its lamé-sheathed waters bell-ringing out-of-time, to right and left for itself. It is not emotions of having reached the goal that foam in the little poodle slipcase of the consummation bed, but the beginnings of desire, the very beginnings, because love does not develop, the emotions do not alter under the influence of life's events, in just the same way as the nature of light does not vary under de Broglie-intermezzos.

In a study entitled *Elegance and Schisma Moralis,* Touqué likewise examined the duality of emotional-ontology and arbitrary-action fiction. In women's fashion, in the style of evening dresses, golf costumes, and, above all, bathing costumes (1933 summer season), he saw the exciting struggle, the wish for futile uniting and penetration into each other of being and fiction, the most humane human and the most stylish human, anatomical human and dehumanized human: in a beachwear costume two phases of being & despotism snaked against each other like the left and right limbs of a figure eight. In ethical life, as opposed to writhing around, after a 'mundane chiasm,' that happened to characterize complete separation: the helpless parallelism of onto-morality & ficto-morality (to make use of compound words redolent of toothpaste ads). Only nowadays do the sort of people who continually commit crimes but are nevertheless good, and those who possibly continually heap correctness on correctness but are nevertheless bad, have a true, almost scientifically experimental, season: simply because not even the faintest connection, the most naïve, thin blood-transfusing little bridge, exists between ontological morality stratum and action stratum.

For Touqué fashion and ethics meant a study of essence since it was there that the bipartition of concrete *Sache*-Person and the fictive Style-Person was most "evident": in fashion they crossed each other in the shape of an x; in ethics they accompanied each other in parallel, or more accurately 'dialectically.' What did that imply for prose? In the past, the milieu and story were together in a lukewarm combination, now the items of the milieu and the story being played out among them separate and thereby they will run next to each other. There will be separate object novels (that is the ontological branch) and hyper-event novels (that is the mania for fictiveness). Touqué had an inclination to write big, mythical catalogue-novels about his favorite objects, like bridges, wells, ships, lakes, and women's stockings.

On the other hand, he also had an inclination to write complicated event novels that combined 17th-century English dramas of blood and guts and all the opportunities for modern detective story complications. After all, that contradiction was also acted out in the strange but related possibilities of the theme and the ship in the two phases of *Scheme of the Beginning*.

This narrative-duality was like the oscillating parts & nodes of electric standing waves: on reflection the waves intersect each other, & non-oscillating points (bridges, wells, ships, etc.) arise at distances of half the length of the wave, whereas by virtue of the reflection the whole phenomenon denotes a double drama (ultra-Webster): infinite passivity and infinite motion assume and generate each other.

Once he had traveled up to Paris in order to watch a performance of a modernized play by Plautus in a small theatre, the director of which was an old acquaintance from Nice. On the train he had read some neo-Thomist reviews that had discussed the most varied neo-realist theories of knowledge, everywhere with the big reality cult of *Veritas fundatur in esse rei*:[9] by the time he stepped down from the train in Paris, porters, Cinzano posters and bar counters surrounded him on all sides, with the pathological wholeness of realism & objectivity independent of him; things were in acute *Esse*-paralysis. That evening he watched the Plautus performance: it was like puppet theater in a madhouse. The characters were made up with deadly ridicule, their voices were the mixed whinings of eunuchs and cretins, their movements the kangaroo epileptic fits of beasts & acrobats, the music a children's song, the text senseless pornography as if he had not found himself among humans but turns of abstract paranoia. The crummy make-up was precisely perceptible: sometimes the index numbers in a formula had to be pushed by one to the left on the bottom (that is how in a big storm the leaves of a swaying tree customarily displace their index number one further on with each leaf), four stepping into three's place, three into two's, or in other words, the signs stay but at the base a total shift is carried out: on the stage, too, the characters somehow remained in a stunning borderline case of identity, but the make-up hung on them exactly like an index number shifted by exactly one person with the deadly ridicule of senseless otherness because the whole game was criticism & death. The dehumanization ridicule-unit in make-up was somehow felt to be exactly one 'person-worth' and he always saw a regular different person on one of the people. Marionettes, buffoons, animals and idiots: when he saw those somersaulting amid the glaringly piebald set scenery, the ontological concepts of the *Bulletin Thomiste* were still stretched out in his brain, and he felt that he would have equal need of both things if not for his entire life, at least for a good few ensuing months of his youth.

II.

Conversation about Leatrice
(a former actress and industrial designer, currently dancer, who wishes to quit nightclub life)

— Sorry, but something is up with Leatrice.

— Leatrice? — he inquired in pained astonishment.

— You see, that's the main thing I hate in my whole so-called Leatrice cult; that people think a sentimental Dostoevskyism is driving me to gad about with those kinds of girls.

— Is it such a dreadful disgrace if a person, God forbid, just by chance, purely out of some sort of dawn-time moment of abstraction, happens to clothe themselves in yesterday's, in a just generally outworn, worldview? — he asked, pursing his lips, dispensing with a stylized mollycoddling smile pseudo-pedagogical rococo bonbons of the sort with which visiting aunties customarily pamper brats who, for ceremony's sake, have been deformed into ultra-tots.

— It's not a fault from the worldview's point of view but it is an affront to my instinct for the chick if people think I am yesterday's person. I don't ascribe any more value to the today than to the yesterday, it is just part of my hygiene that the 'cut' of my thoughts should, as far as possible, be the *dernier cri*.

— You are always so neat and elegant, no doubt about it. But what is the matter with Leatrice?

— She's rebelling.

The response was a scowl.

— Don't laugh. I am well aware in just what bad taste rebellion is as a sport, but now I'll take my chances with your irony & approve of rebelliousness. But then Leatrice's rebelliousness must be a special affront to your sense of form: it's not some kind of refined, inward rebellion, with a disciplined exterior, but a thickset, beastly toadying, 'idealistic' rebelliousness, fed by brazen testimony.

The response was again the pseudo-pedagogical auntie smile with some words quietly muttered with quotation marks emphasis:

— It was not for nothing that our Uñez said about you: "You know, the one with her mouth routinely half-open — in wonderment, of course, we thought, *comme il faut*: though in the end it wasn't a kiss which popped out, but a definition."

— Where did Uñez go?

— To Mexico as an architect: he said that with him that is the transitional condition between mathematics & fashion design. But Leatrice? What's up with her?

— She doesn't want to be a cocotte.

— Mon Dieu, how common. Leatrice has to be saved. Didactic, pedagogical, and moral urges are spurring me to save her.

— Why?

— For the sake of the general education of those corpulent coffee brokers, who only once in their life hear something intellectual, however trivial the affectation, they heard something via Leatrice, saw it, felt it. For these coffee brokers, the cheap, press-stud pathos with which she speaks about her memories of Italy (she was never there in her whole life) counts as the height of their 'wits,' not to say 'soul.'

— A truly fine general education: getting a coffee broker to stomach a fraudulent Venetian cliché.

— There's no need to put on airs! It's what a coffee broker needs; everybody needs the feel, even if only just that once, of intellectual matters: for some that senseless metaphysical libido comes via a Heidelberg literature mystic, for others via a cocotte talking about a Naples she has never seen, but in any case there has to be something for once in their life. A bit of goose flesh that has not been provoked by a woman's foot or some such thing. Sorry, but I'm a pedagogue. I... — at which point he breaks into a laugh. — Never mind! I won't get worked up about it. I also detest Bartley, who won't pay the streetcar conductor a penny for a ticket but gathers the sections of an apology for his existence, and at university for five years has done nothing else but phrase this catechism of the grounds for his existence. I am a pedagogue, and that's an end to it. Leatrice is needed; let her stay a cocotte.

— She doesn't want to. She's had enough of traveling salesmen for coffee. Yesterday she came close to making a scene behind the bar counter.

— *Mon Dieu,* an ideological drama, an ethical Grand Guignol. Poor Leatrice! She's also been infected with gravitas. So is the time over when cocottes had a sentimentality of didactic value about them? She's been infected by refinement, she's been infected by you.

— *Merci.* Do you know Steermans, that wee rubber salesman who has himself analyzed in the surgery room of that shrink Lednitzer and in the evenings is of such joy to Leatrice?

— Meanwhile he writes confused discourses from which all that is clear is that he is offended since some form of schematic university idealists ('professional idealists,' as he wrote in *Mercure Methodized*) with caste-Inquisitional arrogance reduce the big problem-complex of the 'mercantile spirit' (I recollect: he makes constant use of the attributive 'teeming' as in a teeming problem-complex) to the concept of 'salesman.'

— That's just great! Poor Leatrice finds herself mixed up in that tragic shortsightedness; indeed, that's the basis of her revolt, her little rebellion, that I venture to espouse.

— Self-patented patronage mams'elle of revolutions related to the conversion of behind-bar-counter cocottes — a fine occupation! Colossal.

— In plays of old at this point the blushing heroine would say, "How cruel! Mock not," now I am constrained to say something of the kind.

— Let's accord advantage to gossip over metaphysics: how was this whole Steermans-Leatrice affair?

— Then come with me over to *The Perspective.*

— Perspective?

— Yes, Leatrice didn't like the name *Boxico,* and she announced that she would quit the whole business if they didn't change its name to *The Perspective.*

—Leatrice, *mea* Leatrice *peccatrice,*[10] I think your sentimentalism overstepped the mark of its having any pedagogical value from the viewpoint of coffee reps. In any case, at 9:30 in the morning as it is, our friend Leatrice *peccatrice* won't be in the nightclub even if she does rebel and she has ethos-thrombosis of the spinous process.

— She may not be in the bar, but she has an apartment on the floor over the bar; she has locked herself in there, sniveling and quivering with rage. She would like to cry out to the world that she hates the dictatorship of salesmen over her erotic needs. Yesterday evening, when she dragged herself from the nightclub up to her apartment with all the cheap, ready-to-wear 'inhibitions' of her suppressed revolts, who do you think was standing before the door to greet her?

— Well, who?

— A woman from the Sally Army, that's who. I've no idea how news of Leatrice's attempt to raise the roof had spread so fast as it can have been barely three-quarters of an hour since the first symptoms of her moral qualms till her return home; but you couldn't disguise the fact that she had been standing before the door, I have no idea for how long, a cross-eyed little maid from the Salvation Army, with, perched on the bun of her hair, one of those black bonnets that look like a muzzle, epaulettes like Tegethoff-class flyswatters on her shoulders, and clutching a crimson-edged book. Ena was with Leatrice because Lea was ever so slightly sozzled and so could not have got home alone. Ena had talked about the Sally-Army lass's hand, to the point of sculptor snobbism that it was possible to establish from the degree of the luminance of the skin surface and the diameter of any warts the duality which characterizes these dipso dames for one thing, their withdrawal from the world of devotion, for another, the memories of primitive handiwork (both a lily & a wound), going on to apply that repugnant morphology to priestly hands in general.

— You won't credit this, but Ena, Lea's other supporter, has been hanging around in cafés & art galleries for days with that wee, bespectacled Danish sculptor.

— Excellent source research. Suffice it to say that Ena threw the poor Sally Army cherry out, declaring in the stairwell that if someone gets a bellyache that is not in itself going to turn them into an ascetic; if someone is disgusted by an uncivilized coffee dealer, that is not going to make them a wet nurse in a Protestant kindergarten, et cetera, and she was not going to hold her soul out to any fishy cretin of the God squad to crumble dollops of a Bible printed on crimson-edged paper into it.

— That's Ena's style for you; she is the last orator in European literature and in our hotel.

— On that they went to Lea's room and were together until six in the morning.

— My word, that is a great subject for a serenade or an ethical textile pattern or even an as yet undiscovered branch of art: those two women together the whole night on the floor above the nightclub; I have a talent for reconstruction, being able to spin out minuscule scraps of solid gossip into an impudent epic;

I see it all, Lea and Ena on the edge of the bed — Lea is howling, racked by sobbing, the cocktail and the ethical inspiration; beside it Ena, the public speaker: I would never have believed that the most universal negative doubt could encounter such rhetorical health. There is something delightful about Ena; to look at she is life and mechanized sensuality, but to hear the driest of professional nihilists, who does not allow one to relish anything, anything at all. The only thing living about her is her rhetoric. And there on the bed beside her my little Lea!

— Is Leatrice of greater interest to us?

— And you're asking me?

— You practice psychology as an expert, and you know that when human relationships reach a critical point one feels that they are not true relationships, or rather what there is, in fact, is absolute artifice & affectation, there is no space freer of lines of force (and you must surely be aware that I am plagiarizing you with these semi-official metaphors!) than that between protector and protégé.

— Well, of course. I well recollect that before the school leaving examinations, at the closing ceremony for the literary circle, I read out something about a lover leaving a girl and afterwards her feeling something very painful, very new and, for all its indefinability, very concrete, but in no way resembling the conventional notion that up till then she had formed (more on the basis of the sense of the word rather than its content) about 'pain.' My short story had a title something like "The Eclecticism of Pain."

— Why was that?

— The title is a terse reference to the heroine of the story feeling that what is referred to as pain signified a big void, which had to be filled with something; anything; a large abstract hangar into which positive concepts (it didn't matter what) have to be put; a new perspective before there were space and color whereby her perspective could be more objective.

— It's my belief, please excuse me, that you are wrong (*non credo quia credibilis?*).[11] It may be that when I like Leatrice's primitive emotions, which you may see as complicated hysterias, then I am doing something like Rococo or whatever maidens did when they began stroking white lambs, but the fact is that nostalgia sometimes takes hold of me & I swing back from the 'eclecticism of pain' to 'sensation' (but I had difficulty in uttering it & no doubt flushed good and red in doing so, didn't I).

The other knit his brow, and said in imitation of severe, self-important doctors:

— You were quite right to refer to lambkins when you stand beside Leatrice's bed & try with great incredulity to beg some 'feeling' from someone who happens to be uncultured but is just as complicated (on another plane, of course) as others, you are going to create a truly melodramatic impression.

— Well, that's necessary! — the other interjected querulously, signaling with the voice and an ambiguous smile that after those remarks he did not dare take the side of melodrama, yet also did not wish to part company for good with that small point of principle, and so half-apologetically, half-ironically letting drop that little 'that's necessary,' indeed leaving the lips open in the belief that in that way a stronger connection would be left between the words and himself, so the other would not dare give great offense.

— Nothing can be done. New points of reference, more secure pivotal points, have to be sought than those 'feelings,' which have already been modified as much as possible. Poor spontaneity. *Requiescat in pace*. We have to seek out a new inner life, & it would be cowardice coupled with naivety to incessantly run back toward the failed stations of melodrama we long left behind us, merely on the basis of the illusion that those good old, substantial, homogeneous 'feelings' & other categories are — *horribile dictu* — primary or what the hell.

— That is just as if Ena had said it — and incidentally I advise you to get Ena to write the introduction for your psychological thesis: sometimes a bit of metaphor jingling at the head of a dissertation has quite a good effect, and Ena has enough intelligence not to unduly compromise your style of definition. In any case, you yourself are nothing like as cool as you would like to be: your own exactnesses are pathetic exactnesses, indeed the technical part of defining is sweeping you toward new contents (admit it, often pseudo-contents); you pile up two hundred definitions in succession without even suspecting what you want to restrain between the contours, and after such protracted overscaffolding, finally some small realistic content evolves as a by-product (on the basis of intellectual abiogenesis?). That's your way of working, isn't it?

— You know full well, I'm sure, it is a basic law of intellectual life, of creative intellectual life, that one does not fix just one point and endeavor to build that into a reality with words, but a small irrational, yet strong nucleus starts sporulating aimless ideas, and the main idea, that particular leading idea, is an unexpected gift, something totally chance, utterly unexpected. It's not a case of, having found God, one starts praying to Him, but before that, when one as yet has nothing in the least concretely tangible about God, then one prays; we start with a prayer, which leans across from nothing into nothing, and those words create, exude, God from themselves and He springs from the clattering thicket of words — and here he burst out laughing and made a gesture like a magician in whom there is something of the chic of self-irony — like Venus from the water. Every big system and strong positive is a by-product: there is no 'goal' at all, only chasing and galloping into nothingness, apart from which results that were never counted on, never even dreamed of, and that were only in retrospect lied about as being the 'goal' all along.

— Nice! By the way, Touqué's magazine, *Antipsyche*, is full of stuff like that.

— Leville-Touqué is an imbecile, because all that he understands by psyche is psychoanalysis or infantile special needs education, but he has no inventiveness, no feeling for, in the same way as you, pardon me for saying so, you also have no feeling for there being a new opportunity here which is a radical break from categories heretofore, and people are in the process of clarifying a new attitude.

— O, attitudes, o, opportunities: positively prosaic ways of plugging things. I can only guess what joy you get, with your sardonic view on life, from the symbolic nature of our pilgrimage to Leatrice's place: at one end of the street a wee sentimental cocotte, at the other end a sterile rationalist, or whatthehell! someone who doesn't have the guts to launch deliberately into nothingness (in all honesty there is no 'dynamic nucleus' in me) and you prefer to cadge from a person like Leatrice.

— It's not uplifting, I can assure you.

Meanwhile they had arrived at *The Perspective*. It was the kind of house which can be seen in their thousands in a small French town; all that was special about it was that the entire house was squeezed between two staircases that were barely broader than firewalls, as if it had been placed between two desktop printing presses. It was narrower below than higher up, so one really did get the impression that the stairway-stay was squeezed between continuous forces and was bending. The two staircase walls down below naturally jumped a bit forward onto the sidewalk while up above it led to a newly constructed terrace or some kind of hanging garden, which was Leatrice's work. In point of fact, she had studied interior decoration in Paris and the terrace was a modified implementation of her final exam project. This had extended the mansard style of the house with ironical touches, but she had also mixed in a moderation of 'Nordic'-cubism and a Russian folk element. The columns of the terrace were imitations of vast, naïve chimneys (huge Fontainebleau-like dressage for smoke), but on their sides there were small enamel tags with gaudy Russian folk-embroidery patterns. Iron railings were quite modern again: dense bands of horizontal iron bands ran wave-like along them, the distance between them widening and squeezing together (alpha particles in the wild path of deflection of snakes of probability in the meticulously vertiginous space of an atom's nucleus); according to Leatrice, it was all nothing other than an enlargement and isolation of the hair on a Gothic bust of Jesus.

For all the infantile gaudiness it nevertheless made a uniform impression of healthy cynicism spreading in mixed forms. The bar premises were on the ground floor, from which an infinitely narrow spiral staircase led to the upper floor, which was now Leatrice's room; in the place in which the spiral staircase was now located only a big service lift had operated, and after that had fallen into disuse, a staircase had been crammed into the tight tube such that if a person walked up it they appeared to be revolving on one spot. The three flights of stairs looked like three propellers threaded one above the other onto a shared vertical axle.

Leatrice's room could also be reached from the back garden, and that was what Anny & Halbert used. Leatrice's room was very long and very narrow, taking up the entire façade of the house, and it had three large French windows. The furniture was crimson, a garish and yet still agreeable crimson, warm & clean. The vivid carmine furniture agreeably alternated three times with the pale countryside that filtered in through the greenish-grey windows. In front of one of the windows was a horizontal lath into which were set thick wires on the upper ends of which were impaled a row of long, narrow wax heads. They were colored busts; the bespectacled Dane had on one occasion used them to pay Lea; right then she happened to be in the throes of some sort of hyper-baroque Spanish affectation, and the six heads stuck on wires were a souvenir of that. It could be that one day they would acquire historic renown, because Leville-Touqué had made use of the heads in a rhetorically intoned simile at the start of one of his most important leading articles in *Antipsyche*. As it happened, the second head from the left bore a distinct resemblance to Leville-Touqué, and it is not out of the question that the bespectacled wee Dane had fashioned it after him from memory. The resemblance was particularly striking right at that moment, because seated there, at one of the little tables, was the man himself.

description of Leville-Touqué

He had a sallow complexion, almost a lemon color, which in the chin area opalesced into pure green due to a residual tuft of beard. The chin was extremely narrow, in fact no more than a particularly sharp indentation directly under the lower lip, after which there was a pointed little bony prominence. The lower lip was excessively fleshy and light red, like a pale beetroot, and had no wrinkles on it, so that it glittered like the surface of a silk-tie-dyed Easter egg. His upper lip was thin, the nose big and a fraction concave. He had a steep, domed brow, "a Cartesian Turkestani-melon," it was called by someone who loved giving clever-clever definitions of things. He had small eyes of a vivid green; the lids were flat and quite dark brown, setting them in sharp contrast to the pallor of the forehead and face. He wore bottle-lensed eyeglasses set in a spindly black frame that was perched a conspicuous distance from the eyes.

For all the sloppiness, a sort of brisk discipline ran through the man; in point of fact, he was upholding the tradition of the Romantic scholarly type without any of the awkwardness. There was a lisping tang to his voice, but that only served to even better bring out the chiseled yet mouthwateringly delectable precision of his sentences; he stammered a little, but words almost sparkled from the sly positives. He seldom reasoned aloud; he was more full of pathos while still arousing the impression of being a rationalist; everybody sensed his irrationality as being a 'smart' logic, his enthusiasm as being mathematical. His head also embodied that: a mystic mulishness mingled with arid rationalism in his features, his look. He wore loose-fitting collars and stylish neckties, achieving a singular compromise between elegance and clumsiness with his external appearance and gestures. Scrawny hands dangled out of the loose coat sleeves; the palms of the hand were small and puffy, the fingers long and widely separated, the whole looking something like broken bamboo. He sat at the end of the table, legs crossed, and under his arm was a yellow-covered notebook with a red spine carrying in blue Anglo-Gothic lettering the word *Antipsyche*. On his knees was a sheaf of creased printer's proofs.

— Good morning; where's Leatrice?

Leville-Touqué dropped the galley proofs & jumped to his feet.

— Good morning. She's washing.

— Decay, decay — said Halbert in a sarcastically unctuous tone —, she didn't use to pay any attention to personal hygiene. O, those overscrubbed cocottes! I hate them. I have to undertake major excursions until I come across a woman who has even a faint odor of flesh. Embracing one of the hygienic hetaeras you get nowadays is like caressing a bathtub in a druggist's shop. Tiles, cold water, soap — revoltingly clean. Poor Leatrice.

— What are you doing here? — Anny asked Leville without so much as glancing at him. She placed her handbag on the table and in Leatrice's mirror examined the pale-green new tweed jacket with pale grey stripes that she had on; she was wearing a broad antelope-skin belt; the mercury-modesty of the wide, dove-grey surface of the skin was in harmonic contrast to her long, slender cinnabar-red lacquered fingers: the signatures of borrowers tend to be latticed on the pink mermaid tails of bank notes in the same way as Anny's hand was on the belt. In female dressing one of the greatest joys is always feeling the body and garment separately, the fashion and the figure. That trivial fact is the greatest perversity: that dress and woman do not coalesce, that the curves never spill over into creases, and the lapels do not run across into true breasts as in some superficial metaphors but instead stay very much separate in stimulating raw duality. There was something barbaric in the vivacious digits as they danced around the loosened antelope belt.

— Me? — a sloshing of cleansing water now carried to them such a cheerful, clean morning sound that one could not imagine that swimming-bath Triton hooray was brushing against a body in which a 'spiritual struggle' was nesting. — I gave a bundle of page-proofs to Ena, who has meanwhile become a *directrice de conscience*, and instead of correcting the misprints she spent last night with Leatrice. I haven't a clue as to what she had been helping with.

— Where is Ena?

— Inside, in the bathroom.

— What is this? — Halbert asked with evil-minded distaste as he cast a look at the proofs that had been left on the table with a dismissive wave of the hand like a valet tossing dirty napkins into a basket for table linen.

A moment before, Leville-Touqué had glanced at Anny, who, with a skeptical-encouraging smile, responded with something along the lines of: "Go on and slaughter each other, it's my pleasure, though for the sake of convenience I am strictly neutral at present"; from which glance Leville only exploited the encouragement, and said with a smile:

— One of my articles. It bears the title "*Exteriora Imperent*"[12] — I took it from a medieval work on jurisprudence, where it did not have the same meaning as it does for me.

While speaking he was waiting with a petty sneer on his face for Halbert's mimicking response, though in that leer there was a streak of cowardice, in his somewhat awkward brashness, a certain prior defensiveness. Undeniably there was also a lot of sardonic prudishness about Leville, of course carried off very oddly; that was also what guided him even as with the smile he politely and cordially adopted in advance a critic's snigger. He even blushed slightly. Halbert smirked, and he tugged at the end of his nose as though he were taking a sheath away. From the bathroom could be heard the kind of deep gurgling noise that usually accompanies water being run out of a washbasin. Moreover, an unpleasant smell, almost like that of muddy pipes, pervaded the room. The sound of the wooden heels of mules clopping sharply on wooden slats thrown onto the floor, and in the meantime panting deadened by wet toweling.

— *Exteriora Imperent* — he addressed Anny —, are you familiar with those geometrical figures in which the whole structure of the basic figure only gains structural sense on the basis of an outer point, from which various straight lines usually run toward the figure? Well, that is what it is about: our life only becomes constructible (nice and rounded, that is to say) if one finds an external point like that to which to form ourselves. I formulated that radical 'exteriorism' in the April issue. The most radical 'exteriorism' of all is morality. There was a time when the saying went: "Know thyself." That is naivety. Self-knowledge is: death. Forget yourself, forget your mirrors — at this he gulped, a sort of half-swallowing, half-hiccoughing; he was ashamed of his pathos even as he enjoyed it —, renounce the whole lot of intelligent narcissus masks; the lyrical mask and the psychoanalytical mask, and fix on something absolutely alien, a thing that holds no resonance within you and comes from precisely the opposite direction than your soul.

— As far as geometrical diagrams are concerned, you could submit that to a sermonizing journal & their reverends would be thrilled by similes like that. Don't send the technical guff, because they will be less impressed by that. What are you looking to get at with that external point? What kind of illusion is it to talk about an outside at all?

— In the glass there are internal layers, flaws and folds, and there are pictures projected onto it. Both are equally on and in it, yet it is still very much two kinds of a thing: in our souls there are projections and internal autonomic elements. The distinction stands. — There was an undeniable hint of pusillanimity in his emphases.

Leville-Touqué's childhood and youth in parenthesis

Leville-Touqué grew up in southern France; his mother was a simple, highly religious woman who deferred to her husband in all things. He was a semi-cultured writer who took part in a series of lectures in a Lodge run by Spanish Freemasons, the subject of which was how psychoanalysis might be employed to undermine Roman-Catholic morality. In this there were diplomatic and fanatical, pedantic and dilettante plans of methods, all of which made a great impact on the short story writer's father. The son was a marvelous pupil and an excellent pianist.

It came to pass that a strange disorder set in with the boy's sense of rhythm, with him being tormented by neurotic hallucinations of sounds. The father got it into his head that his son was going to hit upon a new rhythmic system and thus tried to inculcate in his son his own obsession of 'an inventor of genius,' whereas the boy merely felt ill and was overpowered by a severe depression. His mother wanted to call in the old family doctor at all costs but the father brought in a Spanish neurologist who awakened in the boy a disgust for the 'psychic life.' He quite literally took to his feet to flee the doctor & for a while he resided with an old aunt. There he wished for nothing more than to forget about any 'psychic life.' He detested the illness, the diagnosis even more, & the treatment most of all. He was well aware that he had something wrong in his mind, his nervous system, but he did not seem to wish to recover. At least not that way.

This all happened during a summer vacation. When he again started attending school (this was when his father took him home), for assignments he wrote essays on subjects like "Superfluous Psyche," "Banished Psyche," et cetera, as a result of which everyone regarded him as a materialist. At the time he was as yet too young to dare deny that openly. He quit piano playing.

It was a confused year. He made the acquaintance of a sixteen-year-old Romanian young woman who had come to France for classes during summer. She became his lover. As a matter of fact, he pursued carnal pleasure like a maniac, virtually non-stop, yet he was nevertheless overcome by a kind of tranquility. He knew it was a pseudo-tranquility, and more numbness than harmony, but he held on tight to it nonetheless. That was when he started to pare self-apology into a dogma, already avowing that *Antipsyche* did not denote materialism.

He was teeming with smoldering psychological confusion and fanatical sensuality but meanwhile denied Psyche & denied materialism. At the age of 24, with a few university students & young priests, he launched *Antipsyche* as a quarterly journal. He sent a copy of the first issue to the Romanian girl who sent back the following response: "Perhaps I am at liberty to accept *Antipsyche* from you in interpreting it as: «*Pro Corpore Meo*» — no?" Leville-Touqué was not surprised that his history teacher and his first lover held him to be a materialist & it was with a wry smile that into the first issue he had slipped a small card with a fountain-penned note: "Sap-head. Maybe I deserve that."[13]

Before one of the windows red & blue lights flashed wanly in the morning sunshine.

— What's that?

— In the neon sign of *Perspective* the tubes for the letters RSPE are on the blink and they are being repaired.

Leville's face was strange in the daytime reflected red-and-blue lights; it was all like the dress rehearsal for an anatomical ceremony. A soft Laue-print[14] slipped over his greenish-yellow chin with cathodic routine, and the anti-psychologist frowned slightly if the upper edge of a wedge of light precisely intersected his eyes, so that the baggy yet taut skin under his eyes, which was somewhat whiter than the other parts of his face, glinted quite silvery, whereas his eyebrows were a darker brown than they had been up till then. The muscles around the eyes had a singular structure of elasticity: he never 'opened' or 'closed' his eyes, it was more a matter of adjusting the muscle threads and skin inlays around the eyes by precise switching of the nerves, leaving the eyeball itself fixed, with only the direction and position where they bunched together altering; the degree of turbidity of the thin capillaries, that fine, reddish-brown network, which was reminiscent of the ribs on the underside of oak leaves: the brown cuticle of some of them could have been scrubbed off with a toothbrush so as to separate the system of vessels like a miniature map. Beady black and green eyes around them huge lids, which were located around the pupils like a beach parasol over a black powder compact; all of that under gigantic spectacles, on the glass lenses of which floated colored bands & rings reflecting the neon sign's lights.

In this theatrical or circus-mystic lighting, Leville-Touqué greatly resembled one of those sculptural heads executed with Spanish mannerism, with the yellow-jacketed journal with the blue of its title lettering under one elbow. He had sparse hair, starting only at the top of the skull and looking as if it had not grown from his head but hovered several millimeters above it, flattened horizontally; if one held one's eyes at the same level as the starting points of his hair, one could have seen between his hair & head.

The way he was now looking in front, he was 'demonic' and idyllic at once; he was a yellow statue onto which one involuntarily imagined a silver wreath provided with some panegyric inscription, a wreath which could be bent with the fingers like the wire cage of a muselet cap on bottles of champagne; there was something morbidly selfish & isolating in his features, the promise of something very urgent and true, but something his audience was unable to capture as thought, to such an extent it was identical to his profile. That is how it is customarily phrased in obituaries: the tragedy of the hero of antipsyche and anti-individualism was that his personality & mental curiosity were marked with such exotic anatomical preordainment that no one reached the tenet that "the salvation of man is a fiction beyond man," or "the soul is not inside us," but they couldn't go further then claiming that "an extraordinary personality represented an interesting reaction at this time," etc.

a comparison to Leatrice stepping out of the bathroom: one of those old postcards of a nude in a lake at night by Stengel & Co. of Dresden & Berlin. The 'morality' of the comparison: infra & ultra are driving normality out of modern thinking

The bathroom door opened: Venus Anadyomene. Ena had her back to it, bent over the washbasin, where she was tidying soap and brushes. She was wearing a morning dress and so moved stiffly, lest she get wet or get soap on her. The big yellow beads of her necklace were hanging down into the porcelain basin and clinked continually. The lively tinkling clatter was a discrete but definite musical accompaniment to the birth of Venus; meanwhile the flickering letters RSPE had immediately taken possession of the threshold of the doorway & the lower half of Venus' body, cutting it from her left hip to the center of the breast on her right, splintering into tiny ancillary undulations to vanish in the region of her right armpit. On her upper body was an ordinary white linen pajama top, which ended above her knees and was clinging to her body in damp grey patches here and there. Her feet were bare and her bathing costume was rolled down below the knees into a sort of double ring of leggings; she was just in the act of heaving and tugging it off when she had nervously nudged open the bathroom door and plunged the world into an all-pervading smell of sponges. The base color of the bathing costume was probably black, but it was covered with jazzy thin horizontal stripes and had balled into fuzzy tufts. A white leather belt was draped over the door handle. She was tall and in her pose she resembled the slim blonde nude bathing in a lake that had been popularized by the Stengel & Co. postcard.

It should be added that the Stengel & Co. postcard was very instructive: amid rings of immense, dark green waves was standing a slim Psyche epigone who managed to prove with her movements, her colors, and her topographical coda, that petty-bourgeois piquancy and petty-bourgeois mysticism are closely related and, besides being psychological blood relations, they did not denote some inferior thing. The long fingers of the young woman covered her lap: her three middle fingers were, so to speak, a coquettish triad of her *mons veneris* in the green silence of the cave or clearing. This bashful gesture at first seems to be just a movement of a freezing cold woman: a twilight breeze swirls forth from the cave's dark dens, the wind-whistles of the trees and grass, so that the bathing young woman first & foremost feels chilly — "*in principio erat* gooseflesh." In the water, too, sudden substantial temperature differences may have arisen: where the sun broke through the selfish counterpoint of the branches, which dismembered the raw and aggressive theme of rays into cool golden slivers of diminutive mirror negations — there the young woman feels the water to be suddenly too warm, whereas where the water shivered from one end to the other under the blue murk — there every grace note of a wavelet was now gradually icy: at sunset everything turns cold within a trice, rather than gradually, with leisurely transitions.

The active hand of the sun still lingered on the upper green organ manuals of the trees, but the lake was cold like a February episode. The leaves, the grass, the stones, the earth, the flowers & her own skin grabbed at separate ice roles: the outset of bashfulness in this picture is undoubtedly improvised coolness, which is shed toward the alarmed target doll of the nude in accordance with the separate personality of every object. As on the occasion of the hydraulic dissection of the water we would find individual sections of water to be sweltering directly after sunset, but others icy, so on the girl's body and skin there were hot and cold spots: the sunlight no longer reached her shoulders, but nevertheless she glowed among the Ariel terrycloth of the breeze as if she had managed to salvage a radiant scrap of the sun. She would have liked to collect her entire body (*pudor est frigidarium glaucum postmeridionale*)[15] into this glowing bit of her shoulder blade; on the other hand she dared not move because she suspected that the warmth that had been left behind would vanish at the first flicker; if she were wishing to make use of it then it would suddenly come to the mind of the departing sun that it had left a scrap of itself behind & would promptly return to make good its absent-mindedness. By now a small, ruddy ray of sunlight gleamed only at the top of the tallest tree, so her eyes were turned that way, which was extremely difficult, as she did not want to move her head together with them. She was rather like a bat pinned alive to a door for purposes of torturing it: with averted eyes fixed on the uppermost branch of a cypress & a shoulder blade in the other direction, clinging to the smuggled residual heat of her body — a piquant borderline value of a caloric function.

The picture displayed a mixture of the realism and outstanding affectation that can be found in so many paintings of the time: the girl's face was a photograph of a Bavarian model from Munich, whereas the endlessly broad and endlessly rhythmic waves lapping around her legs displayed the most acute degree of stylization. Precisely that duality could be of service to a new century. It was decent of the waves to start around the girl's ankles: she was not immersed up to the knees or the waist in the lake, but only to the ankle, so that the endless rings of water and the nude pendulum, slim as a reed in the middle, came into impressive contrast and were likewise in the service of modesty: what on the yellow area of the nude was merely a small modesty spot in the open-handed mirror protocol of the waves was blown up in a monumental melody of modesty, a landscape, the wood's virginal rule of construction. The water's loudspeaker of modesty transmuted the girl's small efforts to cover her lap into the profuse concealing shade of the wood, into rays' vespertine incognito. Indeed, in the final analysis, looking at the whole picture, the pudendum no longer signified even a secretive blot over something that was to be concealed but was itself the necessary form of existence: little shoreline flowers, underwater pebbles, shirts and socks lying on a beach were all happy amulets of modesty — the barely-an-artist managed to emancipate his hero's psychic quivering into the ontological nub of things. (So why do I still say he is barely-an-artist?)

The girl therefore was, above all, cold: that was the beginning of the modesty. Secondly, though, the whole world consisted only of modesty: boughs, clouds, water & four-leaved clovers were all products of modesty — that was the end of modesty. The first, animal shivering: infra-virtue; the other, the pudendal shape of all natural things: ultra-virtue. It would be no wonder to me if historians of the future were to call the twentieth century the century of 'infra-ultra culture': art, science, & fashion all follow that technique (though, more than likely, it is not pure technique) when presented with a theme, be it humankind, a number, or a suit jacket, they do not start out from the average phenomenon in practice but from the preceding, what could be called negative state, which is then supplemented (leaving the 'normal' out of consideration) with the ultraphenomenon, one might say 'transpositive' state: a picture of a leaf will not be a green chlorophyll tray, covered with veins, which hangs from a branch in the picture or a poem but the leaf's logical prefiguration, its foreground (that word is perhaps more precise than the ponderous 'precondition'), connecting to the ultra-leaf, indeed anti-leaf features that can be sucked out of the leaf: the first circumstance is the exalted degree of leaf predestination; the second circumstance, precisely the opposite, is the degree of leaf-superfluity or leaf-universality, by which, that is to say, every imaginable thing is a leaf; or in other words, it can no longer be called a leaf, the word only having any sense to the point that it signified some differentiation from other things in the world.

When one speaks of the style of the infra-leaf and ultra-leaf, in which the 'normal' leaf is completely exterminated from among the brain's notions, then infra-leaf is in no case to be interpreted as meaning, let's say, 'bud,' & ultra-leaf in no case, for example, as 'a fallen yellow dead leaf-feather,' but the leaf's logical necessity, its formal, conceptual determination, and, finally, such generalizations of the form as become senseless or a game: after all, normality consists precisely of keeping a balance of inevitability and frivolous chance (i.e., the infra and ultra), but the twentieth-century's routine of ratiocination is not interested in keeping a balance and instead the lower & upper poles, the big torsos of 'not-yet' and 'not-anymore,' are enticing.

In the art of a century like this not much of a role falls to a person, to souls in general, because the individual is always expressed by the pre-mental (this has no imaginable connection to the 'subconscious,' a notion which typically lies outside the more recent sphere of thought of the 'infra-ultra culture') and post-mental; in other words, the personality, life in its entirety, is omitted. As a matter of fact, the new art can have no kind of theme, for there too ante-theme and post-theme will play a role, but as the ante- & post-theme are also 'something,' a role will again be played by the infra-something and ultra-something with the simple omission of the 'something' — and so on *ad infinitum*, and this whole syntax, indeed lexicology, will have to be recast. Just as we can imagine eyes that see heat and are blind to the visible spectrum, so brains are now being readied that are blind to 'something' but highly sensitive to pre- & post-figurations of that. We have seen the success of this routine in rectified eyes with the vespertine bathing of the Stengel & Co. postcard, but we have to refrain from a pure truthfulness that destroys itself — let us move further into the rich bower of obscure and sustaining moments that precede the truth.

A reddish-golden sunlight shone in the girl's hair and at the top of a cypress and this irradiated a subdued russetiness into the empty blotches of shadow as if one of the characteristic features of bashfulness were autumnal pomp: the girl was nothing but simple shuddering, harsh alarm, and yet, that late brownish-red sunlight gives her body a princely splendor, rank & balmy distinction. The smoldering, late sunlight runs like fiery moss through muscles gone green from cold: every fall '*lucrum cameræ*'[16] and resounding nobility conceit marched by on the Bavarian model of puberty. There is no kinship between these thin bones, immature muscles, and boyish legs & the flickering, splendid sunlight: adolescents and purple do not customarily produce good dialogue: here too each lived its own role, with the light laying out with itself each of its daytime incidents, the girl preserving her simple-minded non-genericness among fantastic sunbeam tactics of love.

In the Leatrice who stepped out of the bathroom there was a lot of this heroine of the Stengel & Co. postcard: her ankles were bogged down in the wet ankle rolls of the peeled-down swimming costume like the ankles of the girl in the picture under the sweeping waves. It is always on the basis of such quite minimal but important similarities that we find the most diverse things as being similar; and justly so, for in fact if a quite 'insignificant' detail of a detail tallies one cannot think of that as a pure accident, but one supposes a common cause must be at work: we always treat the infinitely small detail as a disclosure and on that basis we also try to equate the dissimilar 'significant' parts, in this case the pubescent portrait of the Stengel & Co. postcard from Munich with elements of the profile of a 'cocottoid.'

description of Leatrice

She had long blonde hair, parted not quite in the center. On one side, the longer cascade, there were several large waves running down the hair, perhaps two-and-a-half times larger than normal, but they were so large that, even though the hair came down to her chest there were only two of them altogether. The band of hair had its own particular dynamic scheme: just as bodies often have a center of gravity that lies outside their physical bounds, so too in this case the direction of the line of the wave that was manifested in the hair did not coincide precisely to the actual waves, only in places, and there it was almost audible. But precisely that was what was beautiful, those only occasionally materialized waves, those suggestive half-lines and dissolving trial sinus curves. The other, shorter side was full of little wavelets that were like silk springs, and there seemed to be very little linear about it, because the sun was shining onto it, making the whole look rather like a ball of steam billowing in a headlight, which glowed, shone, steamed, and only here & there showed a hint of a misty-green internal smudging that allowed one to infer a degree of plastic cohesion. The hairline at the parting was pink, like a gently arched rubber cord of rosewood, & beyond it the bifurcated hair rolled down like a dark blonde shadow on the shaded side. People generally called faces like that of Leatrice Achariol-Zaninoff 'regular beauties,' that is the best that can be said, & it also tends to be how they are described in films. Her brow was not big &, seen from the front, it was shaped like the white bone handle of a moustache brush — an anonymous oblong oval.

Her eyes were two smaller-scale repetitions of the same basic form. She had soft, greyish eyebrows, with all the indefiniteness and quiet precision of a shadow: what is beautiful in the pale shadows is that, for all their misty nonchalance and trembling amoeba-like nature, they preserve with such immutable strictness the palpable essence of the tangible object to which they owe their existence, being functions, negative ones at that, and yet proclaiming the formal content of the object more definitively than the object itself. There are also painters who are able to depict edges and intersections far more sharply by eschewing the use of lines and employing the thickening and hatching of certain bands of shade. Leatrice's eyebrows likewise seemed like cunningly placed shadows of a distant little blade: around the nose they suddenly thickened and became like plumply velvet catkins, while toward the temples they stretched out, almost purring, like the brow lines on Egyptian statues, but not at all in those fashionable sharp, skintight streaks, but pliantly and unsculpted. The eyes themselves were also elongated, like the cross sections of glass lenses in a physics textbook, & there was no sharp contrast between the white and the iris of the eyeball.

There are eyes of which the physical surface, and so to say the psychological surface, are entirely identical: those are vacant, insubstantial, & sterile-looking eyes. On the other hand, there are 'deep' eyes where the distance between the two kinds of 'surface' is so big that the physical one virtually completely vanishes, and the eyes as a whole arouse the impression of the last shaded room of an endlessly long enfilade of rooms, or the ceiling of a low room of which there is a fresco in perspective so that the room seems to expand upwards almost to the sky: the eyes come from much further away (from 'more deeply') than the face, and they lose the character of physical simplicity & homogeneity, and instead of that create a special suggestion of space, full of shadows and plastic grades of continual deepening. As if one were looking into the deepest depths of a warm tent in which there is no light, only a sense of distance that is only realizable for us as a ray. Leatrice had 'deep' eyes like that. The rings around her pupils, which rippled and floated in her eyes, were dark grey. When she rolled them there was no sharpness or determination in the movements of the eyes, because somehow they were not reduced to around the pupils but the look was everything from the lower band of the brow to the cheekbones. Just as in modern homes, instead of a light source localized to one lamp, people prefer scattered light pre-filtered from hidden lamps, so too that principle was realized with Leatrice's eyes because the sharp gaze-arrows did not flash from the pupils but the whole of her central face was a rippling, dark-grey gaze area. The irises seemed to float in that twilight tent without any constraint.

It is not impossible that the romantically-decoratively inspired historian of ideas who first radically defined the 'latent Gothic' of the Greek soul in place of long-used poetic allusions, had a face like that to thank for the idea of this perspective. Because there was something 'Greek' in that face, just as there is in many film actresses, broken through all American sentimentalism, metropolitan ultra-hygiene, and English racial conventionalism. The nose could barely be seen, so uniform was its color to the color of her skin, and its modeling stood out so faintly — that just-mentioned paradoxical statuesqueness which owes its contours to its murkiness. The lips right now, in the morning, were pale, like a plump, grey lizard, & as if she were tightly squeezing them together at the two ends, whereas in the middle the lips lay loosely one on top of the other: a person's lips are usually in such a position after a contented swallowing, when one has swallowed a big bite but is already preoccupied with a new thought, yet due to the pressure of bliss this lip gesture is left abstractedly on one's face. Her legs right at the foot were very slim, but higher up they widened with slightly exaggerated eagerness — lower down, they were smooth, gleaming, taut & agile-firm, but above the knees tiny dimples cropped up in the softness: on stepping it was striking how much further the upper parts trembled than the lower.

— Anny? — Her voice was childish, slightly husky, and slightly insincere.

She raised her right foot, leaned on the door, and started to nervously shake and jiggle the foot about in the air, which was her way of dumping on the floor the wet swimming costume clinging to her calves: it did indeed slip down the stiff right leg to her ankle but it stayed on the foot. — Ahh — she ejaculated in frustration, at which Leville-Touqué, who was now seeing Lea for the first time in his life, ran across and pulled the wet costume off. — Thank you. Who are you?

— Leville-Touqué; I need to speak with Ena.

Leville-Touqué pushed up his spectacles with the bone of a flexed thumb then folded the swimming costume, indeed on his own accord wrung it and threw it onto the bathroom floor (meanwhile sensing that however much he might wring and squeeze it the body somehow latently remained in it, in the strict meaning of the word, within a certain time it is not possible to crumple it in such a way that some tangible emptiness was not left in it that could be sensed by a person in the same way as voids in lava in the wake of bodies that disintegrated long ago): that plopping was the end of the Anadyomene scene.

Ena, too, had cleaned out the washbasin, and through the clicking of her beads, the accelerated and suddenly dying clack, one could hear that their wearer had also straightened up.

— I've had a bath. — She threw herself down on a red couch ('la Cardinalle'); where she sat, the cover darkened in a thin band around her because her legs were still wet. — Hand me a blanket, they are in the second of the flat drawers. — Ena squatted, the beads tumbling to the floor and rattling on the handle like hailstones on a window. The light of the letters RSPE went off. With her two flat palms, her fingers pressed together, Leatrice spread on the front of her legs the bottom of some linen pajamas and thrust the bathroom door with the tip of an outstretched right foot. — I am very happy to have the company, I'm delighted to see you all, but may I respectfully ask the gents to go out on the terrace for a couple of minutes. *Au rev.*

Halbert exclaimed plaintively, too loudly:

— *Mea peccatrice,* why are you raising your price? I know everything, and it's all nonsense. The difference between morality and being a tart is only one of price — a virtuous woman is very expensive, a cocotte is cheaper. *Mea peccatrice,* what an anti-democratic streak morality would have in you.

He brightened up so much on his cheap wisecrack that Leville-Touqué clapped him on the shoulder and jerked him out of the room. Ena and Lea called out something, Ena's sentence longer than Leatrice's, and at the end of Ena's sentence Anny also interjected, then all at once silence ruled.

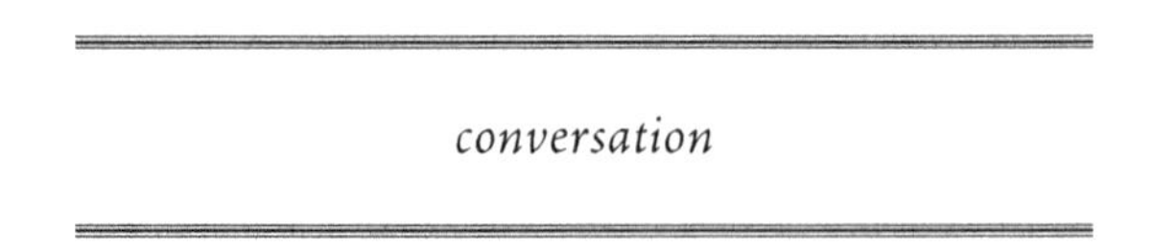

conversation

When they were outside on the terrace any momentary rapture at the jest had slipped away from Halbert and he felt lousy beside Leville-Touqué.

— What do you make of Leatrice?

— It was always my bad luck that despite having just a moment's glance at a woman, I noticed a great many things about her so that when as a naïve boy I passed on my remarks to my friends they always guffawed — and quite rightly so. As a matter of fact a fair woman does not mean for me what she does for a *Lebemann,* a man of the world, and a connoisseur — I have no idea what makes for a lovely leg or a perfect neck, that sort of thing. A fair woman (do excuse me, if I expound at length; that is an intolerable and useful by-product of my craft) is a person who inspires me to invent a special anatomy that I then, once I have worked them out in the workshop of my intellectual and logical desires, relate back to the woman, & I can spread it over her like a sleeping jacket of airy weave but embroidered with patterns of pedantic symmetry. Their true beauty is not in them but in the ability they have to force one to live through and create an unreal anatomic vision; or to put it briefly & laconically for you — female beauty lies in the possibility that on glimpsing it we shall immediately be unfaithful to her for the sake of an unreal, strange, hallucinated woman.

— You're a fine one to talk, dear Touqué; you are incapable of enjoying something without first having convinced yourself that the thing is unreal, remote, constructed & artificial. If you eat an apple you strive to terrorize yourself into the illusion that the only feature that we wish to discover in a natural apple is one which can be found in an artificial wax apple, indeed, in certain respects a genuine apple is more artificial than papier-mâché fruit, and having thus satisfied your perversity you can then go ahead and take a bite of an apple. No?

— You're making fun of me. In times of old the prophets would have been enraged at the jolly jokers who took their thoughts to the point of absurdity and thereby caricatured them. They, however, were naïve and exceedingly undiplomatic prophets. I am grateful for being satirized, in the present case, for instance, because satires express my thoughts much better than I do. If I were to have my complete works published then I would assemble an anthology of the satires and communicate my own works only in the margins or in the form of footnotes. A writer can never take his principles *ad absurdum*, he daydreams vainly in the empty illusion that he is capable of self-parody. My dear Halbert, I await the final formulation of my thoughts in your belle-lettristic frivolity. If by any chance your services were to be enlisted for my journal, I would be deprived of a wonderful propaganda opportunity.

— You put it diplomatically, or in other words, steer clear of the truth. In the end, when your corpse is fished out of the great flood of literary history no one will recognize your face, but a not particularly cunning coroner-philologist will light upon a two-dime popular, selected (selected!) paperback edition of Oscar Wilde in your soggy pockets. What a blunder that will be, Touqué, what a blunder.

— That's very possible, only I don't get why would it be a blunder? By the way, one thing I don't like about you is that for all that you are a gentleman you make use of such unserviceable and demagogic terms as 'truth' & 'diplomacy' — what's the good of that? There are some people who out of a naïve love of convenience identify the truth with ordinary and cheap plausibility, thinking anything that is not plausible cannot be true. That is when those petty-bourgeois legends come upon the opposition of 'artificial' & 'natural,' and other puppet-theater duels. Humans and their mental life are very plausible and tangible, but the matter does not end there.

— You live in an exaggerated anti-truth cult that you are capable of lumping together the cheapest traveling-salesman positivism and most intricate psychoanalysis.

— Aren't they the same? Are they really two different things?

The salty coldness of the sea drifted over from the distance, the rustling of the leaves was like the icy sputtering of little wavelets. The sun was cold and yellow, the terrace was wet from an early-morning sprinkling. It was an ascetic morning, which awakened Leville-Touqué's sensuality. Warmth, 'lush' colors, & glutinous sounds are good for many things, but not for screwing up sensuality: they spread one's desires on the asphalt, onto posters, into darkening windows; by contrast on cold, slightly damp and sunny mornings, the dark fleshiness that accumulates in a person at night is lagged with insulating material, as it were, it does not radiate asunder into the world but sets out from the body and springs back to its source by the outlines of the body in order that it may thereby intensify and tauten even better. It is a mistake to suppose that trees, birds, and all the sets of the Rousseau-esque régime and the *opéra comique* have to participate in true eroticism: it is much better if the body stays in plastic isolation & quietly excludes the aforementioned poor lyric-masked mediator called nature from the game.

— What sort of person is this Leatrice?

Halbert was very crestfallen.

— Ask her yourself.

— Do you want me to make a fool of myself? Fifteen-year-old boys are in the habit of seriously asking street girls to tell them their life story.

— She likes to talk about that, it belongs to the blessed little Romantically-minded bundle of which Ena will deprive her only for Ena's pushy skepticism to fill its place with a banal morality.

— Leatrice is an exceedingly lovely woman — Leville said frankly, with a feeling that rationalist types rarely permit themselves, and if with due discretion they do allow themselves that lyrical mood for a few minutes then, they are very much aware of what they are doing and are pleased that their audience also ascribes to it a special value; should they blush or possibly display some microscopic tear drops in their eyes, then the cause of their emotion is not the lyrical subject but their own ceremonial affectedness.

Leville-Touqué was like that as well when he uttered the word 'lovely.' He even remarked: — How many a time one has fought against the novelistic interpretation of 'loveliness,' how many a time proclaimed the esthetic points of view of negligible quantity, how many a time smashed to pieces the justification for the decorative — and then, what do you know, sometimes, there is a rare moment when something (not necessarily a woman) appears before one's eyes which, with its gentle certainty and provocative definitiveness, demands those few phonemes which make up the word 'lovely.'

— I'm glad of the occasion of being able to see you as a poet. A big Easter celebration.

— You're so sure of yourself — but perhaps there is more shameful and concealed lyricism in your irony than in my pathos. It is not a trembling voice and tears that make one lyrical, and most certainly not the cynical formulas of critical style that make one a stone-hearted intellectual. There are weepy rationalists and ironic Werthers, you should be well aware of this, because as a professional psychologist you pigeonhole people a lot.

— If it comes to hidden illnesses, it is perhaps not malapropos if I make so bold as to point out that you, too, are secreting a psychologist on your person: you may have had psychiatric aspirations, but they have not succeeded, and now that you are sick you have launched *Antipsyche*, which may be none other than a graph of a pathological state of mind deriving from your suppressed psychologist nature. All one has to do is find the key to unlocking the true cause of each rhetorical programmed utterance. You have your nostalgias, so you are a little bit ill, because every desire is a slightly sick state — and you have the talent to work them into a program.

— Perhaps you are right; the difference between us merely consists in how we interpret desire as such. I am at one end of desire; at the other end is the object of my desire. You, on the other hand, trace desire in a circular form, with the ego as a starting point coinciding in the area of the circle with the goal as an end point. I perceive and draw desire as a long straight line: the starting point is inside me & the end point outside, at the antipole, as a horrible fact, an objective external reality. — He broke into a smile, & tweaking the smile further, added softly, in a well-scrubbed, easy trill: — *Exteriores imperent.*

A waiter in shirtsleeves with a white apron & black waistcoat came up onto the terrace seeking to enter Lea's room.

— What do you want? You can't go in — Halbert said with genial emphasis as he felt that the embarrassing dejection that Leville's supercilious manner had aroused in him had relented.

— A whole lot of cocktail mixers from last night are in there.

— I'll have a word — Halbert said, knocking on the door.

— Hang on a tic — the girls roared.

— It's not that we are burning up with longing, just hand out the cocktail glasses and tin shakers that were left in Lea's room last night.

Ena came and gave the waiter four glasses.

— Lea sends the message that if any of the gentlemen are naïve enough to have the idea that Lea is throwing fits of modesty in not permitting you into the room then they are kindly asked to adjust their thinking before they come back.

— Lea did not send that message, my dear Ena — Halbert said with a chuckle —, that's your style, sweet Ena, being as how you are the last of the Mohicans who still seeks to impose some kind of class consciousness on cocottes as if they were immoral in principle.

When Halbert came back Leville asked with childish sheepishness:

— Have you already been with this — Leatrice?

— Yes, I have — he said with a smile and somewhat uncertainly as he did not know what tone Touqué was getting at.

— You think I just want to get you riled, but I can assure you that I am leveling with you: for me women represent the symbolic satisfaction of my thirst for unreality. My thoughts are extremely conventional, and the most perverse paradoxes are prepared from the same colorless-odorless boring material as a caretaker's most half-witted humdrum notion. Prosaic. Concrete. There is something secure in philosophy, something comprehensible and transparently limited from every angle. But when I get near a woman's body I sense the magic of the unreal and transcendental. At first blush, that sounds hopelessly romantic, and I would not disown it at that, it's very à la mode and yet it's not that at all. You yourself had your flirtations with psychoanalysis and know in which line of their Koran cases like mine are dealt with: I saw Leatrice, I have a very dim memory of her, but I see before me all the more strongly and more alluringly a tall, slim woman in a tight and smooth, lemon-yellow frock of balloon cut with a black-lacquer belt and dark bronze hair that looked half-wet — so, on what page of the psychology of associations does that stand?

— I could carry on, so my excuses if I ask: is everything with you of such a 'psychic' stamp, if you will permit me to use that poor expression?

— Call off your hunting hounds, and quit the dreadful lousy mirror mania you guys have about it all being a matter of mirrors and there is no world. You surely don't think that I deny the presence of the psychological? Of course I make no mention of it in my journal and my articles, because I loath such tasteless and gushing compromise-sentences like 'although we emphasize that the true person starts in the remote-external and not in the self, that by no means implies a total & ridiculous denial of the great importance of psychological life,' etc. What would be the point of blunting the shameless bias and frivolous edge of that program? But there are times when I, too, for amusement, make use of your 'psychological life.' At times like that I don't think, just associate. It's a pleasant enough game, though it soon pales, of course. But if a woman is running through my head, I can live for days on associations without thinking of anything. At times like that I am inclined, just for the heck of it, to write a psychological novel. You can imagine how that would be followed in the next issue by a thunderous article about psychological novels. In point of fact the whole issue would be a supplement about psychological novels. If you wanted you could have the right of reply. I regard you as the first chance of Psyche's rule. My role is easy because as a so-called pioneer I have the right to be obscure and undecided. There is a bit too much polemical favor in its tack, but successors may make a Trans-Psyche out of *Antipsyche*.

Halbert drummed nervously on the door.

— It's clear, it's clear — said Leatrice in a brisk tone, and quietly, as if she had not yet completely finished a thought, Ena.

Ena's character

Because Ena did a lot of thinking in general. For her it was a profession in itself, one that she had learnt and applied, that she was proud of and enjoyed. As her university colleagues said, it was not "*l'art de penser*" that was manifested in her but the "*métier de penser*." As someone had previously remarked, her external appearance was in singular contrast to her way of thinking. She was always dressed in the very latest fashion, but deep down she was anti-mondaine by nature, and that was evident just by looking at her. She avoided French fads as far as possible and was always outfitted in the English style. But what on another woman would have looked chic for sure merely seemed to be the consummation of some insipid program on her: "a woman should always be up-to-the-minute in every fiber of her being, in every stitch of clothing" was the dry principle and the highest grade of up-to-dateness. For her dressing was the product of a strictness of worldview, not an ingrained instinct. In any case her whole being was more a slightly anachronistic carrying into effect of the 'female idea' without the least trace of femininity. There was little that was chic in her, but a lot of naïve rhetoric. Many people at the university laughed at her for her ideological way of dressing. For her the woman as a whole meant a 'healthy woman,' so she was also one of those hygiene-obsessed women about whom someone just before made a sarcastic remark. Truly, everything about her smelt of sponges and her skin was rough to the touch from all the cold water it had been scrubbed with.

Her father had died a long time ago, so even in high school she had grappled a lot with poverty and done a lot of tutoring. People were pleased to take lessons with her because she was a 'clever' girl of exceptional memory and impertinence, which impressed many parents. She had an uncle with a huge library that embraced the scholarship of the entire nineteenth century, and she would prepare copious notes late at night in slightly leftward-sloping hand, with horizontally flattened, squat and rounded, separated letters. The uncle was repressed, a tireless utopian, one of those sickly dream-constructors whom only a vogue for positivism is able to breed. He had once written a book with the title *Murderous Sainthood*, which in those times as an as of yet still uncertain vision had been denied distribution rights, but he had lived on in Ena's mind and had blossomed into a dissertation on the concept and practice of marriage among the Scandinavian peoples that she had written as a seminar exercise in her first year at university. She had once had an untidy pseudo-love affair with a man who was employed at the embassy, but whenever the matter of marriage came to the fore he always developed severe peptic ulcers. In her second year she had obtained a grant in Norway to carry on her studies and read law.

Ena was a tragicomic minor heroine of unsanctified work for its own sake: she supported her mother and she paid for her own clothes, as a result of which she had developed a layman's respect for work, which lay just as far from any idea of the acceptance of a religious duty as it did from a wholly brutal 'efficiency'-sentiment, but it was nevertheless something very bleak and aimless. "One has to work" — & Ena was sedulous, tireless, her teeth like scoured porcelain, her clothes puritanical, the latest word in fashion, and unutterably lifeless.

That was why she was standing alone in the railway station at the time. Because she had no women friends. She had students who respected and loathed her, and she had tennis partners who were likewise frightfully bored with her even though she was actually a very good player; but for her tennis was just an arithmetic problem to be solved, and she played like a machine, almost never missing a ball and being highly economical in her movements. When there were tennis contests at the university everyone decided to set her on a par with the Japanese, who were similarly clockwork players, quite inhumanly so.

She set off on her journey alone, with her brand-new yellow leather handbag, in a green herringbone-pattern two-piece suit with a raw-silk fawn blouse and a little brimless cap; a silver lorgnette hung around her neck. Her tragicomedy, which had developed in full-blown form in Norway and was still maintained now, was that in point of fact she deemed to discern in the latest intellectual trends and lifestyles, in the emergence of new types of man, in new styles and institutions that showed the most total dissociation from the principles that she had found conserved on the shelves of her uncle's library, a vindication of his own antiquated views — an enlivening of the library of her childhood. In Norway she had straightaway set to work positively, greedily observing the family with whom she lodged as a paying guest and people in general, while of an evening she would assemble her data and construct myths from them. Like every born positivist observer, she was a hybrid of impressions and legendary inferences. She failed to notice that her colleagues had long got over the demand for 'truth' in the naïve dictionary sense of the word, and, through the very fact that they admitted they wanted 'myths,' came much closer to the true content of certain things than she did with her own bigoted self-delusion.

Her whole awkwardness was evident in relation to Gerda Staalbreck's women's clinic. Ena fell ill in Norway and had to be operated on. At that time a high repute was being built up by the Staalbreck sanatorium, which was situated not far from the seacoast and had only female physicians. The clinic was surrounded by waves of gossip, views of the world, and belles-lettres. The physicians were called a white-coated lesbian league, & Gerda Staalbreck — predictably, and as was only natural — the surgeons' Sappho. Some called the hospital a modern nunnery of a new type of woman where the patients were not only treated but also drawn with the assistance of some sort of mystic suggestion into a secret freemasonry of the 'new woman.'

Ena saw in it nothing less than one of the fortresses of classical feminism *wie's im Buche steht.*[17] When she recovered, it is said, she essentially had no contact with either the clinicians (there were a dozen of them), nor with other patients, but she dictated to a young high school student an essay under the title *Nouvel Embarquement pour Cythère*[18] in which she extolled the clinic, the female physician, lack of illusion, dwindling maternal sentimentalism, etc. Gerda's sanatorium truly did have significance as a view of the world and development of a model, but that had nothing to do with Ena's materialist Cythera; indeed, it was the opposite. When Ena thought that the body cult of the Gerdas of this world was a fight launched against the mind, then these female physicians also 'transcendentalized' the body, & they had reached the point that a millimeter separated them from formulating a new, all-pervading, all self-avowing & self-corroborating program of metaphysical rebirth in the *Gynaikeon*, which was Gerda Staalbreck's medical journal.

The sole person who had an inkling of the true path of Gerda and her supporters was a village preacher, the priest of a village near the sanatorium, the not totally uncultivated population of which, not unnaturally in view of its proximity, had the most to say about the inhabitants of the sanatorium, and in a Christmastide or Advent sermon spoke about the spirit of *Gynaikeon*. The congregation had not understood much of it, & he had written it up as an article, but that could not be published because that would have given the impression that the Church endorsed what many, including Ena, regarded as an anti-Christian totality of 'materialism.' It may have been that, but for that very reason, as a paroxysm of the material, it forced him to face a big metaphysic, which he later had the courage to accept & profess, in contrast to Ena's affected & cowardly *ignorabimus*.[19]

Gerda Staalbreck and her physicians never responded to the reflections relating to them, but later on, in one of the numbers of the rejigged journal, she set off from the lyrical picture (elegant, indisputably elegant, when a surgeon picks up with gloved hands a poetic picture like an excised body part resembling a plant) that the rural parson had made use of: the picture of a convalescing woman buried under thick rugs on the terrace, but the murky-brown morning sun was cutting through the mist to shine on her face: over her head twinkled a mist-shrouded, lusterless yet still burning morning star, and the woman's hair was clouded on the terrace by hoarfrost or powdery snow: she was smiling and carried under her eyelids the possibility of an unknown new morning; it was then that she sensed a connection between the star of Bethlehem and the dull star above a misty sea, etc. Neither by poetic suggestion nor by logical reasoning did those sorts of relations enter Ena's head: she saw nothing of those.

When she returned from Norway she had recovered her strength. It was then that she became truly rhetorical — it was then that her 'symphonic doubt,' as Leville-Touqué called it, developed and, at the same time, her great faith in the material, which had lost its credence. Her world started to crumble at all hands, and she saw ruins as flowers, agony as renaissance. She had met Leatrice about six months before at the *Perspective* nightclub. Ena was a puritanical soul, never flirtatious or coquettish. When she wanted to dissuade Leatrice from giving up her trade, she was not seeking to gratify her own eroticism in continuing to keep a tart as a tart. Ena was rhetorical, but she lacked all passion & sentimentality. She was a rhetorician of doubt, sobriety, and 'principle,' but her life was like that of a Quaker old maid. The concept of 'modesty' slightly bothered her, yet she herself was very prudish — on the other hand, at every step she would protest that with her it was not a principle but selfishness, a reasonable saving, etc. She would have been cut to the quick by anyone who called her 'virtuous,' not to say a 'lady.' When Halbert and Leville-Touqué went in, all three of them were sitting next to one another on the bright-red settee in virtually the same pose: Leatrice, Anny, Ena. It would have made a good cover on a book with a title like 'Profiles & Metaphysics.' Anny was a young, slim girl in the third year of university, but a year younger than she was officially supposed to be. She was rosy cheeked, but that was not a wan, corny, 'discreetly fresh' rosiness, but vivid, vigorous special rose color that shaded almost into lilac whilst differing sharply from a flushing & healthy ruddiness. On it were strongly etched features as if nature had worked over a standard pretty 'blonde-and-blue-eyed' face with a touch of cubism. Her blonde, slightly dry, and fanned-out hair had been trimmed to half-length, but at its ends there were looped-back curls that like tubes of pastry into which cream can be piped had never stiffened but gently come undone and poked forward on either side of her neck.

She had piercing blue eyes that, if she opened them fully, almost led beyond her inasmuch as they gave the impression of just a single light blue, almost silver point of light completely independent of the anatomy of the face, which was not constrained within borderlines: a glittering white sphere around which two blue rings arose in the air like the colored ripples of wavelets in a lake; when laughing, on the other hand, the eyes would be knitted together (half in embarrassment and half in flirtatious irony) at which time all that could be seen between two small frown-wrinkles was an incised blue filament (the eyebrows & skin under the eyes would wrinkle; for a young girl the lachrymal sacs stood out unusually sharply) — and in the corner of the eyes toward the temples the preciously unitary white-and-blue halo seemed to spin apart in the form of minute white globules of mercury. Her lips were narrow, her nose discretely snub, but the nostrils were, so to speak, in special frames, having all around them a fairly complex modeling as of gummed-on miniature pretzels. When she laughed her mouth lengthened. She went through a particular mimicry when she suddenly switched from laughing to paying serious attention: one half of the face stayed in a rigid laugh (the eyes became blue slits as on a special kind of Japanese print; the light on her glasses would break up into tiny lead-shots) while the other half displayed childish naivety mixed with a skeptical fervor that best typified her whole flirtatious being. It all looked like an easy little half-sided smiling fit; the eyelashes were short and reddish, spaced a big distance from one another. Her foxy little face was well suited to the university's new aluminum benches.

Leatrice looked up without moving and in a slightly hoarse voice asked the two men who had entered:

— What's this? Curiosity? A circus? Or university?

With slightly stale humor Halbert noted:

— Don't push your good taste too far, my dear Lea. You need to look out for your future as well for it will be a trifle odd if you are continually going to make *ex cathedra* pronouncements on moral issues and every day make recommendations to the pope on the reform of the monasteries & the constitution. Be at one with your honorable past, not by idealizing it, that would be stupid, but by being modest about it. That is a major virtue — modesty. Your poverty and willingness to help were always conspicuous, even though they had in them a fair dose of mockery and the blasé; but those rebellions of yours were not noncommittal. We are clever. Tell us, what did you do?

— I don't know. There was and is a huge confusion in me. I could say that I feel this & that, or I want this & that, but all I would relate is the lesson that Ena fed into me. I don't know what I want, though I have the feeling that I'm very determined and strong. I am very, very determined & strong.

As she was saying the last sentence she became like a doll: her eyes were fixed remarkably penetratingly and rigidly in an impossible direction whilst her voice was low and singsong, with certain sounds dropping out like on a telephone line when contact is lost for a moment, whereas others burst like bubbles — there was scorn and tired cynicism in the abstracted pronunciation of what she had to say.

— You people have a theory about 'square pegs in round holes' — that's what you call those who do not fit into your little boxes, your tedious branch of learning, and your ideas of marriage, though anyone who accepts that 'square peg in a round hole' whatsit thinking is a coward. What if it's you who are the square pegs in the round holes? — she asked with a grin, pulling all kinds of grimaces. She twitched her nose, crinkled her eyes, and her tongue was pressed up behind her teeth: there was gap enough between the teeth to allow her to wedge her white tongue between them.

Leville-Touqué felt utterly lousy. For him it had always been the greatest mystery of life that there were some people who shamelessly dare to invest all their taste & conceptual abilities into making some trifle the moving force of their lives. If that strange act by any chance happened in front of his eyes he usually became very flustered and began to feel ashamed of himself as if by the very fact of being in the same place he was also responsible for the other's stupidity. At the same time it occurred to him that nobody had yet truly worked out these bestially self-gullible people. Right then that was how he was looking at Lea: like at an unknown animal in an expedition film. The elementary stupidity which shook up the map of her musculature so pathetically only intensified the woman's erotic value in Leville's eyes: the body's extraordinary beauty aroused an impression of improbable intellectuality in him as distinct from the dreadful nonsense of the practical content of the speaking. The body was concrete & yet unreal, its smell, shadow, and weight on top of the settee was pure rationalism, like some higher organization that was entrusted to Lea only for a short time — like a delicate liturgical utensil into the hands of a nervous young boy.

Lea spoke in a whining, arrogant-imploring tone of voice, in what was almost a diphthongal phonetics in the way that great violinists are able to draw the bow in such a way that one has the impression two or even three violins are playing at once, with sentences whirling all along in a weeping-caterwauling scale & simultaneously on a sharp, sulky trail and meanwhile her body writhed under the constraint of a totally superfluous thought. She set her eyes and lips as if the thought were written out on a lath in the air and she were biting it in such a way that she was hanging on by the skin of her teeth and her body was just dangling in the air — if she were to let go of the lath she would fall, but the lath was coated with gall. She would have liked to possibly knead her knee into a ball with her hands. As she looked up toward the ceiling with imploring eyes, she seemed to be relying on some mystical listener who would be able to release her from the burden of thinking & expressing herself and who 'knew & understood her' — the sun shone on her face & the murkiness around her eyes was like the paths in parks on which the shadows of leaves float in hushed sunlight, or like those neon signs on which threads of tulle are made to flicker under frosted glass & the fuzzy-frayed shadow which eerily flickers like the blood in a filmed x-ray of a person's veins. Apart from or rather precisely because of all their triviality, Leville thought some people are able to play their 'not-really-one-of-us-ness' magnificently.

— The two of you are going to explain me, or you want to interrogate me, or laugh at me, or write about me — you want to tell me that it is shameful & ridiculous to want what I very much want, which is why I defended myself and will continue to defend myself against you. It's just that I am very afraid to defend myself. Because one has to be very brave, & what if it's to no avail?

Leville felt that he was faced with some terrible labor, a process of parturition in which the body that had developed as a self-reliant intellect was seeking to shake down the stunted thought: he could almost see as the helpless 'soul' with its rotten roots clung on in an asymmetrical position to this liberated raison body, like a dark crab which nips its claws into the white ankle of a Venus seeking to rise from the sea and does not let her step onto the shore. If he had to decide quickly, on the spot: would he kill the crab with a sharp pebble lying on the shore, or would he possibly twist Venus' other leg toward the crab's mouth in order to wrench it behind the field with the blue murmur?

an examination of styles of desire:
the essentially two kinds of adolescent desire & mature desire

He had the impression that if one were to pull out of the girl's body, in algebraic fashion, in front of the parenthesis of her skin, the biological and esthetic factors, indeed those similar to the rational germs as well, there would still remain within the parentheses of the surface certain palpable entities which, without the least intellectual trait, would resemble truth-like formations. At some point in time the body was propagated as an anti-pope against the soul simply because people sought to take revenge on the haphazard garden of so-called illusions with the homogeneous mechanicalism of material: before any thorough observation of the body, on the grounds of an inflexible prejudice it was perceived as a merely theoretical antithesis of the 'soul,' as a vengeful negative posing as a Parca. All those gloating determinists who formulated their new criticism armed with the new Erynis-mask of the 'body': they worked with a theoretical notion of the body — in natural science material meant nothing other than an abstract-logical antithesis of the spirit, all the complexity of chemistry no more than an idea of the 'fatal function,' as opposed to the self-important free play of the soul, etc.

The more he became immersed in the analysis of pure material, the more he developed matter into a theoretical notion, indeed, an apparition: the pathos of positivist ambition in the end saw in the body only a criticism automat that could flood the pretentious fields of the 'psyche' with a shower of vetoes at any moment. As a result, a kitsch predestination, looming darkly to far and wide, stuck to figures of nude females as mystic embodiments of the concept of abstract material: always with the theatrical bearing of a nihilistic Circe or the sin-hegemonic 'natural force.' In front of him pedants, vapid gigolos, or specima of hereditary transmission: this nude figure was unable to inspire any pleasure because there was nothing truly material in it & thus its 'queue' comprised grey seminars, monotonous revue bars, or logically constructed sick patients.

Leville-Touqué recalled very clearly that his father had still looked at a strange woman as at the badge of an anticlerical club that had the power, with the assistance of a few tickles, to drag a person back to primeval chaos: the primal amorphousness was a great delicacy in his father's eyes to the extent that an entire logical chaos etiquette evolved in his behavior, an *ananke*-routine that the family could also easily learn, and out of convention could accommodate to in the interests of a hypocritical peace. Thus, when Touqué first felt sensual impulses he was already equipped with some ready answers in facing them, which, that being the first occasion, actually did correspond to the stimuli. After all, at that time the entire female circle was of a lamentably antiquarian nature; replica statues, lines of poetry, entries in encyclopedias, snatched keyhole-mosaics, philosophical half-wings: nothing but scrap iron, niggardly compilations like the study of a 17th-century dilettante polymath, in which dried grasshoppers and Italian pictures acquired at auctions are strewn next to each other: through naïve 'home-empiricism.' That is truly detrimental in the head of a youngster even if he does not notice that it is merely a matter of untidiness in which seductive primacy plays no part — and in that way the destiny-clichés heard from his father's lips could easily be assimilated.

That was therefore the first erotic stage: disorderly female-encyclopedism plus theoretical matter-superstition. Into what did that well-known dualism evolve: a lot of erotic data and one erotic faith, which related to each other in the way an incomplete borrowed herbarium of pressed flowers does to a monopolist named Pan of a romantic-colonnade of rhymes? At first sight it may strike one as sensational to call something dualism which is so unitary for everyone, but this separation runs perceptibly all through Touqué's early youth, because what he heard from his father was separated by strict boundaries from himself, and however much he developed those 'thoughts' further and thus, as the saying goes, subsumed them into his own personality, he nevertheless placed them into a separate, foreign plane, which was to his own erotic antique shop what the obliquely slanting, uniform blue of a distant sea is to the randomly planted flowers of a hillside garden.

Of course, the essential difference can be observed in styles of desire: in the starting state every moment is replete with the shy dynamism of possession, which, as it were, develops 'abstract empiricism' in the brain — observes shoulders, hands, & other parts of the body, but in all of those sees only graphs of love, even if not entirely anonymously. What is of interest is always the connection between the distribution of the intensity of desire and the nature of the observing, and only if one examines that relationship will one manage to give an accurate psychological ground for the fact that right then Touqué saw in the female body (and in 'senseless' material in general) a certain truth content, in a trans-rational sense of the expression, as opposed to the paternal tradition, which, in line with the taste of the times, celebrated in the body an elementary denial of every kind of truth, indeed, truth-like thing.

---

simile about adolescent desire

At the time of 'abstract empiricism,' with every woman, indeed fantasy image, love begins again from the beginning: one notices the individual properties of bodies, does not see '*the* shoulders' and '*the* neck' as people like to put it — it is only lacking desire's ability to apportion: the total energy fills every single form as if those were flexible forms into which desire flows as an expanding gas and distorts them into not so much anonymous as over-individual figures — sexual caricatures instead of a sexual portrait.

That age could best be perpetuated with intercommunicating vessels: a tube runs horizontally, and all manner of fantastically winding branches of tubing rise up off of that: if one pours in water, or desire modeled as a fluid, the liquid will stand at exactly the same height in even the most elaborate branches. Maximal desire & maximal object always coincide absurdly so that a person has difficulty distinguishing in this drama the case in which the figure of a woman which crops up immediately elicits the total desire from the state in which desire is stored in the soul in the stylized but individual form of a colossal nude. The fact that it is always nude figures which occur is more logical than natural.

The style of desire when one looks at the soul's content from an intellectual viewpoint and calls it a domesticated and unopinionated antique-shop is best called hieratic, though if, by contrast, one examines the individual erotic elements, then one should make comparisons to a large hall of statues in which the statues grow separately out of the ground, but no kind of system or connection can be seen in their grouping: the forms of the statues represent those particular ceremonial forms of realism which are able to unite baroque epilepsy and the closed nature of Egyptian mummies.

If one now envisages desire as a red tongue of light in the didactic waxworks, then the game will be as follows: a red tongue of light appears above one of the statues & all the other figures will be invisible in the darkness. The flame picks out the head of a single figure and suddenly sinks into the material of that figure; within a few seconds it suffuses the whole body, the figure loses the color and nature of its material, retaining only its form, although a frame of incandescence replaces the line of the boundaries of form (in the way that with certain painters the outline of a foot is not rendered by a single line parallel to the outline but by innumerable perpendicular brushstrokes): that is the sterile moment of the identity of desire and its object — force is no more than an image, and that image is no more than a dynamic scheme. The image is truly maximally clear, but for that very reason there can be no question of observing. In that state desire is aware of the object as a whole, but it cannot observe, only see — like a mask that matches the contours of the face exactly: every detail of the mask can be sensed, but it cannot be observed because it is wholly identical to one's own face. The red flame of desire completely took up the figure so that it knew every atom of it, but only functionally: the red light has filled the figure, but so perfectly that the figure is unable to move in it.

At this degree of desire, therefore, desire and its object are in suffocating balance with each other like two wrestlers stuck together, who tussle with each other, intertwined, and not so much as a hair's breadth of asymmetry arises in their movements, as if they were not wrestling but were made of magnetic materials every point of which would adhere for evermore to every single point of the other. There can be no question of perspective between desire and its object, in the same way as a tourist who has suddenly been transformed into a hill cannot see the landscape.

Truly typical of that drama is the loneliness in which it is played out: it is pitch black in the waxworks, the Magdeburg hemispheres of flame and desire completely exclude all the wing flats of time and space — if only one, infinitesimally small shard of milieu were to fall between, the entire simplicity would be ruined in a trice and the desire style would switch to a higher degree. When it has united in that way with the first figure, the red flame is all at once extinguished, but moments later is playing through the same comedy with another figure: it permeates it, fills it (not surrounding it like a halo, like a cowardly ring does coquettish Saturn) and thus is a radically empiricist fire, though that makes an inverse Narcissus farce insofar as it does not fall in love with itself but greedily feels all over it with its whole body in order to turn completely into it. This tragicomic scene resembles that otherworldly diagram in which it is palpable that God is infinite knowledge & infinite truth in one person. The desire would sometimes like to escape from what is, after all, the slavery into which this greedy possession of objects has led it, but it does not succeed. The way this can be seen in the waxworks is as follows: the red light sometimes lifts a millimeter from the outline of the figure, but the next moment the figure immediately rises after it, and the two forms which briefly slide apart now again completely coincide. The whole thing is like a parody of an animal fable in which the prey pursues a fleeing bearded vulture — or the efforts of a person who does not see objects as if they were located in the outside world but in his own eyeballs & is trying to drag the various objects out into the world with his two hands in order to be able to see them properly.

Interpolation: relation of Prae *to Non-*Prae

Every work develops its organic 'not this work' counterpart. Two comparisons:

from architecture;
from phenomenological Roman Catholic theology.

(Not this; not this! Every thought, every truth, is just a neutral blank wall, an inhibitory frosted glass and meaningless dividing layer between Touqué's two craved and driven 'truths,' between his life and his dreams. Analogies, hypotheses, pedagogical statues, correlations and facts were all just helpless private parties with which he had nothing to do, in any truly wished or even approximately vindicated way. If anything was a matter of life and death for him, it was the incidents in his own life, though those incidents had neither beginning nor end, no time or color, had no sense and were in no way fateful, because these were all already naïve rubrics of 'thought': for a while he was happy enough to spoon the sterile inverse of his life into their toy caskets, but then he soon yearned to be back in 'life's' alien, devastating, self-evident deafness to raison. And alongside the almost unconscious and endless movement denoted by the word 'life' ran that emotional desire-mill of dreams: by day there was the amorphism of the inarticulate deed, by night the colorful composition of pure, absolute emotion.

But thoughts, novels, truths, professorial terminology or poetic lies say nothing, nothing at all, of either the invisible plans of events, or the eternal precision of form and lyricism of dreams. Was what you could read above the essence of adolescent love? No. It was a matter of a million things [though even that is a distortion, because as it happened there were no words at all], but his life never knew anything about such matters as an 'object of desire' or an 'identity of desire.' Here it was not a matter of a naïve counterposing of 'life' and 'consciousness' so much as a universal incongruity of 'an endless but excessively articulated, moving nothingness' [that is in place of 'life'] and 'a finite, tautologically-false something' [that is at the back of 'consciousness']).

The essence was life and dreams, the former with its blind lines of force, the latter with its radiating clusters of emotions, because by day there is no true emotion and desire, whereas by night there is no true endless course, or floating-nowhere in a thousand directions.

There is no maneuvering booby-trap narrative that would be able to salvage anything at all from these two things. At times like this, kind gentlemen and cultivated ladies say with a smile, "after all, literature is one thing and 'real life' is something else," but all art [primarily of the programmatically unrealistic, anti-life, dehumanizing kind] nevertheless seeks the reality of reality, the tangible nub of the everyday — even the most characteristic dream-burlesque is the way it is because it wishes to be 'onto-onto-onto-onto-onto-logy.'

If the title of this writing as a whole is Prae*: does* Prae *have anything to say about what it wants? No. It does not. It does not even come anywhere close to itself. The same thing happens here as with the over-scrupulously penitent: as they pronounce the name of the sin, its place, the number of times, they immediately feel it is untruthful, so unaccustomed is the limited atmosphere of the 'truth' after the infinitely extended nothingness of 'life.' 'Life' itself is truly unrepresentable, but on the other hand this 'unrepresentability' itself ought to be tacked on, as tangible fact, to every representation so as to give, in conjunction with that, a more credible whole. A quite crude way of allowing us to sense the unavoidable content of untruth and prevarication of every representation or thought was Touqué's oscillator, which signals after each 'consistently accomplished thought' that the consistency is merely grammatical, the harmony merely conceptual (in the present context the term is invariably used pejoratively): that the spark of reality which set off the whole thing instantly fell into the depths in a divergent arc, only words remain floating in the logical plane of a neutral horizon like the pictorial remains sketched out of the smoke of exploded form over the downward-scattered spark-parabolas of a firework.*

'Life is inexpressible': that is an intolerable commonplace for everyone. But the massive concreteness of the 'inexpressibility' can be expressed, and a form of expression of this kind, it so happens, would be the polar opposite of a commonplace, because never yet

has it been done radically. Running behind, beside, and around the text of Prae, *is an organic accompanying stream, the 'Non-*Prae,*' inseparable from* Prae, *which, unlike the temporary episodes of the above-mentioned oscillator, is a finite counterpart, complement, fellow balance-pan, or metaphorical arc of commentary to* Prae.

What exists, which is to say Prae *itself, is a continual blunder, institutionalized prevarication ('truths'); what is truly exciting, interesting, the one true faith or the actual, by its very nature lies outside any narrative, and that is the inaccessible, the "Non-Prae," which bears the same relation to* Prae *as a tautened bow string does to the arched shaft of the bow. On statues of Eros the figure of Eros is sometimes shown holding a marble bow; this has no bowstring, to be sure, but the bow is nevertheless arched in such a way that the viewer cannot fail to imagine the non-existent string as being there. In the figure of* Prae *there must, therefore, be some sort of positive signal from which the tensile strength of the 'Non-Prae' that is constantly running in coexistence to* Prae *can be made perceptible, deducible. Principle: to utilize the essential impotence of literature with productive optimism as a useful structural factor: to make the constant ghostly absence and its continuo of otherness a harmonious component, to incorporate the 'Non-*Prae*' into a work's preserve in much the same way as in the Pantheon there also used to be a positive altar to the 'unknown god.'*

The above principle was accomplished equally by architecture and by the new scholastic theology, which incorporated phenomenology. In one corner stands the baptismal basin: its ground plan is a three-leaved (unequal) clover, above which rises the completely smooth and soot-black font wall. Standing out horizontally from the wall of the green font are metallic cloverleaves: their color is incandescent, they are totally without veins, almost immaterial wafers of clubs symbols dissected from the playing cards of archangels. In the wall directly beside the font is a huge window, the dimensions of which are roughly five times that of the font's ground plan, though the shape of the window is absolutely the same as the font's cloverleaf. One third of the window's cloverleaf has been chopped off to fit it onto the wall in such a way so as not to leave enough room up to the corner angle.

What does this black leaf of marble mean and above it this light, translucent giant cloverleaf fragment: what does their close juxtaposition mean? The relationship of Prae *to* '*Non*-Prae'*: the font but, above all, the green clubs-shaped trays horizontally standing out from it signify the real plant, but the perpetual octave further intensified by the window's huge clarity, absolute openness, and severedness signifies the unrepresentability that complements the plant, the perpetual flight, the obvious transcendence which radiates from the cloverleaf denotes that [for empirical eyes or artistic hands] incomprehensible nothingness, negative, or 'anti'-feature which is every object's most positive feature if we approach it with any sort of [theological or horse-feeding] interest. There is no need to emphasize that this 'supplementary organic nihil pendant' happens to be the nidus of values, precisely what we like in the thing, and it is only 'nihil' or negative or 'anti' from the viewpoint of explicit expression. The window cloverleaf must also be sought next to the font cloverleaf in the narrative: the positive form of* '*Non*-Prae,' *which naturally here, too, means the* '*True*-Prae.'

If one wishes to grow said font in rapid kinship with modern phenomenological theology, then one must see in the font the duality of 'in-über'*: the pulling-apart of things to a concentric nucleus of the identity* ['in'] *and to rings of otherness leading out of and away from themselves and receding in transcendent circles* ['über']. [*L. Brehle,* "Heidegger'sche »Sich-vorweg-im-schon-sein-in« und Neue Sachlichkeit: Nichts als Sache." Marburg: 1933.])[20]

the style of mature desire:
its identity with the new pictorial & theological styles.
Relationship of nonsense & truth:
truth value of (absolute) 'disorders' of a certain type'

Over time, however, a few shards of civilization nonetheless drop into that space: the cluttered antique shop starts to transform into a little social novel. That is a fairly poetic stage: in place of bad essays on Rubens steps the social milieu of girls, beside abstract Aphrodite-torsos the cases of women further elaborated in the direction of practical life, though still with many encyclopedic and rarity-value remnants. The idyll is, in point of fact, nothing more than an automatic chemical result of a mixing of incipiently threadbare mythology and incipiently more concrete practical life. How does the relationship of the intensity of desire and the object of desire evolve here, as contrasted to the previous one?

With both things one experiences a duality: thus, desire, like the image of the woman (the 'practical Venus'-iconography) both become stronger & weaken; indeed, it is rather as though weakening were the true form of strength. It seems that this is a basic style of forces in other areas of life as well: gloom intensifies the contours, the initial sculpture of truth consists of a refined compound of errors, the premature fruit of virtue blossoms out among the glittering leafy boughs of zigzag peccadilloes, not on the God-inoculated branches of asceticism. The course of desire does not flow to the last drop into the cup of the female body, but only half of it like a skeptical high tide: the other half overruns the path that winds between the desiring youth and the desired woman, or in other words, not only is it interested in the woman in her own doctrinally isolated reduced-to-Eve state, but also in the small social apparatus which surrounds her, the little social charade which it has to play out in order to reach the woman. Those people who, instead of analyzing, stop at images, might say that the desire, which just before had still been red, now suddenly faded like a lonely initial and, all at once, turned blue then, finally, opalescent. If one perceives that in a naïvely chemical way and not just as a game, one truly gets close to the rhythm of the process.

It is unquestionably a matter of the dispersal of forces: earlier, there were truly gigantic energies looping round the woman's body — the way the claws of birds even while they sleep are automatically curled round the branch they happened to fall asleep on, so, too, is adolescent desire fixated on the goal. Now, though, the desire quantum takes up position in the world in various patches (*ad minorem Heisenbergi gloriam*),[21] and thus naturally much less force reaches certain areas. It is typical of the map of erotic energy that the patches denoting the desires (let's say, with mystic-precision, the blue areas) will never coincide with the real outlines: they never completely fill up the woman's ground plan (or cross section — but then that is the job of a cartographer), nor do they fill in the path indicated by the social network.

Desire hovers above the world like the shadows of small flocks of clouds over a landscape: it covers half a house or garden, etc. Just as many liquids change color if spilled in thinner layers, it is understandable that shades of the color blue should take the place of the crude domination of the carmine of blood: as if in the logic of colors blue were the exact definition of 'intellectual ignition,' combining the most obvious vitality with the most obvious coldness. If the former state has a strongly sculptural quality (after all, on the one hand, sensuality yearns for foolish over-plasticity — but, on the other, it can only find its extremely abstract Eve obsession about women in theoretical-abstract idols), then this later situation points to a strongly impressionistic inclination.

For a long time, Touqué's entire life was composed of nothing other than what one might approximately call the stifling struggle for 'truth as an end in itself' & 'a ramification of *n* ends.' When he dissected tautology with an oscillator; when he broke down the Eve of the adolescent Eve to clothes, social indexes, & half-desires; when in architecture he 'corrupted' the step into a model and promoted mirrors into pillars of essence; and when a few pages later he wanted to make the whole train of thought that has just been described ambiguous or, if possible, utterly senseless with some kind of forcible interpolation: in all these cases he lived out single versions of this bloody alternative.

The instinct that he should etherealize any 'something' straight away into 'something which, as it happens, is not this,' i.e., alienation, has many different forms: there is a musical form when one plays through 'something' in several tonalities, one does not substitute the same architectural form or the same adolescent-homogeneous Eve theme with completely alien themes (for instance, a dining room with a dung beetle, or an Eve with ice cream wafer tubes) but just breaks them up modularly.

Here we have a diagram of a room like that which is not yet 'substance-alienation' (that would be an expression later employed by Touqué), only 'essence-modulation.' The subject matter: parallel, fairly thick and fairly close, red wavy lines. One wall of the room is a wall of broken glass into which a red wave subject has been incorporated by a chemical process: this is the first appearance, when the subject presents itself in a pure species of light. Not far from the wall arises a red grille around a small lakelet (after all, this is a matter of hallway furniture): here all that can be seen from the red wires are the outlines of the wave, empty dimension cases, & sterile hints at a frame: this is the second appearance when the subject still moving in a 'pure-species-of-light' modulates into an 'empty-species-of-space.'

This is the next transposition: against the wall is a chest with red drawers, and around thirty drawers indicate the line of the wave adopted as subject, or in other words, here one sees it in 'material species.' On the far wall, opposite the glass wall, is nothing other than an enormously enlarged half-crest and half-trough from the wave subject, i.e., sounding the triad of a scale hitherto practiced on a cimbalom or an organ, and leaving that to bellow permanently: grandiose fragment as mythical essence. The ceiling of the room is a metallic mirror curved in one direction (the bend in it is the fever chart of a steadily convalescing patient), in which the subject-disruptive aspects of light, space, material & basic chord are all at once reflected in order to give a final but newer modulation. Adolescence (like the malaria season of 'identical truth') is unfamiliar with these essence disruptions: to desire separately from Eve's white naked figure the contour that is just a white line in the air, with no flesh — to desire separately the flesh, which is just an endless row of impersonal instinct drawers — to desire separately the beauty, which has been liberated from flesh and contour, separately the dress, separately the social situation, on the dissociating Bach steps and Bach filters of the modulations: every single 'key' lets through something different from the Eve mass: the *whole* Eve at one and the same time is unbearable once adolescence has passed.

This may be called decadence, compared to what preceded it, but then that, too, is decadence: just before, the sea was as dark as a dreamless sleep into which the spiral foliage of gaudy images does not get to cop a feel. It was blue to the point of blackness. The evening is drawing in: the light is fading, all at once the outlines of hills, palms, villas and the folds of hamlets — the sharp grey slices of gusts of wind flying around in the dusk, the appearance of which was much more active & more surprising than lights going on one by one. The weakening of the light all of a sudden in silence brought a million precisions to the world:

the analysis springing from the stray froth of darkening. The decadence of light? The sea just beforehand was homogeneous like one's first desire. Now, all at once, rose stripes run over it, which offer more excitement of perspective than luxury of color: the sea suddenly becomes an enormous paradox of space-geometry (all without a barbaric dynamic flourish!), because it has ceased being planar without having tipped into three-dimensionality: neither its material, nor its geometrical relations, could be clarified — light & water were totally interchangeable, but, on the other hand, the scurrying novelties of alteration did not spark even the faintest impression of movement: those reflections occurred within the most chaste stability. The lilac 'something,' which essentialized the wind and light, the coolness and the band of the horizon together into a new material, caught the edge of the hills, the slim fingertips of jetties, & the suddenly lacy trees (there are fish which, at an unexpected turn of events, become incandescently the hue of water — their body 'combusts into neutral' — and only the gently rippling miniature reeds of the fish bones turn grey anatomically in their own flesh mist) & created new units.

A crude analogy: as if in places the flesh had easily been stripped from parts of the body of the landscape like an oiled and loose-fitting glove so that in places all that remained were vibrating positives of the structure, in other places, however, rose-colored pluses were still adhering to the flesh as if they were masks; there were only two possibilities in the whole geographical change of fortune: either skeleton or fancy dress — the role of 'normal' landscape was no longer current. This is now one of the world's old techniques &, it seems, one which is repeated with changes in the style of love: the harmony is only found in the fleeting vigil of destruction, in the sensual fulfillment of which the main emphasis is not on a genuine, organic entity but on the nightmarish & hypothetical nature of an entity.

If one were to translate that dusk scene to the historical language of Touqué's life one gets an exact diagnosis of the second (i.e., post-adolescent) degree of love. The circumstances of life form a tangled, fine net scattered through the pencil wires of which are located blots of water color: that technique ultimately culminates in a portrait of a woman, certain parts of which (if possible, not the contours) are marked with pencil, others with blobs of water color.

That red blot, which denotes one of the lips, & that oblique little gallop of the pencil, which represents the other lip, in themselves stand at an absolute distance from what would serve as the representation of a mouth, and maybe by means of their maximal state of having started from the lips they achieved the most incandescent codification of the sensual nature of the mouth. (This is not a pictorial analogy but identity.) What is a mouth? A concept-minimum onto which no end of non-pertinent matters adhere that, simply by virtue of adhering to the concept-minimum, glow into a mouth without formally complying with it. As it is in the figure: the concept-minimum in that case consists of there being a designated place in the image (not an anatomical mouth, merely a small word which defines the place: 'the mouth is here'); the adhering, the compilation, of one of the lips being just an unreal colored blot, more a blot or a squirt of cherry, and not a millimeter of it resembles a mouth, but the logical minimum is that at the geometrical site of the mouth it all at once swells it out with intensified 'mouth-ness'; likewise the pencil line, which is similarly a stub of an alien comet, which on the short bit, which is the place where the mouth is, suddenly, under the influence of mouth suggestion, becomes a lip, even though it came from an entirely different place, & its sprint is rustling toward other targets.

The difference between the present and the preceding state is, in point of fact, the difference between poetic love & mundane love; what is particularly characteristic of the latter, however, is the lack of assertion of total and naïve esthetic and sensual elements. In the latter it is always a matter of this 'impressionist' duality: on the one hand, the fleeting and nevertheless concretely present, ethereal concept formed about women, on the other hand, sensuality as an aimlessly milling pastiche of instincts that never connects to a complete model of women but only juggles around with bits of the form that it has had capriciously pinched off, washing them down with skeptical games of erosion, throwing its waves over the intellectual-type net of the minimal idea of woman. This dispersal and pictorial relativism betoken the entirety of the forces of love.

There was a time when there was a fashion for sentimental novels in which a Christian man, after his conversion, again falls under the spell of paganism, and that pretty-pretty mythology which makes it possible for us to wrap up even our most philistine wishes in the guise of exquisite symbols flooded the soul of the hero anew with hackneyed dreams. Of that type is a Danish novel that is far removed from all pubertal archaizing: the hero is a Roman convert who in the final moment of decadence all at once sees the crumbled culture of his homeland as a system — in a half-visionary, half-syllogistic hour, he sees the mysterious movement by which chaos suddenly exposes the most ancient order of the structure.

Generally, in relation to decadence, people always imagine there is some overproduction of form for its own sake, agglomeration of scenery, and delirious refinement, because they are used to taking art at its own industrial literalness; few brushstrokes — skepticism; plastic cleanness — positive balance; flamboyance — decay of death throes, etc. Yet order, system, a logical core, is not the root of the matter but an end result, the very last, belated fruit or by-product, a geometrical image, the restless and unrestrainable coastal wave as it casts that damp patch on minute pebbles — the wave has by then long gone & its 'ground plan' is only visible for a moment anyway as it immediately dries. When Christianity was still living in the age of foliage and flowers there was not yet any opportunity for internal lines, or even for suspecting them, yet the Roman world stood before it, heaping up all manner of withering so that precisely that clutter should display its puritanical anatomy: there are flowers that are slender-stemmed and of Roman construction which, to all intents and purposes, spring up from the ground only to etch a single soprano contour in the air with shrieking simplicity, and there are complex calices with all kinds of petal eversions, anther secessions, & ovary elephantiasis, in short, a true jumble of forms & a complete lack of 'correlation': all the same, a clearer form, more tangible, & more massive substance emanates from flowers of the latter kind than from the former.

The rigid tracery of fixed stars (for present purposes, the fact that they, too, move can be overlooked) is never felt to be a strict image of divine regularity as after a short time stability arouses an impression of limited one-sidedness; even if the fixed figure is the most perfect expression of symmetry or the scholastic & anano-ethical *ens* [22] axis of 'divine truth' (a borderline case of pathological over-symmetrization), one nevertheless perceives it to be a fortuitous rigidity of a fortuitous situation: the clusters of paralysis of the profile which arise after a stroke are hardly likely to strike one as essential products. Every fixed harmony constantly traces a falling curve in one's soul, starting from the rational balancing of dogmas to the 'rule of eight' of Italian Renaissance architecture: [23] that is approximately how these subordinate symptoms are positioned relative to the domain of the truth, like a tennis ball that is 'out' in relation to lines sketched on the court.

In every proportionality, or numerical serving of essence, there is a sinful materialist feature: there was a time when it was believed that what would make the hundredweight stones of an octagonal baptistry ethereal, indeed, spiritual, was that its ground plan was an octagon, and that textbook arithmetic 'harmony' based on the pupil of the eye would, as it were, christen & absolve material of its own weight, whereas it acts in exactly the opposite way. The eye and the soul do not find a way out of the Pythagorean dungeon of the octagon: the harmony always leads back to the stones, completion finishes everything in the direction of the stones, so that instead of a 'divine'-balance of construction one ought to speak of a 'diabolic'-balance, every trick is so stone-centric and material-canvassing. The soul is always on the move, so such a fixed regularity as a logical truth or a Bernini-church takes up station disproportionately in relation to the soul, whatever the circumstances, because it is like an uncontrollable racing car that is only able to hurtle perpetually in one direction, whereas meanwhile the soul is swinging to and fro. A truly harmonic building, thus, does not suck up the proletarian gestures of the pupil but accommodates to the flashing to and fro of a soul: it counts in advance on the soul's oscillations and with its forms it tries to anticipate them since despite all their freedom the dashing about can take place only within limits. One senses drawings of the intersecting trajectories of five shooting stars as essential because they are truly 'objective': none of the stars wanted the drawing, it was given regardless of them so it has a meaning outside them.

The concept of the essence thus shifted over to the domain of statistics and the calculation of probabilities; the next thing will be having Catholic theology rewritten by sprightly tunesmiths for God into roulette positivism. (A Munich theologian by the name of R.A. Grabmann started off from the bifurcate notion of 'roulette-positivism' in writing two studies about Christ's God-man person, one of which was "*Neue Sachliche Christologie*" in which he stresses the quondam human, the individual, the hazardously unique and unpredictable — the other: *Gott: Limes-Wirr-Warr,*[24] discusses the divine soul as an absolute confusion of contradictory possibilities, a resultant of ideas which flit anarchically all over the place or, more particularly, it leaves the resultant to one side [that is Christ] and only brings out the chaotic collisions of lines. God before becoming Christ: a spin of the roulette wheel, a bacchanal of every possibility. Jesus Christ himself: a sole positive, a number which 'came out right,' not a regular and harmonious resultant [in point of fact, Christ was not 'any man in the street'!], not a geometrical axis of the endless cyclones of possibilities, but an accidental resultant, a dynamic remnant. *Sachlichkeit & 'unstable'* probability go hand in hand, and also in religion, R.A. Grabmann shows fairly convincingly that their joint appearance can be very useful: God all at once becomes recklessly more concrete and recklessly 'more omni- than omni-.')

Two similes were used: that of roulette and that of the capriciously thousand-petalled flower. Both of them signified one possibility of a substitute for essence; in roulette the absolute chanciness of a lonely number, but simultaneously its absolute positivity signified the anti-essential hyper-essence — with the thousand-petalled flower the chance coincidences that remain in the wake of the disintegrating forms of chaos. In both there is something 'predestined' — in one case the sole possibility out of many — in the other, the essence substitute arises from the summated shadow of the total of many possibilities. The single number that emerges in roulette is quite definite, arithmetically sharp, & impenetrable (7, for example), but against that is endlessly lonely, aimless, indeed senseless to the point of idiocy compared to the totality of numbers. With flowers it is the reverse: out of the confusion of petals the eye nevertheless picks out the numerical shadow of synthesis, a secret disease of disorder, of decomposition, or in other words, as a vase or 'order' it creates the impression of divine logic (in contrast to the nonsense courted by № 7), but, on the other hand, it is all just a shadow, an optical illusion, an unstable after product. It looked Romanesque when it disintegrated, the ground plan of the moisture of the wave appeared on the sand of the beach when there was already no wave. Roulette & floral chaos, therefore, signify these two things: on the one hand, positivity + nonsense — on the other, fleeting shadowiness + sense-rich logic.

What do those two propositions signify in love; what is positive cannot be sensible — but what is logical is just an optical trick? In adolescence, at all events, exactly the opposite is true: the statue and the clumsy example of the flame of desire or desire-specimen that completely occupies it shows precisely that every positive (e.g., part of the female body) was immediately stuffed to bursting with intelligence: the woman was symmetrically placed in the boy's life. On modern airplanes as a rule a wholly disjointed string of letters (at least disjointed for outsiders) is usually visible: XXDWR-AF303: in the more developed post-adolescent erotic period, the anatomy of the female body relates to a regular model of Eve like the mishmash of letters and numbers (as in the case of roulette) do to the complete ABC or to an intelligible word such as 'seagull' or *'oiseau de mer'* (as is sometimes seen on other airplanes). The letters in the word 'seagull' lose their positive *'Sache'*-nature: they powder into sense: exactly that happens with women's shoulders, hips, and lips in adolescence. In order that the glowingly concrete reality of the letters should get across, they need to be thrown together with airplane tomfoolery like that: so that the woman's body should be elevated into a truly positive in an atmosphere of love, desire must race all over it, across it, beside it, & half into it for only that way can the redemptory duality be born (in knowledge and at the rendezvous): infinite concreteness — 'infinite nonsense.'

architectural example

This more intelligent desire has its fashion-design or architectural models, which are exceedingly apt for the purposes of elementary demonstration, like gloves, for example, which are produced in the following fashion: the outlines of the hand are traced with a barely visible pencil line, then a single large, slanting band of color is drawn across it, but not as if there was any wish to fill the outlines of the hand with some color or other; quite the contrary, as if there was a wish to draw out of mankind's consciousness, once & for all, as brutally as possible, with a lethal wipe of a sponge, the faintest conceptual epigone of a 'glove.' The design of the glove pattern is thereby complete: the intersecting and murderous blue band of paint running right across the glove is made of blue leather, and those parts untouched by the dye's nihilism are woven from flesh-colored yarn, thin as a hair, in the form of a very loose-spun net. The hand's God-given form is just a kind of artless 'lined paper' of the sort little boys use when they learn how to write: if an adult writes on paper like that they crisscross the simpleminded guidelines with their irregular scrawl. To the intelligent desire the female hand is some such outmoded scribble: the 'form' of the desire is not identical, not even approximately, to the material, 'prescribed' forms of the female body: the two are intersecting.

Any love (or architecture) worth its salt is based on the above-outlined glove craft: first sketching like an anachronistic ghost, a rational Banquo suggestion, the conventional Eve sketch, its Eve outlines, or, as the case may be, the house's naïve-practical foundation walls, its basement rooms, and then completely forget this plan and throw around, in irregular Heisenberg-quanta, desire's broken, Marconi-signal-like pieces or irrational blocks of glass, brick, or concrete: as far as possible, plan and material should stand in relation to each other like the two stems of a gigantic letter 'X.' This kind of architecture is very similar to one of the ways of performing Theremin's aerophonic-music: the performer stands in front of the electronic apparatus and waves his hands around in the air, thereby drawing out extraordinarily high-pitched differential sounds.

There is a room, a dining-room, for instance, where the ghost plan consists of a horizontal prism, the table of a smaller horizontal prism inside this, etc. Let us imagine this framework is floating in space: that is when the gesticulating Theremin-architecture & its squealing form-interference begins. The table is a huge, black extended letter S of the symbol for an integral calculus, which starts outside the wall, under a tree in the street, transects the wall & arches above the room with its Leibnizian intricacy for the far end of its curlicue to loop out into the stairwell. The walls are black, in concordance to the lines of a ghostly plan (those elementary and contemptible rule-lines), all except the fourth, where an unfinished, crudely whitewashed wall rises, and half a meter away from it, in the form of a black glass plate, like a useless folding screen, the fourth black perimeter plate, radically slipping out of its 'designated' place like a chestnut husk beside the chestnut (though here the husk is all!). The fourth wall had to be rendered 'pointless,' lifted out of context, in order to be a genuinely wall-like wall: it is not the fulfillment of utility, or coincidence with sense, there is no 'self-identification' of an infantile sort that makes things concrete or true. Touqué starts to feel Leatrice's body to be 'truth-like' when he sees that repeatedly-mentioned duality of 'positive + nonsense.'

Clearly, the congestion of decadent styles does not betoken a burden for the observer but easiness, because it does not tempt one to accumulation but involuntarily to omission. If there are only four lines, I am obliged to accompany them right to the end without omission, but out of a network of five hundred lines a big leading blot, a synthetic shadow resultant, remains in my eyes. Thus, there is a striking symmetrical relationship between the raging of details of a Baroque tabernacle and a female portrait with the aforesaid couple of lines: Baroque altars elaborate everything in physical reality in order to realize a single contour, a simple confluent silhouette in the beholder's eyes — whereas an Impressionist picture copies that 'order,' that ethereal result, and thereby the beholder automatically imagines, with nervous supplementary play, the entire vibrating host of details around it. In both the 'silhouette' represents the logical positive and the detail the ancillary illusions.

What is it in an Impressionist picture? There is no synthesis because it is replete with opennesses, discontinuities, or hypothetical over-continuations & contour unruliness; nor is there any particularizing, because the details are spots of color as an end in themselves, or the gestural relics of pencil flourishes enjoyed for their own sake — yet, all the same, we enjoy its unity, its coherence, and its richness of detail. Impressionist pictures *ab ovo* are dependent on our eyes: we can imagine that one Renaissance picture or another, if it were installed in nature, would be able to grow into it without any forcible assimilation; the existence of the portrait referred to, however, is fatefully a function of our eyesight, its life-giving atmosphere is the most special human optics — sheer nonsense in the nature of the outside world. By its being ingrown in us, and by the other half of the picture being concealed in our soul, with the blood circulation (the perspective is: optical circulation) at one time crossing the picture, at another one's brain, one eventually has the impression that the picture itself is a fountain of 'rational formulae' (not thoughts and not optical forms). (In parenthesis one may comment on the fact that if someone in his erotic life fairly quickly reaches the point of seeing the female body as a 'rational formula,' this is far from meaning that he lacks raw truth's clown contrasts of syphilis & Arcadia, etc.)

Whither does life move on? Or rather how does life strive to become more life-like? And what particularly is it that causes a sense of the intensity of life? In the beginning, for Touqué there was an Eve whom he wished with concentrated desire for himself: for an Eve like that there were countless women whom in his dreams he obsessively coopted as passive hymen partners. This is the lowliest grade of life: the mist that for millennia in the form of a self-embracing cloud wrestling with itself swirled over valleys, resounding marshes, and sweltering seas — long before the steam engine was invented. The strolls with the girl in point of fact were dithyrambic processions; the conversations were Plotinus hallucinations — in other words, the whole state of love is a perpetual building of bridges: the glistening arch squirts forth from the amorphous fire of extra-vital instinct &, flying over life's wide process at white pace, it drops again among the empty frames of symbols, beyond life. When that grade was sketched in a diorama we said that the red flame of desire was totally filled up to bursting by the statue of Eve which just happened to be in front of it: but that total filling up does not mean that it assumed the structure of Eve's body with its complex details, only en bloc, like someone seeking a 'female body' that could only be utilized erotically, wanting as much 'woman' as possible, & therefore if the Eve sheath were to be pulled from the red fire, all one would obtain would be a purely symbolic mass, consisting only of outlines.

This is the realism of instinct: rite instead of stroll, trance instead of talk — a cliché for all practical purposes instead of a complete woman's body. Naturally, it is not a question here of a 'critique' of instincts, but of the fact that 'life' & 'instinct' are dimensions that are dreadfully far from each other and, as a matter of fact, are in contest against each other in the world.

The aforesaid bridge, which shoots over life at an excessive pace, later shortens: as a band of fountains of white pearls of powder is suddenly rent into glass faucets if one turns the pipes slightly off so, too, does desire break down and start to drop, let fall a pillar, nearer the source. In other words, the 'vital' force apparently begins to weaken, and one will sense the forms of weakening to be intellectual, that intellectuality, however, will anew be a strength: we gradually move away from women, & through the moving away we carry a continually stretching shadow with us, or we see them in an ever-stranger perspective, & we take such a liking to that perverse viewpoint that now it binds us to women much more strongly, by now until old age, when we will again start to move closer to them with the sterile judgment of adolescence, and finally we will again lose all perspective, and with that 'life,' and we shall die with the kiss of a genuine courtesan on our lips but with a lifeless fiction in our soul.

What a naïve reality would the pallid paradox of the 'approaching distance' be if it were possible to express the difference between Touqué's embraces at 16 & 26 years of age: the interior complexion of rapture, that essential change of response of the tactile nerves, which separates the latter from ten years before. Who would see the difference? The same twinkle in his eyes — after all, in expressing 'doubt' in connection to the latter state, naturally it was not to imply that 'as the years progressed he looked on love with ever greater indifference' — nothing of the kind was said; indeed, quite the reverse, as a gourmet spider he waited with wilder hunger for the babes who happened to fall into the lap of his net — the 'doubt' did not relate to the ethical content of life or to women's character but to his own erotic-dream technique.

A book before a kiss, a book after a kiss — that is a day-to-day thing for a person like Touqué. There was a time when he transfused the inspiration-mist of a book to the next kiss, he pressed together all of the book's ideas, figures, & illustrations into a single kiss cloud, & the following kiss (usually purchased in the shop) would almost seem to be a discharge of that tension. A fairly grotesque meteorology: to knead a book of philosophy or novel into an amorphous premise of a kiss, then to jump in a shop for a ready-made conclusion, and to bring the two into an artificial relationship. In a later period he would not have placed a book in the service of a kiss. Let us, for the sake of ease, take a book's ideas & a book's letters as being identical: then, in the case of the adolescent's kiss, Leville-Touqué melted the letters into the shape of a woman's lips — whereas in the case of a later kiss he distorted all the letters into a curved mirror that imitated the form of a woman's lips: the most hysterical reflected forms of distortion, however, are always at an essential distance from the sculptural forms of melting over. And that is the case not only with books but with all the contents of life: in the first period he formed everything into an Eve-shape so that the entire world was a forcibly transformed Eve-forest: every single tree was full of bulging might & circulus vitiosus,[25] which are undoubtedly the most consistent forms of autonomy. Now, however, they had become a single woman-mirror, a curved mirror, he distorted the whole world into the perspective of a masquerade — he cut off from some things, added to others, conjuring a new chaotic landscape around himself of which he was the peak & the starting-point, and the things were filled with much greater delight by not transforming them into Eve-Midas Eves, but only due to an optical whim did their substance become 'spifflicated.'

First Non-Prae diagonal: hotel & seaside sand in the dawn; experimental landscape of the identity of objectivity & unreality

(... He marveled that she had gone off to bathe at such an impossibly early hour as it was barely 3:30. He dressed quickly and glided down between the numbered catacomb graves of closed room doors: here and there a couple of nightlights were still on, which did not betoken light but simply a time from nine to twelve, and then there were burning white flat lamps, which did not denote any time at all, only the sick operating-room light of 'all-night' duty; he encountered complicated candelabras, entirely switched-off, the dense branches of which were entangled in the turns of the staircase like the sagging frames of half-fallen balloons caught in the branches of tall autumnal trees; but even these extinguished electric lamps of frosted glass denoted a positive form of lighting with their little electric bulbs like the eye ovals of Greek statues without pupils: the bronze arms were the liberated and perennial bushes of dreams, while the candles were an indifferent, naïve catalogue of symptoms of a clinical death service.

Elegant hotels always move between Bohemian-idyll and X-ray diagnostics: people give themselves up to the most irresponsible affluence, but their let loose Arcadianism always flows into sanatorium forms. When he first went to sleep with this girl in a third-floor room, he did not know whether it was through his limbs growing weary from pleasure or the tart chemical odor of anesthetic that lulled his eyelids like heat does emery paper.

As he raced down the steps, the gigantic bushes of extinguished electric candles at the turns in the stairs quivered: on each landing there was a bit of the floor on which there was no carpet and he always trod on that with a sharp thump: above his head he saw more and more rough-grey blind electric boughs as if they were the briars of daylight behind which 'precise indifference' were burning with its bloodless face.

That was the most unsettling of the three types of hotel lighting (evening lamp, duty lamp, and extinguished candles): he recollected a feverish dream in which he saw in front of himself an endless and permanent hypodermic needle in which milk, a saline solution, running soda water, and ash blown into spirals circulated, streaming ceaselessly into his veins: the electric candles were exactly like that. Their two kinds of 'sharp blindness' or 'poisonous neutrality' were exciting: the immaculate whiteness of the porcelain candles and the grey buds of mist — he saw that white and grey related to each other in a completely different manner to what he, in his spectral sap-headedness hitherto, had supposed. The dawn's true turn in fortune does not commence with the appearance of the sun's rays but with that universal greyness that is neither 'dark' nor 'light,' just as the colors of the extinguished electric candles did not signify either glitter or dullness: what, then? Perhaps the simple, isolated fact that every object was precisely itself, but in the most extreme moment of self-identity: only just reaching themselves in the chaste Narcissus-glance of identity, with the first, preparatory awareness of outlines, colors, and weights: the shoes lined up in front of the doors to the rooms had just that moment become shoes, the telephone handset had just reached by a whisker's touch that first microsecond of 'objectivity' without having also assumed the ballast of 'reality': from the extinguished candles there almost emanated a counter-X-ray bestowing the minimum of probability.

Because dawn was a counter-X-ray: it did not reveal the structure of objects but their very outermost outside; in the world's ontic symptomatology, it is just as important to see the surface of a surface separately as the inside of things, and the only-outside of the outside of things is just as hard to discern as the hidden pathoscape of their depths.

He thrust against the big revolving door as if he had been a ball dropped before a roulette wheel: was there any way of knowing where he was going to end up, dropped from the hotel's wings? Fair enough that one gets out of it spinning round and not straight: though one knows one is going to end up on the street or the cold morning sand of the beach, there is nevertheless some sort of process of unrealizing that takes place between hotel and street in the dice-rolling jackpot of the revolving door, thanks to which one gets back one's own existence as a magnificent first prize and random luck: when he flew out of the glass plates of the revolving of the big glass catapult he felt like a dice that fell to the ground while showing the six on its back. "Ego jactus est":[26] *he himself was no more than a pure gain for existence. He had had little in the way of life, events, memories or plans, just the concrete advantage of being awake. A person's role at dawn is odd: a shallow-meticulous greyness gives only the* 'gas-mâché' *of the reality of things, whereas the wheel of fortune of the door shoved him into an active, hard, and crude consciousness of life. His surroundings: objective, but of nil build; the fugued-out 'ego': strikingly live, but ludicrously aimless. The confrontation is important: the ripples in the sand all sloped sharply toward the sea and toward billows resembling Arcticly white, snow-covered boughs, but they were so devoid of content, chaste to the point of self-annihilation, that it was impossible to believe in their reality ["... every absolute objectivity will, in itself, become unreality": is dawn supposed to give some such lesson?]; he himself felt within him the almost crystallized mass of life, but no practical or human deed or human profile contributed to it ["... every absolute life-likeness will of itself become an inhuman accumulator of death"?]*

Last night there had been a strong gale that had brushed the sand in the hollow form of sand models onto the flowers, smaller bushes, and ladders of leaves. Now there was not a breath of wind, the Moon had already vanished, but the sand still retained all the beauty of both: it was silvery in color with green here and there, like the divine ground note of immaturity, in other places chalky and nacreous white-gaps, in one place like whipped cream, in another like unswept crumbling plasterwork. But what the linguistic catalogue breaks up, the wind's coordinating waves enticed together: the whole world was a monotonous sea of sand, a tautologous sand dune without any variation. He thought he was in the otherworld and he was late for the last judgment like a globetrotter for a bicycle exhibition which, unknown to him, had closed a day before his arrival; since the flowers were suffocating from being up to their necks in sand, all the leaves had been buried alive, so that only here and there was a coal-black scrap of an ear or finger poking out like the corner of a folded name card of condolence; he had the impression that some kind of sentence had been passed; a stifling moral pressure had gained ground over his own consciousness of life & the world's mimosa-objectivity.

There is no more amorphous sensory impression than exhuming from graves in the dunes, standing tight against their body but slapdash for all that, tiny bushes that have been buried in soft, shifting sand: with one's fingertips one now comes across loops of stems, now grubs in the body of the sand, fluid and easily pushed aside, a body which part crushes, part leaves free, the flower to be buried. When he looked over the black mosaic of those leaves that had been left free, he did not know straight away whether they really were plants: perhaps it was a host of diminutive black hummingbirds, or some charred black scrap paper that had been blown there from far away. Of course, those were in sharp contrast to the undulating forms of silvery blue sand.

In its pushed-apartness, the sand resembled the forms of women's breasts, only the sole points of the nipples were substituted by the long edges of snaking spines; without bearing even an approximate resemblance, nevertheless the troughs & dips, the edges and the areas moved into flatness, gave an image of female breasts which had been separately diversified. The shadows were also the reverse, of course:

there were sloping and globular, so to say 'regional,' patches of darkness, and, scattered between them, the stiffly formalistic shadows of the siblings of the sunken leaves, which related to the former like sudden unconsciousness does to the floating loosening of consciousness in dreams.

It was a dawn in summertime, but the whole gave the impression of a polar ice garden: the sand was cold and white as the most stinging niveous snow, in sharp contrast to the dense greyish-brown walls of the firmament. On the shore, after the wind negatives of the sand mammaries [the previous evening he had seen on a glittering and globular scaffolding of a candelabrum the cut-off breasts of the girl he was now seeking: she had at least nine breasts according to the bends in the candelabrum, some of which were thin as a line, others as fat as a ball, and they were connected in the most fantastic fashion: on the other, the body material from an epaulette, a broad epaulette from a protuberant point of a breast, et cetera], thickening beside the water was a small jungle of palm trees. Since the sunlight was behind them, they were pitch-black, standing out sharply from the two kinds of whiteness of sand and sea. Some of the listless leaves stood apart only at the tip, like the hundred-branched crown of a high aristocratic order on a non-existing person while on others they ran all along the stem like the spines of an ankle-length halo on a statue of the Virgin Mary.

The sea was like a barbed-wire fence comprising both horizontal and parallel lines, heavily packed with snow, and crossed by hanging icicles: the same matutinal duality of colors as on the extinguished electric candles in the hotel; glittering white and water-colored greyness.

Near to the palm-tree grove lay the swim-suited girl, in deep sleep, half-covered with a shawl. Here, too, was a new world of shadows: the Red-Indian feather headdress or Sebastinian arrow-cluster of five palm trees were located on one spot, casting a shadow but not complete darkness. At dawn blackness was not the opposite of lightness (after all, the 'lightness' itself was not light or sun-colored as by day) but a variant of equal rank: no difference could be found between the Moon-colored sand and its strictly self-recurrent existence-glistening and the black air under the palm. One side of the girl's bathing costume was wet through, the other end had been muddied by the sand: the clumsy mud stain gave the impression that the girl had been in an accident; she had fallen, tumbled, and now was lying in a faint among the protruding roots of the palm trees. The projecting breast with the wet and rubber bra (just like with a convex lens), by contrast, gave the impression of clean-cut, indeed, merciless, sportiness: the bra served not just to hold down the breast, but it also tamed the curve into a form which was accessible to the air, to the morning barely-a-draught, and could, so to speak, at the same time, flutter it lightly, and thereby the bounds of the whole grove were transformed into a sort of Venus-pillow. Her face showed the maladroit, unskilled course of her sleep: the wildest lack of vanity.

Unconsciousness, sport, and petty bourgeoisie. One wonders which of that trinity the girl will utilize as the first voice of love! Is everything dreamlike? He felt his own consciousness to be a dream, precisely because the consciousness was such a conscious consciousness and just-consciousness; he felt the sand coverlet, the palms, the sea powdered into snow, to be a dream, because they were excessively realistic and only real; and regardless of that he saw before him the physical dream in its own human, medical factuality like a crushed box of canned food, a discarded tube from which someone had extracted his consciousness and the seashore's impossible possibility in order to make his head spin. It was 3:30 a.m. When is that? He bent down in order to feel the salty-cotton and slightly sweaty fabric on his lips...)

old & new possibilities of the relationship between kiss and intellectuality ('life' & 'logic')

What is the simple pleasure inherent in perspective? No more than that (but it is plenty) it is where the strictness of a sole viewpoint is asserted consistently and to the last molecule (e.g., with the curved mirror), or in other words a higher order; but at the same time it engenders the greatest chaos in the world, plants grow, the Alps look small, blades of grass, dungeons, & giraffes will become earthworms without in the least measure having to truncate their essence. What is life's path? The same as that of algebraic or geometrical series: for a while the emphasis is on 0, 3, 6, 9, 12, et cetera, but later on all the pillars are lost in fog, with 3 remaining as the eternal number of the relationship, like the flower which emits an unexpected fragrance into the air from the sods of a row of flowers. The woman of the initial period can only be called Eve, she of the second period might be called a Hypothetical Lookout Point.

On the other hand, it was quite natural on Touqué's part that, since the world had to thank a woman for such a stylish turmoil, over time he should come to feel that the woman herself was the locus for the game — on the lines of perspective that run from the woman to Touqué and back, from him to the woman, the contents of the world flow into the woman indeed, ultimately the woman herself disappears, & in her place all that remains is the perplexing (but optically entirely logical) world of reflections: that is the ecstasy of love, the pinnacle of life. At that point the woman is just a momentary starting point, the man merely touches her, and the next moment that touch groups the whole world into a new perspective, love is realized in a pathetic relationship to the world, not in total possession of a woman.

But from a practical point of view the woman also profits from this, because obviously this is not a case where the man reads two hundred books and kisses a woman just once a year and distributes the savor of that kiss among the lines of a new set of two hundred books. From a practical point of view one may be the greediest Don Juan even though from a theoretical standpoint the woman largely disappears and Eros ignites at various points in the world: there are pictures in which, for example, a woman is seen in a window — she is sketched in pencil, more a caricature than a portrait, but her hat is worked out with thick paint. Beside her a table has been tossed in with two lines, but a wilting flower is painted in suddenly strident colors. In the background is the sea: an insignificant grey blot; but past the horizon, green hills strut around with glittering concreteness in the same color as the hat. This is a bulletin about Touqué's most civilized embrace: He is holding a bottle-shaped, completely transparent, glass woman (*"Daseinschöpfende Sich-uneigentlich-machen der Frau"?*),[27] but through that touch all of a sudden the world burst into lights at the most diverse points, though those lights are all logical parts, continuations and supplements of that one and only woman, indeed, the one and only possible, definitive sculpture of her: just as 'order' is always only an autumnal by-product, a sophistic shadow, so the woman's true sculpture is never in itself but in those scattered ('disjointed') things, which can be seen from her viewpoint, from that erotic nest of induction where she stands. It is not the nude figure but the cactus dozing at the edge of the table, the green roses of the distant Atlantides,[28] and an unexpected slice of the hat. There is nothing in the woman, but everything relates to the woman, and the relation between the cactus and the woman, the green hills and the woman, the piece of hat and the woman, is always the same: the aim of love (and the whole life) is to create just such permanent tokens of relationship. (This can be an intellectualization of love, but under no circumstances a spiritualization of love.)

What in fact gives the thing its intellectual character, or when do we say decidedly of something that it is intellectual without its having anything to do with some idea? Naturally, that is a matter of psychology and of fairly recent date: in times gone by the 'reason for a kiss' would have found abode at best in mysticism, where indeed a lot was said about such an identity of life & sense, but that was in sharp contrast to a modern sensibility sniffing around for an identity of that kind; in mysticism reason was conceived of as being a doughy mass, the homogeneous tendency of life, so it was just a name, a convenient smear, while in recent times a formula like 'kiss-reason' does not imply the reason is superfluous, because after all the mind is anyway already in a kiss via the chemical route (just as sedatives are often combined with tranquillizers so there is no need to make special provision for them), but a totally new interpretation is demanded of 'reason' as of 'kiss': the difficulty lies precisely in the fact that they are so much functions of each other that the two cannot be separated, because as soon as they are separated I have left on my hands the concepts of the just-concepts of old 'life' & old 'reason.' In mysticism the strictest senses (never the meanings) of 'life' & 'reason' played a role, and the two were simply taken as identical, nothing being easier, after all, than identifying such cavities without profile — now, however (and that 'now' is Touqué's current and most personal 'now' as he stares at Leatrice's body), both 'life' and 'reason,' in the old & inverse senses of the words, are just fictive linguistic deities, and in their place there is something else.

It stands to reason that if two deities lose their authenticity, it is the assistance of those two deities that is required to dethrone themselves: when Touqué gazed at Leatrice's body & felt that it was starting to take on a new meaning, then he was operating with the old senses of 'body' & 'mind,' instinct & sense, life & reason, yet at the same time he did not see the two as identical but perceived them as being an accidental sundering of two alien things which were of quite a different nature. In that sense, Touqué was always anxious to the point of comicality, he was highly preoccupied with the birth of new ideas and the relationship of the new to the heritage taken over from the old, because one thing that filled him with horror was what he styled 'mystic consumer-genesis.' What he meant by that were the method and trend that consist of two concepts fusing like two primitive animals to form a single new figure: this is the true opposite of multiplication by division. Thus, if eight animals like that lived in a glass jar, then there would now be only four, which might be totally new figurations as compared to the original eight, but through 'reproduction' by the metamorphosis of marriage they have halved in number. In the next mating season, two progeny will proliferate out of the four, and finally, at the peak of procreation, the 'proliferation' of the species will come to an end in just a single specimen. If that is transplanted to the domain of concept creation, one comes out with the game that always filled him with horror.

By way of contrast, though, another schematic aquarium game lured all his sympathies, which, to distinguish it from the former, may be entitled 'rational telegenesis.' Here, too, a pair of animals swim around each other with dainty fluttering and an undulating chic of algae before finally intertwining on the eternal bed of waves like a corkscrew sinking precisely into a slim scroll. Prior to that the new pair, with a sudden flicker, were renewed into a single giant flower, but now floated in the water in a passive embrace, stiffly, like two corpses, and gradually became paler and paler. All at once, at the other end of the aquarium, around two meters from the 'parents' on one of the highest rocks, a huge flower animal with flirtatious golden petals and swaying palm trunk is suddenly flung forth like a divine source. Stuck together, two meters away, the parents are by now completely snow-white; they dart on, still for a moment, and then, like air blown underwater, roll apart like diminutive glass marbles.

That is how Touqué would have liked to bring the progeny of the concepts of 'Eros' & 'raison' into the world: to approach the two and thereby bring into the world at an infinite distance to them a new progeny, not one atom of which was derived from the parents but was nonetheless their child. Then, since the intellect, just as the notion of life, both became nonsensical to him: he saw Lea's body at one & the same time as intensely intellectual & lifelike. Sometimes he imagined the thing could be disposed of with such avoiding games: in the past the world was imagined in such a manner that tiny vital and tiny rational units were located mixed up next to one another, but the ultimate 'atom' was always either an only-vital or an only-rational point, so that if one takes the one as being black, the other as white, the world can be depicted as a picture one half of which is a pure black area, the other half pure white. Now, however, we think that the ultimate 'atoms' still consist inseparably of '*vita + ratio*' & therefore the world can only be portrayed as a picture in which there are a million small two-element circles, half of each of which is black, half white.

---

the succession of a sterile 'truth'-climate
and productive 'clarity'-states in Touqué's life.
Worthlessness of primitive composition and
value of absolute dispersion from a logical & artistic point of view

---

He sensed clearly that some inherent sterility was yawning at the bottom of his trains of thought, and without brute force he was never going to manage to close them in an orderly fashion so that many a time he made conditional apologies on behalf of autocracy. It is possible to direct one's thoughts autocratically like the supple stem of a creeper because in whatever direction one rolls up or stretches it, the plane of 'truth' is somehow placed in the world in such a way that we always receive as a projection the same shadow, that same one & only possible truth.

What is in point of fact in question is approximately a gyroscopic coordinate apparatus: however I move about with a point in any plane of the system of coordinates, the system will hover gyroscopically (like a compass in a pitching ship), and in the end I always obtain the same sole signal of the situation, in whatever various positions my point had stopped.

The relationship of error and truth can also be perceived as complementary floras: error is always a colorful flower which, the moment its colored margins have unfurled from the bud, automatically brings about in the garden of 'truth' the birth of another flower which, with physical precision, supplies the complementary color, indeed the complementary form & scent. The more 'absolute' the flower that opens in my brain, the more stunted a small flower will grow in the garden of truth in order to maintain balance, and the more relative the small seedlings that are going to develop on this earth, the more grandiose the flora that would gush forth in that fabulous garden, but the result would always be unchangingly the same.

When cozily manageable optimistic mechanisms like that went through his head, he always hated their symmetry because he felt they had nothing to do with the order of things: he rushed out into the open air and felt a great hunger for more ethereal, more indefinite solutions. He felt that any kind of system which encompassed the totality of the world was not rational in a petty-bourgeois way in nature and had to be discarded: it lacked the clarity, that fresh airiness, which did, indeed, accompany his rational observations. With him those two states of mind were always sharply distinguishable, alternating in waves.

One of those states had been visible up till then: its main feature (not just in relation to Eros, but to every other reflection) comprised the suffocating dualism that the brain develops mathematical and biological forms which culminate in an algebraic formula and a super-flower pressed into a punch. While that process races through the mind (its main feature is precisely the ecstatic tempo: the formulæ expressing the regularities of the hyperbola are immediately identical to an animal system of life, which in its childhood is vertebrate and later loses its spine only for the animal immediately to produce out of itself some postulate pertaining to spherical trigonometry: the exoticism of an exotic animal no longer seems material, but intellectual, so that there is an internal relationship between joke animals, hoax flowers, & arithmetic), a darkness of tragic mania flows over it, and Touqué naturally strove to free himself from it — for a time, it is true, he would have the impression that he was 'spiritualizing' nature, but he would then realize that he was going in the opposite direction; when he recomposed the rose mathematically in his mind and then redid the mathematical scheme into a rose of reason (as if one were to replant a person's skeleton in unknown soil and get the bone branches to flower and leaf as raison-flesh, as if the structural abstract directions hidden in the skeleton were to have continuations and logical consequences that took on a new lease of life as flowers), he did not prepare an intellectual extract of a rose but it was precisely its materiality that he made more material: lines of structure are nothing other than 'grounds' of material, the sensation-humming region in our tactile nerves, etc.

A rose should be imagined as a fresh statue of metal that has had some colored liquid poured over it. At first sight the liquid settles evenly in every (smoke-thin) lamia, but in the ensuing moments the labile paint starts to slip from the edges to the center of the sloping petals (which one can even better imagine as being made from microscopically thin, transparent glass) & in the end, in accordance with gravitation, take up the position that by now represents the threshold of freefall: that gathering of material (paint) in the direction of gravitation is undoubtedly something that one will see in partially abstract, partially vital form for, after all, a line of force is something geometrical, but at the same time also, as energy, something highly vital as well, though nevertheless the essence is that it is just liquid paint that has run together — it was not the structure that separated from the material but the material ran together into denser material — whereas the material, the true abstraction, is identical to the normal image of the rose, just as with vitreous transparency it floats around the thickened paint.

Touqué saw a parody of 'spiritualization' in this conceptual experiment: the structure of things is precisely their outermost outer, their intellectual essence is a total of their surface properties — while the system, that composed game of shadows that forms their internal anatomy, nothing else than that practical trick of the mind by means of which it condenses material into a 'portable'-form the better to work on it and more deeply imbue — common & expressly materialist impression-comfort.

The simple hypocrisy of sensuality naturally did not satisfy him: he wanted something genuinely rational in accordance with sense, an intellectuality that not a cubic millimicron of life could leave even if it were crushed under the greatest conceivable pressure. He looked back at one of the chief symbols of hypocrisy, the picture on which instead of a mouth can be found a red rag of color and a bit of a line shaving. That is the above-mentioned suffocating dualism: an abstraction and a material exotic. Do I have a 'spiritual' image of people if, for one thing, I exaggerate out of a skeleton a nude skein of branches outside the body, &, for a second thing, if I knead a mass from its flesh that I toss beside a grill of bones stylized to the extreme in such a way that half of it gets caught on the branch hedge, the other half flutters about like a flag in the breeze? Because in the picture that is what happened with the woman's mouth. There was an atmosphere of 'truth': all enclosure, sultriness, a pâté of proportions & a graphical asymmetry intensifying the dynamic order. That is what became the fate of that picture, which, not long ago, was a symbol of 'freedom' & 'openness.'

But there was also another state in Touqué's life, a wave crest, which differed sharply from that tropical & consuming 'truth'-climate. That pendant-state might be called the era of 'illumination' — in an optical, not a metaphysical sense, of course. When the preceding inclination had been fully lived out to the furthest limit, when cacti had wriggled out of every abstract system, & out of every miscarried wreck of roe had become a theoretical 'proof' in the mathematical sense of the word, then that whole Sisyphean construction suddenly collapsed, because the totality of synthesis turned nauseating and automatically mendacious. The 'illumination' likewise deemed to discover sense, solution, & tendency in the world, though having nothing to do with the 'truth,' by which only the complex outlined above could be understood.

It took a quite extraordinary strength of character to suppress the leaning toward something like 'truth,' and in its place endorsing a forcible breaking up of 'illumination.' In our half-lit midnight room we always set objects, shadows, and fleeting thoughts objectified as statues into a uniform composition, a comfortable closure of which it is not our thirst for harmony but our momentary laziness that has need. But the morning rays of the sun disrupt that magical conglomeration, and wedge white blades of rays into precisely the place where the shadow of a vase and the delightful, almost fluent denial of an old decision may have grown into twins. Those glowing, white rays were sought out by Touqué, an illumination that was beyond the laws of structure & the monotonous distortions of perspective, so that there was no possibility of creating a 'synthesis,' many sources of light were needed that did not shed light in the geometric directions of searchlights but as unexpected sources, surge forth in the manner of one-sided fountains from the roots of living trees, from the hips of people, & from the most neutral points of the air.

At first sight, Touqué's two mental states appear to be an opposition of 'order' and 'chaos,' but it is more a matter of the psychological difference of 'only-animal, wholly-instinct' & the 'clump dispersing with ideal completeness.' The latter lacked all *l'art pour l'art* creation of disorderliness: in fact, he fled there because in the 'truth'-state untidiness immediately seemed to be a simple & transparent projection of some sort of order, and Touqué sensed a bourgeois comfort of order in all classicism, but in his acceptance of disorderliness he saw the asceticism of the mind. Nor did he seek out mistakes for the purposes of esthetic tricks.

Given a landscape, a slice of happenings from life, or two types of alphabet on a printing-press. The landscape is hanging in the air, trees, lakes, reflex ladders & cloud supplements extending far beyond the water. The mind immediately endeavors to compress this incoherent agglomeration and create connections: to pull in the centrifugally swerving fragments as if the gaze were wishing to create some sort of common denominator. He promptly relates a treetop to the crest of a wave, the two to a reflex-scale, & thus in a couple of shakes he sets up a whole series of relationship-loops within the picture: he senses the absolute of chanciness to be an order-power.

The whole order was born an optical hypothesis and immediately it grows gigantic, yields a composition: yet still he condenses the landscape ever-inwards, tears the landscape away from the living wreath of other tracts of land, & even though the picture comprises just three acts, it is nonetheless condensed into black by the over-ripe system of connections, relationships, proportions & censors of osculation that proliferate within it.

To speak with a cabbalistic grimace: the composition is just a negative isolating avalanche, and for that reason, even though it awakens the most profound senses of 'truth' in one's brain, it is less appropriate for the production of truth. The composition always intensifies things inwards: it is like an animal from which the right leg, left kidney, & one of the tusks has been torn, at which it develops a new biological balance inside its remnant contours; if one were to crop it further, the residue will evolve anew a harmony within the organism: a suspicious animal. The mind snatches at such a compositional routine, & it creates a system within all senseless torsos; the more chaotic or sundered the fragment that it inspects, the greater the pleasure with which it formulates the scheme of order: it supplements the torso, but not outwards, toward the ideal, but inwards, toward the geometrical diagram around the line of gravity. The torso now can not only hope for but actually obtain the missing arm, but the remaining waist will also be reduced to an abstract balance of form, which is indeed ripening with the greedy (because the most stupidly only-biological) tempo of a 'negative avalanche.'

Engineers sometimes draw precise lines, arrows, & strung ellipses above marshy, ruined, half-unearthed and half-natural meadows, and thereby capricious wild countryside gains internal regularity: the above-mentioned fraud is also based on that: one draws up the geometrical substance of some stupid rubble, whereby one will perceive a doubtful relation between substance and rubble, and enjoyment of that primitive relation will make one forget that the rubble is nonsense. What, then, would have happened if Touqué had given way to the burning impulse of 'only-animal, wholly-instinct'? The moment they presented themselves before him he would have condensed straight away every single woman, every single still life, every single molecule of landscape, into tiny medieval logos-princedoms in which in place of the continuation of thought a lie of a refrain would have stepped forward like scenery (a refrain is also thought-inherence), & thus the whole world is an incoherent, absolutely disorderly pile of such little systems which are inwardly ultra-contrived but outwardly totally cut off from each other. The ideal situation, by contrast, is that every single woman, every single still life, every single molecule of landscape, should remain in the order of 'circumstances' that stand over and outside all of us, is not a line-of-force; because those systems, reducing into little buttons, do not, like droplets of water, reflect the whole, as a syrupy simile would have it.[29]

The goal of 'illumination,' therefore, is to hinder from arising what in every detail is an inwardly directed order-thrombosis: when the little red horizon and solitary palm branch, situated far apart, start to converge like a periscope looked at from the ring-shaped end, one immediately starts getting interference from 'illumination,' which does not allow a connection to mature at a place where separateness is the sole positive reality. This a wide, white, biting, stinging whiteness, which exterminates and flamelessly burns down any improvised 'structure'-idyll. All that the 'clump dispersing with ideal completeness' means, therefore, is the intact maintenance of terrain with the assistance of acute 'illumination': it never looked for attempts at life-likeness, did not stylize confusion and other hogwash, but the clear morn of the world that had not yet been touched by a way of looking at things, not been skimmed like a glossing-over wing by a shadow of concept & perspective.

Second Non-Prae-diagonal: Riviera landscape; opalescence of infidelity and fidelity. Mutual exclusion of woman-person & love

(... The napkin ring first uttered a quiet 'goo-goo' sound, was quiet for a moment, then clicked sharply on the pavement, steadily adopted the rhythm of the flight of steps, signaling each of them with a ringing click, and just as precisely in the places where nothing could be seen of the red bricks of the steps, and then fell silent as if someone had pressed on it a chloroformed wad of cotton-wool; a long, long pause, and finally a warm splash like a frog's last swallow before falling asleep. All of a sudden he could choose between three perspectives: he could have grasped the garden around the fish lake like he had hitherto during snacks, or he could have broken it down to the acoustic zigzagging of the napkin ring, and lastly he could have projected the polite racing of the search for the ring, his presentiment of searching into the bushes, slim columns, and wells.

The rolling of the napkin ring down the terrace was, in any event, a betrayal: their secret intimate meeting all at once acquired a new flavor. Until then, in their own eyes, in each other's body, they had the dark-blue foliage similar to a wool of dense volcanic fumes that separated the artificial lake from the God-given sea: the sound of the rolling ring, however, was in the timeless self-explanatoriness of their secret tête-à-tête like the unexpected laddering of a silk stocking, or the second hair into which the end of a single hair splits: the transparent skein of existence that had been imagined as being homogeneous had become unstitched. The question is how long is the thread; how much did it round off from existence into a reality that could not be sewn back?

They suddenly exchanged looks among the yellow mirrors of the afternoon hush, which reflected reality in so many millions of ways that in the end they saw it in just a single form, but, sensing the hazardous route of its dreadful planimetric reflections [what if the many corrections of silence did not return in a single image?]: where on the partner's being-hemophilic body did the wound that had been assailed by the unexpected noise gape? They were sitting on Louis XIV armchairs, but under their feet protruded the coarse red bricks of their rural house, bound by white mortar or glue; so uneven was the ground that the four legs of the chairs were unable to reach the ground simultaneously. He was very glad that they were sitting on indoor chairs, not garden seats; the further pursuit of the flaunting of urbanity is part of the essence of a garden. He felt himself to be a Robinson Crusoe who had managed to rescue a single drawing-room seat for the castaway island.

The stiff landscape, silently standing, was like intersections where waves are thrown back, where there is no vibration but one can sense that both before and behind are rippling lines of big arcs: the four Roman columns, not bound by any horizontal stone band, as if in the slim bend they had swept infinitely far, then had been reflected and, colliding with themselves, had come to rest: there is a steely dogmatic and seasick-inducingly uncertain, crazy streak in silence. The columns were whitish-yellow like the Citroneige skin lotion or Alabaster-brand facial cream advertised in fashion magazines, but at their base they were muddy and overgrown with moss, so that from the terrace they looked as if they were floating in the air like those barely noticeable radiations in some microscope slides which are always visible on the upper or right-hand edge of the picture as they just barely reach into the wide elbow-room of the picture, the fourth of which was like the other three, though the inscription notes that the band marked D is no longer a hydrogen effect but some entirely independent phenomenon. We would only have to have moved a little away not to be at the intersection, and then immediately the columns could have seen double: that would not have been the 'noise' state but an experimental representation of the philosophical ambiguity of existence — not lyrical uncertainty, the threadbare dimensions of moods, but concrete, numerical two.

As the columns lined up flawlessly, clearly, equidistantly on the bank of the fishpond after the steps, the ruination conferred on them a restless hybridism and perfect chic: as they had no purpose, not having to carry anything, their small, wreathed capitals soared into the sky with, so to speak, perfumed nostalgia, but in that slim longing, that stylite tower of mercury, there was no contrition, melancholy, or true faith: it was all crystalline affectation and cosmetic eremitism. One was unable to take one's eyes off those ambi-indices: now he mourned Hellenic culture as they trembled in the sun like the last masts of a sinking ship, now he would have liked to do gymnastics, swim, swing on a horizontal because each and every column represented the muscles of a vestal beach-girl's E-string.

There was something virginally frigid and lesbianly selfish in their distance to each other just as there is asceticism and murder in every perversion. Were they together or separate? Did they cynically deride Hellenic culture, or did they respect it like the pinhead of redness of decorations does the troublesome sea of heroic blood? Their foot was thick moss, their caps an offertory topknot woven from polished snakes toward an impossible high altar: what was being ridiculed here, and to what were prayers offered, he asked himself, and the question that was breathed by the columns hovering in the middle distance; he diverted it onto the girl's face like cigarette smoke. Was that nature or riddle-civilization, leisurely to the point of suicide; love ecstasy or indifference of ultrahigh frequency a million cycles per sec, beyond the hearing range? Was the silence mystifying internal-X-interference what he wanted or precisely the alienation racing alongside the stalks?

"If something very much is, it is not at all" — he thought to himself like a peasant crafting an adage, and he got to his feet in order to

look for the napkin ring that had rolled away. The staircase sloped very gently, so it was very long. His legs may have carried him down, but with his eyes he quickly scanned the far end of the stairs so that the red-brick slices in the end assumed a form like a hammock hung between two trees; he stepped ever-lower but his eyes nevertheless carried him upwards. After that gentle and self-contradictory concavity followed a sharp, smooth slope of the lake: he was surprised that although the perspective contrived that to be as askew as a lounger's backrest set to upright, the water did not run out of it. The water was dirty, stagnant, brown and green, with glistening, muddy, and sharply defined splotches; one did not know whether eternity turned into a poetic idyll, or the precision model of absolute flatness turned into foul marshland. The lake was situated a good deal lower than the end of the steps, but from there it appeared to be higher: the real sea's glassy and drained-of-blue level was already visible at tower height, above everything.

One could choose among the great chances of tranquility beside the basin: the pondweed rocked one into a natural historical-'past' mood, the flatness into a mundane-geometrical mood, the reflections of the columns suggested rest via gentle psychological relativism: everything here was regular and dreamlike, elegant and agonically distributed. It was impossible to separate the lake from the woman and not sense that these variations occurred in his love as well: the woman's beauty was sometimes just an automaton of scintillating health, nickel-plated and taut sporting spring or sometimes floating tiredness, sleeping pondweed, a slowly departing golden net of time-shaped impossibility ['past,' in other words], into which nothing ever gets entangled.

Which of these did his desire seek? How was it possible that the same body could simultaneously be time congealing into a bog and a present flashing like a cigarette lighter? That dual ungraspability & confutation measured out in stanzas which radiated from the lake was latent in every embrace: the woman was swimming a long, long way off like a cast-away reed squandered in the tide, every blood vessel and joint gradually vanished just as over time the spiral cloud mists, grizzling into infinite space, will disappear forever from the weak grip of the lenses of one's telescopes, and at the same time the woman so filled a person out, was so here and now, that she became unconquerable precisely on account of the glass edge of the present.

Weighing on the lake's spotted surface was a red-hot layer of air, fitted precisely to the water, a gas-shaped Helios griddlecake, like a funerary sacrifice beside a grave or food prepared for the road. Was he happy or despondent? When one's emotional life reaches its zenith but the subject of the emotion, its intellectual attendants, is pulled out of it so that one is faced with a virtually pure lyrical pulp, then pain and joy, deadly resignation and screaming delight, organ-playing dubiety and confidence-boosting certainty, are all the same, unrecognizable.

Once, a long time ago, he fell asleep in that very garden: when he woke up around three o'clock in the morning, he could see nothing but the syrupy grey air (a sense of distance, skyscape, and the open underclothes of the breeze's run gathered in a single common impression) and giant black leaves directly above his face: he did not know whether they were pillow tassels or dirt sprinkled in mockery on his forehead or spring leaves of the lilac bush or the loose ribbing of a huge nest among which an unknown bird had kidnapped him.

That was how he was with his lover right then, when he reached the burning-hot bottom of the steps [it was curious that the bricks, despite being glowing-hot, had retained their powdery-unglazed color] and looked around beside the water. The badly painted hair of the nymphs must have looked like the lamely speckled lake: a band was pale green like the Artemis pistils of certain poppies, the other brown, like indigestible walnut oil. Anyway, his love would not see a more amorous day: after all, why should he not look at her in the eyes quite strictly? Did he want anything from the girl in the future?

Nothing. She ransacked his entire life, not so as to meddle in it, but precisely by remaining radically out of it.

He spotted the glittering, scheming little circle of the napkin ring. He made his way round the corner of the lake; the bush vanished from sight for a moment, but in its place his gaze fell on something much more annoying: on the surface of the sleepy lake a flat flower was floating [the water was sleeping in dream centimeters, the flower in millimeters inside the same dream space], between the petals of which lay a blue envelope — the letter that he had received the previous evening from his new flame. How had that got there? It was impossible for him to remove it from there inconspicuously; he would have needed long fishing rods if he wished to extricate it. The girl shouted down from the terrace: — Leave it. — Then, after a short pause: — Got it? — The young man knew that the woman could not yet see it from up there, because it was hidden by large flowering bushes at the corner of the lake; but if a little breeze were to impel it a bit further toward the middle of the lake, facing the steps, then she was bound to notice. He could not throw a stone at it as he would not hit it anyway, and it would be conspicuous. Ecce flos fraudis:[30] *his lie had become an enchanting flower, shoulder strap of the Nereides, and a non-returnable eyeshade of the Tritons. He forgot about the two women; all that he saw was the blue of the letter and the voice of the other: — Got it?*

The napkin ring was under his nose, but it was a physical impossibility to reach for it when all he fervently wanted to grasp was that envelope. What had splashed at the end of the ring's rolling if it was not in the water but under the bush here? Did the two lovers have an objective autonomy, or were the two more the reciprocal relationship of two lies: did they live in relationship to each other like a function, one member of which becomes real by making the other unreal?

He suddenly felt that his whole love life, in which he had never been happy, was composed of nothing other than such lie functions and senseless objects like the blue letter. He looked at his watch and established that his wife had probably been waiting for him a long time at home: the little gold watch on his wrist was like a dog leash; the exact time and measurable minutes always on his skin meant only the wife, the miniature transformer of the big dynamo of suspicion, burning at home: every time he looked at it, it was always later than he expected and wanted; in vain did he try to fit the lake, the columns, or his lover into lateness, he found that the lateness was merely the excrescence on his wrist, like the red scar at the injection site where his wife administered the pungent poison of 'home time.'

He suddenly ducked behind the bush because he felt that he would not be able to avoid being exposed that very day. Who whom with whom? Serially or intermittently? The lover of the wife, the one lover of the other, the wife of both lovers? All three women meant for him something of the sort that could, if it came to it, be recorded as 'absolute joy.' Would he have wished to have any of them for a longer time? No. If only it were possible to say just once and once only to the women without whom "he was unable to live" that the word 'life' should not be understood in a practical, social sense but only in the always isolated plane of love outside life — then, perhaps, he would also be able to pick one for life as understood in the practical sense as well. But that is never said to the face of any of them. The rendezvous is not needed as a symbol or fragment of an eternity spent together, but because it is a rendezvous. This is not a matter of love coming to an end, of love eliciting only intermezzi — just the reverse, love is always everlasting, only not in a social or hands-of-a-clock kind of way.

Beyond a certain point in a love relationship a woman is no longer a person but a relative axis of one's feeling: if one sees the woman in the street or in a social gathering she does not represent the object of one's love but a matter of indifference, a stranger. There is no connection between bonds of affection around spending time together and a woman's social persona; hence, even the greatest passion does not actively want the woman, because when it might wish for her, or in other words, when the woman is absent, then the man, too, is outside love: when, at such times, he phones her in order to arrange the next rendezvous, he does that without any 'passion,' purely out of logic, because he knows that a rendezvous will be good even if he is not feeling anything of the sort right then.

A love story is always bound together from two strange and mutually exclusive materials (in point of fact, it is never a 'story,' just apparently so): the closed love circles of rendezvous' and the logical threads that automatically bind those rendezvous' together, in which there is not one thread from the colored fabric of the rendezvous. When he saw the turquoise cadaver of mendacity on the lake, all three women dropped from the rendezvous-sphere and ended up among the logical threads, i.e., outside love. He had always marveled at those heroes in novels who, when a jealous husband or proud father exposes a forbidden relationship, want the woman even after exposure, even though that at that moment the closed eternity of being together had ceased, and the woman can only mean a social plus the way that, at the end of fairy tales, there are 'two more days' following the end of the world.

Everyone would hold him to be unprincipled if they knew that was how he thought and felt. Looked at superficially, all that is in question is that "the woman will be dropped the minute she occasions social inconvenience, since that is an irritating drag, it's not worth a divorce," etc. ["Where are you hiding?" — and just as the napkin ring had tapped all the way down the scorching-hot steps, now the woman's shoe started off the telltale Morse code on the rapidly reeling telegraphic tape of his conscience.] But that is just a semblance: love never seeks a joint household, sleeping together on the divan, reading together on the beach, and the common planning of journeys — these are all just approximate [to use a baneful word: 'sociomorphic'] metaphors, similes and images, mainly for the sake of the woman's more practical brain, mentioned out of diplomacy. There is no follow-up to a happy rendezvous, everything has happened. "We shall be together again next year in Cannes": in the young man's lingo that meant: "right now that golden red peach suntan under your eyes makes me infinitely happy." If the woman then actually demands a train ticket to Cannes, the young man will be held in a fever by a desire to flee, shabby and primitive plans to escape, he is so much hurt by philological accuracy in a place where no 'logos' was intended.

A love relationship can last until the grave if the fortuitous times spent together are not deliberately transformed into practical time. He would be 'forever' with his lover if he did not have to choose her openly as a person before society, as a statistical, gendered individual. Who were those women if he had looked for a Wasserman-test on their blood? Lies, rendezvous', and demographic factors.

When he saw that so clearly before his eyes, he would have liked to fall asleep from tiredness. If his deceptions were to come out should he carry on lying? For whose sake the lying: for the woman as person or for the anonymous inner magnetic orbit of the rendezvous? It had to be the woman as person, viz. non-love. Was that worth hammering out the most nerve-racking marital epics for years on end? When did he have a positively womanly woman in his hands? Never.

Big shadows fell on him, which saved him, but he could do nothing with them. Now, when, in the trinity of wristwatch, floating letter, and shoes tapping on the steps, his life of lies had become obvious, he nevertheless felt that he was faithful, even a genius of faithfulness, although he was no friend of either lyrical paradoxes or of perpetually-forgiving, cowardly humanism. His own infidelity was no more than demographic infidelity from the aforementioned 'demographic' point of view, one physical man and three physical women. Yet it was a matter of three persons, all three of whom lived their own life.

When that simple thought crossed his mind, he found it stank so much of apology that he rejected it. Where could he flee to? As long as there was no need for him to speak. Was he running away from responsibility? You bet! A love squabble had nothing to do with love. Just because the police were counting on his present persona and that of half an hour ago as being one and the same — he was not going to stick around for that reason. What does deceiving a woman amount to? Had either of his lovers received less than the other? No. If the second one had not been around, he would not have loved the first any better. The anger of both men and women at a rival is, in many cases, pure arithmetic nervousness, abstract anxiety over symmetry: it does not demand more love but more justice, more time, more equality, all of which are notions outside love, and they belong to the epic (i.e., non-amatory) part of love.

One love can never disturb another. Or if it transforms it, then it is the infidelity which shapes a more realistic fidelity toward the person whom one happens to be deceiving: in recent times his wife, for instance, had been nothing other than the geometrical center of absolute fidelity in the domain of love; by continually lying to her, the bushes of lies, day by day yielding a proliferation of perpetually rock-hard buds, in the end had filled all the room with their creaking branches and blind buds, only in the abstract place of his wife did there remain a clearing, a positive space — so that if, from a practical point of view, he became ever more unfaithful, from another point of view [whose? even he did not know] he felt the fact of fidelity much more savagely, albeit negatively and impersonally, yet all the same with near-divine sternness, as an elementary sensation, as light or breathing. What he felt amid the flower-jokes of the busking bushes was that it was not morality which is inside us but, willy-nilly, we who move about in morality.

He thought that he would hide among the dense, dark-blue, nocturnal blue-vitriol bushes, then make off from there to the seashore. The leaves were so dense that if he lifted a foot off the ground in order to leap, the branches would simply hold it up in the air, in exactly the position in which he had thrown himself up, not a millimeter lower. He was barely a few steps away from the lake, but all the same, it was a different world: the water was polished nihilism, the bushes crumpled-constellations of sense. It was alarming to see the whole park the other way round: the four columns in front, then the lake, and finally the empty Louis XIV chairs on the terrace. From here the water's dappling was not apparent: as a whole it was grey, like dim tin-plate. The columns were eerily close, and he was glad only that he was not as visible to the approaching woman as those slender alabaster teeth in the dazzling hair of the vacancy of Villefranche[31] *though the fact that something was that visible, indeed, virtually its whole being was just-visibility like that of the four columns, cold as snakes, greatly disquieted him because when someone is hiding they would like there to be only invisible things in the world. It was impossible to move around between the bushes, with their tiny poisonous-blue leaves, only swim, in the strictest sense of the word. The odd thing was that this primeval forest was barely more than three feet high, so that the body was more in the clear afternoon sea air than among leaves, yet one had to struggle tooth and nail with them as if one were neck-deep in foul mud.*

He saw the whole miniature jungle from above; there was no place for shadows. He wormed on his belly as on a battlefield. What did people expect of him? Was he a misanthrope or a philanthropist? He avoided them, and therefore he took with him only a husk of a husk from their society; he loathed their interiors, because all he found there was gaucheness, wickedness, stereotypes and character-stone flaws. Then, at home, he constructed a marvelous 'misanthropic only-fair anatomy' from the shadows of gloves [the hand was already malevolent], from footprints [the steps were already set halfway toward evil deeds on the points], from the map-like scent of the hair [the hairs were already woven into a fiendish net], and now that three female persons were pursuing him at once he would have liked to escape and throw the new anatomical plan back at them. Today the 'demographics' man might still triumph over the fictions and lies of misanthropes, but by tomorrow his own failed realism would be resurgent. [It seems that the only way he could steel himself was with those kinds of melodramatic images.]

— Hellooooo, hellooo; where are you hiding, this is beyond a joke! — Silence. — Where are you? Uhhhh…

Among the bushes he had stumbled on a small fountain surrounded by a few inches of clear ground. He squatted there as he was dropping from fatigue. He knew that if he was discovered then something highly unlikely would happen. He wanted to sleep and pray. The grass all around him was damp and ice-cold, because water was being sprayed beyond the rim of the fountain. At its center was a statue of a smiling child. He kissed it indiscriminately like someone who loved him the earliest and longest. It was not that he set more store on objects than on people as the etiquette of pessimism stipulates. Quite the reverse: so fond was he of the three pursuing women [the letter was in the middle of the lake, up till then he was an hour and a half late home, and his shoes were by the columns] that he could not have fused them into the red horseshoe of a single kiss, & therefore he showered the strange, water-spouting, grinning young masquerader with the most impossible, inhuman, most unfaithful, and yet the first redeemingly, sensibly intelligent kiss. The approaching girl called out: — Where are you? Oh, there's the ring, by the bush!…)

III.

The Cannes fashion salon of Touqué's mother, the Perroquet Galant.[32]
The connection of modern architecture to the nude figure & death

By somewhat of a simplification, the alternations of phases of stifling-'truth' and phases of open-'lucidity' may be underpinned in that Leville's parents were, by and large, personifications of these two states: his father was a parched 'Logoneiros,' his mother naïve clarity. In adolescence Touqué was naturally very interested in the interplays resulting from inheritance so that he succeeded in adapting himself retrospectively to his father and mother, selecting & forcing upon himself with fussy eclecticism his parents' attributes with which only an imaginary invalid will drill himself task by task into the diagnosis set for him: around that time, he prepared two poetic portraits of his parents in which, notwithstanding the hodgepodges of criticism & adulation, it would have been in no way possible to discover any of the fashionable artificiality of ambivalence-style — at most a boyish clumsiness. (Because clumsiness is just as important a factor as the Protean-bogeyman of instinct or the contrary extreme of stylization: we ought to insert between the Parca-visaged automat of sincerity & the goddess grown into a permanent mask a bit of ersatz mythology about the Guardian Spirit of Stupidity, who plays a role as a positive inspirer & stylistic creator in life, reaching such concrete boundaries that it is all but impossible to treat it merely as an internal mental property.) The two portraits were liberated as two symbolic motif jugs and in the course of the trifling events of life he perfumed himself ad libitum now with the father-elixir, now started a new scene of life with the stamp of mother-style on his brow: that is how parents arise in the head of an adolescent that resembles an egg-hatching machine.

Anyway, his mother and father lived in two geographically totally different environments. His mother had a dress salon at the seafront in Cannes. Near to the promenade an old hotel had a parking garage consisting of a whole row of smaller & larger locations that, since the hotel had been completely remodeled, were no longer used but were rented out as business premises. Touqué's mother had moved into one of those sites from an inner city street.

The shop was fitted out by a Parisian designer who won a prize for the design at some exhibition. He placed in the wide space of the garage a huge 'hanging' glass disc as a free-floating lamp: the walls of the fashion salon were not the walls of the garage but matte-grey glass staves that were broken every now and then by a glittering metal pillar. The manner in which the whole disc was held up was not evident, so craftily was it placed.

In the middle of the street side part of the disc a slim prismatic bronze cage arose, somewhat taller than the staves in which a gaudy bird of speckled enameled porcelain was placed. To the right and left of the slender cage of tubes, as if it were cutting into an iron-rigged wall of frosted glass, were small doors that essentially appeared as the prunings of a graft on a tree trunk.

At both of the two small doors were two glittering metal staircases, leading to the disc-salon hanging in the air and with the stairs not quite reaching the ground, like train-car steps that tend to end in the air. On top of the garage were garish clumps of flowers from each of which dangled a pallid runner, pale green to the point of being almost golden, onto the blind-silvery brow of the shop. At the top of the cage was a little black-marble finial: that was the one and only solid point in the whole floating salon, and it also did not comply in form to the lines typical of "ethereal-cubism" but resembled old-fashioned stairwell space-fillers decorated with minute carving.

For the young Touqué the new premises represented an enormous mental change. The old *Perroquet Galant* had been situated on the north side of a shady street — the cage had stood in one of the shop windows on a little stand covered with velvet and contained a stuffed parrot: it, too, had been narrow and tower-shaped, but its contours had nevertheless stayed within a fundamentally bourgeois framework. In the other window there always lay a dress in front of a grey, buckskin-colored curtain.

When he first saw the giraffe-necked new pseudo-cage in the window, taller than the shop itself, he felt a sort of faintness, a nauseating alarm: he knew that there was an inner kinship between the seaside and the old cage, however glaringly impossible the difference between them might be. When he palpably saw before his own eyes, not in the old window, but in the window of the new shop, that a cage which he believed had been articulated once & for all in the old window could be continued as such an absurdity, he had a sense like coming across a new forbidden splendor.

He had a recurring dream in which it unexpectedly turned out that a town he thought situated a long distance from the place where he currently resided was actually very close, no more than a few steps away; all he had to do was turn into a little side street that up until then he had never noticed, or board a small local railway service that had a branch of which he knew nothing. He was always like that with Paris, sometimes for weeks on end: in the morning he would turn his head with delirious melancholy and incredible thirst toward shady gateways and half-overgrown tracks, pretending that he would see the first houses of Paris.

That dream had another variant in which it turned out that physical joy could not be gratified by those women with whom and in the manner that he had hitherto sought day and night, but that joy was in his own body, only in an unknown spot (a side street leading in five minutes from Avignon to Paris) which had hitherto escaped his attention: he felt a new body part on him which he touched with joy and curiosity as if he touched a box of bonbons that had been hidden as a surprise under his coverlet or a smuggled bouquet of flowers. The new joy was generally free of any guilty conscience; indeed, a kindly priest would often stroll across the scene who, rubbing his hands with a friendly smile on his face, would be delighted that Touqué had found the right road so soon. In the morning he would scratch his head, trying to find the point that made him think that joy was obviously not to be found in the normal practice of love but somewhere else. At times his gaze fell on a palm tree, & all of a sudden he felt that he had hit on the key, but when he looked longer at the nude plant figure taking a nap on the great blue plateau of the sky, he did not know whether he ought to follow its form, parrot its motion, or possibly look its color up in an etymological dictionary.

When the new cage was ready he agitatedly examined the old one and was on the point of saying: "You sure fooled me, looking the way you do. There were so many sins & joys in you, so much space and drunkenness, and I never noticed so gentle (at most refreshed a little with ordinary irony) was your exterior. But now I see clearly the technique of how one can wring another face out of things."

A glimpse of the new forms first and foremost induced a moral seasickness in the boy. He did not know whether the new cage rises to the heavens with an idealist program or with a nihilistic tendency: he sensed the same ambivalent sensual pleasure shivering in his body as in his dreams, when a sense of pleasure and moral satisfaction in point of fact were one and the same thing: about morality it turned out that his fortuitous form of Atlantis Eros and the profile of his heart (how was it possible that he had not noticed it before?) were molded in accordance to the prescriptions of the catechism. As if the piquancy of the new architectural style was to confuse in the soul the sense of redemption and the Fall: what could be the meaning of the glass, and then the frosted glass? Cleanness & lightness, but also a kind of simplicity that no longer had any connection to harmony. What about the whiteness? The transparency? What about the frosted glass? These morally directed issues were always the first for Touqué, who considered that the esthetic experience was the most sensual and therefore the most worthwhile when an absolutely material entity is distorted into a bigoted moral viewpoint to the point of sadism and the esthetic experience spills out like artificial blood under the pressure of that new perspective. That later became a deliberate method for him, but to look at every excitement from the point of view of the conscience was as of yet only an automatic assertion of his upbringing.

All art was a vibration of the law, of the possibilities of sin & the possibilities of virtue: not the subjects but the styles — above all those of architecture. More than that, morality was the sole possible 'viewpoint' for him, for it was that in which he was best able to exhaust his self-importance & critical thirst because, on the one hand, the fewest of his partners and acquaintances used this particular consideration in their judgments; on the other hand, his extraordinarily firm principles permitted him a hysteria of precision.

The small glass doors were glowing in the afternoon sunlight like a field of focus in the disc wall that spread out like huge petals of fog roses & emanated from themselves into Touqué's voracious soul the sort of epilogues that "there is in us a dose of nudity, a degree of naked smoothness, which avoids the games of Elysian puritanicalness & primitive shamelessness and unveils new possibilities of spatial nakedness. Our nudity is provocative: it's as if it united in itself three grades: the deadly cleanness of a body excessively scrubbed before an operation, the further-unstripped nakedness of a body suffering in sensual perversity, & finally, the logical bareness, the rational mathematics, of lust, which evolves involuntarily from these gradations, and which lies far from any love, body, and joy. Boundless clinicization, boundless lesbianization, boundless mere-formalization: those are our glass walls. Set your love novellas in progress among us."

(Nudity nowadays has indeed ceased to be a symbol of lifelikeness or materiality. The clinical picture always indicated death: in the past, death ended rather in 'dance of death' types of diagrams, in which it was not death-like death figured but in general destruction, defeat, misery, shattering of illusions, and, as far as possible, with a social background, in which personalized death was a separate factor.

But what does 'absolute' death have to do with a logical landscape of 'destruction,' alien as that is to it, or with the punishment of society? Or with skeletal-statistics? 'Death' is the body itself, normality itself, or in other words, health: nakedness brushed by ether, whether an outer skin or deathly cold chastity, is already death. This lacks all drama, every Parca gesture, time and emotion. No more than the body's most autonomously glittering white dimension. Physical joy becomes a perversity. But that path is likewise not the path of life or overrated matter; on the contrary: it seeks to whip up pleasure until pure 'intellectuality' is finally excluded from it, that even in its clumsiest adolescent forms it unmistakably suggests it; like a woodpecker he would tap all over his own body as at a maddeningly closed column of bark in order to find the way out of himself.

So-called normal erotic delight leaves the body as a single untidy mass: a perverse person [meaning, of course, an 'ideally' perverse person, as even a petty bourgeoisdom[33] that is pettier than normal flourishes within perversity] grinds the body into a pessimistic mosaic of lust so that the network of lust within which he moves is by now an immaterial 'abstract mask' of lust that is almost independent of the body. In the end [in the third degree of nudity, after death & perversity], the mask crumbles as well, and all that remains is a fantastic inhuman and anti-human schema of man, some kind of 'plant-animal' between madness and rationality. Nakedness, therefore, in its glittering passivity, is already death; in its motion [if it does not promenade but 'moves'], however, is, first of all, an intellectual heretic mask, finally an operation of unknown meaning. That is how the glass walls of the *Perroquet Galant*, & the glass turbines of the French cubists in general, transformed the old-fashioned 'humane & lifelike sensuality' of female nudity.)

Touqué genuinely felt these kinds of things: the openness was more of an aristocratic *odi profanum*,[34] as if the adored nymph, who had hitherto seemed to be a flirtatious ordinary little shepherdess, undressed all at once and froze into a strict question: her nakedness was not the zero layer in the series of layers of clothing but a new beginning, an unknown closed door — the geologist who, after a series of bands of earth progressing to the center of the world, does not come across a new stratum but an unexpected landscape: with unknown islands that swim above the sea, with puzzling clouds that dragged their mobile roots in the sea like disintegrated sticks of asparagus.

associations on the glass walls of the fashion salon;
first association: clinic & moral misgivings

The odd days that he had spent in the clinic came to mind — he apprehended his illness as a divine punishment, & thus white beds and cream lampshades played a role as the furniture of purgatory. These were the colors of penance and cool forgiveness because he felt that God no doubt forgave sins which had been repented and confessed, but only because he decided that repentance should elicit forgiveness with chemical regularity, but there is no true joy for God in that forgiveness. The whole of life, health, & gentle joys were all numb around him in such an atmosphere of 'indifferent clemency': the wafer that he took at Communion was rather a clinical nourishment, a nurse-colored sober tranquillizer that may be the body of God but it lies passively on the tongue like a lifeless, icy, and watery fish.

The white lilacs that could be seen alongside the gravel path from the window started blooming; the leaves were grey from a young age, and the flowers were just greenish-yellow little sponge roots on the branches. Some sort of botanical Jansenism may also exist in these scanty gardens, where spring only works with the cowardly half-delight of convalescence and is similar to the awakening of nervous people: pale sunlight is their every joy, something intellectual that is far from them, because as soon as an association bound to the material is permitted to come forward from the day before, even if just a little bit, then immediately some pains, resting but ready to grow, are associated with the morning — they watch the sun's nascent brightness through an open window and they dare not look at any kind of object in which a dreamily awake bud of pain or fear is lurking.

The fight of destiny and affection here lacked all majesty: they were almost not struggling with each other but appeared in an official capacity, like customs officials of former enemies at a border post, or an aging priest & the devil, who, from the words of confessing believers, every so often would make an appearance before him — trivial sins and absolutions stepped into as meek a relationship as the little wizened vegetable heads sweating in his garden and the helplessly leaking watering can.

Therefore when Touqué looked at the dingy and rugged glass wall of his mother's shop, he was always surrounded by the sadness of medical surgeries & respectable piety devoid of inspiration. Many a time he marveled at those saints who were impelled to sprout the first flowers of their sanctity from the dark wrinkles of their diseases because in his case illness deprived him of exactly that.

In the face of illness his individuality in point of fact was a little fiction, a '*portrait moral*,' which he himself had produced about himself as the practical subject of his prayers, because just as we usually have a need to render God conditionally human for a dialogue to be realizable, so we have to sum ourselves up as a 'human,' and thus evolves the role of prayer, which soon becomes conventional. Big variations of our sins, which differ from one another like the bluely incandescent, opalescent snowy peaks and gentle slopes snoozing in green, lose in the prayer attitude of repentance that true plasticity, and for all the emotional excitement, they only appear as the more abstract zigzags of value of deadly & forgivable sin.

But what happened during and after illness was precisely that real life and a self-portrait life, analyzed for the purposes of prayer, which until then had stood in customary relationship, were brutally jostled apart — the whole thing afforded a spectacle like the scene after an earthquake in which a scrap of garden with a few saplings and paths was all that had remained on the sloping rim of a huge volcanic precipice.

When he wanted to pray, naturally the old 'I-grisaille' immediately sprang to mind, but now he felt it to be a naïve little cirrocumulus cloudlet above a strange and ample 'I-wrinkle.' "I have expanded," he would keep on saying in lamentation, and he would watch and take stock with distracted but constant attention of his growing & changing dimensions, which he could no longer tuck back into the old, outgrown box of his consciousness, and he was not yet at all able to procure a new one as he had no idea how much, in fact, he had changed, where he had grown, where he had lost something. "This may be the revenge of objects on me," he supposed with a smile, "of objects which do not tolerate being projected as routine backdrops on the Lilliputian-film screen of our conscience, and now spring forth like a life-size Gauguin-fresco from a wall papered with pale allegorical figures. If that is so, then it is undoubtedly very boring."

He sprawled listlessly on his pillows and felt bitterness about such a doltish disorder being made of his body without his knowledge or consent. "Because unknown things never attracted me, even just on account of the clumsy homogeneity of the unknown: I like to swim in the thousand-colored waves of known things. I shall give myself a new concept because in my mouth the taste of dust swallowed without a wafer is so stinging that I feel a new anatomy, a new moral anatomy, in my soul. I am not going to take vulgar tricks into consideration."

These were all resolutions, but it was hard work accomplishing them. When he began praying he did not know where to place at least a single one of the slim columns of prayer, and he therefore commenced praying in the air: his old closed consciousness and new physical moral landscape floated separately in his life. The old portrait was now more of a defiant portrait, and he would paw the disjunction between it and his convalescent personality with sour pleasure.

Perhaps Purgatory consists of our substance growing in two directions like a rankly proliferating letter Y: to the left the 'real person' bears fruits with all his whimsical forms, and to the right the separated 'consciousness': a simple face of a person seen from the moral point of view and as regards the etiquette of prayer. (Naturally, this is never a splitting of the ideal man & the sinful man — purgatory, after all, is not a puppet theater of contrasts —, but rather a vandal bifurcation of consciousness, prone to stylization, & the rebellious content of consciousness.)

Meanwhile, there were sometimes anxious periods: hitherto there had been a conversion key between the conscious image of sin and the vital drama of sin, but now he was sometimes irritated by the unmanageable shapelessness of sin & feared that his dimensions were, perhaps, very different from those accepted in his prayers. In the past he had taken a bird's-eye view of himself and was able to see clearly the diameter and ambit of sins. But since falling ill his feeling was that he had sunk into himself like a scraggy-winged bird between high walls.

Examination of the conscience perpetually forced him to make a gesture like that performed by jungle explorers when they have to pry apart the ramparts of trailers which have adhered together. "I have expanded," he would remark sadly on such occasions, too. In our dreams it often occurs that we are incapable of reading something, however much we strain our eyes, or we are unable to make out the contours of a landscape, however much we sense internally its 'præstabilita' nature[35] and thus try all the harder to split our adherent eyelids: Touqué was like that with his sins — he was unable to draw comparisons to them, evaluate or examine them, because the illness cut new erosions between the old relationships. Naturally, the pure beauty of repentance also requires symmetry, a certain harmonious composition of sins — but now that the sins were displaying their most topsy-turvy hill contours, he was unable to get into a uniform mood of repentance, only feel fragments of desolation as the sole possible parallels to sins that have lost their contours. Scrupulousness was also the vengeance of precision, with philological cruelty, but all the same it remained a barren experiment.

It was the time at when the thought of *Antipsyche* was begotten, which was at first only called on to promote his own psychological recovery — understanding by Psyche the new post-sickness mood of consciousness, a positive gloom. How were the saints of old able to utilize illness as a first step toward heaven? He tried to theoretically construct the approximate sanctity of which he could be capable, if he wished — that was how the fragment of self-parody, entitled *Hagio-Parodia*, arose. The 'saint' accumulates the self-torments because he does not know the weight of his sin accurately, he just has a fear of sin '*en bloc*': in his soul live two worlds which have detached themselves from each other, one being a romantic landscape of sins that never had a fixed horizon, the other being a landscape of conciliations by capricious installments, but there is no rational relationship between the two. If the two landscapes were set in parallel, then bleeding whips would end up above gentle-blue lakes of virtues; on the other hand, the long muddy channels of propensity for sin would never come upon cruel criticism, only daisyish unconcern.

The 'saint,' however, is aware that he is a debtor who has plunged into amnesia: he has forgotten his creditors, and now he throws his money all about the place, stuffing thousands into the wallets of people who only lent him pennies. Not for a moment does he know if his penance is at the beginning or the end: whether he was a rich man who could rest, or a poor man who had to Harpagon-together a nook in the forecourt of heaven. His every wish was finding some unit of measurement, but the moment he spotted that possibility, he felt deep disgust in the face of a petty-bourgeois yardstick.

As a result, there develops inside him a pessimism full of hatred against his own soul, then against other people, and finally against God Himself. He has to come to the realization that his asceticisms, which became ever wilder, are in actual fact furious vengeances on God, who created chaos within us. In the twilight of his life, when he already has a reputation as a saint, he goes back to his way of thinking in early childhood & he is already forced to discover there that despairing theophobia at the base of his first self-denials. When he threw away the first cherry from his lips, it was more comfortable not to eat it than to think over for a minute whether or not to eat it — or possibly after eating it to fret over whether next time he should eat one or rather not. Renouncement always preceded the decision to renounce: his entire 'saintly' life was nothing more than a glossing over of his resolve of a saintly life.

His apparent battle was a battle of avoidance — he preferred to become 'saintly' rather than decide in conscious thought that he would be a saint. He went around barefoot for fifty years because in point of fact he very much loathed walking barefoot and therefore he did not have the strength to renounce silk slippers in his mind (it was easy to do in deed), but, on the other hand, in silk slippers the possibility of barefootedness would have irritated him; he inclined toward saintliness, as those who are about to fall jump dizzily into space, which resembles a cyclone magnetizing itself below them, generating a separate anticipated deed (to wit: leaping down) merely to avoid the struggles of deciding. Now, after fifty years, he was bored with that escaping, that flagellating laziness, and he dared at last to undertake the fight of combat, of choice: veritably to decide that he become saintly. What is more, he succeeded in guaranteeing harmony. At the same time, however (as is called for by a sensation-seeking novella), he became unpopular in lay circles just as among his fellow-priests: as they saw it, he became petty bourgeois, bland, turned soft. The halo that he had almost forced onto his head was taken away, but he finished his life as a real saint. (Just as certain pieces of romantic trash came into fashion from the exaggerations of 'psychology' ["Analytical thrills of fatal Phobia,"] so the adolescent Touqué-torso was a moral horror novel — not through its events, of course, but its moral sophistication.)

second association: the Munthausen-portrait

The cause of the scrupulousness was, in the last analysis, sobriety, and only outwardly did it appear to be hysterical: inwardly it was dry. If he had excused himself anything he would have felt that a juryman sentimentality had taken possession of him, so that he exerted a merciless severity vis-à-vis his sins: in his memory was a crudely pressed woodcut which portrayed, half in caricature, a German statesman, Johann Munthausen, *aet. suae* 58,[36] who was famous for quelling with enormous ferocity any demurely budding apology for sin. His face was haggard, & the cheap engraver had indicated it all with just a hollow cleft — in places the black blot looked greyly worn, as if the ink had not been picked up well by the dry paper, so that the huge funnel-shaped wrinkle of a recess did not appear to be part of the skin, just a separate plaster patch, an emblem of severity. By not being thick black but rusty, like a centuries-old ink stain, it gave much more of an impression of his being cruel and harsh: it was not a stagy and festive sternness, but bored, banally and pipsqueakishly cruel, the kind that does not sacrifice on the romantic altar of the concept of 'order' in its judgments and dispositions, but enforces in his office the rottenness that had evolved in the cellar atmosphere of his organism. The compass needle of scrupulousness reacted to two regions — one was the exalted and tropical 'thriller'-world of the *Hagio-Parodia*, the other the tinder-veined bureaucracy of the Munthausen woodcut.

The portrait was mounted in a Renaissance frame and surrounded by angels: the outlines of the angels were also blurred as on blotting paper, the fine network of lines only here and there caught with quite unexpected sharpness, as if the gaunt indifference that emanated from the features nevertheless rose in its final conclusions into a world of such fine & graciously-lined play angels. Behind the head a beamed roof could be seen in abrupt abbreviation: the perspective was uneven but it was broken off close to the frame, otherwise what it sought to sketch would not have fitted in: the fact of perspective per se seemed to be a direct consequence of the white-hot indifference, let alone this violent optic-denying and optic-chasing blunder. Meanwhile everywhere the whiteness of the paper was showing, which by virtue of its coarseness could not be an open space, only a meaningless network of reticulated bands, as if the sole object of the depicted subject were to stack up the most formless 'Gothic' facts in place of all logical illusions.

---

*Third Non-*Prae *diagonal: Yvonne prepares for confession.*
Relation of dehumanized soul and sin.
Morality & sin as non-human components of space-time

(... So she began to look for the phone. At first on the small tables, among cigar boxes, lamps, and fashion magazines, then on the couch, at the bottom of pillows, scarves, dresses laid out by mistake, and blankets. As a matter of fact, she ought to study once, first of all, from precisely what part of the wall did the cable start off; secondly, what was the color of the cable, its feel, and its thickness; thirdly, what was the shape of the new telephone set? Did it have a fixed shape at all, or was it all just perhaps elastic mimicry? As she reached a hand under one of the couch's pillows, she felt around three wires at one and the same time: one a thin green, live, strict viper wire; a shaggy cable resembling a worn-out spring, with remnants of pressed-apart perms in its resigned and cyclical body — and finally a coffee-colored

miniature braid, pedantically plaited as if electricity also sometimes wished to accord a favor to the old-fashioned way for Solveig to stay insulated.[37] *She tried to follow the direction the three wires took in the room by eye, but they managed to vanish with incredible adroitness.*

She thereupon called on psychology for assistance: there was a scheming, evil streak in the green wire, a malevolence, a rationalism, an adroitness, and a truth, so in all likelihood it was not the telephone but a private little bell in her husband's study ["...o sinuous green of serpent's spheric truth: leafy-mad circulation of Paradise's tubular precision..."*]; the big cable, with its disheveled Victorian chignon and badly ironed little aunty-wiles, probably switched on and off electric heaters concealed in the fireplaces; but as for the third? Well, the third was suspect, so she tried tugging it and looking for its termination. She had barely touched it when in doing so, in an impossibly unpredictable corner of the room, she yanked off a glove-box, out of which spilled like a waterfall the warning paws of destiny, in the form of black leather blotches and cigarette smoke divided by millimeter squares: a varied puppet theater of oath, assistance, death, pose, stroke, box and amputation clashed before her eyes in half-a-second, thanks to the first rate theatrical talent of the gloves. That was when she began to get really jumpy, and between the silk pillows she scooped a trench for herself with the eagerness of young Renaissance cardinals when they glimpsed a wavy-bearded portion of a marble bust deep in the earth. She could have chosen a medical instead of an art-historical memento, as after all she was dissecting, examining the green veins and neglected arteries of electricity, but it was better to stay with the cardinals, seeing that it was a matter of confession.*

All at once, the whole salon became an electric breviary: this green, yellow, and brown wiring trinity, the kind of colored bookmark strips which customarily dangle in as much profusion out of prayer books as the number of pages that can be found in them.

Odd that the wires were lying in the room so freely and higgledy-piggledy, like lizards in a wood, yet nevertheless they discharged their obligations so precisely, assuming one found the connecting plugs: how is it that after so many superfluous bends and ludicrous detours, they do not forget that they have to switch on a specific lamp? What haunting environs they pass through from the wall plug to the lamp: they start off from the basket of a woman's hand, then they get lost under a silk coverlet, cross a carpet's flowers, swirl into a pile of books, wind round two vases, warm up by the wall of the fireplace, accompany Andromeda like extras in the neo-Classical dance figure of liberation on the wall tapestry, before reaching the lamp bulb: when they go on there is no trace in their objective light of flowers, books, Crusader mythology, or a fight against temptations — the electric light on the ceiling goes on as if it had been evaporated up there in a beeline.

If she had not had urgent need of a telephone right then, she would undoubtedly have enjoyed their threefold hide-and-seek in her salon: the wires' sloppy parodies of the blood's circulation, irrespective of the supercilious meteorology of the cushions and finally the third independence, the precise timetabling of the changes of light of the lamps. Where in that salon might the boundaries of technology and of artistic convenience be? Perhaps no electronic apparatus had ever sunk as low as here, almost into an organic quagmire, among the irregular objects and movements of domesticity. Every instrument was deprived until the last possible point of any scientific or arithmetical character: instead of the click of the switches there was mute turning, like the bored twisting of the head of a flower on its supple stalk; the form of the switch itself was concealed by all sorts of masks like an escaped prisoner in a detective story: the big disc had become one of Amor's small arrows, the little handle — an enormous soap bubble of iridescent glass. If neither voice nor form resembled even approximately the mechanical system of a switch, where was that in-

finitesimally small area on which a switch has to be of a mechanical form in order to be able to work? The wires [which made one think of telegraph wiring in which clouds and swallows learn the calligraphy of flying in the neutral sky of trains], the wires are draped around the candelabras like a wreath of vines on the brow of Anacreon or they are destroyed completely, which likewise satisfactorily fulfills the textbook conditions of situation comedy: out of – signs come spinning circles, out of + signs cubist muzzles, out of × signs 'mixed pickles,' *and nevertheless the operations are exact to a hair.*

The whole salon was a philosophical identification of a second-long exploding picric acid and an Angora cat yawning for centuries; that automatically determined the movements by which the tenant had been looking for the 'phone': half with an engineer's laying-on of fingers for taking the salon's mercurially unstable pulse, half for the wing-flapping of the raptorial bird as it seeks to pluck a wee fish from the water in order to simplify the multiple equation of water and air.

But now she had found it. She could not feel distinctly which part of its body she was gripping. But the temperature of the object was unmistakably the acute drop in temperature of a telephone, around ten degrees altogether. The whole telephone apparatus was like a spoon that had been picked up out of clotted cream, the gobs of which were adhering to its concealed forms. The bell, hearing device, and mouthpiece were all a single ball. When she moved her mouth over it, it did not look as if she wished to speak into a specific slot, but she only sought out a rough position for speaking into it between the pillow and the fur blanket: in old pictures one can see forest virgins living in the wild (cf. volume 18 of Brehm's Jungfrauleben*),*[38] *who drink from brooks, raising two hands to their lips, and meanwhile, to the right and left, a few tastefully placed half-meter drops splash back into the channel — that was also how Yvonne was with the telephone.*

Meanwhile, with a chance jerk she also switched on the light-blue lamp next to the fireplace. Although the lighting was weak, like a placebo prescribed for a hypochondriac as a formality, it nevertheless gave the room an oblique and unfavorable sharpness. The lamp-shade was an opened parchment accordion with a single cord and with holes punched all along it, like a medieval document with the big ribbon seal of an electricity company. Was the lamp indeed blue, and was the light pouring out of it already white, or was the lamp white and some unexpected celestial bluing dropped its own coloring onto it, like the stepmothers of romantic dramas pour sleeping powder into wine glasses when the drinker turns aside for a second.

"Is that you? Well, I can't come today. No, no. Of course! For that very reason. Actually, I don't believe you: you are too full of yourself to be jealous. Do you want to know? I go to confession. That's it, exactly. Why? Accordingly. My husband's older brother or great uncle comes, and that's what they want, my husband as well. Haven't you got a prayer book? I've got around a dozen of them, it's true, but I have no idea where they are. I'll take your confession. At least that way you'll get to play a role. Is that a strong promise? Insofar as it is up to me. The two of them leave early in the morning, so wait on the other side. Don't be scared. Stop mocking me. I can't stand it. Understood? Hate it. In any case, I'm hardly in the world as it is, because all my relatives are priests: cardinals, bishops, monks. There's a scattering here and there to take care of the succession. Silence, silence, and more silence. You've no idea; just let it go. Tomorrow morning, tomorrow morning! Yes, there. No, it's not worth it, you can be there, the same as always. Bye-bye."

Of course she did not replace the receiver on its hook, only let go of it as, after all, it fitted in anywhere with the colors and shapes of the pillows. It was five-thirty, and confession was scheduled for eight o'clock. She looked out of the window: it was assembled, or rather just strung together, from boards: the individual sheets were barely touching, so that there were small gaps between them where the wind blew in and sliced-up the room into a chess table of draught in its own image. In every glass square was a loosely textured clip or rosette, which more or less held the boards together.

Yvonne's house was oddly homey: at certain points, the homeliness was developed up to the very point of insanity, at others it was lacking to the point of a forbidding bleakness. But it was exactly the right environment to prepare for confession, she thought to herself. The openness of the rattling windows, the Lisieux-blueness of the lighting pointed to loneliness coming of solitude, whereas the couches, bags of feathers, and carpet plasters folding up in amorphous creases called attention to the freedom coming of solitude, to fantastic sincerity. What, in fact, is a home, solitude, independence? Is the principle of "my home is my castle" a hygienic principle? Is it not rather corruptive? She wished to be sincere with herself, wanted to redeem her most personal self from herself: the resolution was strict, light blue, and draughty, but the result was a voluptuous meowing: comfort rang in her muscles like a typewriter bell: her whole body ran along the uninhibited corridor of 'privacy,' and now it tinkled from the absurdity of that's all and yet I am free.

Sin and non-sin did not so much as enter her head; for her confession simply meant 'solitude' and 'sincerity.' She felt that she was already confessing in being deliberately alone. For the first time she recollected her life critically: the critique consisted of not carrying on her memories into the future for a few seconds but closing them in the present: she knew that everything would carry on tomorrow morning exactly the same way as it had done up till then. But she placed those continuations a step higher than where her memories came to an end — the same cloth, the same pattern, only transferred to a new machine. This is sadness, she thought to herself, that one afternoon you mark a little pause between your memories and your immediate future. She delighted in the past, but the truth was that she did not swap pictures for a practical reason; she made the action literally ascetic. The room was cool, so she wrapped up well.

The accordion lampshade gave a grating all along the wall — not so much in the form of shadings but lights, as if all at once the room had so much become the Loyola operating theater of consciousness that it would not tolerate the crude materialism of shade and would only suck the lighting plan out of it. Behind the lamp was a huge folding screen, reaching up to the ceiling, which stood in a snaking line of some twenty twists and turns: it had enormous bends in the middle, which grew slacker toward both ends. A gigantic bunch of flowers was painted onto the whole thing with crude poster strokes like with stage scenery.

Yvonne felt infinitesimally minute among the corrugated lights and primordial flowers, but she knew that in point of fact the late-afternoon disproportionateness was the essence of morality: she felt the size of the painted flower as a twinge in her heart; she could almost have cried. She felt she was at the center of the narrowest ring of the ethos: the highest degree of comfort meant the first degree of solitude; that was surrounded by various topsy-turvy objects, in any case other things than her, that was also closed by the blue-deficient, tail-biting summary snake of absolute strangeness: the pupilless-looking window, the whites of the eye of which is a Venetian platinum heaven and the lampshade's ghostly directional collar; as if it were directing the traffic of damned souls above a suddenly moral valley of 'privacy.'

I am good — she felt with algebraic relief. — The pillar of ethos can be nothing but those two —, she thought to herself as she popped a Frigor-choc[39] *into her mouth —, things are very much OK: I feel how alien, hostile, and different they are, and home is full of uninvited guests: just as water freezes into icicles in winter, so the things form a big candelabrum of conscience, of otherness-taps, of which she, she, Yvonne, was the life-giving current. Secondly, things are all suicidal, inside them is a fine, barely sensible, but destructive shivering, which magicks each and every one of them into the agony of the thinning drop-hips of a fountain: the infuriating positive of comfort runs over into the big lie declinations of daubed flowers;*

the window's Venetian 'theologia negativa' pekineses back into a pottering domestic pet.

And goodness is nothing other than upper-class see-sawing between the two extremes — between the home's orgied homeliness and sentimental annihilation, to and fro. A poor person can never be good, because goodness is not 'the 'soul's business,' as proletarian priests imagine. Goodness is, first and foremost, a 'business of private property,' because only private property unites that indispensable two-branched crown, the 40°C fever of marriage, and the incorruptible Carthusian Guignol of objects. Bit by bit, with the cautious movement of confectioners or young chemists taking examinations with stage fright, she shifted the lyrical humbug *of responsibility into the outer rings of the environment, objects, and world.*

*Once someone said of her, behind her back, that she was '*moral insanity.*' What a ridiculous slander: after all, that worker across the road, where he will meet his sweetheart in the morning, carries the sacks so precisely from the shore onto the boat, balancing himself on a thin log; after all, that wheeling seagull, after prolonged lassoing of hearts, so precisely hit the Byzantine basket of an old statue, and above all, the fact that now, now of all times, that certain 'hic et nunc' surrounds itself with such universal sorrow and an antihuman selfish halo, it just shows that there is only ethics in the world.*

What did she have to confess? Is sin possible? What is sin? Nothing else but an unexpected cutting off of that saccharine-sweet twilight pan-ethics that emanated from lagoons and her own pillows — all in all a shuddering from that "section of a Dedekind-style[40] *sequence of numbers": just as in the sequence of all the real numbers a section can only denote an irrational number, so Yvonne's body and life were an irrational intersection number in the infinitely dense series of the outside world [i.e., ethos dowry]; sin is, in an arithmetical sense, the irrationality of individual life: it intersects the moral duct of the environment, and it does not itself belong to the pieces of duct cut off on either the right- or the left-hand side.*

Sin, therefore, just means the seen, as opposed to invisible, ethics. Why the need for anyone to speak of predestination? A 22-year-old theologian in a play on words in one of Yvonne's light dozes mused about 'existenation': every existence-mimic is a moral-mimic: how is it possible not to notice? There was no idyllic or happy streak in this, on the contrary: the projection of the conscience into the body of objects does not signify relief but more rugged asceticism. In her room there was no furniture, only 'space hangers' and 'space traps' — among the silk clouds of comfort all that was left from her body was the unearthly memory of the voice of the previously sounding telephone: no environment & no person, only space-proofs, misprinted and not as yet proofread, and a few orphaned sentences between, a sort of celestial star monologue beyond the Milky Way. As a whole 'libertinage' *enables the discovery of the ethical face of the world: if anything goes, then the anthropomorphic face stuck on objects, making them ridiculous, peels off completely,' [but cognac bottles have to be dunked deeply into hot water for the paper label to be stripped off of them].*

Poor persons can somehow be 'morally virtuous,' Yvonne said to herself out of honorable democratic loyalty, but they cannot see or experience 'morality' as such, since it is spread in broad strata at exotic points of the world to which poor people never have the fare. And if they have, they can only see bits of the world; that is bourgeois morality: seeing only bits of a wide, exclusively moral world where entry is not permitted; what is not seen is considered a sin.

Prosperity is the pathological superabundance of divine providence in one place: there providence is so dense that whatever a person blessed and ruined by it may do, they will always keep traversing it like a moral torrent of the Danaë — they are soaked by it... Money is not the Devil's invention, but the flitting spore garden of 'eternal goodness' [is that how the Countess of Ségur puts it?].[41] *Should she cancel the ordered confectioner's snack that he had prepared for her? Good Lord! she had not even cancelled Geraldine!*

She looked at her watch: she might still be at home. Both time and the foreign woman friend were just aspects of her ambiguous moral mood: the watch was on her wrist and she was touched by that mundane comfort, feeling herself protected and secure forever. What was comfort? For one thing, free fall, falling wherever, ever-open possibility, thus dizziness, restlessness; for another, security, an 'Assicurazioni Generali' [42] *run wild in theology.*

What's her number? Where is the phone book? Here it is: this luck through comfort had already made her nauseous. "Hello! Is that you? I'm unspeakably, madly, madly ashamed. Why? I'll tell you straight away, but first I'll kick up a little phonetic Canossa [43] *and have myself showered with the spiritual stones of my own membrane-echo — nice, wasn't it, it took some doing, but there you have it — anyway: the wretched self-burnt forelock of conscience, the Atlantic collection of pressed flowers of grief — why do you interrupt me? I'm really offended that my style is not to your taste. Well then, try this,* Miss Matter-of-Fact: *I'm going to confession today, so you can stay at home. I'm going to confession! What is it you don't understand, you anticlerical demon? Seeing that I can't speak puritanese, I can't offer you any enlightenment. Apage Satanas.* [44] *Tomorrow afternoon I shall be at the Azaderos' place. Sure thing! Me precisely. Why me? Goodbye." Out of anger, she accidentally slammed down the receiver on its hook.*

Had she ever done anything in her life? She felt that her whole life, on the one hand, had been an epic dash; on the other, there had been no 'deeds' and 'events': the dream-like magic of remembering consisted particularly in enjoying the surges of the past, as if time were an ever-better acting drug that races toward the depths of ignorance, and she saw events separately as simple formulas, arithmetical representations, of rushing, with which she had nothing to do subjectively: time raced so much that all kinds of inner thickenings arose in it like in that set of vases which she had got the day before yesterday: the fictitious cuffs of velocity turning on-the-spot.

As a matter of fact, this universal dream-mood of time was a much more woeful woe than a woe that had arisen as a result of any special spiritual calisthenics, so the clear situation was that from childhood on she traced a big epicycloid around the circle of a non-existing [and, precisely on account of the absolute definiteness of the non-existence, magnetically attractive] sin: the two things held each other in balance, the certainty of the sin's impossibility holding in check the eternally epicycloidal pathway of woe. There was a time when she would have regarded herself as insane if she had felt anything like a 'contrition of goodness,' but now she felt that she was preparing for confession with a clear head, and her conscience hit upon a single possible handle: it is not goodness and evil that add up to ethics, but the great path of melancholy [time, melancholy, and woe are the naïve little aspect-amulets of a single entity] around the alluring nil of the perpetual 'deed-impossibility' or 'action-senselessness.'

The saints, she thought to herself — meanwhile gradually slipping the coverlet down from her stockings, which resembled bubbling champagne with the consistency of carbonic acid — balanced 10-centimeter 'deeds' with 50-centimeter 'sorrows' in the hair's-breadth contest of morality; I, by contrast, regret, or rather 'exist around,' with all time, space, and the eternal strangeness of existence, a deed that has been annihilated to nothing. She got up from the settee in order to set straight the white lilacs that had just been delivered for her. Which vase to put them in? She looked at the fireplace to check if there was a free one there. Standing on that were just long candles, doubled by a reflection in the mirror, as if they were standing around a bier. The color of the lilac was as if it were surrounded by ten frosted-glass globes and through those ten layers it was reached from outside by tinfoil light: starless intellect, dead illumination. She burst into tears: she was more than a saint, obviously. She thought about confession with particular pleasure as it represented a foreign incision in her new "ultra-sainthood constructed from the differential-equations of plane curves."

She reached for the telephone. "Come over, after all. No way have I yet gone for confession. All the same...")

When Touqué looked at his own sins, he then took that woodcut-face (he avoided mirrors, which would have painfully attested how distant his true face lay from that satirical crust of a mask), and the vocable fragment *'aet. suae'* would keep running nervously through him in his searchings of his conscience and the grandiosely grey sorrows of his wishes: because it was not the name that lodged in his brain, being written in insignificantly small letters into its frame, but the big Antiqua letters, which started straight away by the hair, each different, the initial 'A' spread its legs like an ungainly gatekeeper, the 'E' & 'T' following it were suddenly thinned as if type from another font had mistakenly ended up there, the 'E' of the 'Æ' diphthong was so unexpectedly scrawny as if it had withered away in a trice like an express-sick letter, whereas the 'A' blossomed in sunshine.

This crumpled typography (because it was evident that they were not stylized painted letters but, for all their disproportionateness, typescript) was the culmination of Munthausen's strictness, which was able to humiliate the Roman lettering that started with such military elegance into a grotesque procession of beggars. In any case, the broad initial letters and the subsequent pinched ones were reminiscent of the sick asymmetry of a palsied mouth; besides which in Touqué's head *'ætas'* had coalesced with *'æstas,'*[45] so that with Munthausen the concept of summer signified the bitterness of pessimism and the power of suppressed hatred consuming itself to the point of apoplexy.

third association concerning the glass walls of the fashion salon: illustration in a German magazine

That was how his memories intertwined when, with inquiring and astonished eyes, he sought out the beauty of his mother's new salon and, slightly freezing, hit upon the color of the windows of a provincial small-town hospital, the autumnal face of a life of grace, and the tropical & cold-sensitive flora of misgivings which vegetated behind it. The slightly piercing song about the 'new nudity' of drum skins, which are similar to parchment paper, was still ringing in his ears, & he tried again to compare them to known types of nudity. He was also concerned that he could only bring them into a relationship to nudes, whereas he knew straightway that he could not discover any paradoxical relationship between the bodies of French girls and the scroll nude that could be seen through the Cubo-firescreen: it could be that Jacqueline & crystalline-Cubism branched off from a stock on an infinite genealogical cluster, but that kind of remote possibility was of no interest. In all likelihood, pendant nudity had to be looked for somewhere further north, and a photograph seen in a German fashion magazine entered Touqué's mind.

It was printed on somewhat rough paper, the kind generally used for red-tinted copperplate pictures; indeed, the first and last pages were common or garden newsprint while the cover page resembled slippery, sticky silk. The photograph had been taken somewhere in Danzig[46] and portrayed a seaside nude. The woman was lying in the sand, with sharply shadowed parts of the body akin to a blasted sand dune, except the upper contours: the sun disheveled those, making them look like sparkling silver terry-cloth in the greyness of the background.

The woman was resting her head on one arm, holding a small flower in the other hand & looking at it with a dreamy smile.

Touqué was unable to perceive the figure in any other way than as the prole-mundane result of a cover with the feel of artificial silk and rough-waved sheets of newsprint: after all, decorative pictures are placed in such magazines so as that the turning of the page is already an organic part of the picture and the 'derivation' of the picture on page 2 & page 10 was completely different.

The difference here is not the serial number of the page, of course, but the rhythmic, one could almost say kinetic-art game of turning the page: two slim crumbling pages beleaguer the portraits at the head like a long veil which hitherto had danced freely around a ballerina who is producing a nest on her ankle but now subsides like a dozing horizon, & after it a studio-glitter grey portrait stands before us like the mirror-mute surface of a lake behind the very broad rings made by two half-quivering waves — while, for instance, the motion-color of much turning of pages masks the features of a picture on the inside of a magazine: the hand has long ceased the ceremonial slowness that accompanied the very first pages with the question-mark bridges it had laid down, with the picture appearing among the bushes of a landscape that is zigzag to the touch like an unexpectedly interpolated vision: we await the pictures at the very front so much that when they do appear, they are in fact born from the Venus-wombed shell of expectation — while with the impatient flood-tide of subsequent page-turning from the opposite direction come pictures that induce one to halt, and the hush which looking demands does not follow from the style of page-turning but is the addition of an unfamiliar tonality.

There are two kinds of miracle technology: with one the milieu itself hovers in front of us in magical stillness, in airily gently rocking encumbrance, & should the least puff of breeze run over it, then the miracle is immediately evident, the entire landscape immediately becomes apparition-faced; with the other, the miracle is preceded by all sorts of tiny dramatic twists and complex stories, and when the agitation is at a pinnacle, the miracle appears from an unknown region of the world: the latter is what applies to the pictures that were to be found inside the magazine, hence to that nude in Danzig.

Touqué was unable to cut the body free from the vulgar curtains of newsprint that serially concealed it, & he sensed there was an internal connection between woman and paper prologue: as if, deep down, Eros had sprung from her proletarian roots. There is a nakedness that does not seek to be a ninepin of erotic myths, which avoids the 'dimpled'-immorality of idylls, indeed, which also stands far from the old Baroque conventions of naturalism and only creates an impression of misery, lack of clothes as abject poverty. The plein-air that surrounds it is not the anonymous world of nature but the meadows directly after the suburbs, with scrawny saplings, weekend sandlots, bus & tram stops from which "one can reach the heart of the city in 20–25 minutes." There is the odd store of building materials here & there, with cement-dusted planks and stacks of bricks: in the photo one gets a sense of the mannered tedium of that milieu.

Nature is not simply the antithesis of the 'metropolis' but a foreign material which propagates from the inside outwards, & it can also permeate the metropolis's so-called asphalt jungle (the way that in old physics textbooks the ether pervades every kind of foreign matter), but it may also be lacking completely from romantic tracts: 'nature' is never the primitively formulable antithesis of the city.

The woman's skin resembled house walls injected with mortar, and it likewise seemed to offer an example to the taste that seeks to transform Protestant simplicity into the classicism of proletarian poverty; indeed, to identify every kind of logical clarity with defiant & demonstrative poverty. Thus a Socialist-Dorian style evolved that conceived of poverty as being an intellectual fact: not as a social accident, but one of the perennial constituents of the human soul. And indeed, they construct a concept and style of destitution that have nothing to do with actual poverty, and even luxury villas may be furnished in that kind of proletarian taste so that pomp and suburbs are equally perceptible in applied-art forms.

The woman reclining in the photograph was also filled with this tragicomedy: the lazy but helpless desire seemed to be a social gesture, and it strove to fuse the concepts of eroticism and poverty into theatrical identity. "There is nothing else, only my body": some such cold civil-law formula was the first consequence of that nude. One would have looked to her in vain for the old softness of *perdita*-sentimentality;[47] instead of that one found a statistical arrogance in which body, sin, love, were a fateful industry, a tragic handicraft.

Sin here is part and parcel of love, like a hammer to a worker: a simple, even clean instrument, not in the Russian sense of the word, but in a raw industrial sense. Sin therefore coincides with the old idea of 'sanctified work': it may be the same action which characterized the first Puritan traders sailing toward lay morality and which lives on in this frigid love.

We are therefore confronted with a fine Germanic complex: Hanseatic-Doric *Kontor* castles, *Institutiones Religionis Christianæ*, predestination the homosexuality, puritanical moral hysteria & melancholy 'petty bourgeoisie,' a coalescence of the whole so-called Mediterranean rational purity with the economic nudity of German destitution, the coincidence of the struggling tempo of the narcosis of eroticism with the bleak 'uprightness' of the first Reformed-Church trade guilds, etc.[48] (All these caricature concepts remained in Touqué's memory from a sketch that *Europe Hypochondre* of Nice once brought out as a feuilleton under the title *Gediegene Gomorrha: une hypothèse allemande,*[49] which dealt with a young woman from Frankfurt who in her most extreme sexual 'tics' was following the rigorism of bourgeois morality that emanated from portraits of her merchant grandfather and grandmother, but when she became aware of that, spread the notion of the lower middle class into such a dark mythology that what up till then had been the normal orderliness of sin, its official routine, had ceased to exist, and thus it was being lost in the esthetic hopelessness of dilettantism and guilty conscience.

Hence, when he was scrutinizing the new walls as he walked around the *Perroquet Galant,* the memory of that short story and that photograph also blended into the sour associations. In the early days they were what was dominant for him, and even though they were decidedly unpleasant, he knew that it was just a matter of time (nothing else), that the glass walls would become symbols not of pessimistic but of joyful things: just as fruits came of flowers, a grey association is transformed into a resplendent one by the same pleasant mechanism.

Cannes at dawn.
The philosophical chemistry of time & quiet on the houses

Once, quite soon after daybreak, he had to run down into the new salon to bring a box of odds and ends of clothes into the old place where one of the old ladies was accustomed to working at that time in the morning. The whole shore was still grey from the severe anemia of the night: the hills were just lilac, like evening clouds fallen from the body of the day in which a little of the colors of fire were still flowing, but slowly seasoned time was already padding them out with ashes; the gardens were also patina sponges on which the quiet did not seem to be a lack of sound but a plastic supplement: palms suspended in muteness, flower clocks, loungers forgotten on balconies, white wrought-iron chairs gathered together on the promenade gained new form from being steeped in the alkaline bath of stillness for a night: as if they had lost their spatial dimensions and were only swimming like thin pencil outlines in the looming morning. Only the first stray sounds will unroll the trunks of the palm trees anew from the planimetric spell to which they had been submitted.

Sometimes of an evening a big pile of debris would be put on a sieve so that during the night the moisture in it, which would very slowly ooze through, would trickle into the tub underneath: in the morning the strikingly large mass of water in the basin, which would give concrete length to yesterday night, would always be a delightful surprise: that morning prospect itself looked as if it had percolated down from yesterday's jumbled rubble & glittered in transparent cleanness like a crystalline 'infusion' in the saucer under the summer-breezy apse of horizon of the strainer.

In the cold silver tea of the matutinal air there was something intoxicating for Touqué (he relished the feminine uselessness of the very expression 'silver tea' like a stolen & forbidden cigarette): as if the city dunked in the silence (like the vibrating flower petals which, after having been dipped in mineral founts and withdrawn, have stiffened into porcelain) were a big cover by virtue of which it made clear that the whole of life is an unserious game, walls have no thickness, palm trees no credence, streets and shops no reality; silence has made a masquerade out of everything, made everything smaller, brought them closer to each other.

Our daytime life passes off, basically, in a strict classical style; that is to say, we always have dealings with people, we think of them, calculate with them, meanwhile the lifeless milieu reduces into conventional background spots — that is, assuming we do not humanize it out of its original role. In the morning, though, where there is not a soul abroad in the streets, no "proper study of man": everything is like a thronged panorama rising out of the waves after a flood has retreated, or a glittering & coquettish Pompeii, cleaned of the clods of earth and muddy lumps of excavation work. Only then does one see how much more the 'outside world' that exists is, how astonishingly guaranteed it is, in a quantitative sense — much more than one had imagined yesterday.

By lacking people, the entire city creates the impression of a great negative relief: gardens suddenly sink into vertiginous & clear concavity; the streets over which slim sport cars usually dash around like goldfish are like cavernous boxes out of which a convex object has been lifted — or had the whole body of Cannes become a symbolic bed that still preserved on its sunken pillows and troughed sheet the untimely forms of the people who made their escape from it? Touqué would have liked to reach into all such niches that hitherto had been filled with people — in order to enjoy the city's abrupt porosity, the draughty grill of the at last unblocked milieu gutter.

How unimportant, comical even, the signs on shops are, & every burgher of Cannes would find them just as comical now if they were to stroll alone along the streets, but since they wake up at one and the same time and all at once stroll on the streets in their thousands, the crowd fosters the illusion that these are 'important' things, that this is 'life,' & all that ought to be continued. A city's mute stiffening is much more grotesque, and thus more appropriate for religious contemplation, than its collapse: freezing one hug in an eternal gesture would be more deadly than severing it. But he threw away that trivial thought of immobility practically before he was born as being not born of thought but only the rebounding wreckage of the most primitive religious meditation (i.e., the meditation was primitive, not the religion).

Another such reflex movement of his was to identify the experience of 'truth' with that of 'ontological farce,' & he sniffed in the ancestral myths of logic after a comical Muse as a starting point. He felt that both attitudes were childish alibis, both the raw moralizing & the 'marble-logic,' as he disparagingly called his second, pushy behavior.

church façade

He looked at the church façade, eyes brimming with tears of happiness. Pre-eminent things are denoted by Latin peoples with the attributive '*importans*' — those walls did, indeed, take something upon themselves as if the lack of man were their main staple, like water to plants. In certain rooms one can see a veronica on which an image of Christ's head is painted in deep brown in such a way that if one stares at it, the head will appear to be casting a glance toward the viewer: Touqué felt something of that kind in relationship to the early-morning church. As if an inner wave ran through every column, statue, & stone wreath; mystic breathing, which he had not noticed until then (the 'breathing,' of course, was only the rigidity of the church wall, no more than the expired fiction of the sensory organs behind which the precise arithmetical picture of the reality of mendacious statics (viz. an irregular helix) lives its impertinent course: the deeper the stillness presses the poetic calumnies of stiffness into the narrow stork's beak-shaped vase of the senses, the more Touqué's incorruptible imagination sensed the church's façade as a conch parturition held together by a procession of a thousand paragraphs streaming into each other).

He was skulking quite close to a small relief and was examining the stone's lifelike grass growing or the movements of a mimicry-fish, of which one cannot be sure for certain whether it is a scale or a moth worn away into lead. By day, starting from the human, he always arrived at the stone, but now he looked at the statue from the stone's point of view, and thus its human form was just the most ultimate vague borderline thought with which the aristocratic raw stone had nothing to do.

Just as people are used to being psychoanalyzed, he wished to unmask the smiling figure of the relief down to its ancestral center, the dawn still seeming to offer the most appropriate medical instrument to that end. He put his eyes close to the statue's eyes and tried to imagine the ovally-formed stone details were non-eyes, so that the anthropomorphic form of the eyes was just a feeble disguise, thin as a hair's breadth, on the stone's surface; but the moment he slightly distanced the head, it immediately took on the appearance of human perfection with exaggerated power. Because silence has an enormous strength, much like a huge wind, pinning one to the first resisting wall, or like water, plunging one straight away into the first underpass: Touqué himself felt from one minute to the next that fatalistic urge to penetrate, which must resemble the minutes preceding suffocation.

He was unable to stand in the middle of a street, was constantly having to rush to some object or other in order to stroke it with interrogative-shaped fingers or to smuggle his nose, like a mediocre fake, to the place of the nose of the royal figure slipping out at least for a moment from the relief. The dawn quiet does not tolerate, so it seems, any sort of bungling dualism and sought to fuse Touqué into itself: he was ashamed of himself, just like when he attended a social gathering for the first time — here everyone was either a caryatid or a canal or a window shutter left open, according to the rules of etiquette — he alone was in human dress.

mass & silhouette

He therefore stood face to face with materials on which the energies of millennia, indeed hundreds of thousands of years, had worked: that thought was accompanied by the assumption that in the extraordinary complexity of matter the 'transforming' human will, as it is now customary to put it, would become visible. He stroked the statue, ran a finger along the net of the wire fence, ran his eyes ladder-like, like a monkey, over the meager housing's elongated windows, which seemed as if they were reflected on the necks of flasks, and he felt that anyone possessing only minimally different biological and historical eyes than us would no longer be able to tell the difference between the totality of Cannes' 'refinements' and the wild flowers and minerals of the surrounding landscape. Thus, an infinitesimally small fault in the eye would see the façade of the Regina Hotel turning white from the milky kiss of dawn, the rocks of the nearby shore, & the early, bearded waves similar to blurred portraits of lions, as a coherent, unbroken landscape.

He could not free himself of the impish thought to look at hotels and churches dipped into bottles of the spirit of silence as almost a 'spot check' of civilization. Up until then, during the daytime in the 'study of man' season, he had seen buildings through a human prism, so that his psychological shades, indeed his anatomical complications, were all flung onto buildings & streets in the way that pictures on a glass plate, on being projected, click into place on a film screen and fill it. In that way we imagine the houses as being just as complex in their internal architecture as ourselves, the same chaotic network of capillaries, the dark Styx-games of blood pressure; we conduct our amatory paradoxes and our disturbances of social balance into the seats and wallpapers and by day we genuinely have the impression that they are very good conductors from that point of view.

In the morning, though, we experience the reverse: a complete absence of the complexity of matter. The civilization that had 'completely transformed' it in fact hardly touched it, or, rather, what we imagined to be civilization in and on the lifeless body of matter was no more than a shadow of our spiritual & physical life that fell on it, & therefore, in point of fact, our one-day life was older than suspect civilization with its 'transforming' thousand years. Is our sensitivity the first-born, and civilization just a perennial suckling babe? Do we little mayflies bestow from our ephemeral life the illusion of a 'hundred-thousand-year metamorphosis' on lazy matter day after day, again and again?

When Touqué looked around the small square, on a side street of which the old, ransacked *Perroquet Galant* stood, he felt a single one of its short yesterdays was a historical past, with separate geological phases & stylistic epochs spiced with foundations of religions, whereas on the neighboring houses he felt practically only a few minutes older-being vis-à-vis the untended hillside. In the middle of the day a person could come and go in the organized basin of midday like someone who, on the mystic heights of the peak of hundreds of thousands of years, enjoys the *ne plus ultra* of refinement, while his human present time was just a lucky parvenudom; in the morning, then, a drastic switch of roles takes place insofar as the houses become parvenus, whereas in a single split second a man stretches the dilated channel of one's old age.

In short, by day we place the 'past' in the environment and we take on the role of the present, whereas at sunrise, all at once, we become the overfilled amphoræ of the past, & the environment assumes the microscopically slender role of the present.

The dramatic piquancy of every daybreak lies in this change of roles. The organism of the houses is not complicated: a bit of mortar (where it has become worn one can see the bricks) and after that some wallpaper. Touqué's eyes jumped between these couple of layers as if he were leafing through a book that he had thought was two hundred pages long and only noticed, to his great amazement, that someone had ripped 197 pages out of it. Here time did not have a parallel chemistry. The parts in every building have fallen apart: here a bit of a window frame, there a glass griddle cake that was totally alien, after them bricks that have not come into any biological relationship with the former objects; nothing but jolting foreignness, without the imagined capillary veins of transition. But did civilization nonetheless have an effect, with those melodramatic millennia nonetheless being shifted somewhere?

Did the historical work of a million people consist solely of making naïve ground plans (including the greatest masterpieces of the Baroque), naïve statues, and complication-free machines like that? Because he saw everything relative to the spiritual turmoil closed within himself as such. The main beauty of art, he now thought, was in representing precisely those transitional subtleties that one would look for in vain in material, imagined to be refined by the passing of time. In one picture Adam & the tree, Eve & the snake, the apple & God, represented a biological vicious circle; they were transitions from one toward the other. (Touqué found all that to be so relative to reality, but of course when he looked at art emancipated from reality then he saw the same primitiveness, stiff simplicity, as he did this morning in the real outside world.)

If the passage of time did not create physical complexity; if materials preserved their primitive clumsiness and crudeness so highly (that if architecture did not become a thousand-premised flowering; that unification did not come out of the juxtaposition through a million-fold shades; that angels beating humans by a nose length did not come out of puppets), then maybe the energies deposited on material ought to have become a 'spiritual' surplus in the course of development, and sniffing anew he examined the alphabet of the high roofs of the houses lining up in the blue of morning.

There was nothing to search for in their interiors: as matter is, indeed, composed of billions of electrons, be it invisibly, so Touqué imagined the visible body of matter with some species of decorative logic as an opalescing ray through the continual influence of 'civilization.' If civilization did not transform material inwardly, then it was external, on the surface of the surface. Thus, auroral Cannes would unite the most naïve era of handicraft (homogeneous, 'uncivilizable'-material) and, like a conceptual fata morgana, the system of independently hovering contours (of course, by contour he would have liked to mean something non-architectural). It was then that the silhouette first appeared to him (he liked to call it a 'French national vision') as the vehicle of civilization. There is a current that runs so intensely through a conductor that it is always situated on the surface, almost seeking to leave the conducting material far behind, & in that way it holds only the minimum of which is needed for its running: the intensity of civilization prevailed in similar form on the houses, statues, grids & barricades of closed chairs.

---

women's dress salon, seamstresses

In his hands was the bandbox in which lay the desired, essentially fully ready dress, on which, prior to being sent home, some last-minute change had needed to be made, as the owner-to-be, panting and chirping, had sent word by telephone after midnight. Touqué was fond of listening in the workshop to the excited telephone calls of customers as they sought to reassure themselves or hastily came out with new notions, or declared that there was a veil they thought they would find a piece of but, sadly, there wasn't even an inch, or sometimes they inquired about a handbag that, as memory served them, they had forgotten in the workshop: at times like that Touqué could audibly sense every pallidly trilling heartbeat of the woman's agitation, the incandescent and querulous phase changes of uncertainty, his eyes in the meantime resting on the glittering, strange, ownerless clutch purse, which by its own provocative *fait accompli* stood out sharply among the half-tailored silks, unstrung mistletœ, and tacking-tailed lining torsos — for a few seconds he gloated in the receiver over the imploring of the bird that had fallen into the trap as, in its vibrating, screeching voice, it hopped here & there in the telephone's little night, then slowly, later in detail, told the woman that the handbag was there; he set his eyes on the purse and, at first in generalities, later in detail, described it so that there could be no misunderstanding — he felt how those individualizing details lit up like colored stars in the darkness of the telephone, how, after every detail, the woman's voice calmed down into a harmonious cheeping until finally the telephone's blindness was swimming in the light of the handbag, & at that the bird, with a grateful farewell & a click of the receiver, flew off for ever.

He was never able to free himself of the intrusion of that analogy: the half-ready dress; the seamstresses, whose hair tumbled onto the fashionable materials, bending over the needles; the aristocratic, nay, theological skin (*peau d'ange?*)[50] that they cut with clumsy, rusty scissors, the handles of which were supposedly formed to fit the hand but rather sat in the girls' thin hands like the broad hand guard of an old-fashioned cavalry sword;

the colors that flowed left and right from under the sewing machine's sputtering weapon as if it were a telegraphic set that immediately translated the whirring Morse stabs of the country of colors into big color waves; the fashion magazines, left open and creased all over; the Euclidean dress-pattern diagrams on cardboard paper sheets resembling sackcloth: all that gave the impression of a crowded small garden with blooming flowers and withering leaves, foliage, and nymphs, to which the telephone served the birds' light transcendentalism as a garnish, not so much with its sugary and choked purring in the stifling air of the workshop, like bubbles of carbon dioxide gliding to the top of champagne, but by virtue of the little messages streaming into the business from the telephone, each of which united the airy outlines of another female sound portrait with one of the materials lying in the workshop: one of the girls stood with the telephone, a second worked in her lap on the telephoning owner's dress, and the two of them shuffled around with whichever message they happened to receive there and then. After the message had been passed over the telephone, a portrait of the customer would continue to hover over the material, and with her indecisive personality, would meddle in the strict craftsmanship of the tailoring: the workshop was full of the transparent butterflies and birds of the telephone messages, which cheeped around, making the atmosphere noisy & idyllically nervous.

Sometimes she would melancholically contemplate a stooping seamstress as with her enhanced vermillion face and spectacles from fifty years ago she tinkered away on a glistening piece of silk, while above the naked nape of the neck, which would be horizontal, one could almost see a little bee, which, with its buzzing tyranny, was holding the girl captive & looking at the tacks, now from the height of the ceiling, now alighting directly on a finger.

Who knows what such a small experimental garden can be used for, where the idea of 'human' was present with such tropical maturity, and yet would only be assembled from inhuman masks and the pasteurized spiritual life of the telephone. This labyrinth of torsos, this hanging hypothesis garden of Venus, also gave love a new flavor by seeing only artificial forms and perverse abstract samples on which women wasted only their filtered vocal ladder rather than their bodies during preparation: what a strange alteration every body thought went through in the big white triangles, giant lilac buttons, and the deadly diagrams of the color telegrapher.

How many times had he stolen into the workshop among the half-ready costumes & evening gowns late at night or at sunrise: as they lay there he had the impression that five or ten women had undressed hastily in a narrow little cloakroom and were taking a midnight bath somewhere nearby in the glass-roofed basin of a winter garden that was perhaps illuminated from below; then he again imagined the reality, the concrete future of the dress, the odd role that it would play along with the woman's figure; he experimented with the idea that he paired every dress with a shameless thought, so that when the customer put it on as entirely new, a novella had long been woven into the dress: every adolescent boy always did that exactly the same way.

---

dehumanizing lifestyle & modern ladies' tailoring

He opened the rose-colored tin slightly, in the upper corner of which the minute picture of a colored parrot was embossed like an Egyptian crest: it was a large, yellow coat with a collar of brown leather and with buttons blown up like rubber spheres almost the size of ninepin balls. "That, too, is an idea," he thought to himself, smiling, & he lifted the coat a little: the fabric was much lighter than he had supposed, he almost had a sense of gripping a freshly cropped and as yet unprocessed sheepskin; but the leather collar was conspicuously heavy.

At first, he thought that he had opened a grave in which the long coat was lying like a skeleton, and he immediately tried to connect these Minkowski-forms to a female body.[51]

How different dresses were in reality than how he had dreamed of them in childhood after the coverings of Greek nude statues: there the dress grew out of the body or adhered to it without its becoming an independent system; it was almost an imprint of the imagined embraces of an adolescent love desire: the tailoring took shape from the caresses, the belt from clasping the hip, the buttons and jewels from the bashful-pushy pawings of pubertal doubt — those were always emanations of the nude figure, beginning with the Eve costume to that peculiar décolletage of rococo dames that extended precisely to the nipples yet all the same allowed a view of a smooth slope, an incredibly long, sloping plane, from which it was impossible to imagine any spherical tendency, just as from the slope of a thickly snow-covered roof of a Swiss chalet it is impossible to imagine that in point of fact it is a detail of an Easter egg's ellipse or a section of some horn, with such bravura asymmetry were they able to separate the upper and lower hemispheres of their breasts: outside the dress was a single long and smooth plateau of powder, whereas under the dress was a ludicrously small nipple pedestal: from that Touqué always understood the ancient language of love.

In his dreams there were dresses which, from a certain point of view, were similar to the structure of suits of armor insofar as every body part was given a separate reliquary, and an interconnection of these ornamental sheaths yielded the dress:

special goblet creations for the bosoms, special collar rings for the neck as if it were utilizing the motifs of a column-plinth or a gigantic tile to preserve the neck bone relic of a martyr that had remained intact; the lower limbs were surrounded by leg tubes, the feet by glove-shaped monstrance shoes.

On the other hand, there were masses of stylized dresses, which, in contrast to the previous embalming style, sprang from an anatomy-free mixture of flower motifs and lines of motion, similar to those ornaments that could be seen on furniture, silver paraphernalia, and buildings around 1900: fluttering veils, swimming mud streaks, bands, eel clouds & ultra-mermaids whose hips ended in a languid oceanic tail, which then coils five times round whole fruit bowls, like a hawser, the strands of which happen to be fraying because someone untwisted it in the opposite direction to the twisting; their hair was a giant periwig that had fallen into the water, on which the dissolving form of a knot of hair was still recognizable, but otherwise the long braids spread to all points of the compass like the flame flickering on an infinite candlewick.

It was those two styles that the erotic imagination by and large hit upon in the field of sculpture: either tunics streaming like sea waves, which preserve what is more just a 'spiritual' image of desire, or else an anatomical reliquary, which already pigeonholes the minute joys of possession side by side as dresses. Those dresses that had been prepared in his mother's business, however, were not male-centered in that way. Touqué at first did not even understand why people talked so much about how "women's main ambition is to please men," when he noticed that there was no hint of that in the way they dressed. He saw that when customers discussed matters with the seamstresses how abstractly they would dispute the choice of each tailoring pattern, in which act the desire to please seemed to hover at such an infinite distance that it could safely be ignored.

Women's dresses are not for men, but some unknown female end-in-itself, at the bottom of which can be found a female notion that, at its root, is incommensurate to a man's concept of women. What could an image of woman be without the fateful factor of desire playing a part in it? For a while he was under the illusion that those dresses betrayed something of that as they resembled neither dresses from the anatomical drawer nor petal negligees but had their own geometry. But 'geometry' had already long been suspect: he saw the primitive instincts of life and not the uplifting ornamentation of cleanness.

What he now took pleasure in was rather what he felt in front of the morning-time houses of Cannes: a minimal-prayer, a first intoxicated inspiration of the cult of allusion. What an extraordinary value a 'silhouette' has if it contains everything that civilization has achieved for itself, just as the almost microscopic slivers of diamonds that have been successfully produced with the aid of horrendous electric energies.

Orchids are cultivated into miracles through long years of being taken good care of, propagating them, grafting them, and chemicalizing them, in order that, at the end of an artificially over-aristocratized greenhouse genealogy, after chemical changes of fortune of perverse family complications, there should appear a few everted petals: a couple of little brooms of toothbrushes sybaritized into silk, geodetic frou-frous of a glass saucer's handle, two red copper wires, which tilt forth from the skinless ovary in wild-grape beat, and underneath all that a miniature but all the same clumsy goat's udder, which is patchy, like an English joke dog — that is the outcome. Touqué enjoyed that idiosyncratic balance between precise, ceaseless work and apparently decadent result. After all, at the end of development there could have been a flower that resembles certain neon signs on which, around a latent nucleus, the colors are continually bursting, blacking out, then shrieking off and getting entangled again, even the slimmest connecting thread being concretized forthwith, even the most evanescent stab at an artistic structure immediately receiving material realization; in short, the totality of logical variants at once become identical to precise chemical variations.

relationship of matter & human spirit on the basis of the picture of Cannes at daybreak: a little anti-Hegelian game

But in the real world, so it seems, it is not like that. Idea, intellectual work compressed into matter, or even 'substance' itself, is radically shallow, Don Juan-like phenomena, which touch matter only occasionally, at unpredictable intervals, and thus do not induce a chemical change, only have a minimal superficial wrinkle, a fleeting vibration of a profile: they are like a bird of paradise made from a single hydrogen feather, which, with the majestic curve of a female arrow, only accompanies the course of a quiet river — it may be constantly mirrored in it, but only quite rarely does it brush it with its wings, and all the less does it dip its fan body among the waves.

One is involuntarily inclined to grasp the progress of civilization as the work of several hundred thousands of years: as if during development 'substance' were displaying slave labor to mold the face of the world, which in every cell is alien to its own and, for that reason, would complete goldsmithing work and miniature painting, though in fact it has nothing to do with those kinds of 'work.' The situation is rather one of 'flirt-Hegelianism': this whole historical '*Ur-substanz*'-menstruation[52] is similar to a modern love novella, far from any ritual seriousness. The work may, perhaps, exist, and people may possibly hammer the material, but the work is unable to penetrate it like a greedy X-ray; at best it can only spin around it and turn into individual perfume.

That 'substance' was not a swelling inner artery of material, merely a wave of scent that occasionally drifted toward it by mistake, & thus was accounted for perfectly clearly by the yellow woman's coat in Touqué's hands, from which it was evident that it was not a female sprig that had come into being through a female tree branch but a piece of cloth that had been seesawing on the wings of stray breezes and, quite by chance, got caught on a nude figure that had come into its path, but the next moment it would fly on freely, and it would scatter over unknown islands the barely-forms of women that it had adopted for half a minute. How much careful measuring had been done on it, planning, modifications, criticizing & then re-workings, until in the end there seemed to be just a momentary meeting between the female body as-it-was-in-reality and its 'substance,' living in 'extragalactic isolation.'

The tight connection of substance and object does not assert itself in similarity, not in the thing being a miniature portrait, the substance — a Cubist version of the same picture (that is, at most, a methodological matter of instruction in drawing, and not a matter of meditation), but rather the opposite, in the repulsive force of their otherness, because only through maximal difference can they be homogeneous, in the same way as only mutually repulsive currents can be equally positive or equally negative. The homogeneity corresponds to the fact that one of them is the object and the other is the substance of the same thing; the dynamic juncture of repulsion, on the other hand, corresponds to, let's say, an optical relationship, namely, absolute heteromorphism, being simply the visual difference of an adynamic repulsion. To start with he saw the 'essence' in the silhouette, where the minimum of matter and the minimum of essence coincided, but now this had also switched into a paroxysm of that airiness, when he saw the intensification of 'spiritualizing' (here this is, of course, more a spatiophysical than a moral concept), the next step as: to be wildly different in comparison to the object.

the three relations of substance & day-to-day reality: close kinship, barely touching, absolute otherness

As a matter of fact, he ran through a scale of three: the first step was the 'truth' grade, at which object and its essence were together like the Laocoon Group, where the extremities of the suffering and strangled man are the serpents that squeeze him to death: the state of identity poisoning.

The second step, when the 'substance' is merely reflected on the object and sometimes brushes it: the object endeavors to work its essence out of itself, but in the end it gets no more than a coquettish tongue lashing from its essence: the essence does not infiltrate the pores of the object like bacilli, that would push it into a deadly 'substancitis,' but nibble a bit of it here & there, or keep dropping in strange little puzzle case-endings.

Finally, the third step, a logical culmination of 'identity': in other words, the alterity grade: when the essence is still not airy enough, even in momentary silhouette shape it is still an excessive mimicry of the object, then it hatches out of the empty space of immateriality like a foreign lining that appears on turning a glove inside out (the birth of Venus emerging from the sea is in point of fact a similar kind of lining-disclosure: the reverse of the blind sea being brought to public attention), a second-degree nothing hatching from a first-degree nothing that humiliates the first as a crude 'something'; otherness, which is alone capable of completely meeting the requirements of 'spirituality' (geometry, not ethos), of absurd ethereality; the least common point between object & substance induces thickening, & thus an exacerbation, which cannot happen with the therapy of otherness: if the essence of a woman is a white shoehorn, then the two will never coincide.

He felt that was essentially psychology-free, and moreover French, so he would be able to write a possible local philosophy of French art. Though as yet without the clarified triple scale, he had already experimented with such ideas in an essay produced for *Antipsyche*, but as yet unpublished, under the title "Truth Sentiments as Traps for the Psyche," in which he analyzed above all the first stage, when he suddenly had to learn a direct-turn ski stop on an artificial slope of 'truth.' He had already encountered such a form of differentness of substance that could better illuminate not so much the psychology (that being fashionable) as the logic of Don Juanism (Juanus Logicus?).

---

added to this a new example of dawn from Touqué's life: Jacqueliné's waking up in the hotel room

---

It happened that in Cannes, at the end of the season, indeed virtually after the season, that he made the acquaintance of a woman who, now that the season was over, was willing to breathe in a couple of hazy smudges from the self-serving motifs of love onto the lustrous page of his materialism. Touqué saw how much the girl's manner changed toward the end of the season, how much more she was 'not pressed for time' (because with that type of woman 'not being in a hurry' expresses the maximum of which they are capable emotionally, as if mere time were the opposite of the life and 'love' that they were pursuing), and he looked ahead to the day when he could show up at her place. She had tiny grey eyes, like little berries grey with immaturity, with thin, chalky eyebrows; the paint on her lips was like the color of the petals of certain flowers: near to the stem it is dense and sharp, but it turns pale toward the more distal part of the perianth, like writing when the ink starts to rub out on the pen. She had originally been brunette, but broad bands of dye that were starting to fade snaked in like the lavish space-fever of certain minerals. (This insignificant professional portrait only makes sense here, of course, in order to be able to later differentiate it from another.)

They dined together on a mid-May evening & the woman was still sleeping at seven in the morning when Touqué awoke. The room was in pearl-grey shade, & through the glass of the window, the iron rods of the balcony grill looked like blue flower stems in the fog, the curtain quietly rocking like a hung-out net in which the sea had got caught up as prey, like an indigo-leafed poster lotus, and hills, skew palms in a jumble on the slopes like hairpins pinned in disarray and ready to drop out at any moment. Clouds were dangling from the branches of the sky like laburnum in the spring from bald twigs. A couple of automobile toots could be heard from afar: well-meaning but hesitant injections to awaken a paralyzed sense of space. (The like-like-like determinants of analogies were already running around, bathed & combed, when reality was still stretching with closed eyes in her slothful bed.)

— Are you asleep? — Touqué asked her, with a somewhat awkward smile, because every morning he forgot those mimicking tricks which were indispensable in life but of which he was never spontaneously capable. The girl did not reply or even stir. — Then sleep on — he said, & pressed a kiss between her pushed-up shoulder & her neck, inwardly curved like a saddle, or rather his lips did not even reach the girl's skin only her head was very much cut out for that helmet. The coverlet lay wrinkled and wrung-out on the bed; it was evident that she had never put the whole thing in order but always unconsciously plucked at a piece lying in direct proximity to her fingers, so that one half of it was freely hanging beside the bed down to the floor, like a sail jogged into dejection, the other half was twisted around her waist like a turban.

The mirror over the hand basin was crooked, and in it Touqué saw the woman in an entirely unfamiliar perspective, as if she were dangling down from the coverlet like a suspended relief, the background to which was the morning table of light that had been pushed in from the window: the real light tottering in, in a faded forget-me-not color, burned like a gleaming plate in the mirror. He felt sorry for the housemaid who had taken such pains to make up the bed with fresh linen with the prescribed precision, and he pondered why women crumpled the blankets and pillows so maniacally. Jacqueline (let us call her that) looked like the victim of a catastrophe: limbs flung all over the place, the pillow, like a detached block of ice or spent avalanche, was not so much under her head as in her forehead, so that her picture in the crooked mirror looked more like a scientific photograph taken for police purposes, or for a picture magazine. Greyness had deeply penetrated everything: her lips and hair were, in line with the fashion of the day, grey summer fabrics with a blue cravat to go with them, thus exposing the slumbering embers inside the grey color, and Touqué felt that he was lying beside the woman like a discarded waistcoat that she had been too lazy to put on a coat hanger the previous evening.

He looked at the clock on the night table and with unexpected determination saw on its dial that it was 6:35; that number was a cause of extraordinary joy, as if that small positive fact could have fitted the whole of last night's adventure into the story of his life: the whole game had fluctuated back and forth on the tonogenic steps of the night like a *praesens*-polyp in which minutes and hours are only the sort of rubber branches that do indeed wind all around in the pleonastic water of the night but then find their way back into themselves anew.[53] Now, however, that floral ball will nicely straighten up into a single thread and it will come to a halt on that mile spike of 6:55. The small ticking clock was like a pocket altar in which, on the example of the Roman Penates, the house's private time is present like a device for counting the chapters of a miniature history. What was the last thing? Jacqueline was half asleep; he had taken a glass of cognac to bed and tried to force it into her mouth; the glass had dropped and he had remarked that she should immediately put on her slippers in the morning and not go around barefoot because the splinters might wound her. Then he, too, had lain down and fallen asleep.

But the thing could not be continued anyway. For a start it was 6:55. Would that be a continuation of the cognac fiasco? Was that narrow, whitish ticking the end of that wide-ranging fooling about? He threw off the coverlet, got up, hit his head on the bell & with cautious steps sought the traces of the smashed glass like scattered petals of a mercury flower. The larger pieces, in which one could still feel that they were parts of a spherical form, he threw away into the waste paper basket. The glass resembled the coverlet, a memento of a little idyllic vandalism. Oh, fine matinée soup: this grey lake in the depths of which yesterday's kisses lie like golden-ribbed & purple-bodied triremes in a melodramatic maritime museum — the oars had become coral stems, the wave-moustachioed prow a seaweed monastery: and all that can barely be seen as everything is still shrouded in the semi-transparent, semi-linenizing greyness of dawn, & on top of the lake are swimming the few broken pieces of glass & time, which, so it seems, had trickled on during the embrace like a water tap that someone had forgotten to turn off in the evening.

He looked out through the window: the hotel was on the hillside so that a few house roofs and towers and the May oakum of gangling trees clambered under the window like the branches of a chandelier, the upper ends of which are straight like stuffed bodyguards but lower down all at once take a big curve in order to be able to run their curving roots in good time toward the shared pillar. The streets were dark-blue wells; the roofs were as if they were perukes independent of the houses that the light washed into itself while the walls got soaked in the vitriolic gloom. 'History' and 'its object' fell apart in this grey morning dividing water: yesterday's kisses were legends that may still be salvaged in metaphors, but instead of them there is time, the broken glass, and a landscape, which fall over from the high-frequency spring chaos of the past as strange flowers.

He looked back at Jacqueline sleeping, who meanwhile had turned in bed and showed the tattooing of deep wrinkles on her face that until then had not been visible. "Happening is shed from you, too, like a sloughed mask, & you sprout from it like a tempero-virginal piece of flesh: all told, sleep is for the purpose that the severance should not be drastic." Unfaithfulness starts with the same woman being attractive in the morning, too: no doubt she appeals because she is 'fresh,' not a continuation but a beginning. "Just come, auroral light, just grow tall, toothbrushes of the firmament, splintery celluloid palms, just withdraw into the room, blue-shod sea, and close off the path between yesterday and today, incipiently reverberant light, and with your minute flood-tide sweep away that fictive bridge that still trembles like an obstinate runner between yesterday evening and today, and throw here, onto the magnetic rock of my knees, that woman's body, which has remained as a result of the obsolete procedure of »happening« in an unknown novelty" — that is how Touqué spouted to himself when he pushed aside the folding screen in order to get at the washbasin.

When he opened the hot-water tap and the water sparkled with a transparent tinkle at the porcelain, he again had the impression that he was registering the ultimate results of a derivation as if, after a precise sucking of the kiss, "*quod erat demonstrandum*" — the tap would point with a gesture to the tube of the tap and the water's silky activity. Once that would also be the end of history, he said to himself ironically: just as all that is left of the dramatic Huygens-garden of love is a foreign statue of a female body (yesterday dense blooms on boughs of dense foliage which had mingled in disorderly fashion in the wind like at a masked ball — today: a single long bare branch at the end of which a single unknown fruit was hanging), so, at the end of the world, behind Sylla's dictatorship, one will find a tube of toothpaste; behind the edict of Nantes — red riding tails; and behind history in general, a shop window, as if every 'event' were a purgatory & 'objects' a kingdom of heaven that had fled from it. (See the article: "*Neue Sachlichkeit* as artistic verification of the 'substitution'-theory of substance": object & fragment of material can always be perceived as the residual outcome born from the cocoon of incidence, hence the interest of the photographed heap of stoppers consists of being today's residual substance from yesterday's comedy of a marital squabble.)

When he turned the tap on, he considered it to be very loud, and he was fearful of waking Jacqueline, so he would rather take a bath for preference. Having no wish to disturb the maids so early, he himself set about preparing the bath, but first he left a scrap of paper on the table with the note: "Having a bath." The shoes were still outside in the corridor like the individualizing blazons of an unfamiliar order of knights. He did not know where the bathroom was located, and was even drolly minded to recall a detail from yesterday evening: maybe he would be able to deduce it from that. The lift cables stretched silently in the middle of the spiral stairway as if they were stamen filaments of step corollas: the metaphor is useful in the morning for pacifying a little the big flying asunder of 'past' & 'substance,' because it represents a transition between myth and '*Sache*.' All at once he spotted a glass door, so he hurriedly jumped in. "This is at least regularly new, with exact words and calculated rhymes," and meanwhile filled his nose with the odor of moisture. "Now I'm going to carry out a baptism on myself that will not wash away my sins but will rather bring to the surface their logical kernel" — whereupon with a rapturous Baptist-glance he sought out the shower's downward-pointing tin-flower handle. He turned on the water, which poured intermittently, splutteringly, & unevenly, into the bathtub. The sun shone onto the tiles, filling him with the feeling that hygiene made Eros a lot more poetical than an otherwise commodious Arcadia which lacked running water and central heating. A kiss and its other corollaries makes the body somewhat flowerlike, besmirch it a bit, and it smuggles in among the muscles an awareness of people that is just a marshy botanical plagiarism: the bathroom is of assistance to that, and within a trice it drags an awareness appropriate to humans to the surface.

A naked embrace has roughly the effect of a fever: although a person takes a turn to the right, one nevertheless feels that one's body has stayed on the left side — one feels doubled, and the new Janus-statue would like to confront itself, if that were possible, but the result of that effort is that a third head is born into the bargain: thus, while embracing one occurs in a large number of copies, and one feels oneself to be, in part, a myriapodan caterpillar, in part, a statuette of a hundred-armed Hindu divinity.

In the bathroom that suddenly comes to an end: all that is left of the Facsimile orgy is a single slim sample that has nothing to do with yesterday's mirror image, powdered into the thousand-wave lake of events — that coerced-uniqueness is barely able to retain for itself a recollection of the embrace, just as a cogwheel is also unable to make progress on an ordinary rail. But the new body, which is a negation of yesterday's flamboyant anatomy, does not feel it is an antagonist of its nighttime predecessor but its quintessence, its heir; the more the Aurora-Cubism cubes itself, the deeper the experience of Baroque inheritance ingrains itself. The difference between fidelity and infidelity becomes blurred: he is in love with the soap-dish because it is Jacqueline's quintessence, it was born out of her, she has crystallized into that, and because it is so different, strange, & alpha simultaneously.

---

further exploitation of the seaside dawn:
re-examination of the conventional notion of 'precision'

Shining in through the enormous bathroom window was the sun, which cast its light on the white houses and Schrödinger's Ψ frippery of the bay,[54] which might have served as the starting-point for the ground plan of an elegant hall, as if even nature were displaying the characteristic features of mundaneness: here infinity is rather just an absent-minded gesture of nonchalance as was immediately noticeable in the curve of the shore, having within it the crazy dash of distance and also the curve of muted weariness (in books of mathematical logic one can see diagrams that depict the paths of similar relationships — the whole is much like a thirty-pronged crown, though it has a special trait: the first prong [which denotes the first relationship] is totally vertical, the next prong [which is like the first, but naturally denotes a slightly divergent second relationship] is already leaning outwards a bit, the third even more so, and so on — by the time one reaches the thirtieth prong, which is again directly next to the very first vertical prong on the circularly-shaped crown [in other words, the current of likenesses of the prongs of similar relationship has got back to the starting-point], then this last prong is not just bent to the side but simply extending downwards, deviating 180° from the first prong.

The similarity between each two prongs is so great that the difference in deviation is barely noticeable, though the first and thirtieth prongs let fly their paradoxical aristocratism in the most wildly opposed directions, an aristocratism about which [at least judging from the way the prongs progressively drop down the further round the crown they are] it is impossible to establish whether it was due to strict self-consistency that it had come into self-contradiction, or whether the relay shading of the path of falsehood with spectral transitions had helped it toward the ultimate positive sense of similarity and self-similarity.

The seashore at Cannes traced a logical curve of that kind to Touqué's eyes: the curve of infinity, twisting against itself, evolved from tiny curls of finitude — at every point the glittering cosmetics of finitude, and yet it all ran into the perverse simplicity of infinity through a latent 180° escaping from itself into itself); the hotels seemed to be just momentary flowers as well — though they were strong and bold, statues of foolhardiness, audacity, & white-hot nihilism, with a memory of the houses of Italian villages nonetheless on their faces. The antithesis of sea & houses was like a duel hallowed by aimlessness: the blue was not a sincere color, just a self-consuming mimicry of empty defiance.

Everything was exaggeration, not in a pathetic, more in a cynical direction, as if it just happened to be a peculiarity of the Côte d'Azur that incandescence & vegetation did not idle into romanticism but into irony stimulated by faith. Here, under no circumstances was it possible for the 'natural' and the elegant person to be contrasted; the swell on the sea was measured movements, the brightness of the sunshine was fiery discipline, even the wildest rocks of the hills bear the proud bloom of discretion.

This landscape is only fine in its own entirety because only then does it gain the frivolity almost crystallized into dogma, which represents its essence; that connection which pertains to the extreme whiteness of nothing and the thin edges of almost-something; as if the sea, the hills lying like resting hands, & the vitreous parasol of the sky, went to make up not a geographical but a 'logo-sentimental' landscape: among our emotions, there are some for which the massiveness is in their irresoluteness, & uncertainty is a needle-shaped source of light.

There are moments when the day-to-day linking-together of ideas that normally exist between precision and crystallographic linearity seem to be totally ineffective and completely to miss the point of precision: the Riviera landscape is in fact also a diplomatic intrigue against naïve precision of line in favor of a more elevated symbol of precision which is in the air. There is something recklessly & unforcedly dynamic in the whole thing, similar to the empty craziness of rapture; that craziness seemed to be truer precision than that of constructed lines, and it was one of the most ancient motors of Touqué's feeling of antilogical logic.

All that ceases when one looks at details: the Côte d'Azur is either a recapitulatory blue continuum geyser or nothing. Touqué liked grey picture postcards most of all because they better expressed the super-landscape quality of the scenery than colored pictures, or even paintings, of which he could have viewed a seasonal exhibition almost every summer. There was more clarity in the greyness of such a photograph than in the crumbling proportions of atmosphere of the pictures; it was the prime or background color of neutrality, within or above which flash minimal but concrete fortuities as if the entire Cannes world were an epaulette of grey fog out of which blinding-white sparks flashed forth here and there, occasionally wavy lines or jetty lakes turned inside out, similarly to mirror writing. Infinite indifference filled with fortuitous points: that is the Cannes stage set, and the nearest to that was the style of the black-&-white photo; when he looked at a picture like that he felt that he also ought to base an artistic composition on that kind of thing.

When he abandoned those speculative trajectories, however, he turned affectionately toward painters, who did not reach greyness and the gelatinous, amœba-like form of the essence by stripping off the sensual and colorful exterior, but rather by intensifying that, since masking to the point of absurdity anyway leads to a condition equivalent to rawness.

IV.

The painter Jacques Bournol's pictures of the sea: portrayal of space locally, its connection to the new-'novel' technique & to a new psychological method

Jacques Bournol, for instance, mixed three elements in his pictures of Cannes: first of all, the almost logical biology of sea animals (as was by then fashionable); next, the forms of style of the Romans of yore on the Riviera; and finally, that certain 'innate tragœdia' that can be sensed even in the most laughing tropical flowers & fruits.

The sea was black: just as in our childhood we sketched hundred-towered castles in such a way as first to draw a thick line of ink, &, with a piece of paper placed parallel to that line, we daubed that vertically, so he painted not so much the waves on the water as its overimagined internal transparency, as a result of which the sea became a continually (but not regularly and proportionately) deepening concavity without having assumed the form of a funnel, a maelstrom, or any kind of vessel, being particularly reminiscent of those pictures that aim at optical illusion, on which a flight of stairs is drawn diagonally and it only depends on an alternating internal wrenching of one's imagination whether one sees it as a normal ascending or an inverse staircase: here in the picture distance and depth also colluded; the water was a dark, big foliage, on the branches of which (the original ink lines), now on their heads, now on their tails, the leaves of light (those blotches) were separate brassiere-saucepan concavities, and thus the water became a space of ever-restless self-analyses & lightning-quick totals.

Touqué felt that that was the sea's spatial lesson: both a staircase and a bough of foliage, circles of reflection flung together, which, taken together, yield neither plastic art nor a plane: a glass serpent that slithers in a rapid spiral up high (or deep down?) on both the planar and spatial trees of scales and in the wave mirrors of the sea's meanwhile glistening body, as it simultaneously reflects both — that is roughly what the sea was like in Bournol's pictures.

Plane and space in this seascape seemed to be truly naïve fragmentary notions instead of which a reality of another nature had been smuggled. The sea had no perspective, neither bad, nor good, neither unnaturally naïve nor absurd to the point of theoretical perfection: instead the picture of the water broke up into little space-planets, scattered autonomous space-systems within which it might still have been possible to recognize some mementœs of the 'planar' or 'space-like' or the 'depth' & the 'surface,' but with that same painfully nauseating feeling afflicting the most ancient pillars of one's body, with which one would recognize the disintegrating features of a disfigured face that an enormous iron plate had squashed apart — a giant worm had grown out of one ear, out of the nose, had possibly become a single point of flesh the size of a forget-me-not; a foreign ornamentation snakes over the entire face, but there is still a memory of the original proportions in it, and the two systems of lines torment us in paradoxical balance.

Like in a garden which is subdivided with Versailles precision, one may start to indiscriminately pull out individual flowers (let us assume everything is made of rubber), one to the right, another to the left, press down the trees to the level of the ground, pull up the blades of grass to the clouds: in this new, artificial chaos the original Versailles rule would still prevail, because the roots are in their places, and being a focal point, the plan does not permit dissolution; indeed, if the focal point suddenly ceased to exist, then it would not be this artificial chaos that became definitive, as this present chaos, in the last analysis, nonetheless owes its luxuriating arhythmicity to the fact that every tree, every blade of grass, is fixed at a single point.

With a distorted face it is also possible to imagine three degrees: the original profile; the distorted one, which even in the most twisted caricature-tendril still yields to the fateful cohesion of the original state; and finally, the third position after distortion, when the gravitational pull of the original has already ceased, & ears, nose, mouth & forehead freely bloom like leaning towers under which the earth's attractive force has suddenly been discontinued.

In Bournol's pictures, the planarity & spatiality of the sea stood at the second degree: he had forsaken geometrical perspective, it is true, but had not yet reached totally floriferous space. It was as if space wished to abolish its unity and homogeneity & instead to transform into a complex tree: the individual waves in Bournol's water were independent rotation-leaves & polar-flowers, which would not dream of spatiality in general, instead they championed only little space zones as the sole realistic elements.

Formerly it was possible to fit all the objects in a picture in the rays of perspective; two tangents started off from the eyes like the two wings of an opened pair of compasses clasping objects with systematizing embraces. It seems that with Bournol that optical scheme did not feel comfortable as in his pictures there was no unity of view; if one instinctively rested one's eyes on one of the bands of paint, interpreting that, let's say, as depth, and trying to relate the other bands of paint to that depth, then it occurred that after the next inch the presumed depth altered into an edge without its being truly the edge of anything. That was what happened the whole length of the picture: things became plastic without "having even a minimum of 'corporeality' or 'extension' in them"; things looked planar, posing as blades in the most dogmatic way, but when our eyes groped after the paint, our pupils skimmed thick solid figures.

The waves were not set in a quiet and self-consistent lake of space, but each and every wave developed its own space as an integument for itself, which floated around it like the profile of a dancing scent or swaying mirror-swindle. Besides our calling it a floriated space it could also be called a picaresque space: picaresqueness, after all, is an absolute variation of plot, one living almost beyond humans & human deeds, a movement and proliferation of relationships totally independent of them, and yet the Bournol-type pictorial space is proceeding toward a (biological?) space beyond optics and geometry of that kind which strains as a source of destructive force under the conventional mask of 'plane' & 'space' in order to break out at that certain place, which is third in the analogy of the distorted face and garden, and rule alone.

As Touqué contemplated that new spatial complex in which the individual spaces lined up next to one another like an air balloon collection of alien globes of gas, which, for the time being, were on a shared string but would at some time be released, and then their selfish movements would become apparent — he supposed that if a painter were able to realize in a landscape the innate multiformedness of space, the same could also be applied to psychology, where a principle of 'absolute capriciousness' had hitherto been lacking (though only that could be 'absolute structure').

He attempted to imagine this by conceiving of 'life' as the rotation of a catapult, and, instead of considering the 'harmonic' circle (the suffocating symbol of so-called 'truth') that is constructed by the rotation as the human soul, he rather took as the picture of the soul the innumerable rays in the direction of which the stone would fly if it were freed (of course, that has nothing to do with the barrennesses of 'vital' freedom): the soul decomposed into a forest of scattering lines where the circle had once been.

A person's entire life was a series of starting points or, as Touqué would have liked to put it: a projection of infinite remote actions; when we reach for a glass then a big arrival or meeting scene takes place somewhere in a transcendental drama, of which our reaching for a glass is just a small-scale projection. But that geometrical picture could also be imagined as two rays running from two infinitely distant places and converging infinitesimally close, almost coinciding on the circumference of a circle — to put it another way: on the area of a circle absolute foreignness can be perceived as identity.

What did that denote in Touqué's psychology? In infinity, at an infinite distance to each other, let us say, are two theatrical stages or, to formulate it in a bigoted fashion, two 'absolute happenings,' which are totally alien to each other such that they are mutually irrelevant almost to the point of delirium. Let us suppose that on one of the stages it is about an embryo coming into being from a flower, while on the other it is about a girl stealing from her father's wallet because she wishes to bribe the concave print of a conch in the sand — two, on the whole, rather absurd scenes, which are at an absurd distance to each other in infinity. The two happenings, however, are projected in two rays onto the said area of a circle: infinitely scaled-down and in infinitesimal proximity. We reached for a glass of water (this is the first point on the circumference of the circle, i.e., the story of the embryo flower), after which we drunk up the water (this is the immediately neighboring point on the circle, i.e., a projection of the story relating to the conch print): in these two actions, logically built up in two time measures, reside two actually infinitely different (different both in relation to us and each other) events — when one puts the glass to the lips in reality one does not continue the first movement of reaching for the glass, but a completely new, alien, rootless action begins: our life is apparently a coherent outline, but only apparently: the reality is in dramas that are scalloping in infinity & are infinitely dissimilar to each other, at the ends of centrifugal branches.

Coherence is always a fictive projection of an absolute and genuine incoherence existing in infinity: just as substance is strangeness cultivated to perfection vis-à-vis its own subject, so coherence, logical succession, is no more than the shrinking of infinite distances into naïve optics.

Therefore one is granted the possibility to construct big drama constellations of little acts: instead of reaching for a glass of water and drinking it, the original should be written down, the embryo flower and the bribery of the conch print. Touqué tried to write up his own life in that manner under the title *The Antipsyche Idylls*.

plan of The Antipsyche Idylls
(*"Psychologia De Sitteriana"*)

A small wedge has to be inserted into the joints of logical coherence; a minimal angle is sufficient for the purpose of knocking two nearby, almost identical points into receding directions & thereby falling infinitely far from each other in infinity: that was the structural technique of these idylls — to deduce the original from the projection, from coherence strangeness, from identity mythical dualism. He felt that to be a truly rational world, unlike order systems: raison and logic again excluded each other in his eyes.

Thus, the old scholarly antithesis between 'psychoanalysis' and 'plotliness' ceases altogether: the true analysis will consist (as in the aforesaid idylls) of cultivating the most bizarre plot — Lesage, the psychologist, and Proust, were naïve amateurs:

the former leaps in the endless peak of rays, while the latter moves only on the circumference of the circle: the first is the mill-turning horse at the end of a pole, the second just the stone revolving on the spot. (See "*Quelques remarques concernant la naissance légitime de la poésie narrative ou le roman d'aventure comme l'analyse absolue*": an article of Touqué's that every Parisian magazine had rejected: they all thought it was a game, whereas it was more wilting asceticism or bleeding puritanicalness.)[55]

If an unemployed person has nothing better to do, they could revive some occasionalism for Touqué's 'psychology': after all, what that concerns is that every moment our life is on terms with an endless drama, which is not just a passive projection since an endless 'force' attracts life to these colossal adventure novels (*Psychologia De Sitteriana?*): when we reach for a glass of water, then an infinite force attracts us toward the embryo-staminate flower, in the direction of the centrifugal ray; when we drink the glass of water, a quite different but likewise infinite force attracts us to the tragedy or farce of the conch print — and since we nevertheless reach for the glass of water and nevertheless drink the water, only in that way is it comprehensible that on every occasion just as big a force is countering it: precisely here there would be a spot of renovation work for an occasionalist: the slightest human action is indebted to that continually interfering braking force without which a person would explode into a cosmic narrative: these huge hidden adventures surround one like the hypothesis-roses of a wreath of infinite extension.

There is a paralyzing agent that is granted to art which is able to deactivate that occasional counterforce which holds the soul on the circumference of the circle, thereby allowing two centrifugal-comedies to splutter forth from the same point in life, liberated as a double geyser, the way that in a Bournol picture a hundred kinds of spatial otherness sparked in every direction from the sea. In Cannes-photographs, fortuities flew about like wandering stars under the negative climate of indifference: that mood, or rather administration of fate, lay close to Bournol's painting. Springs have a point of stretching beyond that they are unable to return to: when they are pulled past that point then an odd feeling passes through our hands — in place of the spring's defunct strength, our own strength stumbles forward like a dead body (like a bird that flew toward its goal with proud wings but dropped dead when it reached above it); below us lies the stiffened serpent & above it totters a murderous force.

That relationship made itself felt on the picture postcards, in Bournol's picture, & also in reality: the sea, the arc of the shore, and the resting vanity of the hills were all overstretched springs (Gaea Antigaea?) on that point when even the most frivolous local gesture still strains back with every nerve (like a spring) toward self-identity, but maintaining that state for more than two seconds will bring on paralysis — totality, geological over-sufficiency, tips over into a torso, dark caricature, or, put simply, into no longer concealable otherness.

Space in Cannes (abstraction & trope)

But those two seconds lasted for an eternity, & thus the landscape expressed a perpetual *limit*-excitement between Cannes & something anti-Cannes. When one looked at the countryside from the white walls of Avignon one sensed that this country was the antechamber of Paradise, because it starts losing ground underfoot, while on other landscapes the totality of times finds its poster-style *point* in the heavy statuesqueness of fruit, the

Provençal countryside, by contrast, finds its sole realistic consequence in the movement of annihilation (this is not a naïve-radical 'nothing,' of course, but a precise and rich geometrical nothing). That is why the landscape does not ceaselessly luxuriate in the wildest colors, but dismal white blots of salt lumps, gravelly sand, & dried-out channels mingle in among it — those blemishes and Braille-cosmetics are the first as yet strictly landscape-faced signs of annihilation.

Just as certain rhetorically constructed sentences lose their logical and grammatical character beyond a certain point, and only the dark-waved but sure flow of rhythm asserts itself, so the truth of the subsequent thoughts is assured by no more than the predestined arc of the rhythm before it has been expressed in words: so the quintessence and inevitable tendency of a landscape lying far from the Riviera, as yet barely even resembling it in external features, bursts forth from under it like a crazy heretic current: force-free tension, subjectless-point, a needle-prick hypothesis, spectral greyness, a dogma-meshed nothing.

Nothing which fell into the lap of this landscape by the shore was emptiness or formlessness, it lacked a cliché of *nihil*, a Romantic blank window & sleeping sickness.

On the other hand, where the colors really have continually enhanced themselves almost visibly (a given color transformed from a basin into a river, which, however, dropped into itself, rose up afterwards a fraction darker from the bathing in itself then again rested into a basin [i.e., petal], for the petal to essentialize once more into a pure color fluid and sink into itself the next moment just like a swan, when it pokes its head, together with its neck, under its own wing, as if it were seeking to fit a plug into its body: the self-induction gymnastics of primary, secondary, tertiary, et cetera, color identity), there it was perceptible that the incandescent wildness of color was due to the surrounding emptiness, otherwise its sharpness would have dissolved on the enticing conductors of the surroundings — as it is the garish colors always aroused an impression of intense vacancy, as if it were only possible to protect the color from fading in a metaphysical-thermos flask of the thousand-oscillation 'nothing.' That is how it was possible to 'desensualize' the adored flower petals and make ridiculous in its own eyes the trivial connection that exists in people's heads between tropical matters and sensuality: incandescent colors & spiritually charged space stood in a functional relationship.

As to that 'space' or 'nothing' as he indiscriminately called it, even a poet would have been hard put to say precisely — it was not exactly geographical emptiness, but then nor was it a metaphysical notion either, rather he borrowed it from his own body as a water-colored insulation around the flowers as if there was not only a certain quantity of blood and other chemical materials in one's body, but also a subjective amount of space that could be passed over. With a bit of Leibnizian malevolence he sometimes saw all of Provence as if the earth were just an infinitely fine continuation of the sea, being also conceivable as an infinitely slow and infinitely flat wave of water; the blue tritonia of the sea, on the other hand, was conceivable as an infinitesimally small land, so that even around Avignon, as a matter of fact, the sea waves hover in a sweeping hush, and the Mediterranean's most remote coral shrubbery is also an infinitesimal rose bush.

In point of fact, this is the most important dialogue in this southern border district, the sea twisting around toward Paris and the land sifting apart toward Africa, as their oppositely directed rings continually intersect each other. Making use of the fairly public road displays of the Cannes & Avignon districts in that way, in "absolute lability" he created for the intellect a stage on which it could safely stand, if it sought to be worthy of itself ("*Esquisse d'une topographie transcendantale de la France*").[56]

The kinship between Paris and Venice is conspicuous even from a superficial point of view, but with that Leibnizian correction the kindred relationship became even stronger: the grey houses seemed to float in almost transparent water, the wind which ran along the furrows of the streets was salty and blue. The sea, by contrast, was the genuinely logical arable land, with its perpetually running clods of earth, full of the wind's capricious sowings, which did not crumble the quiet life of crippled seeds but somersaulted and sang between the slithering walls of a dancing womb: a seesaw gesture ran over the soil and an astonishing scintillation of seeds stepped into the place of learned ripening.

The breakdown of landscape & the breakdown of the soul could only take place in accordance to a common rule, only the system of breakdown had to be robbed of the counterweight of geometrical analogy (not because it was geometrical but because it was an analogy). The drawing of the whole centrifuge and perimeter was, in reality, only an inferred auxiliary dream next to the real dream that he felt when listening to music or in his moments of amorous consciousness.

Music acted on him like electrolysis on water: in the very first bars he could feel it was engendering an inner turbulence in his soul, wedging between the cohesive force of molecules that had long fused together; indeed, it strove to split what seemed to be unitary points into two or three, as if the sole chemical purpose of music were to goad the practical but hypocritical unity of our psychological life into reproduction by cell division or into Rutherford-liturgies[57] — the more one gives oneself over to the rollercoaster of music, or in other words, the better one is able to anticipate the next whole row of bars from the present arch, and thus the condensation of force engendered by anticipation swings one with a huge gesture from one's day-to-day watch-towers, the more rapid the complete dispersal, the rocket-like pulverization to disconnected drama planets, which is perhaps similar to tiny scenes of a naïve Shakespeare-imitation, leaving one's old self under oneself in groundless obscurity like a forgotten & clumsy rocket gun with which truly nobody at all can be bothered.

That is why it is so difficult to chat about old topics with old acquaintances after a concert: one does not feel oneself to be integrated and caught among contours; instead, one hovers and seesaws in the cloakroom like a polyp in the sea, which, with its hesitant arms, seeks a safe place for itself, and it is impossible to tell whether it is just coquettishly ballet-dancing with its legs or maybe groping around with pedantic attention. (One's attention has a habit of flagging like that polyp during sleep: one's consciousness touches on the topic, but it immediately slips away from it like a wave licking the shore, only the next moment to lap it anew, though by then its end reaches an inch or so lower.)

One would like to talk in the cloakroom about foreign animals, never discussed but categorically topical tragedies, or astronomical therapies that urgently need to be solved, which jostle and teem around one like new relations, an extended family resurrected from the Pliocene. Cards and chess players tend to branch off like that during play, so that after a game they are incapable of thinking of their own life in any other way than king, ace, jack & seven: if the female table companion by chance inquires about a son who is due to take an exam they immediately jump into a card riposte, and they would like to hand the woman one of the fan of cards they are clutching, and when they are obliged nevertheless to settle back into their so-called real family situation, that seems to be just a trick of etiquette, an artificial convention that was hit upon by a pair of notorious female table companions out of a flair for euphemism.

examples from The Antipsyche Idylls;
first example: suicide in a hotel;
an analysis of the development of pain

At times like that, strange happenings really do come spontaneously, not at the calculated end of centrifugal lines: while one is pulling one's coat above the heads of the crushing crowd, like Menelaus supporting the dead body of Patroclus, one is already pounding in front of a closed door behind which one's suicidal lover is dying — yet no one else in the entire hotel knows a thing about that, the room number and figure of the door had not yet passed through the transformation of sensation under the influence of the attention and the scandal; in time, a waiter appears, carrying a bucket of ice upstairs, takes notice with alarm, and the alarm suddenly conjured on his face (one is amazed how superbly the face 'is able to jump into' a role in life that was as yet unsuspected in the preceding minute: the grimace of the bucket of champagne held in the hands is still the joy that it had assumed as a mask in the kitchen, borrowed from the soul of the couple dining on the fifth floor — & while the waiter perfectly mimics, without prompting, the steadily accelerating misgivings that landed on him at that very moment, the bucket is still sitting in the waiter's hands with its still stereotypical & by now untimely grin & sluggishly assumes a somewhat more agitated profile only when the waiter racing toward the door puts it down next to the wall, at which point one of the bottles tips slightly to one side) will be the first conductor of the headlong current of spectacle: the room's door, which, down to the last fraction of an inch, resembles twenty others that are to be found upstairs, suddenly becomes conspicuous all the same, for the time being with that minimum of intensity which flashes on it from the waiter's exploratory concern & the accompanying surmise of his gaze.

However, the current of excitement of the pounding man (Touqué was pitched into that by the last bar of the concert, now confronting an automatic idyll in place of the edited idylls of *Antipsyche*) acts as a transformer on the waiter, who for the time being is straying in dilettantism: he suddenly thrusts the bucket at the wall & races over to the pounding man like someone who, with a single desperate gear change, is pushing himself over into a wild intensity — that is all the more successful for he is not as yet aware what it is about, and the agitation can gush forth with uninhibited dash without the filter of a precise reason or topic that has been worked out in more detail curbing it, breaking it up, and modeling it.

For several moments more the song that preludes the birth of the scandal arises from those two themes: the man's energetic main subject, in which consciousness compresses the enormous sphere of dread (the lover lying covered with blood on the bed with a revolver) into an infinitesimally small area, &, as a second subject, the waiter's almost *l'art pour l'art* fear, which, in contrast to the first, spreads freely, blossoms opulently, like the ancillary flora lent to the first bloom of fear out of charity or theatrical bravura or possibly sensuality.

The pounding man chokingly stutters: "there's been an accident" not so much to the waiter as to a nameless darkness, as if he were seeking to say something quite different and only out of tiredness was he using those words, which could, at best, be of as much help to him as a bridge that has fallen from its pillars & is dancing like a ripe fruit on the onward-surging waves would be of help to someone drowning in a flood tide; as if with those words he was not even trying to free himself from the growing quagmire of his own desperation but wished to posit the primordial principle of that growing and more and more complex black vegetation, referring to an old destiny that now touched on the sensitive spring of the present minute & thereby unhinged a gigantic structure, so that the waiter, the first time he heard the utterance, did not have the impression (as under normal circumstances in general) that the sounds & sentence were linearly issuing from the mouth of the fuming man, but rather as if he were hearing a negative mirror image, which may have likewise started off from his mouth, somewhere from the extreme borders of the body, like medieval-style speech balloons, but was cast back toward the inner darkness of the soul — he even narrowed his eyes in the first second as if he were seeking to observe a phenomenon in a dimly lit test tube that only lasted for a few moments.

Before he could have continued the attempt to psychologically turn inside out a person who had withdrawn into himself through pain, so that he should clearly see with anatomizing eyes the painful spots on the psychological wall put at the mercy of the crowd, with a deftly improvised atavism he exhorted the man to quietness and silence.

The waiter's face was by then likewise distorted, but in order to be able to enjoin the man to be calm he needed to compel his own face to be composed, which could only be accomplished with an audacious leap, a sportsmanlike throwing on of a mask (the way fugitives roused from their sleep habitually, without any thought of grooming, fling their cloak around themselves with a sudden and intemperate, unmotivated toss), & thus the new portrait is a little badly drawn: the rescue portrait that had overshot the mark with which he strove to aid the moaning man onto his own preserve of discretion as a lever was too stiff; because he had to be suddenly brought to a standstill, or rather the grimace of conditional tranquility had to be caught on the wing in order to be of any use.

The next moment another door opened, and an alarmed male face jumped out like a figure on a spring from a jack-in-the-box in order that from this free staccato, all at once, willy-nilly, there should be a third subject in the strict fugue of widening scandal. The scared face was evidently that of spectators and connoisseurs of sensation, with the precisely measurable delay that was so typical of them, like a club badge: their excitement is always awakened by one of the earlier phases of scandal or disaster, and by the time they reach the site of the trouble, then a much later scene of that is to be seen, whereas in their eyes the interest was fixed in being connected to an even earlier phase, which is unable to run in parallel to the present, & it takes a fairly significant chunk of time for the time-lag that they lugged around with them to be released, & from a certain point they run, with a redeeming lurch, with the Greenwich Mean Time of the present.

The fears of the three faces were not so much in rhyming as in assonance-relationship: everywhere there was something communal that glittered and imposingly moved on them like an express illness that developed in half a minute & immediately leapt into crisis, but at the same time the individual facial features, outstanding as consonants, among which the infecting song of shared anxiety gets stuck, were also definitely effective.

When the waiter warned the desperate person, for a while he did not even listen, at least so it seemed, then all of a sudden he began to whimper, but in order not to tip the balance over on the anxiety scales of pain, he flattened himself to the door as if he were seeking, with his breathing and the words he had long set free to fill the cracks in the door, the way that the openings on a building are glued over with paper when fumigating it with hydrogen cyanide.

Irrespective of the waiter's warning, the dying away of the voice was odd, but that he had actually heard it could be picked up from the fact that after a while, quite inorganically, so to say thrown out of the dissolved material of pain like a stone that had been accidentally mixed up with molten iron, he said this much: "yes, I know." He then began to walk falteringly for a few moments as if he would suddenly still like to lop off the growing branches of scandal in the corridor and to wind back the premise-yellow petals of its flowers into his own body like an old handkerchief that he had lost and of which, due to its grubbiness, he was especially ashamed: not so much because he feared scandal but as if, through its being spread, the logical essence of the event, its coherent content, would also scatter like that of a stage play which, after the second act, instead of being continued on the stage, is tossed into a labyrinth of mirrors where the characters go mad, becoming boundless garlands of reflected flowers, and where, after being moved a quarter of an inch, a hundred more projected duennas would immediately jump onto the walls.

For a while he had no idea what he should do: should he surrender himself to the half-cocked giant seesaw of pain, which perpetually only tumbled downwards, or should he concentrate on his own story, on those novelistic elements on account of which the episode had happened (from the viewpoint of the police and the plot), it is true, but which had not the faintest connection to pain, with the extent of the final phase. For one of the most vital components of pain, and its technical trick, was for a painful episode and the preceding story suddenly to break apart; the dead body, lying covered in blood like the closed formula of a last deed, and the open comb of the preceding little series of events, will never meet any more.

The 'deed' itself is always an unknown third person, who stands apart from the preceding events as from the victim of the deed: after all, if it were somehow possible to bring the decisive revolver shot into a mock-organic and self-deceptive connection to the woman herself and her exposure to life, then the pain would not be so great. The essence of that resides precisely in the extreme disproportionality, in the deliberate fault of composition that he committed at the last minute.

A separation of present & past is what is performed by that certain third person, who is invisible but inferable to the point of positiveness: the present ceases to be time (the first terrorist & revolutionary act of pain consists precisely of the radical extermination of time) & possibly identifies with the dead woman's body, while past, dwindling infinitely as a miniature painting, makes its appearance at the diminishing end of the binoculars, a past which had withered off the woman's body like a pimple constricted by the ligature of a single hair so circulating blood should be unable to pass though it from the body: everything that is occurrence, time, & motivation is lying in the shapeless ubiquity valley of the present in millionfold reduction & with a total absence of life.

On which of the two paths chiseled by the scheming third (i.e., the autonomous 'deed') should he dispatch his soul: should he walk the path of the past, for, after all, the police would be there straight away and they would ask, and he would be hard pressed to relate to the gentlemen the events of the past, events that he could barely see, barely sense; in order to be able to relate to them he would need to take out a magnifying glass that comprised the imaginary lenses of yesterday and the day before yesterday; the image of the dead body and the deed had to be somehow blotted out in order that he be able to swing back into the old optic and thus be able to see events not as microbe-like, senseless, & low-order movements, but as life-sized drama. Or else resign himself to the cone-shaped whirlwind of pain spiraling toward the center of the earth, the sole tumbling wave of the present in which there is such a dazzling guarantee of totality that one believes that, in the final analysis, it leads to joy (the explanation of pain-gravitation is not power either but a deviation of mental space?), the way that those who are operated on while conscious reach such a crescendo of pain that every rising step of pain beyond it no longer strains from sensory impression but from anticipation of the joy that is infallibly and logically bound to be forthcoming — or as the rings of purgatory finally rocked with geographical compulsion into the vestibule of Eden like the grey waters of the Canale Grande before the gate of a romantic place: should he resign himself to that new present and eat with greedy teeth the rootless, branchless, foreign fruit of '*præsens atemporale*' for the sake of a latent core of joy?

The 'deed,' the isolated fact of the suicide, the unknown *deus ex machina*, stood between the wave panorama of the present & the stable little mosaic of the past like a mythological folding screen that can never again be unfolded in life.

Pain is more comfortable than plot: for all its basalt-walled darkness, the present arouses a feeling of freedom, indeed even of repose, unlike the strictness of the little past, with its logarithms calling for close attention, which lie on the far side of the cadaver. One staggers around in pain as in a secretive virgin forest into which one was abducted in a moment like a Ganymede, not knowing whether the nest of snakes hissing at one out of the dark will fall on one like the icy contents of a thousand-mouthed tube, or whether the taste and smell of paradisiacal fruits and artistic flowers await him — nor is one clear about the intention that comes across in this gloomy primitive garden, nor with its ground plan and structure. The deeper and deeper one tumbles in it one does not know if dizziness repels one or one is moving about a conscious path of discovery: with a heightening of the bodily sense of lust one passes the superbly ambiguous moment where the will & automatism are barely distinguishable, & unrestrainable free flying toward an unleashing of pleasure is unable to outstrip the finite will, or on the contrary, as if it were a race in which two galloping horses close in on the finishing point — one occasionally more in front, occasionally more behind — not two independent race lanes, but a racing motion toward a single goal, which at any moment branches into two bogus competitors who execute the cross-movement of two pendulums swinging in opposition to each other. All at once, however, the common root (gravitational pull & volitional impetus) of the two kinds of motion (in lust as in pain) at which, Janus-like, they had accidentally branched in two is revealed.

Just as the movement, the tempo of the waves, is constantly ambiguous, so, too, is the subject of the pain indefinite: is it art, if it comes to it, or a trampling on art? An inspiration, taking that in the most pedantic literalness, or a triumph of prose over Carnival? Is it an eternally illuminating concrete beauty from the dead husk of the past, or does it mark the start of the homogeneous denial of everything?

Is pain pain, in other words? Do we want it or run away from it? And does running make any sense in a dimensionless mental space? When he looked around at the waiters standing in the hotel corridor he felt like a mythological statue standing on a well in the middle of a lake must have felt vis-à-vis guests standing and strolling on the bank: a definitive rigidity, as if everything of its human character had been destroyed and only its weight remained, the anonymous burden (now, instead of a name card he ought to show a slip of paper of the sort that street scales issue, showing only the weight that they have registered), the rest is just reflection in the shivering mirror of the lake at twilight; self-portrait and sensation of weight had not simply separated but, tragically, were also transformed out of pessimistic intrigues: his weight became heavier and multiplied, whereas his portrait (which up until then had, as it were, spread and proportionally distributed the weight) became airy, quivering, uncertain & echoic — still golden-colored on the fleeting strip of the lake, but it will not be for long once the sun has gone down; it will then only be black Leda-crêpe until the Moon finally distorts it into a wraith.

The weight is unvaried and permanent: he would like to speak to the people on the shore who were keeping watch, but the Newtonian-tricks of the nearby lake do not allow him to find room there: his own portrait turned into separatist amoebas, poetic variations, and frivolous water metaphors. Since no sincere social connection could come into existence between the statue and the seashore figures, and the man, trying to orientate in his pain, and the astonished waiters, stood on two banks of a sparkling water, the egotistical muse of pain tried to exploit the isolation. For a while, through a causal relation, the seemingly self-serving colored vortex of pain nonetheless connected to life and thus it could be called sadness: however, the muse, like an underworld gracioso, broke with a gazelle leap the thin glass channel through which the end of practical life poured into pain, which was coming into leaf and seeking again & again to forget all about life: he was nurtured on memories of life through that transparent artery so as to be able to breed his own world independent of life.

A paradoxical game commenced in the development of pain (*dolor autoteleologicus*, Linnean classification): as long as it was merely 'sadness,' or in other words, it was nurtured by the events of life through a thin but sure artery, and was therefore still strongly a function of a positive story, it strove in huge proportions, with jungle-like caprice & chemical inability, toward some sort of art-oriented and joy-like exaggeration; from blood cells of facts it unfolded into a sleep fan that had lost all decency; whereas now that the muse had severed the connection, the pain that foliated into an autonomous being, out of which a perverse esthetic or a pendulum-like exchange of values of joy appeared to be straining to come to life, began to create an idyllic nest in the depths of the maelstrom as if a swift whirling of the tornado around a cone's axis were there merely for peace & quiet to arise alongside the cone's axis and around the apex of the cone — the essence, cause, and aim of every rotation is a silence at the *origo* as a perennial inertia-flower.

The muse's irony consisted of that: hitherto life had nourished pain until it detached from it, but after it had detached, it became a petty-bourgeois nidus of ease — slippered comfort in place of the new esthetic, milk-grey convalescence in place of the joy of new meaning. At the closed edge of the paradise of pain the waves planned in the spirit of 'grand style' were still surging mountainously high, and the darkness was evaporating out of them in similar waves (like profuse perfume from ladies' hair if the wave is slightly readjusted by the distracted plowing of a comb), dark fruits hung from the parturient arms of the branches like poison-containing pendants, but in the center of the garden out of the swirling stack of leaves (fizzling copper coins are constantly showering above themselves in such fashion as a disc in change machines) a little bower emerged as a telltale center for dotards: the pain had become a negative paradise, where the whole garden was full with the sin-resinous trunks of forbidden trees, but in the middle stood a single permitted cherry treelet, with little branches and little-girl tastes.

Just like the apostle on glimpsing the rainbow secrets of a resolving-vision[58] gets mixed up in the fermenting excitement of knowledge and in the middle of the trance all at once exclaims with petty-bourgeois naïveté: "Let us build here a shelter for ourselves," a small rural hut, perhaps, like the one in which pensioner Deucalion[59] took a nap while around him a phosphoric sea of mystery glittered, so pain, left to its own devices, hastened toward the disclosure of an *Innatum Idyllium* of that kind.

The value and decorative utility of that antithesis is well known to interior decorators & fashion designers, when in a Cubist room, where the walls are white & smooth, like canvas stretched to the tearing point, and the table is pure opaline, only here and there is a gleaming little steel spike protruding from it; where the lamp is a network of thin tubes, similar to the millimeter squared paper needed for the sketch of a graph (the hairline tubularity of eroticism is examined with it in rendezvous laboratories): and in a room like that they place in a corner a little rococo porcelain figure from 18th-century Kloster Veilsdorf[60] in which an egg-headed maiden is shielding her maidenhood, fingers stuck together, with a single broach-shaped hand.

pain & life, antithesis of succession & time

Pain is the most life-like thing in the world; it stands closest to that biological center as a result of the magnetic power of which every thing outside it bends toward it with trembling steadfastness like a dutiful & helpless compass needle — hence every consolation is impossible.

The basis of consolation is that it interprets the same facts that were the cause of pain and sorrow in a different fashion; a big role is played in consolation by reference to time, in part as a bitter & protracted cure, in part as a Garden of Eden of unexpected surprises & glittering *chances*. But pain cannot react to that because the hitherto hidden center of magnetism that simultaneously absorbs the unrolled path of days & weeks lining up into the future came into the foreground, & as it is the nature of force, it constructs around itself the glass armor of a globe. As it makes no sense to explain to nervous people to "be strong-willed

& get a hold of yourself," because their nervousness consists of precisely not being able to will anything, so a comforter talks futilely of the future, the passage of time, because the main attribute of pain is precisely the fitful rolling-up of time into the present, as if life and time excluded each other, & in practical life that relationship subsisted between them as between diplomatic etiquette & ethic destiny — time was just a precious Esperanto, an artificial language that could be set aside at any moment.

A flattering form of address for the sultans and sultanas who frequently crop up in *The One Thousand and One Nights*, is that they are 'lord & master of time,' or 'Hail, queen of time': whatever the precise philological meaning of the expression, it awakens a quite different notion of time in the naïve reader than does calendar time. It's as if time were made up of a concentric series of large rings of waves that draw in ever tighter proximity to the king's body and increasingly assume the contours of his body: time is just a more sublimated form of the royal body that will some day be born from it, & as such is therefore merely a prelude to the material; put another way, the waves set off from the sultan's body are, so to say, serial echoes of the subject of his one and only body, which he leaves after himself in people's memory like back-stitched ripples in the wake of the course of an onwards-gliding propeller.

Whether the reader considers time as a by-product streaming from memory or a first try in a particular part of the world, in both cases one feels that it is equally tied to a single individual and in no case to the pushy Nonius horse breed of the diary. In that way a group of people that meets at a hypothetically assumed point called a 'historical date' is a veritable time garden: each & every participant brings the individual rhythm of their own destiny, and these differ from each other like a thousand forms, colors, & scents of flowers.

When people withdraw into themselves and look at themselves, they immediately spot a sort of uncertainty, a seasickness of self-analysis, which derives from consciousness's being a resident in a neutral field onto which the convention of space & time only penetrates, like a droning blur of music through a thick door. One is astonished at one's own soul: motifs; volition springs that have long lost their elasticity & have stiffened into all the more exotic floral forms; thought experiments; pressed samples of memory, and between these incoherent and dead islands of values, the empty running of a constantly fluctuating vital force.

It is as if consciousness were flung over a hanging garden which is full of the most insane colors and internal movements (tropical static) while the world runs around it only as a pale tape, as in film shots a car 'hurtling along at top speed' is in fact stationary, is merely being shaken about a bit; and the streetscape which is visible through the window is a ribbon backdrop that is swiftly wound on further beside it (deceptive mask-kinetics).

Consciousness automatically switches such a bifurcating process on: within a trice, the 'story of the self' suddenly breaks away from the dark hanging garden of the 'self,' in a moment, the 'plot' is shed like an inorganic shell, a useless husk, from the closed sphere of life. One habitually feels that unexpected but radical bifurcation when an airplane rises high up: up to that point the countryside surrounded one like body-fitting clothing, the line and cut of that garment were the accustomed subjective perspective; when one tips up high one feels as if one had suddenly become naked, one is seized by a geographical modesty while one sees the machine has improvised an artificial and unnatural molting when it left on the ground one's landscape clothes and threw into the air its central cells, meager & barely able to move as they are. Pain accomplishes exactly the same with us: one leaves time like a grey telegraphic tap, which, with its senseless clattering and snaking around itself irrespective of itself, winds into the distance below or above one but in any event far from us; we can look at time like at a fish through an aquarium glass, or at a distant panorama from a lookout tower, with binoculars.

That is when it becomes truly apparent how unreal every 'plot,' every life story that is told about one, is in contrast to one's genuine life, which is the movement that avoids progress in time and exchanges in space: so extremely only-spool, never a thread. If I recollect a visit made socially, I see the tangledness of a dripstone cave, where the hours and places, the bus, the residence, the faces of the guests, the afternoon's feeble clarity and the epidemic flood of the closing-in of evening trickle onto and against each other like stalagmites and stalactites, drips & towers that were not constructed to a plan, but by passive dripping (an endless tape of intonation on which a tangled afternoon is a minute wrinkle, et cetera); consciousness always uses bad, shifted emphases. On the other hand, if I relate the story of my visit after it, then (with no little exertion) I cut regular columns and charming plot walls out of thin stone configurations and mud idols with elephantiasis: onto the stems of the capricious cave flowers I stick whatever 'time' is appropriate there (before doing so I make a careful examination of the little bud to check whether time is really needed there), & then I select the 'spaces' from the lump of pressed fruits (likewise with a conscientious magnifying glass), & I collect the two groups in separate racks, and alternately stow them away with checkerboard justice next to each other. The whole regular ornamentation has little to do with my life, but that is how I operate, because my female friend also operates that way, I am only acquainted with her life that way, sorted into a plot, from time immemorial, and I ape the game, trying to set out my life into a 'story.'

Life is like the interior of a wave, a poetic anatomy of it; and a plot dealing with it is the upper contour of the wave, the surface of the surface. There are things for which there is an essential connection between contour and interior, but that is not so with the wave; what has the fortuitous & fugitive azure borderline to do with the interior of the almost anesthetized water's edge: with animalcules, a million tiny shellfish caprices, a sea of microscopic autonomy? Nothing.

Let us compare the hermit crab, which sits in the depths of the sea, squeezed into its gastropod shell, and from there inspects the animal and plant life going on around and above it, then take a swimming-costumed woman, who, her elbows on the white plate of a Monte-Carlo Beach table, gazes at the play of the waves; let us set the two commentaries into glowing simultaneity, and we will then see how in absolutely no way do the surface and depth of the sea have anything in common with each other, so that we could safely denote them with two different nouns, & instead of a single Neptune create two gods for them. There is not a single common point between them; indeed, it could be stated as a rule that with things where contour and content are not connected, this incoherence always pertains with absolute clarity, without transition, and when measuring the independence (Leville-Touqué-type substance strangeness, for example, may have need of that), the antithesis of Neptune glove and Neptune hand could be just as much a unit of measurement or rather point of origin, like the zero point on a thermometer. (The edge of a wave is a source of geometrization: the white surf abandons the water and spreads into an abstract world of self-supporting formulas, whereas the depths of waves are the path to complete biologization, to the point of grotesqueness: a world of caricature-corals, gastric-question marks, and apoplexy-chrysanthemum pseudo-animals, where the notion of 'life' indulges itself to the point of complete buffoonery.

If one compresses the dead-pure equation of a wave-profile and the sticky skin of a balloon-polyp into a single strangeness-constant, then one has the bifurcation handle with which one can feel the irresistible splitting of modern man. That 'constant' or schizophrenia-unit cannot be confused with a connection that played such a major role in Touqué's earlier life: an abstract thought to which a biological simile gave truth-like muscle.) Humans in practical existence are ambiguous beings, hermaphrodites living on the crossroads of time and life who live life, sometimes from the point of view of a hermit crab, sometimes from that of a girl on the beach, without that leading to stereoscopy; rather the opposite. One cannot find a scale between the internal perspective of life & the external perspective of 'plot,' which leads from one to the other.

A person lives through something and relates it: there is no bridge between the two things, only a jump, a blind impetus, just as there is no transition from a German word into the corresponding French, they must be swapped completely. So if it were a matter of a flower, which ought to swing from root into petal, omitting the stem: the root is gigantic, the inflorescence luxuriant in a highly-strung manner, but there is no tree between the two. Is there some kind of transitional picture between a photograph of one diver & a photograph of a yacht? Some call the cause-and-effect relationship merely an optical illusion — that kind of relationship exists between real life and narration: only the usual relationship without any real connection. The way the rocking outline of the sea denotes narrative vis-à-vis life, at the same time it also represents time (that abstract or empty narrative) vis-à-vis the 'chronoid sphere' represented by the interior of the sea: the sole real thing and totally alien to 'time.'

It is now conceivable how helpless a consoler is when faced with a sufferer: for a comforter a fellow-being does not constitute life, only narrative, not 'chronoid sphere' (i.e., the vapor surrounding life), only inhuman time: I wonder whether a sailor, who is at home on the surface of the sea and aware of every artfulness of the waves, could do anything to help the internal problems of an anthozoon in the dark depths of the waters? Can they meet at all, or can they have just a single common point? The man panting in front of the closed door and the waiters standing around in the corridor were face to face, like an inebriated Caliban of the base view & the wavering engineers of an elevated view. They were tragic symbols of the situation that for an individual only two definitive perspectives are available with regard to one's own life: either total chaos, the billowing underworld of infrared consciousness, or time-scaled over-happening, an ultraviolet narrative. Would it be possible to stand between the two & acquire a 'normal' viewpoint? (It is decidedly decent that one always surmises that the impossible is 'normal.')

Obviously, pain lies very close to the center of life, & thus customs of that realm are reflected in it — under the influence of pain a person is all at once transformed into a medium who does not react to the empty rebuses of wandering souls but to the most atavistic suggestions of life. As under the influence of pain one's individuality settles like iron powder in a globular shape on the small central globe of life hidden somewhere in our inside, so it faithfully imitates the movements fashionable in the center like a (shall we say Bergsonian-Order) monk who dons his 'chronoid sphere' cloak instead of time's secular robe. That, however, only happens in the period of absolute maturity of the pain, and until one gets to that point, it is often necessary to wear the forms of narrative & time as a humiliation.

Sometimes the pain does not mature so speedily as it does with the man pounding on the hotel door & the bleak days of amateurish dabbling around have to be recited for a long time like rosary beads: for example in the grieving felt after a person has departed. The moment of taking leave in general does not denote the moment of the ripening of pain, more a flowering, a glittering (but immature) spring. Just as when touching boiling-hot objects one feels pain only some time after touching them, so here as well, at the time of departure, on packing, while standing about at the railway station, one is just gathering material, carrying out a philological study of sources — & just as that historical work will not be the most brilliant in which the data will take their place in the most impeccable ranks, but one in which the data, in an unexpectedly asymmetrical and frivolous moment, will elicit the somersault of a concept which has no evident logical connection to said sources: so, on the occasion of the modeling and planning of pain, it is not the narrative details and the story of departure that in any way constitute the organs of pain, or the temporary torsos of the whole grief-œuvre, but at best the climate, sun, rain & wind under the influence of which the pain-flower will awaken from the transparent field of nothing, in which, naturally, there is no longer any trace of light, wind, or rain.

When the woman we love is still with us but we know that in seven weeks time she will be making a trip to Rigi, admittedly, those are the embryonic days of pain, and we can already sense that we wish to cut ourselves free from the details of departure: the sole fact, the abstract thought, without image or story, of 'the woman departs' is sufficient. That sets off the first germs of pain and will also bring into being the exotic *terminus Ad-Quem*-bloom[61] set as the goal: just as in life one cannot inherit acquired characteristics, only ancestral inclusions, so pain is incapable of merging into its own flower even a millionth of the particles from the external story of the departure — in the external story, there may be episodes which ought, ostensibly, to assuage the pain of parting, yet the suffering soul does not react to them at all, for the incipiently growing embryo of pain is not a function of the details of departure, progressing in parallel to the taxi careening toward the railway station, the porter with his luggage trolley, and finally the slim wagon of the departing train, but merely a function of the aforesaid minimum: '— the woman departs —.'

pain is a fixed system

Just as the development of an actual embryo in the mother's womb is not a function of the man's amorous moods, ecstasies, and doubts running in parallel over nine months, merely the result of a physical minimum, the fertilizing sperm, which during a moment outside the plot, fulfilled everything and induced a bigoted independence. Love and pain play out the same comedy: for a while the characters swagger and gambol in the upper plane of plot, but at some unexpected moment a fraction of an inch drops from that stage (insulated from the magnetic center of life), whereupon the center of life immediately seizes the liberated article (for instance, 'the woman departs' or the fertilizing sperm): it is no use walling in the superficial stage anew with insulating material in order that it be secretly cut off from the central attractive force of life, the bit that was once snipped off from above blossoms to its own ends, and all at once it will stretch its plentiful and strange branches over the insulating wall of the stage into the foreheads of the cast, or in other words, Don Juan finds himself confronted with a child that had no conceivable connection to his amorous plot, & the man, stupefied by the pain of departure, is faced with A Pain quite unlike the woman or their relationship, unlike anything else, but a surprising ready confection from an unknown workshop yet nevertheless addressed to him.

Life obviously plays the role of schemer, the poetic rival of man; both are at work on some play, but life is doing so secretly, on the sly — the man is studying an entire liaison, examining with a lover's misgivings the documented authenticity of the lover's eyes, lips, and gait; observing in the savor of the kisses whether they are truly original and not false papal bulls; with the course of events he takes care to separate the original thread of the story from the subsequent coating of myth, sobriety of inspiration, amatory puritanism, from the stylization of routine, et cetera, and when all that has been peeped through in order to compose the opus of love, there jumps to the front something one calls the magnetic core of life, for which there was no opportunity to keep track of the lover's parts of the body from the viewpoint of authenticity as, after all, they were totally insulated from it, there was only one single moment when a little morsel, nonsensical in itself, dropped from the whole data set of love that he, naturally, greedily seized upon; from this single awkward mosaic he had to create a work to outclass the work of man, to whom a thousand details were available.

Man senses, as has already been mentioned, with a wise and discerning melancholy, that the plot part is not going to be of assistance in finding his style of pain, and for that reason, as he really has no choice, he attempts to imitate the dimly suspected technique of life (his big rival). For example, he would pick out a detail — let's say a picture of the departing railway wagon, the zippy movement of the carriage marked Paris Est, with which the transition from the stationary position to motion is not even apparent: the slim body of the whole is so streamlined, even before starting, and yet, so little is seen during motion from the movement of the wheels, nor does anything stir on the upper body of the carriage, so that it effectuates more of a 'motion-standstill' average than those conceivably opposed states separately; besides, the railway track is set on a long platform, so that the arrow-straight line of the rails already anticipates the train's motion or 'activation of distance,' which is essentially different from motion (both more and less: more because it is 'cleaner,' more independent of physical determinants, and more of an aerial-hot realization of the concept of motion, but less because the notion of a goal has withered from it like a useless leaf and thus it lacks anthropoid drama, thus by the time it actually sets off on the rails, one does not sense any moving away, only an intensification of distance represented by the rails: a departing railway carriage is not motion but no more than the conjuring into life of the lifeless province of the rails, as if every distance were simply an unexpected incandescence of sleeping space, just as in music when one wishes to bring out a sound ever more strongly and there is no other way of solving that than to elongate the duration of the sound: if one emphasizes the spatiality of a small area, pronounces an ictus on it, or animates it from within, it will transform with chemical accuracy into living distance (*ubiquitas inflammatio est hiccitatis*).[62]

That is why the rail branches diverging from the shared trunk of a railway station also possess no geometric or geographic quality, but are at best melancholic petals arising from the excitation of 'being there,' unperturbed reflexes of precise melody (*transfloreatio hiccitatis intentionalis seu de identitate Motu ac Spatii: stabilitas est spatium virtuale, ac Motus semper idem spatium est, sed vivans*).[63]

The ultimate lesson of the 'starting' of the railway wagon, then: motion is non-existent, only two kinds of space: a preformed pseudo-space, which is just a task, so to say, a task to be solved as space rather than a true space (as symbolized by the slim pair of rails vanishing into the distance), and a real, living space, as opposed to the previous dead one: it is the transformation of pseudo-space into real space that looks like motion, which, naturally, is an optical illusion.

But man is not completely duped by that illusion as when the wagon 'started,' he straight away sensed that the phenomenon did not correspond to the clichéd mundane experience of motion. It is no accident that a suffering person loses this random detail so that he could adhere to life's magnetic core, but he himself offers it to life, he himself carves a fissure on the wall of the plot (the story of departure) so that life should capture that detail (the image of the departing wagon, with its opalescent identification of space and motion, seems very suitable for life, which likes such indefinite symptoms, to catch it: one is inclined to believe that the exchanges of values and collisions of proportions which occur in plots are special signs of contact with life, or at least of intention, so to say little slices in the plot which are prepared for assimilating life), but life does not catch it because life does not like sentimentally indefinite entities, it does not like torsos, as understood in a narrative sense, but logical sperms: as much as — 'the woman departs,' & it would be futile for Don Juan to offer the foolhardiest detail from his own story of life, that would still be plot, however indefinite and misty, 'vital' & 'imprecise': no child would come of it — the womb is indifferent to gallant anecdotes.

When the man who has taken leave staggers homewards from the railway station he feels that he cannot truly suffer, because his pain does not yet have a true form — what he feels, that discomfort, is not pain but precisely the absence of pain; sometimes one recollects an old melody with total emotional fervor, feels its rhythm internally, and still cannot sing it — the man feels something like that on his way home from the station: he wants to surrender himself to the clear beats of the waves of pain, but they haven't flared up as yet, so he must struggle in the slight waters, the tiny ripples, of the plot.

Even when he thinks of narcoses, he does not wish to forget pain, but the formlessness of pain; it is vain his pressing and releasing, straining all the locks on his memories, for not one of them would open: a memory is not the inside of a drawer, just an external image — when he tugs on those drawers without a key he is obviously not seeking plot details as those are painted on the outside of the drawers, after all, but their inner contents, of which he can feel only the weight, their nature being perfectly unknown.

It is so clear that the pain is caused by the termination of cohabitation with the woman that it is inconceivable to him that the style and composition of the pain might arise from anything other than the woman's actual body, & that is why he always returns with desperate automatism to that, being unable to persuade himself that a picture of the cause could not count at all on a picture of the effect: to achieve a harmony of pain he is capable of anything (that harmony was a *sine qua non* for pain to be painful at all), except the sole redemption, which is to forget about the cause of the pain: to forget about the brown polka dots of the girl's blouse, the brass buttons of her suit, the whiteness of her beret, the sandal form of her shoes, the morning stroll on the hillside, the evening dialogue in a little urban park, the great adolescent-like recognition of each other on the greedy bridge of a common piece of reading — all that had to be discarded in order for him to be able to find the resolving composition of pain.

But who is able to eradicate what he has lost, even from his memory, just in order that he might, perhaps, truly find it? Instead he becomes immersed in the Baroque esthetic of the memory & thus tries to salvage what is salvageable: the 'story' of a terminated cohabitation with the woman.

Regret puts the man before a crossroad: on the right hand is the opium-laced promenade of memory, to the left the thorny path of forgetting. This would be an opportunity for him to see the essence inherent in love, the essence that had attracted him so far but which he could only reach with the complete suspension of love; it is in the woman alone but can only be possessed without memory of the woman — he needs to become immersed in the woman, but then leave the whole matter behind; in full knowledge of the premeditated infidelity, he needs to make such a big love glow in himself that infidelity will be impossible — who is able to disabuse that example of naïve paradox into practice? (The formulation of pain is not pure work because it involves Janus-facedness: as if the pain were at times the same as the 'essence' of love, & the mind were working on both simultaneously. If he had found the form of pain, he might in addition also have found what comprised the 'essence' in love & in the woman.)

The fact is that through his own efforts there is no way he is capable of forgetting, and his entire life will hang in the air until an outside power makes him do that. Some day, though, he will hear a piece of wonderful music, glimpse a marvelous landscape, or meet a strange & attractive woman, and at that moment he will cease being a slave to his own short novel, forget (from the point of view of assessment, of course, not visually) the episodes, the woman, even himself, and will feel that that is all just a small part of a gigantic structure, of a single living, breathing, & hovering system.

---

the relationship of system & component, a simile of that:
the whole façade of a church & a statue from close-up

If one arrives at a hotel in the evening, one sees only a few windows, a few lampposts, and some white spots on the mudguards of the taxis suggesting a remote star, but in the morning the black wadding of the dark, which protected the whole city against brittleness on the intrepid slope of rushing hours, drops off, though already in the evening had had a presentiment of greater distances and a richer architecture, by morning are nevertheless mechanically prepared for little, suddenly flit over the sea of houses, towers, & bends in the streets as if they were not looking but fluttering this way and that to wherever the rippling wind tossed them over the expanded world: 'vision' is like the electron, so fashionable: it may not be present anywhere, but its waves of probability fill infinite space; it makes a tactile sketch, adjusting to the wind, which likewise embraces the form of objects only by and large, letting them go with sketch-kisses.

If one was placed onto the façade of a cathedral, into the place of a dislodged saint, one may cautiously feel around for the wall of the niche, the middle of the nearest columns, the blind iambics of the acanthuses on the capitals of the columns, and fashion all of that into a nice joined-up nest for oneself. In the morning, however, one would notice that there were another hundred niches like one's own ranged alongside it, and there were another three similar stories below as well as above it. Then one would be obliged to carry out the ambiguous operation of multiplication, which consists of sending off the nocturnal nightclub plasticity from the palpated niche to those lined up into the infinite distance, which is complicated by the fact that the radiating monotonous row of distant niches rains like the sheaf of a fountain toward the one and only niche that has been endured, as if they were seeking to wash out its subjective realism with their own incorporeality — there is no giddier feeling than to learn that something we had initially become acquainted with as a goldsmith's minute work is of unexpectedly endless extent, especially when the extension is mainly due to the multiplication of the known detail.

We shall lay our hands on the head of the statue next to us, and from the depth (that in the case of a church façade we do not feel to be a necessary depth only a contingency of our outlook; under normal circumstances, after all, the perspective is a natural constituent of space, indeed space itself, yet here the perspective is suddenly written to the account of our individuality, a disagreeable disease that we would like to shake off. That is the reason why in some of the statues there is no detail of depth, there is no depth-tendency inherent in the layout of the columns or the ornaments of the rose window, in contrast, for instance, to the details of a cliff wall or waterfall, every atom of which is already 'depth' in the way that every atom of oxygen is oxygen.

The church façade is only so enormously deep by accident, since in the drawing it is not predestined to be vertical: for that matter it might also accomplish that pattern horizontally, as is sometimes also accomplished, for instance, on the internal flooring, where the standing statues are substituted by the reclining figures on the grave plates, so that the whole floor is a reclining façade — &, perhaps most importantly: it could be executed on a smaller scale than with a waterfall and natural precipices) a similar one smiles in our direction: the one standing in the distance will be visible in 'natural' size, but, on the other hand, it only gained that naturalness of proportions through the unreality of perspective, while the giant doll that we have to hand may be surrounded by every minute touch of reality, it is true, yet on account of its proportions it is nevertheless foreign & mendacious.

The two kinds of figures ought to mix in order that a balance may be struck: the figure next to him is more just a massive shadow than a definite likeness, the plinth is just a romantic block of stone on which no purposeful decoration is evident — while in the distance, sunburned, only lines are to be seen with no mass, indeed, the dizziness on high is partly caused by the fact that one is unable to imagine the distant columns to be real material, reliable stone — as if the piece of wall on which one happens to be standing would, over time, be transformed into an airy backdrop, a floating drawing (the way a mermaid's positive breasts and concrete waist transform into a scaly and improbable fish: the simple and reliable forms of the breasts into a glistening, symmetrical and, for that very reason, seemingly frivolous drawing before fraying, even lower down, into faltering foam, the white froth of steam); the lower down one's eyes run, the more games and theoretical friezes there are, the less credible it is as stone, the more one feels that a lead doll & lead forest are hovering on a glass thread that is ready to break at any moment (symmetry's lost respect?).

The amorphous stone shadow next to one relates to the other hundreds and hundreds of its small-scale relatives like a dark tragedy does to an ironic little street romance that used to be written about it, off the top of the head in frivolous short rhymes ("shrewd suggestions of a wanton order..."): & while one bleeds to death from the wound of tragedy, one is obliged to listen to those glib lines, to discover in the gushing caprice of one's blood, the colored and regulated reflection of a hundred similar fountains, to see there a copy of the uncertain gesture of one's agony: the moment when one realizes that one is a member of a big system, and that it always harmonizes from ambiguous songs — only through miniaturization can one be an organic part of the whole, or in other words, turning meaningless leads into a feeling of gigantic intellectual harmony; on the other hand, precisely on account of its decorative perfection, we sense the completeness of intellectual structure, to be an eternal game, just an ironic halo around the formless fixity of one's own position; the plinth, as was said already, is a romantic block of stone on which there is barely any purposeful decoration, but now, when we see that little dent, which we felt was mere decay, a chance trace of time in a hundred copies, we are compelled to feel it as being artistic decoration, a cannelure planned with geometrical precision (the way blurred blotches on the edge of a page in a book cease to be meaningless blotches once the book is closed and they yield a map of fine colored lines, an artistic pattern, along with the others): the dented plinth and the slim lines arising from the repetitions in the distance are separate, but the latter is incapable of penetrating the former, only falling onto it like flirtatious rain or a dancing hypothesis.

The world of one's niche is the world of life, an asymmetrical cave with capricious lights & disheveled shadows, whereas the wall floating below one is the artificial world of truth, order, composition, where perspective rules instead of the unpolished experience of touch: a transition from the small environs of touch and lifelike short-sightedness into the perspectively shortening world of the whole façade (if one bends out from above and looks under, one has the impression that one's own cave is automatically transformed into order, a unitary structure of the façade, by one's mentally plunging down into the depths, through the fall), barely perceptible, which likewise intensifies the feeling of uncertainty: around one mere-life, beneath one mere-perspective — one wonders whether the supporting pillar of life can be a blank piece of sheet music of perspective?

Irony and magnificence encounter in the feeling that awoke in us when we discovered ourselves as a so-called organic part of a system: irony, because the discovered order only just surrounds us and projects its theoretical reflections on us (besides being just cosmetic & fictional in nature!) (so, as far as the 'organic' part of our being is concerned, that is not at all organic, merely optical) — but also magnificence, because with the system being just a visual accompaniment, it gives us a degree of freedom — we rock like a light boat on the buoyant waters of the system: it is thanks to the deeper positiveness of life that the little dinghy of life can sway on the waters of a giant, regular decorum — maybe that is what is magnificent.

The pain, therefore, not a forgotten atom of which could play a part in the preceding story of pain, at last floats before the suffering man's eyes as a self-supporting 'system,' & thus he can inspect it broken into two parts: the events form one step, as if they led somewhere & he stands atop that illusory pyramid of events awaiting the redeeming panorama, awaiting the summary perspective from which, naturally, nothing will come, instead a finished melody will be heard in the distance, from an indefinable place and direction, a rhythmic mere-sense, as if a big stack of words were lying under it, and the 'sense' would radiate toward him, independent of words, from the wandering lap of the distance.

What is the typical characteristic of this simultaneously shallow and precise system which unifies the restless-sharp wave vibration of a microscopic viewpoint & the single-waved gloom of a memory of mood? This unexpectedly incipient order best resembles the situation in which one looks with binoculars at a cluster of bells hanging in a distant tower and at the same time hears the music streaming out of them.

Those kinds of 'order,' like this pain, all go back to those 'binocked carillons': the chaotic motion in the middle, the gleaming ends of the bell clappers, the wobbling shadow of the bowls of large bells, the clockwork-like chatter of lights, of small bells: one sees in the binoculars the most chaotic jumble of largeness and smallness, light and shade, speed & sloth. By contrast, streams of the purest harmonies penetrate our ears like the regularly successive ripples of a lake: the fountain in the middle of the lake is all tiny blobs of water, torso pearls and foam shredding, but close to the bank those capricious twitches of water soften into combed undulations as if it were not a hysterical knot of energy eddying in the center, only the water's absent-minded self-consciousness asserting itself in each such broad and flat wave, in the same way as the self-consciousness of women in a lazy state is expressed in aimless adjusting, with a bare-touch, a wavering wrinkle on the knees of the drapery of a dress.

The autonomously floating pain thus unites in itself every roulette-grimace of lewdness and the closed firmness of recognition: when a suffering person spots the music, the landscape, or the woman-with-a-wonderful-exterior that is eliciting the system of pain, he is unsure offhand whether to reel from inebriation (those dancing bells of caprice) or to plunge to the bottom of contemplation like a body swimming on the water to which has been added that infinitesimal excess weight that all at once pushes it into the deepest of depths (that is the melody that streams from the bells).

That duality determines the ultimate relationship to the faraway woman: up till now he could feel that his relationship to her signified that every point of his individuality was bound to every point of her face, movements, and voice, like every single strand of Gulliver's hair was fastened to the ground in the land of the Lilliputians: now, after the budding of the autonomous pain inflorescence, that image does not correspond to the new impression that is felt about the relationship. Just as the pain is not located in the events, but separately, so love (from the new point of view of pain) is not attracted to certain components of the woman but, with a single magnetic grip, thrusts them en bloc toward the woman: the individual attributes that the woman found worthy of affection flutter around the private-strong idea of 'behold the woman' in the form of merely stylized hypotheses, one-sided sketches.

The way pain is, that might be the picture of the woman in memory: for one thing, just the colorless-odorless, thought-like relationship to her, the immaterial but massive logical line of fatal dependency; for another thing, the stray, torn, exaggerated, or cut-down picture of individual properties, which flutter hesitantly like falling leaves round the strict line of force, & if by any chance they fall very close to it, then they may possibly adhere to the immaterial center, now on its last legs, of 'behold the woman.'

This, too, is a duality of frivolity and precision, as in pain: in disintegrating, the image of the woman fluctuates & seesaws as if released from the shackles of the profile, experiencing an airier, more frivolous, world of free versions of profiles; on the other hand, the woman's attractive force became barer, it is not diffused into her limbs but, being sucked out from them, collects in a separate place; in other words, she attracts the man more strongly and fatally, in a bee line, as it were: that is the intensification of precision.

Hitherto the man had not sensed the two things as being separate: his love was a mass of vision and strength rolled into each other; a situation made possible, of course, by the physical presence of the woman. Now, however, the probable woman had vanished, & all that was left was the man's attitude toward the woman: the sun was no more, but what was left was a sunflower in its own special attitude, that he is unable to recognize, since only the sun had figured in his consciousness hitherto. If one embraces a woman, in truth, one has not the least idea of the self-sufficient gesture of embracing, only of the woman: we don't have the impression that we are laying our arms on her from outside, like an accidental garment, but that one is in the shape of the woman, slightly underlined, systematized, and emphasized. If, all of a sudden, she were to disappear or dissolve in one's arms, and one were to remain stiffened in the model of the embrace, one would have no knowledge at all of the woman's form from one's own gestures; the embrace is not a simple negative of the form but its irregular & incongruent pair.

pain & fidelity.
Absolute fidelity as the formal precursor of infidelity

Now that the woman has departed one sees oneself in one's own eyes in a totally unfamiliar form; one had thought that the woman was a statue, whereas one's self was just a pliant sealant into which her form becomes impressed and thus, if she goes away, an accurate blazon of her absence will remain. Instead of which, however, another statue has remained — one that had been imagined hitherto as being only negative: a self-sufficient, new, unknown positive formation, a completely new plastic costume, so that he does not even recognize himself in his solitude and is incapable of drawing closer to the departed woman in spirit. He is driven near-mad by his desire for her and his pain, but when that pain assumes a realistic form, precisely on account of the pain he feels himself as being so alien vis-à-vis himself that he is unable to envisage a shared past in which his former personality was still face-to-face with the woman. While they were together it was only a matter of a 'love' in which both of them merged and held each other in balance: the 'love' was a joint work that they beheld and enjoyed together, sometimes stretched out on it as in the grass of a jointly owned luxuriant meadow, sometimes they were swept a long way away from it and gazed at it from a distance, but the emphasis was always on that 'love,' that third entity outside themselves.

Now, after the parting, the man notices (of course, the woman may also have noticed, but seeing that up till now the man has been the protagonist of these cogitations, let us stay with him) that the 'love' has disappeared: like a chess player who sees that the board & chessmen are suddenly snatched away from under his nose & instead of the 'game,' which up till then had seemed to be the sole & exclusive reality, suddenly an alien and fundamentally unsympathetic reality is attacking — in point of fact, the reality of the 'player': himself. The man realizes for the first time that he is 'in love' — & that knowledge, the awareness of a new role, betokens such an upheaval for him that it cuts off the way from him, so he could imagine 'love' in his memory: the two are mutually exclusive.

When children rip the head off a hobgoblin, all at once a long wire can be seen sticking out of the beheaded hobgoblin's neck: when the woman was separated from him, the naked & wild line of force tying him to the woman, the energy skeleton of the relationship, could be seen all at once. The head, though, rolls a long way away and becomes a dancing ball in the hands of chance: the woman's face, exterior, her entire concreteness, are not permeated by force (in the way that in the world of atoms there are states in which the concept of 'energy' has no meaning) but hover separated, self-sufficiently, like fleeting reflexes. The system of pain was also followed by the woman's individual image, two 'binocked carillons,' which, naturally, were joined as a third by fidelity's peal of bells (or rather this was already practically in them).

From the very start 'fidelity' was rendered impossible by the great strength of the longing for the woman; that longing and that pain so transformed, distorted, and forcibly renewed the man that in this altered form he was incapable of fitting himself into the old duet — either he would be destroyed completely in the community of 'love,' or he would become absurdly concrete, & thus foreign to himself, in the unknown role of 'lover,' there being no third possibility: this is the dilemma of personality with every love.

Besides the simple fact that pain has erected a dividing wall between the man and the woman (to be pedantic: between the lovers & love), it burnishes and lubricates the slippery path of infidelity (which had already been present in fidelity from the very start): due to the woman's attractive force and her image separating and the fatefulness of love becoming obvious, the image itself became liberated, elastic, & hypothetical.

During the absence, the separate force and image willy-nilly develop independently: the personality of the woman who has gone away is preserved much more by naked power than by visual memory traces relating to the woman. This is surprising because power, due to its abstract nature, seems anonymous, yet nevertheless the reality is that the woman's 'nude figure of force' is more individual during her absence than her 'nude figure of image.' But is there any such thing at all in the memory as a 'nude figure of image'? When people talk about memory traces they are usually thinking of two main traits: their dimness and their synthetic nature. As if they were a matter of sketches of watercolors that merely depict the contours and dominant blotches of an immense wild chestnut tree, that is, the 'essence' taken in a sort of 'optical' sense, but that is only an imagined painterly essence & has nothing to do with the style of memory traces (for example, Constable's sketches unite the relationship between essence & ephemerality, as if the cardinal sense of a landscape were identical to its theatrical 'tic').

People in general do not pay attention to the pictorial aspect, in the strict sense, of their memories, but only bother with the conceptual consequences that a memory has evoked, and therefore by memory 'trace' they mostly imagine a Constable-sketch of that kind when, for instance, they think of a man's memory traces of the departed woman: as if the woman's face were appearing in the air a little hazily but all the more succinctly. In reality, however, it is precisely the opposite: the trace is not hazy and not succinct, because the much talked-of 'stylizing' power of memory does not, in fact, exist.

When the man turns his attention toward the woman with a certain artistic violence, he does not see the outlines of syntheses but, on the contrary, fragments of mosaics, as if chopped-off pieces of a microscopically realistic photograph were lying before him. Or, to stick with the parallel of analogies: while people in general imagine 'memory traces' as being Constable-sketches (as in films, when the main figure recollects a past scene, a much hazier but more succinct image is copied on top of a picture of the present), in reality they are more like Japanese woodcuts: lilies fall from unexpected directions into the center of the picture, or rather sheet of paper, and they run seemingly toward their structural complements beyond the paper — before them is a void, after them a precipice, but in the intervening part glittering cell-realism. Thus, a memory trace will always be a torn-off bit of a photograph: a torso of a movement, a nod of the head, a fragment of a sentence, or detail of a dress, between which there is no connection, and if the man were to lose his rational strength and photograph his memory traces, he would look at them as fragments in a museum cabinet of chess pieces, which do not belong together and have been produced in a hundred different styles, bearing an inscription along the lines of "other finds, which have remained unclassifiable, deriving from various dates and from various sites."

Whilst the desire radiates as a homogeneous ray from the man toward the woman, he is unable to set up a simple, stylistically consistent pictorial equivalent to force, and it would be no use his trying to concentrate the pieces of the torn-up mosaic in the vicinity of the force: a racing railway train might set fallen tree leaves a-dancing around itself over one thousand kilometers, but it will never be able to reconstruct them into a coherent tree. Thus, the memory traces also assist infidelity: memory tries to develop each separate single pictorial fragment further, one by one. A truly 'stylizing' work is set in motion here, though not in the sense adverted to earlier (according to which the constant erosion of time would lap uniformly around the picture of the woman, like water around the oval body of a boat floating in it, or an iceberg that a warm Golf-palm models with synthetic strokes), but every single detail develops further, not by molding its own individuality toward a common form lurking at the bottom of all the details, but, on the contrary, by sharpening its own individuality, distancing it still further from the presumed common (in truth, anyway, non-existent) image of the woman.

The man remembers a kiss gesture: it has no date, nor exposition, nor evolution — an analytical slice of an image hangs in the air: a portion of an arm, the wrinkles of a bending elbow, like the creases in a glove after the first time of use: the skin's positive but inexpressible fragrance; an indistinct portion of the jaw and mouth in an upper corner of the picture, slipped and crooked as on the rainbow periphery of a lens, and a strong bubbling of blood soda around the lips not so much on the chin as on the lower part of the nose; when he recalls these, the few seconds of oscillation consist of this tingling around the lips and the elbow's glove-like wrinkles alternating in his memory (like a French name card and a Sumatran bottle of medicine); while the memory trace appears in movies and in naïve drawings as a miniature picture, here it is a fifty-fold enlargement; he does not read a novel but only looks at two senseless letters through a magnifying glass. But the concentrating power of memory is so weak that he is unable to hold his attention on even those two letters (the way that in a pitch-black room only a fairly small area can be precisely looked at with a dark lantern: it does not conjure up a general semi-gloom instead of the darkness, but an overaccuracy [sense] restricted to a minimal [stupid] area, and that helplessness is already leading to stylization, because the attention is musically varying the two letters), in accordance to their oscillations.

According to the Constable-superstition, the memory would darken the woman's arm black, harmonize it into the ground plan, but reality contrives the opposite — to the given memory of kisses (one of the characteristic features of which is that it does not represent the woman but only a unified picture of the man's lips and the woman's arm, in which even the intensity of the feeling is still contributing in a spatialized form, as is customary in feverish dreams: if the memory trace were photographed, one would not recognize anything human, but it would show a transitional form between a musical score and a hallucination; the realism of memory traces is never identical to the superficial realism shown by an ordinary portrait photograph; among other things, the intensity of the feelings of the one who remembers, strengthened to the point of being graphic, always contributes to the memory trace as, for example, in the present case where the velvety big umbrella of excitement, which, from a photographic viewpoint, may well be an exceedingly imaginary thing, is an anatomical datum, a central part of the body, in the imagined memory photograph) it creates a new woman in time, a woman whose entire arm has come into being from that cell of 'elbow bend + nose tingling + female chin detail,' from which cell, in just the same way, her legs, her back, her whole body, her dress, her character, will also develop.

Relating that to the earlier example: the tree leaves dancing beside the racing railway train will never again be reconstituted into the one & only original contiguous tree crown, but out of each and every tree leaf will develop a new, separate, and entire tree crown on which the individual leaves, branches, roots, blossoms and fruits will all be 'pictological' developments of the original fallen leaf.

This is the real stylizing ability of memory: not to produce a single portrait, but to develop the fragments from a thousand portrait fragments into a thousand entire female figures. Instead of creating a single hazy essence-doll in place of the departed woman, it conjures up an entire picturesque society. With a dark lantern one sees only a small detail of the embroidery of a pitch-black room: one goes home and creates the entire room, all the furniture, frescoes, chandeliers, the contents of the books lying in the bookcases, the guests who will be sitting in the room in the future, into new entities from this bit of embroidery-ornamentation. Afterwards one will again throw light on another detail with the piccolo lantern, e.g., one will see with it just a single Roman numeral on a clock face: once again one will go through the previous game, the whole room will be composed in the style of a Roman numeral (just how 'sound' that work is can be seen from the great facility, without any strain, with which the fever is able to form an entire human from a Roman IX, for instance).

In the same way, one produces an entire palace full of variants of the room on the basis of the little illuminated particles: a female society from a couple of memory shards. The practical upshot of that is that while the synthetic-hazy memory trace of the woman, if it existed, would sharply differ, being unique, from all other women with whom the man, in his loneliness, might meet, those woman variants (in point of fact, barely-variants as they are by now infinitely remote from the subject of the memory) which have developed from the ultraprecise germs of memory, are much likelier to allow newer, strange, genuine, and living women to be interpolated into their company just as yellow, in its own unique character, excludes green, but variants of it can be readily placed into a rough spectrum as a hundred shades of yellow, among which, even red and green may easily appear at the edges.

The roots of trees sometimes stand a long distance apart from each other but the crowns meet. Thus the memory wrecks of the departed woman that have remained may lie at inorganic distances to each other, but the entire new female figures can be set up in rows that easily melt into one another, because the ultra-realism of the germs is unable to reach out at full strength to the perimeter of an entirely new female figure in the same way as a loud green and a loud yellow liquid are totally foreign, but if one makes a fountain out of them, the pearling and powdering crests of the jets of water shade into each other.

If he makes the acquaintance of a new woman, the exterior of the strange woman can always be fitted between two shades, which are two complete female figures developed from two 'faithfully' preserved memory traces: a yellow polka dot pattern on a blouse pulses a million vibrations around itself, which is to say it constructs a million strange female exteriors and characters, among which, naturally, it is easy to fit in anyone, because even a red square pattern can be a wave limit of a 'yellow polka dot' pattern, besides the man recollects a hundred more details — each fragment makes millions & millions of entire female waves pulse around itself; in other words, from a couple of ultraspecial fragments (from the discrete quantum-theoretical '*Eigenbilder*' of fidelity),[64] an entire probable and as yet conceivable female status is automatically created (infidelity's absolutely complete & infinitely continuous series of women): a 'faithful' husband is never caught by surprise when he sees a strange & new woman as that, too, was already among the million stylization-waves of some memory wreck: it was already present in the previous woman.

To put it another way, memory constructs a mechanical fault scale in place of 'synthesis': it prepares fragmentary pictures of the one and only woman with a million misprints, as if a distorting machinery were steadily tracing a single portrait stub a million times over, right, left & center, up & down, but altering the color, form, the outline and the interior just a shade with each & every one of them, so that when the man comes across a strange woman, her specific & living truth instantly fits into one or another of the unintended misprint cases of fidelity.

second example from The Antipsyche Idylls; *analysis of the hush over the lake at night. Introduction to this: the relationship of infinitely many lines & absolute smoothness. Lace on the woman's dress: a million leaves in the nocturnal scene. Simple silk of the woman's dress: absolute hush in the nocturnal scene'*

When the man pulls his coat out of the cloakroom & lugs it, like winged game, over the heads of short women, who moan indignantly like downtrodden branches & knocked-aside foliage, all at once a gaunt woman tumbles out of the slipshod trap of the heavy coat like a startled little fugitive: she hastily cranes her head to and fro, like a wavering beetle wagging its antennæ like little whips; she would like to jump down, feel the air around herself, and for that reason she tries to assume her leanest possible form: around her are nothing but darkly clad men in black and blue jackets that encircle the frolicking little silverfish like inky primitive sponges; the men sway slowly like sunken wineskins which have finally touched the bottom but, with a lazy minimum of elasticity, are unable to rest in one spot but keep on rising above the ground — the little woman, on the other hand, performs in the cloakroom, from down below upwards, those startling movements, reminiscent of a chain of paragraphs, that electric string lizards & glass-*choc*[65] Venus' Girdles customarily perform when they throw themselves like an arrow from the bottom toward the surface — with her ankles she sets a small letter S in train toward the crown of her scalp, and by the time the set-in-train quivering small-S has run lightning-quick to the knees, newer small S-es have been sent on its heels, starting off from the ankles; if one watches among the threads of the corkscrew the one that is at the opening of the bottle, one has the impression that one new replacement after another of the rising, initially observed screw threads is constantly coming from the bottom of the bottle; and in the same way, from the perpetuum-chain of letter S-es, the young-missy paragraph of ever-continuation & long-completedness comes into being: the lean young girl thus danced and struggled from the bottom upwards between the horizontal swaying of torpid male bodies.

Her dress was a light cream color: absolutely smooth & cut to fit, though with the occasional grotesque grimaces of wrinkles running over it, which had nothing to do with the girl's figure, because it was not her muscles which had brought them about but the external pushing & shoving of surrounding people, to the point that it was almost necessary for two people to hold the flailing concert girl up; the abruptly running wrinkles (if one delivers a small rap at the bottom of a large, smooth mirror plate, then lines of newly arising cracks all at once run across the whole mirror) represented an alien figure of force, a detached caricature, which sometimes strove like a parasite to cling to the girl's body: the way historians of art make a distinction between the pleats on a classical chiton which follow the curves of the body, rigid muscles turning into waves as it were, and the folds of a late Gothic mantle, which have nothing to do with an angel's movements but are independent, foreign crumple ornaments, as if an autonomous and parasitic flower of force had taken hold of the angel's body, prompting its petals against it like a spinning top its rotations against the divisions in a parquet floor, so that this duality prevailed here, too: when the men gave a bit of free space to the woman, slippery rings of muscle ran over her body, whereas when they pressed her tightly, then an imposed crease ran over her defunct body like an improvised dress skeleton.

At first one notices nothing on such a pushy and whining little fellow-spectator, but if a snippet of subject from the toccata that one has just heard unexpectedly comes to mind, that sonic memory illuminates objects, people, or thoughts that happen to be in one's proximity: now, too, one is suddenly struck, under the influence of the sounds, by the delicate lace decoration hanging on the girl's smooth dress; until then, it had, in truth, been a matter of indifference to him, but now the two extremes of smoothness and roundaboutness united in algebraic-inebriated harmony; as he saw it, lace and silk, mirror plate and cobweb, glittering and thousand-branched coral, smooth lake surface and complex little well, were closely connected, almost identical: the woman's slim and not smooth body, with its own moss-radial, puritanical, and elastic surfaces, relates to the microbe-designed & thousand-filleted lace collar lying around her neck like a melodic & harmonic variant of the same scale: the network of lines is no more than the harmonic form of the melodic smoothness.

About how many antitheses might it yet turn out which, in point of fact, the difference between them is little more than the exchange or omission of one or two elements, not a radical dissimilitude of all the component elements.

The absolutely smooth and absolutely complicated, therefore, do not proceed against each other in opposite, north-south directions: a smooth whitewashed wall and an Arabian hyper-ornamentation inserted into it do not signify a 180-degree collision, but perhaps just a deviation of a single degree from a parallel. Or to put it genetically, if one takes absolute smoothness as coming first in time, let us say we have the body of a transparent fish resembling a crystal globe, then the minimal developmental step, the smallest possible change of the glass sphere within the shortest detectable time, will be a horrendously lined-over anatomical picture of a ball of cotton, without any transition; what was previously said about foreign wrinkles in the dress can be employed here as well: the least touch immediately elicits the greatest complication — the least rap on the mirror conjures up an enormous network of fine cracks, a complex wound-linearism, not greyish blotches, which for the time being, at least according to our naïve logic, would nevertheless be closer to the mirror's original smoothness.

One is decidedly of the impression that an arabesque was already present in the smoothed-down white wall from the very beginning, and it was necessary to drop in only a spot of foreign material, or set in motion just a puff of a wave for the linearism that is inherent in it to be chemically precipitated instantly: the way a sea of pearls, taking advantage of an easy salvation, will rise with the fizz in carbonated mineral water when a pinch of salt is dropped in it.

The idea that 'complexity' and 'homogeneity' can in no way be opposites, only melodic and harmonic variants of the same thing (two variants that signify no more than one degree of deviation from parallelism, but not in the sense that the two scales thereby intersect at some distance; rather that one of two parallel lines slips on a bit for a moment as if it were being mirrored, but afterwards it carries straight ahead on its way anew), as can also be sensed from their continually appearing together in modern architecture & dress design like a deep mental pressure, space-sapphism simplifying into abstract plains & decoration consisting of minute grids of lines: if one fixes a plane with artistic eyes, a minimal swing of attention immediately sees a chaos of lines in place of the plane; the two styles are the result of a single look, with the difference of an infinitesimal shift.

The woman's body will become ever smoother the more & more it resembles a light drill made of just one ray, which, with its own immaterial clearness S-es, ditches her fatigued body into the depths and fires it on high in order to knock a hole in the night; whereas the lines of the lace collar will become ever more acutely just lines, and the space throws out its hair's breadth thin but needle-hard branches in all directions; the more the girl's body and the lace cage that flutters on her move away from each other, the better one can sense their primordial one nature: in the end, the whole girl is just a lacquer-browed big nocturnal lake, which the light of a single lamp sweeps across (of the shivering paragraphs a single large integral sign remained in the silence), while the lace on her neck turned into ash-green bankside bushes crowded with tiny leaves and with vibrating branch innervation.

As he was lugging toward himself his coat from the counter over the heads of the people, the stump of a theme which had come to mind was still ringing in the concert-listener's ears, but a celestial scenery was already swimming before his eyes, which, however, had preserved with dream-like scrupulousness all of the original woman's influence in love: the woman's flaring muscle-smudges lived on fully in the lake's glittering blindness and the elastic plenitude of its wavelessness, and the naïve-coquettish elegance of the lace collar lived on in the veil exaggeration of trees & bushes. Both water and trees are uniformly stiffened in stillness, yet some kind of suggestion of a sound nevertheless radiates from within them: the water seems as if it would pour into a lower basin of one single deep booming of an organ, & therefore its basic state is not 'down,' but 'lower down,' whereas the trees make up a fizzling silence, a continual upward branching silence, which is always analyzed toward ever-higher harmonics, so that although every leaf and bud has been frozen into immobility on the branch, they nonetheless arouse on high an impression of perpetual attenuation & decay.

If one pays close attention to what our strongest impression is on viewing a nocturnal scene of lake and forest of that kind, or what best arouses a decisive impression of silence and stillness, one will happen upon that latent movement & latent sound: the lake will fall ever lower & lower, contract ever more together on the bottom of a series of basins that are tilting infinitely into the deep, whereas the bushes seem as if they would fly away, as if they were climbing over the water every moment — that is what their 'motionless'-ness consists of; the silence is likewise composed partly of that deepening boom and partly of a continually tapering & ascending, infinitely threaded falsetto.

Stiffness is always composed of the initial points of a million possible points: movement always represents a single drama, whereas stiffness the first aborted glints of the cells of a thousand dramas, the resultant of which is a wavy line of rigidity — thus, midnight muteness and immobility are more complex than simply performed daytime genuine movement & genuine sound; hence, if one is looking at a landscape, one totally has the feeling as in a theater when watching a curtain-raiser: it is not moving, but the knowledge that the curtain might be raised any moment makes one have the curtain raised a hundred times over.

Silence is chokingly exciting because it cannot be continued; silence cannot be 'dragged out' for long in the way that in singing, for instance, just one note is sung after taking a big breath: the silence starts off existing, but the very next moment one expects some sort of change, the silence has slipped out of one's hands and broken like a current — in order for it to continue existing, a renewed, second connection is necessary, then there is silence again for a very short time, though out of that some new direction is automatically effected that does not at all lie in the direction of silence: one's attention is turned in this new direction, though it was only given a blank-charged indication of sound there, the direction of a little hallucinatory spark in which the attention returns, disappointed, to the direction of silence: this game is constantly repeated, &, as mentioned, the irregularly twisting originating line of 'silence' is made up of restless little curves of these hallucinatory sparks. This continually interrupted A.C.-like behavior of silence is felt equally in the lower sphere of the lake as in the upper sphere of the trees, only there happens to be a difference in rhythm between them, the choreography of excitement is different.

If one looks at the lake, one has the impression that the silence-stratum lying in one's immediate proximity slips into the distance and, refreshed, returns again from there: the warm, blackly-glinting zone fogs up, but it reassembles anew at a distance and ripples back toward one imitating the tempo of inspiration and expiration. That rhythm, as a matter of fact, derives from one's sensing the dark-warm surface of the lake, the muddy odor evaporating out of it, as being itself silence, while the next moment, under the influence of an involuntary rationalist goose-bumpiness, one senses one's own human muteness as being silence, and thus consciousness steps into the place of the previous picture, so that it is a matter of an alternation of a silence of human consciousness and a picture silence of the landscape; there is never a true balance of silence, only a constant seesawing of two extremes, an exaggerated relief muteness of landscape silence and an unmimicked muteness of a void sensed in consciousness. Whereas with a lake this ebb-and-flow rhythm prevails (the ebb is the landscape, the flow the empty frame of consciousness), in the domain of bushes and trees capricious foci are scattered from which restlessness radiates in the form of reflex movements: it is as if silence were flitting between the branches in the place of sleeping birds, or the shortcuts of rested lizards were to be assailed by tiny Ampère-arrows of silence between fallen leaves & grasses blinded into crystal.

The silence, then, plays the daytime drama anew in the form of a radical pantomime in which the 'mime' turned out to be mere mental iridescence, of course; in place of waves, consciousness and landscape seesaw across each other; in place of the coruscating wings of birds, a polylogue continually jetting out of the thousand forms and groups of leaves & continually ceasing; as if it was a gigantic society, every member of which pulls the known grimace that is customarily pulled by those who very impatiently wish to say something but must nevertheless swallow back at the last minute because their superior has started to speak: the sea of stiff leaves all make that face, the sputtered words straining their clenched jaw. Beside a tiny zigzag movement, the hush also has a movement suggesting internal incandescence or expansion: when the Moon popped out from behind the trees and clouds, all at once it was suffused by a grey incandescence, but not in the direction of light and clarity but darkness & fogginess.

These alone are the magic minutes of the night during which darkness is truly able to flash over & shine itself into a star colloid, so that it does not awaken an impression of growing lightness, after all, but of growing obscurity: the Moon has no rays at such times, it lacks all of its alpaca routines; it floats solitarily and out of place in the milky-grey gloom powder as if that did not stem from it but were a perfume liberated from the darkness crowding among the trees. The way the deafeningly azure sea water immediately turns white, indeed changes into colorless surf, when a child splashes in it with its legs, so the darkness, as long as it is crushed together like charcoal in a forest, appears black under the great pressure; but if the grip is loosened even just a little bit, it comes out in its true form: glassy flower flour, pale-green moth powder, white ionization-boa.

Just as darkness floats over into this fresh fog blooming in early-spring leaf color, one has a feeling that, aside from its inner movements, as our entire solar system flies *en bloc* toward foreign & remote constellations in space, so this silence-system, aside from being composed of the flitting of little hallucination-orbits, is also flying faster & faster toward a distant, even quieter silence-target.

The shivering shadows on the surface of a lake are the measuring instruments of that dual movement: they perpetually shiver, pull apart, merge, gain independence as waves, but at the same time as they perform a rallying movement, there is also a movement of a single big ascent, of melodic continuation: they outgrow the lake, and, like a spherical lift, they raise the whole landscape on high. One would instinctively like to sing or play the violin, because that way one would be able to run in parallel to the continually ascending silence: in silence one sees everything from an Expressionist worm's eye viewpoint as if one were in the opening of an evenly rising fountain and viewing the ascending column of water from exactly the middle of the starting-point of the water jets — one sees at first only a slim jet and at the end a snap fastener of profligacy, unable to penetrate higher & thus falling back in glittering boughs of water: silence also rises for a while, dizzyingly, straight as an arrow, to the clearest springtime brightness; the pale-green color of the moon, which ever more clearly approaches the luscious pallor of leaf buds, is accomplished so completely in the end that one falls off it like the drunken froth of a reckless water jet, so that, totally losing one's balance, one staggers between the water's black mirrors of confession & apple-silver gloom-fjords.

By then silence is blaring like a triumphant finale: there is no difference at all between the moonlight, tempered into golden air, and the lake — the water appears to rise from unknown depths, at the place where the black tents of the trees cease, the inverted mirror images cling to the edge of the banks like rubber balls which are incapable of remaining in the depths of the water & strive to occupy the highest possible position at all costs, and one has the impression that if the landscape were to be shifted a hair's breadth, those mirror images, which had slid up to the bank on the elastic wall of an infinite vacuum, would suddenly soar high up like air balloons, and most likely they would also take the whole landscape with them.

Because the landscape seems to be a really small ribbon of embankment that was set before the universally rising wave of silence; a pointillist horizon-ornament which is at times a bridge and at times a dike above that crater of fog, which came into being on the site of the lake and thus relates to the bushes of the shore like a soundless night '*train bleu*'[66] does to the missing mute railway station — it is part of the essence of silence that it is always 'in transit,' never in the lake, among the trees, or in an amiable and transparent apse of the heavens, but an alien movement in relation to every single object, which only ever fulfill the role of a precise filter or harp string; the string owes the finest completion of its individuality to encounters with a touch running across it, so the sharp contour of its individuality coincides with every openness of distance.

Every pure sound has that double influence: if a string is twanged, one simultaneously feels the ever-stronger modeling, thickening, and concretization of something, but along with that, the formation of an open path of mood, the amorphous spreading out of one's soul, its tottering indecisiveness: as if the only way to intensify a positive was to intensify the gloom as well, as an unavoidable side-effect. Silence, too, which runs in outer space via an anemic emerald trajectory and brushes *en route* the colored leaf-eyelashes of the trees, sets in motion an ambiguous movement like this on the blind silhouette of the tree — it makes it sound even more black, or coats it in velvet three octaves lower, i.e., banishes it back into its essence but at the same time there remains around it, like an invisible cello bee, the open swish of hurrying on, the humming of distance (just like inside telephone & telegraph posts), the enticing shadow of the forbidden fruit of space.

The soul perceives the ancestral unity of an enhancement-substance and an enhancement-ephemerality as a perpetuum mobile of silence in shifting rhythm, and for that very reason it involuntarily bursts into song: only a melody is capable of imitating that game of ambivalence, which goes on behind the green veils of the night.

But only at a time of complete wakefulness is it necessary for one to imitate the silence with a genuine song, because even if one nods off just a tad on the beach next to the stiflingly phosphorescent current of silence, the landscape, with the charming self-evidence of a dream, will, in any case, be instantly identical to a song. One can almost observe the point in the slumber at which the landscape is still a landscape, and at the next point, following immediately after it, a song: if a croaking frog awakens him for half a tic, then during that half a tic the snoozer will have a sharp sense that the song is again being seen as a landscape; indeed, the sole typical feature of that half a tic of waking is the momentary deafness — one did not awaken because the frog croaked, but because the song-form of the landscape was all at once not heard (as if the door of a room from where a piano could be heard were suddenly closed), though the next moment one again swings back to the staircase of consciousness, whence the song now clearly flows toward one. That half a tic for which one was awake on account of the frog's croaking was in the final analysis much more unconscious than during slumber: precisely when the eyes were open, the ears registered sounds, and one was sensitive to touch, one felt paralyzed; indeed, became unconscious. Those awakening caesuras that keep on breaking the slumber are felt much more as pangs of death than sleep itself.

One suddenly becomes a dual being during a waking start of that kind (no more than a shuddering ripple on the intact lake of dreams); one opens one's eyes but does not allow the seen picture to penetrate to the soul, yet, by what is almost strong muscle work, holds the thread that one had woven in dream and will continue after the awakening pause; on the one hand, one isolates the wakeful state with a bold gesture, on the other, one holds on to the thread of the dream with one's hand, so that one does not mix reality and dream but holds both of them in two directions at the same time: one is neither dreaming nor, practically speaking, living, but grasping the ends of both with an insulator (rather like two fish that one simultaneously pulls up from the water), so that soon (after a deliberate choice) one lets go of the thread of reality, and, after half a tic's delay, sets that of dreams free: kills one of the fish (reality) and throws the other (the dream) back into the water.

At such times one takes especial delight in perverse games, indeed will wager with oneself on whether wakefulness or dream is going to win out after such an airless awakening pause: dreaming can be conceived as a long thread or a branch, the form, thickness, elasticity and durability one senses quite clearly even when one has awakened to the frog's croaking — the dream measurably survives the awakening as if the stage play had lasted a couple of moments after the curtain had been brought down, and one suddenly seizes that piece, hanging as it is into the space of wakefulness, and only in that way does one succeed in holding the whole dream for a moment, like clasping the end of the skirt of a woman who is seeking to escape, but at the same time the sharp blade of reality is also approaching at near-infinite velocity in order to quickly cut the little connecting bit (thread or branch) between the whole dream and one's hands. It is an amusing sport to hold that appendage of a dream before the blade of approaching reality to the last minute, thereby, so to say, exciting or tempting reality to rush even faster toward one, then at the last moment, when the blade is on the point of severing the thread, to suddenly snatch it away from the roused blade of reality and carry on safely dreaming further, and instead of cutting it off, to bring forth a gigantic new flower on the salvaged old branch, delighting to have gained a wager with oneself

— the dream won and continues. (However, if, on another occasion, one hears a fine song, one immediately senses the outlines of the awakening midnight silence landscape, so one might write on the music score in restaurant menu language: '*paysage y compris.*')[67]

relating to the analysis of silence: the dilemmas of longing & their resolution in dream

All this signifies the unveiled delights of darkness: similarly to unveiled sensual love. Sometimes one goes to sleep by preparing a planned dollop, a pastiche which rocks us out of the portrait of the desired woman and the raw material of one's cravings, and on that account some brake on desire always plays a part: one's own personality and the woman's personality are two big obstacles that do not allow the desire to reach its target at its own pace, approaching the speed of light. Indeed, in a conscious state, one does not even feel the positive percussive force of desire, only the negative of oneself and the woman's personality, so that on the occasion of an unexpected encounter, bouncing back immediately after an elastic collision is a natural reaction, and an 'all the same' approach is already a mental assault.

The woman's physical picture (because it is a picture, not a desire-rack) stands at the center of big repulsive forces; for a while the arrow of desire can fly straight toward her, but when it comes close to the whirlwind-like circle of desire, the vortex takes hold of it and, like some headstrong switch mechanism, diverts it to a broad bend out of her path. And while at first one imagined a situation in which the goal of one's desire was hovering like a magnetic statue in front of one, I don't see one soon has the feeling that the statue is behind one and is holding the arrow which is seeking to fly: in the 'first half' desire truly arouses the feeling that one wishes for something, but afterwards all one sees is that the target is a paralyzing injection in one's soul, which does not permit it to run to the end of its original course.

Picture a legendary traveler who glimpses from a long way off, in a valley, the foaming outlines of a city of one thousand towers: the traveler's heart soars high and he spurs his mount; a sudden momentum, an attractive force, sends him speeding straight toward the city as the crow flies. In the very next moments, however, the city flies into the traveler's soul, or the traveler's soul unites with the city, so that in point of fact he has reached the goal 'in spirit': but his horse, turned wild by the spurring, carries on galloping at the old pace. On the other hand, the goal is no longer ahead of him and can no longer denote a direction, and the traveler is also unable to get his bearings: that is the stubbornly anticipated goal's vengeance. The genuine city vanishes & into its place steps a hallucinated labyrinth, which, of course, is a stylized & enlarged picture of the genuine one: while at first the outlines form a little isolated system in the distance, now the stifling high water of towers, cupolas, streets & dead-end streets billow round the traveler, who is unable to proceed further with his rearing horse.

The inner comedy of desire is that only two images are at its disposal: a little sketch hovering on the horizon and a diagram that has over-flourished & over-accumulated in the soul of the desirer — the 'truth' always drops out. When Romeo glimpsed Juliet, in point of fact it was not a burning chandelier that he caught sight of, it was only the index number of a voltmeter (the way the traveler of legend only spotted an abstract formula-city in the trembling depths of the valley); when he longed for her, then he no longer saw even the chandelier, only the senseless, chandelier-less-Juliet-less blue-green spots in his eyes, caused by its light.

Desire, in the sense of both resolute and purposive flight, was actually attained for just a single moment: at the instant the woman was glimpsed. At that point the spirit crashed on her like a wave crashing on coastal rocks: the very first glimpse forgets the social obstacles and flies to the woman's outlines in the knowledge of possession. The subsequent desire is actually just nostalgia for the golden age implicit in that atavistic moment: there was an entire history in that glimpse, the Arcadian variants of games of love, an entire landscape, a lot of traveling and shared adventures.

For that very reason there is always a defiant streak in desire: the desiring man always feels that the woman is wrongfully holding herself aloof since, after all, she has already once been his. The first glance, then, was already the first embrace, and desire always seeks the second embrace, not the first, which had already occurred at first sight, along with an entire associated novel. Desire increasingly assumes that nature of a 'legal relationship,' in contrast to the character of a natural relationship; one's own body and soul behave as if a woman simply 'attracts,' but if one looks at a woman, one cannot perceive her in any way other than as a structure that is equipped with the most refined repulsive organs; the whole woman is an automatic sentinel who will indefatigably defend whatever she is hiding behind it.

Attraction therefore cannot take her as the starting point, because, like 'half' of something, the desire has no complementary half in the woman, and thus it is of compromisingly unreal character. It is there much better to form a 'right' to the woman than to rely on the illusion of natural attraction.

The reason one thinks that way is because one humanizes women excessively: one supposes that beauty is of their doing, created in order to attract men. One cannot conceive that there would be no personal attractive will in the attractive force of a seductively lovely woman; one thinks that if a girl is fair then that equates to her being sure to want one. Yet volition and beauty may be infinitely remote to each other in the way the glittering façade of a superb castle and an eccentric proprietor may be infinitely remote to each other. However, one customarily overhumanizes not only the sham-blood smeared on the lips like butter, but also articles of clothing, indeed, objects which are no more than the woman's personal property and lie far from her (a handbag, for example), every pretty detail; a dress pattern or thinness of fabric can each separately be imagined as being attractive little personal characters which knowingly summon one.

Thus, if one is confronted with a pretty woman, one might break her up in one's fantasy into ten or twenty street girls: the hat, a flower on the hat, the veil, the velvet patches on the veil, the cunning relationship of one velvet patch to another, the eyelashes, the movement of the eyelashes, the shadow made by an eyelash — each one of those signifies a miniature woman, each separately (just as with memory, as we have seen before), behaving like the most vulgar cocotte and inviting one, tooth & nail, by deploying their whole personality. The purse lying on the kitchen table while the woman has gone out of the room completely represents the woman: the shape of its fastener, the glistening of its lacquer inlay, all seem to be personal beauties, addressed to oneself, seeking to attract one to her, though that is a grotesque assumption not only for the lifeless purse but also for the living woman, in whom volition and knowledge are not scattered in a concentrated manner throughout every part of the body, so little cocotte buds should spring forth, but, on the contrary, they are located in a very small area, pressed up close together, like a little spider in a hidden corner of a net of an unknown material. That is the main reason why the female body represents a constant of negative value in the history of desire: indeed, desire itself also seems to be a kaleidoscope of aimlessness: one's own body and soul are totally permeated by desire, one's last cell and thought are saturated by it, and one involuntarily thinks the same about the woman as well; the way that a woodpecker's imagination is full to bursting with edible beetles & it believes that the bottom of a tree's bark is similarly crammed, but its impatient tapping convinces it of the reverse.

Just so the man, when he symbolically 'taps' the woman's blue eyes, merely responds to an imagined call by her; so much does he feel her initial desire only as a 'response' that he perceives the fact of beauty simply as a visible picture of the woman's desire — when he steeps his soul in the fog-azure petals of the twinkling eyes, in point of fact he is discoursing with the improvised ambassadors of desire. He soon notices, however, that the 'blue eyes' are not a promising landscape but a lifeless ornament in which there is no soul: it is simply there, but the woman does not reside in that 'blue eyes' garden. The ground attracts a dropped vase as well, but when they meet the latter smashes. It seems as though people discovered 'charity' earlier than impersonal & subconscious magnetism and therefore were unable to imagine that a pair of blue eyes can exist without a knowledge and plan of enticement being behind them.

Desire, therefore, continues to fondle female beauty like a blind person would an unknown statue: it feels more & more that 'beauty' & 'woman' are separate entities, or rather, that the desire was not aimed at that woman-person but at the beauty homunculi created from elements of beauty.

Desire is able to construct the ethical equivalents of esthetic qualities, and it always seeks the resonance of theses in a woman: the woman is just an inferred phantom. The rapture of the very first glimpse consists of a coincidence of beauty and that translation of 'charity': there is an ethical feature in blue eyes, a psychological element that the desiring man senses not just as a surplus radiating from the local esthetic of the blue eyes, but as the center of the woman; similarly, for him the character detail and volitional fragment of drama which can be read from the snake coral of the lips is not a forced experiment at selecting the ethic that inheres in the esthetic, but signifies an accurate and faithful expression of the woman's total personality — only later does he notice that the moral personality which can be constructed with mathematical accuracy from the woman's outer appearance is not at all identical to her true personality.

At the center stands the woman's body; to the left of that is the ethical portrait constructed from it, the most characteristic feature of which is that it strongly seeks to invite one; to the right is the true ethical face, which bears no relation to the external beauty. The man, however, has only the exterior to go on, starting from where the woman ends and where her personality no longer plays even a part or, if it does, then it is ridiculously slim and glaring; it is only natural that every conclusion will be in a mere ornamental relation to the woman's body.

If one hears a melody and it peels off with melancholic lethargy from the violin's body like a heavy husk, one instantly sees behind it the likeness & pose of a melancholic composer, and justifiably so, but that method leads one down the totally wrong track in enjoying beauty. The basic mistake desire makes, then, is that it tunes the external portrait that is built up of the woman and the inner character sketch into compositional affinity; the indicators of beauty are constantly pursued as ethic, & it strives to force that as 'soul' onto the woman in whom the soul is a mere inorganic stain, an irregular and independent blotch.

If it is not intended directly for us, beauty is of course worth nothing; the only way one can call a woman beautiful is by imagining her as one's own property for a moment (sometimes an equation can only be solved by division with *n*: here, too, an '*n*' of that kind is needed for a verdict on beauty to come into being; the '*n*' = 'the woman loves me'). If the desiring man should wish to conquer the woman rationally, he ought to accomplish two jumps: shake off the enthrallment of masks and head for the center. That is impossible, however, because there is nothing pointing towards the center; one cannot even hazard a guess as to its whereabouts. When a man in love tells a woman what her qualities are, she usually listens with pungent disgust like to the description of a strange woman; she senses that the desire (however flattering) is addressed to a big & complicated structure, a big feminine system, patched together from a mouth, shoulders, knees, sounds & seamstress tricks, which bears no resemblance at all to the small, monochrome, non-decorative, almost pointillist picture of her own consciousness, her own consciousness as a woman. In practice, of course, it does not matter whether the confession of desire addresses that little point of consciousness or a false soul contrived from externalities: what is important is that the man will be attached to her in the eyes of others — that is why for the woman no particular problem generally stems from this.

As noted, before falling asleep, we are sometimes wont to make a half-pathetic, half-resigned mixture of our own desire and the woman's body; we bathe the woman's body in desire without the desire being able to penetrate even a merely imagined image of the woman.

At night, after a longer period of sleep, one suddenly awakens as if to an unexpected pistol shot: one pricks up one's ears in agitation as to whether a further noise will be heard before starting to wrack one's brain as to whether something might have broken down, perhaps that was what wakened one up, but there is no question of its being anything of the sort. One then notices that desire is coursing through one's body like a loosened mountain stream with an unrestrained hurtling, & it was on that sudden rupturing of desire one had been awakened: in those moments desire is, indeed, a one-way flight toward the image of the woman, at which, under the influence of sleep, the portrait of an ethical invitation emanating from the merely-picture and the real inner portrait have totally coincided, allowing desire a free run.

At that point, the 'blue eyes' are no isolated moral mask inviting one's body without volitional consent, but a genuine summons: the unbroken call of a 'charity cocotte'; beauty as a whole is no longer a tapping bark that protects the woman's hidden wishes, but sparkling proof of the calling spirit: whereas up till then the body had been a statue of distance, now it is a logical by-product of union (in a volitional, not a physical sense), a precise projection of understanding.

If blue eyes signified a gentle harvest of desire after a past childhood when we twisted the withered necks of lilac tresses with cowardly gloves, then the whole woman is now truly an intact harvest, intact gloves, and intact grapes, & desire can freely spill out on the countryside which had been so longed-for; if the mouth's sliver shaped haemo-bluff was a simple warning-light of desire, now the whole woman's soul is dazed by this scarlet, and the man can fall into her like water from a higher basin into a lower collecting dish. Hence the dizzying speed & homogeneous unidirectionality of the concurrences of unexpected nocturnal desire in contrast to diurnal desire, the tension of which may have been enormous, but it did not have a speedy straight track.

People often say that men are looking for something in women which is not human & have done with the matter at that, but they fail to notice how extraordinarily odd it is that one half of the human race should look on those human beings, women, as absolutely non-human. For the emphasis is not simply on the beauty side of women (as if there were another side somewhere), it is purely & simply that only their beauty comes into the question, one does not seek a millimicron of the 'human' in them.

It is unlikely that in this world there is some sort of beauty independent of women which attracts people, & since nature has a need for women to attract men, well, it vested that beauty with women as well so that it should function as a lure for men: women's beauty is not a particle of beauty dispensed from the big common ground of beauty (so that they could be looked on as a 'human being + beauty') but they are themselves beauty (i.e., 'beauty – human being').

The moment a pretty woman makes an appearance at the table every thought of human purpose in one ceases; everything about her is only of interest as beauty, and human form only hovers over her like a paper mask dropped on the waves of the sea. Desire is always targeted at this radical dehumanization, whereas women remain human beings and live their life as human beings.

What is strange is not that non-human dream functions should be interwoven around a human being, not that the woman's humanity means for the man a Dirac q-number,[68] a number the explicit purpose of which is to represent something unnumerical, an active non-number, but the fact that certain of her most concrete and solely practical properties cannot be grasped as concrete entities: a lovely human leg is only comprehensible as beauty, however much it is a means of walking for the woman. During an awakening at night, when one is roused by the changing of the desire switch, the desire is such a stifling delight because then one sees the woman herself as if she did not even feel herself as being human and this beauty were also her inner vital principle; as if her every movement, sound, thought, digestion and kidney function were not 'human'-functions but 'beauty'-functions.

Men frequently advise women that they look in the mirror a lot: one can understand from this that men have a feeling women are not sufficiently aware of their 'just beauty' (in practice, of course, women are well aware that "I am beautiful" — or rather "I am attractive to men" — only they don't know they are just beauties & as 'humans' negligible quantities), or rather, their life is not applied entirely to their exterior — they are constantly concerned with their exterior, but never as their sole spiritual center; beauty is always just one of the instruments, parts, or purposes of their life, but they always feel they are humans who happen to be beautiful, not just beauties who happen to resemble humans. The men hope that if women look at a mirror the mirror image takes the place of human awareness, because men feel a woman's soul (the only authorized soul) is a mirror image, therefore they strive to impress it into a woman in place of the naïvely plagiarized & incongruent 'human' awareness.

That is why, although with a lesbian woman a man may have less chance, that sort of woman is more 'ideal' for him because he reckons that those women see a female body the way a man does, and the way a normal woman never does: as an esthetic quality. Women who cling with naïve stubbornness to their 'human' character reach only as far as the stage of cosmetics in front of a mirror, but a man wants to instill a Sapphic relationship between the woman & the mirror so that there is no need to explain his desire separately to the woman, but it should be taken by the woman as natural; if, however, the lesbianization has succeeded, the man drops out of the game.

Dreams, though, present the man with precisely a woman who is 'beauty'-conscious to a lesbian degree, in contrast to an unjustified human awareness, yet still inviting to the man: from that comes the magical galloping of desire. The way the clear, free, and absolute flight of desire sometimes nevertheless frees itself from its bound, arithmetically irrational, form, overfiltered by human obstacles, so the clean flow of darkness, impartial & devoid of moral interference, streamed forth from the heavily barred depths of a forest, like a gigantic white fish through the fresh opening in a tightly meshed net torn in two: a whitish-green, infinite, but still numerically 'simplex' arch above the black valley of silence.

connection of the two examples to Bournol's painting

This is how *The Antipsyche Idylls* alternated in the cloakroom: suicide in the hotel, the constellation of pain (it was referred to as a composition, yet it was a constellation) outside the soul, then the two kinds of motor models of silence that were equally foreign and related to each other, equally signaled the closeness of projections on the imagined ring of projections of the soul & the distance of projected things in infinity. For in vain are the centrifugal fugitive branches of the eternally radiating tree of Antipsyche absolutely foreign, as they seek to sling their buds apart toward antipoles, they still approach each other, act on each other, and thus the hotel detective adventure, the constellation of pain, & the atomic physics of silence, however far they may find themselves, or whatever foreignness they might mirror on the glass wall of '*homo anti-psychicus*'; since it is '*homo*,' this smuggles an inevitable shadow of a common denominator beneath them all the same.

In Bournol's painting, as well, which led Touqué to work out a series of soul-ionizing idylls of this kind, the countless autonomous space-knots and wave-selfishnesses nonetheless showed a certain collectivity inasmuch as the foreignness may be endless, but the alienating relations barely show a couple of changes that soon become apparent as a fairly naïve schismatizing routine: total foreignness always remains just a hypothesis and approximation, because the job of alienation can only be half done, in the same way as two planes vertical to one another do indeed intersect each other, but a third plane, which is, again, equally vertical to the previous two, is merely a fiction & only expressible in roundabout mathematical ways in which complete foreignness & ineradicable similarity prevail equally.

Touqué so despised morphological logic & psychology that he did not simply content himself with dispersal, but wished every dispersed element to be equally inverse in relation to all the others, so after a + would be a –, after the – an alternus that was opposed to the previous two in the way that they were complete opposites of one another, and after the alternus a fourth sign of alienus that was the complete opposite of all three, then the *contrarius, antius, sineus,* et cetera, forms of foreignness, the 'idyll of the endless dilemma of configuration,' where the bidirectionality of 'either-or' is substituted by a million alternatives or pluralities. The world has tired of antitheses & attempts to help itself in two ways: it fuses the + & –, or rather, it becomes insensitive to such opposition, so that all struggles, dramas, and tests of strength are for him incomprehensible naiveties (that is one of the ways out) — and, on the other hand, it creates limitless oppositions such as + & –, there is & there isn't, this & not-this, so that the limitation of opposition to just a binary one likewise ceases here.

Bournol strove with the greatest asceticism to give expression to the latter version in his picture of the sea: a dark-blue – wave pushed across a light-blue + wave, whereupon he was obliged, for instance, to suggest a third, absurd but indispensable logical procedure by leaving the two colored waves to be crossed by a white one, then a fourth would be a hundred percent opposite in that he stretched a white thread next to that, at some distance, a fifth by fastening a thin magnifying strip to the frame, where the foregoing waves, inverted and enlarged, were mirrored, & so on.

one of Bournol's paintings

At the top of the picture lay yellow hills, roughly sketched, as if with pincers and chalk which draws intermittently (an omission is always an easy route to possibilities of complete opposites beyond identity and contradiction). On the expanse of sea, as on the hills, Roman memorials, columns, triumphal arches and tympanum entablatures are etched into the soft paint with the tip of a wicker cane, without any geographical justification, like a watermark in paper. The negative technique of etching makes these architectural forms even more compelling: the whole thing is pure cheerfulness, tendrilling frivolity, without the engineering impression of architecture vanishing.

The entire Roman culture, which in Touqué's head consisted, nevertheless, of ablative absolutes & the inorganic curio of Scævola's virtue,[69] all at once identified with the sea's economy of 'leafy-bough crystal' (that is the transitional Riviera spatial unit), with the organza dance-lines; as the wicker ran along its intaglio path in the paint: like a zephyr in its liveliness and immateriality, but implacable as the law in its chiseled nature and its character of seceding from paint — when had he been able to sense both of those simultaneously? (Bournol taught him that even classical philology encloses a butterfly inside itself. In one little poem, "Histoire Fleur," he wrote in resonant axioms that historical mementos were just as much flowers as were the products of nature: ruins were therefore not miserable fragments but the optimistic & mature fruit of time, etc.)

Grammatical and virtuous Rome all at once became flowerlike and fashionable Rome: the amphitheater's memories filled with the lights of nature and elegance; it is true, however, that in the calices of the flowers there remained a touch of the Scævola-shade, some grammatical rigor in the irresponsible glitter of a monocle. At the bottom of the picture, in what was virtually a very Dutch manner, were strewn fish, snails, anthozoans, sponges and crabs like a crowded pyre or crumpled garden the smoke or scent of which was, in point of fact, the etched Roman commemorative series.

Bournol painted these aquarium models with great naturalist gusto: it was the antithesis of the barely-technique of etching — all thick splotches, the entire lot almost a carton relief which had been stuck onto it. The scales stood out from the bodies of the fishes like the seed scales on a pine cone or the edible fleshy bracts on an artichoke, slippery through moisture which had turned them into silver casings in the light. The diabolo wheels of the snails were sheer mother-of-pearl in the prodigal colors of the rainbow, their tentacles proud masts. The anthozoans were giant powder puffs or fountains turned into statues: on the whole, they looked more like the entrée trolley of a luxury hotel than a poetic science.

The entire right half of the painting was taken up by what might be called a mythological figure of a woman: the dress comprised fairly spiritual rags, more a mix of dirt and semiglass, but the head was contrived all the more humanly. It had enormous eyes, and one could not differentiate the nonsense of the dimensions from the marvelous clarity of the gaze. In it was a goodly dash of a Greek statue's poison of white irises which has cleared into blindness & of a longing gaze fixed to concrete objects of life: the two vision-magnets floated in huge white ovals like the black discs of a never-ending pendulum with all the bliss of fixedness & the psychological cataract of nostalgia.

Bournol went through an expressionist phase where he worked out every mechanizable flower of distortion, and after that, in a magical moment, in an unexpected scene of 'realization,' he confronted the Greek type of physiognomy: the grimace of distortion & a Greek head floating like a drop of oil in a water of silence were able to unite.

It could be sensed from every charm of the face that this was not a matter of synthesis but a 'miracle' which was of an entirely different nature than ordinary compromises of style. The loveliness of the face preserved an almost impossible moment from which a painful feeling of uncertainty would eternally radiate. Up till then he had painted big-idol skulls reminiscent of the heads of embryos, huge polyp fetishes (the woman's hands and feet were likewise ungainly impediments as in Aztec reliefs), and now it was precisely that clumsy, merely dimensional magnitude, which nevertheless evoked a head resting on motionless seagull wings of proportions, as if in the mass *per se* there were likewise a harmony that might come about at unexpected moments: it looms out of the ungainliness in much the same way as that band of red wax that one sought to knead into a big white wax ball when one played with sculptor's wax as a child in order to end up with pink-colored material, but instead, after half an hour of prolonged pressing & flattening out, all one got was a stubborn red wax strip which one thought broke up long ago: so here as well the unexpected harmony appears to separate out from a lucky variation of the raw magnitude that will disappear the next moment, & in the future it will not be possible to base a theory of 'mass-harmony' or 'cretin-Apollonian' duality on that, or guess its technique, only wait for another chance, just as one cannot set up a rule for kneading a wax ball with a red stripe but trust to fate. What made the face uneasy was precisely that it was evidently not a station on the swelling slope of development, just a roulette-constellation among others.

That momentary interchangeability of barbarian quantum and Greek dream of proportions, though, was useful for Touqué insofar as it made him perceive the possibility in the so-called 'equilibrium' of Greek statues that, through a psychological vibration, they, too, might be pathological fetishes, and therefore it was not a spirit of 'proportion' and 'harmony' that informed them, as one retrospectively pictures it (as if a pseudo-Plato had carved each & every Greek sculpture), but someone who at all events carried in himself a fair dose of the Polynesian or Iroquois. In Aphrodite's lips one does not sense the mouth substance but the form of an Attic peasant girl — just as in geometrical lines one generally senses not a neutral combing of space but the living landscapes of the River Meander. (Was Euclid an impressionist painter?) None of that is worth a lot — he thought to himself; at most a presumption like that, he repeated: "— every harmony is a matter of chance; harmony is an X-ray of chance: there is nothing else in the world than just composition & just harmony — " etc.

---

remarks on Greek sagas in connection to a mythological figure

---

There was a time when people used to divert themselves with a form of patience which amounted to their coloring in with chalks in the way children do, humanizing to death, and kneading into novellas portraits of the gods that consisted of abstractions & dignities, without being able to understand Olympus a scrap better.

The essential in those gods (and perhaps an incidental lesson in Bournol's picture) was maybe that they were able to be concrete without the paraphernalia which one now holds to be indispensable to concreteness. The broadest variability, lack of contour, and self-contradiction did not render the divine figures uncertain and drained of essence: it was as if they were able to play a game of chess with them in which the white and black squares on the chess board seesawed like the continually changing waves of the sea, and the figures themselves also swapped roles, clothes, and personalities among themselves at every moment. Despite that, they were able to play the game with mathematical precision and dry sobriety. There is no sense, then, in rouging Aphrodite's lips in the manner of the ethnology of a hypothetical Attic peasant girl: one rather ought to disperse the face into fleeting moods, the tragedy of Phædra, the self-serving chuckles of an auroral little girl, into a score or two dozen lines of poetry, the hallucinatory outlines of a city, or a hidden pendulum of semiphilosophy. Chaos needs to be conjured up behind it, albeit independently of our partly scientific, partly esthetic concept of 'chaos,' constructing from that the antique concept of 'concrete,' 'precise,' and 'positive,' or the lack of those concepts (cf. L. Kramer, *Über ontologische Maskierung der Hysterie in der modernen Mythus-Interpretation*. Heidelberg, 1932).[70]

the ideal relation of order & chaos according to Touqué

For Touqué, as he looked affectionately at the giant head, the enticing prospect presented itself to construct a world where an infinitesimally small but eternally moving spark of order flittered in the chaos, whereas a minimal inducer of chaos hummed in the order — because he was disgusted by a 'chaocosmic' world, where by virtue of a petty bourgeois automat, confusion and harmony were always unequivocal & identical.

He feared chaos because it was too easy to perceive it as order, whereas if that notion were denied, then it would once more become self-serving confusion, a vitalist bluff, which is similarly intolerable: how are order and confusion supposed to relate to each other, he asked himself with the inflections of arithmetical riddles. He also sensed that composition and confusion ought to stand in an actively dramatic relationship: the balance needed to be replayed in time again and again.

Sometimes he simply thought that between a geometric series and a random series obtained through spins of a roulette wheel he was going to find a third kind of series. The mind seeks, with a single Tantalus-gesture, the maximum order and pure chaos. A great mind rejects sophists and sophistry but feels an eternal attraction to a world order the center of which is active ur-sophism. Touqué imagined the temporal relationship and alternation of order and irregularity as ordinary circuit breakers in which it is precisely an interruption that causes a solenoid to become magnetized & break the circuit, while the passage of a current stops the magnetism and thus again induces closure and so on *ad infinitum*. At the moment when absolute chaos reaches its maximum point, that maximum ties it into an order, but the maximum of order automatically breaks up into chaos, and that vibrating (the interrupted buzzing of electric doorbells) can go on without end, one is the precondition and goal of the other in the most extreme connection: the closing & breaking of an electric current are inseparable, perspective-vibrations, the sole function of order & chaos.

Eros & Einstein idyll, end of the digression relating to Bournol

---

So in adolescence desire cancelled him into blind identity with the girl, later desire did not fill out the woman's body but the paths that led to her, apparently indifferent objects that lay around her, i.e., he saw substance flare up in logical and erotic foci at foreign points, but now, when he listened to Leatrice's hysterical clichés, and meanwhile he considered that it was precisely her sheer stupidity that was placing Leatrice's body in the most intellectual pose, he felt that even alienation of essence was an excessively coarse expression for what was being enacted before his eyes. Even active non-Leatrice and anti-Leatrice were too Leatrice-shaped in relation to the new feminine-something that he saw through Leatrice and for which he yearned with all his senses.

He felt he was facing a process of labor but did not know to what precise end; he thought that he had already pulled interminably on the inseparable love parallel of sensuality and abstraction, male lust and female fiction, but it seemed that no: desire directed at the woman could be even more bestial, and the woman herself could be even more fictitious than any fiction, emptier than a diagram of nothing.

He paid attention to his associations: what happened to them? They jostled each other apart; where there was a target there was no direction, and where there was a kiss, there was no mouth. Yet all the same there were mouths and kisses, targets and directions, albeit in alienating counter-chastities, and Touqué considered that his spiritual life, his love, and his idea of women were behind these, so that if he wished to find the essence, it was not sufficient to frequent a world of absolute foreignnesses, but he needed to find a drama-free, pictureless basic situation from where insubstantial things were no longer too materialistic, their truth-cancerous states were not apparent.

He paid attention to his associations: it was as if he had been placed on the surface of a gigantic soap bubble which was continually expanding and dilating. As a result he likewise took on color, sweated, and lost sense, turning into just space. A picture of a poppy in his adolescence was a double poppy (a bold typewriter letter struck twice over, one on top of the other), in his substance-alienating period the poppy picture was a blue bottle stopper with no poppy (a typo on the typewriter in place of the 'real' letter), but now (although the condition was much more exploratory than to be able to map it against the other two with a demarcated 'now') the poppy is reflected on a bubble, where its color alters all at once into a pseudo-celestial madness of light beyond color, & its form into an infinite spatial detail — not a double flower, not an anti-flower, but life's divine glitter (so far still with God) coupled with space itself.

Touqué strove for an intellectual virginity of Byzantine logic, so that he was unable to rest satisfied with self-torment, with the eradication, the annihilation, of the organs of instinct, but he had to become identical to what was virtually a momentary grace note of the very first notion of God, of existence, where there were perhaps these two things about poppies: an incandescent ultra-light (instinct? love? ethos?) & an empty frame (space? logic? number?). None of that was mystic convergence, the poppy's wave-bath renovated nirvana — on the contrary, it was its most precise formulation, because the continually expanding soap bubble is not a space but a regular sphere with which it is easy to reckon. Touqué, however, was thereby finally rid of the hated some-sortnesses of certain after-images (the 'materialism of sensibility'): the hospital in his childhood, a German periodical, a Munthausen woodcut, an end-of-season lover & a glittering bathroom — one and all found their way onto the bubble's surface, & there they did not turn into kind-of-transient images, nor counter images, but into the sphere's geometrical curves, equators, and Arctic Circles, so that all the wrinkles of neurasthenia became regular bridges of a giant space balloon, growing into infinite geometrical absoluteness until the emotional stains, colors of desire, & willpowers separated into light oceans & rainbow pajamas along the same curves.

When Touqué saw that his tiny associations were suddenly just-space properties of some sort of divine space, he was far from delighted that his 'little personality' had faded into some sort of 'big unit' (as such that would be an unwise thing, for sure), merely that in his love instinct and abstraction had come into even fiercer opposition and exaggeration than hitherto. His desire and love for Leatrice were, on the one hand, nothing else but one perspective of the space of existence (an abstract meridian of the soap bubble), himself and the woman together are just perspectives, nothing more (that was the most logical imaginable opposite to the hated Baroque dynamic), on the other hand, their love is a huge rocket, a separately flowering, aimless, womanless, just-life beyond Eros (a themeless color-narcotic of the soap bubble).

Whether that state did conceal anything really new, or was just bad Pythagoras-allure, a variation on the old official and bourgeois essence-schizophrenia, he was unable to say exactly. After all, there was nothing truly new in the separation of a biological spot and a logical line; he had lived through that, reworded & reiterated it to the point of boredom. He had talked about paintings in which the mouth consisted of a pencil and a crimson spurting, etc. Now, however, he felt the matter from a theological or absolute geometric viewpoint: Leatrice and Touqué, desire, life and thought all finally vanished, only space and color energy were left without any approximate sense (cf. Karl F. Langhofer, *Hamilton'sche Differentialrechnung der transerotischen Liebe oder die symmetrischen Kœffizienten der Raumsexualität und die antisymmetrischen Kœffizienten der anti-vitalen Bio-Sexualität.* Leipzig, 1929).[71]

In any case, there is no need to turn to the Einstein-idyllic example of the soap bubble for Leatrice, being an industrial designer in glass factories, had often blown sphere vases in the inside of which poppies were floated. If two poppies were set in around the equator of a globe, naturally they could float separately in the water at just as great a distance as Leatrice & Touqué's bodies were from each other in the room on the floor over the nightclub. If, however, a dark background or shadow lining ended up in the sphere of the vase, then the poppies were thrown back on the glass wall and in such a way as Touqué imagined and sought dynamic, Baroque-spurning desire: the two poppies suddenly elongated in the glass curve, the dramatic and plastic forms of petals, stems, leaves and poppy stockings clarified in a single shared band, an abstract geometrical symbol, the two isolated poppies converged, not after naïve struggles of forces, desires, and movements, but simply by virtue of the form of the vase, the optical tailoring of space.

It would have been ludicrous to talk about the two flower reflexes interacting by the procuring technique of magnet courtesans; they did not even run to each other, but if they happened to come into precisely that spatial perspective, they were simply one. The situation of flowers in vases like that was also very erotically logical. The flowers were on the inside of the vases, it is true, but since the transparency of the glass was all but the same as that of air, the concept of 'on the inside' was uneasily modified: the flower was set off in the direction of the adverb of place ('on the inside'), and when it genuinely started to slip on the slope of sense, then it suddenly twisted that being-inside in the direction of an electrically neutral and snake-humbug 'anywhere': it was not the 'inside' that became 'anywhere,' but the whole meaning of the inside was turned back in all conceivable 'not inside' positions, but in such a way that the 'inside' did not lose even a fraction of its meaning.

Things like that helped Touqué to a better understanding of the desired woman's physical situation than when he was hiding in the tangled spaces of 'placing' by eyesight & desire. The glass vase was half-filled with water, but the empty upper half of the sphere was nevertheless over the water, so that the air cupola was just as important as the poppy; indeed, the flower became more of a bit player, a statistic of a stereometric knick-knack: people decorate their homes with space, and in order to give these ripped-away spaces more taste, they are placed in or on flowers.

Water half-filled the vase, and the use of the fact & notion of 'half' was likewise a smart eroticism-plagiarism: it emphasizes that the so-called torso is in itself unitary; the fragment is not a fraction in an arithmetical sense, the lack does not indicate any subtraction, the nonsense is in no way anti-truthful. Indeed, precisely that 'semi'-positivism arouses in people an algebraic sensitivity toward absolute unity and absolute totality, though not in the primitive direction of supplementation but toward itself: whole and isolated, uniform and asymmetrical, absolute and localized — they will become similar in meaning.

In the half quality that Touqué savored in the vase with the sunken water level he saw the fiasco classicism of love: an accurate 'semi-eroticism' in point of fact is a God-given elementary unit of Eros (two 'semi-eroticisms' added together is a naïve calculator game, not true mathematics). Only the heads of flowers were thrown into the water, and if the leaves were, too, they would be separately torn away from the stem because a new vase is not a little totem of organic life, not a relic of rational interconnection; to the contrary, it is a model of frivolity, and although nature produces flowers with roots, stem, leaves, and maybe also with a sunshade, it was only our naïve logic that saw those roots and stems as 'interconnections' and secretly colluding organisms, when they were nothing of the kind: the maimed flower of the vase is a truer nature, its rootless and foolhardy luxury a more true-to-life state. Leatrice! Leatrice!

V.

Return to the situation outlined on page 90

He agitatedly pushed up the spectacles on his nose and looked at the other guests in the room. How many times he had ridiculed the apologies of the instinct-doctrine lyricist, but now they appealed to him. Only on condition, of course, that the whole problem of 'instinct vs. intellect' was somehow revised from an entirely new point of view (he did not insist on the last, of course), some entirely 'inner horizon' as journalists were in the habit of saying. — Halbert? ruled over? No. Leatrice is a sick woman, hysterical, & that illness carries a big esthetic cachet — that is just childish romanticism, and the only reason he does not reject it was that it concerned a woman.

A woman. What if we were to begin at the beginning, this fact: a woman? A woman: a frightful unknown; the science of women: a frightful lie. But that is the path of all knowledge: the parallel of the big unknown & the big imputation — how stupid had those become who were irritated by that. Because behind all such things there is some truth; the entire truth.

So? He would have liked to kiss Lea: to scrape out of the ice cream dish the streak of strawberry chocolate that had stuck to it. Lea began everything at the beginning — that is why she would manage to arise from the waves. Because so far no woman had ever managed to arise from the waves. What from a scholastic point of view was called 'rationality' held them back in the dark. In other words, that was my discovery: "Let women remain stupid"? or what? A metaphor, a picture, a new picture: Anadyomene? All my searching ends either in a triviality or a well-worn metaphor. Because I want to discover, because I search, because deep down I am not antipsyche. He agitatedly flared and pulled at his nostrils. Probably nothing in Leatrice altered, but within a couple of seconds she became odious in Leville's eyes, because a theoretical conclusion could not be coaxed from her. He despised her. He despised the whole world, which is thrown together from trivialities & metaphors. Perhaps everybody in that room was a born maniac, but they had not found anything meritorious enough to be worth the large amount of precision-demanding work called for by a mania, which was why they were agitated.

— Yesterday, when I was with Steermans, I was already unable to withstand my new strength and new world; they triumphed over me. But the day before yesterday I had a much better day being with a young boy who was very afraid of me: his hands were trembling, his heart was pounding, & he was so cold that he was only able to conceal his shivering by continually saying with forced nonchalance, "Pooh-Pooh." I enjoyed it that he believed I was what I seemed to be.

— Leatrice, *mea peccatrice*, are you sloshed? It's not a good show at all to put on such airs. Where on earth did you learn to put on those affectations?

Halbert was really angry. The more fool him — Leville thought —, he fails to see it may be about much more than affectation, him, a psychologist and all. Or perhaps it's really about nothing, and how mortifying it is that something a psychologist by profession can dispose of with a couple of rude remarks, he, the one who is anti-psyche, considers to be an oddity & is all but set to psychologizing.

What fearsome possibilities there are for dilettantism if a fanatical denier of psychology deems to discern a psychological discovery in a momentary erotic transport. He was irritated by his own perpetual lack of an attitude. He would fain have strangled Lea and shot Halbert dead. But then there wasn't a gulf between him & Halbert: Leville had merely crisply formulated a program, but naturally that did not amount to each and every precept being equivalent to a cell of his blood & reason; he, too, was a psychologist, but he wished to be freed of the demon of his chronic selfishness, and he had issued a watchword to which he himself still had to adjust: the program's framer did not formulate an outcome into a redeeming principle but strove, thereby self-delusively, but not entirely irrationally, to justify kicking a goal into the distance & to try to reach that goal and convince himself of its truth.

Producing truth is not like a tree putting out foliage from which flowers and fruit are produced: on the contrary, a germ of uncertain direction but positive strength vibrates in the earth, then on a quite distant horizon a poised, mature, fictional fruit has to be produced, & roots, tree, & branches grow nostalgically toward this distant hypothetical-flavored fruit.

There is no natural development in the nature of the production of thoughts, only violence and compulsion. The most forceful thoughts from a biological point of view later give the illusion of precisely the most natural logical order. That was the fundamental difference between Halbert and Leville: Halbert started from the inside and his thoughts multiplied virtually by cell division like certain protozoa — whereas Leville forced his thoughts around irrational 'external' points, as if carrying deduction to a fantastic *ad absurdum* of which he made no secret, indeed (with a certain childish-cynical smile) he bragged about it. Despite that he deeply yearned for people like Halbert or rather admired them because they were so much able to be themselves (not in the naïve sense of 'they found themselves'), because there was no canon between their sentences and the center of gravity of their own personalities.

Leville was well aware that never in his life would he have that harmony-feeling of identifying with what he said: even if he gave complete intellectual assent to his own thoughts he would never have the primitive certainty that his entire life would be devoted as a cover for his thinking. It was also odd that precisely someone like Halbert, who, whenever he said anything, did not produce any distinct thought of his own but simply illuminated an organic component of himself like the local brightness of a small electric light bulb on a complex machine: it is precisely those people who arouse an impression of theatricality in the most gradual measure. Because an actor always engages in a more sincere relationship (identity) with a role than does a normal intelligent person in general, to say nothing of those Leville-types. Leville always viewed that theatrical sincerity with disgust and amazement, and out of that twofold attitude stemmed, on the one hand, the journal *Antipsyche*, and on the other, the intriguing problem of completely clarifying the psychology of romantically self-identical people — in other words, his strong interest in Halbert & his sympathy toward Leatrice.

---

relationship of women & objects

Leatrice got up and childishly hissed ("you have no idea what this is about"), looking straight ahead, though not a long way off but as if someone was really standing close by. On her neck were hanging some kind of real pearls: pearls of disparate sizes hung down asymmetrically on threads of various lengths from the main row, and when she moved it appeared as if balls of mercury were rolling about in all directions from her chest to her shoulders, yet all the same some attractive force was holding them together in particular directions, because however much the pearls scattered, a little twitch of the most distant one would immediately pull after itself another lying quite a long distance away. Opposite one of the tall, narrow windows stood a mirror of exactly the same shape, which therefore gave the impression of a window — under it was a small fireplace that looked more like the ankle-high drawer of a bedroom standing mirror, the whole thing no more than a little china table. She picked up a vase and sat down in its place: her back and its mirror image looked like two petals forking away from each other, whereas the forelocks of her fair hair fell toward her lap like the overburdened arched stamens in a 250-fold magnification in a German *'sachlich'* journal.

Leville looked for a while at the vase in Lea's hand. There was an odd disjunction between a woman and the objects around her, a foreignness which, from certain points of view, pertains to a child and his or her toys: that conspicuous incongruence that is perceptible between gesture and object is present more progressively and in modified form with a woman. Even if she strokes a flower, even if she creates some strange & new object between her fingers through her own devout diligence, a relationship will be lacking, and that foreignness is almost tantamount to destruction.

A much greater isolation exists around objects surrounding a woman than a man: because there is a greater otherness and more intrinsic foreignness. He felt the same between a female body and dress, even between a woman and the food that she was consuming. A woman is always a dilettante and untimely amateur in a man's material world. Exploring that difference naturally coincides with the exploration of 'personality': actually, the reason for the condition that one does not dare finalize one's own personality into a self-identity is, in part, that one does not feel oneself to be sufficiently isolated but is, in some measure, scattered in various relationships and various dimensions in the surrounding world: as if one were moving around in a hall of mirrors, surrounded by various troublesome shadow and mirror images that, in the end, one is already confusing with oneself and is gripped by a giddiness arising from omnipresence when he tries to move the right leg not on his body but on the left leg of a distant image.

When Leatrice set the vase to one side Leville, for a moment, pitied it on account of the foreign, almost antagonistic touch: he himself had much the same relationship to flowers, books, and water as one conventionally supposes of a godly medieval master craftsman; he somehow felt himself to be their possible creator, and the notion of work and love was also associated with them. But just because he was connected to them he was not entirely free among them, and because he was acquainted with them in that manner, he also bore some skepticism toward them. There was none of that in Leatrice. Women always carry an unknown milieu around them like the vacuum in a Thermos flask: that milieu was not necessarily the same as the banal backdrops of untouched, primal nature; it could be that this was just an approximate mark of their foreignness, but it might be the truth itself.

The natural history of that intimated milieu ought to be written down — that would be, perhaps, a genetic elaboration of 'instinct' at the base of which, or so Leville wanted, a form of intellect would be found again. When he looked at that blue-colored flower, one end of which was bent over toward the mirrored landscape amidst the indistinct sea, the sun stifled in steam, and the seagulls indistinguishable from the whiteness of the sea's spume, as a gigantic swaying flower — while the other petal, enriched by the mythical complementation of mirroring, let itself down among them: he was swamped by an overbrimming sensuality because, as he saw it, the glaringly concrete conclusion of his own nebulous thoughts was blossoming before his own feet, & when his mouth trembled from the skin of an imagined Leatrice on his tongue, actually he would have liked to cry out with the healthy intellectualism of an experimenting scientist: *quod erat demonstrandum.*

Leatrice and the mirror. Mirror & space

Actually he was faced with the common chord of love, the root of sensuality: he saw the image of Leatrice's back in the mirror, saw Leatrice herself (though the word 'herself' does not necessarily concern the second voicing of *ens*) & finally he saw the 'foreign' vase in her hand (though he is not sure that the word 'foreign' is still valid in this scene). What was the relationship between these three Leatrices as, after all, the vase also belonged to her body: did the sinuous weight of the infinitely clear arch of the back in the mirror and the body leaning in front of it represent the two sides of an equation? Was the whole thing a weight-equation reduced to one motion, a body-theorem transcribed to light, with the seemingly 'foreign' vase as an unexpected value? What is a body? Did it make any sense?

Would he have been able to say, if it came down to it, which of the three bodies evoked sensuality: the reflected one, the living one, or the chance vase? The vase, too, had turned organic, and the living Leatrice had become an optical screen on which foreign rays danced, obstructed on their way: sensuality did not desire flesh but the polarizing mirror-fiction of reality, & reason did not seek the Leatrice-cache legible in the mirror, but a solitary kiss. Leatrice was no longer a 'living body,' sensuality no longer 'vital-energy.'

What had happened? The arching back in the mirror was surrounded by a mirrored setting that Touqué, who was facing the mirror, was naturally unable to see in the original, so that the back was like an image he was dreaming up, for in dreams, after all, there is a well-known fragment of narrative in a mythical milieu: he recognized the flesh color and the textile weave, but no longer the deep picture of the room that surrounded her: flowers on the wallpaper confronted him in the opposite perspective with the pace of an intricate dream, as if a mute person were all at once hearing their thoughts in the form of a sharp echo. His own sensuality and those parts of the room that were only visible from the mirror immediately became competitors since it looked as if Leatrice had long been destined for that reflecting world: a reflection always looks older than an object, secondariness is the exact clock-ornament of fate.

On the other hand, inasmuch as Leatrice's back in the mirror was a dreamlike, indeed historical antiquity, it was algebraic at the same time: as if, by the simple fact of his not seeing her back in reality, the vision had already, straightway, become arithmetically-flavored by the 'featherweight of unfamiliarity': the numerical event was nothing other than a momentary shot of unreality. The two big leaves of irreality: the geometrical & the dreamlike, therefore, nodded uniformly in the mirror. The space itself, after all, the deepening space of the room, unseen, only projected that kind of double nature: every space is simultaneously a dream and a number, stupor and proportion, nothing and absolute — yet sensuality could find much more satisfying nourishment in that than in raw bodies and bulky nudes.

The colors were more colorful in the mirror, the forms sharper, and on precisely that account they swung over into mathematics: a regular pentangle is a long way off being as good a symbol of geometric proportionality as an irregular crest of a wave or scrap of a flower, though the latter are photographed with extreme clarity. Leatrice's back, therefore, was at once in its material brutality and its geometric abstractness. Geometricality does not mean 'regular' in the sense of the word applicable to engineering drawings but the energy superlative that absolutely pries apart every irregular object to its own contour — the contour on which one can sense the infinite tension of a boundary: that contour tension yields the true geometric illusion. In the mirror, though, the contours were much more visible than they were in reality, & that did not exclude dreamlikeness: anyone who sees the essence of dreams in blurriness at best defined them but never dreamed: the essence of a dream is precisely this terror of the contour, which also holds objects back only so that their borders should be able to burn more tragically with their geometric blaze. A relationship of simple oppositeness of direction never exists between a mirror image & its reality: one of them to the right, the other to the left; the one above zero degrees, the other below it.

The back of Leatrice seen in the mirror did not simply go in another direction from the genuine one, but it was exactly twice as large as the living inflection: the living Leatrice inclined to the right at an angle of 45° from the surface of the mirror, but the projected Leatrice did so at an angle of 90° according to the dogmatic physics of illusion: the mirror copied the curving back in the other direction, but then it inserted in addition, as a separately perceptible and sensible +, the curve independent of the back and the pure opposite direction independent of the back, so that when Touqué compared the back bending in the mirror he saw in the mirror a nostalgic double of the genuine motion. He later realized that the curve of the back with the mirror's added curve did not show a doubling of reality, but in reality the curve was zero, whereas there was already a curve in the mirror: Leatrice was genuinely sitting aslant, with her back bent, but in reality one did not notice that some spatial situation, an embryonic geometric gesture, was being enacted here, a living person can never be perceived as something fitting dimensions: it is the mirror that will first reveal one's hidden 'algebrosis,' which is why one senses Leatrice's back to be so excessive, a bridge bending to infinity, as if the projection were a tonal scale whereas the living body was a theme written in that key with a cluster of resolving marks.

A difference cannot be drawn here between ontological bigotry and patience with empty symbols: if the mirror intensifies the material, it immediately tips over into abstract figurations — if I search for the start of those numerical figurations, I shall have straightway reached into the body's biological pack of cards: I lay out five cards, their backs facing me, and I pick one up, now seeing the face value — I wonder if in such a game the important feature is the abstract geometrical place or the individual face value? If I play cards, Touqué wondered, and among the cards turned up toward me I see the uniform backs of the opponent's cards, what is the main point here: the eight, for me uniform, abstract backs of the cards that I merely calculate, or the 'inner' cards privy to me but which only win value from the calculated backs of the cards?

That was somehow the way that mirror-Leatrice and Leatrice-Leatrice related to each other, like fans of cards seen from inside and from their backs. The mirror was not completely vertical, though its slant was quite minimal. However, that couple of degrees of inclination was sufficient for it to perfectly effectuate the two branches of unreality, the geometrical and the fantastical. Through the little angle, objects in the mirror all deviated from reality, tilting into leaning backs of Pisa, leaning palms, and leaning lamps, and that universality of leaningness, which seemed uniform in every small detail, awakened the impression that, according to some scientific viewpoint, the objects are tilted in a geometrical perspective: if a statue were to become animated and were to perform a three-degree tilt to the right with its muscles, one would not notice anything, but if its pedestal were to tilt by the same amount, and the still rigid statue with it, then one would sense the alteration of basic principles in the direction of either scientific over-accuracy or general upheaval.

That latter feel is perpetually employed by contemporary sculpture & poster printing: it is not the objects that are tilted but the entire space is set crooked in the frame. The space becomes a perceptible space by being aslant: the whole technique is employed for want of a better one, and that technique is employed for the expression of simple space (which actually lacks all crookedness). Leatrice's hips were pressed completely against the mirror so that at the bottom of the picture something resembling a double cactus or a duplicated palm could be seen: the two hips fused, were almost one, the thick hip trunk being rent right and left by an invisible dimension thunderbolt, but while one of the flaps of the hip cactus entirely resembled its trunk, the flap that continued in the mirror suddenly swung over into a pure spatial flap precisely by virtue of the three-degree minimal tilt, so that the sudden shift from palm trunk into an abstract dimension, from the stub of a nude figure into a slim parabola, was very enjoyable to Touqué's eyes: it was as if the fireworks had come off well & it were a matter of two sparklers that had gone off blindly with a bang; the mirror Leatrice arched with an endless curve into the world of clouds, whereas straight after being launched into the air, the living Leatrice spattered asunder somewhere on the ground.

But dreamlikeness is just a step away from the harmonization of dimensions for its own sake, which plays a part in geometry: that little bit of lopsidedness, which with its barely Euclidean-lever tipped every object in its basic principles — that lopsidedness set off objects on a slippery slope on which they would never again come to a halt. If I have a photograph printed crookedly on the white page of a periodical, then that slantedness at first isolates the picture, in other words, scientifically objectifies it, arouses the cool experience of 'angle' — yet at the same time it sets it on a slope so that it does not remain in the world of 'icy' objectivity, in the strict net of projection-echoes, but constantly slips, & this unending tobogganing (which can only happen on a minimal slope that is just barely oblique) is already the most characteristic dreaming-motion: though nothing might have moved in the mirror, neither Leatrice's back, nor flowers or lamp, nevertheless it all elicited an impression of eternal hovering, bending, mute sliding onward: the movement does not occur in space, but absolute spatial-space is linked to stationary objects as an opalescent surplus, and the perpetually restless, dreamily swaying, spreading latter entity, gives an illusion of motion.

He looked at the mute and dead petals of the flowers in the mirror, on which not a single speck of dust stirred, but it was surrounded by the slanted space in the mirror: the flower received from that shadow-phosphorated spatial ring floating content like a goldfish swimming dancingly in water that is rippling here and there. He had seen solutions of radium salts in glass beakers set next to each other in a laboratory: in places where the solution was in direct contact with the glass no change was visible, but the glass beyond the surface of the liquid had acquired a coloring. Those flowers behaved in the same way in the mirror: they themselves were stiff, but above them the most spatial-space existed (this was elicited by the slantedness in the same way as in the inflexion of nouns it is the genitive, not the nominative, which causes stems & roots to explode), and it was that pure space that aroused, together with the stiff flowers, the impression of dreamlike onward navigation, of floating forever in one direction.

This, therefore, could no longer be 'motion' as it was deemed in the old sense: objects had become more inert and stiffer than ever, they paralyzed gravitation into a lethal stroke (that is a great deal more than simple staticness) — but the space surrounding them became much more spatial (through the infinitesimal distortion), it protruded aslant toward objects like the colored rings above radium salts, and the movement was nothing more than, on the one hand, absurd stiffness, and, on the other, the joint co-existence of absurd spatial-space that evaded the object; thus 'movement' and stillness coincided in the mirror. That can be experienced especially with palm-house artificial lakes, where water plants remain permanently in one spot on a still and standing sheet of water: yet they seem to float slowly because the surface of the water emanates such a pure spatial-space that it is movement in and of itself. When Touqué had thought through all that, he felt that his amorous sensuality was running in a good place. (L. Klebenhayer, *Erotische Syllogistik des Spiegels* I–II. Göttingen, 1933.)[72]

Leatrice soliloquizes & cries

She was perched there, on the little fireplace, like a stray animal: women always arouse the impression that they are the offspring of the present minute, while the surroundings are always terribly ancient next to them, even if, in line with the latest fashion, a trendy interior decorator only finished work on it yesterday. Leatrice suddenly jumped to her feet & looked with anger & lust into the mirror: in the mirror, the gulls flittering above the sea looked like small white flowers that she had just shaken out of her hair.

— I can still be compared to myself, and that is my curse: that is why you can still address me by my old name even though I share nothing in common with that mask that is dangling on my face, nothing to do with it. How dreadful it is that that cannot be ripped off from one day to the next, that I have to tolerate that I turn round on hearing the name of my mask. That my mask continues to elbow its way in front of me. Yesterday, or at the time of voluptuousness, that mad guy wanted to paw me on my face: how startled he would have been if he had noticed my new, my true face, my old face.

She leaned near the mirror so her nose pressed on an indistinct spot above the sea like a huge hovering cotton-wool flower. With her two index fingers she pulled down the skin under her eyes, like young children do when they want to play a monstrous Chinese dragon: the flesh on the inside was yellowish, & there were big spots toward her nose (especially under her right eye) like the brown spots that multiply on the green petal of a tiger lily toward the interior of the corolla; in contrast to this brutal anatomical revelation was the 'spiritual' darkness of the eyes. Before she was able to continue her oration, she took an offbeat breath then set to it:

— Because here it is underneath. — She suddenly turned her head back toward the audience with an idiotic angularity, with her fingers continuing to grip toward her cheekbones: — Here it is, only you can't see it. I'm discarding the mask: it will wear down like a thin, cracking husk behind which a broader fruit is ripening. It will fade, flake off, and everybody will talk about death, despite my new face being in labor behind it like a flower that bursts its vase. That was how my father spoke, and I never understood, yet from now on I shall hear those words as if it were not him talking, but — (at this point she scowled as if fixing her eyes on a very small hard-to-explain thing, with her voice also taking on a quieter, discursive tone, like someone seeking to illuminate something very precisely & from many sides) —, but his voice was on my lips, and I was only moving my lips after him, I can't even hear the sounds just as I can't feel objects with my fingers if they go numb; I only hear my father's voice, but it's coming out of me.

On the last few words the many tiny wrinkles smoothed out on her face, which had accompanied the nervous explanations, her fingers (with which she made complicated gestures as if she had to set out tiny mosaics in the air, but the small pieces of stone were in the hollow of the same hand as the fingers that had to accomplish the inlaying work) leveled gracefully to her knees as well, like flattened-out wild chestnut leaves in a passing wind: her deportment, now equally distant to the pathos of the first shrill-unctuous tirade and the suddenly inserted explanatory, analytical mimicry, became sleepy and dreamy. Her chest slumped, and it looked as if her entire bearing was set for the pleasure caused by the imagined situation that, by and large, her body was held suspended, as it were, by the muscle tension of the eyes turned up under the eyelids; indeed, the work of the eye muscles required so much physical concentration that all her other appendages, including her legs, listlessly 'drifted.'

She looked like a single rigid wave (one which was paralyzed not just on the surface, but, in fakir-like fashion, right through to the inside) that had been lifted out of the sea and set up in a room; still booming & buzzing with it was the scrap of sound that was a thousandth or ten-thousandth of the universal 'sea-booming,' about which some philosopher or other spoke: the foam (the longish whites of his eyes, which for the first time looked white because they were turned in front to unused surfaces as a result of excessive looking upwards) was extremely small, as is generally the case with the parts of all such objects the bulk of which is usually hidden in the depths, underground or elsewhere, & that hidden part unexpectedly surfaces.

Anny would have liked to blab something but she felt that Leatrice had overshot the mark & was descending toward awkward mysticism: she looked at Lea as on an elevator that was gliding down under her nose toward the lower floors and which she could no longer board.

— But my father did not want this — at that second Lea was virtually dragged back into the world by her own voice, it was perceptible from her emphases how a statement that starts off vacuously is filled with humaneness, like a railway train passing under a coal-feeding crane into the first carriage of which the coal dust is only drizzle, then into subsequent ones is released as a dense flood, and into the last carriage is dumped in the form of a single tight mass: by the time of the final sounds Lea was already weeping. But when she fell silent she controlled the crying for a second, as it were, examining the words she had delivered as if she were thinking it was not worth her weeping on account of such transient matters as her voice, which was floating in the distance like the pallid sail of a sinking yacht.

Halbert started something in the form of coughing: — But… — whereupon the distant sail abruptly swelled, all of a sudden ran at her face, and Lea cried franticly.

A big relief overcame the audience: weeping always sounds as if somebody were pleading her way back into life, & that was particularly so in Lea's case. She took fright, was terribly scared at her own forced yet wished-for mysticism, and she cried like a child who is afraid of ghosts. Everyone in the room was happy, like people who had won quite unexpectedly at precisely the moment when they were already in a major crisis of doubt in relation to their own identity, but now there was no need for doubt, there was no reason to screw their eyes into unknown and sickly perspectives as the little dilettante-mystic (she was that, wasn't she?) was weeping, that is to say, had returned among them.

That crying retrospectively made everything that had happened before uninteresting: it seems that the screaming pathos, then uneasy explaining away, and finally the wave of repose, had no other goal or content than temporarily preparing for that lamentation, as if the crying had to go through this triple transformation in order to finally reach tears, like wheat going through a succession of grinding rolls until it becomes flour. Laughter does not have that retrospective destructive effect, but a single burst of crying washes everything away and makes everything impossible.

Anny had the feeling that the moment had come for her to be able to have that pretend mysteriousness cooled down into what it was originally, namely, "she'd had enough of cretinous traveling salesmen for coffee, whether husbands or nightclubbers: more beauty and morality" — Ena, however, completely stiffened like someone who will immediately make an apodictic statement.

Lea observed all that. She saw that her crying was being exploited, and she immediately sensed that what she had said up to that point was no longer behind her in the air. All of a sudden she was overcome by despair and felt that she had to raise her words from under the stratum of crying, from the sinking ground of the past minutes: she was irritated that she could go no further forward in speaking because with each new sentence she could at best only exhume an older one. She tightened her lips and every syllable she uttered was in an unnaturally miaowing voice:

— I am not yours. I am a lot better, or at least want to be a lot better than you lot. I can never be as good as I want to be, but at least I envisage the good, dream about it — (she said the word 'dream' sharply, in italics, like a political orator) — I look, look, constantly look: I forget myself, become totally part of my dream; I dream goodness, all the saints, though I myself am no saint, never shall be, but I see more of it than the saints do, I shall enjoy sainthood more than the saints, who had no time for it, & I now collect that big-big amount of missed enjoyment...

She looked into the mirror: to do that she had to turn round, but in turning her mimicry did not slip a fraction, she managed it carefully like a wobbling, fragile fruit basket in which not a single vine leaf is allowed to stir or a hazelnut to slip; the sole surplus was that she looked at herself in the mirror — as if she sensed that her face was precisely the way she did not want. She went on looking at her face for a few more seconds; her friends also watched the soliloquy body. Her back was very real, her head very unreal. They sensed her as sharply dual: in reality, her head could not be seen; in the mirror, her body was forgotten. She was beheaded like a martyr who had the sea and the sky floating between her neck and her head. Suddenly, she turned toward them again, whereupon her head flared back in all its plasticity onto her neck, and an end came to the double life: the spirit in the mirror, its husk in the room.

— But I shall be sad as well — (she said that with an odd gaiety, like a child who, after staring for a long time at a speeding train, suddenly exclaims, "I'm going to be a locomotive driver") — : Sadness, which exists because pleasure cannot be so very great, that it, too, comes to an end, will be mine. I shall be like a devotional picture that Father was unwilling to buy off Pridatiev, who painted it, because he was insane: a martyr sat on a tree trunk, holding his smiling head with one hand like a water bottle. And in his other hand he was holding fruit in a bouquet, and offered it to his head, which leaned over the fruit with a smile. The ground was full of snow, blood, & summer flowers, blooms were out on the trees like candy on a Christmas tree, the sun was shining, and ice was dangling: Papa said that it was bosh, unproductive, desperate struggling, though real life is like that, my life, a life of the greatest joy & greatest sadness.

Leville noted none too quietly, nonchalantly clapping a hand on his knees and while he was speaking, smoothed over with outstretched fingers the place he had struck on his trousers: — People ruin everything by searching for the maximum with naïve obstinacy. They suppose the maximum will be reached if they continually include it in a program and they do mental acrobatics to reach it.

He pushed his chin with a smile between the gap of his collar toward his Adam's apple, trying to blunt the edge of his sentence with this only subjectively perceptible double chin. Then, feigning indifference, he looked up at the lamp: a couple of dim light bulbs between two parallel opaline sheets at the end of a long nickel tube, like a glass model of mechanized grapes.

Leville was greatly taken by the room: there had been a time when its underlying style was petty-bourgeois Rococo, & that had been converted with ironic taste to an exaggerated, puffy red hemisphere-system of furniture, while a number of pieces, among them this latest light fixture, were absolutely up-to-date. A pleasant combination sprang up from the sensuality of the covers and the lamp's mathematical coolness (he soon came to realize, of course, that said 'sensual' feature and said 'algebraic' feature were not opposites but a pair of extremes of a single root). The bar's proprietor even remarked that when the house and nightclub were converted, it was all like a clinic over which flooded the lighting of a stage melodrama. In any case there was a shade of a difference between the styles of each place, and Leville wanted to establish what was the minimum ('style-threshold' as he called it in sarcastic psychological lingo) necessary for the difference between two similar rooms to nevertheless be noticeable.

Every room can be traced back to a basic structure: Leatrice's could be conceived as a grey prism at the foot of which red balls were resting (a bunch of cherries, say) around & between them, glass tubes (gigantic thermometers, on which the centigrade markings were represented by window bars and wallpaper stripes). If one wanted to sketch that one could ripple sea breezes across with blue chalk, signaling that the room was tugged at indiscriminately by sea reflexes, like a manuscript inordinately corrected with blue ink.

Ena commented in dry, staccato tones: — It is beside the point whether the search for the maximum is rational or not, the fact is that people look for the maximum, there are elemental forces in people that cannot be understood but which seek the maximum.

— Where? — Leville-Touqué yelped — saints in the Middle Ages also wanted the maximum, but they managed to reach that, too, because there was always something numerical, positive, and healthily human in their ideal of the maximum: ten thousand Hail Marys, kissing of boils, God's feet, hands, heart — that ecstasy is full of, so to say, decent bourgeois specifics. But that perverse grandiloquence, which has an agonizing negative, a lack of purpose, as its sole content is — excuse me Leatrice — sick & sterile.

Leatrice, when Leville started the sentence, wanted to give a sarcastic riposte, but then Leville's determined, reedy voice somewhat won her over and half cynically, half through the instincts of a schoolgirl, which sometimes crop up in even the most intelligent women alongside a man of affirmative character, paid attention to what he had to say.

— A lack of purpose? Those forces, about which Ena spoke as well, shove one toward very anonymous places. You said this was indecisiveness? It is most decisive, even though there is no word for it, and it is impossible to tell how it arises or where it goes: many of the things that I am able to explain to myself are very weak and indecisive, but these instinctive matters...

— *Voilà le mot!* — Leville uttered quietly, making a gesture with his right hand like a conjuror who has just pulled out of an egg the signet ring of a spectator sitting in the gallery — instinct! The instinct is so simple, so disenchantingly irrelevant a matter, this certain snobbish obscurity that does not derive from the density of complexity but from the vacuity of the great big nothingness. The whole thing is some superfluous energy, and you consider it an inner proclamation, as if you were founding a religion on your thirst instead of drinking a glass of lemonade, resting your elbows on the counter of *Perspective*, and courting the bargirls.

He sensed that the matter was not as simple as all that, but it was absurd for him to say anything else, so odious did he find the pitiful apology of 'internal forces.' In any case, he again thought that in Lea's case grandiose stupidity was united with a precise beauty of an entirely revolutionary character, & for the time being those were disturbing each other as reflected together in his sympathy. Halbert gave a cough in his habitual manner, raising his right hand three feet from his mouth because he was too lazy to bring it nearer.

— *Mea peccatrice*, I was much fonder of you downstairs in the bar, because however much I may be acquainted with such mental states, it is somehow not to my taste, which means nothing, of course. Still, given that we are now here with you, speak, try to say what you want, or what you don't want, whichever is easier; what those last points were at when you were still in the down-to-earth world, so to say, but from where you proceeded toward your so-called 'new paths.'

— Are you a medic? What do you want? What will you achieve if I tell you this or that? I loathe your deductions along with your psychology. I am precisely not what follows, & specifically not what you think I am.

Anny asked in her ever-dissonant voice:

— But what are you going to do?

— I'm under a great temptation. You know that not far away, in Staak Lemoullis, the 'priest's Venice,' lives my uncle, who was very fond of me and whom I left. Not for any money do I wish to go back to him, but it is possible that out of weakness I shall do so nonetheless. For the time being, I'm quitting the *Perspective* & going to live on my own. Not in this town, though.

In a quiet, murmuring voice Halbert remarked:

— Look here, Lea, you haven't changed in the course of a few hours into a mystic who lives in a trance. You may want to be a mystic, and you could very easily become one, but meanwhile I beg your pardon, you are only being secretive; all you want is to move somewhere else, just a little. Admittedly you sincerely want that, but you are playing the mystic all the same.

Ena and Leatrice wanted to get a word in at the same time. Ena jabbered:

— What an unnecessary distinction that is: 'sincere mystic' & 'pretend mystic' — as if concepts like sincerity and pretense existed in psychology. I have talked with Lea for hours on end, and I very much understand her.

A bit flustered, and out of exaggerated modesty, Halbert replied with a breezy emphasis:

— Trust me to make those distinctions. I'm aware that shamming is undeniably important, & the fact that you sham something is just as important as perchance another's sincerity, but if, in the end, I am able to establish that it's a matter of pretense and lying, I shall in any event be examining something other than in a person for whom the matter is sincere. You speak in the same tone of voice as a person who pretends that they are having spasms of appendicitis and looks to having immediate surgery, because making a distinction between 'pretense' and 'sincerity' is naïve and unpsychological, isn't it.

Leatrice said in a wistful singing voice:

— You talk about me, and you believe that I am the subject. Look, the reason I want to move is because there is nothing I wish to say, because you misunderstand, you misunderstand what I have to say, because there's no other way of understanding than misunderstanding; there's no other way of seeing than mis-seeing. Because you want to impose yesterday's Lea on me, the day-before-yesterday's Lea, who is not me, but who is familiar to you: and I see in your eyes with horror, disgust, and impatience my repudiated, reprehended, & abandoned yesterday-image. What you have to say is not current, it is comically yesterday's and the day-before-yesterday's, as if you had chatted yesterday with an acquaintance at the beach, and you were thinking of going out there again, & started conversing airily: toward yesterday. Of course, you can't help it. At such moments you always lure me back to yesterday, & when a sound passes my lips I sense with disgust my yesterday voice when my own is already different. You know — (she again adopted that explanatory tone of a young girl who reels off to her friends an extraordinary adventure of hers in a whisper) — it is rather like hearing a melody clearly in one's head but being unable to sing it vocally: the inability one feels at a time like that is awful.

Leville looked at Leatrice, seeing in her nothing other than her being extraordinarily lovely. He then noticed that when Lea had talked about a 'new me' being in the process of evolving inside that was going to burst the outside husk, she had imagined precisely the opposite of what was really taking place in her; actually it was more a matter of her whole personality wasting away, or rather, she was being absorbed into the surface, the body, in other words, into all that Lea called her 'yesterday me.' He attempted to assume her self-image and look at Lea as something non-current, but that only heightened the delight in that body. That was not yesterday, or if you prefer, it was yesterday, but even so, definitive & unique.

This was a special cleansing: while a woman's brain concerns itself with the minuscule matters of real life, she is, as it were, inserting her body into the world and into 'life,' but when something irrational gets under way in her brain, which is naturally homogeneous and one-tracked, then those thoughts are like an ice-breaking needle on a ship's bow — they cut life in order to open up a fresh and absolutely free path for the body.

When Leatrice had been a courtesan she could not have been anything like as erotic as she was now, since concerning herself with her body took up her spirit in countless tiny little intellectual directions, but now by not uttering a word to anyone, by breaking her connection with the room, with time, & with her own divergent thoughts, her body was endowed with a particularly pure impetus & gained a new weight in its neglect; 'mystical' one-sidedness was a tilting rope straight as an arrow on which she slipped with impudent speed like a suspension railway.

The starting and departure nature was undeniable, and there were various opportunities for metaphor to perceive that: *'la Cardinalle'*[73] was like a sliding trough from which a new yacht is let fly onto the water (1°), or like a flower from the rim of which a butterfly flies off (2°): the latter of which Leville felt very plastically in himself because the whole house was narrow and around the story seemed to broaden like an unfolding flower on its stem — through so much of the country being sliced through the opened window among the parts of the room, the whole little apartment had a floating and open character, and it felt quite unreal that underneath it was still a building & not a springy stalk or trunk on which the room swayed in the slow rhythm of a boat that had been recently anchored.

Between the two similes he then naturally found a most expressive and unmentioned third, namely, rail junctions branching away from each other at railway stations, switch buds from which open the lavish rail flowers of unknown directions: within an inch or two it still seems as if the new rail was just a nervous flickering of the eyes, then it bends sharply away, & although it only started at the switch point, one nevertheless feels that the new branch was already present in the single old rail from the very beginning. The branches of trees are always surpluses of lines that have sprung up by summation, arising by a process of biological interest, while the leaves are compound interests which continually add & summate — rail tracks, however, even if a single pair of rails suddenly branch in five directions, always remain one; it is only that identity may accidentally land itself in a playful configuration in space in which, through reflection, it looks five-branched in the same way that a straight stick under water will appear to have broken in two.

Touqué rejoiced in those changes, in which the only purpose of a flower, a blossoming bundle of petals, is for it to better define the shape of the bud: stamens, colors, and a series of artificial shade, which are located in the calyx in the way that lenses of various shapes are distributed in binocular tubes, like the belated definition of an expired bud which, of course, cannot thrive at the same time as the bud: it is either the adolescent carbuncle of the bud or the tropical sophistry of definition.

---

role of sensuality between ontology and fiction,
between an exaggeration of precision & Romantic bluff

When Leatrice's body was partly divided up into an optical quantum-pagoda of the mirror and had partly run aground, on the other hand, in crude 'mystic' kitsch, then Touqué experienced the pleasant development in the domain of eroticism which extended from existence to his own definition, at which it turned out how alien definition is next to the defined; there is no blood relationship between them, but since one's brain links the defined and the definition out of a superstitious love of tradition, it sees the two alien entities together in a delicious, crazy identity. When the butterfly flies away from a flower and the flower afterwards oscillates to and fro from the final thrust, then the pendulum swing in which the butterfly's distance is measured as the flower rocked was for Touqué the ticking of its identity: the better the petals' manometric pose expressed the butterfly's departing withdrawal, the better the flower was absorbed into its own flower nature: any alteration whatever is definition-flavored & reactive.

As if women and things in general had only overtaken their definition in the most recent times, and they were now fitting their form to primitive specifications with belated Lamarckian-tricks, now medically, also demonstrably, the elementary '*genus proximum*' and '*differentia specifica*';[74] indeed, only those two can now be seen, and they counterbalance one another like a positive and negative charging of form. "Leatrice is a creature of female gender with blonde hair, so and so; arms, so and so long, etc." — a definition that has two blots, two energy kernels: one of those is the living being (the *genus*), the other are the data specifically indicative of form (the *differentia*) — in the new anatomy, above all the erotic physical structure, those two extremes continue to develop along their own paths, accommodating, breaking up the body's unity, taking literally the conspicuous anarchistically disruptive character of every definition.

The intensely consistent continuation of the living being, or in other words, the genus, is histrionic bluster, a belletristic general hysteria that manifested in Leatrice's words & acts, for every affected vitalism immediately swings over into hysteria if it has even only a bit of sincere belief in its program; on the other hand, the data specifically indicative of form, the totality of little prerequisites of *differentia*, refined into abstract numbers and constellations of algebraic functions in an ecstasy of individualization; in a sick forcing of individualization they molded a supra-individual precision masquerade, an 'overidentifying alibi-motor,' so to say.

Sensuality was not directed at a uniform woman but at two antithetically foreign things, both of which were already beyond a mundane average or stereotyped-Leatrice: one was the line world, broken up into layers of the mirror and fluorescent in higgledy-piggledy fashion, the other was Leatrice's 'spiritual life,' though as a consequence of its extraordinary strength, inflamed to the point of caricature, tumbled out of the woman as it were: hysteria is like a lump of black iron, hidden in a bouquet of flowers, which will drop to the ground any time it is clumsily shaken — entirely savage and disproportionate feelings, wild charity, logical love or hysterical play-acting, virtually separate out from the body and may be examined independently in space — and sensuality is a double-pillared arch based on inhuman sentiment & inhuman physical appearance.

Infinite precision, which can no longer define anything precisely on account of its endlessness, plus its necessary counterpart, infinite vitalist instinctive bluff, were best symbolized by, or rather illustrated for Touqué, the detective thriller that he had found late at night on the seat of a bus: the novel was about a murder that had been committed in a bathing resort, and the aforementioned two Leatrice-extremes perpetually figured together. It was precisely that constant coexistence that was important from the viewpoint of Touqué's love, much more important than to derive the two extremes through the use of the entire box of tricks of absurdizing cosmetic surgery.

The similarity could immediately be acknowledged in all its crudity: Leatrice's immaterial muscle-parallaxes, which he put down to the mirror's grey glint, corresponded to the girls in swimming costumes who (there were some four of them) committed a murder in a distant changing cubicle, and above all the waves of the water, the seesawing Ionian exercises of sun & sea; the bloody cadaver of the murdered person, on the other hand, that the girls, swimming underwater, had lugged into a lateral channel yards away, signified an independent block of feelings that had fallen from Leatrice's body.

For years on end Touqué was unable to rid himself of that double spectacle, these two antithetical branches of the deed: the slim American girls zigzagging so that the greenness of the water made their bodies abstract as they circled in nervous circuits around the hundredweight reality of a dark cadaver. During the court hearing on the crime, the individual witnesses tried in their statements to link with almost scientific mania a given specific to a given abstract phenomenon; one spoke of a hair's breadth of a footprint pressed in the mud, which was maybe the shadow of a cathode ray and not far from which she had seen a long trail of blood; a second mentioned that she had seen a colored bubble on the water, like a half-built soap bubble, which was perhaps a mother-of-pearl case of a last breath, exactly as big as the last section of a soul, but she also recollected a dark, sack-like thing under the rainbow ball of foam; a third had seen a brick-red swimsuit belt from the back, then heard sharp laughter, but that evening she had not found her vanished friend's big briefcase, and so on.

The figures of the perpetrators became ever-more linear, evanescent, little more than amalgams of seconds, shadows, and fragments of spectra, in parallel to which the dead body had become ever-more massive, uneven, and definite material: nowadays cylindrical clocks are made on the wall of which the hand is a single fixed arrow, whereas a ring of numbers is constantly rotating in a strip around the cylinder — the dead body was a stiff and unmoving indicator needle like that at the bottom of the water, while the homicidal girls and interfering waves of minutes revolved around it like a ribbon of numbers with an opalescent scale. (A German philosophical thesis expounded the necessary parallel and mutual presumptiveness of absolute instinct & absolute artificiality, not as accurately as the detective thriller, but with a degree of good fortune, Hartländer, *Über morbide Hyperontik und polylineare Zeroskopie als neurotische Dual-Konstanten.* Greifswald: 1933.)[75]

When he ran his eyes over the gathering, it was hard to retrain his instinct to carry on into the immoral poetic world of symbols and allegories, taking one of the above similes as his basis. His eyes passed from the nickel chandeliers to the small electric candles along the wall: once upon a time those had been meek and shabby Rococo mountings, with gilding and white; Lea, however, had painted them in color, the moderately out-of-style floral forms had been painted back into colorful meadow flowers, so that an indistinct cartouche or a curlicue that had become completely detached from nature suddenly resumed the form of a pea blossom or vine tendril. Underneath them, on the wall, were four plaques as colorful as outdoor terrace columns. The room was of great appeal to Leville; there were heaps of impertinence about it, an obstinate female dilettantism, which may possibly be worth more than true competence.

Suddenly he was struck by the thought as to what would be the best surroundings for Leatrice: an abstract background, say, a grey wall and opaline firescreen, or plein-air; or perhaps that eclectic little room in which there was laughter at the mix of styles, too.

There was a knock on the door. Leatrice said quietly:

— The owner is coming to check up, talk me round, snoop. I have nothing to do with him. Everything will be left for him; he can turn my room into a museum, and my clothes will be gifted to the couple of dancers with whom I have made friends.

— Turning to Anny, she added: — I'll only take that two-piece hunting suit with me, you know the one I mean.

Halbert answered the door. A young man was standing in the doorway: plump, with a low forehead, and a dry, stuffed tuxedo waistcoat of black wire gauze and a stiff tux front, over which a striped pajama jacket had been pulled; his skin was brown, & the way he looked was part obsequious, part cocky: he resembled a Black-Jewish half-breed.

— Oh, Monsieur Halbert, you're here! You know, what my girl is playing at, my one and only girl, the ungrateful little baggage. But can a child be ungrateful?

He stepped toward Leatrice, thrusting his left hand in his pocket and making a move as if he wanted to pinch her face between the index & middle fingers of his right hand: "What's that, then? Uh! Temper, temper!" At which he burst out laughing and started looking about the room for accomplices as if he had discovered a quite extraordinary tortoise under the corner of a rock. — Flash company this girl keeps. When another of my girls had that howd'yecall it, that whatsit, 'that get-up-and-go' — (in so saying he slightly crouched and chuckled as he imitated Lea's mimicry of yesterday right under Lea's nose) —, then the entire university wouldn't pay a call on her — (the word 'university' was pronounced with the cheeks puffed out & both hands raised to the heavens: his shirt sleeves were strained to bursting at the wrists) —, but she'd just ask a manicurist to drop by or go to a hairdresser and get her hair waved. But then you were different, still are, heaven knows. — All of a sudden, he lowered his voice, as a signal, so to speak, that they had long had a good, confidential relationship and yesterday's semi-scandal had only been a temporary 'bellyache' & not a serious, terminal row: — You know, afterwards Steermans came round to me to moan, he's in the habit of putting on that childish & fresh tone when he speaks — (when the owner was among 'college' types out of a confused sense of politeness he would have liked to speak in definitions, & he tried with all kinds of the snappy gestures intellectuals adopt to make good his mediocre range of verbal expressions, in the same way as in front of foreign guests he hid his lack of proficiency in languages by his jumbled employment of the conversational gambits of the language in question) —, as if the starter course were bad or the wine had a sour, 'gone-off' taste.

— No doubt moaned that one of his girls had happened by accident to come over all moral, eh? — Halbert muttered in jest with a wink at Lea. Lea was evidently taking the whole conversation like an impatient lady in the vestibule whom the footman was in any case going to divest of her fur coat in a second but she had a 'business-like' glitter in her eyes which detained her on petty duties like that.

The owner carried on:

— To the chortles of the girls he came after me into the office & continually demanded something, talking about his rights, he was drunk as a fiddler, and he ended up half-whining, half-yelling (a duality that he put over like pianists do when they suddenly swing their right hand to the left, over the left hand, and with a dreamy but quick glance he ran his eyes over the audience, for whose benefit the punctilious gesture had been intended) declaiming an entire invocation to order & order about.

Halbert turned with a smile toward Touqué:

— The legal nicety of obese little salesmen like that amuses me: They seem to think that the whole notion of 'justice' is nothing other than guaranteeing a profit margin and prompt delivery of a measure of vulgar titillation to what at root, as in the present case, are petty-bourgeois-minded shopkeepers. I have already had the good fortune to listen to Steersman's outpourings about 'order': when we talked about conservatism he was almost overcome with tears in defending the old régime, by which he meant some variant of free trade; 'bourgeoisly' romantic little chunks of profit that it is impermissible to disturb; freedom to do business, & a small family which lives on that freedom: that's 'order' & 'truth' for you.

Leatrice meanwhile went over to the owner (her movements by now were totally 'this worldly': indeed, it was perceptible how, by an action like a jolt, she switched from her mystic to her practical style as red and blue alternate every second on the same spot on neon advertising signs, & when one is illuminated the other skulks palely underneath, though more in memory than in sight).

Leville felt that he would like to find a point of view from which he would be able to condense his lengthy series of impressions of the woman into a coherent unit: the marveling observation and intensive material loyalty, which manifested in exaggerated peeping, always led to mystery, distorted everything into the form of a question as, after all, observing was no more than waiting for the next second and reaching a solution by fitting its supplementary future conditional to the memory in such a way that the whole woman was a function of that perpetual next second and thus could not be confined in a mental Thermos flask that does not permit the future to intrude: he would have liked to leave the whole scene behind to be able to think something definite about her, which he could not do any other way than by cutting through the thread of life and, by that Parca-esque gesture, setting about creative recollection: he would have been able to sketch the Y-shaped diagram, which with heroic pedantry would have shown how reality and appearance coincided for a while (maybe even that was not a true and accurate mutual cover) and later, after a forcible interruption, Leatrice would go to the right and the Leatrice-memory & Leatrice-modification would go to the left.

Leville would already have very much liked to remember Leatrice, because in that way he could have felt that the woman was his captive, whereas at present she kept continually slipping out of his grasp like an eel of which only the tail end is in one hand, but its head is constantly being swallowed up by the next second, from which it cannot be snatched, pulled back, and brought to a standstill. To be sure, some people kicked up a big tragedy about how positive observation excluded completion and, therefore, the possibility of coming to a conclusion, whereas memory (which is often no more than an artificial flight from looking at real life, i.e., burying one's head in the sand) bases its conclusions on a shard of life, with its being at last in possession of an isolated & finished residue of life — but then how much despotism prevails in that.

'eternity routine' of
Leatrice life-image & Leatrice memory-image

When he kept a watch on Leatrice he was seized by the same nervousness as when he sat on the seashore and looked at consecutive incoming flat wave endings: each one flowed into another, & he felt a physical agony at being unable to isolate them so that he had to shut his eyes in order to be able to picture a single wave, but on the other hand he was unable to bring the waves to a halt in his imaginative memory — the movement remained in his memory against his will. Either ungraspable eternal undulation or graspable memory, which, on the other hand, was not undulating: that was the trashy dilemma of experiencing and remembrance ("let's be honest," Leville said to himself, "that's not particularly disturbing"). If that's what one sees, then there's nothing to do but smoothly fictionalize it.

The sole interesting thing about it all is that one has an obsession about 'reality' when one proclaims the tyranny of fiction: one establishes that the living Leatrice is not 'real,' that the Leatrice preserved in the artificial atmosphere of the memory is likewise not 'real': but when there are only these two, & exclusively these two, Leatrice-possibilities, from where does any kind of true Leatrice at all come into one's head? There is something touching about this superstitious desire for the 'real' Leatrice — that nervous, sentimental, & anxious scrupulousness over not feeling the two given females to be 'real' enough — that whatever may turn up one will always sense, on the basis of a lurking & strong criterion, that it is not the 'real' one: that is some sort of endearing honest streak on the part of people. All of these only seem so in the paradoxical mirror of the spirit, & of course life hardly maintains fellowship with that: it would be interesting if the relativity on which one always insists & points to were, for once, to be manifest in the world's physical outer form — then it would turn out crudely and in its material grotesqueness how absolute, how simple, & how clearly structured the world is, or if you like, how much it is, all the same, 'reality' — how concrete something is, in a petty-bourgeois sense, which has borders where a rehabilitated János Hári hangs his legs, in the scientifically literal sense of the word, to the great amazement of nebulous relativists.[76]

Leville had a draughtsman's acquaintance and it came to mind that he would ask him to paint a sequence of pictures under the title *The Relativists' Big Picture Book*: in this the two Leatrices would be drawn —the observed Leatrice, the Leatrice who was scattered in time and thus could not be constrained between lines of synthesis — and the fictive Leatrice-memory-model. Down in the right-hand corner (as in American two-page colored advertisements, where the main picture represents a tobogganing party, but lower down, under a dotted line, is seen a little tube of toothpaste as being the 'true' essence of the above picture) is a miniature photograph of Leatrice, the purpose of which will be to remind people of the positive, peasant-style positive, character of life.

Actually, those two Leatrice-pictures portray the two perpetuity routines with graphic rawness: in a movement of the observed Leatrice, drawn from life, the next movement is always already germinating, her body forever arching and coiling into movements each more different than the last; just a single random slice of the movement of the Leatrice living in memory, however, will develop that fragment further, more similar to itself, toward the pattern of its pattern, and when it has reached that, too, in the tight tube of memory, then it will still be forever shoving it likewise toward ever-newer patterns.

Both of them signify 'perpetual motion,' though this does not correspond to either of the average conceptions one has formed of motion: the eternally continuing in life as difference, though every movement brings something essentially new to the gestures hitherto, it nevertheless makes itself uniformly felt as if it were not movement but a fortunate point of view about stability from which multiple dimensions of stability are visible at one & the same time, much as that of a complicated grouping of statues; on the other hand, the memory trace that adds nothing new, which does not continue perpetually in other movements but, on the contrary, declines into the perversity of identity, that memory trace does, indeed, always furnish newer and newer surprises that is to say, the paradoxical situation pertains: while reality is continually altering, one does not sense that variation as movement but as four or five passive and stationary dimensions of stability, and whereas memory preserves a single rigid excised stump that is perceived by identity-sensuality in constant development, in the form of newer upon newer decorations, each more alien than the last.

Life is constantly dissolving and expanding a 'moving' body, because every subsequent movement is a wider ring of a wave following behind the previous one, as if the gesture-waves would always strive toward a regular circle: the raising of a saucer and a subsequent search for a handkerchief relate to each other like a sketched saucer around which is a line that only roughly follows the saucer's outline and thus approximates to a regular circle, and, because every movement dissolves the previous one in the overall balance of the full circle, every movement in life seems to be well-set dimensions of a single stationary position. Memory, by contrast, progresses inward from the outline to the point, it sucks up the saucer inwardly to the substance-point, but that is attended by eternal distortion, mask-swapping.

The artistic construction should one day be of benefit to this double way of looking at things: at a place where in reality a million changes occur, one always sees a single stationary condition, and where truly rigid fragments occur (in memory) one jerks from otherness to otherness in the most unpredictable leaps. An actress makes thousands upon thousands of movements in the course of a stage play, she fills out thousands upon thousands of positions with her body, yet one constantly senses her to be a statue, of which these shifts are just bits of space, colors, bulges, or diagonals, merely juxtaposed (never after one another!): it is as if we would totally & naturally lack a sense of time, and we were seeing every drama simultaneously, from beginning to end, in a synthetic space moment. That is why one can never take an action in practical life: one perpetually sees oneself & one's partner distributed in the past & future, and 'tomorrow,' 'the day after tomorrow,' & 'in two years' time' are also already now present in one's field of vision, so there is no room for active movement. One is unable to prophesy, one cannot see into the future, yet, all the same, if one looks at a woman with whom one is in love, one distributes her in some form into the space of the future: one surrounds her physique with expanding rings, with copies of outlines which, step by step, are more inaccurate, the expanding curves of which break through the walls of today and tomorrow, the barriers of years.

The more disconnected the movements (seemingly 'one after the other') that a woman makes in the course of life, the sooner she will attain a time-free stability without drama; if one takes as an example said raising of a saucer & the subsequent search for a handkerchief, then one can clarify that in a sketch: the raising of the saucer is portrayed as an equilateral triangle, and the subsequent search for the handkerchief as a totally irregular little smudged area next to it, it is obvious that one feels the alienage between the two diagrams is maximal. But if I should wish to see the two diagrams occupying a common frame which, as far as possible, is parallel to the outlines of the two plane figures and at the same time mediates them in a unit within the frame's moderating-recapitulatory course, then this will much, much more quickly reach the frame of the regular circle, as if they were not such disparate figures — so, it is the most disparate real-life gestures that we believe explode drama and time most concentratedly out of themselves, precisely they fly toward absolute stability.

When all is said and done, Touqué reached exactly the opposite of what he had imagined at first, which had been to continue the real Leatrice's movements forever, thinking that those could not be set between 'synthesis-lines,' but the continuation, the maximum of change, reached exactly the absolutely static, which is the ideal form of synthesis, as everything is so evidently one that a synthesis is superfluous, the concept has become meaningless. Expressions of the kind that he had used beforehand: 'scattered in time' either had no kind of real content or the scattering had to be taken *ad absurdum*, & then it would have had an essentially different content, precisely its opposite: perpetual standstill.

As far as the other illustration in *The Relativists' Big Picture Book* is concerned, viz. the scheme of the fictive Leatrice-memory (as he had just said), it likewise turned out that precisely because he wanted to capture the absolute of the scheme, the most vital logical central organ of the essence (i.e., self-identity), he never reached anything definable, but ever-stranger constellations passed before his eyes: instead of a model, unexpected & individual random-portraits; in place of essence, a perpetual diaspora of flickering masks, as if the memory-trace-atoms of Leatrice were all at once decomposing to newer-atoms of unknown women, and the most-Leatrice of Leatrices would suddenly disperse at the last moment into a bunch of other bar dancers: *Memory and Rutherford or the two Noble Kinsmen.*[77]

---

conversation about the periodical Antipsyche

— I am amused by Leatrice's unfathomability; I am amused by any psychological game; even my own craziness would amuse me because I am unable to imagine any other calling for *Psyche* than that kind of decorative-entertaining calling: it grants playful, gaudy, confused perspectives, like a colored lamp that is swaying to and fro and thus shows a different-colored and different-shaped world every moment, but I feel (forget for now the sentimental and 'unscientific' sense of the word) that this is just a game, and the world is not now red, now green, now trapezoid, now hyperbolic, but much simpler. It doesn't dishearten me at all that I can report in words, or think with thoughts, only my toy picture; that I have names for a trapezium and hyperbola, for red and green — on the other hand I have no name for the world's simple form & simple shade: I shall take pains to create for myself a language that will express this absolute and exclusive monosemy, but I can say in advance that this will be neither some affected pseudo-mathematical hieroglyphic language nor a futurists' childishly monist expression-scale; rather, what it will be about is that it should be perceptible within the available words and signs that it is not a detail, but a whole, that the detail, precisely by virtue of its character as detail, constantly hints at, indeed uncovers, a whole. For that, though, it is necessary, naturally, to break from the temptation to decorativeness of Psyche's rule. Skepticism is a decorative instinct, not an intellectual activity. I have the psychological fact of relativism to thank for my faith (the interim word 'faith,' as with 'feeling' before, is to be forgotten) in the whole and the simple (I cannot think these words 'whole' and 'simple' in small enough lower-case letters to avoid molding some sort of colportage-myth from these notions). Notwithstanding which I have no desire to be a philosopher of the doctrine of the Absolute; I wish for something simpler than thought and better than instinct.

(Leville looked around, automatically, to check whether anyone had noticed that he had maybe demanded an ethics right then. He was not cowardly, but at that moment he was scared of it, though it had been an axiom of *Antipsyche*; sometimes, however, it is necessary to avow a principle for years until it coincides fully with one's thinking & inclinations, in the same way as a machine will sometimes function well for years on end, but a time comes when, due to an accidental bump, a switch is shifted and work with the machine flows with an utterly mysteriously increased facility and speed, and one senses directly in one's own body that only now is there complete confluence in a matter in which hitherto, so it seems, there had been disharmony even though it had functioned well.)

— At all events it is necessary to free oneself of the seaweed of impressions, however great the intellectual patience with which those are processed & however much they are transmuted into precise and logical products, they remain nonetheless in their irrational rootedness, and even if the results that proliferate from them may appear to be of hard, rational soundness taken by themselves, the moment one touches them, particularly when one seeks to take nourishment from them: straightway the sourish taste of superfluity can be tasted and they crumble as dust between one's gums.

(Marvelous fruits, those: when he called to mind Leatrice's many images, he truly had the feeling that he had reached into Flora's dark fruit basket, among which had grown superhuman fruits, the scents of which were heavy on the eyelids, like the fumes of some narcotic, and now hastily rushed out from that forest like a small boy who has been lured to an opium den and, after the first few puffs, the first furtive intrusions of sleep, dashes into the open air — half-enjoying, half driving-out the unfolding & fraying gifts of the vision.)

— To be simple and short, I don't want impressions: I have no wish to fall for such bad sirens. It may well be that it is a paradoxical struggle, but that is the least of its faults.

His resolutions were not psychic stirrings but concrete visions insofar as he saw them printed on the pages of *Antipsyche*: indeed, a picture of the printed pamphlet actually preceded his thoughts. (People talk sarcastically about those for whom words precede thoughts — yet sometimes precisely the greatest thoughts are born from the obligatory routine of holding forth, as if the mechanical whirling of words were the electric tingling that is needed for a liquid's chemical composition to vary — words agitate that 'silent mirror' of the spirit, and often, with a single magical touch, the redeeming enchantment of a word, it is completely reordered, regroups down to its atoms, and displays miraculous new systems.)

In any case 'impression' was a highly alluring Circe, so that a crude, colorless pure intention would not have been enough to suppress it (which is why so many good intentions and such good will take a tumble: because they are so impossibly abstract, such vision-free psychological experiences, like a strong wind that blows on an imaginary terrain on which there is not even a single blade of grass, on which its blowing would show and could be checked); an impression has to be counterbalanced by an impression (*"la impresión con la impresión"?*), and it is more worthwhile to hang on to typography than to colorless, odorless moral impulses; the new leading article dropped like a merciless curtain on the effeminate basket of impressions.

"We are a movement, the tendency of which is fairly clear and concrete for it to be necessary to bother designating its precise position in the geography of the mind. We are not so girlish & agoraphobic as to shrink from not being able to state our names, only our addresses. It may not be the most elegant way of introducing ourselves, but we will try to make up for that negligence later. We confess that we have deliberated on whether we are science, literature, or whimsical pastiche, but we realized that, although we do not fit any straightforward category (we are not proud of that, because all kinds of out-law romances disagree with our taste), we represent something just as positive, resolute, and sharply circumscribed as so-called pure artistic forms. Perhaps it is a question of a dynamic unity — of course in the intellectual, not the pathetic sense of the word.

If, in the columns of our paper, we shall abhor pathos, right to the point of vulgar pretentiousness & soulless affectation: be so good as to take it as scandalizing eccentricity without which a serious line of thought is unimaginable. We set ourselves up against Psyche: understanding by that a respect for the soul in the sense that the notion of man would be identical to the notion of the richness of so-called psychological life; that richness identical to the infinite accumulation and complex interweaving of psychological nuances; art identical to progress toward the soul: accordingly, we set ourselves up against the medical, esthetic, & philosophical overestimation of the soul.

We are not physicians, esthetes, or philosophers, but we know that a histrionic dilettantism is occasionally required so that this universal and holy amateurism that we accomplish should carry experts along with it, or rather embrace in a unity, even if only retrospectively, those scientists & artists who have already been working in that direction for some time, and sometimes — being well versed in the vanities of scholars & artists — even embrace them symbolically, despite themselves, into *Antipsyche*'s provocative constellation. We are not inclined to grant our antagonists the pleasure of being able to say of us »what a superfluous & tragicomic struggle it is that cynically professed amateurism proclaims against specialized branches of learning & the arts« — we do not permit that because, after all, this is about anything else but that.

Though kitsch and works of art do not live at a snobbish distance to each other in our brain, strife of that kind would, indeed, be unjustified kitsch. All that is in question is that we shout out the kind of thing that the noble and often suffocating discretion of science does not dare shout out. We are, at most, *enfants terribles*, but in no way illegitimate children. It is more a matter of casting principles before us and throwing out the question as to whether those can be proved, or rather: demanding proof. Let philology and hysteria, anxious moral philosophizing and instinctive lyrical impromptu, be together on these pages: admittedly, this is not our pride but possibly our tragedy.

We demand proof: that truly sounds insolent, but our experience is that an invitation brings the guest; it is not guests who constrain on us a wish to invite them. We believe that there is a need to set down these principles. Why? It could be that at root »an instinct for contradiction« lies against psychologists: only that »instinct for contradiction« is not so much sentimental sulkiness or something of the kind — as is generally supposed —, but a strongly intellectual factor. Our instincts are guided by our habitual trains of thought — thus, perceiving intuition in that way (not just scientific intuition, but also the intuition that satisfies our everyday needs), we have no need to fear that the use of the term »feeling« could belittle us. In other words, there is no need to picture the matter as though one could only give a technical response to a technical query: as we see it, it is possible to reply to a discourse on medical science in an architectural style as a party of equal rank, just as it is possible to refute the concept of a historical figure with a hat creation or a bacterial discovery — the »meaning« alone being important everywhere: the »meaning,« however, is a neutral material in which there is not even a trace of architectural or medical concreteness, it is almost like an international language, diplomatically colorless, in the plane of which a medical institution and the contour of a neoprimitive temple have at their disposal exactly the same projection image, which is to say they can be treated as homogeneous. So much by way of an apology for our authority, etc."

When Leville-Touqué thought this over for a few seconds, he believed he had satisfied the interest of the 'struggle against impressions': he had done something against them intellectually, so he could surrender to them sensually; indeed, it was almost for that reason that he wracked his brains over this mind game after which he could safely enjoy his 'impressions.' An impression did not have universal significance, it had no significance: if one takes this into account, if one writes it down and edits a polemical journal for that purpose, then one's conscience can be untroubled and one can enjoy one's impression: Leatrice.

Halbert & the nightclub owner

The owner spoke quietly to Lea: on such occasions he gathered his body into a reverent and soft composition, thereby signaling that this was a serious business matter. People like that have, by and large, two sorts of sentimentalism: one sort, which tends to well up in the midst of 'serious' work, actual business negotiations, when they are moved, so to say, by the fact that they are now engaged in something entirely positive and are making entirely definitive decisions about some matter — thus it happens that they will state the driest rattling-off of contractual facts in a soft, melodic, gushing tone of voice, speaking with genuine inspiration (that was the case here with this owner, gesticulating quietly with his chubby-wristed and cigar-shaped fingers); the other condition of sentiment can be observed when the person is faced with some detail of art or heroic life, stylized history: at a time like that they have only entirely primitive feelings, though with snobbish obstinacy they feel this latter condition to be a culmination of their emotional life — yet those culminations are only ever reached in a sensual knowledge of work and which are much more akin, for all their petty-bourgeois sense of security, to true esthetic feelings than those enthusiasms & stirrings which they are accustomed to display on stage or in book reviews.

— Come, my dear Mr. Halbert, come. Escort me down. I have to look over how the bathroom in the basement was built. Come.

Halbert winced, with a bored & sarcastic expression on his face, thrust his hands in his pants, and slumped his chest in such a way that his necktie assumed the form of a cynical gesture:

Halbert was one of those rather taciturn people who make up for their uncommunicativeness by constantly expressing their opinion with their clothes and bearing and thus develop a quite special clothes-mimicry, a plastic language of which one could even draw up the imagery quite accurately. There was something troubled and ponderous about Halbert's movement, but at the same time he had the fortunate habit that when he executed the clumsiest superfluous stretchings and initially awkward shiftings, then a counter gesture would unexpectedly develop on the other side of his body so that it all swung surprisingly into balance, creating an appearance of lazy nonchalance. ("I can never ascertain — Touqué remarked —, whether your colleague is an imbecile or aristocratically blasé.")

On this occasion, also, when he followed the owner through the door, he described with his foot a circle in the air as if he wished to tip a heavy piece of iron to the side — meanwhile he lost balance but afterwards, with a swing of the head, he tossed his hair behind his ear and by so doing his whole body snuggled back into an orderly gait with that corrective movement. As soon as they were outside the boss started to splutter.

— Right now I have so many worries all at once; you have no idea that I'm getting married. That's right, married. I'm getting hitched to that Spanish girl from the *Evergreen*; an odd setup, wouldn't you say? Diplomatic embarrassments, the boss and owner of one nightspot gets spliced to one of the star dancing girls of a competitor; I'm not kidding, I really did have to cut a deal with old Tuflin — poor Fridolin! — that's what we called him, you know, because his mustache drooped on both sides like that vaudeville actor — I'm sure you remember him — but now poor Fridolin has snipped them off, perhaps thinking that he would have a better chance of winning her back with a shaven mug, but the cosmetic trickery got him nowhere because the Muchachita (you may know that in the *Evergreen* they are in the habit of calling the girls of all the different nationalities 'Miss' in their own lingo) told him that the skin under his forty-year-old whisker has an entirely different color, & now his face looks like cheap crèpe de Chine, one half of which has been faded by the sun and the other half of which is still fresh because it had a strip of advertising tied round it; great, wouldn't you say? Fridolin... — he muttered.

— I don't get it; sorry! How can one get married like that?

— Like that? What do you mean by 'like that'? The woman? A woman like that? I could tell you, God knows — or what are you driving at?

— I don't know, I am only asking, I don't understand... Yes, that's it, a woman like that and you...

— You know... what can I say? I have women continually circulating round me. I'm up to my neck in them, I see them constantly, and then, all of a sudden, one of them somehow ends up with me — it's not so much a matter of honor. No, not that, look, I have no illusions. But there are times when that, too, is what one needs. It's hard to know what to say precisely: in some way I am turned on by her spiciness, I want to be with her all the time... no, not always that way, of course...

Halbert struck the bannister rail and, eyes rolled upwards, said in a self-ironic, censorious voice (his way of trying to gloss over or bridge the distance between him & the owner): — In other words, the old tried and tested perversity: marriage is more perverse than the girls being on tap...

— It may be that, I don't know — at which point he adopted an amiable, humble air, which in point of fact was just a knack for smuggling himself onto the level of an 'exchange between friends' & discussing serious matters on a 'collegial' basis.

Halbert, a smile on his face, looked straight ahead: he had extraordinarily long, white teeth but a small mouth, with the lips thin and colorless to the point of greyness.

— All the same, that kind of thing is interesting, a marriage like that, love, or whatever, of that kind — what are you after? Not a family, not passion, not fidelity, not a flirtation: just marriage. A totally abstract marriage — this last sentence was placed in the air so as to speedily fly off since he had a feeling that it was not a continuation of his train of thought, just of speech. Suddenly his face was wreathed by the shadow of a deep inner smile as if he were bending over a memory that had assumed symbolic significance, then just as abruptly he snatched up his head, as if in the depths he had seen the opposite of that see-sawingly seductive symbol & had burst out laughing: his buck-teeth gleamed, and his whole mouth gave a vertical rather than a horizontal impression.

reason & culture

In truth, his mimicry represented a bit of an antithesis: the shadowy & gently grave smile spoke to his hidden ideal of love (Tristan?), the laughter to that ironic playful love, that unreal jest, which was more a parodic but sentimental prelude on the subject of love than true love. Leville-Touqué immediately came to mind: sallow, abstract-sensual face, greenish chin, and thick spectacles dangling on flimsy wires, big, yellow, fanlike eyelids and, stuck under them, beady twitching-penetrating eyes: a banal mask for a schemer, which straightway, with the sardonic concern of seeking to irritate, went into refined rhapsodies about this marriage (at that moment he noticed that 'abstract marriage' was in itself already an involuntary aping of Leville's style): he would have been able to spout Leville's essay of apology word for word, still without saying anything on Tristan's side.

All one has to keep an eye on on one's fellow-person is a wrinkle, a mimic nuance or tone of voice for, in the face of life's events and phenomena, that alien wrinkle and the alien conceptual standpoint which is hypothetically, but in minute detail, derived from it, always first spring to mind like one's own inner attachment: because alien thinking is always connected to a face, a look in the eyes, or a handhold, so as to appear as a strong, visible, and statuesque reality, unlike one's own thoughts, which are always shapeless waves, and if they ever reach the stage of being cast in definite form, will still lack the necessary clean character, untrammelled by origin, to have any authority.

On the whole, Halbert did not hold Leville to be a bright spark, feeling rather that he spoke in a foreign language that he treated with nervous meticulousness, but those striking results about which his university colleagues spoke were not personal but the virtually natural consequences of a fashionable thinking-technique (Touqué's 'logo-jargon'). He was in the habit of calling trains of thought like that (they were represented in the university not by Touqué alone) with an English pronunciation, '*floraison*,' thereby in some measure honoring that style of thinking's fresh pomp and paradoxical play of colors or mimesis, but at the same time downgrading it as adolescent bragging motivated by beauty. None of that was expressed in the true sense of '*floraison*,' of course, but in the word's distorted, Anglicized pronunciation: his face was a clear, unbroken smile, whereas the word was scrappy, primitive, & held in ever-so-slight contempt.

Halbert felt that he was different from Touqué in an elemental fashion, and thus there was no possibility of debating with him as it would rarely have been the case that they were of 'opposing' opinion: it was more a matter of 'differences in attitude' or else they were interested in entirely different things and would feel one another superfluous. Touqué, naturally, did not resign himself to the distinction of 'rational opinion' and 'attitude,' and once, in a long tirade, he expounded that an attitude was in point of fact something rational, too, just reason or a train of thought enlivened, and racial determinations came later than intellectual standpoints, i.e., racial features by blood were just pure intellectual standpoints, later rendered automatic, the results of which remained in the form of 'culture-attitude,' but the causative and intellectual contrivances of which sank into oblivion: thus, a 'racial attitude' considered to be irrational was on a footing of equality to 'pure reason,' etc. (cf. *Kultur-attitude und sogenannte Reine Vernunft*, übersetzt von Richard T. Klingel. Bonn: 1931.)[78]

Halbert did not feel a need to worm a way into everything, and, like a noxious but extraordinarily prolific plant, to throw out near-immaterially thin tendrils far and wide on things: he preferred to roll between things with a laden and floating calm like a ship wallowing on swollen waters & could swing to shore at any minute if the tide were just half an inch higher: 'complexity' and 'simplicity' did not signify much to Halbert, because he co-existed in listless but colossal homogeneity with things — the contact was cool but of sickly cohesion, and he felt things differing from him protruded only with pallid semi-plasticity.

description of the bathroom under construction

They reached the basement: torn crimson carpets hung on the walls like antiquated banners, stiffened virtually into stalactites from the clustered columns of Gothic cathedrals, behind which were pink & white raw-plaster walls & brickwork, quicklime powder and mud on the floor, and most horribly of all: all manner of pipes, thick & thin, black & grey, which burst forth at the bottom of the walls, giving them an entirely human anatomy: they were arteries and veins, skin and membrane, as if they were a symbol of a young woman who is lounging on a divan with a film-Greek face; but her waist was torn asunder so that insides & blood vessels jutted out like buckled rifle barrels.

The corridor was, moreover, extremely narrow, and there was only a dim electric bulb burning in the ceiling — the whole giving an impression of being at the bottom of the sea, with big, pressed leaves of scarlet unfurling at the sides, which had grown onto a porous-checkered crystal (which was not pink in much the same way as the Doge's palace in Venice), but up above (where the wallpaper had been torn off like an outdated election poster) the corridor twisted into big rings & hanging flares in order that fish (which, to be sure, would arrive the very next moment) should be able to swim through them like a subway.

If one has looked at that called-off corridor it would have been easier to understand why some artists preferred to paint churches which had been boarded up and were under construction, or the hulls of ships hidden in a network of scaffolding (thick flowers that can be seen only indistinctly behind the pages of a math exercise book of squared paper), to painting figures stretched in space in engineering symmetry. If one really fixes our film-Greek young miss whose head is like a marble bust but whose lower body is opened up — the brutal forethought of 'how dreadfully different' her insides are from her face, and at the same time the imperative fact that nevertheless brings this intestinal network into the most organic connection to the face, indeed, one takes to be identical to that, gives the whole impression a perverse statuesqueness. Like those textiles the insides of which display other patterns than the outsides owe the impression of concreteness & massiveness to precisely that paradoxical connection which subsists between the two kinds of patterns — the suddenly glimpsed picture of the inner side or anatomical picture unexpectedly tossed before us seems to come from an extraordinarily remote future yet mystically appropriate explanation.

This spectacle was also like that: every revealed inner part immediately creates the illusion that one has somewhat discovered the secret cause of things, somewhat — and in close connection to that — the symbolic character of it all: the cause, an excavated root, a violently ripped-down curtain, suddenly creates unity between scattered superficial phenomena; suddenly all figures drop into a chasm (into a causal precipice like toppled chess pieces); a capriciously wriggling reducing storm runs through the things, and all are traced back to a root cause, dwarfed in ironic perspective, or in other words, hovering on the spot where they will fall prey either to irony or to the self-important horizon of the allegorical over-connection. Sudden stumbling on a cause, premature symbolic synthesis, and finally slighting irony are also closely related in the most down-to-earth life: some experience it as a self-conscious sensation, some as rational repeated nodding, but at all events it is a continually appearing trinity.

Halbert, too, felt that he had discovered the root of *The Perspective* nightclub in the way one usually examines cadavers for the summary sense of life — as if in a human being there would be a stubborn compulsion to search for and drive out the ground plan and meaning of the preceding state from absolute antitheses and 360° turns: we tend not to establish the personal identity of things, with triumphant eagerness, on the basis of themselves, but on the basis of an unexpectedly emerged unknown profile.

It all seemed to Halbert like a gloomy aquarium into which a toy cupboard had been built so that the fish should be perceived on more facetious paths & from multilateral viewpoints: Leatrice's room, the roof terrace, the girls, the owner, were all just small fry which ran about in naïve zigzags; on the whole, it was a very vulgar view, barely differing from that of a person who sees big cities as 'bustling ant hills': it is the most primitive form of a said symbolic-ironic summary outlook that the discovery of an unexpected cause or pseudo-cause elicits (that cause is immediately identified with the entire internal structure of the effect) but which at the same time is one of the archetypes of the most elevated artistic approach. (L. Ernst Widlowsky: *Kausalität, Ironie und Symbolik in der Klassik*. Heidelberg: 1926.)

On one occasion, a prose poem of Halbert's about the sea was published in which similarly belittling phrases were encountered: in that connection Leville-Touqué noted that hidden at the bottom of that kind of style was a naïve consideration that dimension is more important than plasticity: notions of length, deepness, etc., were richer than the complicated texture of Gothic buildings, which filled the blind nude figures of dimensions with a dash of blood. To lament houses for dimensions? To discover a 'connection' & incinerate living elements on the altar of that pallid geometry of cause: what vacuous snobbery. (Anyway, there are two types of that sort of approach, & Halbert undoubtedly represented the more attractive of them: there are German and English forms. In the English one there is always a naively concrete, honestly sentimental facet: when Halbert described the vast ocean on which the small ship was rolling, at the end of the day he was giving voice to a petty-bourgeois religious attitude — the basis of such Halbertian-syntheses, whether decorative or scientific, which came down to much the same thing, was never metaphysical but moral.)

At the university, people had derived much fun from a debate that had been organized at the initiative of a small 'artists' club' and had taken place mainly between Halbert & Leville: the main subject was allegorical painting, and here Leville immediately came out with his distinctions between German allegory and English allegory, and gave a fiery apology for the petty-bourgeois English postcards and fantastic landscapes, which are much more humane than those which are just dry illustrations of a system that does not coincide with humanity's one & only true philistine metaphysics. (Needless to say, of course, Halbert understood little of that apologia, & what little he did understand he found insulting — but for that reason Leville found Halbert's standpoint all the worthier of defense.)

They got down right as far as the bathroom — loud laughter and noise could be heard from inside. The proprietor drew aside the door, the latch of which was glittering and homely, as if chambermaids had long been cleaning it, though the door itself was still full of splinters, so rough a state had it been left in. The door creaked in the dust and shavings. Opposite it stretched a long, horizontal window: ocher and light-brown stripes alternated on the glass in waves like bands swirled on bookbinding cloth with a comb; the ocher part was opaque, the brown slightly translucent.

— Actually, this was a dining room window, but I had it put here. Looks good, don't you think?

Before every sentence, Halbert stretched & fidgeted, there was a measure of disconcerted and lazy pride in his homing-in, with him responding as follows: — Yes, it has something about it. The bands resemble the seascapes that posh fashion journals usually use for their covers if they publish a swimsuit issue in the spring, and it also fits in very well here.

The bathtub was trough-shaped, or rather, a yellow shell that grew out of the wall without any break & closely fitted to the floor in the form of three seashore waves — not exactly practical, but handsome. It was suspended, as it were, on the window wall right down to the bottom, like a huge stoop of holy water in which there was not a single sharp angle, only a wavy-inclined slippery surface, so that if one took a bath one's limbs, ending up extra-gravitation, were thrown into the most unexpected disarray. Both to the right and left of the yellow basin, almost up to the ceiling, were two enormous majolica flowers combined with tinplate ribbons and huge dislocated springs: they were asymmetric sunflowers mangled in cretinous Gothic taste — one of them had a giant black ovary and short, stubby petals — the second was small, but had huge petals, shaped like the tongues of krampuses, hanging down from it. The soap & sponge trays were likewise the same sort of half-tinplate, half-porcelain flowers — only their petals were silvery and their insides crimson.

The walls were rough and dirty, the taps lay on the ground, so that only crude holes could be seen in the plaster, in intriguing contrast to the harmonious piquancy of window, basin, and the two candelabra. The walls were soon to be tiled, and the work of art would then blend into the room's homogeneous tone: the basin will not have the fiercely sharp demarcation and intense isolation that it had now — to that extent it resembled those highly colored flowers with complexly tortuous forms that grow in the most desolate environments as if they had not sprouted from there but had been dropped by someone.

The presence of those deranged, cross-eyed flowers was interesting: as if it justified the flower's indispensability, its constant necessity. However much art may distance itself from sentimentalism and the natural: there is no urbanity so naïve or over-psychologizing, so artificial, as to fail to find its own beauty and creative will in flowers. Flowers are a mysterious center, which is omnipresent: at the bottom of books, women, or the bespectacled or fashionable denials of romanticism (or flowers), is this redeeming, healthy obsession — the flower. It would be tiring, perhaps, to carry responsibility for a sentence like " — at the bottom of every creative function lurks a flower myth as sole end-cause, and beauty streaming into all material can be traced back to that —," but still that stubborn echoing of the same form

— *in principium erat flos* — is genuinely moving.[79] Women, deductions, illnesses, divinities and unfolding abstractions are all born under a flower constellation and vary that basic pattern.

Quite unexpectedly they glimpsed Ena in a corner as she spoke with a short blonde girl who could have been a clown of her gender; she paid close attention to what Ena had to say, but in the meantime she was constantly tidying something on herself without for one second taking her eyes off Ena. She was most likely a bar dancer, wearing a short pink silk dress with big black dots and a belt of black lacquer; in one hand she was jiggling a black velvet hat and a pair of dirty white gloves: when she dropped the gloves she just yelped once and, without looking at the floor, only at Ena, she squatted down to reach for them. In the meantime, she shook the dust off them, still goggling with animal naivety at Ena, like a dog on the watch for whether its owner is going to throw away a stone that it will have to fetch. Her hair, the color of egg yolks, was heaped in a bouffant, so that when one tried to picture the little black hat on her head she looked like the sort of Rococo satire that was turned out in truckloads by porcelain works. Her eyes were light grey, but she had a slight squint, not fixedly but willowy — if she looked attentively she would wrinkle her brow a bit, with an old but small hand she would clutch at a shoulder in order to draw a slipped strap back under her dress (that movement, too, was like that of a dog snapping at a beetle around its thighs while lying down), when her left eye would slip slightly inwards and up, with the unsettling result that at precisely the moment when she was concentrating most strongly, there was no positive spot of any kind in her face — it was full of unhealthy tensions, but intelligence was spread over it by virtue of the strabismus: one had the impression that her countenance was made up of two or three intensely attentive faces in various poses as in some classical Cubist experiments.

Ena, who was fairly tall, stood in front of her, hands on hips and slightly leaning forward, her pearls hanging, in the pose of a professor who has left the operating theater for a moment and right now a short physician was cursorily consulting him about the condition of another patient.

— Do you think the apartment is neat? Have you seen it?

— I've seen it — the little blonde said, almost weeping with vitality —, it's superb, it opens onto the garden, it's magnificently furnished, the biggest settee I have ever seen. And the housewife is kindness itself, so kindly.

— What woman are you talking about? Who is still living there? You do realize that Lea's position would be impossible among narrow-minded neighbors?

— Of course. I heard that not long ago old Stessy from *The Evergreen* wanted to buy a condominium, and a majority of the other residents voted against that idea. Plumb crazy!

— I'm going to make a phone call. That's a bit odd. Hang on, I'll go out on my own. Thanks, goodbye for now.

— Tell me — the little blonde said entreatingly —, is Leatrice really leaving? Why? What's wrong? — There was something about the stresses put on the words that is only found with women like that: if they don't understand something, or they wonder with an interrogative accent, they display a failure to understand other people, other relations, & other claims, a failure to understand of such supernatural clarity from a psychological point of view that the mimicry, expressing complete incomprehension, must be declared a museum piece. Her face was distorted, almost to the point of crying, in critical and alarmed astonishment, when she asked why Leatrice was going away. That ideal form of a failure to grasp, when a person with a querying expression grows completely stupid, is contorted by the disgust that she or he feels in the face of all the things that are currently impossible for that person, is seen at most on the faces of foreigners as they gawp at each other in a coffee house or on a bus, or sometimes on the faces of healthy people who look at a fellow-human who has suddenly been taken ill.

— What were you looking for out there, Ena? — Halbert asked.

— I wanted to make a phone call, but the box upstairs is occupied because your workmen stuck water pipes and electric cables in the wall, and in doing so I think they've gone and put the phone out of action, indeed all the electrics: none of the lights are working — and with her left hand still on her hip and her right hand reaching with disparaging flippancy but determinedly (her veins over the hand suddenly popped out like a cat's claws amid the cushions) for the white-colored temporary switch on the bathroom's wet wall, screwing it just once, casting a weary glance at the ceiling.

— Oh, this phone doesn't work even when all the others are in order.

— Go into my room. That one is sure to be working — the proprietor said.

— Are you looking for an apartment? — Halbert asked as he fidgeted in his accustomed slow and perplexed manner.

— That I am — for Lea, given that she has to move away from here. It doesn't matter what's up with her, what she feels, what she wants or doesn't want (she recited this trenchantly, eyes swiveling, as if she were addressing a gathering), she can't stay here. Everyone is astounded and everyone asks why. It's very true that at a time like this, only in order to give some kind of response, she utters something that she has nothing to do with and out of which trouble always comes. Among the Jews a sick person was always taken a long way away from a camp so that others were not infected — why should not someone in an indefinable crisis withdraw into seclusion — perhaps precisely so that the person should not gain health from his or her fellow humans? — (The owner merely grinned.) — Because all you lot do is gawp: Leville impertinently, you yourself melancholically. And Anny?... ahh, Anny!

— What have you to say about this bathroom? — a smiling Halbert asked Ena, who was speaking like a Morse-tapper.

— Like that of an Italian prince: splendid luxury, work, art — it's like being thrown into the middle of the Renaissance — Ena chuckled.

— Right, I'm leaving. — At which he spoke to one of the workmen: — Go and call a taxi, if you don't mind. It should not pull up right here, in front of *Perspective*, but on the far side & a little bit further down. Thank you.

Ena & Leatrice's conversation

Halbert kept looking at Ena for a long time: her bearing was singular, indeed slightly stooped, because she was so imbued with the primitive joy of activity that one moment she would dance, the next she would be coiled up in herself in reflective delight. She struck out the beat of all her actions accurately & with childish pedantry: she made fists of her hands, rough from washing, and struck them against each other; indeed, she oscillated a long, thin index finger in front of herself like a restless and self-centered compass needle or metronome. Ena hurried up the narrow stairwell, which displayed a distinctive dual style: the velvet stairs runner with the narrow white protective strip (like a used towel slid under straps) was reminiscent of the primitive elegance of an Italian hotel, whereas the gaping windows forced into the wall yawned above them like openings cut by a surgical intervention, only with the oversensitive several-hours-old skin of their scab (viz. the glass), which would shatter straightway if the wall were to budge even a fraction of an inch — those windows, however, testified to fast modernization & poured such big shafts of light onto the antiquated tidiness of the little stairs at the corners that this undersized and museum-piece detail of the hotel became highly comical in this broad-rimmed lighting system more suited to bulky masses: as if one wanted to fit a room from a doll's house into the celestial turbine of the ecliptic.

Ena teetered her way up the steps, and at the turns of the landings, the incident morning sunshine would always suddenly throw a golden cape on her shoulder that it would pluck back in a trice two and a half steps further on and allow her to shabbily pass up the petty rise. Leatrice was left alone in the room & dressed.

— Come with me & look at the rooms. The taxi's waiting down on the street, we can talk more there, but you can't stay here, there's no sense in being tormented, for one thing, by business, for another by those university types, & you should have a word with them, & if by any chance you don't talk decently to them, then you pick a fight or kick up a fuss. You know you have to tread your own path; even if you don't see it clearly beneath the soles of your feet you can sense that where you are standing right now won't be solid ground for you any more. I was saying as much for hours on end, but I'm now going to take radical steps and shake you out of your passivity. Any fuss you might kick up here is not going to be useful activity, just a humiliation.

Lea was standing in front of the mirror and was raking her hair with an utterly senselessly large, giant yellow comb: her whole demeanor, the faded energy, showed a great tiredness that, before the mirror, she was trying to distribute to her limbs like a decorative burden, hard to fit on, but, when it came down to it, a cloak tailored to her body; the hair which seethed between the floodgates of the comb appeared to be a strength-splendor quite irrespective of that tiredness: in front of the teeth it flowed into big clump-spools like partially frozen, partially crumbling snow in front of a snow plow — behind the comb, however, it ran like big fields of ribbons of wheat — full of the wind's whimsical lines, but equally maintaining the regular forms of unending parallelism that were predestined by the line of seeds on being sowed. The room was gloomy: Leatrice's face and figure did not look malleable, just a piece here and there floated or vibrated like remnant leaves on the top of a long-dwindling spring of water.

— What's the shouting for? — Lea asked wearily —, you're doing what they do in some families when something critical has happened; in one go they give it everything, not as if the matter required it of them, but because they have learned that 'something needs to be done,' so they hustle & bustle, leave no stone unturned, just because it's something that 'needs to be done at a time like this.' Is it absolutely necessary to do something? No doubt it is, but all the same, the way you imagine, Ena, is no way to set about it, because somehow this is very humiliating for me. The way you think is that there is some psychological foible at work here, some kind of mania, frailty, or sickness that has to be respected as, after all, it's the doing of a force of nature that has to be protected against citizens and has to be set on a purpose-built location like an extra-special flower that has no place among the others. But, Ena, it's not like that. Excuse me if it's ungrateful of me, but as best I know you are not an advocate of mine when it comes to pleading my case. It pains me that it is no more than a platform for you, and from that I can see that you don't deeply understand.

Leatrice apathetically tossed the comb into the mirror's drawer: it was a long, narrow drawer, like the gutter of a water-spout jutting out on a cornice of a medieval building (a clumsy injection tube in the mirror's outermost lights), she irritably let the comb drop like a charitable gift to a pestering beggar.

— Those who want to disavow me, who deride me, are my partners in this life. Only they, my enemies, are able to assist me. That was how I heard it back home, and I understood straight away when I heard it in church. I cannot have partners either, nor do I need them, because they are not able to give me strength. The new life that I preach to myself is meant for, suited for me alone. God so wills it that in certain people everything should blossom that He let fall for us on earth: somehow those are flowers that only find infinitude between the four walls of a single soul; the more souls want all at once and together to receive God's flower within themselves, the more does heaven's lot contract: the souls of two persons together would be half as wide as one person's, three of them a third as wide, Ena. What good would I get from looking for a troupe? The business of fraternity is that of a bad Christian: every fraternization diminishes God — narrows His garden. I see a lot of priests, a very great many priests together, & apostles, as they await the Holy Spirit — but together, in a crowded collegial gathering: they labor, they supplicate, they virtually shrivel up from the great compulsion in their wish together to coax the Spirit from heaven, like toothpaste from a gummed-up tube. You're familiar with that bad Pentecostal Catholic comedy, which is why I have no desire to have protectors. I'm well aware that you have no wish to melt into me spiritually, and you stand up for me only as a cause, only as a presumed sibling — my feeling is that we don't have a lot in common — don't get me wrong, as friends & socially, there can be no distance between us, but from my own drifting perspectives… — Lea broke into a smile and threw herself down on the sofa as if she wanted to frolic, and in dragging Ena down as well she caught hold of her bony, angular shoulders. — Don't you get it? — and at that her face grew more serious, though in an odd spot, in a few wrinkles and the more carefree corners of her face, there had remained a few glimmers from the smile that had suddenly been poured on it, like raindrops on a leaf from a long-forgotten shower. — Don't you get it? The Christians say that Jesus will come to them if two or three of them congregate in his name, but they have got it all wrong — (she again said that in a twinkling-jabbering manner like a gossipy-aged woman who has come upon a secret midnight rendezvous at the corner beyond the burgomaster's villa) —: God comes only to the solitary, and there is no other love than that between me and God — anything else is just hypocrisy. And yet, and yet, I have no wish to retreat, it is not permissible for me to retreat, because then everything would immediately become a lie, which it is not permitted to be, because not even the greatest solitude, the most desolate cloisteredness-within-myself, can be egotism — (in saying that she adopted a mollycoddling tone of voice and, bending forwards, pushed her brow under Ena's drooping head, as is customarily done by those who wish to intrude under a sulkily sniveling face in order to look them in the eyes: she could just as well have said in that mollycoddling child's voice that "you mustn't warm the coffee too long because little Tess will get her mouth burned") —: I must collect my uniqueness from others, I must ransack my fellow humans in order to acquire in myself a wholly one-to-one kinship with God: via them I have to see myself alone.

Ena got up from the sofa and, hands on hips, looked down at Leatrice. — Why did you kick up a fuss? How come you moaned about quitting the house if you now see it as being part of your very essence to be with them? — and with that query on her face she fell to the combing chair.

The sun shone outside, and the sea rumbled from afar, like a huge block of paper being torn or rolled in the safe hands of the winds. The quietly rolling sea sounds defined the wallowing Leatrice in roughly the following way: "an art-loving mystic, sickened by self-criticism, saw in a flash her forces of deepest inspiration as being transparent Sybilline tricks, & meanwhile felt that the mystery had been accomplished in the outside world with far more peasant devices, in a much more honest and sober manner (with the good-natured grandeur of self-explanatoriness) than in her inner monastery of humbug embroidered from fish-bones." The alternation of the sea's roaring and hissing stood out, sharply set apart, on the empty chart of silence; as if the roars, which came less often, were minute hands, and the hisses second hands: they signaled to Lea seriously, but with the forgiving, almost affectionate irony of old people, that the 'mystery' did not attain its degree of bounding maturity in the caprices of the soul but was already long ready and now worked in day labor like precise clockwork, but even its mechanization was unable to take away its ancient magic.

Lea elbowed her way next to Ena & indicated with her eyes (they were tearful) toward the sounds of the sea: — Perhaps it's just jealousy at work inside me, maybe I only want to compete with the sea, the trees, the hills that people (with the easiness of holidaymakers & poets) apostrophize as being the "mysteries of nature" — yet I have no wish, am unable to hand over that work, the great task of seeing & being a mystery, to anyone else, only to myself, not even to nature or even — yes, perhaps even — to God. — (Meanwhile the screw clapper swung into action once anew, disinterestedly & solemnly, in Neptune's blue bell.) — I'll leave these things here, but I'm not going into seclusion. I shall stay among people; I am together with them, without brother or sister, somehow like the stars appear to be a big flock in the sky. At the same time, one can sense how solitarily the stars of the Big Dipper twinkle, how much they are themselves, self-standing and not in love with each other. I don't suppose — she said while getting to her feet and, moving ahead of the sound of the sea, like swimmers ahead of a wave —, that the miracle would be the sea's & not mine. It is lazy self-deception to listen to that booming and shift the responsibility for every secret onto it and suggest that this is something private and uncertain. Everything in the world is just a call, and one must assume to seek out the genuine one: that to which I am called, over and above the call. Having been expelled from paradise, Adam and Eve have to labor by the sweat of their brow: that work is nothing else but daring and acknowledging that the sea is only a limp foretaste or a slipshod reference so that one unearths it, insists on it, wishes like grim death that the sea, God, everything, was inside one. For me every flower is a flinging down of a gauntlet that challenges me to that duel of acknowledging and proving that I am a flower, the true one, and with that humiliate the intrusive allusion to the point of withering.

She began to pace up and down in the room: her steps were hesitant, but a hard beat seemed to be in charge in her insides — as if one were to place a machine of precise & definite movement onto an unsteady table: at this the force of the machine keeps continually shaking the table, whereas the machine itself slips about here & there on the table, so that a peculiar double motion arises from the machine's regular grinding and the table's capricious wobbling. Ena, somewhat miffed, was sitting on the sofa, staring ahead of her, not making a move, started to speak so softly that at first one might not notice she was speaking; all one heard was the slow drip of a mild sound:

— Are you telling me you are a program for me? I'm not one of your sisters, I'm not the same as you, but I don't have any need of that. To my way of thinking you are jittery, and are not able to say why. You don't want to; you're being secretive about something. Earlier (but not now) you set off with the intention of saying something, but then you suddenly took fright, you commenced violently twisting and flustering as if you were a lunatic sexton dashing half-crazed toward the altar because a draught fluttered a wrinkle on the curtain of the chancel. You really could not expect me to do anything other than a nurse does with an unknown wound. If in my tour route I had by any chance happened to spot Francis with his stigmata, I would have dug out a roll of gauze from the first-aid pack, bound his hands, and put him on the first wagon that passed by. Full stop.

Lea jumped over to Ena and sat in her lap. With the index finger of her left hand she started to push Ena's nose upwards: she distorted Ena's face into a Breughelian snub. — How about that!

— Don't take me for a full-blown miracle, so to say; none of the being loyal and at the same time critical, because that would be far too genteel to me, if you don't mind. What I'm trying to explain to you is that miracles have to be fought for, have to be wanted, have to be stolen from God. Sometimes it is to no avail urging with the tower of your virtues that you slap on each other, like conductors slap farthings on the counter at bus stops so that they tickle God's chin: God does not care about your virtues, or at least not always. You have to outwit him, have to wheedle it out of him with the help of some trick or perversity. Once upon a time it may have been possible to persuade him to sift some flower or other through the net of his stingy fingers to the earth by climbing onto a pillar, by shedding blood, by winning a battle, or by preaching a few trite adages about virtue. But God, so it seems, lost interest in blood, virtue, and oily Byzantine science. — (All that was said in Lea's characteristic greedy-gossipy manner: it was precisely in this that she differed from Ena, who always vignetted to death the minute futilities of practical life with dry rhetoric, with garish '*obstat*'-labels [the kind of thing that is placed on a door behind which a patient with a contagious disease is lying] — all Lea did was ruffle her face into a peasant grimace, shuffling the inner roughness of the muscles with mundane mechanical plasticity, as if two smoke-thin masks which, flexible as they might be, nevertheless retained their form, were being squeezed on top of each other and alternated in ending up one on top of another: that of a superstitious Russian peasant girl who stutters out her account of last night's nightmare to the other maids and a blasé Parisian actress who generously scatters among her words her various salon dodges of technically perfect mimicry.) — In olden days virtue was fine, because God carved it mottled with miracles: if a meek scholar exhorted a pompous emperor to be good, then a diamond crown would be let flying at Emperor-Exculpating Eusebius right before the front gate of the palace. When he left in order to return to his simple room, angels seesawed around him, & even God talked, so not even a quarter-mile of film reel was enough for the painter in order for him to dangle all God's words in one band under His beard, when He said: "I am crowning you as the true emperor: my angels mined for you a blue-diamond crown from the deep-blue mine of the sky with the pickaxes & harpoons with which you stabbed and larded Satan's bloated belly; now, look at you, you go in, etc., etc." — said Leatrice, letting her hands fall into her lap.

She recited the quotation ironically, holding her arms aloft, her eyes tear-filled: rapture and irony endowed her face with a measure of harmony, the anxiety of desire & the semi-nobility of renouncement rippled together on it.

— But it's not like that now, you know. Had you seen the fleeing priests whom I once saw on a highway in Russia: I was acquainted with some of them; how fine and holy they were. Their beards hung and dangled in the dark as if they were incense-burners suspended from a roof pole: their eyes were dimmed by cataracts from all the exercising of their virtues, they hummed to themselves, and they were pallid, but God never gave them anything fair to contemplate. Their church was tedious, its sole adornment the cost-free darkness, but they did not spend a lot of time there either, and they filled them with monotonous furniture; into the old monastery they carried stacks of clothes, filing cabinets, and roughly polished writing-tables with green baize of exactly the same form as can be seen in tax offices and the waiting-rooms of hospital offices — they were saints, but they had seen nothing and therefore had done nothing either. They were semi-official ascetics, you know, and therefore God did not concern himself with their virtues, though take it from me, Ena, they were a hundred times more virtuous than the marvel-steeped menfolk of Byzantium, much more.

Ena rose to her feet. — I don't know if you are of a mind to come outside with me toward Martonne and take a look at an apartment in a villa there, or should I send the taxi away?

— I'll come with you. I want to tell you everything, everything.

Ena was suddenly touched by the childishly gleeful gravity of the manner in which Lea said that "everything-everything" and quite forgot that in her eyes, from time to time, her friend inflated into an allegory of 'decorative bigotry' under the influence of her obstinate inspiration, so that she linked arms with Lea in the instinctive solidarity of girls. When they had just gone through the door they met Leville-Touqué, still clutching a red-bordered issue of *Antipsyche* under one arm.

— What a pretty sight! Mysticism and skepticism arm in arm! A bit cheap for an allegory, but if it were to be daubed as a fresco in the Sunday assembly room of a humble religious society, an art-loving parson would look on it as a case of, make no mistake, "only the Roman Catholic Church can provide art with true subjects." Wouldn't you agree, Ena *chère*?

Leville-Touqué was very much aware that for him not writing a satire was not hard, but not writing an allegory was, because he perceived every phenomenon as a symbol, & that mechanical symbol-optics was always a great burden for him, which is why he once said what a great tragedy it was if a German synthesis-cataract grew on the eyes of an out-and-out Frenchman when physicians had not yet discovered lenses that, if placed before the eyes, inflamed with synthesis-cataracts of German pathology, then they would counteract the divergence due to allegory and show objects in their caliberless bourgeois solitude. "Altogether, there has been a spread of this strange mania (syn-opia):[80] if something is peculiar, then it should be grasped immediately as a concentrated formula; that is how 'Music,' 'Work,' & other nonsenses came to be out of concertina-playing mailmen." (Admittedly, on other occasions, it was precisely the encounter of abstraction and brutal fact, et cetera, which he considered magnificent.)

Leville was well aware that every remark he made, essentially without exception, was of the above type: he defined something and in doing so straight away raised it into a symbol. In that there was a lot of intellectual routine, a depressing fact with which he tried to come to terms in the weak form of immediately calling it 'cheap' and reciting it in a stutter as a ridiculous quotation. Many was the time when he complained that he had a murderous curse of perspective on him against which he had to struggle, because it was an infinitely trifling and barren affair, indeed diabolically humiliating; the whole thing was only the mind's instinctive search for comfort, a species of romantic laziness: one avoided the complex interweaving of facts and rather escaped into superficially recapitulatory, so-called recapitulatory morphology: every search for form, symbol, or '*morphē*'[81] arises from atrophy of the mind: neurasthenia. It may be that Touqué was now laying that down anew, but when for one quarter of a second Leatrice and Ena appeared in front of him, the first sentence that sprang to his lips, automatically and with sensual malice, was once again a symbol witticism of that kind, the 'cheapest,' as he added.

The entire university laughed at Leville when out of some neoprimitive affectation a Portuguese painter (he was nicknamed

Wasziljewa Pintor) started to immortalize his friends in one of the rooms of the Hotel Miramar (to the proprietor's great consternation) in sorts of small allegorical frescoes — boys and girls with an object characteristic of them and beneath it a ribbon denoting typical thoughts: at that time Leville would race around frenziedly and whining, rubbing his eyes to restore the images of his relations anew into their original confusion from the simplifying pattern for which a lazy soul is so hungry by nature — that soul which is fond of packing things in one piece so that they do not branch off from one compartment of the brain to another, &, for that reason, snips confusing threads off (covers things with lies) like the branches of a slim pine tree and stacks them, trimmed like that, in themselves; this was a wearying, enervating battle, as those small fresco images of his friends had been imprinted in his mind, naked, slippery, though he did not wish to remember images of his friends like that but together with all their boughs, their troublesome roots, or their colored plumage, which he did not allow to turn into a spectrum swindled into proportions in himself. "Every symbol signifies lethal planimetry: only an unscientific, allegory-free, synthesis-ignorant naïve way of looking at things can offer wild plasticity. I shall not permit my friends to be reduced to a plane: my beloved *bratyi,*[82] I, & not that dozy Wasziljewa Pintor, will preserve you."

---

the meaning of nature & history on tourist posters

Squinting, Lea looked at Leville, who, on other hand, opened his eyes so that he could be taken as a mystic poet & the girl as a blasé esthete-cocotte. Touqué thereby wanted to cover up his earlier weak witticism by slapping *Antipsyche* on his thigh, then waving it in the air, before hurrying over. Lea & Ena crossed to the other side; they did not immediately get into the taxi, however, but at Lea's actively sniveling, they walked to the corner from where one could take a turn & get down onto the beach. It was not cool; indeed, their skin was assailed by a steamy, salty tang.

The high-heeled, streamlined women's shoes were curious between the sand and the thin layer of water: on the beach they almost symbolically sealed the mentality that perceived nature and history as ironic décor around one's own life — the majority of tourist posters present primitively stylized maps and towns in pseudo-grotesque perspective, because the offices do not promote the culture & unspotted nature of the world with claims of streaming into the soul as a redeemer & 'shaping the soul,' only little symbolic, minute tradition-hallowed monograms (tracery on the cornice of the Doge's Palace, a crooked cactus, et cetera): these tourist posters mark two healthy extremes: if instead of '*Venise*' they only give '*un coup de Venise*,'[83] if instead of Rheims cathedral only a shepherd's crook as a '*coup de blasphémie*,'[84] then that means that the extremes of absolute convention and absolute cynicism, both extreme demands that have put on muscle as instinct and the most frivolous travesty, signify two sides of the same feeling: to travel to Venice is just as much an instinctual act as it is for a migratory bird to fly to Egypt, but, on the other hand, the forms of Venice are not objects of adoration but of impudent laughter, & this '*adoratio calumnians*' is a healthy state.[85]

The mind works in two directions at once: routine will always be more mechanical and blinder, whereas on the other hand, this darkening into instinct points to ever-newer projections, hallucinatory distortions mutate each detail of Venice (not so-called 'typical' [?] details but some little scrap, nuller than nothing): they are placed in the field of force of growing convention, of incandescent neutrality (hitherto it was supposed that only interest, love, craving, etc. possess object-modifying lines of force, though indifference, fashionable apathy, & inactive conventionalism have just as much their own fields of force, that certain radiation of stationary energy or zero-point energy of which physics speaks), and therefore in place of towns one gets these ironic monograms, a cross section of a corolla as Ceylon, a sixteenth-century Portuguese tapestry map below which is inscribed the name of a Mediterranean shipping company. When Venice shall intensify in people to a vital function and physicians demonstrate its presence in the blood as Veneto-globulin, then Venice will be just a small watering vase with a single Arabic grille, a sort of algebraic mark on the Adriatic.

The same relationship prevails between the sea's conservative-bushy 'infinity' & snub-tailed town shoes: and this relationship is of much more profound value in which the 'sea's infinity' & the 'artificial creations of art' dwindle into a pair of characteristic symbols, because they eliminate that self-important and superficial dualism between humans and nature, citizen and art, present & past, which typified the pathetic way of looking at things; in this fashionable-cynical notion, everything sweeps into one plane: doges, cacti, gentians and king figurations gambol in amiable friendship. That is more ethereal than the pursuit of myth every step of the way: one ought to be on good terms with nature, which is to say, it is even possible to be flippant with it; indeed, it is obligatory, because in absence of that there can be no true love (that injunction is all the more so in relation to the arts).

Leatrice's shoe at present represented that Rococo indolence in the face of infinity; with her eyes, however, still scenting the ancestral, maybe official transcendentalism, above the billows.

Ena & Leatrice's conversation continued by the sea (mysticism & conversion)

— This Leville is an interesting fellow, you know; I would like to talk with him once, just show him who I am. (If a mystic is taken away from his monologues, he thrashes about like a fish out of water.) Just before, when Halbert was also there, I thought there was already a bit of the marvel inside me; I felt I could already scatter the flowers that I wanted to plant and that I see as colorful and great; I wanted to show myself off to you both, but that wasn't to be. Perhaps it's going to take an incredibly long time until the miraculous apparition in me is strong enough for me to tell others, and for others to believe that I know something like that. Somehow the apparition has to knead through one's body: only dreams are able to bestow flesh in place of the one we are sick and tired of. Indeed, the main pleasure in dreaming is that under its influence I feel my body melting across into a new state. It would be no use my hitting or torturing it or having it kissed: by doing that I would only be forcing it into the old state, more tedious than it ever was — every kiss is to my body just a nail with which I hammer it into its antiquity; every self-torturing slash of the whip is a hammer blow with which I drive the nail deeper so as not to allow me to get near my new body. But work is needed on that birth-transforming new dream, and every failure horribly dispirits and disheartens me. I always think that my eyes, my voice, my whole body, are so permeated with my dream that I am fermenting and dripping with it, and then I see that you all still have the upper hand, and the terror of the dream has still not arrived above that of wide-awakeness.

The sea reached a long way up over the sand in the form of paper-thin wave pages — it barely seemed to be water, more materialized wind; it was only at the fringes that there was a thin thread of spume, a shivering differential sign of the sea's existence. Seawards from the spume-wind, soft troughs, barely surmisable but nevertheless positive, crept in the sand in the direction of the water as it billowed back: mysterious forms on the borderline of 'material' & 'force,' exhibiting the co-existence of ethereality and definiteness, which is maybe one of the most fundamental paradoxical forms of nature & of life in general: contourless precision.

— Interesting what you say about dreams, Leatrice. One can sense, with the precision of a medical diagnosis, that you lug that Russian demand with yourself like the other items in your wardrobe. Take it from me, people here are never going to believe you, because they long ago pigeonholed you to a place where typical Russian dreamers are stored, the drawer on which 'Byzantium' and '*nihil*' are inscribed, and you are not going to be assigned a separate place. No reason to be affronted on that score: you carry the determinations of your type, which are well known to us. You have to be that way because in your woods the trees have those shapes, the moon reflects so and so, I don't know how, but you can find it in specialist works, as best I recall, Rhode & Egger published in the *Geopsychiches Jahrbuch* (sadly, it has been discontinued since then) the treatise in which you will find two-column pages like in most encyclopedias, and on the left-hand side are descriptions of individual Central & East Asian areas; on the right are the religious customs, architectural forms, and artistic motifs. Each province had its own visual stereotypes from which a long string of generations were unable to free themselves. Cases are listed when, as revolts break out against the compulsory apparitions in ancient priestly codices, and Rhode & Egger (primarily Rhode) demonstrated that the new counter-visions of the revolts from which they produced the symbols of their side stood under exactly the same basic constraint as the old ones: even reform cannot free itself from that inner fate, even cynicism is irretrievably orthodox, their criticism, too — ancient superstition.

In Ena, naturally, that standpoint to Lea was twofold — on the one hand, she loathed the religious streak in her, and she tried to handle that as simply a nervous mechanism, and in so doing, of course, she was insulting Lea, though not excessively (after all, she found that this mechanism was the common fate of people expelled from Paradise, which compulsively drives them toward 'miracles' and 'apparitions': both of the latter were mingled in Lea, albeit not excessively, as the desire for logicality may possibly burn with an even stronger fanaticism in mystics, given their proneness to chaos — on the other hand, she defended her against Leville-Touqué, who was condescending to the mysticism in Lea just as much as to the hysteria, when Ena defended the self-centeredness and justification of illness as a 'natural force.' First of all, she had to reduce Lea to a neurasthenic in order to be capable of apology as a cultural factor. Ena was slightly excited by the brochure for the determinist encyclopedia, so she carried on as follows:

— You get a lot further by seeing yourself as a sick bourgeoise who somehow has to position herself without, in extirpating the illness, turning her bourgeoisness into narrow-minded petty-bourgeoiseness, or, on the other hand, exaggerating the illness into mysticism and turning deities out of yourself like some sort of hieratic discharge. You must realistically take account of the racial endowment that you carry in your blood: don't believe it in the first place, secondly don't throw it away because you have a right to your national disease; indeed, it is obligatory for you — in other words: you have to exploit it, you have to position yourself on a utilitarian standpoint in relation to your visions. Be an eccentric or an artist, but if you dream of a yellow flower, don't translate it in the morning to a moral, not to any kind of moral, understood? not to a symbol of either a practical, a philosophical, or a painterly moral, no moral of any kind — (in the meantime she got out of breath & pulled a face as if she were eagerly beginning a sentence while swallowing, but with a sour-choking mien was obliged to give up, signaling to her table companions with the details of every grimace that no one should make use of that forced silence of the forced swallowing because she was going to continue straight away) —, and if you dream of a red flower, don't with girlish obstinacy interpret that into a deity.

To finish off, Ena wanted to flip a small pebble with the toecap of a shoe into the sea, but the pebble plopped to the ground so that after being kicked into the air it all but rolled over on the sandy ground like a badly recoiling cannon. On the virtually abstract-smooth watery sand (one particularly enjoys the smoothness of such things which are not made of hard and coherent material, like a mirror or marble, but of a million tiny granules heaped together and therefore meaning a million maximal possibilities in regard to never at all being smooth: they were only smooth if a single widespread, gentle, monumental force held them together, and then they would constitute reliefs if that embracing-osculating force, demonstrating an idiosyncratic surface modeling, the eternal piquancy which consisted of one's seeing that it is not assembled from tiny acts, but a single superhuman force has smoothed them out into a gigantic space wave [a precise energy mask or pure spatial X-ray, a diagnosis diagram of the category], like it does the sand here or snow elsewhere) the stumbling footprint inflicted a comical wound, sharply displaying the two kinds of plasticity: the human and the aqueous — the stumbling heel hole is entirely the same thing to the most artistic relief that a holidaying sculptor may plaster up on the beach:

all fingerprints and mosaic patchwork, every piece of form tattered and crumbling, in contrast to the enormous sand layers of the enormous seashore, which in their thinness virtually floated above the ground and thus bestowed on the enormous force its amorphous embossing: as an absolute to a hair's breadth, in place of the doctrinaire & Baroque-grocer agonies of exertion, an abstract & therefore striking portrait of force.

It is possible to assemble a stylistics of life in this way, everywhere the fundamental forms of life: the intellectual romanticism of *Sachlichkeit* is not a bad path, and it is unnecessary to be concerned that it is just hypocrisy at the bottom of which the old naturalism is at work. Why shouldn't it be possible to set the formal language of life as well in a dogmatic stylistic — a book like that would be nice even if its tender precepts did wander over into a garden of German terminology. The same fanlike, condensing-expanding sculpture of projection which, with its resonant monotony, smooths across into a platform of uniformity; the same lines and movements also vibrate under a microscope, and the industrial designer who modeled a black-and-white lace shawl on the magnification of a microbe was a bright spark: at an individual level that might be extravagance, indeed a stupid provocation of the 'petty bourgeois,' but that kind of childishness clouds the style as a whole.

Symmetry, picturesqueness, plasticity, contour, stratification: all those notions are imbued with new content if one examines their biological sense, and the 'gateways of new perspectives open up' if one's viewpoint innervates into itself these basic forms of life and assimilates them into optical preconceptions, indeed into logical maps, for reason. On that basis a new pathos can evolve, full of precision, which with smart evenness holds itself far from two mythologies: romantic natural history and poetic indicative-bookkeeping. These are bad mythologies: the new viewpoint is also mythological, but it is possible to generate a mythology by rational love.

coastal waves: relationship of decadent impressionism & scientific Sachlichkeit. *Identity of 'primitive'-nature & 'artificial' 17th-century art. Science & poetry (geometry & metaphor)*

Leatrice and Ena went just a few steps further (the taxi driver, hands in pockets, gaped as he paced up and down); the huge strip of sand was stretched out like an enormous flatfish on the blue serving dish of the morning: the rocks and detritus from the cliffs lying a little further off looked like the fish's greenish-white skin which a waiter has peeled off with a spoon when it is warm so that the fish is now glistening on the dish with its frothy whitish-yellow flesh; it is quite flat, with just a minimal curvature in the center, in the infinite distance it gently narrows and pushes its invisible head straight into the whimsically served eschatological salad of sky and clouds. The edges of the salty waves did not arouse the impression that they had come from the sea but had welled forth out of the sand: silvery cracks suddenly sprang up in the sand, thin as a hair, snaking softly, but quickly, right across the surface like the remnant wake of a shooting star in the sky when seen in a slow-motion film.

It is a fairly untactical step to make a toast-style apology for a new way of looking at things and immediately afterwards to take steps toward accomplishing a new pupil-convention of the eye, which has not yet found its own true language and thus can easily relapse to the language of the old type of seeing. Both I and my deceased lyrical predecessors to some degree watch 'in parts': the sensitive paralytic of last year's season could have seen this sand on the sea coast — but he always saw something melancholically ephemeral, a programmatic counter-picture of the 'heroic,' and in that he was led merely by affected estheticism: his weak nerves could not stand the rational commentary on the sand, only lazy apperception suited him & therefore he created the Neuron-Rococo, where the sculpture only existed in the form of an *'aperçu,'*[86] and he perceived the whole of nature as an auction of industrial design — he had a filigree, hypochondriac, bric-a-brac-maker point of view.

An air of braggadacio in music making also made the predecessor antipathetic: he always rinsed his little landscapes and fragments of portraits in pseudo-music, and that melodic point weakened the natural strength of the theme. He always had a sickly preconception of 'beauty,' by which he meant the ornamental in its most bourgeois sense, despite all his petty-bourgeois nervousness: as opposed to our stance, which through perspective sees everything as beautiful, or rather: it does not see the object but the perspective itself.

My predecessor's perspective had been shortsighted, guided by dreams: two paths at once, which were conducive to conventionalism; after all, 'perspective' means a big surplus: active instead of passive vision — all things considered, my predecessor saw himself as being fine, and he used the outside world as jewelry, but I plunged naked into the waters of scientific wonderment: both ancestor & successor are materiophiles, but the successor inhabits an identity of scientific and esthetic viewpoints without that being a matter of some sort of compromise to popularity or a gushing cooperation.

Perspective and wakefulness are two tolerable contents for a style: a cowardly hypocrisy in dreamlike, plastic wording was in overabundance in the old way of looking at material, and that concealed an enervated sensuality: portraits dashed off 'with a few lines,' little medallions of poetry which take in Paris or old-time Vienna, were always obvious associations of unaligned sensuality, they lacked the strength of creation, true brave artificiality; the sense of material became an enfeebled symbol, & thus it could only become the style of pseudo-precision, which did not extend to a love of material for its own sake: it is typical that the predecessor, who resorted to 'material' (to '*Sache*') on the basis of so many 'psychological motifs,' exhibited the most monotonous materialism whereas our present-day viewpoint, which enjoys material as such, presents itself as the most spiritual possible style.

That notion is what was also at work in Leville-Touqué when he felt Leatrice's physical beauty, her material metrics, to be spiritual beauty: not with last year's cliché of sensuality, which saw in female material only a few degrees of heat and a few degrees of convexity (warm, rounded, white, undulating, swollen, curly-haired, soft, et cetera), but a million microscopic pieces of data, the style formula of 'life' & not its sensual mood. Material, not as a grip on individual sensuality that first comes to hand, but as an objective grammar of life: a symbol not of our feelings but of the process of life, thus, precise material in its most material form is the language of an irrational endeavor.

In the olden days, when looking at nature, people immediately thought of allegorical meanings instead of closely examining the formal language of nature & looking for answers there — as if it were to be established on the basis of a big lamella of hieroglyphs that the spirit of 'History' were hovering behind it, which is nothing more than a baby-Hegelian bluff instead of striving to trace out the concrete face of events analytically on the basis of a particular knowledge of every single character.

The new way of looking at things avoids the primitive antithesis of concrete and transcendental and, seeing the two as one, knowing how close word & meaning were, so that the formal language of life was an immediate expression of fundamental meaning (where possible: meaning is not behind language, but language itself is a sense-organism), not a pale allusion in the way it was imagined in the Romanticist era.

It is interesting that this 'absolutely lifelike' form of looking is completely identical to that of the intellectual Baroque era of the 16–17th century, to which it is usual to append the disdainful epithet of 'artificiality': it truly was artificial (that was its sense, its justification, its value), & it approached the material forms of nature precisely through its affectation, its 'anti-nature' — the most extreme thought-mannerism & picture-chemistry already long ago reached our own viewpoint. When one speaks of the basic forms of life and the appearance-style of material and force, it cannot be a matter of Greco-Germanic affectation, according to which the totality of life is only to be found in commentary-free appearance, in identity with itself, as the latter would be none other than stagey-monism or poetic and barren substance-frippery: the new approach does not seek to force a synthesis rhythmicized together from naïve analogies in the hollow frameworks of 'essence' — on the contrary, it analyzes, dissects, prepares microscope slides.

When a folk song or classicizing 'essentializing' poem says, I don't know, "Dawn flutters a golden shawl over the meadowlands," it is not expressing the primal form of life, at most the primal form of a naïve person's way of looking at things: that can be a classical, ideal, or hygienic state, but in no event does it lead to a recognition of material diagrams arising in the wake of the active forces of life. It quickly turns out that the artificial scenery and visions of female bodies that 'forced' material into a perverse structure stood closer to life's basic tendencies (the ornamentation-laws included by biology in picture books), i.e., they are simpler or, if you will, 'more naïve' than "the people's voices in their songs" (the latter are color-blind simplifications, stunted syntheses, fakes).

In the final analysis, what could the uniform, necessarily parallel use of the 'scientific' & 'poetic' ways of looking at things have signified in the way of looking at the world's affairs to which Touqué turned his thoughts with such adolescent pleasure in recent days? Here was the sand of the seashore, which seemed to be at once a supplement of projection science & a wild metaphor, at once an exact sample of philosophical 'space' &, at the same time, something foreign (the hotel fish all served up) that already had nothing to do with the sands. By 'science' is meant, in the first place, an abstract formula that combines the characteristic tricks of geometry & logic: half-drawing, half-rational precept; by poetry, in the first place, a thing that avows itself with ostensive heterodoxy to be something other than it is and thereby nevertheless accounts for itself. First and foremost, the sand is absent from the sands: sand, salt, stinging foam and water tracks cease to exist in their own certified identity, and they will be there, in part as geometrical projection lines, in part as something entirely foreign (e.g., *Dover Sole à la Reine*).

A projection of something exotically directed & suited for an exotically voluted surface, and the obligatory-absorption of the same thing into an inorganic metaphor are totally equivalent abstract operations: the projection, with its own geometrical precision, all the same gives a caricature (e.g., the projection of a circle onto an opalizing wave surface), & the metaphor, with its own absolute strangeness, nonetheless forces dogmatically strict congruences between itself & other things.

The thing has to be pictured quite raw: title "Seashore Sand," containing two pictures on two opposite pages. On one, for example (this can be an impudent schema of 'science'), is a sketch which depicts the evolution of rings around an outer planet: in the center is the Sun, around it is an ellipse of Earth, & around that is another ellipse — the orbit of the outer planet. If one projects certain positions of the planet from the appropriate positions of Earth onto an imaginary plane, then the orbit of that planet is seen as looped in respect to the stationary stars: it is precisely the geometrical precision of the projection-lines that creates this orbital somersault, this frivolous star-farce.

On the other side, in a glaring color photo, the snow-white body of the flat fish can be seen between glistening jewel salads and pickled checks of parsley (this is the impertinent schema of 'poetry'): under the "seashore sand" inscription the viewer sees an appetizing colored starter, which is to say one can already sense in one's mouth the fresh taste of the fish, the pepper of the salads, the coolness of the green garnishes, the Gregorian perfume of lemon, though one is forbidden from relating that to the food as it is not food, after all, but a poetic representation of "Seashore Sand," that is, one's sensory impression will be all the more titillating as the pepper, salad, lemon and a host of glistening motley colors are, so to say, hanging in the air and are obliged willy-nilly to adhere to the notion of 'seashore sand.'

One sees nothing of the 'seashore sand,' of course, since the fish has been pulled in front of it so that what drops out of sight is supplemented by a wholly monomaniac reinforcement of the concept, so illustration and concept are unified: the notion is absolutely strong, sandier than sand, and it adjusts to this empty but glowing logical frame without any of the foodiness of the similarly glowing strange vision of a starter. The unification of an outsize notion and a sensory impression of alien purpose, heightened into being artificially non-fitting: for Touqué that was one of the basic rules of the new sport.

Every ontology has to be based on that dual tension: on projection and metaphor, or in other words on two technical stratagems of 'other'-ness, on geometric alteration (this is scientific projection onto an arbitrary plane) and metaphoric alteration (i.e., exaggeration of poetic simile).

There is, however, a third form for processing "Seashore Sand," not to say an 'ontological chance': that is taking a microscopic photograph. In point of fact, the above dual ontology is also based upon this photograph — what figured together in the photograph is here separated into pure projection-geometry

& pure alienating-simile. If one examines the most elementary forms of life under a microscope one always finds together an unpredictable linearity and active materiality: as if the root of roots were composed of an uncertain scarce balance of hypocrisy and energy, fiction and absolute; they are reminiscent of those numbers before which '+' & '–' signs are both written at once. For that very reason the Teutonic-flavored expression 'bio-ornamentation' is accurate, with the ancestral activity of life & the hypothetical frivolity of its forms finding expression equally.

Above, two methods of fiction were referred to: the organized and deliberate strictness of falsehood of projection and metaphor, which make the probability of reality grow stronger, or which declare themselves to be the genuine reality in place of reality. In contrast, exact biology supplies those forms and nature-stylistic and life-graphological motifs that denote the most elementary jargon of irrationality, uncertainty, and conditionality. The game is regular enough to be suspect & yet engrossing: the basis of ontology is two breeds of fiction; the basis of the irrational game is positive physiology.

Ena & Leatrice in a taxi, mask & wound pain

Ena & Leatrice turned back and got into the taxi: Lea was hanging her head, Ena was arm in arm with her; when Lea bent down so as not to hit her head, her hair fell over her forehead as if she had wanted to hide her face from the sun. When she was seated inside she flung her head back. It rested on the canvas of the lowered roof like the freshly decapitated head of a martyr — her hair became tousled around her like a straw basket into which the martyr's relatives stowed the head to prevent the blood from running too fiercely. There was a hint of defiance in the head gesture: as if she wished to throw to the sun the semi-sculpture idol of her face as a self-tormenting victim, so the sun should either demolish every cowardly contour completely to ash pastel, or alternatively burn her face hard between wildly positive boundaries: there are moments when we expect everything from our profile, when we make our whole personality dependent on how we feel the plasticity of our face, or in other words, the mask that the outside world has hung on us and to which a wonderful diction, gestures, an entire character, a past, ancestors and a complicated family history, must be composed; this is not a moment in which to discover one's innermost I, the 'ego of one's ego,' indeed quite the reverse: one's entire existence reduces to a strange mask, and a life has to be selected for that, it has to be filled however one can; at such moments one is filled by a consciousness that one has to create everything, everything depends on one, everything is inside out, tears of remorse yield the dead, too, by an artificial, mechanical route, etc. Indeed, one is even able to swap masks: one feels one's nose to be different when looking at a chessboard or at Hobbema's avenue;[87] one can precisely delineate the profile-variants that various objects evoke in one's senses about the form of one's brow, lips, & chin.

A distinctive struggle was being waged on Leatrice's face: as if the sunlight sought to separate two elements of her face — the dimly and patchily hovering urban forms and a naïve peasantry manifested as a wood carving. Her deep-set eyes were nests of shadows: even now her look was more a softly expansive 'vision' than a definite fixing onto something; the morning sun whispering in her face sprinkled deeply into those nests as if seeking to wash out the little shadows, huddling together in alarm (a nest to which only the shadows of birds gather together as if they would have to scatter in a hurry); either the lovely eyes adopt a brave plasticity or they burn to dust in the demanding light:

dogged determination and redemptive cruelty like that are felt by a person into whose eyes a hard implement is poked — it is the white-hot precision of pain, an imposing transgression within a trice of everything that even the most artificial sleep was capable of imagining: fantasy is never able to imagine the pain that the active intervention of a foreign body signifies in the inside of the body — in the imagination one always traces pains back from oneself, always from the body's inner viewpoint, & therefore the imagined foreign body is naturally only schematic: when it really does intervene (not translatably or assimilably to inner-body pain) then the horror of foreignness is the main pain, as if one's own body ought to cease to exist within seconds in order that some concrete foreignness can replace it.

Under normal circumstances body-consciousness is evenly distributed in our limbs and thus reflects a "realistic" image of the outside world: on a foreign body's penetrating inside, all the consciousness-mirrors converge in one place and thus naturally give an unduly magnified image of the outside world — in our eyes a needle prick renders the entire body a single gigantic wound as all the 'mirrors' (scattered consciousness-fragments) reflect a single object in thousandfold magnification: the plasticity of the painful part also grows as in a feverish dream and we feel giant pain-frescoes and pain-reliefs (photographing those pain-drawings would likewise enrich one's knowledge of 'bio-ornamentation'); when the pain desists one marvels afterwards that only the eyes are bloodshot whereas one's hands and legs are totally intact, and how small the instrument is, even how ludicrously small the entire external world is, the physicians who are around one, the tables, windows and everything, because the consciousness-mirror has again scattered into a thous-& parts, into every part of one's body, so that the magnification ceases, which is, of course, comically unusual.

One almost imagines that in moments when the local wound pain suddenly strengthens the eyes into an ultraprecise microscope one could even see bacilli in all their motley splendor, or the hills and dales of the Moon's surface, with the unaided (i.e., infinitely painful) eye; without consulting real microbes or precise maps of heavenly bodies the visual forms of pain (the aforementioned 'pain-sketches') are wholly identical to them: fever and pain, which automatically spatialize (a tactical stratagem: one considers pain to be thereby more readily avoided or vanquished) in their Baroque system of lines they are identical to the system of lines of cells and tissues (these lines perhaps run at the bottom of every poetic creation or beauty which materializes).

When Leatrice opened her eyes the sea and taxi were small, she herself was dreadfully small — she felt both her eyes to be wounds (as if they had never existed before and only now had the Sun drilled two fresh apertures in her forehead), but those, too, were diminutive: she suddenly closed them in order to feel their monumentality afresh, but by then she had already taken with her the proportions of the external world, reduced in size, into the dark of closedness, and therefore she was no longer able to feel the first eye-overgrowth, only imagine it.

She pressed her hands on her burning eyelids; she felt them in all their ridiculous paltriness like a naïve hunter who looked at the approaching game with a telescope: huge wings flickered in front of the lens, she aimed and shot, and in front of her feet lay two miniature sparrows. She pressed and massaged her eyes; in vain, they were two small bullets. It was vividly in her recollection that the sun had burned them almost to wounds and thereby had made them grow huge; on the other hand, she now saw herself before herself: the consciousness of having a giant body did not square with the dimensions of her diminished body, & that grotesque dissonance between her colossal self-perspective and her hummingbird-sized body irritated her; she tried to reconcile the two, but failed; she writhed in her thousandfold awareness of her body like a foreign little insect that had fallen into a gigantic glass basin.

— What are you doing? — Ena asked. — Why are you throwing yourself all over the place? Either blood will rush to your head or you'll hit yourself against this crummy thing — whereupon she started pressing and tugging away at one of the iron rods that was holding the roof canvas; every exertion that takes place within the framework of a much bigger force is strange: the tension of the arms while the car races with a wild power; it is impossible to imagine that they are able to exert force on a definite place in a definite direction: it's as if the entire operation were to be spread out into a weak plane of force, flattened out in the course taken by the car.

— This is how I used to fry my eyes in the sun at home when I was a young girl —, said Leatrice. — For me it was the greatest joy, my favorite game: I would get onto a hillside and spread myself out on a meadow, then look at the green and red circles that spread up within the blackness of my eyes. It was not so much that which interested me, though, but afterwards I was always so big on the inside, so enormous over myself, over everyone and the woods as far as I could see. My eyes were often filled with tears and red, properly inflamed, and people didn't know why, because of course I never let on. Once I did blurt out the secret when a peasant boy was going to be thrown off the farm for having red and watery eyes, and then they thought it must have been something I had caught from him — I let on then but was laughed at. Admittedly, I was also praised, with them saying what a good girl I must be for making up a story like that in order to be nice to the young peasant boy — but they still went ahead and moved him to another farm.

— How long did you live in the country?

— A long time. Until I was nineteen. Not in one place, mind you, and not always with my parents.

Lea looked out of the car: the sea was a good bit away, but there was nothing to hide the distance between the road & the seashore. The sea looked like a lake, or at most a tightly closed bay, and because there was a broad strip of coast between the water & the car, it seemed to be elevated as if it were resting in a huge, flat clay calyx, and it was just a hair's breadth away from running over the edges. Lea wanted to put on a contemplative face but the wind immediately wiped those gentle, melancholic features from her face as a hairdo, rearranged into languid waves within moments, is blown away, so that her mournful features were tied more tightly and composed of different, longer-lasting wrinkles.

— I once lived by a lake and read about the lives of saints. That was the first time I wanted to be a saint, at a time when I did not have the foggiest idea of morality, and that was perhaps my luck. Don't think that the book was a pure adventure story for me: I loved miracles somehow for their own beauty; they combined both God's and my own body. Many was the time I got young boys and girls to flock together from far-flung farmsteads to play at being 'saints.' I went off with my 'disciples' to deserted trees, and with a flourish of the hand magicked up fruit and branches: of course, that was done by going on further from the withered tree into the garden. Yet by then I could hardly wait to be able to die like a great saint: sometimes I wanted to die immediately after the first miracle so that I could lie down and the girls would kiss my body and clothes. A big quarrel broke out: I would announce that I was dead, and they would yell that I should do a bit more miracle making. Sometimes, indeed a lot of times, I was a martyr; sometimes I would tell them of the miracles of saints who had never lived.

— That's only natural — Ena commented drily.

landscape & 'landscape-ethics' from Leatrice's childhood. The lake of the 'coin of virtue'

Leatrice pondered. She saw that cold, blue lake on the bank of which silver-leaved dwarf bushes grew: at a regular distance to each other, as if they were toy poplar trees of doll's house proportions; the leaves rustle, and she believes, wants to believe, that angels are rattling distractedly on tambourines. Because the true sacred daydreaming did not take place during play: she did not dare to be so theatrical among the children (she would have liked, for example, to be kissed ten thousand times on a naked knee onto which she had placed a stone frame: this was the reliquary), and the looks that she could set on her face were not as sanctimonious as she would have liked — so that whenever possible she would steal away to this blue-black water in the evening: even her stomach would be nauseous from fear of herself, but she would risk it.

At first she would just stand beside the infinitely mute water: the smeared black-&-white ovals of the swell resembled badly baked spongecake that had overrun the mold and which gave a minimum scale of peace and quiet: but she was already picturing even those silver and clotted-blue smudges as a manifestation of the way black moths & white moths appeared to Hermit St. X... — and brought him various messages. She imagined that those were coins, black and white coins in her big treasury. She related them to the value of psychological goods: these coins were her virtues. When she squatted down she dipped her hand into it and rubbed the water like Harpagon did his money: she stretched her hand voluptuously above the lake, signaling to herself that it was all hers, and when she got home it was still just that glittering water that she saw, without any bank, tree, or landscape garnish — only that elastic golden-green and moral-ringed water. When the peasant children went by the lake on Sunday morning in order to reach church, she took pleasure in knowing that, by the light of day, the children could not see the coins of virtue of which she had so many in the evening that by day she had no need to go to prayers with a prayer book.

Already then the two kinds of religiosity were sharply divided in her brain; she considered the other children peasant-like and vulgar because they prayed in church. Her way of explaining the lives of saints was that one had to be on the lookout for God, one had to discover Him somewhere, and then everything was in order: miracles would shower down and human beings would rule in their dominion. Death, suffering, and self-denial dropped from her memory, or rather she called certain things, and more rarely, certain feelings, 'death' and 'suffering' according to which kinds of miraculous objects a martyr had been in contact with after death or during his or her sufferings. Her 'virtues' as well were like that when she regarded the vespertine reflections of the lake's waves as being that; thus a ruddy cloud would be 'death,' on which she would cast her eyes upward as on a *comme il faut*-escort[88] who was needed, so it seemed, in the grand procession of life and sainthood; she would speak about it with the stresses on the words with which children as a rule pronounce the names of what to them are unknown illnesses; naturally 'death' was not an 'end,' and suffering was not subjective pain, but these were just constants, death was a permanent background, or rather a gigantic figure of secondary significance, within life.

vespertine trees; movement in a standstill, simile about a docking ship

As far as that goes, death was a flowery meadow of miracles, albeit that was not the way adults saw it. When she had lived by the lake an upstanding farm manager had been her best friend (she was living at the place of her father's elder brother; her mother was no longer alive). When beside the lake her teeth would be chattering with fear, she would scamper home madly (or, on the contrary, with legs almost paralyzed into slowness), her eyes downcast, continually looking at the ground because at the end of the road, on the side of a slope, stood a little chapel white as snow with a little black spiral dome: when the Moon shone on it she was blinded by its whiteness, and when touched by only the dull rays of evening, it was green like a ghost which, out of a diabolical irony, had placed a black radish on its head.

Everything there was her treasure: the crystalline midnight flight of the vector of the transparent blue sky, the minute little arrows of the stars, the squeaking flight of which was jumbled by the muddy nets of the roadside tree boughs; the trees were as if laths had been poked into a stake horizontally, at regular distances, to the right and left, & a black pulp had been hung onto these girders, which were like the rungs of a ladder, leaving out a lot of the tendrils and allowing half of the thick pulp to stick to the laths, the other half of it dripping down slowly onto the road: as a result those skeletal trunks looked like a stalactite figure that guides point to under the name of 'Flag.'

It's as if every evening a board game was staged in the sky: the stars had to be shot like arrows in such a way so as not to be blotted out by the shaky semaphores of the avenue of trees —

if a star could only be spotted due to a bough being swept aside by the wind, that did not count as a winning number. At times like that, when filled with dread, she groped or somersaulted her way home, she was tormented by the thought that the treasure was not hers after all, that there was a huge split between the lake & herself, the whole thing was an awful lie. In her brain images of the lake, the line of trees, and the white chapel rippled, one above the other, like a three-branched millwheel: she felt that she had stolen something — a huge treasure that was swallowing & wrecking her.

She ran to the farm manager while he was dining & started crying. She was asked what was wrong; she would dream something up, a big man with a stick coming after her on the road, or a gigantic cat leaping into her lap. When the bell was tolled in the little chapel on the walls of which the white Moon raised dust like a sack of flour thrown against the wall — he and the farm manager's wife said grace before the evening meal. The tolling bell had a strange sound: broad and warm, but it had an inappropriate edge (as if a trashy tin fringe were to be sewn onto a big black velvet shawl), close to sarcastic gloating. The farm manager & his wife meekly prayed, and Lea also put her hands together: she felt very much at home there in that convivial room and the prayer was to her taste — it was like wearing a warm lambskin jacket as a protection against wind flurries at night.

When the farm manager went over to the window in order to open it, shivers ran down Lea's spine as if some crime she had committed were about to be revealed: the freshly fallen moonlight was lying finger-deep on the small bushes down by the lake, the trailing roadside trees with their hair hanging loose (in the room upstairs there was a coat of arms on which thick hair like that was dangling from a skull stuck onto the end of a sword), the hillside chapel (like a candle stub on which the dome was a forgotten snuffer) — all of that was as if it had been her fault that they had become so eerie, and that would make Michæl angry.

As he opened the window the wind virtually drove the landscape, too, into the room like a loosely hung carpet, & all Michæl said was "Wonderful evening this is!" A quiet shudder ran through Lea (her blood was at the stage of being shivery like carbonated water from which the fierce fizz has gone after being left standing for a day or two) — if she had been a cat no doubt she would have set to ecstatic purring. Through the fact that Michæl summed up the whole weird landscape-miracle in a placid, almost cheerful sentence, the world gained an entirely new meaning in her eyes — idyllic ordinariness and a mysterious insistence on miracles were far from being intertwined in her sentiment: all told it somehow reassured her that the world (the lake, the avenue, the chapel) was a simple thing for another person, so that she felt a gushing fellowship with Michæl in that 'work' community that both of them were fond of looking at the 'world,' only Michæl saw it one way, she differently; true, her own way of looking at things differed sharply from that of others, but, on the other hand, she was not excommunicated from other people as a result, as she had so feared in her lakeside solitude.

She suddenly became loquacious & started to say loads of mundane things about the roadside trees and the church only in order to reassure herself that these were not necessarily haunting her, or rather that, even if they were, they did not have to be regarded with any air of mystery.

When the farm manager then accompanied her through the grounds to the villa, with tears of pleasure glistening in Lea's eyes: these were rare moments when she was conscious of all the mysteriousness of the landscape & her own life without feeling any fear — it was not that the tension of mystery resolved into the idyllic, just that she was able to settle down by the idyll with a childish sense of security: stubbornly selfish though children can be, they are sometimes just as sensual in dividing things — they may repeat the partitioning of two dice an infinite number of times & take pleasure in sentences like "This is mine, that's yours!" A sense of dividing up like that functioned in Lea & it filled her with an overflowing mood of "everything is OK"; she prevailed on Michæl to relate all kinds of rural and woodland peculiarities, though details like that were of no real interest to her, only it was gratifying to hear the calm drift of his words as she gaily looked back on the avenue of trees: they could now be seen from the back and that physical change superbly fitted Lea's change of mood — she remembered the avenue of trees like that even after she had grown up: the joyous-miracle side of the approach from the villa and the dark-miracle side of the approach from the lake.

The boughs hung quietly over the road; not one of the leaves rustled, as if they had attained the acme of their positional harmony; the complete standstill sketched new melody courses on the sky: the restless rings of stillness; there are objects which, if they come to a halt after slow or stormy movement, the fact of standing virtually transubstantiates them, they all but float above themselves — as big ships, which come to a stop after long and slow swinging round: at first one does not even notice that they are stopping, all one senses is a mystic cleansing and tension, but without any dynamic tenseness; the new state absorbs and resolves the totality of forward movements; while the boat was still turning there had been something ruggedly predictable in its movement, because every single state had been a 'situation' that was in a definite relationship to the waterside warehouses, jetties, or cloud compasses, which stroked the ship's shoulder like glowing direction fans: sea, buoys, minute propellers, diminutive porters were all just little dashes on the face of the scenery so that the gigantic clock hand should turn over them.

When it had suddenly come to a halt, the ship's 'situation' ceased: one expected that now it would finally be fixed, though the opposite happened — one's eyes suddenly gave it great pushes, as if they were trying with their look to shove it here and there in order to ascertain whether it had stopped or was still moving; suddenly everything that had no direction, only force, was seized by a peaceful dizziness, lifting into the air all at once ship, tower, cranes and bridges: the irregular undulation of 'standing on the spot' commences, the ship loses its positive outlines, its weight, its sense, and due to standing it near enough wastes away, becomes transparent like a logical paper model, so that all statics simultaneously lead to the most neurasthenic-improbabilization and to the sweetest mâché-logicization.

That was also the case with those trees which had been quivering in Lea's soul like whirlpools: now that they had all at once stopped, every deceitful mask of movement, the distortion of drama, had fallen from them, or as provincial orators would put it: 'chaos spawned virginal form' from itself, but she did not truly sense that, it was more a case of thinking the process in principle, because in reality precisely the opposite was the case: while the boughs scattered their icy value patches here and there in the wind, those images of boughs were all exceedingly determined and understandable: in their total rigidity, however, they radiated a constant uneasiness, like a self-contradictory fountain: they were less, a great deal less than themselves, but they thereby set off into the twilight waves which were much cleaner, clean to the point of stupefying: they themselves became thinner, but they spread invisibly in the telltale ether of the quiet, like the eternally swelling floodtide of 'halting.'

If the ship docks in the bay, or the wind pushes back the appropriate foliage on the relevant branch anew, or in other words something 'stops,' then pure bipartition happens: the foliage shrinks to the minimum possible of existence, its material just a fleeting aspirated sound above its notion of itself — the movement, on the other hand, spreads out all the way to infinity, filling the entire sky with its regular rings: the movement will be eternal and certain, & the essence will become an orthographic whim or a misfiring cigarette lighter.

It is also exciting and mysterious that this 'stopping' does not contribute a single new element; it is like a kaleidoscope: the exact same pieces are featured the next time it is turned, and that endows it with the mysterious effect of one's seeking an essential, regular connection between two successive configurations, as if the second had uncovered the essence of the first; however, on turning a third time, to one's even greater surprise, the latest one seemed to be the disclosure of the essence: the illusion of the 'essence' arises not through abstraction but by rearranging the same elements.

The becoming quiet of crying faces and the dying of living faces evoke the same feeling. When one discerns a new gesture, an unusual intonation, a snippet of a demeanor of unknown origin on an old figure, one has the impression that one has come across a deeper stratum, indeed the most central causative chamber of character, that the figure has divulged itself, and, on the basis of a new comment or indeed the old one, is regarded as merely an external front that dances as a hypocritical calyx on the conventionally coerced stem that is nourished by the newly discovered strength of the root of character. Sequential differentness gives an illusion of gradual deepening and one therefore endowed with an infinitely curving series of commentaries raised to a higher power.

The first such disclosing-commenting state of the trees was that coming from the garden: when the mass of coal and water, black and ruffled into itself, was slowly lifted by the ironic-well-intentioned chemistry of the thin strands of the Moon (as when light shines onto a thick book that one had seen on the table in the evening merely as a black blotch & one is thereupon able to make out the title page, indeed later, with the light taking heart, even the microscopic typographic lace of the footnotes); all at once, with gently perverse untimeliness, the forms of individual leafs separated out in every little detail, carrying on their edges the silvery buds of scientific and metaphorical possibilities; there was no transition between the crucible-black and the pale contour areas; the light touched certain areas, others it left in bituminous perdition, which for Lea was a great miracle because she had always thought of lightness as being uncertain, a diffuse, perpetual, and amorphous thing, because it was like space: always there, but like nothing at all. Now the great mummy owls of fate (because that is what the oval blots of foliage looked like as they perched on the wall bars: their shoulders oval, their bottom mattedly fibrous like the tassels of an old-fashioned shawl that have been dipped in water) were X-rayed: for Lea that was not unduly surprising, an abyss miracle, because for children there is never a 'disclosure,' only an enchanting change which takes place within the elastic area of constant wonderment.

The second metamorphosis, however, had taken place around dawn: the site of the vespertine ink statues was supplanted by a million little reliefs that seesawed between the counterpoles of identity & perfect strangeness; every single cut of lace (which bore on itself the duality of abstract-quality crystallinity & life-quality uncertainty, a Touqué-tailored mixture of proportion and unbalancedness) almost self-consciously enjoyed its linearity and convexity, shadow and leaf entanglement (Linea Anadyomene):[89] all this related to the mythical evening monochromaticity like a sharp negative to an incinerated black film: every imaginable angle was intensified; indeed, a clutter of abstract edges and surfaces certainly governed (just as on a photographic negative where 'reality' is total yet everything is composed in the cool net of a system of lines), covering up that compromise state that the daytime appearance exhibits.

Leatrice's uncle (ex-soldier, has-been intellectual)

In those dawn hours there was also another notable event: that was the time Leatrice's uncle returned home from nearby R*** when he was living on the farmstead. He was a Jewish-born but christened bachelor, & all his efforts lay in entering fully into Christian heroism: he made up for "Jewish-amorality with healthy Christian-immortality." For a while he was an army officer, but he was booted out of the army because he wrote a play with the title *Heroes* for his hoofer flame, into which he condensed all his 'nostalgia' for an overcondensed 'Baroque' (the whole neurasthenia-masque had about it a certain whiff of the history of ideas). Since then he had been unable to live in any other way but one of having written that; he disappeared and wasted away in that one possible formula, plagiarizing his own myth in desperate self-infection.

The fact is the performance was seen to the end by a colonel who was greatly taken by it. He applauded and fell in love with the actress; the next day, for form's sake, he inquired into who the author had been & when he learned that he became glum, struck up a conversation with the sole cultured fellow officer in his class who explained that the piece was a parody of all true heroism; he did not know what was Baroque and what wasn't but it all seemed to be the love-rhetoric of an impotent man, full of all the condensed atmosphere of love that only distance is able to create. The colonel watched the piece for a second time & did, indeed, notice those things; a week later the author was fired, contemplating "what a deep crevasse separates the heroes themselves, who bring about their own 'Baroque' in animal-ignorance, and the hero-immortalizing heroic consciousness, which caps all that into a steely synthesis with the mortar of eternity."

The gods are monstrously ungrateful: instead of becoming intoxicated by the fine statues and precise-piquant legends that are constructed about them by mythopoetic humanity, they prefer to turn away from those ornamental ready-made boxes into which they could squeeze their senseless-amorphous mist-existences and chaoticize without consciousness.

If those soldiers had sensed the pedagogical power of their synthesis their mythology would have had the strength of a magnetic drill; that vision, with the obligatory strength of symbol, the intoxicated prestige of legend, could have been an active ailment of discipline. But they remained 'soldiers.' While she watched their army exercises from a distance, she did not see in them anything other than engineers and officials who with maps and protractors, statistics & budgets, trample underfoot their own raison d'être.

When Lea's mother died he went to the burial in full military dress: his uniform was made theatrical partly by its outmodedness, partly by his own eccentricity. That funeral was the first time Leatrice took a fancy to Uncle Péter; he had held one of her hands. The small group walked on a narrow, stony path, only Péter's garb gleamed in the late afternoon mist. He talked a lot: he was the first person to have a strong influence on Lea's style. "In times gone by a military burial was splendid," he recounted with almost tearful eyes — "when a dead body was borne on an almost tower-high trestle, with so many red flags after it as there had been wounds from which the person had perished, and even if the person had not died of wounds, then a red flag was carried in front with a black circle around it — the 'wounds' were carried by seminarists, from whose arms dangled red-dyed cuffs: like red smoke, like burning slaves — that's how the redeeming wounds stepped after the corpse; if the body resting on the moving platform of the catafalque could have opened its eyes, it would have seen only the flapping row of flags without poles, as if carmine seagulls were accompanying it on its last journey. There were two sorts of red flags: unattached or semi-attached — the first sort comprising loosely dangling triangles, given to those who had died in a victorious engagement."

If in the meantime Leatrice turned aside she would have heard something to the effect of: "Poor woman, only a week ago she was going out to peasant families, taking food to them, and bustling about to make up a dowry for one of the girls... You know that when she went to her neighbor, the landowner, he was unwilling to admit her, and that exasperated the poor woman... interesting that she did them nothing but good, yet the peasants still did not like her... They felt something..."

Péter, on the other hand, said nothing about that kind of thing: he felt dreadfully chilly, he was greatly touched, although it was not personal pain but an abstract thesis play to evoke sympathy, a form of the fear of death that had been melodized to bits. Lea already considered she was seeing the red birds, and if a shaggy or chic black bird flew away, cawing or mute (imitating the swish of mackintoshes hastily put on by guests as they hurried off), she put it onto the list of participants at the burial: if they flew a long way, then she imagined them as kinds of outliers and pageboys, nervous and too far-sighted ministrants, who were making arrangements that all should be in apple-pie order in even distant streets where the procession was going to pass. If a dark-clothed elderly lady or man approached her & stroked her cheek, their freshly dyed & still moist mourning garments and cheese-colored cheeks (the green of mold still on them) would throw her into such a fright that she burst into tears.

Péter went on speaking, however: "The soldiers were followed by three groups: there was a group of mourners in black, which symbolized the family's grief, and then there would be a group of jubilation in white, composed of monastics, Franciscan

& Dominican novitiates, who would mark the ascension of the spirit to heaven and would be called 'angels' on such occasions. Between these two groups, in slow march, would come soldiers with masked faces: each of them gripping the sword of his neighbor as a sign of blind obedience and the automatism of impersonal duty, From time to time the mourners would crouch down, drop to their knees, and shout "*Ver*," which is Latin for 'spring,' thereby symbolizing that at the bottom of even the celebrated rebirth of nature lurks pallid death: on the other hand the young monastics sang from sheets of music, then at the end of each line, their right hands held aloft waving the scroll of music, they sang out in bright tenor voices "*Mors*," which is the Latin for 'death' (at the same time the black-dressed monastics, or rather every other one would, in checkerboard order, crouch and growl "*Ver*" in a plaintive-reproachful voice). At that time people called military burials "the wanderings of the red and white birds," because from afar that was all that could be seen: the red flags aloft & under them the white sheet-music crowd like a flock of birds, white as snow, which had been panicked into flying up by a stone plopping into the water."

---

his intoxication

Péter couldn't hold wine, didn't like it at that, but he was learning how to get soused: he occasionally participated in big drinking bouts in the neighboring small town, and around then he was in the habit of returning home from those binges when the first light of dawn encompassed the villa and its grounds. Objects just hovered in the otherworldly silence: while the rose-colored light gradually called forth the microscopic outlines of the flowers, the terrible nullity of tension, of the silence, completely corroded the material of the objects internally & densely filled the space that intervened between them; dawn was a paradoxical narcotic which made one dizzy & fall into an intense buzzing, at the same time making one's eyes keener: only dawn stillness was able to give the parallel bounties of intoxication and precision. In the evening the garden was mere material without form, a chaos of dense materials, whereas at dawn everything was form without materiality, as if the plastic barks of the trees, the boughs, the grasses, the fence posts, were all empty, like a collection of hollow-sounding statues made of sheets of a hair's breadth thickness.

Péter's cart burst into this organic unity of the 'plasticity of stillness' at around 4–5 o'clock in the morning, like an otherworldly malapropos miracle: the noise developed in terrible isolation, from the very first faint rustling to the breaking sigh of arrival; it was not accompanied by an echo, the thousand tiny ornaments of noise by day did not associate themselves with it; it did not mix with other sounds but developed separately in its material rigidity, like an autonomous body that could be sketched and set on weighing scales.

It was all like a transcendental experiment, let us say studying the chariot of the prophet Elijah in airless space. As it happens the lesson of 'monumental simplicity' could also be deduced from it; the clear tread, the clear cough, the clear snorting of the horses were all audible, magnified one thousandfold. Lea listened at such times. She looked at the low mountains in the distance, which were hiding on the horizon in silvery disorder and in random contexts because of the white rokima flowers, between heaven and earth, like snow-covered eels that the morning flux of the sky sometimes tosses onto the shore, but they immediately flee back; in front of her was the long road turned pink in the middle of the meadow with the piquant irrationality of novelty, beside it, nearby two trees plunging into the middle of the landscape with the docility of absentminded barely-anchoredness and futile half-docking, like the Virgin Mary visiting Elizabeth; the two trees were full of chaste freshness and mature optimism; morning well-scrubbedness and October harmony, and Lea delved with eyes wide-open in the meadow and in her soul, in search and understanding of a connection between the noise of the approaching cart and the marvelous balance of the scenery.

Péter liked to come home alone, he drunkenly urged the horses onwards, and when he arrived he was half-dead from fear of himself just as Lea was when she scurried home from the lakeside in the evening. Péter was blond-haired, soft, with a pointed, Vandyke beard and slightly confused grey eyes; his skin was greasy and pink, always with a glistening layer of sweat. He spoke with a slight lisp, leaving a lot of saliva on his chin: while speaking brown filaments were strung across his mouth; he had small, thick lips, which he pursed & meanwhile breathed by slurping up the air. His cadences were a little melodic: they had that air of serious emotion, which derived from his liking the content of his own sentences with nostalgic warmth: this was some kind of pleasure in his imagined self-evidence, so that he did not report on even his own 'Baroque'-visions with loud & vehement pathos, more in a quiet, mawkish-logical manner (that was also the intonation, albeit a degree or two more baritone, of the proprietor of *The Perspective*).

His drunkenness was also very odd: he smiled sleepily, his hands trembled, a forced humor struggled in his features, and he hummed in a stertorously deep voice, as if he were bemoaning and whistling the flop that had come of his personality: unexpectedly, his essential being was let free, then in hindsight he would wish to keep it secret, and in doing so he overdid precisely those gestures that he wanted to conceal; afterwards he would suddenly become sullen, with deep loathing & a hesitant, mordant melancholy running across his face.

In every drunkard or dying person there is some such inner tectonic battle of waves, as if it were not a matter of the simple twitching of muscles but of the anatomical separation of layers of character, the breaking-up of masks and sincerities that had long agglomerated into each other: within a single person a whole group of people is jostling, like the possibilities of fleeting forms belched back in a melting-wax-torso — the whole thing a grotesque labor in which one is a tearing sack that is tipped over by the figures tussling to be born; when Péter suddenly stuck out his belly so that the buttons popped off his trousers and, grinning as he wept, threw his head back, it did not seem as if he was nauseated by the whole affair but as if a giant of a man were seeking to burst out (a child who is already wrestling its mother to the ground in the womb): now he strains Péter's stomach by pressing it with his shoulder blades, but since he could not break free there he suddenly thrust his head on Péter's throat like a battering ram so that he was obliged to snigger with a gargling sound & stretch his neck forward as if he were being strangled; it is possible to see the anatomical proportions of the inner person exactly from the various protuberances of the body in parturition: the nude in epilepsy is a new style of sculpture that provocatively crosses the healthy body.

Péter forbade anyone from coming to his aid on such occasions. He struggled solitarily with himself: he did feel himself to be alone, because his every movement was so strong, unusual, hard and sharp that he did not feel them as being movements but foreign ghosts which he subsequently recalled (like fever patients) as if they had been strangers (was Eve nothing more than an unusual muscle twitch of that sort in Adam?)

his monologue (his grotesque & estheticizing yearning for a 'heroic' life)

Lea saw none of that, she only heard the sounds: the stamping of the horses and Péter's monologue. At times like that Péter always felt that his hiccups, his vomiting, the belches which threatened to burst his whole body apart were, actually, the vengeance of his own mask: the coarse irony of the infuriated 'hero' hatching so grossly in the face of the intrusive esthetician so that a monologue like that meant tiring intellectual work & amateur dramatics for him; at one moment explaining to his own hiccups in a whining voice, with diplomatic craftiness, (as to a Breughel-mercenary independent of him) the relationship of his personality to heroism, at another assuming the role of the hiccup and justifying himself with all sorts of military pass-words; of course, this internal dialogue took all kinds of forms: quarrel, mollycoddling compromise, small-shopkeeper tricks for bribing, bureaucratic '*viribus unitis*,'[90] contract pathos, defiant separation, & arrogant resignation.

"It's an old custom, we know... to create someone and the ungratefulness... the gods as well slay theologians with a rain of fire... sodomites, fair enough, but slaying theologians and apologists?... dogmas..., the first good and tight corset into which they fitted; with their spreading stupid sky..., old Jewish *Ewigkeit*,[91] suitable for prophets..., but dogma clipped stupid *tateleh*[92] God-the-Father's beard, though it was fine like it was, he was a somebody... Ah! Was it me who challenged you heroes, huh? You don't want to be heroes..., not just soldiers, to drop dead just like that, in accordance with regulations, the wounds also official, the most tedious wounds... Die a hero's death?

Poppycock, they are cretins, they die like a lesson, as if a blank in a tax return ought to be filled, ... you like that, don't you, cretins! Jordan & belles-lettres! Who was it invented heroes? Jesuits and crusaders, was that a ghetto? Kaftan *à bouillon*, no?... Thickheads, you dismissed it from your minds, but it's not even necessary..., I gave it, I showed the big gesture, it's not necessary, clots, not in the regulations... circus pathos? right? Clots with no fantasy... just like the gods: riled up about theology — soldiers about the knowledge of heroism, their own materialized conscience, but of course that's not enough conscience, rhetorical, slobbery, infra dig? Office, office... the *Champs de Mars* is needed like hell: a green blot on a map, so and so many acres, this is where you will stand... Mars? Who needs that? 'Tenshun, hup-two-three, briefcase, mechanical engineers — *Champs de Mars*? Mars? *abzúg* Mars,[93] theatrical god. Phoœy! Is that your principle?... Peasants and counts, you're going to croak without knowing what that is — I've explained, written it down, no need for amateurish bragging, cretinous bard, phoœy! Sweethearts, how could you have become such imbeciles as not to want your own beauties? Destructive parody... How can you babble on so, my darling lovey-dovies: you trample on the past, you've scrubbed the memory of Christianity, I'll resurrect it for you, & that makes me the murderer? A tradition-trampling charlatan? What asses! The lot of you ought to be crushed, once & for all time, & held under holy terror in the yoke of beauty, cretins... If beauty is not inspiration, not desire, then it's terror... The old, eternal rule of gesture, the grand liturgy, a liturgical death in place of a boring death by the book... Muscle is no hero, peasant power — nothing... Spirit, spirit... but to you that is decadent, destructive... The militarism of imbeciles, where blasphemy is the hankerer after the past... Envy, primitive revenge, because I saw more than them, they can't bear that, but I know, my whole life long I knew

Christianity, me, me the Jordan and belles-lettres (I only know, I knew, even if I were to bite the dust, even then... Jew? Shush! What do you know?... Baroque!... Have you any idea what Baroque is?... You don't know, pickled mercenary, short-sighted soldier... I'll give you Christian heroism!... I gave my life for a poem in which I assembled everything fine for you to see your beauty, I humbly held a mirror to your face, your mind, your heart, I never had a part of it, I am not from this family, but then families become extinct or decadent, but the memoirs of private tutors & boudoir secretaries live on — is that a fine thing when a successor kicks & humiliates a chronicler simply for adverting to the past with love & affection? Sweethearts, did I wish any bad to come of this? Is this intrusive? I have never made any secret of your not being of the same blood as me, but I'm better acquainted with your blood, & don't be so naïve as to believe it's intrusion: there is no one humbler than I am... I want to finish my business with you, my 'intrusion'... (Lea heard sounds as if someone were sneezing, coughing, and groaning at the same time: Péter was blubbing) — I shall assemble my siblings, yes the *sidelocked* lot, the *hondlers,*[94] the intellectuals, & we'll go in front of the tsar. Us! Us! Because we're the only ones who can dream & who can see... That's a holy legacy, not an official, not an engineer, not kicking & empty elegance: yes, they will go off to the tsar, take your pick between stylish spurs & heroic dream: we can talk about Baroque heroes, we are alive, we have vitality in us, impetus, and past... us, the crucifiers of Christ, we have more right than them to holler Pro Christo with the chaplains general, salon ministers, and their words. Phooey! Tollbooth lackeys... Soldiers? Salon padding!... Don Antonio: in his left hand the letter he received from his wife telling him his child has been born, & in his right hand a reliquary bawling across to the traitorous bishop, "I have no dilemma, thief of the purple: Church and state do not fight, it's only your grief-stricken old man's avenging fist striking you!..." Antonio, the way they recited that — for them, that was a parody, idiots... we will go off to the tsar, to rouse them, dozy cretinous officers, financial bishops, & office monasteries, my Jews, crawling with lice, are going to humiliate them... their elegance, their manner, their vainglory, & their genealogy can come, but we know everything, we know what beauty is... here they cannot set dolled-up, booted ankles against flat feet, that's a cheap trick..., there the tsar will see the erudition and the stupidity, the pathos and the boredom, the Baroque and the salon... Tsar?... One cannot have confidence, he will also say that it's a parody, & what do you people know about this... idiots. Ah!..."

Lea, holding her breath, was standing by the open window: Péter's words panted in great solitude; it was as if several people were speaking, each hiccup or reel rolled out another layer of speech register (a millwheel patched together from various paddleboards that is pushed round not by the water of an evenly gurgling source but by fitful geyser-like spouts); the hiccups were audible, afterwards a couple of moments of silence, whispering, then a half-cough, half-shout, a hoarse jabbering, which had not the slightest thing in common with the whispering person: Lea just listened and looked at the countryside, the rising sun, the first yellow streaks, which did not look as if they were coming in parallel from the sun but were breaking through higgledy-piggledy, crosswise, diagonally, and vertically, scattering onto forest and meadow; as if the whole dawn were a miracle-stage paradise-floor on which God was holding a levée, while down below, on the low shelf of hell, a soul that had set out for damnation was fuming, striving, toward salvation.

It was strange that anything could exist apart from the great unity of dawn, that the trees, on the canopy of which God's breakfast underlinen was already gleaming yellow, were displaying total indifference to anyone else and not attracting the life of all strangers into their own performance. From that minute on, nature was imbued with a gentle demonism and slowly fulfilled irony: the growing yellow light was like an immaterial flood which threatened to inundate the villa's yard where Péter was drowning because the yellow water had already reached his mouth; the same yellow glinted everywhere as it did in the evening on the ripples of his lake (it was linked in ladyfinger-biscuit ellipses, but all the same basically in checkerboard sequence); the morning radiation was triumphant, ironic, & destructive, its treasure, its 'virtue' was — there you are! — about to swamp Péter in the yard; awakening, for its completeness, called for Péter's soul as its victim.

(At all events, that excitation of the rays into a fluid is an old technique: as if the wave were shaking up the more traditional prestige, the gazelle-tempos of the fountain shaking up the more alluring hints of the mystic-game — although the basic excitement of the growing colors of the irradiation lay precisely in that the stronger they were, the more they became one with the objects that they surrounded: at first a stand-alone little watercolor appendage at the edge of the horizon, but later it all of a sudden stops pouring in from outside and seems to be radiating much rather from the inside of objects, as if it were supplying data for an anatomy of their essence, suggesting the Ur-acts of self-revelation: not a shallow amalgam, but the one and only authentic language of substance-nakedness.

At times like that one senses the light's obscene forcedness [the season of *ne-plus* gold on the tree boughs at dawn, for example] and self-evidence. That duality [which is sharply opposed to any sort of faking into a 'flood'] is experienced most often on the stage: a green light gradually starts to diffuse onto the line of girls dancing in yellow, and one enjoys the change with the liveliest sensual reactions, but by the time the green attains the ultimate degree of its plenitude, of harmony, one senses the pre-Creation silence of the essence of the line of girls.

If the first endeavors of the yellow of dawn by Leatrice at the same time represented the first contents of her moral life, it should be remarked that yellow, in any case, was one of the most rational of colors: as if it belonged among the most notable elements of spring, summer, & autumn, and thus would have the greatest role in these three naïve seasons being in addition the three parvenu-hypotheses of a sense of life — that the georgic was not, first and foremost, a natural-historical or nature-caressing genre, but a metaphysical technique.

It is maybe not such a perverse logomania to pose the question of which of the three seasons is right: for it is hard to presume that nature was engaged in the infantile tastelessness of adorning itself apart as a three-headed Janus, which three heads would depict three aspects of its uniform value [both 'aspect' & 'depiction' are two comical symptoms of the tiredness of the brain], the decoration crisis was most recently the central topic of discussion at a midnight synod of crocuses. So that the concept of 'beauty' could be laicized & limited to no more than a superficial petal cult, some people imposed on flowers the old wives' superstition of 'decorativeness,' and with time the flowers themselves believed it and carried on their lives in accordance to that superstition. In the end a couple of pedantic and arch-conservative seminarist crocuses driven by a loathing of 'decorativeness' convoked a conference at which puritanical 'metapetalism' was inserted in place of multicolored petalocentric pseudo-empiricism.

Is life, one wonders, an abstract chorus of power [in accordance to spring's style], or a boastful collection of the irrational power crystals of deeds [in accordance to summer's style], or possibly a lethal vintage of values, a kind of axiological puppet show [in accordance to the ultimate style of fall]? Power, deed, and value: abstractions like that are to be seen in the seasons, nevertheless to group those abstractions into a georgic — are not things like that called 'onto-etymological *gundolfica*'[95] in some of the more modernly equipped internal medicine clinics?

By autumn golden yellow has long monopolized the totality, uniting that with the symbol of value as if it were simply the oxidation of time; in summer the blazing of the sun and the show-off focus of noon is nevertheless one of yellow's essential roles; and in springtime as well the first adolescent allures on the branches all unfold with the reassuring yellow of daylight. On the other hand, it can be seen precisely from Leatrice's example that 'power,' 'deed,' & 'value' were notions that were the antitheses of the metaphysical georgic; as if, although during the centuries there were buds of reason, positive and tangible foci, they were scattered in the basin of the soul and started to bloom there, kicking up hypocritical springs from those strange plants, which represent the most tragicomic flora of human life. For Leatrice autumnal gold [which was the same as stereotyped Byzantine-gold backgrounds] meant the dead time below life & the value beyond life, or in other words, precisely the lack of life; however, it nevertheless became a life surplus, because the dead past [the 'time gold'] as well as the illuminating truth over life ['value gold'] was gone about with the greatest excitement.

There are conditions in which analysis and the production of symbols are barely distinguishable from each other, just as certain states of nerviness can show a cross-opalization of blind sensitivity and strict rationalism: in Lea's autumnitis & auréalgia it was barely possible to decide whether it was a matter of the rapture of reason or the academicism of rapture. At all events, the mind in which there are these kinds of mirrorings fails to find the truth.)

Of course, all this lived only dimly in Lea's brain, but Péter became a big 'saint' in her eyes. Later she entered his room: he was sprawled on the settee half naked, half in a whalebone corset like a box of sugar-plum candies that on one side has already been greedily and clumsily ripped open, so that the paper seal, the outer wrapper, the inner glue, the cardboard of the box, the lining paper & the tinfoil were to be seen one by one, whereas at the other end the intact packaging, touched by no one, stretches brightly. Britches & boots were resplendent on his legs, but on his chest the jacket had been unbuttoned. The landscape's trembling security, which had nothing to do with this man, could be seen through the window.

the body in the Middle Ages, Touqué's four points of view

An odd meaning of the concept 'human being' occurred to Lea — maybe the one that was expressed with such certainty at a number of points in the Middle Ages: on the one hand, a burlesque picture of human mediocrity, its anatomical comicality, for another, its weird strangeness; it is a way of looking at things that is far from any childish naturalism or soft-headed philanthropy; it is perhaps the most idealistic (to say nothing of the most feasible) vision of material: legends, in which ampoules grow from thighs, ears of wheat from ears, and models of monasteries are built in wombs, with the umbilical cord as the bell, et cetera, represent one half of this sense of corporeality, whereas the second half is represented by books of quackery and magic formulas: the concrete and separate sense, the tragic loneliness of the individual limbs. The hands, the ears, the loins and the kneecaps were separate little principalities that legend elevated into symbolic exaggerations, giving them a fantastic architecture due to a decadent starvation for symmetry; on the other hand, the medicine-man verses for healing and putting a spell on people were shrouded in the grotesque obscurity of illness.

The two tendencies together elaborated the Gothic perception of the body that best displays the origin of humans from Adam: the body was a proletarian wound & fairy-flower.

(All of which Leville-Touqué was writing about in an article for *Antipsyche* entitled: From *Humanitas toward Hominitas*. In the first section of this he detailed the influence of the medieval notion of Adam on the awareness of the body [I. Adam *Nudus*], then he examined the influence of the various forms of martyrdom on the average awareness of the body [II. *Anatomia Martyrologica*], the veneration of relics as the promoter of a symbolic anatomy and the mythical emancipation of certain body parts [III. Hagio-materialismus], & finally he analyzed the various notions on illness and the parallels of naïve chemistry and formalist prayer [IV. Ethico-Diagnosis].

Later, by the time Leatrice was embellishing her own 'religiosity' into precepts [not intellectual but visual precepts: pictorial dogmatics], she invented a special rite exclusively for persons suffering from pure body awareness: the priest would lie down in front of the altar, his head would be covered, then he would likewise be covered from his belly to the heels of his feet, so that only the chest was left naked: this body part, rendered impassive, would be mourned on one side by the first deacon [poor Lea had little idea who that could be] while the second, on the opposite side, worshipped it: that is how she perpetuated the memory of drunken Péter; of course, it was an open-air ceremony, because only there could one feel the unbridgeable emptiness between a wriggling little body and nature hovering in scintillating indifference. Beside a plainly spreading dawn, the insensibly sprawling body reeked of repulsive, petty-minded egotism, an abominable self-centeredness over and above the landscape's attainment of its goal, indeed, its aimlessness, so that the lamenting priest pondered on the hard selfishness of the body freed from the mind, the worshipper, by contrast, on the blind loneliness of the body, and in the end both of them pleaded that nature take unto itself the body, & that there should be no contradiction between an individual's stifling goals & Nature's perpetually expanding self-identity.)

on the structure of the new-'novel.'
Against chronological order, antigenetic story-telling.
The 'classicism of dispersion'; architectural example'

Ostensibly, the traces of Leatrice's memories have been sketched, but that was more in the nature of a reluctant dissemblance: details of Leatrice's past were not needed to provide a 'motive' in the present, nor so that the present, maligned quite irrationally as overly lackluster, should acquire some genetic plumpness (as if there were any need of the 'dogmatic' quinine of 'cause' in order that the present's supposed superficiality and uncertainty should pass as a pathological symptom): the aim was more the reverse.

History's successive time-brackets and stairs of otherness are not interesting and important because the prior prepares the latter and thus a naïve 'organicism' can be smuggled into the process, but precisely because it is scattered all over the place, every era sweeps toward different dimensions and, instead of arousing an impression of a 'temporal process,' it seems more like anti-temporal flashing apart: here and there events and styles happen to be parallel to the empty stair carpet runners of time, bureaucratically rolled up in one direction and in the same width, but they are mostly situated outside that strip, haphazardly, like the fluctuating waves and splenetic-mist of a fever as it wanders in vessels which lie a long way from a thermometer scale.

Precisely through their lack of connection an old event and a more recent scene in Leatrice's life, when juxtaposed like this, can be used to confer a characteristically non-historical harmony by virtue of their shameless antagonism to genetics: the relationship of past and present has been reduced or come to perfection exclusively in music. The right hand repeats two notes almost to infinity (this is the present), whereas the left hand hits ever-differing tones, chords, and snatches of themes, which allude to the sound vibration kept up by the right hand as the trajectory of a distant parabola that at one point brushes against one only to run off again into the infinite distance (that is the past); the two portions of time are not in biological but harmonic relation.

Past and present pursue a chance contact sport: a billiard-ball-harmony of foreignness. The internal paradox of harmony is precisely that it expresses maximum security with minimal antipathy: the kernel of an experience is always an enjoyment of antipathy, not to say dissonance. Leatrice's past is also an artificial possibility of harmony of this kind, as for a moment she runs toward it from an unfamiliar direction, only to forsake it again: the past is always wider than the present.

But then there is no sense in using the term 'the past' when the only reason for evoking Leatrice's childhood was to point to an unfamiliar area, a disorganized plane, of such a nature as being suitable to bestow on her a richer plumpness of foreign harmony through its foreignness. Memory adverts to a 'precedent,' whereas here we only wanted to indicate a deviating plane that, by chance, happens to intersect the other Leatrice plane and thereby reinforces her profile in the lines of intersection while at the same time smearing it in the unknown direction of the second plane. To use the language of a pedantic witchdoctor: the old narrative, which utilized the technique of memory, got stuck in the tedium of anemic time-monism; another experimental narrative strives to accomplish the absurdity of placing the various events, totally free of time, as pure spatial elements with the most capricious architectural tricks possible.

Leatrice's past needs to be fitted to her present in such a way that past and present are not in the relationship of a consecutive barely-relationship as recorded, but, let's say, the present is a horizontal sheet and the past is a parabolically curved plate which collides with the present at one point: one almost feels like resorting to that lethally primitive trick (if such it can be called) of having the part generally referred to as 'past' printed out on different paper, and not printing it in book form but in the form of an architectural construction, so that the texts at least relate to each other in angular relationships in space and not in the monotony of suffocating epic gravitation. The papyrus, which was fashionable before the book, that occasionally rolled up at both ends simultaneously, making the oppositely wound up ends collide in the middle, in its own crude external appearance was closer to the narrative experiment that we are trying to achieve, which is to tear narrative into pieces: to make more directions felt in time's place.

A second childish outward appearance: if we are not building walls from bodies of text, but a book, then at least let one connected part run on the left-hand pages and another connected part on the right-hand pages; the two unfamiliar details would thus externally signal the time-negating technique of 'colliding parallelism' or 'repellent harmony.' Instead of time-monism a schizophrenic aquarium: the individual narrative details swim to and fro in a free water of space instead of a paralyzing trough of time, like distracted fishes that constantly change their relationship to one another.

In a narrative forced into the time tunnel or the trap of plot there is no possibility of setting a couple of elements in various relationships: all the elements cling to the preceding one, unable to move. Yet it would be desirable that there be a void between Leatrice's past & present, so that the new narrative should effectuate the dramatic negative, the empty & unsubstantial narrative angles, the distancing space between events. Then Leatrice's past would be more of a factor leading out of Leatrice and would also accomplish narratively that which architecture has long cultivated: instead of gathering the branching parts of a building together into the closed form of an internal structure, it would lead them still further apart, so that a building would become a veritable center for dispersal rather than a collection.

Not long ago a glass church was built in the neighborhood: the left-hand glass wall swept like a huge frozen wave across toward the right-hand side (there was no difference between wall and roof), but there it did not bend inwards but stretched out a good distance until, all of a sudden, it broke off (naturally without any terminal frame): the only aim of the left-hand glass wall, therefore, was to leap to the right-hand side and into horizontality; on the right-hand side, by contrast, there rose gigantic black iron columns which pierced the glass roof and suddenly, with their bare and, from a practical point of view, meaningless ends, leaned to the left: they were like hockey sticks or those curved posts from which lifeboats are suspended — instead of supporting something in the manner of conservative pillars, they were aimless luxury giraffes and stretched apart the glass sail opposite them. Frivolous chiasmus in place of walls: the whole building served the purpose of unloosening itself to bits, harrowing across itself, properly contradicting itself with algebraic scruples — all in accordance to the taste of minus-sensitivity.

Is there any practical hope that sometime we will be able to feature two narrative details in such a way as, let's say, non-coplanar vectors: that they should not, despite translation (as mathematicians put it), fit into a single shared perspective-spasm?

Two kinds of distribution of space play a part in the classicism of dispersal: one of them is the fish promenade in an aquarium; the other is the exploding glass church. With the first the essential thing is that every narrative detail should move freely, that no element should have a fixed spot, that they perpetually perform the most radical Brownian-dance;[96] with the second, on the other hand, it is a matter of a couple of unfixed elements of this group being set, for the purpose of harmonization, in a unique spatial situation so as to be able to cast cunning shadows on each other, and be able by diagrams of self-avoidance and self-withdrawal to render a new-tasting sensual substance perceptible.

In the new narrative there is no kind of succession: If a narrative should by chance appear in book form, that is only because of constraint and powerlessness; in truth, any detail might occur anywhere; the whole work might be rearranged at any time. A novel's scope is not identical to the sum range of its narrative elements, but is much greater, just as the basin of an aquarium is greater than the mass of the fishes in it. The unity of a structure does not manifest in the geometrical assemblage of its component elements, but in part in the extreme *& non-plus* volatility of the totality of component elements, in part in the infinite extent of the wave-space suggested by them. That Leatrice past also has the sense that, according to old *bon ton*,[97] it is novelistic at precisely the time when she wishes to strip off from herself the last strap of the narrative combination underskirt, so that it can also be treated as the customary etiquette expected on saying farewell to a style: perhaps the last polite hypocrisy, a *narratomorphia hypocritica*.

Ena & Leatrice's intermittent chat in the taxi

The car turned toward the sea again, next to the beach. White crests of waves on the light-blue water: not lacey-frothy surf, but sharp and regular thin cords, the curved teeth of an enormous comb, which slowly, in parallel, in the rhythm of a paternoster elevator, approach the shore, where they come to an end mutely, without any uncertain flattening out & nirvana-frippery.

— The water *per se* would make a fine sample for a material: blue, light blue, densely waved bands molded on its own account & going through that, those white snaking lines similar to nets of brash machine stitching.

— To my way of thinking that's... er... what'sit, what's she called, that little hotel proprietress...

— Who? Lemonier's wife, you mean?

— No way! Lemonier's wife was never able to dress well, she never had the dresses — no, that little woman whose husband we used to say puts on weight day after day, in the morning...

— Oh, yeah, Myra Fritz. Yes, but that was sewed on.

— The hell it was! She had a long yellow coat with light-green zigzags in sort of triangles — (she demonstrated on her knees with a fingernail) —, like parquet tiles, out and then in, like so. Indeed, now it comes to my mind, it wasn't parallel at the end, but somehow widened — (her voice mused & she wearily pulled her finger from her knees) —, or else it got wider on the way down. Yes, of course, because patterns as huge as that are not made on a dress...

— Well, there's nothing to stop one just like that being made, but I can't be sure of that. You're wrong, though, about that being a pattern because it was all sewn on, I remember that quite definitely. It was all hand-stitched; after all, I was still chatting with her.

— I didn't know that. Were you acquainted with her? She was one of those morning women, with every dress she had being suitable as morning wear.

— Yes?

— She was always striking in the morning; she did not so much as show herself in the evening.

— I had talks with her in the evening — on more than one occasion. Not at our place.

— It could be that it was only me who didn't see her, but others also say that she was atrocious in the evenings. She had on ghastly slips with two kinds of shoulder straps, one of them being broad as a driving belt.

— Oh, sure! She wore that in the daytime as well. She had a lace blouse that I could see through. An ivory-colored bit of trash.

— But she was impeccably dressed in the morning. That yellow coat also.

— No question, somehow the whole woman was a morning type.

— Haha, Donna A.M., ante meridiem?

— Admittedly it has somehow now become a widespread type of fashion & woman, maybe via sport. It has given rise to ante meridiem-people.

— Still, the evening dresses are also very...

— Yes, but they somehow look odd on them.

— Nah.

— But, my dear, the day before yesterday, hang on, the day before yesterday? When was it that the proprietor announced he was going to get married?

— What do I know, it's not important.

— You're right, but the weather was great. I went down to the beach here. And I had seen the same girls dancing the evening before at the club's supper evening. Firm sunburned skins & pink lingerie.

— Pink?

— What do I know, one of those slick salon colors.

— Yes, there are lots of people who say that they have no place, but then, that's fashion for you! Wearing untanned leather on lace, silk on lacquer, terry cloth on taffeta, and things like that, so a decadent Brussels-cobweb appliquéd to a peeling pattern, sports-red skin is like a breath of fresh air, isn't it?

— I don't know, on her the dress hung weirdly, like a liturgical masquerade on a priest — somehow nothing, but nothing, to do with one another; the whole get up shrieks of external appearance.

— That's exactly what I find attractive: when my parents and I were in Moscow I saw some big ceremony for the very first time and the priest did not look as if he was wearing anything but as if he was walled between four giant osculatories so that he could hardly move — what was good about it was that he was suffocated behind the symbol, he disappeared and died in his own allegorical masquerade. Of course, you use the term 'masquerade' sarcastically.

— Of course I do. Everything that does not come from inside one, measured to one, tailored from one's body, related to one, is a mask. Those are naïve ambitions, dissolving the body in symbols, and that kind of thing; the fact is all symbols are nonsensical & dead burdens under which a person breaks up, and there is no sense in allegory having its fill of human flesh, quite irrespective of the fact that a sleeping naked person is much more...

— Yes, I'm well aware, but you don't understand.

— I have seen human beauty, life, nature, in short everything, most perfectly in the north.

— You can see that here, on the beach. Are the Smith girls still down there?

— I don't know, or rather I only saw the younger one, imagine, in a new swimsuit.

— Does that mean goodbye to the green and silver?

— Not quite, because she bought a green one this time, too, or rather it's made of a peculiar opalescent material that I have only seen before in raincoats; it has a belt made up of wide bone plates, almost as big as a lifejacket or whatsit made of 'blocks' of cork.

— Yes, that reminds me, the older one became melancholic or whatever, that's what I heard, it could be...

— The young one was also very downbeat. Flatfooted.

— Yes, a person gets a sinking feeling going about on sand anyway, but she always went around even more clumsily, downright tenderizing the sand with every step she made, like those tamping bars with which flagstones are rammed into the ground, biff-bam! Bim-bam.

— Here the body is somehow turned into a cult, & for that reason alone one can't really talk about it. What is going on here, when it comes down to it?

— Well now, what is there? — Lea laughed, and she wanted to slap both hands on her thighs like a triumphantly mocking statistician who is slapping a hand on a directory when someone doubts to his face in certain data. Then, with a sense of melody, she sought some asymmetrical counter-subject to the jeering-mirthful — What is there? — and, smiling melancholically, repeated quite drily, sniffing the air back in official knowledge of expertise: — What is there? Enakins, what is there? There is something.

This time, because the slapping of the thighs had not come off due to the shaking of the car, she now, by way of a correction, tapped her pressed-together legs with little pats and strokes.

— Now then, that's something else, but it's still not what I saw there and want: neither flirting nor mysticism leads to the body.

Both were looking toward the beach: the sea was slanting like a furrier's table — dense blue streaks from 'it's own,' with big white fringes, a bit convexly, disturbing parallelism with a wattless thread of power à la Mainbocher or Augusta Bernard[98] — the minimal modification of external geometrical-symmetry, perversely, is likewise one of the basic schools of bio-ornamentation.

— Hey! Isn't that Fritz — Myra Fritz?

— The one on the beach who is putting on her shoes, further away from the water?

— Where? I can't see that. Oh! Yes, the one in checks or whatever. Her? No. I don't think so, it wasn't her I was thinking of, but... oh dear! That's put paid to that. Are we now going to walk with the fence on the side all the way?

— No, you'll be able to get a view again right away; indeed, an even better one to the best of my recollection. I've come this way a lot of times; in fact one can see back as far as being able to look into the street where *The Perspective* is located; in any case it protrudes as far as the sidewalk.

---

lessons of the coastal waves for the history of ideas,
simile from the science of electricity:
the separation of power & intensity; success in fashionableness

---

The leaves of the tree branches sputtered as they rapped on the roof of the car; indeed, the branches themselves almost got caught in Lea's hair like an inverse Absalom. The sputtering, damp coolness and concentrated noise of the car ceased a few seconds later and the friction of the rubber tires ran out again into infinity while Lea and Ena shrank back from life size to seaboard dwarfishness. They jumped to beside the sea abruptly and suddenly, this time quite close; at the same time, a white line clang close to the shore and vanished; the hiss of the tunnel of trees and the honking of the car were still clamoring in their ears, so they were under the impression that it was just due to deafness on their part that they could not hear the disappearing white band of waves; the obliquely smooth sea as a whole was incompatible with muteness, so that Ena even rubbed her ears in order to hear the blue-dimensional phalanx. It remained silent, however, like a vigorous orchestra behind double glazing — the white-flecked flat blue steps, which seemed to be continually swelling and yet stayed strictly horizontal, came one after another, spread themselves, collided, became nothing in an abstract tempo, reminiscent of the Capitoline steps in Rome.

One of the basic stratagems of their mysticism was that the wind-generated waves were not parallel to the shore, so that they were slightly askew when they hit the mirror-smooth watery sand: there was maybe two-and-a-half meters deflection for every hundred meters of shore line, but that was just enough for the element each time it went into a dizzy spell to express its monumental foreignness. The coastal strips were far from each other, with the far ones drawing more closely together (but keeping up their skewedness throughout) so that as a whole it reminded one of some form of line spectrum — with those, a similar sort of rhythm predominates in the lines — broad bands are rare, but thinner ones are densely packed, to the extent that life scans those shadow trochees. Wattless running on zero power was, in any event, very characteristic of them because it counterbalanced the clumsy logicality of the Neptunian 'primeval element' with incisive coquetry: everyone expects chaotic feats of strength from the sea, theatrical pushing forward of Noah's vintage, high-tide baroquery, or rather those are what one senses, but the mute &

millimetrically slanting surf-*rayé* flatly denied all such things & for preference gave finicky answers that would pass muster in salon society.

Of course, 'salon society' & 'finickiness' could only come to mind at all as long as the childish myth of the sea lived in one's memories — once that had been forgotten the slim lines had nothing to do with 'finickiness.' If the phase difference of intensity & electromotive force in A.C. electric power comes to precisely 90°, then the expended positive and negative energies will continually alternate with each other, and therefore, naturally, no work is performed: the impression Lea had was that something of that kind was also taking place in those endless wires of surf and endless blue space resonators, in Neptune's fashionable electricity plant: for one thing, the intensity and power weave separately, or in other words, both the power & the intensity can be seen in their absolute nakedness, their impossible logicality — for another thing, as a consequence of precisely this purification to absoluteness, the net work is zero.

As she watched the dumb sinus lianas swerving to the coast, she perceived that duality involuntarily trying to imitate the sea in her eyes and in her willing muscles as positive: absolute power and zero work. The rare lines of surf and the blue mass of water beneath them were also in some kind of relationship of 90° delay in respect to each other: both radiated an infinitely pure tension, but the two performers were timed so grotesquely that perfect inactivity, empty impotence, came of their seesawing to-and-fro. That forcible time-extinction, or delay-injection, can be smuggled into any conceivable orgy of power, and that bifurcation will occur: absolute power one way and current separately, the edge of a wave one way and the blue block of power separately, thought one way and action separately, so that there is no force in the surf linearity of a thought, whereas there is not so much as an atom of thought in the naked force diagram of a deed.

The sea, then, is in no case uniform: the waves go one way and the power meanders another; precisely the most banal symbols of power turn out to contain absolutely no power, they are just abstract intensity-specters. On the other hand, where the most muscular Tritons have a fling of their infinitely free strength, nothing happens, at most the great amphitheater of passivity can be seen in one singular place. (A young professor at the University of Halle, R. Klotz, saw the phase delay of intensity & power as being the crux of 20th-century thinking as expressed in the electrodynamic simile dimly suspected by Leatrice, the essence of which is the phase delay of intensity and power: *XX. Jahrhundert: eine radikale Gegen-isolierung von I und E.*)[99]

What she suspected to be the essence of the sea was also the essence of elegance: an elegant dress always entails the aforementioned delay-injection, or, in other words, pushes one's intensity-curve and power-curve far apart, and thereby simultaneously suggests absolute energy and absolute impotence: in the movements of an elegant woman one has a permanent sense that there is no force in them, the whole lot is abstract geometrical mimicry (Klotz's isolated absolute I), which, senselessly and in complete transparency, is hanging in the air, however, somewhere nearby, a few meters from the woman, the delayed force can be found as an absolute but invisible wave (Klotz's eternally deflected E). The closing account here, too, is the same as by the seacoast: mimicry absolute, power absolute, outcome zero. Leatrice, it should be added, adored dresses with lined patterns: she had a morning frock that was full of dense little black waves (an erotic SW radio transmitter of sorts), while on another coat five or six broad and horizontal stripes were circling round: on the first a zebra neurosis of undulatoriness came across, on the latter, a grandiose zero work.

— You can see her now — that white one.

— Lovely! She's got an American bathing suit on.

— No, not in the least! It's an ordinary white tricot, just a bit shorter than normal, which is why you dare not think it is just a tricot. But that's not Fritz.

— No, I can see it's not. But who is it? German, isn't she?

Unexpectedly, a roar got under way from the direction of the sea as if a load of pebbles were clattering along a tin slope onto which they were being dropped by a slowly bending crane. Was it the wind? Water? In any event it came from the direction of the sea, and what was striking is that its rhythm was not in the least parallel to the rhythm of the waves: under the influence of the rumbling the eyes immediately imagined more quickly accelerating waves, yet they continued to retain their slow streaming as if the visual part of a loud movie had been slowed to one-twentieth speed but the water-noise had not been synchronized.

To Leatrice this duality was almost impossible, as if she had had to play the piano in a different tempo than that layed down by a metronome. All the same, she voluptuously narcoticized herself in these asymmetries, in the slow multiplication by zero of the waves; as if the rings were just those outermost circles that had been struck by a god, given birth to millennia ago on splashing into time's enormous lake: the body fell as far into the sea as the distance of the focus of an eternal parabola. Yet still, on these virtually level waves, one could feel the gentle curve that carried within itself with such certainty the possibility of a focus existing infinitely far away, as if the place onto which Leatrice had just now hurled a skipping stone was just a couple of meters away.

Given that certainty she felt as if the car were running on the edge of a gigantic circle: a catapult into which two crammed together stones strained alongside each other. Ena and her. Another movement was the flood-like crescendo of the rumbling, then the evenly-gliding easy speed of the car as it ran across the paths of the dead-born waves and the sea din that had been connected to the wrong speed like a delicate moving instrument (an odometer dependent on the revolutions of the wheels) which the dense rule of the identical little lines of the display brings to a common denominator.

lessons of a swimsuited woman for the history of ideas ("movement history" & bio-ornamentation)

A tall, slim woman stood on top of a rock on the shore: as she slowly pulled off or put on her shoes, it was evident from her clumsiness that all her muscles were still set to ward off the swirling azure buffeting of the waters; birds, too, once they have alighted, carry on reflexly fanning the air with a splashing so as they can switch from the stability of flitting about to the uncertainty of calmly standing around. She had on a tight, white bathing costume which crinkled into tiny grey wrinkles between her belly and her breasts as she bent down, but those vesicular, air-filled wrinkles were even better at bringing out the plasticity of her body (there is something vulgar, with a whiff of the waxworks, about the very word 'plasticity') than if it had been stretched on to her. The sea behind her seemed almost vertical as in those pictures of Bathsheba and Susannah[100] where the woman is standing at the very bottom of the painting and the bathwater stretches almost to the top and the horizon is only visible in a supernatural attic room a few millimeters under the upper frame: Waszilljewa Pintor[101] painted a picture of this kind entitled *Annunciation-Anadyomene*, in which the birth of Venus & the announcement by the angel Gabriel were combined into one moment (with an awkwardness typical of blasphemy):

a hermaphrodite Gabriel arriving from on high was at one and the same time Venus and the Virgin Mary, who has been bathing on the beach, is awaiting with widened eyes the message in which the Holy Ghost is bearing love.

The woman was standing on one leg and with the other she was starting to seek out the shoe that she was dangling from her hands — her muscular leg was wiggling about after her shoe, fluttering as a butterfly, like an old donkey that can only be prompted into moving by dangling a thistle in front of his nose from a long wand over its head. Leatrice had carried out similar movements in the morning when she had come out of the bathroom & attempted to peel off her swimsuit, which had coiled around her like the host of car tires on an abstract driver in Michelin-tire ads. She had to totter a bit, move around a bit by reflex, so that her body's autonomy could assert itself in a movement: these momentary spasms of asymmetries that flicker through muscles are a better expression of the type of autonomy on which Leville sought to base a neo-sensual '*Amour Thèse*.'[102]

A movement is the most evanescent entity but at the same time the most realistic & therefore most important feature of a person or a historical era: one gets nowhere with such nonsenses as 'muscular-spirited Renaissance' or 'preening Rococo,' but it would still be useful to deduce the characteristic system of gestures, the broad network of body rhythms, of an epoch as, after all, this is the most exalted possibility for the so-called Zeitgeist, to turn the tempo of a gait into a body posture and discover its last step in a huge pantomime. Of course, only naïve symmetrizing will spring up from parallels of 'spiritual life' & 'expression,' opposed to which it is a matter of precisely nonexpressive movements, of a bodily character independent of the soul, of nuances that may have a spiritual cause but, actually, are self-standing dramas. If I read a book on theoretical physics, before I work out the ultimate meaning & consequences of it all, it already somehow rises into my muscles and prepares new trajectories in my gestures and my handling of balance. "Movement is superior to character, the movement of an era superior to the spirit of the age; movement that we try to interpret independently of the soul is, if you will, absurd, but nevertheless based on some autonomy"— that was Leville's *introibo*-declaration[103] in connection to love. To locate the typical muscle tempo of an era, to systematize that into some sort of form, to take stock of it: a book like that (or a series of pictures? sculptural variations? There are certain synthesis plans about which we do not know whether they should be written, built, or given birth to by mothers?), if it is not just a variety show, it would be a worthy companion of the great Bio-Ornamentation.

Leatrice looked passionately at the shoe-donning woman: because her vanity was strong, in spite of all forcing-on; there was some rustic, boorish conceit in her — she groomed her body like a blasé dentist does an anonymous jawbone; that was why there had always been a brutal, medical quality to her whimsical theatrical elegance. When she dusted talcum powder under her arms, she did it with the motion a peasant girl makes on wiping the scum from her eyes. Later it may become clearer how peasant 'simplicity' (that is only an approximate word), poetic fantasy, and fashionable tricks snatched together with envious greed mingled in every piece of her clothing, her primping gesture, her measuring up of female companions, the tempo of her criticisms & her tone of voice.

It is unpleasant slicing Leatrice into summarizing ribbons of geological strata like this, but this is the way everybody constructs a senseless Gothic-residue of a 'personality' as best they can: encyclopedia-style paragraphs, lyrical tries at a theory, photographs and the wreckage of plays, embryonic-symbols and stylized monologues, sham activities and decorative crises, dry academic commentaries and popular portrayals, where, for the sake of lucidity (as in German textbooks), drastic simplifications & naïvely proportioned classifications are to be found — but maybe this methodological confusion in the approach to a person better expresses the individual's dimension-harem. It could be that the trinity adverted to above does not exist at all in Leatrice's vanity & dressing style: peasantry, fashionableness, and mysteriousness may only be pictorial concepts forced onto her, which stand here merely for the sake of mechanically respected analysis & are pure preconceptions; but just as there is no way of knowing beforehand the foodstuffs and appetites of an unknown animal, so the self-indulgence exhibited vis-à-vis her own nature can likewise not exactly be seen with Leatrice, so that all kinds of test foods have to be shoved before her lips, big mulberry leaves before a fussy caterpillar, in order to be able to see what she will take a bite of, how much she eats, & when she desists, and in that way she gradually eats out a colorful character-menu for herself, in much the same way as one cuts out houses & manikins from children's comics.

---

rationalism & the alluvial age.
Heideggerian-love & Carnapian-love

Leatrice looked covetously at the white-swimsuited woman. In the distance one could not distinguish the water from the sand drifting in alluvial motions: it was as if the infinitely slow drama of the geological rhythm of the Earth's surface were taking place before them — the sea and land rocking in a single wave community, the silent seesawing to and fro, united all the ancient burden and youthful fluctuation of material. The main sense of the shifting of these spreading superficial waves (sand wasteland, dunes, grit, snow cover, shore-side mud) is this gently perfect paradox (the conceptual center of the Lyell-chorus): blind antiquity, Cyclops-antiqueness, heaviness in timelessness, with silky streaming in parallel, mirrored-airy motion, tortoise-rhythm revolution.

The poised white-swimsuited woman streaked above all these like a Dea Alluvialis who united in her person the branches of Touquéian culture: bio-ornamented predestination and absolutely fortuitous-mimicry. His more naïve colleagues, naturally, considered Touqué to be a simple automaton of 'rationalism' & were somewhat surprised when he treated culture like a plant or mineral formation: they did not notice that rationalism and psychologized nature (lyrical or deist 'bellevues') really did exclude each other, but ether-breathed intellectualism and the primordial forms of the alluvial age never did. What is nowadays called 'nature' by laboratory assistants or highbrow woman shopkeepers is just as specially structured, datable an invention, as the steam engine, or Pasteur's vaccination, and it has nothing rational or even metaphorical in common with the waters, fish, and plants of the alluvial age. Touqué enjoyed precisely that lyrical and metaphorical virginity in the forms of prehistoric ages (of course, here and there, that virginity was similarly steeped a bit in sauce): although the dimensions were much larger than in the 150-year-old version of 'nature,' it was nonetheless a much airier, more abstract, & flexible world than the Shelley-Charcot 'nature.'

When in days gone by poets wished to rebuild the sanatorium of Arcadia, the big nihil barracks of the Celts or the rustic idyll, so that the foundations of a counter-citadel of 'rationalism' should finally be laid, they made the mistake of not keeping a smug quarantine, and thus the occasional component of rationalism was dragged into the above institutions with resulting confusion. There is no doubt that in every absolute rationalism there is a logical schizophrenia, as a result of which the brain seeks to swing into total irrationality: the aforementioned poets only half-recognized, or even only one-eighth-recognized, the essence of rationalism, and therefore they could only half-imagine, or just one-eighth-imagine, the opposite, much less accomplish it.

Touqué did not see any kind of god, the tyrannical energies of life, or the 'brain's solace' in the reconstructed areas of prehistory, but pure nonsense, an unknown farce which knew nothing about people, and he very much needed that. The more autonomous and passionate Touqué's hunt for rationality became, the clearer it was to him — precisely as a consequence of the abnormally intact autonomy — that some 'other' direction existed: if a person walked in a single direction for hours on end, then one would physically feel like a slur, in the strictest sense of the word, in one's innermost muscles, like hypnotic magnetic hooks in the convolutions of one's brain: the unknown directions in which one does not go, so that the true target and the path leading to it become a little ludicrous flourish in a line (in vain does one 'know for sure' that one is walking on the one & only right path) around which the unknown paths revolve as booming & mottled waves, as a positive and homogeneous 'other-land,' or more precisely a 'non-land.'

If one is an analyst who has run wild, then one notices, for one thing, the basic mechanism of the analysis, the mechanism no longer being rational and analyzable, but a biological endowment, a senseless strength spoof, like the dozy reflex twitchings of starfish; for another, one suspects increasingly that if one is so analytical and only-reason, then some material or sphere ought to exist in relation to which one feels oneself as being so analytical, so that one willy-nilly develops a pro-analytical peri-rational milieu that will not become the polemical counterpart of reason but its negative pair, a necessary concomitant, viz. irrationality.

One of the chief comic elements of the Romantic 'nature'-concept is that it is brimful of rational bacteria and yet seeks to eradicate rationality; in prehistoric lands and in extinct animals, all rationality is missing, yet with their own logical anarchy they give rationality all the sharper plasticity, indeed, they develop and stimulate it. A swimsuited woman hovering above the prehistoric forms of the dunes is a good experimental constellation to signal a necessary alternation of blind alluvium & capillary-casuistics to the world of love (*"Impromptu Alluviale ou amour heideggerisant — Impromptu Néo-rationnel ou amour carnapisant."*)[104]

Ena & Leatrice carry on chatting in the taxi

Leatrice and Ena felt that when they spoke about matters of indifference to each other, the whole thing was just a labored intermezzo, and thus they also used different voices: that soft voice without emphases or punctuation which expresses that whatever they say is all in parenthesis and no more than a bored brushing of the consciousness for hygienic purposes; sometimes the sea is in the business of displaying such a not-so-much intermezzo as supramezzo: its top is a thin, garish green, transparent & porous layer of water that slides to & fro whereas a dense, dark-yellow, almost grey mass is stretched under it like a dead elephant.

— She could be German, I don't know her, *fesch.*[105]

— What stupidity it used to be when people were always harping on about German women not being attractive, & yet...

— The difference comes out best if you look at a French drawing and a German photograph.

— I admit that German fashion and German coquetry...

— Such a thing as coquetry is unknown to Germans.

— You mean with them frivolity also rests on a Hegelian base? But take it from me it is naïve to think that this abstract and scientific fashionability (an engineer's clothing instead of a dressmaker's, eroticism building on clinical accuracy instead of naïve Latin lewdness), a mistake to think something is wrong or unnatural because it is programmatic, because it is Hegelian or engineers' linen-ish…

— Maybe a bit of untidiness or irregularity is needed for there to be anything truly interesting in fashion.

— You know, for instance, I was starting to say just now, you remember, I was up north in the Staalbreck women's clinic; never mind that it's not German, Scandinavian things as well are largely like that: well, that was scientific, a sanatorium, medical matter, but the perfection that could be brought out of the body there…

— What? What could be brought out of the body?

— Some of them were highly strung, others with organic diseases, and the female physicians: together they formed a tight unit, and out of diseases and medical science they created a life based on a body awareness on which combined…

— Trust me, it must have been very boring if it combined everything; harmonies of that kind…

— Don't suppose it was based on simple hygiene, on general health…

— What was good about it then was not due to the hygiene but to the old disharmonies. Harmony? With the body? I have to laugh when you come up with sexual panaceas and psychic life preservers. The sole nutrient that fully satisfies our bodies and makes them flower is catastrophe, physical catastrophe! But the idea is precisely to place those physical matters that, up till now, have been called catastrophes in such a perspective that their strength, which was possibly due to a certain moral or other conceptual involvement, should be a pure internal physical game, a physical drama.

— Oh, Lord, just because you kiss each other in glass hangars and musical instruments assembled from curettes, those crises are still...

— Crisis! Who's impressed by yesterday's type of crisis, those 'struggles,' Biedermeier and *spieß*-dilemmas?[106] The new 'crisis,' if that's what you need, lies in the direction of satisfaction; besides which, I consider the crisis-fashions of the day before yesterday to be mystic-masked ribaldry of no caliber; on the other hand, if you lie down naked in the sun in cold air...

— Cubist concrete-altar, neo-Gothic glass letters?

— Knowing everything, which is chemistry, geology...

— What? Now you're coming with that stuff Leville sputtered the other day in the classroom doorway about deliberateness increasing pleasure rather than inhibiting it?

— Far from it, because on that point Touqué happens to have exactly the same opinion as you, & he also says that my notion of eroticism is the most pedantic philosophical-system, a boring rigorism, and when we are drowning in lesbianism we don't know whether we have a body at all and we are merely celebrating the cold paragraph-fetishes of a lesbian esthetic.

— Yes, I remember when he spread his arms wide; that German periodical on photography was lying near the doorkeeper on the windowsill of the cubicle, and it was open on the page where there was a picture entitled 'Visitation.'

— It was magnificent.

— Two unclothed women meet on the shore of a lake. And Touqué exclaimed: Let the theoreticians of Lesbos come unto me, because theirs is the kingdom of heaven, for they are innocent like a seventy-year-old virgin astronomer who has not seen his own loins; they prostrate themselves before Sappho because to them she signifies a hypothesis, a decorative concept, and a system.

— Leville's irony does not mean anything: when my Swedish recollections come to mind, then the whole thing is ridiculous; if I juxtapose Leville's weedy little French aphorisms with those marvelous facts ... Leville always clings to words, and with him everything is riding on that primitive scheme: to call sensualism algebra, rationalism eroticism and that's that; he gives himself airs with the towns of the south of France and their both naïve-refined culture.

— I don't know. I suspect I would not feel comfortable in them.

— I'm of the belief that the most ideal land for one to find everything harmonious is the low North: the Latin south and Russian east are bad exaggerations, but a southern Swedish sun, a single ...

— Don't think for one minute that is how it is, Ena; everyone says that this or that is extreme, that here mysticism is carried too far, there petty bourgeoisness is carried too far: in the abstract these are truly exaggerations, but only when you ponder on some imagined balance, a harmony taken in an arithmetical sense, and you make an abstract theory of that and then compare those 'exaggerations' to that; but in reality harmony and one-sidedness are not opposites, or rather they do not exist as such when taken separately, because genuine harmony comes from centuries of practice of exaggeration; after all, Ena, it is not a matter of there being harmony when there is mind alongside feeling, soul next to body, I don't know what next to something else again, which is its opposite, because those are just theoretical symmetries and arithmetical means, whereas passionateness in life, one-sided passionateness, from an abstract point of view, if it is a constant attribute of a people or a person, bestows on that people or person the strictest internal unity; indeed, it can only be harmonious if it makes one-sidedness of that sort its own, adjusts everything to that, judges and lives from that point of view, and in that way a Spaniard is harmonious and a Finn is harmonious because they have both made one-sidedness their daily bread.

Lea was able to deliver the lesson so well because the contemplative nuns had once been attacked (how many times?), and one of her priest relatives had defended those girls in the monastery against the accusation of 'one-sidedness.' There was a lot of childish humility and superstitious respect for grown-ups in Lea, so that the old gentleman's defense document made a deep impression on her, especially because she perceived it as excusing her own faults, and she was able to perceive even her hysteria to be a harmony, which was nothing other than a unified viewpoint; however capricious she might be, she was nevertheless capable of setting all the other things in life into that structure with the greatest spontaneity. It is a small-minded idea that the ideally harmonious in life would be to reconcile the most diverse concepts, all conceivable possibilities: that would only be a dull pastiche or 'quantitative synthesis,' but under no circumstances harmony. The fact that the qualities of a Latin and a Germanic 'soul,' for example, cannot be brought into harmony, did not signify a renewed recording of a well-known racial & psychological absurdity for Uncle B., but a fight against the abstract ideal according to which we should try to reconcile the one-sidednesss of different cultures within ourselves, for the sake of humanity, of so-called higher interests, which naturally can only lead to dilettantism & a show-off humbug balance (to the official pseudo-Greek pseudo-order). In other words, there was nothing special in the article, but enough for a girl to get by on until the day she died.

the significance of 'oïd' thinking ('logoïd' instead of logos, *et cetera).* Mal-à-propos *& structure. The flirtations of title & subject*

The fleeting recollection of B.'s article was maybe not entirely *mal-à-propos* (it is possible for precisely the *mal-à-propos* to be the main determinant of the rhythm of a structure), because when we need to insert in gross summary a few of Ena's memories, then there is a conspicuous peril of cobbler's antitheses: on one side, Lea's recollections as a stylized symmetrical '*enfance de…*';[107] on the other side, the counter-picture, the psychological contrast-ornament. What it concerns, in truth, is that many perspectives & contradictions should be united, and to do that perhaps a naïve step, a prelude, is necessary when one presents as yet prepared and primitively regular contradictions, drastic symbols & raw summaries.

It is as if a bidirectional clarification were starting in the new narrative: one of them, veering on even more naïve than the naïve, where only raw consciousness is present and, by virtue of that, only crude schematics, tables of people, outlines of plants, and cadastral situations are to be found, without the least lifelikeness: this is a state of a maniacal table of contents. Running opposite that naïve consciousness is the other direction of narrative that one might dub the all-elucidating and all-destabilizing direction of dream, where every detail is for itself & free not only of stereotypes but of life itself.

Consciousness and dream, stereotype and irresponsible unhingedness, are the two specific points of the compass between which experimental narrative is located, but in such a way that with every move of any significance it orients toward both poles simultaneously. What happens, what kinds of movements take place, within those limits? First of all, there is a need to fashion the fundamentals and then for a first, temporary synthesis of those fundamentals. Of fundamental elements, ordered with dogmatic impertinence, there are three: human, thought, landscape. One instantly notices, however, that one of the fundamental elements is not human but only a 'barely confined homoïd'; the second element is not a thought but a 'logoïd,' frizzing yet weaving itself as an endless, flowerless plant, and, finally, the third basic element is not a landscape, just a blasé & misprinted astronomical plagiarism, a sort of 'geoïd.'

(If someone characterized the culture of the 20th century by saying that it turned away from the normal and concerned itself solely with the world of infras and ultras, they might just as well characterize it with the collective name of '-oïd thinking,' since at first we perceive everything in an amœba-like swaying to & fro of identity, and construct strict individuals out of that constant oscillation: false sand statues from a concrete fog of homoïds, the sensible-fictive loneliness of *logos* from the eternal and nonsensical-true lace of logoïds, etc.)

A human being is his own horrible plasticity, in his bizarre totality, with his physical concreteness, is already a possibility of fantastic pseudo-anatomy. Homoïds are just centers from which rings run away and around which rings press close together, or in other words, they concretize mystically, for another thing, they grow dim and melt away: this is the normal course of the crisis of plasticization; it is not the individual people who are still important but the notion of 'human plasticity.' That state does not suggest outlines, but inorganic details, hyperplastic features, and tries to summarize these capriciously dashed-off details (not skeletons of compositions but precisely the reverse) in accordance to a forced synthesis-logic as if those details had originally been born in the spirit of some far-reaching broad concept. The 'impromptu' quality remains, then: wild-thrombosis of detail in pale-glass veins.

Besides which the logoïd lives as a tendency: alongside horrible anatomical precision (i.e., fantastic and decorative body-analysis, improbable soul-luxury), extreme abstraction, rhetorical program, scientific reflection, prayer and other things. On the left, masquerade, on the right, speculation: by now that is no longer a human nor a thought, still less a harmonious union of the two, but two isolated extremes: the human, distorted by a desire for 'precision,' demonic hyperplasticity — the thought that is mechanized apart by barbarian and naked speculation for its own sake. Certain speculations sometimes encounter certain masquerades: theories develop organs, profile-orders, and gesture-constellations, in accordance with an epic Lamarckism; noses, ears, and kneecaps, on the other hand, noses, ears, and kneecaps suddenly transform into syllogisms through pathological consistency. But considering that the time for the first maturing of the fundamental elements, it is widely reckoned, is characterized by impatience, the naïve parallel between profile and theory is not permanent: thoughts that should only be free to line up under a certain definite mask-emblem stick to other narrative embryos & thus a form of drawing up is engendered that is propelled by the natural force of Mal-À-Propos: a hodgepodge of scraps of photographs and segments of leading articles in 500-fold enlargement, X-ray negatives, erroneously glued-on aphorisms & overhasty diagnoses.

That still leaves the 'geoïd': the indefinite geological backdrop. Of course, that is just as much an exaggeration as the plastic cell comedy with the creation of the human. There masquerade instead of human, here, too, geo-anatomical bluff instead of 'landscape': land masquerade instead of land. If one is so polite as to perceive this phase as a narrative spring-stage, then this chaos can also receive a bit of advantageous coloring, the poetic quality of *Ludus Preliminaris.*[108] By poetic we mean, exceptionally, a precisely defined thing: the notion of chaotic associations as fresh flowers, a way of looking at an undulating cultural hodgepodge that one can only call 'charming.' 'Flower': that has a degrading metaphorical quality, but that has to be disregarded, and, if possible, think of, e.g., a complete German content for the flower concept: this includes a scientific description of entelechial development, the rapture of smell, diversity, and concreteness, raw rigorism and decorative frivolity, the theological burden and sense-flipping elegance of life.

(Before a distinction was made in the new narrative between the 'consciousness'-stratum & the 'dream'-stratum, which alternate in the same way as a warm and a cold wave, or a jasmine-scented and a gas-smelling band of air in a spring breeze: the sudden enforcement of flowerness on intellectual confusion is, actually, one of the manifestations of a dream-tendency. For a while one takes pedantic words and fancy distinctions strictly in accordance with their meaning, but then, all of a sudden, the words are released from the pathological blood pressure of sense, and weightlessly they blossom higgledy-piggledy like surprise flowers: this is not lazing into decorativeness but a fateful transformation.)

Free from estheticism, a Reims cathedral and a flower that answers to the name of orchid (true, there is a repellently cheap phonetic prancing about the very word 'orchid') may be treated alike on that basis: almost humorously interpret Gothic art in its entirety, in which the holiest content of life & most capricious game are united — the humor of Gothic art is far from what can be seen in sculptures of chess-playing monkeys and the figures of eel-devouring nuns, but it is precisely in the most abstract construction that the eternally-tragic Propos and the flitting Mal-À-Propos unite.

If, for example, one were to discover a document in which the work of the architect of a Gothic church was not named the Church of St. John the Baptist (as it has been styled for 500 years) but Convallaria Majalis or Cyclamen: what a revolution in outlook we would go through. Scholastic dark ponderables, conceptual sketches pregnant with God's gestures, the mass of centuries, an affected notion of history: hitherto the church had been assembled of these. And now appears the strange-sounding name of a flower, a strange-looking form of plant: that was the architect's intention. So why did he not draw the flower itself, or carve it out, or why did he not have it planted with a cloister garth, or why did he not have an enamel medal minted and found an order to go with it? He built a church.

The struggle between object and title now gets going: if the directory of titles for the totality of memorials of the Middle Ages were to be discovered, what surprises would be in store for us, what conceptual constraints. We would learn of the baptismal font in the Baptistry of St. John in Sienna that it represents an aridly open-eye of sleeplessness; about a monstrance decorated with waves that it represents the last rings of the river Piave lapping above a drowned brother; about the cathedral at Orvieto that it signifies a boyhood sin omitted from a general confession, and so on: from similitude (which is as yet a primitive state) to a fierce and irrational wordplay.

History could also be rewritten, as well as cityscapes: instead of saying (& seeing) that "from the church and over the bridge we reach the Well of St. Basil" we would say (& see) "after the washout of the sowing of the crop, impoverished priests were supported by migratory birds deviated from their path," etc. A dictionary of historical 'floral-irony' ought to be compiled: the Ferrante, the butcher of Naples, would be denoted by a dewy daisy, Mme de Maintenon by a cotton thistle, and the destruction of the grand Armada by the momentary leaning into the shade of two irises. This '*ironica infloreatio*' is the opposite and redeeming extreme of the vulgar products of consciousness like, e.g., a Hegel-tailored '*kultur-schematische Defloreation*.'[109]

Before us, then, we have the basic material for prose in its initial state: without forcing on it the 'flower'-concept it is just a neurasthenic schema, a raw-intellectual torso. (An evil-minded person, of course, will be of the opinion that a muddled state either suggests the 'awakening of spring,' i.e., the poetry concentrated in the 'flower'-concept, or will see in it only disintegrating rubble and not manage to impose a new meaning with a new label, in just the same way as bad genres cannot be ennobled into pure type with an ironic-sincere confession-definition. That is true, but what if the onlooker is nonetheless taken in and that person keeps on trying to fit the Reims cathedral into the unnatural orchid until in a fortunate moment that person has the unexpected impression that this way of looking at things is the only 'objective' one: St. John's Cathedral, or Reims Cathedral, is truly a flower, truly humorous, a darkly chaotic altar-swirl: a radiant satyr-somersault — one is aware of more than one such miraculous cure.)

Ena & Leatrice carry on chatting

— Well OK, but you have to admit that one person is like so & another like so, and a third will then unify the properties of the other two, not on a path of theoretical deliberation; that is stuff & nonsense, of course, but it's simply in it as a uniform…

— How did you find your way there? I know, I heard something, the young Behrens girl also made a bid for it; then there were no more lawyers than you & her?

— She wasn't even a lawyer, she studied economy or commerce, and only took that on as a luxury or, if it comes to it, as a compulsory private lesson, I don't know, those shared lessons & links in the syllabus were always murky — but still, yes, I know she also applied but she wanted something different from me, something else, because mine was paid for by the Norwegians, hers by the domestic authorities — I don't know...

— It's odd, but I can nevertheless understand perhaps best of all that your illness gave you so many ideas. You were operated on as well, I seem to recall.

— Sure.

— For you that was the reason and basis for your happiness, that's how you put it. Yes, it's rather like with saints, they often fell ill, and that was when they first began to contemplate, & that's how they became...

— Yes, I was only a bit smarter and the reverse of Ignatius and others: in point of fact, illness delivered me back to the body, it was in illness that I definitively felt that material might; when I was very poor I felt a kind of gleefulness, and while I was recovering I became melancholic. That *Embarquement*, which I wrote around then, was nonetheless cast in a cheery spirit.

— No doubt your suffering was, so to say, 'pure.' Because some are dirty. Some sufferings are hygienic, regular, and abstract, like martyrdom, self-flagellation, fasting, and all manner of self-inquisitional gymnastic exercises; there are much the same in illness, and it is then that one can reflect on them and possibly accept them, but the whole thing is of no importance, and I above all don't want that. I must particularly not want it, because back home there is a mindset according to which the only thing of importance is that melodious acquiescence.

— Yes, perhaps those two poles are most in existence where you come from; I don't know whether you personally are truly representative, but with you, too, wouldn't you say, miracles and sufferings are oddly associated, I mean, on the one hand, the darkest suffering as a need, the great epileptic canonization of misery — &, on the other hand, saints, miracles, and legends;

or in other words, the heavenly diversions of gentlefolk, a Christo-aulic, miracle-privileged aristocracy, no?

— That's a bit wide of the mark; don't take it amiss, but maybe things are not quite like that. How long were you in the hospital?

— It was a fabulous, new building, haven't you seen it yet? Of course you have.

— I have, but I was not paying attention then, I did not truly feel how much it was a part of itself, house or landscape is a living organ of one's person, no? Either I had no such feeling, or I did not take it seriously; I know, you pointed it out, but we still thought it was a German observatory.

---

from Ena's past: the origins of the G. Staalbreck clinic; three buildings: 17th century, the first modern (myth & microscope), & second modern buildings, leading into those: prose & suffocating 'quiddity'; how is it to be avoided?

"O God, plumassier most orthodox, why did you plunge plumbeous turrets in conical stars?": those were the lines that Halbert wrote in response to one of Ena's Norwegian photographs, which she had thrust under his bench during class, while Leville derived from them, via Halbert, the entire 'English mentality': myth, irony, meekness, naïve destruction, heroic stupidity, phlegm, saga, *spieß*-pantheism. Gerda Staalbreck's clinic was in Romsdal, but the hospital's history did not start with her.

Roughly two kilometers from the present-day clinic stands P*** Castle, fashioned by immigrant Germans into the way it looks now; the castle used to belong to a family of rich peasants, but marrying into the family was a German aristocrat who had all his relations brought there. Examination of the nature of such peasant strongholds and their socio-legal significance was an open question in Norwegian historical seminars and a flourishing subject for dissertations: how did these pass from aristocrats to peasant families, and were they truly castles, true residential centers, or rather neglected big storehouses that immigrants had fashioned into castles, adopting the names of native peasant families, et cetera?

The castle was located on a mountainside and its most characteristic part was a church: its long nave projected far out of the extraordinarily steep mountain face like a huge drawer pulled out of a cliff cupboard; at its end were two cylindrical towers, like two untrimmed candles or mythical ninepins, on top of which were entirely flat, 17th-century onion domes. The church nave was slightly bent, so from certain angles it gave the impression of a stone railway train racing out of a tunnel under which a viaduct had disappeared, and it was now for ever half-stiffened in the air. Only half a block of wall, because the pulled-out church had a support, albeit one shorter than the base of the church. Two flying cylinders at the end of the supporting globe supported the towers but were a good deal skinnier and thus they bore a relationship to the cylinders of the upper bastion like the thinner tube does to the thicker outer one in a telescope that can accommodate it at any time.

Not only was the church crooked, but up at the front end, by the towers, it was also broader than where it started out of the mountain. The upper section (i.e., the church itself) was a whitish yellow; some patches of wall were zinc white, other sections were egg-yolk yellow; in contrast, the supporting mass, which could be inhabited, was of natural stone and brick, in sharp contrast to the whitewashed towers. It was all like a torn-out root which was now accidentally on display, or the parts of an electricity pole raised from the sidewalk, the above-ground part of which has assumed the street's facial features and color, while its long iron root is full of rust & earth, and, besides that, is slender, as if it had withered underground. The little black caps later attached to the tops of the towers resembled a stylized high fur cap with a coronet (which was no more than two crosswise bands that at their intersection were pressed down deeply & had a small cross over the indentation: a type of coronet like that); dark, ribbed umbrils of white-stalked mushrooms. The roof was not as dark as the tiles on the towers so that the whole building was overall reminiscent of the face of a fair-haired person with black eyebrows.

Lower down than this church was the actual 'castle' and roughly on the same level as the church was a third, largely windowless building. The three buildings, which, so to speak, hovered in the air next to the mountain like three cable-railway carriages, were connected by a serpentine road.

Here, once upon a time, two sisters lived in the greatest concord. One of them then married a parson, the other a German physician. The parson and his wife did not live in the castle, but in the village, yet a year later they decided to turn the castle into a hospital, and that duly happened. After three years Gerda returned (that was what the physician's wife was called): her husband had died but Gerda brought with her one of his female assistants and wanted to take over the hospital's management from her younger sister and the parson.

Gerda had completely changed in Berlin, so the two sisters now faced each other as opponents. From dawn to dusk she talked about not being able to build up a hospital with dilettante physicians starting off from piety: the building had to be converted, the whole thing commenced again completely from the beginning, and it was not permissible to adopt the naïve attitude that if someone is ill, they will be treated and that was that, for the whole person had to be transformed and the barbarian borderlines between disease and health had to be erased; a person's life should be redeemed with a consciousness of biological functions in which the difference between a sick and a healthy state would not have such a crude effect on the individual as it had done hitherto; people had to be persuaded to have the analogy of nature and body with the most extreme radicalism, etc.

Eight months after her husband's death a posthumous child was born: en route, in a peasants' house, with old women assisting, etc. (She had her son brought up in Southern France, by relatives of her husband who lived there, and who had asked for the child to be brought there.) In her mind raged the new 'body concept' that had been implanted by her female assistant (her dissertation had been on something called *'Metasomatische Therapie'*), whereas around her were superstitious crones with their folklore recipes for childbirth. In any case, having a child in her body for nine months was an irksome anachronism while in the meantime she was setting sail toward a new love with her female assistant: the attainment of motherhood and Sappho in parallel set up cunning interferences in her psyche.

Meanwhile in Kristiana she carried on the medical studies that she had started in Berlin and, after selling off part of the property she had inherited (in line with one of the clauses in the will she needed the agreement of her younger sister, but she forced it out of her) she built up the new clinic, where Ena had been among the patients.

The new wing was designed by a Belgian architect (he was acquainted with Gerda's young son) in tune with Scandinavian Cubist taste, and for precisely that reason it was closely connected to the old building, particularly to the church. The building consisted of three parts & as a matter of fact resembled a giant three-flight staircase that nestled sideways up against the foot of the mountain & was made of concrete: the walls were smooth, as if they had been cast in bronze. The windows were placed in canellure-like troughs; the fact that there was no edge at all in the building only reinforced the impression that this was not a matter of a building but of a molded iron skeleton or an abandoned casting. The embrasures of the windows showed the oval sweeps of human eyes and were reminiscent of the windows of racing cars and the cabin windows of zeppelin airships; even the window glasses were convex, as if they had been fitted with a Zeiss meniscus lens.

The architect had anyway always been partial to statue-like houses; indeed, he had carried out lengthy chemical experiments in order to devise as plastic a material as he could for his houses, in which he took as his starting-point drawings that depicted the regularity of certain curved bodies and figures, and he twisted round that basic balance all kinds of helix-variants as if a tube of toothpaste had been squeezed on them. As a result, he succeeded in creating the same abstract-erotic impression as was exhibited by the Gerda Staalbreck clinic: a Rodin statue that represented the regularity of the hyperbola based on a drawing in a geometry textbook.

The whole thing was egg-yolk yellow and shivered in the air almost like aspic, as if it had been tipped out from its mold that second, which no doubt was still lying somewhere near at hand. The square before the main entrance was one of the organs of the building's living body: the gate gave the shape of a barely opened mouth, the upper jaw jutted forward like a melting concrete petal, the lower one (like the hugely jutting lower jaw of an African lip-plate tribesman) protruded a long way forward, furnishing a semi-oval area, so that if one stepped fifteen meters onto the small terrace, one immediately came under the gate's magnetic sphere, because it sucked in the whole little forecourt, like a shovelnose fish draws in water. The entrance hall inside the gateway came next with its enormous glass windows, which were stave-like and enclosed the hall like a barrel.

The entrance hall represented legendary Ginnunga Gap in the following manner: both to the left and right there were six stained-glass windows that were broad at the top and narrowing lower down like the blades of a fan, whereas inlaid patterns of the stone floor picked up the outlines of the windows where the glass had left off, and all twelve met in the middle in 12 peaks like in a roulette wheel: the peaks really did each run into a colored and rotatable wheel of neon tubes. In that way the 12 images divided into three parts: a stained-glass image, floor mosaics, and a neon-tube whirligig center. The left-hand series of images portrayed the following: the sea, the meadow, the hill, the blue sky, the clouds — all of which were, in fact, sheets of gigantic colored photographs. On the right-hand side, by contrast, were red blood cells in colossal magnification, muscle fibers, microscope pictures of cross-sections of bones, skull X-rays, & finally cerebral convolutions. Legend has it that the giant Ymir was thrown into the primeval maelstrom of Ginnunga Gap, & from his body parts (blood, muscle, etc.) arose the Earth (water, land, et cetera). That was what was illustrated by the double series of stained-glass windows in the hall: in the middle was a little basin (a stylish porcelain chaos-figurine), above which spun the wheel of light.

The analogy that prevailed in this saga, and which Gerda had pictured with the above-described pedantry, represented the basis of her whole concept of medicine: by the connection of blood & sea, flesh & earth, hair & forest, she wanted to monumentalize a body awareness as well as to intimize an awareness of nature and thus to create a new monistic basic mood between human beings and landscapes. It was easy to criticize that radical mythology. She was upbraided for the most obvious consideration that it was not possible to make a metaphor, and furthermore such a trivial metaphor, the basic therapeutic principle, & if therapy was not the goal, it was not permissible to utilize a hospital for what was no more than developing a decorative human type, to treat sick people as rhymes, to mix up art & suffering, etc.

As an apology, Gerda launched a periodical in which everyone found only an unsettling mix of squirming compromises and awkward audacities. It was also soon evident that only so-called 'modernist' & 'esthete' patients who were anyway already brimming with faith in the reality of all sorts of metaphors checked in for treatment, so that the whole sanatorium became an ill-reputed casino for decadent girls.

Internal conflicts also emerged between Gerda and the female doctor in Berlin: both started out from an emphasis on 'materia' (though it signified an attack on materialism), but subsequently the Berliner woman hardened into dogmatic vitalism, sorts of pedantic-Nietzschean hygienic-principles (Nursery Dionysos!), whereas Gerda became more doubtful and poetic, and intellectually freer precisely on account of her melancholy.

Ena did not spot that crisis and unintentionally only perceived from it the Berliner voice (because Gerda herself, out of sentimental benevolence and a wearily assumed official intention: "in the interest of my clinic," often adopted the Berlin woman's words and principles, as it were, deceiving or reassuring herself that there was nothing that did not concur with her thinking), and the *Embarquement* essay that she wrote about her impressions here were totally not in Gerda's spirit (indeed, were more naïve & simplistic than the Berliner's). That is far from suggesting that Gerda was in some ways more 'conservative': behind her slightly fatigued ostensible-patience were much more radical inclinations than in the active cult of her female partner.

Even the very thought is stifling that in prose works of old a scene should remain forever in a so called definitive formulation, a tempest should forever be enacted in the same way, a building should slice up the rays of a setting sun in the same way (those rays reach among the columns of a glittering peristyle like the energetic fingers of the right hand into the corners of the fingers of the left when flexing a new pair of gloves: the line of columns is also a new order of stacking, the rays straining between them also give a palm-like form of hand, the fleeting spokes of shadow likewise give a velvet dactylocopy of fugitive Selene) instead of becoming instantly nonsensical on account of the description, useless by virtue of concrete visibility.

The above description of a clinic so much denotes that one specific clinic which, pulled by its own weight, suddenly sinks to a much deeper level of narrative, like a balance pan onto which one has shaken out a milligram more medicine than is needed: the whole building falls away and emptiness is left behind, but that emptiness is a hundred times more useful thing, belonging more to the place than one which is excessively 'some kind' of clinic.

Just as in nature there are 'material-colors' & 'space-colors,' so in literature there are 'crystalline' & 'gaseous' basic elements. There's a bundle of green-gold branches the color of which is perceived materially, as if the color were identical to the body of the leaf: it does not mean an artistic surplus, just the equalizing marking of material. On the other hand, there are some pine bushes the lower parts of which are dark green whereas their tips are golden green: here the color no longer denotes the material of the bush but is a dispersing ray, an immaterial foam of light that the eyes are incapable of squeezing between outlines, it all being so fountain-like & airy. The latter colors are, in fact, the true colors, which relate to the materialistic as whipped cream does to unbeaten liquid: clean whorls of space, unexpected springs & burst-open moraines, of the '*Welträumlichkeit*'[110] of German philosophers. Those light yellow pine branches are nothing other than fortunately placed space polarizers and dimension-free '*Um-uns-herum*'-traps,[111] with the help of which, all of a sudden, the most elementary space will become visible: they make a magic paper for children on which one merely has to trace with a pencil a drawing that, up till then, could not be seen to fill out; the more furiously one scribbles, the freer the picture becomes as a result of the irritation.

That 'space-catching'-role is conspicuous on the branches: one can sense that the golden green color is not at all theirs, only a foreign frolicking, a whooping spiral of agony, which is unable to sit back into the invisible phenomenon-nude of 'space,' any more than a wriggling fish into the Galathea-ton-weight nothingness of the sea. The space that gets caught up in the unexpected compulsory pseudo-masks of color on the Husserlian hooks of pine needles is not, of course, either geometrical or philosophical space, not a category or a number, but an elementary endowment that its own absolute being makes an entirely opalescent hypocritical '*umbra mendax*.'[112]

But if one strolls in a park, and the Dorian summits of dark oaks express nature's meaning with all kinds of impressive integers, and evidence-whealed roses splutter life's stabbing-truths with the assistance of ads: it is nonetheless not in those that one sees the main, the most positive value of life and nature, but in those pine branches sizzling with outgoing space in which the alcoholic dance of uncertainty and the corrosive consistency of essentiality are present to an equal degree. It is a fact that a person's first reaction to rebarbative words such as '*Welträumlichkeit*' is to cast them aside in disgust, but it's a shame to act so rashly on the matter, because it soon becomes clear that that primeval space is something very impish, putto-esque, coquettish, and mischievous; ordinary as the name may be, that '*umbra mendax*' itself is charming & illustrious. (A new Isidore of Seville would no doubt find something to ponder upon in regard to 'proton' & 'Proteus' being such close namesakes.)

As it happens, the above-described sanatorium bears no resemblance to 'space-colors,' but very much to 'material-colors,' insofar as it did not enable one to escape from the Amphitrite's possibility-seals (let us stay in the environs of Proteus), but depicted a genuine material, just a single one, that its individuality immediately plucked from the sphere of narrative.

The individual details (including the description of the hospital) have to take up a position in the work like those bent strips of wood that motor boats tow around in the bays of fashionable seaside resorts: only constant racing along and an acute independence from the water surface make it possible for a person to remain standing on the speeding and inclined strips: as soon as that stops the whole machinery is instantly submersed, person, strips, and rope together. The old prose works, actually, are all deeply underwater, just as the sanatorium would also end up underwater if it did not race ahead, i.e., if its place were not taken by another, a newer one, which holds it up in narrative waters. Actually, a scene or building does necessarily have to be sustained at the narrative level in such a way that afterwards the same scene or background is described differently, then a third, a fourth time, (a single theme) differently in perpetuity, but even with one and only description is it possible to single out the narrative angle in which the description remained open, the leaden spine of identity does not straight away wrench it vertically downwards but finds its balance freely.

Descriptions like that are similar to trees bent by the wind, with leaves turned back: the leaves have almost separated from the branches; in place of their obverse their blind reverse side, with sharp veins, is showing; the tree virtually lets itself go & turns into a disheveled gorgonian stack of petal negatives (death is just a 180° turning of the body around the fixed axis of the soul): the description of the whole scene, actually, is a rear view, and in that way it manages to leave the unseen front view for ever open, to push the center of gravity into infinity & hold the present tense at water level. A rigid tree is a 'crystalline' affair; a negative tree turned inside out in the wind, with its perpetual movement of escaping and inversion of identity, is reminiscent of volatile gases, which is why the constituent elements of the new prose were called (analogous to the vibrating vacuity of 'space colors') 'gaseous.'

If, after the above description of the sanatorium, is put a second, which suddenly thrusts horizontally onwards & ahead of the fatal burden of the first, which had been torpedoed down, the excitement of the game can be heightened by the second sanatorium, over and above being the second, having a description which in itself is able to express the aforementioned 'negative openness' (like the tilting tree bough pressed against the wind); indeed, it may even have a third advantage in that, concerning as it does a building, it can in fact immediately represent most obviously and schematically what previously could barely be denoted in the form of a simile of a sizzling bough. If one seeks to immediately designate the difference between the old and the new sanatorium, then reference can be made to a pamphlet by R. Trübner, entitled *Erotik der Ortbestimmtheit und Asketik der Raumbestimmheit,*[113] published by the Polytechnic Institute (ETH) of Zurich.

The aforementioned sanatorium evolved in a Cartesian climate: it was true to its material and represented its own extent. The new, second sanatorium, by contrast, did not represent itself, but space, and for that reason contained only those minima that were necessary in order for space to be perceptible: barely an antenna living incognito, which caught space's most elementary waves of being.

The horizontal glass benches and glass ceilings intersected the vertical walls and went beyond them; the vertical walls intersected the flat roof and rose beyond it. A final façade or outer wall was not to be found between the vertical walls: they grew shorter one after another, and the vertical walls did likewise. There is an ascending scale of mirrors and an intersecting comb of ordinates: walls & roofs only denote a two-way stratification, but they do not finish it — the basic symbol of this division of walls is the arithmetic sign for addition; horizontality and verticality thrown onto each other without any framing square.

The operating room is totally transparent, its ceiling and four walls are glass: clouds, rocks, eagles, fog cords & antelope & glacé-stars can be seen through it — the woman under operation is almost fanned with the wing beats of birds on the glass: is that operating theater a triumph of geometry or nature romanticism, one wonders? If a surgeon takes an instrument from one of the operating tables, in fact he or she does not take that from an 80-centimeter stand but from a 1,400-meter rock tower, because he or she sees nothing, but nothing room-like around themselves: all around is loud sky and an almost maddening free fall of vision — in this operating theater one feels as if one were floating over snowy alps on a single bundle of thread. The walls, after all, are only reflex-curtains of uncertain width, a species of 'handmade resistances' (the end of these space wafers resembles the enlarged ends of handmade paper: unleavened walls in the pre-transformational state), one only notices them when one knocks against them.

One half of the spiral thread of the steps runs inside the building, the other half outside the walls: those inside the walls are likewise wholly transparent as rigid (not frozen!) water, whereas those in the fresh air are made of some dazzling-white, lethally-homogeneous material, as if an improvised magnesium flare had been ironed into the segments of the fan. Besides being made of two kinds of material, their spirals are also of different wavelengths: the transparent steps form broad & dense winds, like the body bow of a decaying giant snake — whereas the outside porcelain steps cling to the interior half of the staircase in sparse and extraordinarily steep winds like the checkered right leg of medieval harlequins did to the dark green left leg.

The elevator is transparent: people ascend in it like X-rayed *'billets doux'*[114] in a mail-chute apparatus; from a certain distance it is possible to see, at one and the same time, visitors in civvies in the ascending lift (a mechanized tempo of blasphemous secular Host-elevation) and the bleeding body on the operating table; the blood spilled from the wounds runs down the thin pipe beside the elevator: a single red capillary tube in the enormous transparency structure, as if the space measurer of the most abstract and most non-human absolute 'space' were nevertheless carmine-blood spilling from the most human suffering.

Suffering was an organic ornament of that space-chromaticism: not only is the Christian and telltale mercury of blood visible as it sharply intersects the gramophone records of the floors but the wound parts of the operated bodies are also cast across onto a reflecting wall, having already been brought out by a magnifying glass: veins, blood, bones, medicine and thread darted about on the enlarged wall like a morphinist-fresco: red lakes, blue floating plants, with expressionist jetties & dancing flags.

The single concrete thing falling outside this building was the colored projection wall, which was completely filled by a pointlessly mobile magnification: in the way certain architects place glittering lines of Rococo furniture in Cubist villas in order to enjoy the balance of naked plane surfaces and the bustling-pleonasm of lines, so here a spatial style going far beyond Cubism (*'fenomeno-logische Räumlichkeit-allusion'*)[115] found its own complementary opposite in the glittering play of the pointlessly magnified operated bodies on a distant wall isolated for that purpose. The extreme degree of Cubism really was the 'vector-nothingness' described here: in other words, the most embryonic experience of space, with a measure of dynamic marks and rough direction al torsos. On the other hand, at the same time as geometricality was carried to excess in architecture to the point of the crystalline essence of nothingness, the other extreme appeared in vernal freshness: natural elements in their own hysterical-true polychromy and plasticity. Natural entities (flowers, fruits, etc.) are in two senses the opposites of the 'nothing over nothing plus nothing times nothing' style: firstly as line-rich things, i.e., 'a line against zero,' secondly as the naïve things of life, i.e., '*A Shepherd's Calendar* against phenomenological thinking.'

The architect of the sanatorium, for instance, put this duality into practice in a private villa in the following manner: the south-facing wall of one room was made of thick, half-translucent golden-yellow glass, moreover in the form of a glass relief, which from one end to the other depicted springtime pentangular leaves with a thousand perforations. If the sun shone on the wall (there was no window in that room) then all manner of vernal shade of gold, from shrill yellow to a warm topaz, could be seen: the leaves of the statue that were protruding a long way away cast shadows onto each other while between them sprang up glittering pearls of fire. The wall's material was not homogeneous, so that by thickening and thinning the glass within the wall, a counter-foliage was outlined from murky rings like a sculptural watermark. The wall facing that was totally smooth, like a cinema screen, & at most had yellow reflections dancing on it. In fashion, in a similar manner, the 'nihilitive space-strewer' & the 'wild plum's-mesh-is-blue'-style[116] go together: there are hats which are just virginal asteroids or suicidal fakir-coordinates, but there are some on which no sort of form can be seen, the whole thing being a crowded pâté of cherries or narcissi.

On the walls of the glass sanatorium (the Milky Way's safety-deposit?), however, there was also an opaque area: two giant, recumbent, black letter U's. It has become fashionable nowadays to adhere a small stand onto the display windows of shops and to place a book or bowtie there: up till then articles had lain far away from the glass, but now, with the assistance of a stand that sticks tightly to the glass (like flies' legs to a flytrap), the novelties can all be pressed on the street, like a signet ring into wax. Those two giant, recumbent letter U's were stuck to the glass in similar fashion, at right angles to each other: one of them, the larger, on the wall facing the sea, the other, the thinner one, on the wall facing the mountain — the two touching each other at the bends of the U's.

The two giant monograms had no meaning, because not one of the words that had any relation to the sanatorium started with a letter U. They were needed in part in order to bestow an ironic and uselessly massive spine to the glass calculuses, but that spine was stuck on from the outside and almost tipped the whole building on one side (*Karthothek der Schein-Entia?*):[117] an unanticipated weight in one of the balance pans which, in the end, nudged the clinic into the flashing awkwardness of irrationality.

The stretching stems of the letter U's (especially those of the thin one: a methodically mistuned logical tuning fork) were decidedly direction indicators, strict pointers of the sharpest directions, but on the other hand, since they were letters, that is to say signs, as it happens they could not mean anything at all in the world here, they displayed a duality of energetic pointing to the goal and absolute meaninglessness. At first glance one could believe of the black letters that their blind tubes would finally disclose something about the clinic's incessantly self-deceptive thwartings of space: the brain greedily reached for the intellectual lure of the letter, the obscene drawing of the meaning, but precisely the alphabet cheated the most, because the sole letter, selected without any logical reason, was the cynical crown of meaninglessness, an Act of Nonsense. (It is interesting that girls would stick nickel-monograms on their caps when essayists talked about 'dehumanization.') In any case, this sort of placing of letters (naturally meaningful) is mostly seen on posters for international fairs, where the initial letter of the city can be seen leaning with Mercurian arrogance against the Earth's globe.

dawn on the Norwegian seacoast
as seen from the Staalbreck clinic, the Moon

The mornings of her convalescence came to Ena's mind: the dense fog that lay over the sea like an undergarment left behind by the departing darkness, a grotesque and telltale by-product that was invisibly deposited, selected from the night, & only in the morning, when the self-important demon raised his backside from his throne, was it noticed; long, curly bands reminiscent of the wrinkling of glaciers photographed from too close at hand, and as one could not see their gradual genesis, they pushed under the mountains with unearthly arrogance, signaling with *fait accompli*-hostility, putsch-like, that their world does not concern itself at all with ours as they raised that gigantic cloud-phalanx & vapor-fauna against us while we slept, without so much as a by your leave.

By day, however irrespective of us meteorological dramas might proceed, by virtue of the fact that one is immediately apprised of, and accommodates to, their slightest changes, the quietest climatic forgeries, one's impression is that one is very much an invited and important participant in the game: by contrast, awakening in the morning is horribly disenchanting, confronting one with radical change. One instantly imagines the outcome in its preceding details, in the minute phases of development at night, in none of which we took part: one feels jealousy, a cosmic jealousy one might say, similar to the sensation that awakens in one when a woman, after retiring for the night, appears before one in a complete change of clothes — however much that might be 'for your sake' just imagining all those fiddly little unbuttoning and buttoning actions that were needed to bring about the festive change is painful.

The great fog-archipelago appeared in part to be a secretion of the night, in part to be the primeval material of the morning lightness, as if the lightness, if pressed, were composed of some such greyish cotton-wool material and only a wind would drive it apart to the extent that it would fray into lightness, a daytime atmosphere: an optical Pandora's box from which all lightness would emerge just as transparent light nets are produced from the ends of tulle pressed until it becomes marble-like.

The sea spread under the fog darkly & stiffly, like a cadaver, or a person's face bandaged up after an operation: the last time one saw it, it had still been full of a million agonizing wrinkles, folded clothes, & one could affix a long commentary and clear rationale to every ripped torso of a gesture — but now, totally transformed all of a sudden, the person stands before one: the voice that hitherto one had felt to be one's own now came from totally different directions, formed under another influence (within half an hour it had become unfaithful to the family and become the surgeons' white relative); his movements, that through familiarity one had virtually come to pass on, now reflect the customs of an unknown corner of the world, and his gaze also had truly gained autonomy only now, become exclusively his own: it is for the first time that the neglected fact that individuality exists outside of us occurs to us with a sense of painful reality.

With people in large measure that is brought to mind only in death: at that point death, or in other words the perfect gesture of egotism, of not caring about one, is radiated retrospectively into the past, and then in those intonations, looks, and manners of speaking with which the deceased formed a link to one, one discovers, or rather: realizes with a self-tormenting consistency, the alienating, equalizing nature of death: death has shown one that the member of one's family had a totally different path; if death is an organic part of life, then the whole of life is wandering on eerie tracks, & its cohabitation with oneself, the love it avowed to one, was just hypocrisy: at the bier one always feels outwitted & cheated.

When the fog had sundered here and there, the sea's new face made an appearance: stiffly, with tiny creases, with a big crash (in much the same way as in an autumnal park even a slight rustling of leaves is accompanied by a huge gust of wind), with a wholly new anaplasty. The following state pertains in place of the big daytime openness: the fog avalanches are like mountains, and between bursts the sea looks like five, six, or seven lakes or tarns — the mountains are soft, the lakes steely: as if an Emmenthaler perruke were lying on the massive skull of chaos. When that spectacle unfolds before one's eyes on waking, one feels what Winkle must have felt after sleeping through at least two geological eras and now, in the third, had come to his senses: the taste of yesterday's supper is still in one's mouth, the intentions that were set in motion in one's mind and muscles during the starter course and ought to accomplish today, but it is comical to think of all that after such a change in the earth's surface, it is just as ridiculous as the ringing of an alarm-clock bell that one may have wound yesterday in all seriousness, but in the morning the trumpets of the end of the world are barking.

All of a sudden the world has grown richer: a new endlessness has stepped in place of yesterday's *comme-il-faut* 'endlessness' — spatial boundlessness was substituted by the stifling absurdity of overly folded forms, endless richness of movement and change. The picture showed an idiosyncratic mixture of the ephemeral & infinite: certain configurations of fog moved now as well (they expanded, changed color), they changed more and more extremely, & every second one was under the impression that they were now achieving the final stage of the form toward which they seemed to be proceeding and with the changes occurring only to adjust to it, when all at once a completely new shape, radically different from the old, materialized from it, although the old form made itself felt through all the changes up till the last moment: the whole thing was a paradoxical mime of entelechy: perfect fulfillment is also actual annihilation; the fateful filling up of the preformed figure is equally a universal denial of the surmised figure.

Above the central layer of fog drifted wisps of vapor: that is a singular combination, when a ready contour and a fluctuating curl of fog are juxtaposed (like a freshly baked tart on being turned out of its mold: plastic art & vapor): the geological elements assembled for a diluvial council in order to formulate their steamingly mutinous Tridentine definition on that primeval dawn. The restless parties were represented on the horizontal tribunes of the early dawn, as trivial yet punctiliously loyal symbols by a dogmatic sea, a skeptical fog, a mystic Moon, & a scholastic Sun. The fog cliffs narrowed and started to rise up high as columns, in a sharp orange color, like pale dolomite walls at sunset: it was curious to see, or rather to infer the distance between sea level and the lowest base stratum of the banks of fog, as if the mountains in a Carinthian landscape were all at once to rise and stop at 150–200 meters while the lakes stayed in their original place.

It was a particularly exciting version of the contour sensation (that magnificent sweet-sure sensation): one could sense the uninterrupted continuation of the sea under the covering-stalactites of the clouds, but on the other hand it could be seen that it is these pseudo-bodies, representing indefinite, volatile, and more just notional colors rather than implacable plasticity, which determine it, cutting out their outlines from a height of 200 meters above sea level — eclipses of the sun and moon offer a similar impression, when shadow (that immaterial, dreamlike, negative entity) excises the hard outlines on celestial bodies carved out of hard materials (an eclipse of the sea?). The Moon was still hovering in the distance: in absolutely the same color as the waves of fog, and the paler it grew, the more discernible were the black spots and wrinkles in it, so that there was a point in time when the whitish green, smooth sky has completely absorbed into itself the silvery patch, like a sugar cube absorbs water dripped onto it, and only the black points could be seen in its place, like birds migrating into the interminable distance that carry the annunciation of an unknown world that has been kept secret to one.

It was now possible to see for the first time the celestial map of the stars in its totality & its reality, because one did not feel oneself to be at a place that bore a lot number on a topographic map or an entry in a land registry: the whole architecture was given over to a schema of emerging worlds, and thus it unified naïveté and horror; by moving over so huge and free a space the Moon was given the stage its style demanded: it became smaller, more playful, simpler, but, above all, more concretely globelike than in the city or a small civilized-idyllic landscape, precisely because that way its spherical nature was detected (that, in the end, had always been known to one from textbooks, but it had been felt to be more of a schema, a simplification, than a genuine spherical nature), all at once an awful grandeur has been conferred on the whole phenomenon: it is always extraordinarily touching if a structure which, through one's intelligence, one had imagined to be much more complex than one finds it analyzed and portrayed in the writings of pedagogues, nonetheless all at once appears before one in such simplicity as was shown by those primitive diagrams.

Hitherto there was only a dim or gleaming blot above one that one did not even imagine as being a single individual: one has seen it on the left and on the right, white and red, in every kind of color, every form and every situation, as if it was ten or fifteen different images, each one of which is highly complex in movement and form, and it is impossible to believe that this protean figure is identical to that white, regularly rounded, simple body, which runs on a simple track above the horizon: it is just as difficult to get used to that identification as the ground-plan of one's apartment or bird's eye view of one's ship — in our lives, our own rooms could be seen in a thousand perspectives in various colors, in shortenings & recapitulations, so it is absurd that all those pictures should be no more than three rectangles; that the many decks, cabins, bridges, sails, salons and smokestacks should be no more up and down than the naïve-unique form of a simpleminded sardine.

If those cosmic affairs are so simple and only fantastic in their dimensions, but so dazzlingly simple in their construction principles (because such a discovery is truly attended by a sense of stupefaction: when the gigantic Systema Mundi[118] becomes identical to the most childish metaphor that one had always supposed was a mere ode-like game of posturing: "they rotate in front of you like stray balls ..." et cetera), then perhaps a naïve rhythm & primitive motion like that lies concealed at the base of all the philosophies put together, behind even the extreme confusions of the mind.

At the same time, one is seized by a frightening sense of loneliness: hitherto the Moon had been a diffuse concept, one's mind, one's favorite poets, the parks of one's city, & the walls of the art galleries of distant lands were full of it; the old Moon had a chaotic but comfortable ubiquity. Now, however, it had become clear that there was just one, one and one only, in a single form, on an unalterable orbit, in white & in spherical form —

no escape, that and never anything else. While on one's travels one senses that agonizing & suffocating atmosphere, the mood of '*reductio ad unicum*':[119] when, after a thousand reproduction efforts, one sees the one true building or sculpture in its frightening puritanicalness, in its uniqueness; from that moment on it is not possible to scatter it to the winds, to diasporize it, because that is the endpoint, the last edition, defined by the almost suicidal taciturnity of uniqueness. Hitherto the Moon or the Doge's palace had betokened a forest-like wealth: now, all at once, the entire forest was reduced to a single lonely, measurable tree, the world around it became empty.

On the enormous pale-green sky, which was now truly space (which related to the evening skies like the infinitely outflung circus-stage of an amphitheater to a restricted movie screen), the Moon ran solitarily: the world became measurable, and that awakened the sadness of solitude, the spacelessness of outer space, emptiness. (If three books are sprawled on one's writing table they are always treated as a patchy-plural: 'books' are sprawled before one, and that tepid, self-deceptive plural spreads the atmosphere of 'books' beyond the material outlines of individual books, the plural creates a veritable magnetic space, which transforms any other objects or tiny happenings falling within its environs: if one should ever think tenaciously that there are no 'books' spreading in every direction in one's room, like the generously perfunctory rain & wind-bands of weather maps, but altogether three independent and finite bundles of paper, all at once, one is surrounded by an unexpected emptiness; three dead aberrations, in all their frightening thinness, and an interminably uninhabited space are suddenly precipitated from the magnetic solution of objects. The same thing happens in one's childhood when, from the million-dimensional tent notion of 'parents' all of a sudden there precipitates, with shocking speed, the startlingly slender inventory of 'just two people.')

That resembles the regret when one imagines death in oneself rather than in one's environs: one is inclined to regard annihilation as the cessation of one's favorite books, one's parents, one's wife and landscapes, instead of within one's own body, developing the blind branches of that knowledge from one's own anatomical centers, not starting from outside in that psychological territory in which every shadow and startlement is the outer world's, someone else's, a stranger's. If one divests oneself of all impressions (the one & only sphere of the Moon from all other impressions of a mundane Moon) and gets to a nameless dark awareness of the body, then one can feel that sheer, absurd solitude that a glimpse of the grey and bleak Moon brings into the dawn over the sea. And the Sun was already rising at the other end of the sea: a crimson, shapeless incandescence has attacked the acute greyness of the horizon, the helical corridors of the catarrhal cockleshells of the clouds have been given brick-colored stains; indeed, when the Sun's inherent incandescence was covered by a sluggish cloud and the Archean-rays that had soared to the clouds, so to say, were cut off from their source, they unexpectedly became linear, giving a zebra pattern to the side of the clouds.

conversation between Ena & the female surgeon (prehistoric ages & modern therapy)

A female physician stood on the terrace in a baggy white, thick-knit pullover, which was turned down and black round the neck; her chest was sunken, but along with the sunkenness she was nevertheless showing some plasticity emerging from wrinkles, which looked more pleasing than brutal tenseness, because that whimsical semi-convex, semi-concave shaping by textile brought the breasts closer to the individuality of the body than the locomotive peaks swelling through excessive 'home rule,' which are virtually self-supporting appendages that take no part in the body's individual dance of the muscles: just as the cupolas of certain temples are just gigantic & inorganic 'Sunday supplements' (architectural elephantiasis), against which an entire flat roof bump (no more than the protuberance of a magnifying glass) is an organic wave of the whole stone structure and likewise was already predestined in the basement wall and, as a matter of course, swells in all of its columns.

Her face was slightly greasy and perspiring, totally unwashed, in sharp contrast to the cool gymnasticizing freshness of the external world. Her big black head of hair also seemed to be still totally permeated by the night and sleep, not allowing through its oily hedge the frosty openness of the morning: indeed, her hair was unwilling not only to come undone in the transparent ice area of the morning wind but was also at variance with the sportiveness of her own pullover; her looks, her weariness, and the dowdiness of her body lay about in her sweater with a coquettish-harsh unsuitability like a puny and sickly cousin of Joan of Arc who secretly tried on her relative's chainmail vest.

She thrust her hands in her pockets and gazed at the nascent world so. It was then that Ena, who for a long time had been looking at the physician's back from a leather armchair in the corridor, or rather the drawing room, came out: at the shoulder blades, which occasionally moved under the sweater and are so estranged from the owner that if one were in a position to say something confidential to a person at whose back one has looked at for five minutes, one would no doubt not say it, because one would lose confidence on the basis of the person's shoulder blades: they are so strange, displaying a new and unknown person, that by comparison the face, for all its benevolence, would seem ridiculous hypocrisy. Ena herself felt the same in relation to the white-sweatered back: how many times she had talked with the woman in confidence, but now, seeing her alone, and just her back at that, though as good as completely motionless, she saw in her a selfish, indeed, hostile, person. That was intensified by the fact that the young female physician was beyond the pane of the balcony door, and the wind (which did not reach Ena) and the plein-air set her on the esoteric stage of an unknown world.

Ena had a camelhair rug over her legs, even though the drawing room was well heated and she was sitting by the yellow spool of tubes, painted a butter color, of the radiator; the flattened tubes of two air-conditioning heaters were fitted onto the dark-blue wall paper of the drawing room in such a manner as to be organically part of the decor of the reception room, or more particularly a repetition of the themes, written for other instruments, of the huge rectangular vases (set on their long sides) in the center of the tables and the lamps (their bases were likewise yellow and their shape seemed as though finger-thick ceramic macaroni had been screwed onto a smooth board); the lampshades were a slightly darker yellow, of a shape likewise like a cigar box, sutured at the edges with a crude fiber. The lamp bulb in one of them was switched on, and Ena was sitting by that, looking at the morning and at the physician.

A chambermaid passed through the sitting room as in the first scene of a stage play of old.

— How early it is for Mam'selle W. to be up.

— Yes, she was on night duty, so now she can relax a bit.

— Did anything happen?

— Yes, the woman who paints was in a poorly condition & had to be given an injection, though that did not help too much. I had to stay by her.

— I've heard she has hysterical tendencies.

— Too right she does, that's what tired out poor Mam'selle W*, having to struggle with that.

— Really? Then I did hear it right, because last night I heard a muffled crump.

— It could also have been the boiler for the hot water, because there is a backup on the first floor, but that is not quite right, because it makes a loud humming noise. It could have been that.

— Yes, that, too, gets on my nerves.

— They're coming round to replace that or repair it.

— But that can't have been it, because in fact I did not hear the noise from my room but from the corridor. Please don't tell on me; I know it's not permitted, but I am leaving here anyway, tomorrow or the day after.

— In any case, you may catch a cold, I know I once saw the Mam'selle on the balcony one evening in a light negligee when I was warming my hands down below, on the car's engine, with the chauffeur.

— That chauffeur has some cheek. He made comments about me to your colleague. About the pajamas. In any case he behaves as if he were one of a hotel's staff.

— He was down there, in a hotel, right up to now.

— Do you know what he said about me?

(Ena was unattractive enough that she took pleasure in quoting the witticism of a driver with which she could make a chambermaid jealous or at least suspicious.)

— He's always shooting his mouth. — She ran a dustcloth round the lampstand: it was a pleasure to watch how impossible it was with such an absent-minded flick (the casualness of which was increased still further by the fluttering of the soft cloth) to shift from its place a lamp, weighing a double brick. A delicate balancing game arose between the massive weight of the ceramic's mass & the weightlessness of light made still lighter by virtue of the little parchment filter. The symmetry of the Roman scales was this: on the one hand was the gigantic weight (gigantic relative to light) but small area of the lampstand — on the other hand (the other branch of the scales) the extraordinary lightness but (relative to the base of the lamp) huge area of light.

— Very cheeky.

Ena gloated in saying that, deliberately letting a delicate jolt of vanity shudder through herself as if she had set it off by turning a switch: she was looking in front of her and slightly upwards and whispered in short breaths, constricting the sounds, saving to the end a suddenly ascending burst of laughter so that it all came out as just one long syllable, something like: "ve-eeek."

— He said — (now as well the last syllable was rising, succeeded by a pause, pressing a bony forefinger on her knee as if she were readying a typewriter shift key without knowing which capital letter to strike) —, that pretty girls should not be allowed to stand around on balconies in their nighttime pajamas; you're right about that, he did not say it about pajamas but about negligees (& mine is not light, as you yourself have noted, but thick. Like a stuffed & stitched down comforter). He said that anyone who stood outside, if people were passing by...

— But no one was passing...

— They would think that...

Pause. Refrain: "ve-eeek."

W* turned her back. It could be seen in her eyes that, due to the reflection of the window, she could not see Ena because she was slipping her gaze with constricted pupils here and there through the glass with a facial movement like that ophthalmologists or opticians make in rotating eye glasses in front of the eyes in order to establish their data; for a few seconds Ena felt fine in that optical casing, because she knew how sure that immaterial defensive wall was — how many times she had maneuvered in the city in front of enormous shop windows filled with mirror images of the street in such a way that however she screened and shaded the envious plates, she always saw a portrait gallery of people hurrying behind her back. She would have liked to make use of her invisibility, but W*, with a laugh, opened the door and spoke:

— Come out. What are you lazy? You're behaving like a truant. I'll show you something that'll bring about a miraculous recovery.

— I think 'I'll show you something &...' is a basic principle here. How many a time has one heard that, but...

— All big things consist of driving something, anything, a flower of speech, a banal social formality or the title of a statue into stubborn tautology.

— You got that right, I don't know if you read, hang on a tic, his name doesn't come to mind, a German writer, drat, it'll come to me later, you have read him for sure, that in point of fact all science and all art is a matter of etymology — when it comes down to it, that's more or less what you yourself expressed.

— I can't say, when was that, in what way?

— You know, about setting forth a concept, a word, an entire...

— Yeah yes, I get you now, in other words, one can etymologize from it an entire system or scheme of life.

— I'm going to freeze.

— Come off it, quit moaning. Tell you what, though: you know that if you were to catch a cold, a touch of flu, that would do you good after the illness you have had? Eh, I'll say nothing, but it would be good.

Ena smiled & stepped timidly onto the balcony like someone dipping a first toe into cold water. Moved, she stared off:

— Ugh, it's...

W* again adopted an expression appropriate to the morning pantomime, in which there was a lot of the artificial superficiality of medical expertise with which she looked at the sea's sprouting and scaling Neptune-enamel, the brick-powdered foliage of the clouds, and the slight blondness of the rolling-away Moon (*o enumeratio miserrima*),[120] like the face of a patient on whom she has carried out successful surgery and is afterwards accomplishing movements with hands & eyes like ordinary people in order that they should marvel at them all the more. With some people the emotion of being moved always consists of battling against it, it being patently obvious that they are curbing their feelings of pathos, and precisely by doing so, they will be moved. Both in voice and looks W* became conspicuously solemn, precisely on account of their dryness, their studied puritanicalness.

— You never did like it, perhaps out of pride, if our sanatorium sought as a matter of fundamental principle to treat your worldview, if I may put it so.

— It's something like that. Don't be mad at me, but it was immediately clear what your intentions were, and it was very burdensome for me to see them being applied. Quite apart from that, though, I had no wish to adopt those views myself.

— You may have seen that no one attempted to force them on you either. If I show you that natural beauty again you would feel that was some kind of hocus-pocus evangelizing gesture, yet it is only the most foolish wonderment speaking out from me when I ask you, too, to marvel with me. — She suddenly laughed. — I was lying. I can't, I just can't look at this without seeking to impose upon my fellow human beings the faith, the worship of the Earth, which a morning like this suggests. What am I saying? It doesn't just suggest, it's no longer just a suggestion, those are just letters that need to be read.

The fog on the shore, directly under the terrace, broke up and there appeared a white, dazzling-white stretch of pebbles. Up till then they had been able to feel as though they were hovering between the sea and the clouds because the seacoast had not been visible, & therefore it had been possible, just as easily, to suppose that the domain of fog and water continued under the balcony, but now that white shore had glimmered through, which there, with an infinitesimal slope, had ducked under the water but was still gleaming from below, at most more palely, instead of a chalky scintillation similar to the honeycombed skin of a silvery lizard, a grey pearl fabric: now they felt that the balcony had reached the shore — glimpsing the incandescent-matte whiteness provoked in them an almost jolting sensation, as if they had run aground. The strip of pebbles was like a fissure starting out from which the morning's entire chaos and parturition could be unraveled within a couple of minutes: the swirling lasted for hours on end, but from the minute that shining reality sliced through it, the whole scene turned into an otherworldly statue of a map on which, as a matter of fact, everything could be seen in the dramatic turbulence of old, but in one corner a spark had already flared, signaling the fuse that was going to bring about the detonation. From that moment, one can already see a rhythm in the drama, the pulses of creation are replaced by second-long bars; those primeval forms in which one had seen life's automatic god-statues were now just a discredited set of playful backdrops & discarded masks.

— Those are our true ancestors, those departing forms, & I want to get those ancestors to come back as 'homecoming bodies' in our bodies. Aristocrats are proud to show off 500- or 1,000-year-old family trees, the ancestors' heroic deeds, preserving their first acts in a concise hieroglyphic language — but I am calling for the attention of a more ancient ancestor, a collective, more democratic ancestor: the earth. One ought not to be allowed to break away from that, it is on that material tradition, on that 'continuity of earth' if I may put it that way, that (the word?) 'geo-cracy' is founded.

Ena wearily remarked:

— Adam in the Bible as well, till thou return unto the ground...

— Yes, and it's incredible what comical inferences, reeking of death, people drew from that instead of founding their pride on it. Earth denotes the real ancestor because only in that is there, at one and the same time, inexpressible old age and blooming youth. With me what was evinced in me when we learned about the 'younger' days of the Earth was, at first, a primitive, I might almost say poetic, impression that it had begun at much the same time as when mankind appeared on Earth. What a stupendous time, with the Earth nevertheless contemporary and in its youth. Like I said, that was a matter of my naïve temperament back then, but I have acquired a few facts, & I live in a world of monumental youth. How much finer the notion is here, in the morning, when the clouds look like huge snails, like fossil animals, and one expects the appearance of trilobites and lingulids, nautiluses and obolids, how much finer the notion of 'eternal youth' than any infinity or even "*Wunderwerk der Endlichkeit.*"[121] The Earth is a fundamental fact: this is where we started, we have been inoculated into this, so we must deliberately innervate into ourselves that solidarity, our body's community of land, its terrestrial identity, in the strictest sense of the term. Medical anatomy starts with geology, and every diagnosis starts, as a result of the precise, the brutally precise hereditary scheme of things, with the palpation of the earth: you, Ena, start there, in those pebbles, waters, corals, stars.

— Instead of crusader heroes & martyred kings, Ethelreds and Wulfstans, I don't know how you put it, highly resonant terms: obolids or -lubas.

— That's exactly how it is. The earth is the most universal, the commonest ancestor.

— But for people it is precisely the distinctive ancestors...

— Yes, but there are two kinds of anthropic cults; one is a cult of people who are eccentrified, isolated, draw strength only from specialties: that can be called an aristocratic taste — whereas the other always designates the new concept of a person, in other words, there is always an intellectual rationale behind it, and you are trying to put across that new notion of humans, a universal hypothesis: you might call that an ethical, indeed, religious human concept.

— So, your people are the founders of a religion? After all...

— Yes, in a qualified sense of the term. As a matter of fact there is a new concept of a person at the root of all religions, & that later comes to be symbolized in all manner of legendary-dogmatic products, totally swamping its naïve bud. For that reason all religions are ethical and every ethic is identical to some concept of humans, or more properly, a sense of humanity: an obsessional idea ("*this* is a human") and the reflex-acts which stem from that (there are very few such acts, as there are for a primitive animal); much later, those ancient deeds are made conscious, and they are formed and stylized further only logically, and from then on every so-called moral rule is merely a theoretical decision, a theoretical descendant of the first actions to be recorded in writing.

— In other words, you somehow imagine the matter like this: *in principio erat* whim, which is to say that you suppose or sense something about yourself, let's say you are overcome by a strong sensation that, for instance, you are dreadfully alone in the forest and looking for a partner in the sky, remote, energetic assistance, or, to take another example, you feel yourself to be very much at one with the forest, indeed, you feel the evening firmament to be a part of yourself like your language: that is the first impulse — you act on the basis of the stubbornness of this mood; it becomes equivalent to animal instinct; you live without any particularly delineated consciousness: you just function — that is an 'ethical *life*' in your view, something like that, no? I am systematizing it a bit, & that, I have to admit, knowing my own nature, makes me skeptical; after that came the intellectual organization, the...

— That's right, that's how it is. It is now a matter of what is the pedagogics of reducing people to their 'ancestral-moods' in that way? As it is, it is fearfully similar to some sort of 'return to nature': and it is that, after all, but much, very much more nature-slanted. In the end, you can pin on us Rousseauism, pantheism, Earth religion, laboratory idyllicism and who knows what else — all of them, given that it concerns 'nature,' 'humanity,' the 'body' & the relationship of those, only the question is precisely how one saturates those basic notions and relations if one gets to the bottom of certain concepts & certain demands with exaggerated radicalism. You are suggesting that the whole trend is disastrously individualistic, it has no social program, naturally, because ethics can only start out from the concept of a 'new-person,' & this can only begin with you, W* said suddenly, laughingly squeezing Ena's throat. — Oh, dearest — she said after that as she had squeezed Ena's throat more much tightly than she intended, and in her mortification she felt that she needed to append some words. — Oh, dearest, you yourself know how awful and wearisome is the life of a style when people are still forced to fiddle around with old notions and foresee that, on that account, its first critic is immediately going to assign the thinking to some old school as a naïve epigone, because nothing flatters a critic more than the feeling that he or she is not going to be taken in by novelties, they have a historical refinement & know there is nothing new under the sun.

— I'm familiar with them, dear W*, they are in the habit of saying things like: "Don't try to pull the wool over our eyes when, instead of a sentimental picture of nature, we find enlargements of X-rays stuck on top of each other & stickers of the Triassic rock system: that, too, is just an old and barren pseudo-concept of 'nature' at the bottom of which is hidden a petty-bourgeois tendency to laziness, or at best the self-interested vision of a few souls with some poetic talent."

Ena was being somewhat frank, because W*'s prettiness irritated her: her physical appearance gave credence to her whole sort of theory; that was really something that she imagined to be an 'ethical function' — the girl could not be separated from her words, they formed such a unity: her baggy pullover, her untidy, radiant and warm hair, really did lead one's fantasy on to a Mesozoic sponge, a direct physical component of which is this multitude of words, which did not demonstrate the objective transparency of ideas but only the inside of her pullover or the current style of her hair; it was precisely this that made her attractive, as if her speech were just an exotic balm exuded by her body in order to protect it; in the preceding minutes that baggy and crocheted white-and-black sweater had been just an enviable textile article, but W*'s words totally permeated it with an invisible material that, in the manner of certain waters, immortalize flowers which are soaked in them into statues, tempered the garment into a living formula, maybe permeating it with a pregnant humanity, so that it was no longer possible to desire the sweater in the way that one woman will desire another's blouse because it was no longer a garment.

That a person's words should be identical to their physique, indeed their clothing, would not have been a surprise to Ena in any case since the triad of 'clothing-body-sentence' is a pretty ordinary matter, but that everyday connection now symbolized the proximity and naïve relationship which there was in W*'s brain between one's elemental body-sense & elemental action; that was why as a whole W* was elegant, because she was an archaic plant, because that reduction to a plant necessarily radiated from her; she felt her thoughts were just reflex movements like an amoeba's expansion; everything was a zigzagging game (Oh dear! *Urspiel?*) — the basic triangle of elemental being, elemental consciousness, and elemental action. Ena envied her that, without being able to formulate it for herself.

— That's a great pullover — she remarked in torment as way of separating sweater and woman with her own words, but still more with W*'s possible response, and thus breaking the beastly harmony. The sun sparkled on the scene as though mirror-shrapnels & mirror-seagulls were zigzagging in the air; the sun glistened on the horizon, on certain points of the sea, and on the walls of the sanatorium as if a proud knockout blow were bursting out of the inside of the Earth, and the morning was by now nothing more than those concentrated wounds of light flowing into steady daylight; nodes of light and spumes of time are distributed in a landscape, with the self-centeredness of sharp interpolations, like some cloud-like mountains in Oriental pictures: superimposed, with those behind each other being mystified into being superimposed — sea and light displaying a system of layering comprised of such Japanese axioms about lamps.

— This thing? — asked W*, digging her long nails into the knitted jersey over her chest & pulling it forward. — I bought it in Switzerland, a cherished memento: I spotted it on one of the loveliest mornings; it was brightly sunny, with everything frightfully crystal clear, though there was no crudeness about it, like there is here right now; the sky was pale green, silvery blond & imperceptibly green, & meanwhile huge flakes of snow were falling sporadically, which were entirely black against the light, though in the shade they were white, like a stylish veil that is woven black on top and white lower down; the mountains were, so to say, absorbed into the exquisite sky while the glaciers reflected it all and were like the hairnets of time; it was then that I saw the sweater in the depot of a French firm. I had the feeling it was a statue of the morning in the way that in the olden days statues used to be made of the allegory of morning.

— It's more that you are the symbol if you put it on, isn't it?

— Well yes. But not entirely; it is a statue in and of itself:

elegant and unwieldy. I'm very fond of it; Cubist, Frenchifiedly, self-ironically Cubist, and yet it has a feel like that, seriously, try taking hold of it like this, doesn't it? Like a flower, an edelweiss — I very much like the two together.

— You pulled it in the way some people lift dogs up by the scruff of the neck and then dangle them in their own pelt like in a sticky & loose bag...

---

return to Ena & Leatrice in the taxi (p. 435).
Arrival at the guesthouse. Two girls

When Ena sped along the seaboard with Leatrice, that morning appeared to her along with the other that W* spoke about & the three united in her soul, intensifying, deifying, and distorting each other. A snowy white motorboat anchored at the quay alongside them — nestling against the little jetty like a sledge which is seeking to turn round but meanwhile is very much slipping along: it was knocking against the shore with an exaggerated slant, with the uncertain, cross-eyed speed of toboggans sliding crosswise. Two women in swimsuits disembarked from it; they had put on bathrobes, & one of them was swinging in front of herself a small bunch of keys with which she then locked the engine or a door.

— There are unknown types nosing about here, aren't there?

— Yes, my girl, but we are here at your guesthouse, where I was anxious to have you looked after —, Ena said with a wry smile.

Leatrice was sharp & weary, with an "Is this it?" she climbed out of the car like a butterfly picking its way out of its cocoon. Not far from the seashore stood a two-story white villa, the glass panes of which, from stair carpet & plasterwork tapes, led up a free-standing spiral staircase to a roof terrace and a huge circular balcony that was like a titanic gramophone record spiked onto one end of a bamboo stick.

— The villa used to belong to an architect; he designed it, and now that he's dead, his widow has turned it into a guest-house; she only rents it out to women, I believe I'm right in saying there are no more than four rooms to let, but they are magnificent, you'll see.

Leatrice looked at the sea: the motorboat was still throbbing for a while, & as its throbbing mingled with the murmuring, moldering sound of the water, she had the feeling that the sharp noise of the motor was not finding a solid enough resistance in the water's sibilant lapping countervoice — an electric tarmac drill that by mistake had been stuck into wax. The two women were walking in the same direction as Leatrice & Ena.

— Hey, look, aren't they coming here?

— Maybe, for certain, probably, because I remember now that the woman who owns the place said something about a couple of sisters.

— Do you know who else is here?

— Well, one room is vacant, yours, and then as best I know, another girl who will be going to university but wants first to get a rest or whatever here at the seaside, is likewise due to arrive today; then there's one elderly lady, and also a second.

— Only contrasts like that will be left here: the young & the old? Not bad at all.

The two girls walked round a shaded little tennis court, with one of them popping in for a second through the wire-mesh door, like into a poultry cage, and snatching into her hand a racquet that was lying there, and in a shrill voice, as if a glass cane were being hammered on porcelain teeth, shouted out to the other: "I'll pick the tennis racquet up because you've left it outside again and didn't screw it into its press." A dense garden stretched behind the tennis court, sudden and unexpected after the dizzying luxury of space of the area over the sea: one might expect a transition between the dazzling expanse of the sea and the spatial deformations of the crowded park; the eyes trip on it like a foot stepping from a solid floor onto a plank which unexpectedly waggles here & there.

How quickly everything can be: there is no need for connecting forms that have already left the boundlessness of the sky and the water stadium but are still far from the zigzag small sculptures of the foliage — leaves that simultaneously display the forms of plants and clouds (so to say, precisely the allegories of infinity resigning itself to a contour); an entire flora and fauna could be devised in which the affectation-choked plastic art of flowers and open space distilled into time were mixed, but the world has no need for any of that — the sea is at an end and immediately anything can come, just as in the middle of Europe, without need for a transition.

When one travels and suddenly speeds into the heart of a long-desired city, all at once everything is there, in incredible detail and morbid lay-out, after the unconstrained homogeneity of a railway night train (an anthill unexpectedly bustling above after one has accidentally overturned a mute covering stone) — at times like this a pre-Paris or half-Venice is grievously missing in which the symbolic directrixes of the domestic landscape and the first outline '*Schlagbild*'-s [122] of the new world are united.

(A German critic wrote essays under the title "*Zwischen See und Ufer*" about German writers who had never lived; [123] he took the view that the history of literature fitted individual writers and poets into an artificial rhythm of continuity, so that when the profiles and the years yielded an overarching unity of rhythm, they were, naturally enough, lying, because continuity was an imaginary matter, there are always black chasms between individual writers on a chronological map: those black ditches were filled by such imagined portraits, which, if one fits them among the genuine ones, will yield a genuine continuity and transition — if not, those imagined surrogate-puppets had to be smuggled into portraits of, in part, a predecessor, in part, a successor, so that the illusion of progress could be preserved.)

The basic pattern of that unsettling lack of transition is shown by Venice's watery streets: in the middle, amorphous water, on either side, decorated stone façades, pictures, chandeliers, furniture darkling through the windows; here and there it happens that steps and water will scour for themselves a binding material from the mud, which is no longer water but not yet architecture — but usually the topmost step is never submerged by water but hovers just a few centimeters above water level in a nothingness cut off from every possibility of merger.

The main staircase of the villa was placed in a glass tube, like a stretched spring in a thermometer; the steps wound around the axis in the same way as the segments of a fan. At the bottom of all Cubism blooms German Platonism; those stairs were also totally abstract, but that abstractness was expressed by the most tangible plastic art: Teutonic definition in which the most obscure, most elemental features were realized in the most strikingly marked, most contour-intoxicated formulation ('sharpest contour,' or 'conceptual plastic art' are far from meaning precision or truth). The ground plan of the glass cylinder was oval, so that the two stories of stairs must have been slightly tilted — indeed, stretched so much in the oval incline so as not to look geometrically planned but like naïve steps cut into a hillside, turning with delicate irresoluteness.

— Good looking, no? — Ena asked.

— Good looking, but not practical: broad steps, stretching so far that one gets as tired as when walking down five flights. What kind of person is the proprietress?

— Pleasant, or rather nothing in particular, neither friendly, nor…

— Did you ask about prices?

— No, but I know the prices, if they are still the same, because I originally saw a photograph of this villa in a newspaper ad, and the prices were also there, & I did have the thought of coming here myself, but then that somehow didn't come about, & just now all I asked when I telephoned was if there was a free room, but I have seen the villa many times on walks out this way.

Down below the door to the stairwell slammed noisily because the two girls from the motorboat had arrived — talking loudly, their heelless rubber flip-flop sandals slapping on the steps: the body has some kind of heavy, almost uncouth charm when the weight does not swing on the needle tips of slim evening shoes (although even then the main beauty of that concealed and seldom enjoyed game is that which stands in the heightened contest of the muscles when it is sought to keep the body in artificial balance: in contrast to the perverse flip-flopping of the center of gravity of the shoe above the asymmetric bridge which takes its start at the toes, imitating the slightly rising line of the tail of a Chinese dragon, then all of a sudden, after a little bend at its peak, dropping onto the pillar of the pencil tip-like heel — the tendons above the zigzag line of that bridging arch bulge in brutal crudeness, with a lurking-flashing curvature and a snuggling anew under the skin as if the enraged flesh were seeking at any moment to burst asunder the shoe's overswinging laying down of lines of tendrils — when the feet of a dancing couple are filmed then one can see that struggle in impersonal clarity) but falls flatly, with its entire weight on the ground, & chicness-searching vanity can barely stand somehow to ease and etherealize that slipshod-slapping way of walking.

The sense of delight that she had felt in the car when she spotted the girl in the white knitted swimsuit pulling on a shoe on the seashore again ran through Leatrice; again a frolicsome, sweet, yet strict rhythm had seized hold of her body to mimic the two sisters. A certain hardness, a rugged fracture, was always strongly tangible in Leatrice: just as there was always a raw, almost peasant-like faltering in the movement of the prima ballerina in a Russian dance troupe — ballet always showed redoubled the seductive game which was just hinted at, between the over-ornamented line of movement, the ideal plucking of a string, and the body's undisciplined weightiness and thick-set obstinacy like a block of wood. In the ballet the survival of the squatting and kicking of peasant dances was particularly perceptible, even in the most ethereal movements. Their long, white, naked legs jumped over the broad, flat steps like a white pair of compasses opened to an obtuse angle, and the flesh kept on quivering on them — not flabbily and easily, but tautly, like a metal string during a pizzicato; muscles and bones did not wobble under the skin with lazy uncertainty and blurriness, but precisely and swiftly, without any conspicuous protuberances, and in giving a singular rustling inside the body, only displaying in the displacement of certain shadows the paper-like folding of muscle fibers.

As Leatrice looked down on them, they spun around the axis of the snaking steps like a propeller: the big drill of the staircase seemed to rotate under their own spiral dashing. All that lasted only a few seconds because they, too, got to the top, and now four of them were standing in front of the white door, looking at one another. One of them said with a laugh to Lea:

— A new resident perchance?

— Perhaps.

— Summer vacation, recreation, university, or what? — the other asked in an ironic detective voice.

— That remains to be seen.

— Both of you?

— No, just my girlfriend.

— Yvonne Valmian —, the first of them said, holding out her hand and laughing as if to say, "I can't help it, in any case I've said it, I wash my hands of it, whatever will be will be." She shrugged her shoulders, offering her hand in such a way that it exuded benevolent impudence. With a smile Leatrice replied:

— I've got a long name. For now, this is all: Leatrice. To be continued in installments —, she added with a hooting laugh. Ena also introduced herself, & the second in the knitted swimsuit: Hilde Strauss.

— They haven't even opened the door yet.

— I don't know what's up.

— Yet here we are behaving like conspirators.

— When a person gives their name I always get a sense that they are muttering a secret password, a ...

— I like introductions —, said Yvonne, — though it's not fashionable nowadays: I like being pushy, being human. I know from myself what a hollow mask a person is, if I don't know their name; I don't want to be like that in front of others. We are stupid like that — a person becomes genuine once one associates the face with words such as Tatanabu Waga Toto.

Yvonne was moving just as freely and easily now as when down below on the beach, but Hilde was shuffling on the spot as if her swimsuit were still wringing wet & she was dreadfully freezing, rather as if she suddenly felt naked beside fully dressed Lea.

Someone called up inarticulately from the bottom of the staircase.

What is it? — Yvonne screeched back, clapping the palms of her hands like mock hearing horns.

— Come down, I pray, and enter downstairs, because madam put the key to the upper door on one side and then went off; she may have taken it with her, so one can't go in that way.

— Why didn't you say so earlier?

They went down.

— Hey, my swimsuit is still wet — said Hilde. She had on a worn greyish-green tricot swimming costume with bands where it had been overexposed to the sun and two thin shoulder straps holding it up, but it was very loose fitting right before the edge, along which ran a string-like wrinkle, or rather curling back: that sloppy frieze, the blotchiness of the whole, and the two crookedly put on shoulder straps, gave the costume something of the nature of a tree branch or a leaf; it was a mixture of moldedness to the body and sylvan sloppiness, taut in some places, dangling in others, in any event inviting form; even where it was taut it had an easy air about it, like a trivial dryad's garland of leaves, whereas in the parts where it was loosely clinging and creased like a sodden leaf, some kind of permanent body shape was ironed into it — however Hilde tossed on that 'Brother Ass' like a 'patina,' the long service to the body always made itself felt, so much so that it sketched out, indeed carved out, the woman even when Hilde wrung it out into a braid.

The fresh dress, and the very old one, have their own equally definite, body-oriented strength: the old one is completely permeated by the body like a highly veined leaf in fall that is more richly saturated with the essence of summer than a ball of boughs in early-July (*autumnus æstas introversus*);[124] indeed, just as a denser fluid of life (maybe of youth as well) is absorbed into the strong features of the faces of women who are beginning to age and wrinkle than into the flesh of young girls, where time has not yet transformed into noble material as in wine: it is as though in those worn-out women's dresses the body's power were multiplied as many times as the woman had put it on, and thus the chemical compound of time and body were bestowing the most erotic emphasis on an item of clothing (*vestimenteros corpotemp.*)[125] — while with brand new dresses the opposite phenomenon is the case: in the former case, the garment absorbed the body's memory of form through the mediatory veins of time, like a new material diffusing everywhere into the stuff, in other words, body, dress, and time are united in it — whereas here, it's precisely the division, the striking incongruence between woman and tweed that points toward the body; one can still perfectly feel the draper, the dressmaker, the fashion magazine and tailor's dummy rather than its having anything to do with a woman, so that attention is immediately diverted to nakedness, for the new dress is quite inorganic and almost wrongly made-up, like a mask used in the ritual dances of savages; no compromise had as of yet arisen through friction between the skin and the inside surface of the dress in order to obscure the cut-out boundaries of nudity and cloth — a female body stood reduced to itself like that in a homespun coat like a lonely flower stalk in a dimly walled vase; a shadow as slim as an X-ray on the wall of the jug if light falls on it.

Ena and Lea talked over the matter of the apartment with the proprietress (she herself looked like a serving girl: white apron, black skirt; her glistening black hair cut into an Eton crop; big, black-framed glasses, one of the lenses of which was a lot more convex than the other), as a result of which Lea booked herself in for two weeks. When Lea entered her name into the register and announced that she would pay that afternoon, she felt that she had tied a civil marriage knot with ecclesiastic solitude.

— Perhaps this afternoon I shall have enough time to think over the reasons that prompted me to come here — she said with a laugh to Ena, but also a little toward Hilde as well in order to create a discreet air of mystery about herself. — I don't know if my seclusion will serve the purpose, because I don't know exactly what the purpose is.

the guesthouse from an architectural point of view (modern space & modern morality)

The whole guesthouse, in point of fact, was nothing more than a single big apartment, so it bore no hotel character; from a small, white, furnished entrance-hall (a set of cognac glasses stood on the table, white earthenware shot glasses, a flask resembling a huge cucumber or a cactus protuberance in the middle, all very low down, so that the black spots of the shadows that one saw in the glasses, viewed necessarily from above, were taken into account in the design of the impact plan of the whole set of ninepins [which is what it resembled]) one reached a big hall where majolica objects combining lilac and gold predominated; in the middle was a small mythological scene of proletarian figures, as if they were embalmed embryos — Nausicaä holding out a ball and a gawping Odysseus: the girl is a Mecklenberg slut[126] on which the lilac & gold rays, which could be imagined as being frozen fire, glinted oddly; those delicate lights nevertheless bestowed a subaqueous gracefulness on all its muddy awkwardness; on Odysseus's head a Doge's cap, crumpled into a fur cap, and his opened lips no longer proclaimed desirous amazement swollen into pain but nonsense almost finalized into dogma. Its creator himself probably wanted the mixture of clumsiness and aquamarine grace that he did, indeed, achieve, though not by means of the devices that the maker used for the purpose, but precisely because he was unable to achieve his goal with those means, and that little flop was truly primitive and charming. In the four corners were four standard lamps; in fact enlarged table lamps that had been only chest-high — giant smooth brass spheres above which the shades were lilac-and-gold truncated cones. From that hall opened the dining room and two more guesthouse rooms.

The whole apartment was full of openness, as if vertical walls were totally negligible with this construction: a big axis was taken, parallel covers inserted successively at certain intervals, and it was left at that. What it had in the way of vertical walls seemed more like a chunk of a folding screen that had been tipped there at random, or a glass rind that the peeler had pared off in regular strips here and there.

As if the demon of horizontality had taken possession of the architect: that planimetric sodomy (there are certain architectural forms with which a monotony of individual elements for its own sake is related to the more complex old proportions like a homosexual sensitivity to heterosexuality; when Leatrice strolled around in the low, but extraordinarily broad and long rooms, she felt she was surrounded by a perverse joy in space & passion that had lost its balance; as if in architecture only verticals were assurances of morality and normality — horizontality was self-serving [space-serving] barrenness, Dorian-flavored frivolity: thus do 'homo-architectural' & 'hetero-architectural' love stand opposed in the domain of the morality of buildings) straight away took hold of Leatrice's body & forced a new self-consciousness into her; she completely accepted the flat promptings, her gaze grew accustomed to wandering close to the floor, to looking at objects only at a distance lying on that plane, never on top of each other.

Those tray-leaved water plants came to mind (Tanagra figurines of the deity of flatness), the stems of which creep under the water from deep down toward the surface and there finally debouch in flat leaves, which, by having such perfect absurdity on the surface of the water (a completely sodden sheet of paper not a single tip of which has as yet drooped under water) seem to be still a millimeter lower than the water's surface without being swamped by the surrounding water: this is a provocative and poetic perversity as in the open air; in bright yellow light they are so horizontal as to give an impression of an already sinking tilt and thus self-betraying and self-deluding essence, as opposed to the upwardly winding stems plunged in the shade which are mere wraiths of the morality of verticality, as if they were not nourishing veins but just nervous stem-scruples, just as in many human souls religious and moral verticality is just that kind of shadow-stem, neurasthenia-drawing & fear.

The launching into planarity, the magnetic space suggesting recumbent positions, awakened a nihilist frame of mind in Lea. These gratings, low settees, recumbent oblong pieces of furniture parallel to the ground, and only horizontally twisting cacti, very much suited the sea's flatness; the shadows, too, became elongated, eerily empty, which is to say sensual; when one stepped into a room like that, one of the walls of which was glass, with 'healthy' sunlight streaming through that, neither the light nor the shade was anthropomorphous — in reality the light did not stream but was 'present,' with painful exaggeration, as luminousness, without any dramatic turbulence, as some sort of nakedness that ensues after nakedness itself as if there were some sort of prism which instead of decomposing light, on the contrary made it whiter, more homogeneous, so that a person's body loses any sense of weight and uniform plenitude (the old window light was a man-mimicking statue of light); the shadows are also not siblings of one's body but mocking-erotic projections in the hygienic and fatefully horizontal mirror of nirvana. The sea illuminated through a long, horizontal window like a Cubist Neptune-carpet; its blueness was the inherent heraldic color of impatient horizontality, while the precise skyline between water and sky was a cosmic advertising formulation, a terse codification, of the villa's architectural proportions.

sonic portrait of the two neighbors

The two girls were Lea's neighbors; she could hear their voices, the tugging on drawers, slamming of doors, and that deep, charged-rustling sound that invisible human bodies emit as mysterious sonic shadows: one would be able to reconstruct from those muffled sounds a quite different body than a person really is if one's memories did not inhibit it. For Lea it was strange to hear that resonant friction & their meanwhile chirruping voices at one and the same time, as if lead-fanned tree boughs rustling above somersaulting hummingbirds — but sometimes the voices assumed a tragic huskiness, at which times they were no doubt lacing their shoes, squatting & with the throat pressed onto the knees: through the wall, the whole process of dressing turned into a panting of damned angels.

It was a strange drama; she was constantly deducing what they might be doing, and she ran those imagined scenes in her brain in parallel to the dark and deep, Roman-style shaping of the voice; the little reconstructed pictures were full of ironic idyllism, and lost in the huge, outsized vaults of the voices which filtered over — puzzle, comedy, and mystery were united in them. She heard a drawer being pulled open: all at once the whole stage was transformed into a huge drawer; the drawer burst out of nothing (after all Lea had no knowledge, as of yet, of the furniture there) like the bursting cork of the whole villa — after that the voices of rummaging appeared before her as the impatient waves of chirping and gabbing champagne. She also pictured the room as being overcrowded, because, being ignorant of its furniture and where the windows were located, she filled out everything with sounds or tangible images of movements suggested by the sounds, furnishing as it were an abstract arena with those, roughly with the insensitivity to perspective with which medieval miniaturists painted their pictures (a castle tower and a human, a far-away mountain range and a nearby hunting dog flourished in naïve coordination): in Lea's brain every sound in fact suggested a picture of uniform size, the least friction signified just as great a shift in the fate of a movement as the noises accompanying a genuinely significant motion.

She did not have any instrument to measure the value of those far off sounds, not knowing which the subject, which the predicate, so she resembled those who pay attention to a poem's meter all alone, and, irrespective of the thought, reconstruct some kind of graphical image of the poem, then from the system of graphs, some kind of graphic logic, graphic ethics, etc. Lea felt that having those neighbors was a blessing for her; she needed, and indeed would have needed, this dancing dispersion, a disintegrating garland, to accompany her construction of herself in her solitude.

---

the triad of 'ego,' 'people,' & 'objects' in the guesthouse'

That tripartition clearly asserts itself in a guesthouse like that which continually accompanies one through life, only not so scientifically separated, isolated like a specimen, but tossed into each other, with coda-like fracturing: the disposition of one's own individuality (it is usually in hotel rooms that the undisturbed fragrance of the 'ego'-monologue rises from the human chalice, now independent), then that of the 'company' or even 'society' (the salon and the historical classes perform the same game), and finally the disposition of 'lifeless objects,' the mute surroundings.

One enjoys this particularly in hotels: on awakening one feels only the weight, extent, and amorphousness (that certain yet to be mentioned embryonic movement) of the ego, the one and only person, that in the morning hours one may change over into enjoyment of 'other people,' the activity of the lounge; one realizes that the one and only person (e.g., 'me') is a living being of a totally different category than 'other people,' 'other people' is not even put together from people but is a homogeneous being of a different nature that one sometimes, quite unjustifiably and clumsily, labels with the word 'person.' It could be that there was a time in a mythological prehistoric age when 'a person' & 'people' were molded from a common material, but that kinship has since become blurred like that between Sanskrit & Swedish. Just as the function of the third factor, 'lifeless objects,' may once have been identical to one's human functions, but nowadays it has independent goals.

A human being in some manner betokens pure strength, a high tide filled with possibility; society betokens constant motion, games, and zigzagging; and finally, the lifeless milieu (objects and scenery) expresses meanings, truths, and principles unsullied by reason. The chief virtue of these three functions is discretion: strength, game, and principle are all just indications, but they cannot be made tangible as thoughts. (*"Kommt nach Swinemünde: Kraft, Spiel und Principia! Strengste Diskretion!"*)[127]

In any case, one of Lea's favorite Japanese pictures could have been a marvelous symbol of that guesthouse triad: in the foreground stood an enormous black vase, behind it blue sky with the star-soda of the Milky Way, while on the right-hand side hung a long text as if printed with a typewriter, the columns of letters imitating the dangling branches of a weeping willow in long and short versions. The 'ego,' the one and only person, corresponded to the dark monologue-vase; 'other people' to the white acid-pearls of the Milky Way, and last of all the logical character of the surroundings found expression in the thick sentence-curtains of the Japanese text. It was obvious that this was a mythological time when vase and Milky Way were still made of a shared material. The human being was lost since an exclusive hotel administration ruled out *ab ovo* any second-hand anthropomorphism: the monologue was not a self-portrait, only a dim shadow of one's net weight and resources, and the company has no relationship to a person, even after chemical analysis.

VI.

A great example of 'people': from the lives of two guests, Veronica Chamædrys & Ulva di Chara; Veronica in the restaurant, her relationship to nature

Lea (Homessa Lea Contranthropa) searched for solitude and independence in the guesthouse: 'living only for oneself' in places like that tends to start with one's soul being filled with the life of strange people from the first moment; at home, when she was working, she was full of perpetual egoism, though officially she was concerned with the business of others; now, at her holiday place, when she wanted to live a life of luxury, everyone, from the doorman to the small pooch who had run away from the nearby hotel, was pouring into her brain and keeping her busy like the most scrupulous maiden functionary for a charity league. Lea's solitude started with strangers' narratives.

In the guesthouse lived Veronica Chamædrys, the protagonist of a big scandal. Lea had seen her that morning in her new spring costume: a blood-red, close-fitting jacket, which was finished off at the back in a tiny pointed flap like the little uniform of an elevator boy; on the front were sewn big, white, gleaming nickel buttons, two rows of them at that, which ended very wide apart at the exceptionally broad padded shoulders, though above the chest, where they approached the hips, they grew ever-closer together, so that at the bottom they met in one button. On her head was a small black cap, rather as if a rubber ball that had been forcibly stretched had been placed at the nape of her neck — it had been run over her head (it was so thin that it looked like little more than the sheath for a hairnet) and it was fastened down above the forehead: if the fastening loosened, the whole cap would snap back to the nape. She greeted Lea like an old acquaintance, holding a saucer to her lips with the left hand and gesturing with the right at Lea, who at first thought it must have been by error, but having looked around, saw that the confidential greeting was addressed to her.

The 'solitude' was therefore intoned, the mystical eremitism had started, Lea = Veronica. Round Veronica's neck was a riding shawl, on her feet black boots. Lea later learned that the reason the woman had got up so early was because she had been given a horse as a gift and she wanted to try it out straightaway inasmuch as she had made an excursion to her younger sister's place in Streluuds (a fair hike). Her mother would make the same journey by car.

Lea sensed that the day would be working for that woman's pleasure, not for her; the sun may have been shining for Lea, but she felt that it was just pain compensation, because later on luster and time would be standing in the service of Veronica. It is not possible to share the day; when Lea had entered the breakfast room the whole day had, as yet, been hers, as if the sandglass's trickling eyes did not form a simple layer in the lower glass bulb but cohered in the form of a female nude, with every trickling second bringing a newer figure or embellishment of an old figure.

The sea was grey, with the thin fence stealthily forming a grid along the promenade, like the first geometrical temptation in God's soul; the gold of dawn had difficulty in separating from the greyness and lay in slovenly stillbirths sprawled on trees, on benches, on telephone wires. Lea recognized herself in that scattering, and for precisely that reason felt in her pocket the safety key to the Garden of Eden, because even up to that point, only in such tattered spaces could she feel most at home. The sharp colors of the flowers fell on the Sun's waterproof envelope as if they were some kind of sealing wax test sample; some people were awake in that sleepy morning like a healthily awakening wife next to a dead husband, proving the first point of the anti-Hyppolites, which relates to the absolute ineffectiveness of the milieu.

Lea would have liked it if the flowers had adapted themselves a bit to her as well, but they proclaimed pure phrases of selfishness: "egoism, thy name is color" — she remarked with a Hamletian equation. However, what was the icy flower-autarchy next to a suddenly materializing Veronica! Lea could not have seen her immediately because she was sitting behind a column. But when she did spot her she would have preferred to rush out onto the street, pleading on her knees to the Sun not to loop its gallant equatorial lasso around Veronica's waist; imploring the sea not to make a free loan of its enormous blue backdrop as a comfortable support and an attorney's speech for the defense behind Veronica's frivolous life; and asking the doorman not to allow her to telephone, to jumble up the exchange switchboard's jacks & not hand them over to her post; asking the tram conductor, who usually took guests across to Walsebrool in his rattling sardine box, to order her off because her season ticket had expired on the weekend: she wanted to warn the whole world to snap out of their half-witted loyalty & play havoc with Veronica.

Two things were certain: Veronica was bad & she had not as yet been touched by misfortune in her life. Veronica at once sucked sun, time, flowers and seas into herself; it was then that it became clear that those sober-minded & alert painted flowers were not self-centered but were only waiting to be of service to Veronica. How naïve those romantic souls who grumble about their minor complaints to the diverse founding, honorary,

& corresponding members of nature — to big, fat mountains, highly strung clouds, or lonely trees in orchard steppes, believing them to sympathize with her. Right then, at the present moment, Lea had the opportunity to experience that nature's leaders and employees alike were merely seeking backstairs influence, with people snuggling up even to the skirt of Spinoza's landlady with the most hypocritical grimaces, because they knew that pantheism was tantamount to a pay raise — nature could forever only be bothered with advancement and money.

Forget Spinoza, but what hope can there be for this rose in the little garden in front of the hotel — from Veronica Chamædrys? Nature, like every trueborn financier, is inclined to be more a sentimentalist than an empiricist and feels extraordinarily good next to elegant people even before she is clear about what profit can be drawn from it within the next week. How was there so much strength in the Chamædrys girl as to be able to elicit in Leatrice a charge of the most hominoid materialism? Lea would have liked to institute legal proceedings against every single woodruff, stonecrop, and yellow bedstraw for deception and fraud.

It gradually began raining: the sandglass's nude-forming property came to mind. The rain was maybe the time-metering material in the spinning blue bulb of the firmament that was now going to bless Veronica. Why did it take away from Lea the whole day, the whole restaurant, the whole world? When she looked at a vegetable trolley that was moving away she could see from the sardonic mute reply of the savoy cabbages that Veronica had already greased their palms yesterday evening. Lea thought that there is nothing else for the rain to do but to pray to God that He would not tolerate that total injustice. A mission ought to be set up in the corrupt world of nature in order to convert & enlighten them — only yesterday that rose had embezzled, this cloud had committed incest, & every *Ranunculus* was as stingy as a cowardly speculator in crises. Veronica had carried all that out in secret. Why not unmask her?

Veronica wanted to get married: she had black eyebrows and rosy cheeks with a tint of the lilac with which rationalist and neo-kitschist Parisian painters are in the habit of representing a damp dawn as it flutters like a pink underskirt put out to dry among the trees of the Luxembourg Gardens. She was reminded of her Uncle Péter's influenza-sweethearts: the bench was wet, rain was dripping off the branches, the sweethearts blew huge handkerchiefs full within seconds, they devoured pills, through kissing they raised to the power of infinity the colds they passed on to one another like a relay baton, while the next day they set down the essential things they had forgotten to say on paper about exactly what lilac shade the Boreal western sky & their noses had been the day before. The head cold-heraldics of the skin of her cheeks stood in odd contrast to the ferocious redness of the coat (a color-muzzle ought to have been placed on it — to *abblenden*[214] it so it was not so irritating to the eyes) and the sharp coal cutting of her eyebrows. Veronica was certainly bad, and the worst of her badness was the sentimentality that could be brought out on cue. That, even if she suspected it with crude moralism, Leatrice sensed well.

The afternoon of the day just gone by, Veronica and her mother had been in the neighboring garden where an inaugural ball had been organized and where the two women had made the acquaintance of the husband-to-be. Her mother often played bridge with the man; numbers, tricks, diamonds and robbers all gave definition to the obscure joy of marrying off her daughter — she discovered unsuspected dimensions of this pleasure in a fresh page, a fresh round. In the buffet, she mentally felt her way once more through the memory of the tricks like the numbered cards of the joy-crystal.

Veronica herself was not a good, just a passionate player; she wanted in any event to beat her husband-to-be and so was continually teasing him into big stakes. During play she was pale and ate all the time just out of excitement: she had no idea why she wanted to win half the riches belonging to the man whom she wanted to marry, whether out of joy or regret. "We must realize that we are living through moments of joyous despair" — an old partner had said when Veronica's thrill had become all too obvious. To begin with she and her Mama had played against the man together, then just the mother, and the third time just Veronica.

The big excitement had arisen at that third game. Veronica had all at once felt a girlish fear about her mother having left her high and dry, and pubescent pride that she was on her own playing cards with three grownup men. She did not succeed in beating her husband-to-be, or rather just once only, and then she had clapped her hands loudly in exultation. The man had smiled like someone who was gently re-ascertaining the validity of an old diagnosis. Veronica announced that she was going home but the man urged her to stay for one more game, which he was obliged to play with a distinguished client, after which he would accompany her back home. But she declared that she would not accept the perverse loyalty of a losing dueling partner: "You're bleeding and are looking to accompany a healthy opponent while you have a bandage that is showing the red seeping through? That's a lot of politeness." The man smiled as though he was well aware that women have a gross and a net understanding: the gross understanding was his own, which was why the net understanding wriggled so impossibly.

Veronica & her acquaintance in the cloakroom

When Veronica went down into the cloakroom, into the big butcher's stall of masks for the whole body, and shivered among two hundred winter overcoats in search of the cloakroom attendant, snatching both her hands from the pipes of the central heating like a self-tormenting snail its eyestalks, she had the impression that she was moving about in a strange crypt where people who believed they were still living up above had long been buried down there, signaling with huge numbers so that they might be graded in the tumult of the resurrection: poor Nigella, how merrily she had danced up above — her hat, shawl, and fur coat, in contrast, were lying there mutely and lifelessly on a shared hook among the other fallen top hats & decomposing overcoats. She rubbed her eyes, and with her handkerchief she pulled out her own doomsday ticket from her narrow handbag. At that point a fair-haired young fellow jumped over and passed it up to her. Veronica was happy to recognize him for an old friend.

— What's this? You're here as well? Why are you coming here right now? Look, I'm incapable of finding the woman or whoever can hand out my coat.

Veronica saw around two hundred coats, so she was freezing roughly two hundred times as much as she had any right to by the thermometer. The cloakroom attendant turned up, and while he was handing over the coat, something crossed her mind that she would have found hard to say to the newly arrived boy, because while she was continually adding a new item to her body, the man was continually shedding items as if he were a continually diminishing reel, the threads of which were winding across with mechanical speed to the woman. Her own female brain was being strangled by one new layer after another, and if her thoughts were able to penetrate those impediments, the man had no resistance massive enough to bore into: if she addressed her speech to his shawl, the next moment it became detached from him like the over-tetchy stem of a poppy; and if to his jacket, it became unbuttoned, and a waistcoat that made him even slimmer took its place.

— I know you play magnificently, so I would make one request of you.

— Who do you want me to beat up?

— That's it. Wallop L*** soundly, really soundly. I hope you are not dependent on him or anything like that.

— Not in the least, I am not even acquainted with the fellow, and I'll do as you ask. Incidentally, though, why do you have such bloodthirsty designs? If you are going to take offence do so now, and energetically if possible, because I am going to ask things which are designed to offend you: should I give you anything from the booty? Or is the vengeance entirely holy idealism? A Bridge Crusade or whatever?

— The latter, the latter. No, I've no need of booty — she said, blushing.

When Veronica herself worked with money, she was normally pale, nervous, and totally forgot about her glances, her movements; true, the reason for that was not rudimentary avarice, but a naïve respect for money; at home she had heard so much about money being the greatest positive in life, compared to which life and death, God & love, were just inconsequential variations, so that when the smallest amount came before her eyes she got stage fright and became anxious, though not as if she had perceived its value sensorially, but because she had respect for the romantic theory of money and feared the prestige of the concept. She did not see the disturbing opalization of pettiness even in financial wranglings of the lowest caliber but imagined them as the mystic endowment of male life, indeed as the natural rhythm of 'life' in general. Both her mother and she felt that menfolk had to be supported in the struggle for and against money and therefore by charitable softening of the heart & sensitive homeliness, out of a tearful love of 'the home,' they, too, concerned themselves with all sorts of shady deals.

At first with excitement & maidenly fluster, in the way first-time hunters tend to behave: if Veronica had had to forge a bill of exchange she would not have had the foggiest notion that this was a crime or crookedness, just: "Heavens! Life is so exciting, men have such special tricks: how odd it is that money is so important in life." For both women money was a curio: they feared it as the most sharply drawn sketch of alienness; they looked at it childishly, as a blue mountain lake, the water of which is always refreshing; and they kept close watch on it, nursed it like a chronically dying person who would be annihilated the moment they took their eyes off him.

When Veronica played cards upstairs she would feel the agonizing role of money by her side: she wanted to win because a good little girl's place was next to a sick patient. Now, when the fair-haired boy asked whether she needed anything from the booty, she sensed money as a blue mountain lake before her eyes, so she merely blushed demurely as if she had heard a racy but obsequious compliment.

The sweetest moments of all for Veronica were when money was the subject of the conversation of others: then she was brought into an ethereal, angelic connection to the concept of money as if she were conjuring up for herself agreeable memories of a trip of old. Then the lilac-pink color of her cheeks much more closely resembled itself than now, at the end of the restaurant, barely twenty paces away from Leatrice.

— What's this?! You taking your summer holiday here as well?

With a chuckle, the man said:

— Holidaying — that would be a slightly exaggerated way of putting it. I arrived today, but incidentally I was in Streluuds, and there I bumped into your younger sister. Is she together again with that lecturer-to-be & PhD, and funded and heaven knows what kind of level he's operating at.

— Him, him? — she asked with a listless and forced smile, because it came to mind that the guy had already once persuaded her sister to protest against the fact that her older sister (i.e., Veronica) allowed her ephemeral lovers to handle assets that constituted the sister's own future dowry. What if they were to pay off any grudges by laying hands on not just the younger sister's dowry but also her own? She decided that the next day she would travel over to Streluuds with her mother.

Veronica in the hotel door; architecture & morality; architectural suggestion & transformation of the 'hero of the novel'

When she got down to the hotel entrance she leaned out from between the glass doors with a motion, as if water had taken the place of asphalt and her gondola were exasperatingly late: if she took one step lower she would be ankle-deep in water, but there was no going back because the extraordinarily wide glass doors were folded like draught-screens, in multiple layers, as if the whole thing were a machine that had been designed so it had a tendency to push departing guests into ever more external spheres — a negative trap, which thrust them outwards, step by step, in such a way that under no circumstances should they be able to get back. The ground-plan of the exit was a quarter circle, & there were doors placed along three of the radii: with the innermost one there were lots of minute folds with the goal of, as it were, making a twelve-meter long glass plate 'portable'; on the second door the folds were much broader, while on the third there were just wafer-thin nickel straws, but that aside, the whole thing was the end of a single enormous stretch of glass: the guests therefore passed through a three-stage '*Gradus ex Parnasso*.'[129] The attendant plays of chiaroscuro were best known to drivers in the cab rank across the road: when the innermost door tilted and a human figure was not yet visible, only the glittering shadow of the glass plates swinging to & fro on the two glass walls in front, they would promptly jump to the driving wheel in order to swing their cab round in front of the entrance; this had a sort of religious character, the way they would leap into the cab at such murky light signals rather than starting off at a human call. In any event, the three-stage space school (by way of analogy a 'hopscotch' for children) represented by the exit had spiritual consequences.

In her childhood (not so long ago), Veronica had a sock suspender on which thin black vertical lines were drawn: if out of playfulness that rubber strap were stretched out so far as almost to snap, those preciously vertical lines would spread into wide bands; indeed, they would take up position on the whole strap not as vertical bands, but, like enlarged telegraphic signs, as horizontal bands parallel to the strap. Between the first exit and the third pane of glass the relationship of the two states signaled by that old sock suspender held true: horizontality was just an oscillatory phase of verticality.

But what to make of it if at the first exit-door, which is composed purely of a vertical plate, like the patented pleat of a glassworks, one thinks of marrying a man who one hopes will lose much more than hitherto in the card room — and has exactly the same thought at the third glass strip on which it is obvious that the 'way up' was just a momentary condition of the horizontal, and the horizontal was a much more typical state of the vertical than the vertical. Because such very concrete matters as marriage or card playing occur in the mind both vertically and horizontally; so what will Veronica's marital thought be at the third door?

Or: what solace does a seasick ocean seafarer find in the discovery that the endless horizontal line of the sea is not the antithesis of vertical but just a variant, let us say, its greatest amplitude?

Just imagine any musical theme being performed with infinite speed or infinite slowness: in the first case all one would hear would be a momentary rustling, in the latter case the endless protraction of a single tone: one wonders who would be able, or dare, to declare that they were hearing the same theme, first as an absurd presto, then as an absurd Cantorian adagio? Who would dare to affirm that the point heard first and the subsequent line, or, to take the antithesis drastically further: an abstraction (the point) and an everlasting reality (the line) were two tempos of one and the same theme (and the logical deception with the antithesis of point and line which had to be committed temporarily in the interest of Veronica's marriage can now be beautifully expressed): body and soul, God and material, are altogether two tempos of a single theme: the soul is an infinitely fast material, the material is an infinitely slow soul. Veronica's sock suspender intimated some such theology: *honny soit qui mal y pense.*[130]

Up till now we have been trying to imagine a musical motif being performed at infinite speed, which is to say, the distances between the individual notes are infinitesimally small — in the endless adagio, on the other hand, the individual notes will be separated from one another by an infinity (will this adagio ever at all reach the second note? A scholastic and a Cantorian answer can be given, but both play only a distant role as marriage brokers for Veronica, so they can be neglected). Let us replace the musical notes by a human action, and not a neutral but a moral one.

An action of this kind is just as much composed of various partial actions, as a musical theme is of various notes: for example, a donation to the poor is always a moral triplet comprising reaching into a pocket, holding out the money, and dropping the money into a hat. Exceedingly interesting things can be experienced if that happens infinitely quickly (coincidence of intention and deed, et cetera), but since Veronica was moving away from the manifold vertical door toward the infinitely horizontal, let us rather look at what happens if a moral deed becomes infinitely slow. Reaching into the pocket lasts forever; another infinity intervenes between reaching into the pocket and holding out the money, and so on: that is to say, the single triplet, the single moral deed, only the last phase of which makes it a moral *deed*, ceases to be moral and to be shaped like a deed since it expands through multiple endless lines to turn indifferent, just as in infinite stretching a blood-red rubber strap turns pink and eventually colorless. The point that makes the moral deed genuinely a moral deed projects far into the infinite, & no one in the world will or can notice from the part that falls within finite human boundaries that it is the infinitely slowed-down first movement of a moral deed.

Veronica knew in the first exit door that she was going to marry the man her mother had come across, she knew not how, but in the third door that thought had slipped into a mirror which infinitely extended it so that only a part of that thought was sighted by Veronica, and naturally that part did not at all resemble the whole thought, so that by the time she had reached the street, getting married signified something completely new & alien to her. It could be the seaside scenery: if the vertical could become horizontal through simple stretching, why couldn't the thought of marriage become a coastal scene through the third glass door?

When Veronica left the hotel it may have officially been evening, but there are cases when calendric consistency becomes impossible: now a morning landscape belonged to her. Only by & large at that: after all, those landscapes which are not proposed by nature as a table d'hôte background but created by our own soul around itself are independent from the schemata of physical geography; the morning dangles from a flower like an endless stamen, on the other bench glows the freshly expired moonlight while the noonday sunlight ennobles a solitarily strolling girl's golf club into a double bargain. Every single object, indeed every little particle of a single object, conjures up a different period around itself: certain parts of the human body suggest night, others lunchtime, still others early spring. So Veronica was unable to resign herself to the night: she undoubtedly had a lot of thoughts that could be marked as 'night' above her mental tracks, but there were a lot that called for other seasons with the least conscientious parallelism.

dawn in the small harbor, Veronica & her woman friend

At dawn the whole world is like an uncleared table: one wakes up and sees dirty glasses, crumpled napkins, and plates of fish bones from the previous evening's supper on the table. It is odd that one should find precisely that to be attractive: according to noble moralists, everything commences anew with dawn; in place of the time-lapsed omegas, the sprucely waxed alphas on the chests of larks which are stretching themselves. As they themselves say: "Everything starts new."

What is exciting about mornings, however, is that nothing at all new starts in them, but the past has remained: at dawn, if one opens one's eyes, the initial feeling, having cast a glance at one's surroundings, is that yesterday's feelings are totally valid today as well, and that one's past, like a safe gilt-edged stock, has not lost half-a-percent of its value, nothing has changed. All that is new is that one has a past, that one can pronounce the word 'yesterday' intelligibly, but even that rather means that all of one's actions are turned to yesterday and, if it were up to us, we would press the whole of today into the tight box of yesterday, and the only reason for living in the today is that, due to physical circumstances, one has been squeezed out of yesterday like out of an overcrowded bus: "the next bus is right behind."

On every newly succeeding day one wants to drill back into the layer of preceding days, and it is entirely immaterial that the train is racing along northwards & we are, nonetheless, walking southwards, if the dining car so happens to have been coupled to the train. One senses that one's path is almost physically tracing a wavy resultant on the calendar temperature chart of the days: time, raw time, is always forward, a human being is always facing backward like a stubborn drill, at each & every dawn nearer the sought-for past that one wishes were eternal. Life thus makes itself felt as if it was forever running late: one ought to have already been somewhere yesterday, and one can, perchance, reach it only today — that can be seen most clearly from the 'time tests' of lovers: actually, they do not wish to add today's new kiss to yesterday's kiss but to continue yesterday's kiss, or rather to run back to yesterday, though the wind of time is blowing straight against them. The concept of the 'future,' the theatrical stunt of 'starting over anew,' is no more than a pedagogic trick, alphaist hypocrisy against the one & only omega.

The greenish murk of dawn stood in the small harbor like a balloon in a body-fitting hangar. Between the spherical closed body of fog and the low hills that served to contain it, there barely remained a free strip that was neither fog nor hill — in that narrow strip the morning was already gleaming, in that strip objects became axioms of conceited time, shadows were sharp as lock-gates capable of keeping up torrents in a single geometrical straight line — that wisp of blue-blond smoke that soared up high from tiny ships (the various wisps of smoke ought to have been ticketed, like coats in a cloakroom, because they had crept quite far from the funnels to which they belonged and it was impossible to tell from which ship they came even though they did not get mixed up) teetered in the largely parallel strands of the gossamer threads like the first tortuous & uncertain big letters in an elementary school child's lined book.

According to some, jetties are horizontal whereas ship's funnels are vertical: in the morning, however, light would slice the shadow from a jetty in such a way that the jetty as well seemed to be standing vertically to the water surface just like a funnel: they were raised frivolous barrier gates which permitted the approaching morning as a Flying Scotsman, though the hotel guests were still lying across the tracks, unconscious and unprotected, in their hundreds. A single living woman was stirring on the shore, who, being awake, might be able to jump out of the way of the full-tilt thrusting arms of dawn. That was whom Veronica encountered on coming out of the hotel.

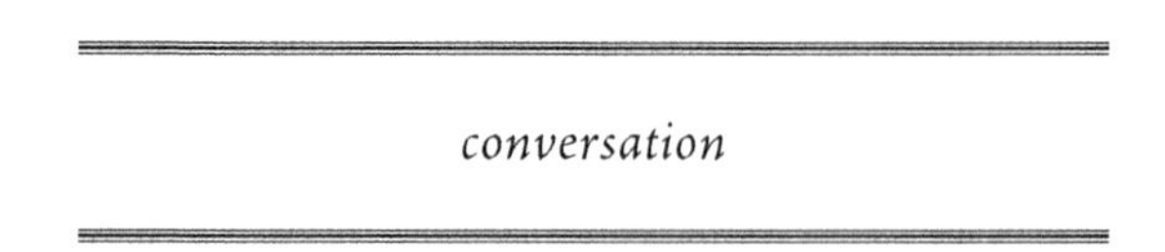

conversation

She recognized her woman friend. She was dressed confusedly: a white rubber raincoat and a big fox fur round her neck, with no hat. The light was shining so slantwise that the whole landscape was ending up well over their heads: the shadows slithered down the white sides of the ships in such a way that they saw them in bottom view — the black lower hulls of yachts through a golden, transparent water layer. No specific sense of underwater diving, however, attended all that perspective: they were not at the bottom of the water but under a strip of water, which was like an upper-story glass floor that left those underneath it untouched.

— Where did you come from? — Veronica asked. She saw that her woman friend was extremely depressed and sad, and somehow she took that to be a good portent.

— Have you been crying? — she asked her, moved almost to tears, though not as if she felt any sympathy but was overcome by tenderness in view of the fact that fate had sent a suffering woman to cross her path so as the better to feel her own joy. Joy is anyway such an insubstantial thing, like dancing, where form represents content: she could make a statue to that out of this female (Ulva di Chara).

— I was in the harbor — Ulva said, and as if that remark was not yet a proper tone, only the flat or sharp, she declared loudly: — Hello.

— Hello. What were you looking for there? — and Veronica looked along the ships hovering above her head: the many anchor chain cables were swimming in the body of the water like aerial roots. The water was quietly lapping because of standing still, whereas the longitudinal sections of the ships were swinging to and fro through being motionless; in just the way that micrographic photos of razor edges are printed in illustrated weekly magazines to show that "this is what a sharp line looks like in reality" (in fact it is full of zigzags & lumps) so those unruly ship's bottoms appeared as such 'silences in enlargement': "this is how stillness looks like viewed through 'scientific eyes'" (in fact it is full of oscillation & swaying). The ships, the columns on the shore, and the fog, were in solidarity, they had only excluded Ulva from their midst.

— Don't you want to sit down on a bench? — asked Ulva.

— To be sure, come here. Will it be OK there, or this one here?

— That one would be better, only the back is rusty all over, see? I sat down there this morning and afterwards this is how my coat looked. — Meanwhile she was twisting her head to examine the rust stains on her trench coat.

— Well alright, then come over here. Tell me, what happened, what is it?

Ulva pooh-poohed in order to avoid any pathos, and said with clumsy dryness:

— He left.

Veronica again looked at the ships; the white walls, made more elegant by the minimum of dirt taking off the edge, quivered in the air as if painted on the green auroral daylight's thousand-slatted window blind, making them vibrate apart interminably — the ship vibrated beyond the ship funnel's black border of soot, in thinned parallel streaks upwards to the disk of the sun. She saw an endlessly silent triumph in that white ladder of bands at the base of which the genuine ship filled a role like a stack of planks slid together at the foot of a ladder with moveable rungs. The entire world, and primarily her, was continually climbing upwards, landscapes were nothing more than indigestible stubs and lumps that cannot filter through the blue sieve of angelicness. Veronica was the volatile water that escapes through a hair-thin tube into a higher basin of joy whereas Ulva was a clumsy fish that had got caught, and while the water slipped away she was left kicking about there until she was stifled, like a stopper that is thicker than a bath drain.

Aqua ad piscem:[131]

— Tell me everything. Even yesterday afternoon there was nothing wrong.

— As a matter of fact something had already happened by then; at most you didn't spot it, and anyway that wasn't important, it wasn't the reason for his going.

The excessive melancholy started to become suspicious to Veronica, so she asked:

— That's the golf nut, wasn't it, who did not let you back?

Ulva laughed out loud, with a grey, awkward laugh as if she had wanted to pull on a glove in a preposterous fashion & was now noticing that the fingers were inside out.

— The golf nut? Not likely! He's fine as he is, but that isn't what this is about either. — She chuckled quietly, without the seams. — No, not him. It's stupid of me, isn't it, to announce just like that, without any ceremony, that 'he left.' I think you didn't even know about this.

— I never even saw him! How did you manage to find the time?

— That's just it, I didn't have time for him, and that spoiled everything, I reckon. Admittedly, he said something to the effect that, thank God we didn't have much time, at least it didn't cross our minds to tinker around with our time and maybe inadvertently flatten out what started as love, and seeks to be that too, into a flirtation.

— That's not so bad. But tell me, how many times have you seen what d'you call him since there was that whatever it was?

— The whole thing didn't last more than ten days. He came onto a yacht with a friend who had some business inland, among the mountains, while he stayed put here, in the harbor. He can't stand holidaymakers.

Veronica suddenly interjected:

— Tell me, did he take off once & for all, have you finished for good?

— Nothing was said about that in such definite form — Ulva said in a raised, sharper voice as a signal that she was only replying in quotation marks for the sake of the interruption & not voluntarily —, it was somehow self-explanatory. He doesn't like things being stretched out.

— That is rather a brutal sailor's pace: to mete out love to exactly the time a ship puts in to port.

— Believe me, that may be how it sounds, but he wasn't anything like that. He was very far from being brutal; in fact, if anything, he was a bit affected. Perhaps even that in itself was only affectation, that he hated flirting and only liked love: somehow he came to the realization that love is the main thing, & since then he has been a pedant about clinging to that.

— But that can't have been all that amusing, from your point of view, knowing how much he was a stickler for procedure.

— No, no — said Ulva, squinting outwards a little, as if she were looking at a portrait of the vanished young fellow and could see how much clearer the face was than all that she was rambling on about him to Veronica and was consoling herself with the recalled face —, there was nothing outrageous about the program. Or rather, I admit that I felt much the same way, but then I came to see that it's not like that, and even if it is, it's not important anyway.

description of Ulva di Chara

What goes for the seasons or times of day goes even more for clothes: before Ulva had on a grey raincoat, but now it was a long red cloth coat that the young fellow of the imagined portrait had given her. Ulva was fairly short and slightly pudgy but with a deftly salvaged hip (certain crystals, however impossible the parts they get squeezed into, nevertheless develop 'in the nick of time' the special form which is their own. Ulva's hip seemed to be a salvage action of the same kind, deriving from a shrewd, ingenious woman who, with her own modest but clean ways, procures with scintillating economy the beauty accoutrements indispensable to her one minute before closing time for the cosmetics shops), with short-fingered pudgy little hands, a round, very rounded head on which the hair, cropped too short, hung like a Franciscan friar's toupee in the theater, with a little tonsure with the hair standing out from the scalp in various colors from blond to grey. The sole linear part was her nose: thin and slightly broken. Her eyes were big and, normally speaking, fisheyes, void of expression, without eyelashes, but even if she only frowned a little, a fine refreshing wrinkle of quite unexpected body would run across it. Those two things, the thin, angularly profiled nose, and the minute tracks of reason on the skin, were unexpected.

In physical geography lessons one sees globes on which a wavy-edged plate is fitted, sundial fashion (like the axe in the skull of a martyr): one cannot imagine a greater contrast than the silly-slippery surface of a globe and against it this strongly marked flat portion. A whole repertoire of grimace phenomena ran across her face like reflections: it wasn't her muscles, or her nerves, which had become retuned; it was just the speckled psychic-shadows passing above her skin being reflected on it. Those reflections, though, were more perfect than the visceral mimicry of other people: a million shadows can be projected on a sketchily formed mask that will express a much richer, so-called 'psychic life' than a living and sensitive, real face. If there were no shadows and the psycho-quartz did not chop up her face into being intelligent, then it was a dead Mongol pod, Max or Moritz from the book by Wilhelm Busch:[132] a globe, or rather a horizontally flattened egg, with short-cropped hair atop, stuck on the head at just one point.

Ulva reached into her handbag and produced a thick letter.

— St. Stephen, that lengthy an adieu? — Veronica asked, taking care that not a single cell in her entire body should be startled toward the sheets of paper as if she were curious; her eyes seemed to be glinting excessively toward the letter precisely because her body was all of a sudden crippled: what was the point of casting naïve solidarity into the air?

— Now you are again going to misunderstand something — Ulva said, pressing Veronica's knee with the tip of a finger, which tilted outwards with conspicuous ease —, the lad was very fond of talking, but I never had the impression that he was *saying* anything (do you get me?), that he was telling me something, words and thoughts, but he really did mean what he was saying because the scoundrel was a bit conceited, but nicely so, darkly & adolescently so, with a growl — (Ulva supposed that if those epithets could mingle with the objects rattling in her purse: a cigarette case, comb sheath, powder compact, keychain — then they would lose their pathetic-swaggering successiveness: that was why she smeared each word in the air and simultaneously poked her fingers into her handbag, as if a practical object could substitute for modesty) —, saying that speech is simply a second dimension of happiness & in part — (here she struck a theatrical pose) — is a piece of my body.

love & talking

When Ulva said that with a snort of laughter, the Sun shining in her eyes like an eyelash brush, her walk in the autumnal wood came to mind: truly how strange speech was there. When two people do not talk to each other but are satiated with each other and staggering on account of the mute metabolism that comes with their new organism, then speech erupts in disconnected pieces; heavy sentences, whining fragments of adoration (*Kosmöschen, Panette*),[133] undertones, unexpectedly intoned homiletics, just as discontinuously as bare branch ladders, plump foliage dumplings, flowers, leaf litter, dust & aloes come one after the other.

What do those speeches have to do with the sentences that one is accustomed to say at other times? These woodland words do not rise from one's body but remain under the skin — instead of planting themselves in the air crystally, they just make waves on one's existence (*autogyro d'existence*), strive against oneself, as if the grapes themselves were getting drunk on the juice springing from within them, as if one's mood rejoiced in breaking though hedgerows, in ripping up bushes, and that was why one created from one's own words a training flora in which one can pitch and toss & suffocate.

What does all that have to do with talking? with expressing oneself? But maybe it does have something to do with another sense of 'expression' (to use a clumsy word: 'deeper'); for at times like that one has a feeling that one's body has lost its balance & needs to be suddenly tipped back into place: that is when the words come that restore one with fabulous speed, rebuild the precarious floors of one's muscles: why?

And why is that necessary? The lovers fell in love because the condition they were in at present appealed to each other: when they become aware of that, then they (especially boys) begin to reconstruct themselves as if what had provoked love in the first place had immediately worn away, and therefore they push a big talking-mask in place of their own personality, a melting tank of words, because they are so modest and bashful that they always see their yesterday self as bacterium-small, and even so stripped to the skin.

Ulva realized how much the talk of her friend was different from *'tel qu'on parle'* when recollecting her stroll; she was not able to accurately tell from a yellow leaf wire whether it was a real tree leaf or one of the man's remarks. How much he struggled (the fellow was a deep shade of pedantic) to explain that, although his words conformed to the branches fluttering up as the ancillary goals of trees, he still did not mingle with nature but strictly preserved his urban character: he denied himself from one minute to the next, and only with the intervention of gestures and mollycoddling nursery rhymes was he able to damp that tiring zigzagging.

Ulva had felt that every one of the boy's faults (pedantry, preciosity, flaunted cowardice, self-complimentary self-mockery, indiscreetly managed, albeit genuine precocity, etc.) were pardonable; yet she was not satisfied with him. He stretched love so far that it could no longer be operated on on an experiential plane; he tossed so many possible attitudes of love into a quarter of an hour that the girl would grow dizzy, not knowing where to look, and would have liked to urgently become his lover in order to quench a little the variation-parade. It was also evident that the parading was sincere: it was not mixed with a single false note, pose, or clumsy-atavism of adolescence. However, it was a lot; just as Ulva muddled up the young fellow's sentences with the forms of rock plants and looked even for the live Moon in a dictionary, she also confused the local love directed at her with the young guy's passive (non-amatory) glow. It was always about her, but with such analytical furor, with such inversions of objectivity, that her empirical self changed into her 'true self,' & a woman never has anything sensible to do with that (the height of objectivity is always fiction).

The mixing up in love of empiricist Ulva and the capricious fluctuation of the 'true self' came to fruition perhaps even more perfectly than during the walk in the woods on a much later afternoon-liaison, when love for him suddenly branched from the girl a two-pronged genus-fork: they were sprawled on a light-green couch in a corner right near a window, so that the room was full of filtered light whereas the couch remained in shadow. As the guy stroked her body with cramp-ridden fingers, throwing, turning, and pulling her about to and fro, she felt she was becoming a helpless doll, an unfinished block of a statue: all the fine salon-humanity which she had compiled with the collecting zeal and jealousy of a medieval encyclopedist with girlish parsimony from books, unexpected sentiments, tourist-trade landscapes and monthly-melancholy: all that was at once futile under what were almost the embraces of a pugilist; alongside the aphrodisiac KO-blow of every embrace, he also felt the plastic of the couch with her head knocking against now a spring that was jutting out, now a rung behind the cushion, now the wall; sometimes she rested a hand, fingers separated on the floor like a goose's foot so that on the couch he might be able to fit his lips more comfortably between the sole and heel of the high-heeled slipper; sometimes she had to sling her legs into the display hanging above their heads (like an umbrella into an entrance-hall umbrella rack), so that he (who would change the direction of kisses from one moment to the next like someone testing whether or not he would grow dizzy in a looping airplane) would be able to kiss her hand, which was entangled at that moment in the earth line of the radio receiver.

Only rag dolls are usually pulled about like that by the extremities, she thought to herself, not anthropomorphious women. On the other hand, the boy, & life in general, has taken care that there should also be an antidote to total dollness: the guy talked so much, told the girl so many jokes, prayers, hors d'oeuvre mythology, anatomical surprises, laws of psychology and formulae of annihilation (those, roughly speaking, are the topics of amorous conversation), that she felt each joke, prayer, and ironically served up slice of mythology was linked to an ever-new individual; the sculptural crudeness of the embraces may have simplified & stiffened her into a single Romanesque cathedral doll, but the talking, on the other hand, scattered her into a thousand souls — she was both a fully grown flashy-yellow dandelion and the blown-away silky-grey pappus, the faltering bit of fluff after the flower has withered.

the two extremes of 'doll'-person & 'infinite nuance'-person;
their relationship to love;
Touqué's plan for Tailor's Dummy and Phantom

Love has long accomplished these two kinds of disintegration with people: it was one of Touqué's favorite topics in *Antipsyche*. The new 'hominity' signified in part *Adam Nudus*, or in other words a puppet, an anatomical curio-like body barely acquainted with psychological life; on the other hand, though, also a richness of psychic life, an intentional multiplication, which was just as 'antipsyche' as the primitive puppet: one gets dispersed into ten, twenty, or a thousand persons, their analytical psychic life has penetrated so deeply into the 'self' that it has finally managed to get out of itself, just as the very deepest point of the inferno is already the start of a new, foreign world; alongside the puppet-type there evolves a flexibly outlined 'anyone'- or 'everyone'-type: a localized, not to say over-localized, person-puppet & the totally boundless, ever-changing person-fog are of perfectly equal-ranking, with a single purpose, and presupposing each other in 20th-century society & culture.

That, incidentally, was evident from the dress of the woman sprawled on the green couch: according to the blind positivism of *Adam Nudus*, some of the individual stripes of the fabric almost encased a selected, raw muscle in a black reliquary; in other areas swirling silks, lengths of twine, and ring buttons served the body's distribution, its lavish multiplication of doubt. That certain salon-humanity, which girls in particular represent in its entire purity, was equally acquainted with the positivist & the skeptic nuances, let's say, the relationship of religious dogma & subjectivist doubt, but it did not carry those to extremes (after all, by then there would have been neither salon nor humanity left in it): according to Touqué, however, it was now simply a matter of one's igniting these opposites to the utmost religious dogma, to the point of crude superstition, subjectivist doubt, to the sick dispersal of the soul (truncating the female body down to a puppet-show log of wood as well: that is the counterpart of superstition; and in part dispersing it over all the objects in the world: that corresponds to absolute dispersal) — if those opposites are pursued to extremes, they cease to be opposites, there will simply be 'two of them.' The fundamental unit of new culture, of artistic composition and of human character, is 'two-essentiality,' the absolute otherness of which does not mean antithesis or paradox, nor does it mean sentimental compromise, as at the time of salon-humanity.

Photographers of the most vulgar tabloid newspapers are slaves to 'mirror-realism': they photograph everyone with a mirror; mirrors conjure up for us a maelstrom of reflexes profuse with doubt — shadows, repetitions, negatives and omissions, divisions & fusions, all serve the dispersal of the figure, but it makes the first face, the original subject of the photograph, all the sharper, harder, and superstitiously more objective on this paranoia-frieze of uncertainty; one is consciously 'two-essence': a log of wood and ether rings, a butcher's shop nude figure & a beam of light interrupted a million times on undulating water. This two-pronged genus-fork will immediately modify two important motifs of love: the transformation of salon-anatomy into a primitive puppet implies the transformation of sensuality, but on the other hand the transformation of the vulgar salon-psyche into a flickering, foreign, and fraying profile implies a radical reinterpretation of fidelity; in other words, instinct and individual develop into something else, and their relationship to one another will be much healthier. The double-essence stepping into the place of the one-woman of old ought to be represented propagandistically by an old-fashioned stage burlesque entitled *Tailor's Dummy and Phantom*: the first would correspond to the new body superstition, to primitive puppet eroticism — the second, the phantom, would mean the new thousand-psychicalness, forever undulating psyche-dumping. All this is just a theoretical hunch, an advance-décor, & it becomes interesting only if it produces new formalities and customs in practical morality and social intercourse to which even the backmost seamstress, who can have no suspicion of the new dualism of 'puppet + mottled everything,' will adapt.

the radical difference of the picture of a woman
& the mood that remains after the same woman.
The impossibility of fidelity

Here, for instance, is a ghost scene from the twoness of *Tailor's Dummy and Phantom*: here Ulva di Chara cannot be fair-haired, only black; she cannot be plump, but slim and skinny, she cannot be wearing a red coat, but dark blue with a big yellow fox fur with a light blue hat and a red ribbon threaded though a glass ring. These changes of clothes occur in the interest of objectivity:

in one's relationship to a woman, whether she be one's lover or the subject of a book, the most realistic aspect is always the feeling or mass of moods that she left behind in one's soul after her departure or a minute or two of her vanishing; and those moods are abstract architectural forms, mental walls, mental basins, mental elevator cylinders and mental ground plans that have to be filled with mental frescœs & mental waters that naturally have to fit into the abstract, rigid outlines planned in one's mind in advance.

The woman who signifies the most, the one & only, in one's life, can do nothing other than leave in one's soul such abstract figures, such peremptory engineer sketches — she herself would never be capable of filling out those mood diagrams and sentiment-hypotheses with real colors & living figures, or indeed, if she were capable, she would prove she did not signify the most, the one and only. Because the industrious and industrial filling out of mood-models is a task for other objects: other clothes, other women, other objects & landscapes accomplish that.

That is the sole authorized official job of objective fidelity: the woman's red dress that one adores, signifying as it does a great love, leaves only an empty color skeleton in one's mind, an abstract framework of redness, & if one wishes to remain faithful to one's great love, or rather to her red dress, then it's no use summoning the exact spectrum of the red dress to one's memory, the memory's empty game is not going to fit into the frame that has remained in one's mind and is not at all a plaything but very much real, the framework of redness: that framework, in its own objective, one might say legal continuity, can only be kept in life by another color (e.g., blue), another object (e.g., a glass ring on a straw hat), and another woman.

If I continued to get Ulva di Chara to move around in her old dress and have her appear with her previous musculature, then I would fall into the childish error of self-delusive pseudo-fidelity: I would have stayed faithful to a few ridiculous externalities while I would have become unfaithful to the essential thing, which is to say to those internal configurations of mood and geometric blank forms of sentiment which Ulva's old figure was no longer able to fill. It is obvious, therefore, that a real woman and the frame of mind about her that has remained in one's mind (what has been called the 'abstract framework') are not the same: the frame of mind is not an emotional copy, not a translation transposed to the language of moods, of the first object or novel of love, but a surplus, something else, so that the mood can no longer be traced back to the woman.

If the woman is a circle, then she does not press another, similar circle into one's mind, but possibly three points or eight ellipses, and if one carries on seeking to anneal those points or ellipses into reality even after the woman has departed, then fidelity is not going to be fed by traces in one's memory, as three points or eight ellipses cannot bring themselves to life in the form of a circle, but they are going to seek to replace the by now false memory trace in the company of other, strange women whose actual physical constitution corresponds to the theoretical figure of the three points or eight ellipses.

Fidelity therefore displays three stages: the true object of true love; the sentiment or mood evoked by it, which is not a memory trace-photograph but a system of abstract mental frameworks, strength-frames that bear no resemblance to the object of love — and thirdly the woman, or regularly the women, who by their physical appearance match the mood sketches formed at the second stage and fill them, keep it alive by, so to say, a blood transfusion, of which, as said, the true woman of true love would not be capable. That is why now, when Ulva produces the ghost branch out of the two-pronged genus-fork, it is a completely honorable process to grant her a new muscle-trousseau.

Ulva & a young fellow together in the wood (as Leatrice's solitude changed into Veronica's story, Veronica's solitude necessarily changed into Ulva's story, & so on ad infinitum*). Rain*

Late one afternoon Ulva went for a walk among the hills of the district with her friend. The world was already lilac when they set off: the rocks encompassed the horizon's clumsily cut edges (the pages of books freshly cut with a thumb rather than a knife look like that) like a giant violet, one of whose petals is grey, like a shadow ironed out of dust, the other dark and sweet, like the velvet tongue of the snake in the Garden of Eden. The sky was light like a sitting-room lamp, its light moving not a millimeter ahead of its color; a couple of minutes earlier the fluffy peaks of the hills and the unfastened edge of the clouds mingled in a shared celestial compote, but now sky and hill suddenly separated, the clouds vanished, a big gap arose between hill & firmament, the hills moved closer and the sky drew back as if the cup of a foreign world were yawning with an invisible interior and a crater only inferred behind the dolomite chain.

In the last act of a play from the Elizabethan era nothing else happens than that the characters in the piece watch the puppets in a booth playing the story they themselves have lived through in the previous four acts: in fact, their life in the previous acts had itself been a stylized puppet life, at the end of which the puppets watch a puppet play about themselves or a recurrent puppet play. Those hills mystified as violets, that yellow sky pursing its mute light lips, giving light & yet lusterless, the turf's damp patches and the solitary pine trees suddenly separated from their shadows (in the manner of infants who are no longer sucking) related to the previous minutes in their new minutes like the last act of that Elizabethan-era play to the preceding acts: the solution consisted of performing the insolubility in the form of a puppet play; nature solved its thousand-prickled optical misgivings by repeating the same misgivings in a rigid marionette-style.

The flat blueness of the distant sea and its still saving daylight surface lay deep under sea level: that was its Neptunian coquetry to place its white-grey back under its own level. The evening was already hanging like viscous ash among the black pine needles; in the middle of the sea the daylight still shivered like a lonely fountain or a swimsuited woman in a January frost.

When in a revolution everything is taken away from everyone in order to scatter as an idealistic present to a non-existent other humanity, those who had a very great deal of belongings would still be left with a couple of lace-trimmed shirts or an unharmed wig: the sea aroused the impression of such an infinitely wealthy magnate to whom, at the time of the lyrical terror of nightfall, there had remained from Phaëthon's ancien régime a white pearl, light-blue gloves, and a glossy-leaved candleholder. But this small geyser of sun in the middle of the blue victoria regia became ever tighter. On dry land the epic conflict between daylight and night could not be seen, all the more so on the sea, in the way that at the time of a revolution such brutal contrasts do not rage in the circle of the bourgeois element as in the hacked-up and diabolically frou-froued gardens of the country houses of the aristocracy.

The middle of the sea was white; each wave, each spray, was precisely visible like a prima donna's face illuminated by a special spotlight; whereas on the lilac horizon, gigantic brown and yellow crests dangled, they barely had any color, let alone shape; on dry land objects promptly absorb the darkness like parched ground does rain, and that is how it yields the budding dreams of the night — while at sea the darkness lies like an unworked raw material & cannot find even its color in its shapeless solitude.

The Moon could already be seen on high; not at the top of the sky or even on one side, nor in the posturing monstrances of mountain saddles, but 'somewhere': after all, evening bestows on these uncertain identifications of place their own true meaning (i.e., their original uncertainty), because by day one has not the vaguest idea about how, in what a mythical manner, the position of a place can be indefinable. The Moon's small silver fingernail clipping did not relate to anything: sky, pine trees, sea, hills, all left its poised and aimless omniscience intact of dimensions. It was not a center around which the Ophelia-chaplet of hills could have floated in the sky's lethal water; it was not a glittering and asymmetric beauty spot on a tricked-out portrait of Thanatos that the sky was displaying; it was no runaway treasure which, in consequence of Ulva's clumsiness, had flown to the divine ceiling from the blind Pandora's box of pinewoods — it was none of that, and yet, or for that reason, it was the most essential, most transformed character of the landscape, love and the evanescent womb of time.

When Ulva and the boy had already walked a good way alongside each other, dark clouds began to gather around them: truly around them and not in the sky. The sky remained steadily clear, transparent and mute like the dead face of Greek women in the travelogues of topographers of the history of ideas — the clouds were floating a good deal lower than the sky, almost among the pine trees, just like horizontal layers of fog. The sea all at once grew red and the Moon began to fly straight above them like a vertical arrow. When their clothes got damp they realized that it was not the Moon that had suddenly broken into a run on high, but downward falling parallel lines of rain were hurtling into the deep. What rainfall could this be, coming not from the sky but from an area just about the middle of the pine trees? There was not a whisper of wind; the light did not become a shade stingier (a needle thin Moon-sliver); the surface of the sea, on which one and the same surf works, stood so rigidly on one spot like the names and dates on horizontal gravestones; the paralyzed branches, the modest eyelashes of the leaves and the green needles, the pebbles, sand, & the eyes of daisies held open and not startled, even under water — all indicated that the merriest, cleanest evening of the world is fragrant in the armpit of the golden age of the sea and hills: on the other hand, the swishing water burnt their skin like alum & their clothes were drenched like the hair knot of a Nereid.

They scarcely saw each other, but distant things sparkled in untouched purity: the creases of the mountains, the evenly distributed sky as good as an unleashed modesty-lamp, many hundreds of houses of a distant small town looking like sparrow droppings, and the scattered flowers of far valleys looking even cleaner than before the rain. For whom is that rain meant? For them? Not for the trees: after all, they stand untouched in the grey cascade like a church staircase under the swaying flags of a procession; likewise not for Moon, sea, meadows and enchanting Basedow-frogs since they do not even bother themselves with it, like those girls who jabbed themselves in the belly with a contraceptive injection of mystic perfection à la Cleopatra Prophylacta[134] and now with unmanageable irresponsibility offer their body as a screen before the racing stream of every type of love.

In the boy's hands all that could be felt of the woman's body was the thinness of her waist, and even that not as an accurate datum of shape but the knowledge that if he pushed her hips inwards they could still always be pushed more and more inwards so that her sole anatomical treasure was more just the marvelous possibility of a movement. Now the landscape was his, or rather all landscapes were: because a true landscape is always the sum of all landscapes and its beauty starts when the sea's floodtide starts to inundate the shore of Bohemia, when the War of the Roses, the red Sun, and the white Moon are together in the sky, when time goes forwards & backwards in a floating and criss-crossing *tour-retour*, like a chain railway above the hillside; when it is both day & night concurrently. What one's eyes see is never a 'real' landscape: in a landscape stars & daylight illuminate simultaneously, in 'real' nature a thick but light snow trembles on every petal in a pale rose-colored forest of azaleas, the red stems of poppy reeds branch forth from the green of lakes — not in order to build up the pattern of a tale, the scholastic impossibilities of a work with technical irrationality, but in order to explore, elicit, and divulge the essential components of nature.

When the boy had stood among the water combs of the rain and the water had woven new and dense cross fibers into the monochrome fabric of his body on its hissing loom, he had felt that he was in possession of all nature: the blinding bands of water scattered his brain, but out of that muddy, miry derangement, the lines & forms of a new certainty were born before him: a bad checkerboard of day and night, muteness & glass-walled deafness, narrowing hips & eyeless seaface, on which five black cubes ended up beside each other, then two white ones, without any regularity; they showed him new figures, legible & comprehensible figures, such as a 'good' chessboard had never shown him.

He had never adored Ulva as he did now, when he could feel only the quietly whistling ice of Oberon faucets adhering to his head like a mock peruke of caterpillars and glass-hooks (he had not brought a hat with him), and the woman was just a leaf lashed this way and that, a single leaf on an invisible branch, just the reverse side of which occasionally gave some light in the racing mirror of vertical rain. That was the finest-looking Sposalizio:[135] the water did not strike the crumbling body of the woman's dubious Ararat but screwed like a bedraggled braid into the bed sheet of grasses, the birdcage of hills, the strange straitjackets of moonrise & sunset, from which he was not able to reach out for the girl.

They ran home like mad in the restricted rain, which left the countryside in peace (if one can call turning into 'all landscapes' peace) and only lashed them together and apart: sometimes they raced across small clearings where there were not even trees to protect them and tiny bushes withdrew like hunchbacked rabbits under the shower of grey fog; here all the air was grey from the mute sketch-insanity of water, which did not get caught in the reproachful *flauto traversos*[136] of trees — the water struck so profusely on the grass, twisted, eroded, & steam-iodized into a point of the meadow as if it were a horizontal press and not a vertical legion of needles; crystalline water grasshoppers that chomp the oasis into debris.

The boy had never as yet kissed Ulva, and now, in the repainted green smoke of water and leaves, he felt that he was swimming in the big vats or in the parrot-walled crematorium of kisses: in his hands he did not feel a tiring and painful desire (something similar to muscle strain) after embracing, because the mildewed rain that fell into his arms like a curtain torn to shreds cured him like an erotic cold compress; the air in its entirety turned into a gigantic body with the uncertainty, brute force, and dancing mournfulness typical of such a thing. Those who have been drenched together once are affianced forever: how ridiculous those banquets with electric candles where, between two waiters, someone with a push cart carrying a starter course utters the customary inanities about 'the young couple,' so the young fellow thought to himself.

embracing & rain

All of a sudden they found themselves on a steep, slippery, and muddy path: the wind was blowing in their eyes so that they caught the rain not in the form of crowded parallel hydrogen-arrows but in scattered great gouts of water, which were dashed apart on the sponges of their faces. In the valley a tranquil clarity and hotel precision reigned. Beside them a swollen spring scattered foam above its own head as if it were washing its foamy hair with shampoo twenty times over; there was not a thimbleful of water in its channel, it had all transformed into froth, a blue mush, an intermittent-*pleureuse,*[137] leaving the channel dry, and therefore it was protected against the rain by those soda water air balloons.

They did not know whether they had landed in the middle of infinite silence or in a pocket of noise: the big acid paddles of the spring grinding itself conjured snow-white brightness in the fog-colored rain — their bodies being pimpled from the downpour, they sensed that they were in the very middle of the spring and saw the distant pines on the peeks of invisible hills through those pearls of water as being similar to roller bearings. The finest moments of love are the very first, when one sees a woman for the first time, speaks to her for the first time, and it is precisely at such a time that the woman can be least persuaded to go on a very long walk, or to participate in very long embraces; when the finest form of longing resides in one, the girls will not abandon even their most insignificant program for him (since "I hardly know him"), not even those they had only agreed to themselves, such as to carry on reading a book in the afternoon, or to finish a piece of needlework.

Fresh desires seldom gain satisfaction, so that Ulva's new friend was boundlessly happy since his helpless limbs were twisted here & there by the continually shifting wind & helter-skelter rain: sometimes big chunks of rain fell on his chest as if water were pouring out of a pitcher in such a way as if a hard glass punch that had retained the exact form of the jug were falling out of it all at once; at other times his ears filled up with tiny crumbs of a watch-glass which the wind blew into them like a sprinkler; his own words & movements would have been unable to express the thousand-sidedness of desire, & now on his behalf the entire world was pouring the varying forms of desire onto the girl's body, besmirched into a fish. An embrace seeks to be both a shove & a sucking up, a dressmaker's prosaic measuring up of the body and a gesture of declaiming for its own sake, pampering & childish dissection: the result of all that is usually great clumsiness, a sleepy, blurred movement from which he was now absolved by the rain, in the cross-phrases of which mighty celestial movements expressed every shade with clear objections.

An embrace is always impossible because it seeks to simultaneously accomplish two gestures which are mutually exclusive: one is preparing the girl's exact mummy case, the other is a demented flinging-around of one's own body; the first feels a need to evenly cover the girl's shoulders and waist like the ritual black moss of Byzantium — the second wishes to tear one's own body into a thousand pieces with the profligate rapture of joy. As one's arms run around the girl's waist like crooked, decayed Iron-Age scissors in the display cases of museums, one's legs and back wish to scatter in the world, to dance at once in a thousand widely separated places. That was not impossible in the rain: one moment the body was clinging together like a snowball in preparation, clutched between the cupped palms of the hands — the next it was exploding like the lines of hanging green ducks in game dealer's shops that looters pillage around in streets forking out of the northern, southern, & eastern outskirts.

further rain

The path along which they were walking all at once narrowed a lot & diverged from the spring's holy English horns of Sienna. They arrived among profuse bushes where they could not see each other. The foliage overhead was so thick as not to allow access to the heavenly Vichy water, not even filtered, so that instead of an even downpour, quite dry areas alternated with thick columns of water: water would accumulate in the massive cups of the spring offered by the foliage & then suddenly spill out as from a perforated rain pipe. Two chaos accompaniments could be heard and distinctly distinguished from afar: the Stuart-ruffed bear dance of the spring and the rain's pizzicato on the unrosined strings of the branches. Through the rain's spilling there in only isolated patches toward its tyrannical christening of the bushes he felt that they had got into a deeper stratum of nature in which the laws of the upper strata were gradually ceasing, leading them over into God's secret modesty-domain.

The boy sensed that transition for the first time when he learned in school that musical natural signs, mentioned in the chapters of scripture textbooks which discuss miracles, are put in front of the snub-nosed green of the leaves, that alongside planar triangles there were also spherical triangles; indeed, not only did these exist but one could also count with them, although he imagined with his child's head that space was outside numbers, especially the sphere; spherical triangles seemed to him to be some sort of optical illusion, a sliding game, a tendentious toppling of geometry, and he was greatly astounded that there, too, there were rules.

Leaves, branches, bushes, the last percentages of the sky, which still showed through the armor gauze of the leaves like blood through an over-thick dressing — there in the depths, where even the longest strands of rain scarcely reached the crowns of their heads, they seemed as if they were clinging to the gradually arching surface of an invisible sphere; giddiness and sphere are closely connected, which is fairly odd, because giddiness is the pathological label of uncertainty, whereas the sphere is a proud blazon of divine self-centeredness & perfect definitiveness. The spherical triangle, however, did not signify termination, only a more refined law, and thus the forest under rain, with its boughs of black shrapnel, its lonely water annunciations, and its sweaty smell of warm dung likewise (alongside the breath of dizziness, close to fainting) hinted at a new certainty; the certainty of the sweetest embrace, the most loving love.

It started to grow very dark, and the sudden quiet, the canal-diameter muteness, and the likeness of a tunnel, made any talk between the boy and girl impossible. That is when it entered the boy's mind to escape from the girl: he didn't mind if the girl was lost, got pneumonia, or fell into a trench like a fish that had jumped out of water and plopped into a bird trap on the shore — none of that bothered him, because he was much more in love with this azalea-ciliate nude that groped between the soaking-wet gunpowder of branches and flowers, by now not the slightest bit afraid of spring's glossy, beetle-inhabited-pistols, the six-shooter blunderbuss of gian, or the bullets of the trees of heaven (O, *nomen numen!*):[138] that entire precious arsenal is soaked, & there is no way of knowing when it will be possible to shoot with it again. The boy knew for certain that the rain's thousand-tasseled holy water had affianced him forever to the girl; indeed, not just betrothed but molded into one: the water kneaded the girl's body so much into himself, into his own body, that he no longer had any need of her, he just wanted to dance alone as Venus' insane hermit in the damp cellars of the forest.

Therefore, the boy suddenly began running lest the girl be able to find him: in his hands there was still a memory of embracing, just like the charming rough sketch of a corset, a brown cardboard pattern, may remain in a corset-maker's hands, but that did not signify much (the boy had once sat at a table in a hotel vestibule making some notes about the schedule: the girl had been standing by his seat, she too was leaning over the table, then the boy had hugged her waist to him with his left hand as if an embrace were a girth for women), because the forest endowed his love with boundless freedom: there was neither spatial nor temporal obstacle, there were no tedious tennis matches at which the word 'ready' had the effect on him of the bloodthirsty death-argot of an Amazon; there were no diaries in her purse from which it would transpire that the girl had already weeks before promised to pay a visit to a woman friend today, when the desire inside one was spilling out like a cyclamen as it reached its peak — there was none of that, because the water so mixed his body up with the forest that he did not need to aim himself at the girl's body with the trembling hands and cross-eyed look of desire on account of which one is already eliminated at the semifinal stage.

After prolonged running he reached a clearing: he was confronted with an alien world. The sea, the hills, the slope running under him, which unwound from his love spine in the way a thread is drawn in a moment from thick spools in spinning mills by another racing wheel (of course, the slimmed-down spools prepare bodies of optical blots for themselves from the humming tempo of the spinning in the same way as the vibrating cords of twine train their whole amplitude into optical muscles), and so he suddenly drew his rain-self into a single long thread from the hilltop clearing to the sea coast five kilometers away; the cindery fibrils of the sky looked as if they were the remnants of some Artemis Usitatissima;[139] a quiet mountain brook which, despite falling downwards on an almost vertical wall, was nevertheless as silent and waveless as those broad silk ribbons on which a bell hangs beside the sacristy door to summon people to mass.

Previously he had sensed love; now he saw it. In the air a couple of black birds were clearing off as if they were rusty wash-basins being tossed out of the attic. Everything was his, every-where and at all times, unlike the girl's girl figure, which was so rarely completely his, existing eternally in every nook of space and time. Because such concepts as 'eternally' and 'everywhere' can never be eliminated from love: every love is bad, because it has its interruptions; if a boy and a girl are together twenty-three hours each day, then they might as well never be together because the one missing hour exasperates the other twenty-three & multiplies all their pleasures into pain.

---

the woman's brief absences from the boy as true tragedies

The great tragedies of love are the minutes that the woman spends tidying her hair before the mirror in the room next door; the minutes that she spends in a shop for toiletries, where men would make themselves ridiculous by entering; the minutes for which she pops into a sanatorium to see her mother's brother and bring flowers following surgery; the minutes spent with a tennis trainer in the porter's lodge talking over when they would make up for the last lesson, missed due to rain; the minutes when a letter has to be urgently written to a woman friend who has already written twice, sending a snapshot of her second child; the minutes spent at the railway station to which they had accompanied a relative who hated to see the girl speaking with us: precisely those short minutes are the surest crumble-ups and torments of love because in big stretches of time, desire evolves into a broad melodic structure, like the million years of the gradual wrinkling of hills which faint into the magnificent drawings of their own weight — whereas under the minute hammers & the stinging lead shot of the minutes, all that is left is stone rubble and a fast moraine. Those brief absences cannot even be called absences because it is not time that breaks, but the hook that had been swallowed, is torn out of one's body — just as rough fishermen do not remove the hook from the lips of a fish (unbuttoning the cold death-buffet, so to speak) but simply tear it out so that the still living fish lies on the shore with torn apart bleeding lips like Neptune's broken-sealed somersaulting letters: that was how the boy always felt when ever-newer arrangements and appointments of a few minutes kept continually springing up for the girl.

Time does not spring up immediately when the girl goes away but a good deal later: until then one has to gasp for air and wait despondently for time's compensating action to take effect. That moment when, after the start of the absence, a separate sense of 'time' finally first appears besides the absence's sense of a wound, that moment does not commence in the middle of a faint daze, but in a very distinct and precise form, as if in a harmonic composition of death. Because there is either constant presence, unbroken, stifling, and disquieting presence, or death written in a melodious, prolonged time-minor: love has those two possibilities; what people actually experience and is broken by hours, indeed even by days, is not even a parody of love (in the same way as infinity cannot be travestied with finitude, at most with a yet larger infinity; in the way a crooked nose is also mocked with an overcrookedness of helices).

The alternative of eternal presence or time-sheathed death is nothing more than the alternative of total identification or total desire: those bitter and lethal minutes, or indeed hours, when the woman is not present, are unable to delight us with the broad beauty of desire, because desire is a fruit of the ray-centered flower of time, and for time, for the creation of time, as the saying goes — time is needed. If the woman goes away this evening and will return only tomorrow afternoon, then in between there is no time, no desire: embracing (if there has already been any such thing) has become impressed so keenly in one's arms, like a narrow dog collar that is given as a present to a dog, and thus prepared without taking measure; that red abrasion, or the rashes of ownership, are not traces in the memory in the same way as the red spots of a child with scarlet fever are not Platonic revisitations of an otherworldly rose garden: the scarlet fever of one's own is something too excessively excruciating & physical to be a memory trace.

At the center of one's consciousness is not a synthetic picture of the woman, nor the whole sea of love with its built-up shores, but a single raw and foolish datum: tomorrow and one minute of it — one is incapable of carrying the woman and one's love that far, like through a little puddle one forgot to put a duckboard over; that calendar date (e.g., April 22nd Jubilate, sunrise 05:11, sunset 18:50) looms with such disproportionate brutality before one that any sort of preliminary calculation or adjustment to it is impossible. One believes with incomprehensible and superstitious stubbornness that the new rendezvous will happen in the future: whether near at hand or far, and what one can do until then, one has not the least idea.

A point in time after such a break does, in all actuality, exist, but it has no rational relation to anything else: it lies beyond every imaginable direction as the paper-thin sickle of the Moon before rain lay beyond the claws of every up and down, every north and every other point of the compass, hungry for better. One has no memories, then, which could tempt one into the sweet harbor of the past; and one has none of the guiding stars

(Stella Temporis), timely in time, which might light up the path ahead; only a girl leaving for a long time leaves in one's hands some kind of compass needle tuned to desire & time. Reality is over, and the dream (whispering chiasm of time and death) has not started yet: to experience that from day to day is, as the boy said now on the pasture, "something disgusting."

---

the color lilac

Everything around him was wet, or rather, everything was built from water, and only at the very top of water trees, water hills, water stars, and water waters, was a thin costume of objects drawn up: a tree suit, hill suit, et cetera, though so true to life that nothing, not even a drop of the water, could be seen. It had a long, long time ago stopped raining in the world while in the dense forest, where he deliberately went astray, it was still pouring down with big tar gestures from the upper onto the lower ledges of the canopy: outside the forest it hurried to the ground by elevator, whereas in the forest the decelerated flow hobbled down the endless staircase winding and upper-story corridors of the canopy.

Never before had he been so alone in his love, never before had he seen with such horrifying clarity that his whole life was for love, that he did not have a single interest that at bottom was not set in the lilac basket of love.

Why is lilac so pleasant for wholehearted love? A layperson will make do with red, but this bourgeois and shoddy heretic hue is more of a bureaucratic marriage-broker color. Lilac is first of all darkness, secondly artificiality, thirdly modesty, fourthly God, fifthly death, sixthly Cherubin & Augustine simultaneously.

Without night there is no love, which does not mean, of course, as to cocottes and virgins, that amorous acts, like fresh butter, are "to be stored in a dark and cool place," but the inner darkness (Oh, Europa!) that is caused by wholehearted love for the woman: the awkward insensitivity that seized the boy at dinner, when for around half an hour he kept on pushing a single cherry around the rim of his dish with his coffee spoon, and when the waiter had already reached over three times in order to take the used stewed-fruit dish away, angrily dressed him down for the third time: "Can't you see that I haven't yet eaten up?" — cherry-charming was the fakir technique by which he sought to melt his natural listlessness into the artistic passivity of a dream. Everything in front of him was gloomy and silent, but that was the resigned gloom of the lilac hue, which was nonetheless replete with the silver atoms and aromatic veins of promise; in the color lilac two backs are resting on each other: that of the departing world and that of the approaching dream; this is how they rest halfway, hating and helping each other.

Every color is like a wee stepsister from a Grimms' fairytale, who, one evening, secretly stole for herself a marvelous film actress's most imposing evening gown; in a color there are small analytic granules, tiny crumbs, which are usually scattered into the balance pan when precisely weighing things in order to obtain the perplexing mosaic of balance, and that little grain is surrounded by the train of a dress or a ray cut from a worn, plush foreign symbol. Thus, when he wished to render to himself in the ice-cool short brush of the clearing an account of why he demanded the color lilac for himself with such obstinate insatiability, all of a sudden a senseless fragment of a word rushed into his brain, a little yelp of the sort one habitually utters when one notices at the last second that the word one had wished to say is not, actually, going to come to mind — a great longing to weep had been attached to the little syllable, pronounced with sure emphasis but no sense, as if he were wishing to turn his entire body into a continually loosening mourning (the way a dry cough is loosened).

---

weeping as an absolute 'Sache' *of love*

One is redeemed only by whole sentiment, 'absolute idyll,' and there is nothing more agonizing than to endure joy in silence without expression. What is weeping? A desire that has left one's body, has not reached its goal (or it may just have touched the goal but promptly bounced off it), and on the way between one's body and the goal it is poised in a regular rebound, self-sufficiently, in sick emigration. The scientific and lyrical value of weeping lies precisely in the fact that one can feel desire becoming independent in it, precipitated, virtually condensed into material, what with desire being the most important part of a person's body: what could be more exciting than to independently examine desire, which appears as an object in the form of crying.

Thus, the obsession of lilacness suggested to the boy a fragmented name and universal weeping as the crudest way of enjoying pure sentiment. What a tormenting comedy that at the very time he was living through the most rational moment of his life he had nothing at hand except the roundabout metaphor of the color lilac. It was useless his telling himself that lilacness was here the prescribed official color of the essence; he would have preferred to look for something surer in which to decant his joy. Every imbecility has its social dramaturgy, only the boundless joy of all things does not have a refuge in action: could the most burning love consist of the fact that it can't do anything?

That love doesn't have a true face and is nothing more than an apocalyptic Bunbury?

He labored in downcast evening solitude like a necromancer who does not abandon his magick implements until the spirit he has summoned appears: he wanted to see his happiness at last and, like Thomas, feel around the unknown charms of joy in love. "If you are a redeemer, what is the air of secrecy for, if you are everything, why are you not swaggering with your matchless profile?" the boy asked his captivating happiness. What is all that erotic infinity worth if it is perpetually incognito on opening the gates of Elysium, between the wings of which joys are packed like the red seeds in the peel of an opened pomegranate? He wanted to deprive happiness in love of any narrative and pictorial trait: to strip the kisses from his lips like the horse chestnut's spiny glove from the brown body of the chestnut; he wanted to delete the woman's figure from the dialogue like a horn from the orchestra so that all there would be was a pale backstage murmuring; with depraved, unhealthy rationalism he wanted to corrode the positive figures of Eve and Adam, the snake and the tree, from the Garden of Eden sketch of sin so all that remained were the tooth marks that were first imprinted in the apple's Satanic snow (like in a detective thriller where the whole plot, from start to finish, revolves around such a dental impression); wasn't this madness? for perhaps the very essence of love is that, that it only exists together with the woman and cannot be contemplated in and of itself.

He tried to devote all his strength to crying: to that disdained, ridiculed, 18th-century instrument which ought to be rehabilitated. Just as the greatest works of music have sometimes been written for sniveling pipsqueaks, so the most celestial girders of love are formed from the particular material of crying. Crying, in all likelihood, is not childish alarm or a loosening of old wives' lachrymal sacs, but a vigorous material: if you like, a '*neue*

Sache' in the style of the sentiments. When he sought the forms of 'absolute idyll' in the frigid uniqueness of the clearing, crying was the sole real and quelling thing that came into his hands: he threw himself into it with greedy materialism. Crying occupied his whole body, the only psychic act that filled every muscle with as much life as the girl's embrace, yet the girl was not there, and the body movements evoked by crying did not resemble the actions of kissing or stroking. Through crying, therefore, he was in possession of a physical action which concretely interested his senses, which in its totality related to the woman and which completely snatched him away from the divine calisthenics of lovemaking; in the realm of love, the *'neue Sachlichkeit'* should maybe take up the lost thread with Werther if it truly wanted '*Sache*-Eros' and not a melodrama. (Cf. Kleberhain's book *'Beiträge zur neupositivistischen Lacrymologie.*)[140]

If the new '*Sache*' always means that it represents the material essence of something, the most positive part of its reality, in a way that it almost exaggerates it against itself, alienates it from its own concept, so that the '*Sachlich* God' is at one and the same time the most absolute heresy, then crying is truly the most remarkable raw material of love (in other words, it sees psychic lisping), because it reinforces longing for the woman or happiness in love in a way that it becomes so solitary as to become detached from all women, scattering its crystals alone. Crying was a white bush of crystal on the shores of the approaching night: the missing girl melted into the night like one of the pages of a book which, of its own accord, has accidentally snapped shut and whose number one has forgotten, irretrievably melts back among the other pages of the text — and in that chilly gloom after the rain, only the sparkling glass buds of crying, its white enamel shoots and its stinging flowers flying upwards and powdering like snow, denoted love's isolated life. Crying did not signify the hemophilic bleeding of a weak person, as, after all, it was not very human, the man was at best the springboard from which it shone like an inhuman, self-sufficient, and hard creature.

Charity and eroticism are the two sick forms of objectivity: the manias of factivity. When the boy looked at crying like at a strange flower construction and felt his sense of being drowned by love had let up, if he set up the slim, springtime lilac bush of crying as a fountain, or instead of a fountain into the entrance hall of the night: then his soul was driven by the divine malady of objectification. Because the soul wishes to become truly a soul by viewing every shade of its vanity as a material standing outside itself: all joys & sufferings, actually, are such construction devices, not to say '*Sache*'-instincts, which spur one to build love and thus love it separately. For one wants to love love anew, and thus again to love this love directed toward love, so that love forms an eternal chain, and each link in it is swollen with the fad of objectification. Even with the sickest will one cannot call the 'glass bush' or 'pearl-syringa' of crying, therefore, the Taulerian[141] and pasted-paper-stigma of sniveling which wishes to conceal something; quite the contrary, it was a first trial of the constructive will of love.

— If, all at once, boundless love has become my craft — he thought to himself —, if all at once I have forgotten everything but everything in the world, and in order to adore the one & only Ulva di Chara, then at least let me do that perfectly. — Of course, he was a little bit of the mind that if someone has gone to the trouble of preparing a splendid bath for him he shall not be making the best use of it, or acknowledging it best, if he washes himself white as snow in it, but if, without getting himself clean, he drowns himself in the water. Under no circumstances did he wish to go home in such a way that love should not be evident on him: because that was very different from people simply noticing that he was in love.

Love usually only makes use of a ridiculously small fraction of the resources of charity, so the rest has to be brought to the surface with violent explosions, and that is what the boy did next, when he ran the sharp spines of crying toward the deepest lying sacks of his soul so that those, too, should burst: average love is a well-mannered breathing-in and a well-mannered breathing-out of the minimum of charity, whereas wholehearted love is an explosion of the lungs to all points of the compass. (The word 'explosion' has a demagogic, carousing flavor that needs to be stifled immediately: wholehearted love lacks every gesture, every flaunting of strength, pose, weightlifting and heroism.) One can encounter persons in love in any hostelry or bus, but those who have taken 'objectified' love upon themselves alongside the feeling of love as a separate lethal supplement, or in other words, not just the few spoonsful of the mouthwash of love, but the entire huge source to boot — one may not encounter such a person in a whole lifetime. The boy, however, was only disposed to return to the hotel as just such a person.

---

women merely 'take cognizance' of a profession of love, yet boys want to remodel the female body chemically

---

He looked with disgust at his hands and trousers, his shoes and wallet, which had not been transformed by love: he would have liked to carry out various self-mutilations, not so that he would suffer but for the sake of reality; to scratch the outer half of his hand on a tree trunk's Wooden Age rasper so that the factory signs of the wounds should shine for him. One of the ideas of asceticism is that one has to change in the redeeming pillory of love; if God's love surrounds us like string leggings do an Easter ham, then one cannot loaf about with one's idiotic anatomy on the stone floor of a church: one has to change, and if one could become better looking, then probably out of love for God one would become better looking, but since one can only accomplish significant change on one's naked body in the wrong direction, one is therefore forced, for want of something better, to disfigure oneself.

A love which is not visible is worth nothing, is not even love: there are only externals or nothing; no third is given. Is there a more pitiful comedy than to turn one's entire life inside out in the form of a confession of love for a woman as if one were standing before the world's strictest shark to whom everything needs to be declared (the best confessions do not consist of confessions of feeling, of specious analyses of craving, but of a strained inventory of the man's life, of that incomprehensible necessity to detail the events of one's own days because one has the impression that the woman's peculiarity consists in one's breakfast, typescript files, and one's father's picture postcard of Lisbon from 1893 found in the drawer, all necessarily signifying the woman), while one notices no change of any kind in the woman: when one says to a beautiful woman how much one craves her miraculous beauty, one usually remarks with distaste that the woman has not become disfigured at all during one's confession, she had not got damaged or grown threadbare. At such times one is seized by frightful doubt and tearful dread that perhaps love does not exist if it's as powerless as that, that it is only by mediation of the mind that it can be grasped, or rather 'noticed': most tragic is precisely that mere taking notice, that non-physical transformation under the severe lashes of love. Love does not penetrate into the woman's body as some sort of ray but is to be understood as a thought that is directed toward her, she always just 'learns' it; female intuition is a wholly rational technique, having no physical character.

Yet one wishes to see love; not the loved woman's pirated little charity-fiddling but the bare water of love the way God from His side sprinkles it on us, and we lob it on, like tennis balls of prayer, toward the bodies of unfamiliar girls with the naïve instinct of passing it on. Everything that represented the object of one's love can be the target of desires only once: for a second time, desire is not directed at a thing it was incapable of transforming the first time round. A yellow fox fur, a glass-ringed, blue straw hat, placed flat with a strange horizontality above the twisted bun, flaps of white gloves: only once could they be the three pipes of prayer into which love blew hard but which never ever made a sound. When one gazes at the departing girth and sees the shop-ready and mercantile exactitude and intactness of fox fur, hat, and gloves, then desire turns against them and is nauseous if by any chance one happens to see those the next day.

What is all love worth if it is unable to turn water into wine or one fish into many? Love does not want the woman herself but the impossible woman transfigured by love: nor the kiss want the lips but the ex-lips kissed into a kiss under the kiss's influence — and if it does not get that (a bunch of women preserve exactly the day-to-day forms of their lips even during kissing), then it suddenly falls back like a creeper whose sole root was on the top of a high tower and which had now suddenly broken away. So if the boy could not see the persecuted face of love in Ulva's existing body, the never-touched nightmare sculpture of charity, how could he have hoped to find it in the desertedness of the clearing? Was it not an absurd and self-tormenting undertaking to feel out there the 'constitution' of love: *auscultatio infuriata?*[142] The love was in him, so he needed to quite radically search only himself, not the woman into whom not so much as a smuggled ion could have been transferred; there was more pure eroticism in crying than in any deceptive duo.

the eternal schism of 'woman's presence' & love

Perhaps it is most imperative that feelings of love relating to the woman, the fantasy part of eroticism and the physical existence of the woman herself, should separate, i.e., when one is together with the woman, then no feeling, fantasy, or tactics of one's ego should disturb the accumulated secrets of the physical present; on the other hand, when the woman is not present, then feeling and fantasy should accomplish variations so extreme on their own subject (which is not the memory trace of the woman) that it has no kind of connection to the living woman, because if even the slenderest hair's breadth connection to her remains, then the lethal contagion of missing will promptly spread into his soul and humiliate the proud quasi of the private feeling into pain.

What everyone has tried so many times, consciously or unconsciously: which is to experience love and woman separately as unrelated elements — finally that should be achieved, the boy thought to himself; he strove to mold the joy of love caused by his engagement in the rain into an absurd fantasticality: after positivist crying that was the second *'sachlich'*-artifice in his construction of love. When he was going to be with the girl again, then that adored body should be hovering in an airless or rather soulless space, not a single notion should cross via its zigzagging winged leaf into the woman's body, every association would run back into itself, the joy-vision would be a parasite of the joy-vision, and the more recent joy would be its more recent parasite: anything, villus and fluff, which might float from the edge of the soul in the woman's direction on the breath of undiplomatic desire, now reattaches to the boy.

Because presence will only become truly presence if it is not related to either the past or the future, but is preserved on the abstract territory of the present in soulless clarity. One's life will be an opiated dense tissue that conceals the whole world from us, but when one has a date with the girl then that blind tapestry is cut with scissors so that under it the woman's real body can be seen through a narrow opening: when a jib door, the decoration of which matches the surrounding walls exactly, suddenly opens and a girl appears, then the door's decorations are not going to run across the girl's body but she will exist independently of them. This has to be accomplished in life so that joy in love should not always turn into pain.

One quite prosaic method, for instance, would be to sleep through all the time not spent together with the girl: if waking up from sleep were to coincide with the initial moments of the girl's being present, then one would very soon learn the pleasure of the girl's presence, her absolute reality (*præsens plus quam logicum*).[143] It would be a very futile and incompetent method to look for similes for the girl's eyelids in the leaves of the trees in that forest clearing: rather, the leaves ought to be forced into being even leafier so as to squeeze the girl out of one's mind, and thus the energies wasted on the barren dilettantism of remembrance are devoted to making future presence even more absolute.

One has to see in remembering a hidden solitary sin of adolescent boys & forbear from it forever if one wishes to achieve some sort of result with the barely manageable machinery of love. In order that the woman's presence should be completely different from one's own love life and bad posters of our desires, the soul should either be blank like death or crowded like a checked cloth or a splitting peapod. Which lies closer to hand there in the clearing's solitude?

the boy alone in the clearing. End of the Ulva episode

When he first formulated for himself the sharp difference between presence & love he did not, as yet, sense its huge ascetic streak; now, when he wanted for the first time to fill his solitude to suffocation with materials of pure solitude, he felt he had died. His first thought had been to reach for a telephone in the street to call Ulva, but it then struck him that the time he would spend from the birth of the thought until the girl arrived was more terrible than death.

There are two stages of the woman's non-existence: one is the man's passive solitude, the other (a new death within death: a two-sixteenths death falling onto a one-eighth death) the solitude to come — the two are sharply different. He supposed that he had discovered a new method of happiness in love, whereas, actually, he felt the shivering of death. There was not even a single point in his surroundings which could have proved to him that he was alive; there was nothing consoling in the lilac depths of the leaves (was he happy? was he dead?); they were set above each other as densely and uniformly as the scales of tiles on village housetops; the stars illuminated uncertainly, their topsy-turvy-light dangled on the pasture like a mass of overstrung or fully relaxed strings from the enormous projecting pegs of a ten-stringed fiddle, one string being a thin steel hair, the other a thick gut cord, one peg ended in a black knob, another was a gilded Arabic handgrip. He was incapable of hearing out of that complex instrument of rays and star shapes a reassuring madrigal of life. (He fared similarly in the morning with the twittering of birds: that, too, reminded him of death with its total scattering

& untunedness; trills, cockcrowing, ceaseless humming and thumping ding-dong drew his attention to the final dissolution.)

Besides feeling dead, he had the impression that he had been ruined from a material point of view, as if the pinnacle of love was to feel oneself to be proletarian. He felt that the laces had fallen out of his shoes, his socks were in rags, the buttons had dropped off his pants, his suspenders were completely loose, he had no handkerchief, he had been wearing the same shirt for three months, his neck was showing between shirt and collar, and his bow tie was slippery with grease: whence the sudden social ostracism? He had a fair amount of money in his wallet, but he was certain that new notes had been issued since he was last a resident in the hotel. He searched for a sure definition of joy, life's masterstrokes, and got stuck on the oddest, uniformly annihilating forms of death: logical solitude, lyrical desolation, & complete impoverishment.

He decided to spend the whole night in the open; maybe he would succeed in discovering something about love. Is there such a thing? Is it a joy? Is it worth it? What is it? Just as rain was his first true embrace, so only-the-night was going to be his nuptials. He only pronounced the word 'nuptials' out of conventionalism; because, chronologically, the nuptials were the last note in the scale of love, albeit not its fundamental note. The moment he decided to spend the night there, instead of the gooseflesh of mortal fear, his soul was filled by the little domestic movements of a dog seeking a resting place; he rummaged in the wet grass and in muddy lairs. He was coughing strongly but he strove to make the cough yet scratchier so as that some significant change would occur in his body. Did he want love or to shake it off? He started running toward the sea, but he would have been unable to tell whether he was running toward an answer or whether he wanted to avoid the source of the question...

if, therefore, Veronica & Ulva come from Leatrice's 'loneliness,' thus from her 'self,' what need is there for the 'self' at all? The impossibility of the 'self.' An illustration of that with the subject of a novella: Queen I., Queen II., Statue and He.

That is how the imagination of Veronica was replete with the life of Ulva to the point that Leatrice went on to accommodate both: as resting people who enjoy 'solitude' and at a certain point become replete with foreign fates like the concave pieces of a craps game with painted dice. Is there any point in listing the commercial names of the 'solitude'-mirrors that mirror each other? The escaping boy was the most lexical Narcissus (for him, love can exist only in three mutually independent forms: some illiterate hocus-pocus around the genitalia, without any 'person' at all, organ for organ; meticulous portrait painting, delirious miniaturism, a woman-annihilating analysis of the external appearances of women; and lastly, a psychological relationship with the woman, an exotic social tie or moral constraint, where neither genitalia nor woman as a person is allowed to appear, only 'soul' lifted from parentheses, which when emphasized that way always means Secession and hysteria — isolated sensuality, fierce reduction to the exterior, and permutated mental disorder: is it not natural that anyone for whom love can only mean one of these should flee from his fiancée? N.B. the boy is not in the last 'perverted' — the above love options are the healthy forms for a solitary person, only characterizing them as described above sounds like calling for disciplinary punishments. Narcissus? A lovely flower. In the language school: "Do you like daffodils? — O, yes, I do. — Have you seen my daffodils in the garden? — No, but I have bought yesterday some at the corner. — I gave him three daffodils." Mythology!), Ulva di Chara, the humble and helpful snob; Veronica, the superstitious and hypnotized servant of Mercury, desired and surmised, and what of Leatrice? With her maybe let's wait with the name.

Isn't it nice when all these are reflected in each other? People give the story of their life to one another like a poorly thought-out, rough-and-ready translation of an Assyrian text — they feel no sympathy for one another, not because they are not acquainted with each other but, on the contrary, because they are *only* acquainted with each other. They know everything about one another, endlessly branched-plots, but they were not eyewitnesses to even a single one of those actual experiences; things are there only as they figured in conversation. Communal dining, sports, promenades and identical rooms make the supposedly individual credence of fates impossible.

What is individuality good for, after all, the sculpture of the 'self,' so accustomed for oneself and yet unsculpted? That a person can never be understood perfectly by another; that the gap between the individual and any sort of community is unbridgeable is something everyone could experience at all times, but as yet no one attempted in the past to found their, say, metaphysical anthropology on that. It was chiefly the vacuum between a great individual and the insignificant mass that was examined, like Sunday tourists examining a miraculous chasm next to town, but naturally any surprise of that kind in regard to the substance of the question is useless. The individual is not incomprehensible to the mass but the embodiment of incomprehensibility; indeed, impossibility — everybody lives from the self, even though that self never exists: it is always classically not there. Individuality has no sense, no place, no purpose — if it runs into the least crisis that immediately becomes obvious.

Leatrice felt that she was unable to find an analogy to the present inner modeling of her self either in the material external world or among the psychological fashions known to her. "Is it so different from the rest?" When she had engraved that sentence on her consciousness like an errand boy chalking a donkey on a stair wall, she involuntarily broke out into a sarcastic & scornful "oh!" against herself. She felt that her individual life did not 'differ' from that of her fellow beings, was not 'other' than theirs, because difference and otherness are too low-key and idyllic kinship-epithets as compared to that self-referencing which she felt in the guesthouse.

Her own solitude was somewhat better expressed by 'concrete absurdity.' She wanted something, but if she examined it precisely there was no impulse in the 'will,' no goal, no propensity for action, for intervention in her own consciousness, or in the lives of others. Is that volition? What occupied her at present was, at its root, something impossible; it did not have any one point (yet it was not just a mental plane but a sculpture coming into leaf, or so she felt) that coincided to a point of 'psychological life' or action. She muttered obsessively to herself: "It's not something inexpressible but the snake-green icy skin of inexpressibility and impossibility in the middle of the self."

What, then, is society, cooperating humanity? Millions of such eddies of absurdity that inane falsehoods nevertheless somehow bind into an aggregate? But then language does not lie because it has not even the faintest notion about anything that nullifies the self into a self; there really is a community, however, that's not a community of people but an abstract group of community elements independent of them.

'Two persons': that is maybe the most brazen self-contradiction in the world, as there are either two of something, or it's a person, but if those two things are persons, there cannot be two of them. The impossibility of the individual is almost something dynamic, it becomes ever more impossible: the first, quite rudimentary stage, is when one examines self-definitions most accurately and finds that those do not define the self. That is the departure, the naïve and well-known break from characterization, the most faithful characterization — the defined casts off the definition with abhorrence, illness repudiates precise diagnosis with disgust and is thus left to its own devices. But by knowingly and necessarily separating from rational expression of the self, it has not gained access to the innermost center of the rationality of individuality. Simple knowledge of irrationality is something excruciatingly rational; the mind therefore wants to be rid of that, too, as falsehood relating to the self — & so it goes on forever.

The soul is always known, or rather can be experienced by us as a momentary state of mind; a 'state' like that, however, is felt from the very beginning to be untrue vis-à-vis the constant motion of the mind: the 'state' is itself already an arbitrary rigidifying of psychological life, consciousness is already a preparation, 'something' already, a ludicrous mis-stylizing of a positively perceived nothing. In this case 'nothing' does not mean non-existence; on the contrary, the highest degree or, if you prefer (oh, sweet language!), the one and only existence, seeking thereby to express the autonomous and solitary character of existence beyond all some-sort-of-ness. The world's sole concretes (what has metaphorically been called 'nothing'), the eternal formations of the impossibility of individuality therefore remain forever invisible, unknown; not a word will be said, no music will gossip about that. That was symbolized quite crudely, not even suspecting the possibilities of the metaphysical usury of the thing, by an American novella, one that a periodical named *Mind* also concerned itself with (Halbert was in the habit of doing work for it) a title like *Queen I., Queen II., Statue and He.*

The whole novella was written in a diaristic style, moreover from the pen of a peculiar prime minister. He writes his records in prison, because his successor in power had condemned him to death, though the execution would only happen on the day marking the third month of the new queen's reign. During those three months he wants to give an account of why, actually, he had engaged in politics, for whom he had struggled, with whom he was in love, what he had believed in: what sounds so harshly in the long shadow of death, horizontal to the point of logicality — what is history? what is life? what is what?

What could be more natural than that he is unable to give an answer to all those things; anything he reaches for promptly turns at his touch into something other than it was, nothing at all is something. He was ostensibly the political protector and lover of a deranged queen. The queen lived in an enormous castle, completely cut off from the world, surrounded by servants whose tongues had been cut out — from the age of twenty she never saw a stranger, the sole exception being this prime minister whose journal is the narrative. The prime minister also lives in the palace, a fanatic royalist, a lover of the insane woman without ever falling in love with her. The queen never receives guests; the prime minister (the *He* of the novella) is always the intermediary. The cabinet wants to be rid of the mad queen by fair means or foul; *He* wants the same thing but he knows that there is no similarity between his loathing and that of the cabinet. The queen's only harmonic state is when she is in *His* arms, at which times her entire body and pallid face are permeated by celestial good cheer, and (farce!) he does not speak of her lover but of her adored, never seen people. The speeches are declaimed at length by the prime minister (though no one believes him) on the queen's behalf.

Question for men: What to do with a woman whose hysterias he loathes as deeply as his lover's ravings, as politically he adores the queen's holy nonsense, and whom as a lover he considers the woman worthiest of adoration in his life when she is in his arms. Why does he take her in his arms if he hates her, and if in his arms she is kindly and beautiful as a goddess, why let her go? Does he love her or not, is it not precisely the doubt clinging to her that he loves most of all? (In the American novella, of course, it is mainly banal psychoanalytical 'paradoxes' that play a part, which does not matter because it serves as a reminder that Viennese psychoanalysis is at a crossroads — either it would fall back into the most barbarous materialistic atomism, or by working out the 'absolute paradox' it would build a path toward a new, perhaps the first true metaphysics.) Is it possible to be changed by a woman whose redeeming ability is closely bound to one's personal existence-by-her?

At the same time, basic excitements of politics and history: an insane queen's insane devotion to the people signifies the forever bubbling, reveling senseless-vital part of the story; the cabinet where *He* orates so much, the attempts of law & rationality at organizing society. But if 'irrationality' makes a greater impression on rationality than does rationality, then is there any sense in rationality? On the other hand, if rationality understands 'irrationality' so well, then that 'irrationality' contains enough rationality not to be irrationality at all. Questions of love, politics, and logic all overturn at once in the time bow of the three months prior to death: the days are the string, stretched continually further back, with which *He* arrows his own life into the "fundamental unfounded impossibility" of his self (as the writer put it).

The only "founded" and certain thing in his life is the huge equestrian statue that stands in the queen's park, yet nobody knows whom it portrays, a king or rebel, priest or divinity, but which inevitably awakens in everyone nostalgia for inalterable certainty. The prime minister was accustomed to spend his evenings at that statue, marveling at the eternally extinct mythology of 'certainty.' Meanwhile he was falling in love with the new designate queen picked by the cabinet, who really was a scion of the people — which is the more plebeian plebs, the mad people that, logically and mystically, had become absolute through degeneracy, or this peasant girl who, besides all her 'primary' racial purity, makes a vacant, doctrinaire impression?

That is how he leaped from question to question, getting caught at every hand on the 'impossibility' of an individual life, seeing everything in everything, defending and attacking, loving & killing everyone. *Pro domo?*[144] There was no *domus*. For whom was he dying? This was not 'skepticism' and 'relativism' (it did not have a single point in common with those), but an acceptance of, make no bones about it, the huge pointlessness of an individual life (which in turn was no disparagement or disillusionment!). That when he would be executed he thought about the equestrian statue's immovable fixity of purpose is an understandable atavism, but the universality of uncertainty alike would soon become a dogmatically fixed point in the country of *Queen II*.

"Halbert will probably mean more to me — thought Leatrice —, than Leville-Touqué."

VII.

Return to Leatrice in the guesthouse (V, p. 488)
Halbert's poem about the sea

While she looked at the sea, Halbert's poems about the sea came to mind (in the car her mind could not work in that context) — she may have felt that the proportions of the apartment reharmonized the sea, too, in new spatial fans (like ordinates & abscissæ scratched above a landscape on the lenses of a pair of military binoculars), but for a while the service regulations of associations still remained valid. Short & broad striped canvas deckchairs stood on the big terrace. The fence was made up of four horizontal iron pipes that were not at equal distances from the edge of the terrace: the bars of the vertical lattice were initially bent a short distance from the terrace and only then pointed upwards. Lea thought that was very bad (indeed, absurd for children) & for that reason did not take her own deckchair anywhere near the edge.

When she was still spending more time on applied art she steered fairly wide of that geometrical style which replaced 'plastic' form with 'pure' form — she preferred to develop folk-art motifs into a cynically-sentimental style (as was evidenced by the furniture of 'la Cardinalle' room), which of course often coincided with that Nordic-platonic taste; the red settees and plumped-up pillows could, with dreamlike exaggeration, as easily have been peasant ovens & rural quilts as pinnings down of the 'absolute circle' (a concept?) or the 'cube entelechy.'

Those shapely figures were in a dreamlike way both mendacious in character and idealistically saturated with realism, which may bring pleasure to some because it illustrates again that the distortions of nightmares & the most accurate pictures of scale in geometry are in an incandescent, paradoxical balance, or, as estheticians are accustomed to banally put it: "the most maniacal lie, an ultraviolet degree of mendacity, already coincides with the truth, indeed only that is identical to that particular truth." *Veritas vos liberabit?*[145]

Those kinds of catechism-aphorisms, for all their meek clichédness, are naturally true, but interesting problems arise only with the most idiosyncratic, individual cases, such as a fence, windowpane, or belt buckle: what are the genuinely tangible points where the duality of the joke of 'fantastic form' & 'pure form' occurs? What are the positive elements that force one to regard certain objects as ideally self-contained or uproarious caricatures? What, if it comes to that, makes up the process that led to us feeling that caricature and idealization were identical? A cartoon is accompanied by solemn belief, platonic ideas (or drawings imitating them) with a decided snort of laughter, and in that duality we see the basis of every kind of symbolism. When Leatrice laughed at her own folk stylization she took that to be natural because *'amor nescit reverentiam'*[146] toward her own people asserted itself in it.

In that villa, however, she found it odd that she had to smile, because there she did not have the feeling that the designer wanted to be deliberately ironic about anything, but she also felt that her smile was not a disparaging disagreement with that style, more an identification with it.

Halbert was fond of ironic archaisms, which is why the title he gave to a cycle of his poems linked to the sea was *Sea-Trinitie that is Some Scholastickally Shaped Reflectiouns upon the most Salient Meanings of the above mentioned Water viz., his Youth Matinall, his Tragicall Burden & his Ymageblossoming Yrresponsibilitie by* G.W. Halbert. A geometrical sea and a poetic sea struggled in Lea's eyes when she sat in her red, blue, and yellow striped recliner in the morning sunshine (lying in it, one could regulate the degree to which one was leaning backwards with a minor movement of the foot: as if that, too, was a magic seat of horizontality — with a small movement it immediately flattened into a stretcher), but they soon coalesced as there was no true antagonism between them. (O blueish fan of horizont-azure...)

Azure fan of the horizons
Swishing as you shade the face of many a doleful divinity
On the seagull'd carriage of matutinal breezes
To the shore you proclaim renewed hostility
The leaden-blue armor of waves rings out
Above it the shade of Sky's Vase swirls
Rooting about the vortex nest bubbling up from daybreak
Skeptical wings of monotone birds unfurl.

One expressed pure rhythm ("... too — a hidden number inspires the shapeless escapade — too ..."), the other the most analytical image of the surface: an ad for Agfa film represents the ultraviolet grade (the state of ultrafactivity), rhythm, infrafactivity. Lea knew that the sea & her own solitude would be in a much stronger relationship than to be reducible to a naïve formula of the kind: "abandonedness — concrete endlessness — barren strength," etc.

When she observed herself she sensed that same duality (with her that might have been a forced refinement of parallels, not that that meant anything: those kinds of wild self-acquaintances and 'objective' conscience-examinations always start out from the mystic material of fiction and a stylized portrait only in order to totter again into the adumbrated scheme of 'via mask toward the face'): her self-consciousness was a dark mass controlled by a moving yet somewhere bound proportion — but irrespective of that a flitter of little scenes were moving before him: the pictures relating to the rhythmic sense of the burden of self-consciousness like small geometrical film clips to a shapeless jungle, such a contrast that it was already kitsch. She had already experienced that sort of schism on the sea when they had been traveling in the car: the image of the waves had run in sharp dissonance alongside the rhythm of the changes in sound — she now lived through a newer version of that typical schismatism in herself.

Perhaps all self-discovery begins with an experience like that — what is, in fact, the 'conventional' person absents itself (Leville-Touqué would occasionally enthuse about that in his article for *Antipsyché*: "... we have no need of self-consciousness or self-knowledge; we call for self-unconsciousness and self-ignorance in the interest of culture, the eradication of examinations of the conscience, if that implies psychological peering into the self — it can stay, if it implies dry self-inspection from the outside, looking at movements and not motives —, because while in geography the filling in of blank spaces on a map signifies progress, in human cultural life the most hygienic, most extremely practical endeavor, is: that there be a lot of blank areas in the mind, a great classical mental ignorance..." et cetera), & in its stead only the chaos-state exists, the infra, which is just blind, embryonic movement, and along with that, the state of decadence, the ultra, which only reflects the frivolous Gothicism of memory (*reminiscere non est humanum*),[147] life's perfidious afterplay: both of them lack what a person instinctively senses is the most genuine part of being human & of life.

The frescoes in her room were replaced by three gigantic photographs on glistening, shiny-grey paper that stretched from floor to ceiling. The first of these represented the surface of the sea. The picture was so narrow & tall that the waves which had been lined up crosswise, above one another, had an all the more grotesque effect — it was a snapshot of incoming lines of wave caps just as they happened to reach shore; between shore and swell were feathery-light waves, as if textures of light or sheets of shade had been laid on top of each other (they gave an impression almost of X-rays because it was possible to sense that to anyone standing on the beach and looking with an unaided eye, those abstract waves may just look like blurred water stains, but here their regularity, their dynamic rhyming, was revealed); beyond the cord of surf, right up to the upper edge of the picture, lay short-term samples of water, formed from thicker material, which displayed dense, comb-like lines in the direction in which they were racing.

As if the sea, too, were a human creation, like art, which likewise has its own Romanesque or Gothic periods, and that photograph were displaying a '*fin de siècle*' era of the sea, a stage of intellectual fiddling after which 'the sea' would wither away as a style only to be replaced by something new, like what came after flamboyant architecture.

Leatrice thinks about her past: performing in Timon of Athens *in Moscow. The 'identity of antitheses' problem in parenthesis*

When she was an actress in Moscow one performance of *Timon of Athens* created a big furor. In Moscow she had become acquainted with a director who was also a painter and stage designer in the T** Theater — together with him she put on that performance. The T** Theater had once upon a time been a hospital; it was a tall, narrow, grey house, built out into the street, with tiny, longish, widely separated windows, a flat, ill-fitting tympanum on the roof (it was a good deal shorter than the house) with some sort of heraldic stub in the middle (with present-day houses one gets the impression that the walls are no more than the outer packaging of rooms that were long destined to be there, whereas with old houses the opposite is true: the rooms and windows seem to have been forced into a homogeneous monolith only by the tenacious drilling work of miners, for which reason a cross-section of the latter always resembles the inside of a molehill, while the former is more of a sparsely lined net).

In front of it stood a small bronze fountain with a rapturous cherub, which made the whole façade of the theater acceptable; it was strange that its shape was unchanged even when it heavily rained or snowed; while on neighboring houses, signboards, lampposts and cars, the black splash of water or white mound of snow somehow united with the object it embraced, thus, they formed a shared picture, with the object taking on the imperious direction of the rain's lines of force or forming pairs to the swellings of snow, this Cupid stood in glaring contrast to the weather. If one looked at it at times like that, it was in no way possible to draw such optimistic conclusions as "Look here! An eternal smile," or "An unbreakable toy!" It was more a matter of seeing the coarse, indeed cretinous indifference, of death. Even though it had nothing to do with it, that little statue at once gave structure to the whole building in much the same way as a Japanese character, dashed off solitarily in the corner of a sheet of paper, turns a previously meaningless area of paper into an arranged space.

Maybe the same compositional form runs through every art and psychology, indeed nature, too, with a foreign, insignificant element always insinuating a rhythm into an unstructured landscape or body of feelings and thoughts. Nowadays that is done in industrial ways: huge walls are electrified till they become organic (an almost chemical process) with a distant triad of lamps; meaningless ground plans are ineluctably cajoled into order by the form of a distant basin. That is what the laughing bronze putto in the middle of the road did with the unwieldy castle walls of the old hospital; what intensified it all was that these represented two different worlds and styles, one the Middle Ages, the other the Late Rococo, so it is no good pedantically preserving the so-called harmony of style of particular streets and squares, because if a Cubist department store is placed next to an onion-domed Russian Orthodox church, that will not only be enjoyed as a dumb contrast by primitive people but they etch out with their own peculiar chemistry, from one to the other, structural lines that one would not have noticed unaided — as if every building or style were an artistic lock, the keys to which only the house next door or a subsequent era would mature out of itself.

She was playing *Timon of Athens* in that theater: she sneaked in under the hard mask of conventional male pessimism as a woman, and she molded the whole type to her own naïve-doubting, naïve-bigoted young womanhood. The whole idea was rooted in this: one evening she had read the play on the side of a small artificial pond, when she got to a simple, puritanical stage direction: *near the seashore.* All at once the brown mirror of the private luxury basin grew in her eyes (only in intensity, which does not burst contours in the manner of official hallucinations, indeed rather glues them together like a porcelain oven and blindingly insulates them) and suffused the whole drama, she became the hero and her beauty also became the content of hatred — the pessimistic rhetoric was all a reflection of that glittering and solitary water, and that is how the idea was born of an overbearing, mendacious, rather affected and yet nevertheless duly brutish performance of *Timon*: pain & despair fitted into a Garden of Eden landscape half in a Rococo-gleefulness of waters, clouds, winds and birds (of course, in that Rococo-gleefulness there is a lot of stubborn cynicism, just as in Voltaire's exotic room in Sans Souci: parrots & frivolous joke-fruit are its declining motifs), half in jungle darkness.

The next morning she immediately rushed to the director and set forth her plan: she wanted to play Timon of Athens, with scenery painted according to her instructions. As in every perversity, in this, too, there was something mystically bracing and creakily intellectual; as, before a mirror, in her light and loose Greek costume, she sought out the movements and intonations with which she would best be able to express the 'demonstrandum' that individual suffering and despair, fitting between sea, trees, and clouds, was actually also a hymn of a happy life; that the psychological inner darkness is essentially likewise a splash of color in the whole mirthful masquerade (nature is an eternal form: *et forma ex definitione semper ridens*;[148] the mind is eternal content: *et quidditas fixata ex definitione semper tragica est*)[149] — there was an undeniable childish sensuality, a sweet ass's game of tag over beauty, an attractive selfishness which seeks, with greater or lesser success, to press her own sensuality, which she had kneaded into art, into every beer glass, arithmetical theorem, or retired old man: all that for a few seconds, until it is just an unkempt inspiration, might even be fairly sympathetic, but, when in executing it, it is bound to become 'a scenic interpretation,' when 'directors' in turtlenecks work a fugitive impression into consistent harmony, by then, of course, it only arouses the impression of a forced & superfluous thesis.

Ever since humanity has chattered about itself and has hastily conducted its indisposition into poetry or certain systems, it has constantly thrown up that identity of 'pain as pleasure' or 'suffering is also a radiant flower,' sometimes as lazy pantheism or even lazier monism, sometimes as the basis of an esthetics or the essence of Christian ethics à la Saint Julien — flowers and God are born from the embrace of lepers. Leatrice also traveled on that line when she lent her femininity and a fantastic landscape to Timon's shaggy-grunting sadness.

This 'identity of antitheses' is a pleasant thing. Here we have Timon's despairing soul and the elementary cheerfulness of a Florida seacoast landscape. It is obvious that the two facts are not identical. That the two notions denoting the two facts are also not identical is not so obvious, because notions are never made visible, only their linguistic expression, about which it is habitually said that it is inaccurate in comparison to the clarity of the notion — though the clarity of the notion is doubtful since it has not yet occurred without language or some other mark, the clarity of a language-free notion could easily be a superstition. But whether notion or just linguistic symbol, the instant two opposed things are seen as two they necessarily are two. Here it is pointless talking about the difference between appearance & the reality hidden behind it; the sole difference about which one can speak is 'thinking something at all' and 'thinking absolutely nothing.'

What can be meant by my saying that a matter is conceptually and linguistically two kinds of things and 'appear' to be antithetical when they are in fact not: the reality behind it is one and the same thing, without any antithesis. What it means is that I have reached the center of 'reality,' & I am looking at the matter from there; if indeed an intellectual declaration of the kind 'I see one thing' makes any sense at the center of 'reality.' If, however, reality shows 'one' at a point where thought, by contrast, shows two, then in no way will that at all be a mixing of the two realities denoted by the two notions (e.g., landscape & despair), because it will be so uniformly, one might say infinitely, one that the sense of any 'identity' is lost.

If all at once I look at the matter from the perspective of reality (which is a pure phantasmagoria, as being reality means precisely 'not looking,' 'not thinking,' 'universal indifference'), then — from a human point of view — I have reached nothing at all. A person is not a realistic being (not even remotely logomorph); a person is a thinking, rational, or truthful being and is mistaken to believe of themselves that they can escape from their intellectual, conceptual prison into reality, for instance by declaring disparagingly that two different concepts are only formulated differently but in reality are the same. The alternative is this: either entities expressed by signs (e.g., a landscape and despair), or complete nothingness, the blindness of reality. Signs, though, are impenetrable, rigid, one cannot perceive one and two, landscape & despair, 'monistically.' In the interest of the 'identity of antitheses,' the thought may arise that landscape & despair are two opposed properties, two mutually alien aspects of a common entity behind both. But that is again superstition. To a human mind, landscape & despair are two separate things, and anyone who suspects that the same identical entity is behind them (or more precisely, not behind them, but in their continuations, as if they were the two stems of a letter 'V' meeting somewhere) — they only feel the abstract notion of 'one thing' behind them, not some kind of reality; they do not put a reality behind landscape & despair, but the empty concept of 'one,' and arbitrarily at that, because they have a psychic propensity for it ('monolatry' in psychology?). Anyone who grandly complains that language and calculuses are imprecise as compared to reality is no friend of reality, but a naïve snob who has failed to notice that for humans only language exists, only grammar, which is very precise if one sets aside the hollow hallucination of 'one,' which is not identical to reality.

The 'director' in the turtleneck soon got into a routine, and while Lea only wanted a stretching of the anger scenes toward delight, he immediately softened the merry banquet scenes into a haze, so that the whole play was given a regular line with a regular moral: "'life's delights' mean death, so that the darkest point of the tragedy is at the very beginning, and from then onwards it rises toward bright altitudes, the colorful paradise of suffering, the vernal 'happy end' of death."

Suffering is found to be fine by people who have been lifelong hypochondriacs; those who have truly been acquainted with suffering usually think of it in a very petty-bourgeois manner: what they saw in it as being 'fine' was more just an ethical consideration, otherwise suffering was held to be very much suffering, tasteless work. We were somewhat put off by the refined & childish equations of legends: 'axe = golden rod,' 'wound = rose,' et cetera, the martyrs were profusely decked out — most likely there was more there in the way of suffering stripped of decorum and flowerless wounds. It could be. But from that performance on Leatrice got very much used to that easy vice versa; stylizing suffering into rapture, old men into young girls, angels into chatterboxes, etc.

It is undeniable that inside us we have a strong, primitive sort of instinct that is only satisfied by such 180° turns: this is one of the forms of extreme thirst for stereoscopy, which has no liking for discrete oppositions (not the breath of joviality on Dolorosa's lip, not the fugitive shade of melancholy in the eyes of the enthroned Savior), but dazed counter images, dancing mourners, bridal couples tumbling about on a catafalque. Of course, what makes a bluff like that possible is that one does not consider suffering to be a springtime salon, drinking aperitifs is not exactly felt to be a Loreto litany — if those things were actually seen as that, it would all be tiresomely boring.

In any case, the foundation of all arts is this: a vision never expresses what the creators see but what they do not see at all. Nothing is more alien to them than the world of their own imagination — they are least at home in those particular worlds, and thus they are the world's biggest philistines and patsies, because they are the most astonished by strangers, & they base all their creations on knowing full well how things 'normally' & ordinarily look in the world. However much sadness that sort of thing may cause, very few of us are honest fools.

It is undeniable, Leatrice was being 'unfair,' stupid when she played *Timon of Athens* to the end; she felt that she had come closer to the meaning of life (if not imagining she had got to the very foundations: there are women like that), because she realized something dazzlingly foreign — the rhythmic principle that the most whimsically arbitrary things always give the illusion of stumbling upon the essence prevailed here as well: it could be that this is how it is (after all, Artificiality messianism is nowadays especially fashionable: *ego sum artificialis, ergo veritas et vita*),[150] but then it is a fact that the truth is the strangest possible thing in the world; indeed, it is the totality of all that we are not, a flawless minus-person. On the other hand, a minus-person again annoyingly resembles a human in the same way as one again sees England on a map in an endless blue of sea, if exactly that has been cut out of it.

Lea was dreadfully astonished by the new world (the first 'paradox' for everyone is, actually, a sexual sin) and precisely this showed that every nerve in her body belonged to the old world; indeed, it was only now that she became truly old-fashioned, & astonishment, in the literal sense of the word, redefined her into her past: every new acquisition explorers make is just a further weight with which to press themselves back in their state of old — transforming oneself is tantamount to making the outlines of one's identity sharper.

Her way of playing *Timon* greatly resembled Halbert's concept of the sea: as if there, too, a storm at sea were its brightness, & night's blind darkness were a collection of colored dolphins.

That in those minutes she needed thoughts like this, when she was truly alone for the first time, alone in a professional way, was very natural: this was just like a need for a military or funeral march. That duality: 'Timon's sorrow and a charm of whistling hummingbirds' is nothing other than 'Timon's sorrow and funeral march,' actually the enormous efficacy of music can only be reached in narrative or painting if one creates an antithesis to the thing that one wishes to accompany.

In music, the parallel (sorrowful for sorrow, a merry tune for merriness) is enough to achieve the same melodic effect; the parallel has to be annealed in the image, right up to the point of antithesis — only then will it be a perfect partner to the power of the melody. In that way it may become clear that the antithetical visions that had been leading Lea as well were none other than ordinary nostalgias for music: melodramatic at root. That was exactly what she could experience at other times also; at times of great joy she would start whistling, but when she sat down in order to visually record them she did not sketch reveling dryads (that would have been precisely one-half of the music's value), but black vases and dismally flat plates (that, on the other hand, was twice the dryads, i.e., exactly equal to the joy of melody); of course, with 'spring' or 'hypothetical joy' always tagged on, because without that it would not have turned out to be the statue of joy that has the value of melody.

There are weights which can only be supported in such a way that the support rhythmically oscillates backwards & forwards, otherwise the whole weight would drop straightway: that was how it also was with her current sense of being moved: she sought a musical rhythm that could in some way hold in balance the sprawling blackness of 'self.' In the wild yellow clarity of the morning she felt like a heavy shadow, as if her own body were in the way: when a person has no thought of any kind, all of a sudden she feels her body is superfluous, like a clumsy wall behind which she can at best only get a peek, like rigidly recumbent patients get a peek from behind bandages. It is not a case of 'the soul wishing to soar,' more of its seeking annihilation. One is ashamed of one's past, one's many minuscule memories; in any case, in face of the sea and new times, the new landscape does not permit even the smallest shred of memory to find a connection to the external world and thereby release & make one lighter: on the contrary, it presses all of one's memories into oneself so that one has the feeling of wearing all of one's clothes at the same time & giving everyone a good laugh.

Memories constituted a regular hierarchical order as long as the plasticity of everyday life could be used as a sure unit of measurement: now, however, the totality of memories have all at once become equivalent vis-à-vis the new world, because every single memory trace was the same distance to the new backdrop. They have become clearer, but, by virtue of that very clarity, have flown back into an impossible remoteness, i.e., they were not in permanent connection to life, and thus the possibility of being spread had ceased: sharp frames had taken its place.

After traveling, when one first makes an appearance in an unfamiliar restaurant, one constantly has the feeling that a parvenu must have among gentlemen, except in inverse form: one is ashamed of a past stemming from aristocratic ancestors, sensing that the totality of one's non-pertinent memories are written on one's face, and thus however much one tidies one's hair, however smoothly one's evening jacket has been ironed, one feels inside oneself a struggling chaos, a swarm unable to extricate from itself the unusable past, which is so massive precisely on account of its unusability, unexpectedly overlogical as a result of its meaninglessness. One would not like to have much connection to the new milieu, only to be completely without a past, light and transparent as one imagines the new environment to be. In that way a certain duality will arise: the past's weight as something detached, and the past's weightless but over precise little pictures.

She insisted on the sea because through it she nevertheless tried to link past and present into an organic whole, a continuity: Halbert's poem was also about the sea, and maybe the real sea itself was a sea. She herself found it odd that she imagined the break as so definitive and profound, as if she had retired to a convent and there would no longer be even the faintest possibility of turning back, but with decisions like that so much energy is devoted to ripening it, yet the ripening consists of nothing more than an extraordinarily intensive and unbroken notion of life after the break, so that a person completely identifies with the vision, with the imagination taking the whole thing more seriously than the intellect and will: stemming from that, therefore, is that since an entire future is anticipated at all moments, this imagined future actually sprawls in the present moments, stretching them into decades, and one totally forgets that it still lies within one's power to alter the thing. She sought Halbert's eyes above the waves in the sea: she was troubled & humiliated that she had a need for that.

---

another memory: meeting the Englishman Halbert in the Woodcut *nightclub. Art historical reflections in the context of describing the nightclub*

She had met Halbert in the *Woodcut* nightclub. Its name came from the fact that an old woodcut had hung in its doorway, which depicted under glass the wedding at Cana in the olden days. There had been nothing special about the furnishing of the nightclub in the past but then it was taken over by a new proprietor, with a new designer, who, starting off from the unassuming black-&-whiteness of the little old woodcut, checkered the whole room with black and white. The wallpaper was black with, in places, metal tubs resembling gauntlets, raising a dual impression of luxury and barbarity, which may well be the basis of all elegance. White porcelain lamps with black lampshades with thick white stitching were placed on black tablecloths; the lamps were not uniform in size, but any differences were slight, so that, ultimately, they were a source of considerable uneasiness. A black doorman in a white suit stood at the entrance; inside, hanging on the walls on black cords, were white chalk masks. The dancing girls were also dressed in black & white, with their lips painted black.

In a way, the relationship of the set-up and the naïve woodcut hanging outside was symbolic of modern art as a whole. As if the new art were effectuating what people *said* about the old creations: they said about the old woodcut that its creator "rhythmatizes the black and white staves in masterly fashion in a raw-knitted, wild harmony," et cetera; today's artist will fall in love with this *sentence*, simplifying as it does to the limit, and sets to work to accomplish that sentence and nothing else. In that way a story with quite a humorous lilt stands before one: in the front, pictures, after them, their descriptions, then the descriptions turned into pictures and written down anew, & again... In that manner there arose a conceptual art that does not portray dynamic forms but dynamics itself: a gigantic metronome without any music.

Yet it will be ecstatically *'sachlich'* in this way, on the route of large-scale abstraction (the most naïve object representing the most mathematical definition) — if all conceptual art recognizes of the colors of an antiquated painter is his 'wild greens,' then naturally the subject area will be replaced by materials, raw material, one will get snakes of pigment from ten tubes squeezed on top of each other, chlorophyll paste & little malachite-loafs. Copying Giotto & '*Sache*' may be polar opposites, but both of them represent some sort of *concept*-puritanicalness: one merely portrays the structural lines (without needing to construct anything), the other portrays the detail under a microscope (as if it belonged to something); one, just a splinter, the other, just a scale in 20× magnification, but both seeking to delineate only 'Fish' — never an epic theme, always the essence.

In this respect, modern art is very similar to medieval heraldic formulation: in that, too, certain heroic deeds, famous places, or implements are reduced to hieroglyphs — here it is also a matter of a heraldic handling of everyday life, everyday implements, so that the Ancient Classical '*pars pro toto*'[151] may often come to mind on seeing arbitrarily cropped photographs or paintings; the game will perhaps be slightly interesting when this *sachlich*-heraldic style proves to be identical to the most primitive biological cellular-phantoms of life. All this is full of inconsistencies & a superfluous symmetry-mania, because the harmful passion for puppetry quickly takes one over if one discriminatingly masks the facts a little bit: on the one hand, *Neoprimitivus*, on the other, *Sachlich*; with one, *Hypersystema pro toto*, with the other, *Pars pro toto* — and in the middle the dead *Totus*,[152] in the air, suspicious *Bio-Ornamenticus*; one is inclined to perceive the relationship of these not logically but on the basis of a nightmare drama or morality, &, more important than that, to mix up the roles.

Architecture and interior furnishing are of interest inasmuch as they unify the characters of the above-mentioned protagonists — pure geometrical construction and '*Sachlich*'-*ness* applied with the greatest lavishness: the *Woodcut* nightclub was no exception, in it were united naïve simplification & barbaric material prejudice; instead of room, table, and chair, roomness, tableness, and chairness were together here, meted out next to each other with codex-awkwardness.

This was her first serious meeting with Halbert. "Was." One of the reasons for pressing things into the past is that one always reserves the future for an extraordinarily major, unsuspectable event in the narrative: if one has something of a plot-like nature so to say, one is always reluctant to set it in the untrodden place reserved for the future; one would rather cram it into the anyway already bloated past; if one takes a thermometer as an example, the novel sets off from zero degrees, continually swells in the minus direction (that back-direction itself can only be a matter of an external and hypocritical stability that actually plays out in several places, a direction-free accumulation of the present) and never dares to ever go forward: even the most critical changes are shunted into the past with obstinate cowardice, as if that were irresponsible territory, whereas the future, the actual narrative territory, is left as a probably eternally untouched void.

At first glance, the nightclub aroused a crude, even vulgar impression; it was reminiscent of the painted statues and colorful boats of primitive peoples, the way that a continually-present primitive roughness, Papuan 'tastelessness,' is felt in Parisian shop window dressings and show-window colorings of the 'finest' rank, moreover (as indicated), that is exactly the essence of their elegance: barbarism and blatant simple-mindedness; where people see 'fineness,' discretion, a perverse moderation of implements, actually, a matter of gruff yelps and bestial twitches — a brutal, wild buffoonery is at work at the bottom of *'charme' & 'chic.'*

When Lea stepped into the raging spell of contrasts of white and black squares she felt a Carnival-time slap, that it was a matter of a consistent carnivalesque gesture (about beauty, not taste) and, along with that, all of her thoughts up till then had been permanently compromised, and, further, in a burlesque manner, it was no longer possible for her body posture and clothes to be in season there; after all, any worthwhile artistic creation immediately makes one anachronistic before oneself, but this now hit Lea quite unexpectedly, even though she had already maneuvered among a lot of fantastic scenery.

the color black. Bluff & love

This was a very good place for love, in its blackness there was a boastful pornography, a naïve, shoddy hellishness, but it seems that at the bottom of every artificial intellectual artistic influence one has to refer to a Brueghelian root, a vulgarity, low-grade notions of sensationalism, and that is how the drunken soldiers in public parks and the great artist are bound into a common guild by the stubby threads of a healthy fraternity, in the name of bluff.

Bluff is a big inspiration for love, and Lea gave herself entrance into that blackness; for a second she stood rigidly on the threshold, indeed, she hunched herself up entirely, but then she let herself go, unfolded, burst black buds out of herself on the walls of the room, conquered it, felt the room to be her own body through her mental dispersedness, so it would have caused her no trouble to scratch a shoulder with one of the corner lamps, or to use a lamp instead of a word; in nature it is often the case (although in matters of metaphors nature sometimes unexpectedly falls into a quite irrational prudery) that complete retraction & compliant dilatation to the point of overflowing are alongside each other — when Lea set off toward one of the tables she was utterly sure of herself; with a paradoxical certainty befitting of the nightclub, which is composed precisely of our being knowingly inebriated and giddy, so that sharp-sightedness and playful hallucinations run through us in uncertain alternation as if sagacity and stupidity were two different fluids that have been mixed together but are unable to mingle (when one is very sleepy one feels that dream is something purely material, rushing into one's head from below upwards, behind one's eyes in the form of a concrete wave) — it is that internal undulation, strengthening into the physical, that one channels into one's gait, resulting in that rhythm of hesitation and determination so advantageous in nightclubs. An inspiring bluff and a rhythm that immediately adapted to the local weather were sure conditions for Lea's happiness.

She felt the room around her like a mask or a darkly phosphorescent flower (as one is well aware, flower and mask are the same, for if one sticks a giant dahlia in one's buttonhole, its effect on one is that of a perfect mask, and one behaves as if one had been given a totally new autonomy, having no idea that one's head is showing the old front page; by the way, any unaccustomed garment or piece of jewelry grows into such a mask for the whole body); that slightly sentimental reaction of hers, a feminine half-sharing in her environment was, actually, a logical preparation for the fundamental duality of lovemaking: hypocrisy & bestiality.

An environment felt to be a mask immediately sweeps one onto irresponsible ground; beauty itself, with its elementary effect, promptly arouses the impression of some kind of sin in moralized souls, who prepare and give birth in their pallid and solitary wombs to a darkly flourished Antichrist — Lea was like that, a sensitive Antichrist capsule who always transcribed her joys onto a dark scroll and converted her resentments into deliberately polished shrieks of joy (informing on Lea, why?) with the slight surplus that she possessed a certain intelligence, which sometimes brought the fundamentally mechanical seesawing of opposites to her attention without, however, having protected her against it.

An art-dabbling Apocalypse is quite bad (yet maybe, nevertheless, better than a professional one as it can more easily reach the goal, viz. a stilted muscle display of ancestral strengths), but it can be utilized for a woman's grooming. Lea also got to grips with some kind of an Apocalypse, the love-apocalypse; looked at with sagacious eyes, this is a glittering impossibility, but if perceived as a female appurtenance, like a powder compact or ankle straps, it is quite acceptable. All Apocalypses consist of an institutional translation to images of strict symmetries of thought, so that it is not at all possible to speak of a sincere pictorialism. Of course, Lea was driven by a certain 'notion' of love when realizing her desires (is that still a word?) in certain planned pseudo-hallucinations. An honest person can never speak about visions as primary entities. It is inconvenient of course if a mystic notices this in midlife, when he has already adapted his fare, his daily newspaper, and his vocabulary of rhymes to his own 'visions' — it is exactly that kind of inconvenience that from the very beginning has occupied us in relation to Lea as well, & this love scene is actually a setting of two styles of mysticism in parallel to purposes of experimentation (the 'experiment' here is not literary cowardice, nor is it scientific in meaning inasmuch as it is a form for its own sake, seeking nothing and not being something that prepares a later 'truth').

Lea made her way between the tables, carrying the Antichrist embryo inside her like an English miss her bushy poodle in a park, and finally took her seat in the embellishing darkness. She did not even notice that Halbert was not yet there, so preoccupied was she by a burning joy; naïvely, she felt that she was facing "life's big forces" (that sort of thing may even suit a woman) and straightway took her red lipstick out of her purse in order to paint her lips when she spotted the whitewashed women with black lips.

That was when she was annihilated for a second time: all at once the white walls of the church of her girlhood days came to mind (which was of little relevance), and she suspected that somehow she needed to turn herself even more fully inside out, even though she felt she had undergone perfect annihilation when she had stepped between the black walls and the lamps looking like black tuberco-cactuses.

In fireworks displays it happens that after the third or fourth forking in the break-up of a rocket we feel that the pattern compacted into the rocket must have reached its end limit when all at once a redeeming fifth form appears that humiliates its predecessor into a torso — at that time one is filled with a half-triumphant, half-doubtful sensation that the last configuration does not perhaps represent totality but a perverse beyond-form of totality that now bears no relation to the developmental trend of the forms hitherto and will bloom, solitarily, on a new plane. Lea, too, had the feeling that these doll-like women were luring her into a world of excessive symbol-sensuality, which lay beyond the normal (mundane) Apocalypse-dose & turned colorless the illusion of quitting-herself which had up till then crystallized in the tube of lipstick.

Leatrice in a hand mirror

In the small hand mirror the lipstick tube itself looked like a huge iron roller, or like the tubes of a water supply system in scientific films (the world's biggest, etc.), while light from her face fell into the mirror at such a crooked perspective as though it were a snapshot made of a drowning person's last moment; a nearby lamp made a giant light sponge swim across the stage of the little mirror; in the distance, at the edge of the mirror, the faces of the whitewashed women flitted across as pale, greenish-grey extras, and, however much they hurried, the paleness of their reflections in the mirror did nonetheless slow them down; small female Buddhas, who have combined in themselves the raw mask drunkenness of farces and operettas made up of the most trivial Buddhist philosophy, the aroma of tea, and angularized waltzes — because love, the totality and impossibility of which Lea wanted to celebrate, always has need of a bit of prepared historical background, some China, Greece, and anonymous Cubism, the way periodicals have already ingrained that in girls: in the lower left corner (with no margin, of course), a giant Venus de Milo head turned downwards, continued by the half-profile of a 'modern' girl, with hair an explosion of light & eyelashes like centipedes — the Venus photo on pastel-tinted bromide paper, positive due to its shadows, the face of the new girl almost resembling the incandescently white spotlight trained on it, making every little blood vessel of her irises so sharp one had the feeling that, after this ecstatic precision, only the clear chaos of light itself could follow; from the upper right corner of the picture, on the other hand, the head of a French Gothic Madonna was hanging down like the awkward lolling head of a doll. Lea had also learned that montage or synthesis & desired it for certain notable points of her life like a slice of toast with a cup of tea. What could better suit love then that neurasthenic pseudo-synthesis, signaled by her little hand mirror with its crude perspectival humbugs: the huge stick of pigment, the crooked head, a senseless chunk of lampshade & scattered little blots of light which floated over her like big powder-puffs dropped onto distant water, dragging after them the grotesque white women, who, with their provocative masks, soon set Lea on the road of culture fantasizing, which served as an ambassador of love.

the relation of the history of ideas, orthodox philology, & a showgirl

To accept a culture, whether it be of one's own day or of others: that can never be done as sincerely as in the case of preparing for love; those are the hours & days when one does not feel that the concepts of comedy & reality are either contradictory or an elegantly suspected identity, but one unconsciously undulates in them, failing to notice the troubled transitions between one's naïve needs and run-of-the-mill symbols, transitions of which 'culture' actually consists: what one's descendants will call one's 'most characteristic culture' only seems artificial forced labor to those who are living now — one sees the "true expression of one's blood" as only the fads of artists (buffoons), and on that account one stays internally clear of them, sensing them to be mere curios.

A festival or market frame of mind is needed to enjoy the typical forms of one's culture, and even an eros of medium strength can acquire that. Two forms of enjoying culture in that way can be especially recommended: absolutely idiotic variety shows and absolutely orthodox nut-mincing philology. Most deleterious of all is the 'mind-synthesis' that was still being vigorously advertised not long ago — there is too much pathos in that, and in spite of all its apparent poly-chromaticism, it is unbearably monotonous, because it is nothing other than the definition-myth of central concepts, which is never capable of real diversity since notions of cultural history (these layman's deities: a uniformed 'logo-lympus') are always made of the same material: my pinning on a Spanish codex illuminator that he represents 'Gothic ascetic-sculptability' + 'Baroque intellectual rhythm' + 'Moslem proportion-eroticism' + 'brutal court elegance' + etc. is futile — those are all cold glass tubes in which only the monochromatic or colorless water of the notion is sleeping in an immeasurable distance from true multicoloredness: it pursues antithesis (not free 'other'-ness) so hard that when it comes across a new color it immediately wrenches it out & names it, or in other words, discolors it, as if its green & red otherness were greedily reduced to an empty pseudo-battle of 'One Color' & 'Opposite Color.' Perspective and abundance of color, wide horizons and real variegation, naturally exclude each other: in order to get a real hold of acerbic whiffs of culture, one has to turn from the frosted-glass Cubo-tables of denominators to the shady-philological Tanagra-witticisms of numerators.

Only the showgirl stands as an equal-ranking partner alongside the oval-bespectacled domestic small-scale connoisseur: the way she wears blazon-shaped garter-belt armor on her naked thighs, with red-tailed, prostrate lions, highly medieval (they do not resemble animals so much as the letters of the oldest Arabic script), with lutes and half-moons, wearing on their heads the red-braided auntie caps of guards on the Tower, with a wrinkled-taut cover like the parchment on bottles of preserves; meanwhile she kicks out, lashes, hiccups and rocks with her permanently bare legs — like a garish signboard of blasphemy, above her chest dances the provocative pewter plate of the historiographic Antichrist: every symbol of heroism, the hallowed heraldics of Christian crusaders and melancholy battle cubs, flicked, cynical, and yet thereby most faithful to the original. Someone should compile a big conversational book to illustrate how a gathering of people destroys (resurrects) the entire past, every culture, into witticisms, playful allusions, bedroom ornaments and letterheads — a history of the world assembled from frivolous aphorisms, holiday picture postcards, banal recollections: martyrs negotiating at afternoon tea (*Martyrologicum Nizzaicum Five O'clock*),[153] a great migration in the vestibule of the cinema (*Cimber Ciné*),[154] God in the mind of a bored young lady (*Theos à l'Ennui Seigneurial*), etc.

the identity of epistemological realism & distorting artistic styles

The black-lipped women greatly excited her acting ability: she perceived in them the same sort of heroism of distortion with which trapeze artists risk their lives — religious fanaticism and stern acrobatics simultaneously: one never knows whether to see ascetic humility or cynical programming-delirium in a face daubed into a doll's looks — those women, too, bore their paints with a distinctive rigidity, with arrogance, with bashfulness, as if they wished to retain for themselves their old civilian smiles, but did not want to reveal the full effect of masquerade in front of strangers: alongside all their joke-demoniacality they also had a naïve air about them as newly hired serving girls whom a firm has donned with unusual uniforms.

One of them was sitting not far from Lea; her hair was like a model head in the window of a hairdressing salon that exhibits how to rub a layer of refining cream into the skin — it slowly rotates behind the glass, rigid & idealized, its outlines showing endless refinement without resembling dolls (dolls which imitate the sketchily drawn heads of fashion magazines and strive to achieve sculpturally the extra-pair-of-lines technique designers cultivate); the crude layer of cream spread on her constitutes a painful contrast to the airy beauty of the outlines, being reminiscent of a death mask, a mummy, or a body part that is to be operated on.

The nearby woman made that kind of impression on Lea. Only her eyes were ferociously unfitting (not being able to make the eyes doll-like is a basic problem in painting masks) — that is when it becomes evident just what a complex, innumerably multilayered life there is in a human eye, when the skin is deprived of its elasticity & caught in stiff armor; indeed, that concealment may display the life of the skin even more: apparently, the surfaces that one thought were just stiff extras for our speech accompany our words with hundreds & hundreds of nuancing gestures; those girls, too, spoke with an odd pronunciation, instinctively feeling that speech comprised of minute intellectual and accentual mosaics was absurd in relation to their white faces, and instead they should employ Cubist grammar & Cubist accents.

The whole comedy seemed extremely superfluous, superfluity to the point of nauseousness, though it was also attractive, like the running depths of towers. She felt the same thrill that she had felt as a child on the shore of a lake in the evening: a wonder that was frightening, foreign, & hostile, yet full of contra tyranny. As if the most logical form of damnation were to be painted in a mask: the denial and extirpation of psychology are symbolized in it, the fatal opposites of doll and psyche, symbol and image analysis. The struggle of restless eyes and facial skins of reptilian smoothness showed the battle that Leville-Touqué analyzed (amidst a stack of marginal notes on much the same subject) in *Psychology and Gesture*.

Lea sensed the last phase of transhumanization, for a moment seeing the perpetual burden of Mimicry in parallel to the secure line of the racial continuity of bourgeois race-preservation; every period sifts out for its own entertainment something 'genuine' about the supposed essence of human beings, and it expresses that in masquerade (cf. L. Klausenbeck-Hentzke, *Einleitung zum Parallelismus zwischen realistischen Erkenntnistheorien und absichtlichen Deformations-Tendenzen in der bildenden Kunst*. Berlin: Schwachtner & Co., 1931).[155] There is a long gallery in Ardglass Castle: on one side (which has no windows) are busts of philosophers beneath which are long quotations from the theory of knowledge, while on the windowed side, between enormous, ground-length, almost insanely oblong clefts, are paintings, or reproductions of them, corresponding to individual theories; that was the way a naïve pedant realized the parallels of the distortion of anatomy & logical cognition even before any systematic study of it had been published.

an 'arithmetic' synthesis & a 'biologist' synthesis (example: a classification of nightclubs)

A thought passed through Lea's mind relating to Halbert's lateness, but only cursorily, as she was still greatly preoccupied by the nightclub's arrangements. She saw before herself an immense series, a universal album of honky-tonks in which every imaginable nightclub was photographed with encyclopedic precision in accordance to a scholastic classification, divided into subspecies and subordinate groups. The distinctions by which the so-called spirit of the age & 'externalities' & knick-knacks of the age were differentiated was quite demented — as if backdrops were less period-steeped than the plays themselves. The word 'album' in connection to Lea is not typical because the individual nightclubs that she had seen opened out one from another like flowers falling apart from one metamorphosis to another, but alongside all her association-frivolity she also had about her a strict, even an accompanying philological mood.

One needs to reconcile those two things that arose in natural partnership in Lea's mind: a distinctive hierarchy of visions, the order of sections by which they were assembled into a malleable structure, and the crumbling capriciousness, the psychological indiscipline of the same visions that they developed. Or one might possibly stumble on the raw dilemma of 'synthesis':

shall we signal it with sliding-ratios and coincidences based on arithmetic (like the sections and subsections, Roman & Greek initials, or symbolic headings of a legal system) — or in the form of a fluctuating, continually transforming watercolor & delirium? Or by a not overly difficult compromise unify an overly adorned Thomist classification with a vulgarly vitalist photographing into each other?

In any event, only those two pictures are of interest: Aquinas and a drunken Panopticon, which sometimes is driven only by the frequently reviled instinct of antithesis. On the one hand a mythological trans-Linnaeus in which the flowers are arranged in accordance to the most perverse considerations of classification: a system caricature, a system for which neurotics, above all, yearn, and is normally found only by those who are healthily predisposed; on the other hand, a carpet whisked up from floral debris on which lie ochre petals resembling giant ass's ears among Técla-camillas & strips of Virginia-creepers resembling a cardiac chart-mâché — *Flos Dogmatica & Flos Hypochondrica*: on one side (some day they will stand on the right hand...) a critical ordering of bars and honky-tonks according to style, location, popularity, owner, era, dishes, shows, closing time and employees, in clear-cut print, with pictures of uniform size, explanations of uniform length, & a chemical index of contents in which the individual entries are placed in parallel to the figures of an astronomical map, so that the 'closure' thereby gives a still more demagogically plastic suggestion — the nightclubs specializing in the celebrated oyster, lobster, sole & turbot will pertain to the Crab (Cancer) of the zodiac, while at the same time the four letters of Crab will also be utilized, and the nightclubs of Cremona, Rome, Antwerp and Budapest will be included in a newer unit, a horoscope based on the history of ideas will be compiled from the background of places that coincide in alphabetical order (neo-pagan, proto-Flemish influences in Báthory's private correspondence in Polish, etc.) in order to thus exemplify the ideal learning, the connection of the most whimsical arbitrariness and the most profound historical curetting of the womb — all this will anyway be made obvious by the heraldic style of the illustrations; on the other hand (some day they will stand on the left hand…), a vitalist machinery in which, in one respect, the basic stylistic forms are given (Rococo clichéd-elegance; German Schelling-Cubism; French glass-Cubism; Flemish redbrick-domesticity; English Tudor-zebra; Italian mortar-masquerade; international club-comfort, et cetera), in a second respect, dancing girls (average evening fillers; an expressionist demon after Apocalypse codex-miniatures; a naïve acrobat; a dancing flirt-automat, et cetera); in a third respect, the company, in a fourth, food, etc. — by now the entire machinery is nothing other than a mathematized kaleidoscope, which in accordance to the order of variations, permutations, & combinations (in the lower right corner of the apparatus, on a small ebonite plaque, three red letters: *V, P, K*: of course, it is a mistake that in that way there should be any system about it, but the inventors realized that the viewer would thereby be able to discover a lot more versions than with a completely free kaleidoscope: that is merely a practical observation, of course, & in the instructions for use, under the heading "Warning!" one can also read a comment that "inferences of the kind 'organized chaos' or 'chaoticized chaos' *cannot* be drawn from the machinery; if they can, then friction is arising in the clamp of the upper switch bar, et cetera, repair of which will involve substantial costs, compelling a total rebuilding of the vitalizing 'Synthèse' cathode-mixer, which will take a long time") gives nightclubs their inexhaustible variants of light, planar & plastic elements, & food smells. One of the statues of an ironically Greek-style nightclub can be assembled from yellow light (*We* have the famous Girgenti yellow…), its tympanum from a small Meccano-strip,[156] its metopes smelling of apple, to say nothing of that most vulgar possibility that bar walls assembled from lamp stands with steel bracelets should be continued in a tank of a counter standing on Byzantine icons.

Here, then, are Scylla & Scylla: two methods which for a practical person or an artist revolving without centrifugality do not tower into such extremely rigid allegories, because they work with few objects (e.g., few nightclubs), & system and chaos are actually identical to few objects (just as in his most recent booklet the mathematician Widmer nicely expounded those trans-algebraic figures that yield a picture of groups, that yield order and 'whimsical' symmetry in accordance to the same rule, and chance juxtapositions also always yield the same basic figure, etc. Likewise pertinent here is one of the sentences in a caricature-like book by Pezay: *Dogmatique artificielle et approximative du* Common Sense *anglais ou Burghes' Empiricism: Celui-ci me parle de la synthèse et l'autre me peint le désordre pittoresque: moi, j'avoue, je ne vois ni polyrythmie composée ni chaos vitalistique — je vois quelques choses qui s'ordonnent et puis se dissolvent, où il ne s'agit point des extrémités, mais du simple* mouvement *quotidien. Mouvement: garantie vulgaire du rythme synthétique*).[157]

'human' (logic) & 'character' (irrationality)
the decisive significance of this duality in love

The encounter of Leatrice & Halbert was born of love; it was not human. Quite drastic devices are needed to express the difference between the two. When one makes that distinction, then character and human come up against each other: 'character' is an unending accumulation of irrationality; the 'human' an unending cleaning of logic, rendering it ever more logical.

There is a woman who has a very determined 'character' (it may be better to employ the word 'quality' since it features here without any moral bearing, whereas the old concept of character is of so little interest that as the word is anyway devoid of content, it is better to fill it with interesting content than use another): her actions, habits, her movement, the humanist tone of her life, are not in the least special, there is no striking or odd feature about them — looking at the matter from the viewpoint of the average person. There is another woman: every one of her deeds, gestures, sentences and cursive capital letter K is striking & provocatively individual, her naked body is a white glove stuck on the viscous brow of convention.

The everyday functioning of the first ('normal') woman from one moment to the next is nevertheless a riddle, a hundred percent motor of irrationality, every twitch she makes, her intonation, is a thing in and of itself, & cannot be approached by word or number, by psychology or physics — in a manner that is stereotyped to the point of tedium, her life conforms to the order of society, official life, and street traffic, and meanwhile her every atom is anarchy, creation of a new person, a breathtaking, unbroken refutation of everything. (That "the chief mystery of all is in banality" — put that way the statement is a banality about which there is truly no mystery.)

The other woman, the 'odd' one, so to say, if one looks at the outcome, the result, or rather the surface of her acts, she genuinely does make herself conspicuous from the squared-paper notebook of everyday life with her exotic lines, but on the other hand, each of her steps is comprehensible, simple, logical and automatically predestined. The latter is what we are currently calling 'human,' while the other, the normal, consisting of the non-ending waves of anarchy, is what we are calling 'character' — 'character' will be appropriate for love, never the 'human.'

In Leatrice there was a possibility of both roles, but when she waited for Halbert in the nightclub, it was likely that the first role (character) was going to be triumphant. Character blossoms from passivity in its own perfection: when she decided (that word, actually, does not fit in with the current notion of 'character') that she would meet Halbert, she was lying on big red pillows, her feet held up high, her head down low, on her legs pink stockings the color of a dying fire, with grey street shoes, the phalanxsterian flat pose which was in contradiction to the 'sample of no value' comfort of the pillows, taken in the literal dictionary sense; her hair half undone, like the columns of gold coins and the ribbons round the stock shares in the barely split cabinet of a Wertheim-safe when burglars were surprised in the middle of breaking into it & thus forced to leave everything behind, having made just a little mess, like naughty children; clothed in a pink garment, neither an evening dress nor a nightdress, just a material that had slipped apart, with barely visible black lace running from her chest to her knees.

She lay that way for one hour on end: she would occasionally push her legs a little bit further away, spreading the stale oxygen of a warm trough and sucking a thermometer's worth of the cold of new surfaces into her thighs, 'drumming' her finger on the pillows (it was more just the hypochondriac heartbeat of feathers than 'drumming'); taking a puff from a cigarette that had got between her lips from she knew not where: her hand was so far from herself, in such an unfamiliar place, and such unaccustomed weight relationships were keeping a secret diary of shadows on her shoulders that she was always amazed that a cigarette had nonetheless ended up between her lips from such impossible places — as for pressures, she did not know whether one of her internal organs was weighing heavily on the grumpy weighing scales of another internal organ or if a book had slipped from her bedside table & was pressing on her arm.

But whenever she wanted, the cigarette set off, together with her hand; it set off before she even knew whether she had emerged from Adam's rib to the point that she could have arms at all.

In fact, in such a listless lounging pose, especially if the legs are fixed slightly higher than the chest (a 'bad' position is more truly relaxing), only will and unknown movement exist: one's intentions are not addressed to extremities but to movements, and when one brings a cigarette closer to one's lips, it is not one's arm & hand that are drawn there but the unkempt hypothesis-bird of solitary, bodiless movement, with all the excitements of hunting with a falcon. When she accidentally brushed her two legs together, she simultaneously felt in her body the rough, silky texture of her stockings, the soft seal-like bumping of the skin, the late braking of muscles — while with her eyes all she was seeing was the vowel-like pink color of her dress, she had no knowledge of legs, dress, muscles, or a rule of the spectrum, only of a stain in which something tactile & something visual are in the tightest relationship, indeed, are identical.

That 'stain' is indeterminate compared to the anatomy of schools and the colorful signboards of sign painters, but for Leatrice it was something very positive and circumscribed. 'Character' is composed of stains like that. Anyone who is worth anything cares only about that, believes only in those stains, adapts only to them — and only that makes love possible. In some ways it is the tale of Sleeping Beauty — the mindless compasses of wild roses coil and form figures of eight around the needle-oblivious body of the sleeping princess as if seeking to loop above her the world's biggest number consisting solely of eights: 88888888... Likewise these 'stains,' which typically were not tailored to humans, surrounded the passive Leatrice's body (the clumsy Impressionist tang is to be extracted): a smoking, deception-gourmet host of colors, sensations, anatomical 'blunders,' wires of volition and movement-sludges — each one an autonomous, 'sensible-nonsensical' constellation that has nothing to do with any kind of human, life, thought, feeling or anything at all, each one a new start of a world, a blind & ephemeral creation. Only the whole (let's say one hundred thousand 'stains' or unnameable constellations of that kind) will somehow be intelligible, for example in Leatrice's case: 'an hour's rest on a pillow in the afternoon.' Leatrice didn't care about that, however.

Leatrice as a 'character'
(*the* absolute *degree of irrationality*)

This state is not a withdrawal into the self or a passive acceptance of the external world: during Leatrice's siesta neither an internal life nor the external world have any meaning. For the time being that state can only be enveloped in an ugly negationhood, of 'neither this, nor that, nor this either, nor that either,' like bodies that are to be operated on, the sacks of sterilized towels are a metaphor of uncertain convalescence (bad blotting paper of death). The whole situation is the most consistent sport-form of flight, ceaseless flight from every kind of whatsoeverness, ceaseless flight from even the inquisitional-ring category of 'ceaseless flight,' naturally. Leatrice was a little thrilled when she noticed that existence was such a tireless incense burner of nameless novelties, out of which the mass of clouds of unknownness would rise until her death: a new Io who was not surrounded by a deity who vaporizes calling cards but the unknownness of her own existence for an unknown purpose — whether out of a wish to conquer, play pranks on, reinforce or annihilate she did not know.

Needless to say the 'unknownness of existence' was not a meek lamentation for want of self-knowledge. She was no silly ass of a young lady, so she was also interested in how the suffocating & blossoming irrationality of her existence might nevertheless be related to the bourgeois staidness of her 'external' life? At the same time, whilst her life was breaking up like a statue into unknown 'stains,' she also knew that she, a woman, Leatrice, would have her tea; if she wished, she would start up with Halbert, if she wished, then not; she was in a fantastic housecoat, only her street shoes preserved a record of the morning, just as the frescœs at Herculaneum do a record of Roman life in a fourth-year secondary school pupil's textbook: she knew all that 'normally' — how did this stolid and the other impossible arc fit together in her life? That those stains were only psychological reflections, a twilight card game of solitaire, of light, of consciousness, there could be no question of that, since she directly and unglossably felt that for her they were extraordinarily important, decisive, and essential: the part of her that was 'interesting' was located there. Was it only the empty prestige, mocked-to-death, of dream & uncertainty that she had fallen for? Up till now it had been easy to mock the dream & the uncertainty, because only artificial dreams & contrived uncertainties had been in circulation — nobody portrayed or intimated true irrationalism.

Character, then, is composed of the constant emission of clouds of individual irrationality, an ability for a wealth of anarchy (here, of course, anarchy has no revolutionary nature). Character is not a moral or human attribute but a meaningless sensation, like beauty. The more characterful characters are those on whom the secrecy and inexplicability of their life (those words should be taken in the commonest, most picture-magazine sense) is more obvious than on others.

'Personality' is not someone who is carved out of the keyboard of other people with special outlines, who is a closed statue, a fixed place among the waves of society: on the contrary, personality means precisely the highest possible degree of openness, someone who is surrounded by an endless irrational 'stain,' in which (as has already been indicated) human & world, soul and foreign soul, this and that, have no sense, everything goes through that willy-nilly like a vernal creator spiritus through an endless big tree bough; an individual 'blue eye' is not one which has no pair or formal relative at a ball, but one which splashes the radical senselessness of blueness in our eyes like a fountain, and, through that elementary, alphabetic senselessness, the unknownness and remoteness of all 'whatsoeverness' of things. The close connection of individuality and self, character and persona, is gradually fading from metaphysical fashion magazines. Leatrice is individual because she has no bony 'I' but is a sparkling geyser of the world's irrationality; Leatrice is a character because she is not a personality but an inexhaustible slim glass of the foaming nonsense structure of all human functions.

When she was on the settee that way, on her own, she sometimes did not know whether she was in her right mind or mad — but then that distinction has no meaning in radical lonesomeness; an individual has nothing to do with the social game of reason, has no need of it. Leatrice sensed that she was breaking up, but she was sensing exactly the opposite of what one is used to calling annihilation. She did not think of herself as being mad because 'odd' things were coming into her mind, but because what came to mind had no echo anywhere.

On their own everyone is crazy, Leatrice thought, and that was a fairly big surprise for her. In contrast to the common routines of crazinesses of a psychological nature, how was it possible to reach an intelligent madness?

A more pronounced sense of the solitude of an individual life is already madness — every 'one' thing has to be senseless by definition, whether that is a number, a human being, or any realm of lonely perception. She watched the latter: she hummed a tune to herself, the notes following nicely one after the other, sensing at modulations the lines of two foreign scales dipping into each other like two long rapiers at the point where only the fists or cups of the hilts touch each other (that is the chief pleasure in modulation — to feel from a tone, a point of sound, an entire sonic line or plane, an entire outgoing level of foreignness); after that she only sang the last note, it may have been an F# as her faint-hearted hearing reported, although that soon stopped feeling like a member of the previous tune, its loneliness finally breaking from the row of the other notes, and it could no longer return although it had not changed a jot; later the 'F#' signature also had no meaning, & soon even the 'note' would have none either, in the bubbling, effervescing, & cheery nirvana of solitude.

It was exactly the same with colors: her pink dress was 'pink' for some more time, as long as she was also conscious of the social concepts, masquerades of artificial etiquette, of green, yellow, and blue, but when those started to melt away from her like muscles from a post-nuptial embrace, then the sole remaining color was naturally not pink, not a color at all, just a specific, vertiginous, meaningless thing that is the world's cause and complement but never occurs in one's life and actions. Leatrice considered 'pure sensation' to be a congenial form of madness, and she had a penchant for rocking her nude figure of an oarless skiff in a 'pan-*F#*'-world like that. Lesson of a sort: here a single sensation denotes the sources of the eternal senselessness of life; with 'character' a million complicated situations, a kaleidoscope of chances. These are the exclusively permitted academics of love — far from 'humans.'

Can movements of the soul that arise from madness of that kind, from madness of the most individual personal existence, still truly be called love? Do they have anything to do with the 'human' practice called by that name? Very often, with almost ridiculous regularity, ordinary humans have ecstasies of love, however, those do not resemble the feelings that Leatrice experienced when she lolled on the sofa in her pink dress. The shifts in the psyche's over-relativized 'depth' (it is best to steer well clear of the word feeling) are not energetic; indeed, they are rather hieratic maps of inertia. Those mean love if I wish, religion if I wish, or art if I wish, the selfishness of digestion.

It suffices to let the logical notion of love flit across one's mind for only a second for one to believe of the entire constellation that it is love even though it is merely a matter of the distant friction of two stockinged-legs and a glimpse of a pink dress. The whole possible Halbert experience is already present in the solitude of the settee: the living Halbert is just a grey bird in the crowded & fragrant world of unfamiliar character boughs.

If my body and life are profusely surrounded by the theological perfume of my own meaninglessness, that perfume layer is the best guide for every impression, because it enlarges each one of them, develops it out of its interconnection, elevates it into a deity. In the most irrational mirror-valleys of the psyche the most banal movement of a man is the whole world, an arched bridge, an eternal bird, a thousand-budded moral. Is that love?

Leatrice does not find that movement nice; it is not her imagination that stylizes, let's say, the rolling of a cigarette into a celestial ceremony, since the most heavenly ceremony is a pointless banality for this most irresponsible mirror; she leaves the impression as merely an impression, forgetting everything intelligent about it. If one gets absorbed in the spring-stimulated unfamiliarity of one's own existence, one all at once knows everybody and enters into close & naïve connection with everybody &

everything: universal anonymity creates a new sentimental flock out of men, hormones, myth previews, landscapes & numbers. Going back into the checkered unknown, from the inner escape of the soul to the bilges of a ship (a ship painted 'human'), and a seemingly suicidal springing of a leak, there is immediately already love, or rather a sense of coexistence with every existence, traveling at the speed of light.

If that is 'mysticism,' too bad — words are anyway being squeezed out of the new Noah's ark, sailing tomorrow.

With lengthy angel-treatments, old mysticism had step by step reached into the soul's most irrational scallop, in which only Jesus swims, like a lost goldfish in a pupilless basin: between this so-called bottom and the surface of the heart there was a big distance that one might possibly have had to walk across for years, choking sensations in turn, until finally reaching the naked soul, the only-soul.

Compared to that, the new withdrawal into oneself is in no way similar. It does not speak of body or soul, their existence is taken for granted, so that they are uninteresting to the same extent as nonexistence — it does not bother with them, the distinction is of no use. The deepest layer (or mirror, or water-holding scallop, or possibly valley: in the pedagogic bordello of metaphors one soon muddles up the artificial pseudonyms of the inhabitants) does not mean distance to the surface, it is already on the surface, only it has no name. It is like a map, but one does not know of a river that it's the Volga, that it is elsewhere than the Amazon, that it is greyish-green, and that differs from bluish brown, et cetera: one perceives in the most doltish fashion possible — that is all. A person's 'character': the constantly undulating mass of the most doltish, cheapjack perceptions of it. And those always relate to the exterior, the wrinkling of dresses, the bitterish rime or electioneering hoarfrost of a kiss on the make-up of the lips: only the most striking layers of things are irrational, logically invisible — a millimeter further inwards everything is comprehensible, & the mental 'depth' of journalists & obsolete mystics (the most distant from externals) is so 'visible' that it is too childish even for a teaching diagram in kindergarten.

Humanity never yet had a superficial epoch because the surface is so close to one, its white-hot irrationality so strains and tightens that it gets behind one's eyes, so to say, and we always see the layers of things that start under their husks. From a practical point of view, it was much easier to record how it was necessary to forget the facial features of the world so that we would finally arrive at the soul's bare branch resplendent with the buds of God, after all the technology is better than what one observes with a strange identification of intensity and helplessness, the run of a ribbon of black lace on a pink silk dress, or the cut on one's heels, which begins where the thicker fabric follows after the thinner fabric of the stockings: in such a way as to forget any meaning, utility, human index, or clever coordinate; one's whole body, all one's organs, unified into a single animal sac that is filled out by impressions, as a pressure, as a suffocating incognito.

A 'doltish' perception like that is in essence a paradox, which is why it is difficult to write a recipe for it: in order that one may sense the redeeming and love-creating nonsensicality of black lace on the basis of an extraordinarily strong impression, actually a person equipped with all the rationalist exquisiteness and intellectual tricks of the intellect is required, the only one who senses the green of the color green as solely green, mono-green, and theo-green, is someone who has examined it to excess on every rationalist step of analysis — that avoidance of meaning by only-sensation is, perhaps, the most intellectual invention in the history of European thinking hitherto. This does not matter at all, and it is unnecessary to hold forth in the form of malicious exposure. That only makes describing it difficult: I can only render the absurdity of analyzability palpable with a higher grade of analysis, for the time being there is no other possibility. Anonymity with a roll call? Yes. In the olden days something was 'mystified' (and that is no more than one is seeking now with the notion of 'character') by sketching it in sand and then gently beginning to shake it, or quietly running water onto it, thereby breaking up what just beforehand had still been a fixed picture — now, conversely, Leatrice will not become first a black bush, then a ball of black oakum, and finally a grey mist (the etiquette of old-fashioned 'depth'), but a still more precise lace, still more 'thatish' than it is — and thus the spark of intelligence will truly render it meaningless. (Big things are paradoxical, but very cheaply so.)

---

how can that be expressed in art?

What sort of style or symbolic utterance can it be that makes an attempt to unify an elementarily ignorant perception and the elementary analytic delicacy that is required for that? Leatrice is lying down in her pink dress, her head slung back and legs held high: in the prank idiom of an old parlor game that was: "someone is proceeding in some kind of something, with some kind of something & with something that is proceeding somewhere" — that is the most abstract linguistic scheme of the thing, the ritual language of ignorance. Is it truly abstract, or the peak of perception?

I grasp colors so colorfully that I do not even know the name for them, only that they are 'something' — although (as has already been indicated) the 'something' is already itself a redundant and disturbing nuisance in the clarity of the impression. Of course even a child's brain can work out that if I express any elementary impression, the selfish and insane autonomy of impression ceases in being expressed. On the other hand, it is possible to intimate maximally to an 'innocent simpleton' the non-female, non-chromatic, non-objective, non-action, etc. nature of a situation like: "Leatrice is lying down in her pink dress, her head slung back & legs held high." It may be that nothing else is at one's disposal than an inflated style of simile: instead of about Leatrice one speaks about things that are recumbent, pouring, like a waterfall, fish-shaped, geometric, or in the form of a time-gland; one writes of Rococo tragedies, salon martyrs, or hermit-arteries instead of pink, et cetera, seeking out with sardonic punctiliousness the simile that least corresponds to the 'sense' of the thing.

Does one have to accept as a final solution that fine arts style that represents female breasts by drawing an endless wavy line, then the distorted projections of touch, marine figure eights, then Oxford lawn finger biscuits, unifying the aspects of the "someone is proceeding in some kind of something" & the machinating, anarchizing style of simile? It is especially important that one divests human actions of their conventional meaning — let there not be 'derisive laughter' and 'cherry-indexed regret' in a work of art; deeds, too, should only make vacuous impressions of movement in one without reason or real purpose. It is not just a problem of expression but of life, as always.

---

how does 'human'-love kill? example: fragment of a short story in which a boy waits on the seashore' for his fiancé to arrive on a ship & later meets her: the woman feels she is a concrete person and that is also how she treats the boy — the death of love'

Love is thereby always present — the greatest intellectual indifference, naturally, is the greatest ecstasy. Crudely maybe, but everyone has long been trying this in the proper direction when they proclaim "we live for today," being unconcerned with the continuation: that is only possible by disconnecting an experience from the sensible chain of life & treating it anonymously — either as 'somebody sometime' or as a maniacal simile. 'Behaviorism' may just be a passing nervousness of philosophy, but in love it is the best life-technique, undoubtedly. Some people react to declarations like "psychology without psyche" with an elegant smile, but love is wont to live not out of truths but plausiblenesses.

Carnal pleasure is highly suitable for forgetting woman's human nature and character, observing and enjoying just her beauty and, isolated from all things human, her 'behavior.' As the desire in women for physical pleasure is, to all intents and purposes, negligibly small, it goes without saying that they are incapable of the above-mentioned forms of love — for preference they look for the human. Leatrice stood at a crossroad when she thought of Halbert & the meeting in the *Woodcut*: should she be in love in such a way that actually she gave no regard to the man and only twist the warm green snakes of her own unknownness around herself, or (in true female fashion) should she bother with the man's character, taken in the mundane sense, with their meetings, and with engaging with him personally?

If one takes raw sexual instinct in the biological sense as a starting-point in every observation relating to love (as is proper for a polite point of origin), the role of that instinct is nil — love delighting in 'behavior' ripples well beneath it with its dark-green Atlantic nihilism, whereas love delighting in the 'person' (found primarily in women) ripples well above it, among purely social categories. If, therefore, one were to look for a symbol for incipient 'humanizing' love (dead at the moment of its birth), those figuring in it would have to be eunuchs & blind-wombed. (Physical pleasure is a good preparation for love of 'behavior,' as has been noted, & seems to be a contradiction to the latter remark that that kind of love is well beneath instincts, has no connection to it. The fact is that in love of 'behavior' ecstasy is not caused by biological pleasure but by the total rejection of the intellect, of all logical relationships, & for that, even suburban hedonism is a good school, a naïve and stammering course of instruction.)

The whore of Babylon is a bad symbol if she is genuinely able to enjoy sex — if she really is able, then she is quite surely a male harlot of Babylon with a badly stuck on mask. For that reason, in a plan for a comedy that is intended to mock the hunger for 'human' love, the whore of Babylon is not appropriate for any sort of carnal pleasure, for she does not have any organ or nerve fiber that would be able to enjoy it. That type is not so general in men, but in a comedy that should be played by a eunuch for whom woman, love, & marriage only mean a new person — *homo ad hominem*, never *homo ad feminam*.[158] All that is so only on account of exaggeration, since in the past it was possible to write that type of thing as a novel: every old relationship or marriage ends with that situation, it is not sexes, only human beings, who confront each other.

The blithe formula should start as follows: a fairly young lad is waiting for his fiancée on the seashore. As it is getting on toward evening he sits down by the water on wet sand in an armchair taken out of the salon, not in the harbor but in a deserted bay which had been bitten out by a juvenile Neptune. The four legs of the chair at times sink deeply into the soaking-wet, mushy, goose-fleshed sand, like the tongue of a feather-brained girl into the mouth of a youth the moment he has a slack-mouthed look, & sometimes they stick out high as if they were not standing in one plane but on a small globe on which all four would not fit simultaneously.

Behind him, like an abstract cupbearer of morality & logic, is an elderly male-duenna, in front a raging storm, with rain, mist, deceptive colors, and skin-tight curtains of sodium, of salt whipped out of the water. The elderly man is poking his stovepipe hat against the rain like one customarily drives a nail into a resisting wall and meanwhile gives a precise explanation of the character of the fiancée arriving from the sea — which in this case naturally means a group of virtuous, intelligent, social features. The sun has long set, but the rain is illuminating — there is no way of knowing whether that is due to its velocity or the holy leanness of the threads of rain.

The storm destroys, it is stupid, confuses everything, & it is full of printing errors — that is why many people have a habit of calling it tragic. Yet that young 15-year-old boy sitting in the water-swept armchair knows that rain can never be tragic, precisely because it is so gloriously nonsense, replete with Spanish etiquette. He recognizes colors, the green of hope, the yellow of envy, the white of virtues — but now, in the storm, they have all cast aside the roles that the study-keen chancellor standing behind him had drummed into them for years on end: the green was as sharp as a blade wedged into an artery & accurate as the shriek of a dying person — it sucked out the horizon's distorting poisons with its light in order to squeeze in its place the forms of lined and columned death; here & there blinded seagulls idled in it like balls over a playground when the Earth loses its attractive force. No doubt the storm would wreck ships, not the sea's brutal seesaw or the glassily transparent press of the winds, but this narrow, glaring-green band in place of the horizon, where both water and sky have ceased to exist under its diabolical hygiene. Perhaps this lemon-reasoned brightness will suck his fiancée's boat into itself & he is waiting in vain here in the storm.

How could the storm ever be pictured tragically? What a wire-like, precisely tuned death is the green of hope. Perhaps what is tragic is if the green can only be hope, the way it was imagined by the elderly man, who does not now even see the green diagonal on the Protean nude of the storm as a ribbon that by chance had got caught on the shoulders of an absent-minded body escaping into his bed. The yellow of envy illuminates from the left as if all imaginable ethics & love had squeezed into a single foggy flower lamp, a lonely kiss of light over the surf that had maybe been buttoned up by the serpentine fingers of the winds like snowballs. The elderly man spoke a vast amount about the fiancée who was due to arrive as being a 'good woman,' but that probably had not much to do with the almost nauseating goodness of the yellow fog that was clinging close to the billows.

The boy did not yearn for the storm, he merely suspected that that was where big and worthy fiancées lived, and the one whom he was waiting for was just a newer page of a notebook from the chancellor's records. The evening darkened, and the ship did not come. Had it gone astray? Had they died? Had they moored elsewhere? The elderly man had said something of the kind, that the woman would sacrifice her life for him. The wind was so strong and scurried in such sharply distinguishable material bands in front of and around them (sterile consciousness-searchlights of space?) that he did not hear that sentence directly from the elderly man's mouth but from an ingot of wind that was being cut in his brow: when the *duennus* articulated the sentence,[159] the high tide of the gust of wind immediately snatched it, wrested it from his lips like an alarmed housewife's greedy coffee spoon the debris of fruit dropped on a white tablecloth, taking it far off and leaving it there for awhile before another gust, coming toward him, carried it back (*physis non physica*).[160]

The boy replied automatically, without the least hint of sarcasm, "I, too, shall sacrifice my own for her." While the elderly man's utterance was immediately scoured off by a wind vertical to the words as they issued forth, the boy's answer ended up in an airless corridor between two massive walls of wind, so that in all likelihood, it never reached the ears of his instructor: he was thus in a position to feel simultaneously that his words were very loud, whereas his ears were nevertheless totally deaf. The spatial position of the two stray sentences as they were broke on the complex angles of the wind crystals and projected ever more strangely further onwards, also symbolized their content: how can the human wire of sacrifice take up position among nature's dark-blue cyclone roses? He felt he was a weary shopper who is offered various wedding samples and does not know which to buy, because they are all strange and fit him badly; he sees the storm blindly because he is a eunuch; he is groping skeptically at the phonetic threads of 'self-sacrifice' because he believes in nothing.

The gaffer lit a big candle — impossible in a storm like that, but needed in the comedy. After all, to sit and wait on the seashore is just as impossible, and yet they sit and wait. The boy is half asleep: the subsiding storm roars in his ears like a black bumblebee under the transparent glass of a tumbler that has been turned onto it, and the sentence: "I, too, shall sacrifice my own for her" left its caustic taste in his mouth like medicine, prescribed for others, which had been taken by mistake. He sometimes awoke — most often because the word 'self-sacrifice,' which for a long time wandered about only in his memory, all at once also began to dangle in his consciousness as well and there took fright, like a delicate woman's leg if, accidentally, it slips into a cold basin. The candle's clumsy flame quietly warmed his ear, while all his clothes actually formed a beard of water on his chest, dented as a soup spoon. The candle's skin-striping warmth, or the storm's fleeting last trail, sometimes filled the hollow syllables of the word 'self-sacrifice' with content &, half-asleep, he would believe that maybe the two could be connected, but when the sweet swooning of his slowly bending head all of a sudden became a standing burden from which he would wake up — he would again find them to be two incompatible worlds.

The chancellor did not sleep but interpreted. He spoke such a lot that the dense layers of sentences protected his back from freezing, like the nearby mountains protect Davos from bad winds. "You will have breakfast together, you will stroll together, you will pray together, you will sleep together, you will be separate together." Always together, always together: when one is half-asleep every word carries within itself the perspective that determines its distance laid down from one's consciousness — as if they were horse-chestnut capsules provided with thorns of various lengths, the short ones coming near, the long ones already halting a long way away. 'Together' therefore sounded utterly different from 'self-sacrifice': its shape & color was different. At a time like this, central point & circumference are meaningless words; the geography of the soul is a lot more volatile.

What is that together? Is two so important? In what way does it differ from the dual number of Ancient Greek conjugation? His destiny will be one number, one number that he had always feared, although he knew it was blood-suckingly important. This utter strangeness, that there on the shore he was waiting for a number, the dual number and nothing else, and that would be his life until the grave: he was almost filled with delight, it all looked like a big adolescent sensation. As his joy became a shade stronger he awoke again, but then, of course, the dual number did not denote anything joyous. "The girl has been writing letters to me for months saying that she has been longing for you, she wants only you, no one else, she has left everyone, thrown away everything from her money to her memory, apart from you. You are her dream, her language, her dress, and the time within which she passes. No person had yet been loved like you. She is familiar with every one of your features, she knows by heart every word you have said."

The boy listened in amazement: "Familiar with me? Remembers every one of my features?" Just beforehand, when he had not yet heard that, even if he had nothing to do with the bright mix of colors the storm had painted up with a sponge, he at least felt he was among them as if he had a white mask on, ego-blunting gloves that protected his whole consciousness, & kept him aloof from himself, but when he learned that somebody, a woman, was very acquainted with him, the gloves of anonymity were suddenly torn, his ego sharpened into an ego did not fit among nature's gaps. Is the world everywhere arranged in such a manner that a far-off woman, by having a fanatically sharp memory, always has the right to force our ego into an ego when we ourselves possibly do not want that? But why should he not accept his ego since, in any case, he has nothing else?

The conical-silk-hatted court monkey produced a thick wad of papers from his inorganic funnel pocket (in the winter of 1933–34 women wore that sort of thing on their shoulders) & read out sentences from them: "Every day I invite someone else as my guest since I am a sociable woman — this afternoon your eyes were invited, after dinner I will chat with your hair till midnight. I like those tiny wrinkles around your eyes, those tangled drawings with which your nerves signal your thoughts in minute caricatures; no sound has issued from your mouth, but the tempo of your wrinkles already precisely shows the slender trough of the sentence. Those wrinkles by your nose are still quite stiff, but then they are all the more restless & colorful toward the corners of your eyes. One is brownish, the other bluish, one silky, the other like paper, the minute sheet music of looking that in my solitude I also transcribe to other senses."

One would imagine that a 'loving' description like that could only make the addressee more plastic in his own eyes, but the reverse was the case: after reading it out, the boy felt that he had gone blind. He saw, though not with his eyes but with a definition that he perceived as rough glass on his skull, not lachrymatory eyeglasses cut for him. He rubbed them with his hands, and it was obvious that the former were of flesh, the latter of unsolicited words. But their reactions, as always, were weak — at first he was alarmed when his eyes were stolen in that way by yearning for them, but then he gave himself up to the spirit of dependence, as if his eyesight were just a clipped-off signature on the back of an indifferent group photograph. Why deny it? Indeed, he asked for the courtier to read out more from the letters.

The night was spent like that; the woman did not arrive, but the boy knew his own features by heart. When morning's golden greyness was gradually pulled out from the night like a narrow and flat drawer from an enormous cupboard (somehow like, according to the method of "extensive abstraction" advocated by Whitehead & company, the origin of a point: cubes that can be placed inside each other converge toward a point-like ultimate cube, thus a point is, in fact, just a sign of the relationship of the diminishing tendency of that diminishing series of cubes — the yellowish-grey plane of dawn above the sea is nothing other than the very last of night's nesting boxes of darkness, which, due to its infinite flatness, is so transparent), he found he had experienced the essence of love & marriage once & for all time.

His wet clothes dried into hard creases and dug deep into his body with their concertina edges. The huge candle was still burning, but the flame flickered quite a long way from the wick as if there were something missing between the end of the candle and the tongue of fire — it was like a three-syllable word, the center bit of which is missing, Dina instead of Diana. That is also what irritated him about pictures by painters in which the arrival of the Holy Spirit was represented: the too highly printed Slavonic inverted circumflexes of truth (the twelve Apostles were like a long Czech word *žřžřw̍čšĭťŭžy̍* — a little tongue of fire over every single letter...) were so alien to the Apostles, which they illuminated from so far away that one could almost fear they would be unable to fall on their foreheads. Of course, the more daylight there was the greater grew the gap between the candle and its light.

They both set off home, leaving the tall armchair on the shore as an artificial nest for awkward time. The boy was king of the country. His palace comprised two parts, the two blocks being separated by a very, very narrow channel, which extended from the sea into the city right up to the palace. The channel was not visible now, & the palace appeared as if it were a single block of a building. Both of them began to hurry in order to have a better look. When they got close they noticed that the channel was completely filled by a huge, extraordinarily high-masted, half-smashed boat, as if the palaces on the two banks were enormous presses, and the yacht — a big, half-crushed bunch of grapes. That was the fiancée's ship. The storm had cast it into the narrow gap between the two palaces in such a manner that a large part of its hull stood out of the water, and it seemed that the thin black-pupilled channel water had acquired enough of the chancellor's pedantry to try, with a flood tide & huge waves, to extemporize a forced, artificial high tide with which it could reach the ship, and that brought an end to the lapse in etiquette of having a yacht dangle above the water as if the body of the ship had the magnetic strength to perpetually absorb long cones of water from the channel's udderless waist.

She arrived. It did not so much as cross their minds to enter the palace, but they jumped from the channel's narrow path onto the boat: what a splendid, fantastic stairwell. They felt they should not take the boat away, and if it began to decay they would get their engineers to construct the proud trapezes of the wreckage precisely there. The snapped or fallen masts inscribed yellow W's, Y's, and X's into the gap between the two walls; the rope ladders formed single-storied hammocks, the white sails leafy boughs and flying icebergs, while the black flag with the green lions was like the artificial waterfall of a park, with black foam and black spray, in which the green masquerade of spring mirrors itself into a heraldic accordion. What a splendid invention is that shattered boat, stuck in mid-air: neither landscape nor building, but finer and truer than both. Naturally, most of the windows & doors had been smashed by the masts, which had penetrated deep inside the palace on both sides, like crowbars or a pair of scissors that had started to be cut but were forgotten in a roll of broadcloth that a tailor had left on his table because he heard a superb customer had come by.

It was very clear that the odd shipwreck constellation was an organic part of his wedding, consisting as it did of futile waiting, the verbose codification of his own character, and a bloodless program of self-sacrifice. Cautiously, stumbling badly, and slipping back every now and then, they clambered up, occasionally looking in through a window. They sometimes became entangled in immense nets, which down at the bottom, in the shadows, were wet and heavy, as if they had been wreaths woven from copper coins, but higher up they were white as snow, scorching-hot from the morning sun, and salt-steamed. It was through a white net coffin like that that the boy glimpsed his fiancée in a room on the uppermost floor. One of the walls and part of the ceiling were completely missing, because the giant anchor that had struck into it had crumbled it to dust. How had the anchor managed to get to the very top? He tried, insofar as it was possible through the square-gloves of the white net, to follow the anchor chain downwards between the perpetually wet lips of the channel & he found that the chain was not broken, it had just taken an enormous swing like an enraged clock pendulum, which all at once throws the weight dangling at its end above its own face — maybe that dreadfully big anchor had tugged the boat into the air above the channel, like Baron Münchhausen pulling himself out of a swamp by his pigtail.

The boy tried to enter the room, insofar as the herring veils around him permitted. The woman was sitting in front of a mirror in a black dress with two white shoulders, like white-water taps that had been left running, one warm, the other cold (one powdered, the other still naturally brunette). The boy became increasingly entangled in the white twine, so that the fiancée jumped up from by the mirror, picked up a pair of scissors, and started to snip at the squares around her betrothed's body. That caused the boy pain as if his blood vessels were being slashed — the netting had been his last chance to hide from his wife, and now she was shredding it strand by strand. The chancellor stumbled outside and with a whistle began to plunge in the air and he was finally caught at the bottom of a net like a stone in a slingshot. Meanwhile the woman had ripped away every strand of netting from around her affianced & taken him into her lap — the boy was fifteen years old, the woman thirty-two.

That signaled the start of the three days of nuptials: they talked for seventy-two hours straight. That was a second annihilation for the boy — the first had been the night he had listened to the woman's letters, but now he was standing face to face with the will that had all been directed at him. That had not been fidelity, but then he had not wanted infidelity either. It was not a question of the woman becoming a burden to him through wanting to be with him constantly & never leaving him alone. Loneliness was not the objective of his yearnings — that is liked only by people whose instincts at a time like that blossom into nothingness like an overgrown creeper into forbidden water.

two styles: the strict parallelism of the absolute rationalist (e.g., Carnap's mathematical logic), & the absolute irrationalist (e.g., Surrealism); two imagined saints: rationalist & irrationalist, characterized by plans for two churches

When Leatrice saw before herself love feeding on irrationality, and a human-searching, continually 'talking'-love, then she saw a typical excised detail of the dialectics of total lifelikeness & total rationality in general. She dimly remembered in this connection a conversation that had gone on between Halbert and Touqué in which Halbert, speaking about his father, said that everyone had considered his father to be a repugnant & cowardly skirt-chaser because he made a pass at every woman and from even the most abstract topic he would immediately get round to women, although women were not important to him, or at least they were not the goal, merely instruments with which his father tried to express the 'deepest' shifts of his soul, the vast loam of absurdities and ornament-artists that steam around an individual life. Neither literary, nor mathematical language, was appropriate for expressing the most ancient spiritual allures of the spirit, so he was looking for a new dictionary, a new grammar, & it seems that he found them in the girls of Exeter & a number of nearby towns. So, it was not the women who aroused amorous instincts in him (in Halbert's view, there was no question of that), but the drive to express & portray the perfect a-rationality of the soul that created women, in part invented figures, in part living ones. Not Don Juanism, then, but linguistic creativity.

Three things are closely interrelated, & Halbert's father (as is evident from his diary) was already well aware of that at a time when those interrelationships were not fashion items in Europe:

the life of protozoa (which consists primarily of movements), the a-rational life of the soul, and the form of women, the totality of their outward appearances in general. The curlicues, relaxations, the stroke diagrams of protozoa and their inaction-calligraphy (e.g., in a drop of water under a microscope) seem to be life's most authentic pantomime, from which the (sensory and sensual) life of the soul barely differs & only the more complex expression of which is the rhythm of female body forms. If among the three participants one watches the soul and the woman, then one can see the totality of a woman in elegant beauty, the totality of the soul in sensory and sensual life rendered absolute, or put another way, in a certain kind of hysteria.

Souls have states that cannot be denoted with any word or sign but can be eminently characterized, for instance, by a blond girl's hairstyle (the million shades of combing *per se* can alone be accounted a perfect language from the point of view of the soul's need for irrationality) and by the half-open, white velvet coat, with giant turned-back linings and giant buttons that she wears over her swimsuit: the relation of gold and snow, the affinity & antithesis of blondeness and white moss, the mixed-up sense of openness since the taut drum of tricot that can be seen behind the coat is not 'after' it in the first instance but at some n-th instance of 'after' without its being nakedness — neither a nude figure, nor a dress, neither 'inside' nor 'behind,' a relation of outside and inside with which language and geometry are not at all acquainted, but the soul is acquainted all the more. And if the soul again makes a change on this 'impossible' space sensation, it is sufficient to make the blonde hair a shade more bronze, or the hip a notch more spiral, and the particular relationship of outer husk and inner seed is also immediately modified in expression (the woman).

The female body is an ever-blossoming dictionary of curved forms, and it is in a much more biological connection to dress than a man (a woman is in every case thereby at least two women) — those two properties make it especially appropriate to express the gymnastics of the soul's protozoon with it, or at least that was the opinion of Halbert's father about the matter.

If novels about women, or rather opalinely changing women's catalogues, were at some time to step into the place of love novels, then old Halbert's type of thinking would in any event figure among the many reasons for that: the linguistic construction of forms of the soul that have hitherto not been given expression. That is happening at the same time as reasoning, too, is corroding itself to innocence with new signs of mathematical logic. On the one hand, there is a film actress who plays all the way through a 90-minute film, the sole topic of which is her face, with a hundred thousand variants of mimicry that never express feelings (joy, pain, fright, etc.) but anonymous shifts of the soul. On the other hand, there is a certain *Überwindung der Metaphysik durch logische Analyse der Sprache,*[161] with characters of the type: '— P. Q. e. Q.,' or 'P > Q — P — Q. e. P.' When such opposed forms of expression are demanded with the same voracity, then every kind of love and literature, morality & religion, must also sense it.

Just as the Middle Ages produced Saint Thomas & Saint Francis (the antithesis of the two, of course, should be taken in a banal sense as one is well aware that there was plenty of mysticism in Aquinas and plenty of logic in Assisi), so the Roman Catholic Church could produce two characteristic 20th-century saints, one of whom would represent with his life the soul's infinite 'irrationality,' the other: the new metaphysics with Carnapian anti-metaphysical signs.

Instead of the imagined outline of the two figures one would rather indicate their schematic casings: the churches that might be constructed in their honor. One of them (let it be named after a place-value notation: the Saint of Reason, Sanctus Hyper textus) will have a simple glass cube, which has a single piece of furniture, fresco, vault and cellar, confessional and lamp: an infinitely dense series of letters. The row starts on the altar's glass screen, being fitted onto the glass as half-meter high letters made from black lamina, which imprint part of the gospels onto the transparent wall with their edges, but by the time they have returned from the far side onto the altar screen again, they contain only the above-indicated calculi of relations. The whole church looks like six grids of black letters hanging in the air.

The church dedicated to the other saint (the temporary name of which, even though it might be misunderstood, is Sanctus Hypocondrus, since he was always going about in a world of the inner life deeply below sentiments, showing the comedian completeness of the idea "*homo* non *ordinatur ad proximum sicut in finem*")[162] is a jet-black, windowless blind cylinder where the middle of the base rises conically (evenly, starting from the circumference of the circle): the huge bulge is half-transparent, made from thick, reddish-lilac glass, under which is placed the only dimly visible altar table. There is nothing else in the church. The congregation can sit as in a circus, in a circle on the rim of the cone's downward slope, since only the shadows of priest and altar can be seen, and with that there is no difference between frontal and rear view (the matter of holy communion is somehow soluble even with that architectural trick). The two elements of the church are the windowless night & the solitary hump of color: a single sensory impression, which always implies the peak of 'madness' (Leatrice herself also contemplated that when she was lying on the divan and thinking about her meeting with Halbert).

the cantus firmus *of No-Word in an abundance of words*

If one does not utilize women to express the irrational side of life, and not the marks of mathematical logic to portray the rational side, but the words of some kind of language for both, then naturally one is going to struggle a great deal — since Adam & Eve were first born that has been the 'difficulty' of expression. If the person seeking expression is really excited by the absolute poles of life's intelligence and lack of intelligence, then he will usually become talkative, 'verbose,' rousing the impression that he cherishes words, though it is precisely his tautology (to repeat: only if he is extraordinarily sensitive and on that account a person seeking to express himself with extraordinary power) which demonstrates that precisely the word is his biggest foe. A person like that very much senses that 'thought' is a tenth-rate phenomenon in comparison to 'cogitation' so that he constantly pays attention, both in writing and speech, to his cogitations, which is naturally a giant, unbroken thread, with regressions, stutterings, overhaulings and unpredictable flourishes extending until the nearest period of unconsciousness (dreamless sleep, death).

In the prolixity of such a style it is precisely the No-Word that is the garish *cantus firmus* — one senses in the ridiculous accumulation of attributives, not a proliferation but rather a diminution, with the consecutive words referring ever-increasingly to one and the same content, each newer attributive obscuring even more, along with itself, the preceding ones as well: the hundredth dress renders the woman naked, the whole is some sort of negative malignancy. If one has some kind of guarantee in relation to a great intelligence being behind somebody's prolixity, then it is most definitely desirable that the person in question is not tempted by a banal ideal of 'classicism,' which 'seeks pure thought in pure sentences,' but takes his words with him as an ever-fertile litter, because that tautology best corresponds to the brain's basic mode of operation, which consists not just of the production of ideas but thinking without contours (that is a psychological advantage), and, aside from that, succeeds best in making one forget words and making one conscious of their irrelevance to their multiplicity (as if every dictionary were just small change withdrawn from circulation), thereby drawing attention to the content behind them (that is a logical advantage).

When Leatrice was wondering where, actually, her quality of being able to see so well the difference of 'behavior'-love & 'anthropo'-love (the difference of irrational psychic-life and rational brain-mechanics) might come from, then by a bit of baby-Freudianism she came across one of her very early trips to Venice, out of which the necessary motifs could be extracted with some tasteful applied-art symbolics. The perpetual undulation of water, or simply its watery nature, indicated the swirling senselessness of life, the 'soul,' & the slim columns of the Gothic houses, or simply their stony nature — life's rationalities, 'humans' in the social sense. The rose and black lacy dress, the street shoes that were not removed, and the motions of smoking a cigarette, or projections taken from them that made them meaningless, were the start of her siesta. When she set her legs down from on high and stubbed out the cigarette in the ashtray like amalgam in a decayed tooth, or a tiny seedling in hard soil, she felt she was identical to Venice: her general condition, the half-suspected internal friction of her muscles, the gradual balancing of the sweet fog of well-restedness in the hollows between the big organs, the gull-like wheeling of the weight of the dress on her shoulders and knees — all that was like the softness, museum-piece mendacity, & hemorrhaging of color of childhood rivers, while her memories and her plans, associations & wishes, ruled lines above her like the spear-wrinkled façades of palaces and human formulae of stone and compass.

VIII.

return to Leatrice's second memory: waiting for Halbert in the Woodcut nightclub (p. 566). Halbert makes an appearance.

While waiting for Halbert she was obliged to order something. From the next room she heard the sharp tinkling of a telephone, a nervous, lengthy, and ceremonious ringing in which desperation and the ringing of altar bells at mass were united. While the waiter set down his broad tray with the slim glass of raspberry syrup he signaled to the other waiter with his eyes with restrained concern, to which the other responded with a twitch of the eyes, but he passed on the message with a snap of a napkin (the white table napkin was flourished for a moment from under his left arm before he thrust it back under his arm with an uncertain but emphatic gesture: there was no question of beckoning), two waiters were bent over an account book by the door with one of them quietly whispering something like soldiers do on changing the guard, or a priest to a clumsy altar boy during mass, whereupon one of them signaled toward an invisible place, whence a few seconds later a new waiter made an appearance and with scurrying steps hastened further, most likely to a telephone: that jingled shrilly, dramatically made its presence known like a bloody fountain among tiny waves, which to start with evoked only a silent grimace, then a loud grimace and, in the third instance, quiet speech, before leading to actual action in the services of the orthodox & titular Order of the Knights of Hors d'Œuvre: Lea took the whole thing as being a festive preparation for her own *'eros kai anteros'* [163] soirée — perhaps all they ordered by phone was gelatin & Spanish onions, but she felt that the dinner ceremony of 'finding and renouncing' had begun with that.

Suddenly, with a crackle on lifting the receiver, the ring ceased: as if the fountain had been abruptly stifled, leaving silence instead, as symbolized by the gleaming plateau of the enormous tray, in one upper corner of which stood, not unlike a tube, the drinking glass, and in the corner diagonally opposite, some sugar and wafers. That was the Order of the Hors d'Œuvre's coat of arms: a clear silver field with a red globe in the right corner and a white one with a brown baton in the other.

If one drinks a cordial from a little round saucer, one is quite close to the drink and can help oneself without loss, but to do so from a tray like that, from the allegorical statue of open country, one only helps oneself to an insignificant portion whereas the rest, the essence, remains unconquerable, with the tray's perspective directly siphoning it away. That is the essential quality of 'elegant' serving, hence of 'elegant' eating: an abiding heraldic tenor: space, distance, perspective, a spirit of empty, self-servingly empty, heraldic fields. When one arrives at a silver surface, coming after crowded blazons (that, too, is a fertile variety, after all), birds, swords, lions & crowned chess tables, one sees just a single red globe in the field: all at once the space that has been disdainfully left unused raises a stimulating giddiness, and that kind of 'heraldic vacuum' makes the table setting stylish. The Russians have a folk custom (maybe just some of their writers do) that roughly consists of being able to attain genuine purity only by experiencing sin, or rather, it ripens parallel to sin while committing sin, and thus sensuality & asceticism are, at root, the same — sin becomes the possibility of the sentimental, pseudo-metaphysical 'completeness' of one's human nature. Lea had quite a big penchant for that, or rather she very much made it a part of her, and it was on that account that she had come this time as well (as has already been indicated several times), in order to put into practice, by the book, the ceremony of love and renunciation: it may be that this strikes one as highly improbable for a young woman, given all the artificial decadence she had forced on herself and practiced as a hard lesson; it may be that the asceticism only figured as a stimulating 'pickle' for love, as has often been claimed about the Middle Ages with such childish naivety — it might be a lot of things when an enormous number of diagnoses are made about all sorts of 'dual' people, with whom it is customary to be drunkenly obstinate about causality, in linking an abstract hieroglyph to a tedious obscenity; with Lea, for example, a kind of theory about goodness as being first and foremost a visionary need, a stagy (hagio-kitsch?) system of morality, a regular hypocrisy of renouncing and experiencing, and a naïve piglet's ear canal shivering under them.

Halbert made an appearance at the side door; he was not in a tuxedo, just in a dark-blue suit with a big, soft blue necktie almost like a hair ribbon. A small, red-haired, snub-nosed little girl, powdered deadly pale, was just in the process of taking her coat off in one corner and phlegmatically only wanted to put it on the back of the chair. The fur coat was so short that it could not be folded, she was squeezing the furry whatnot with one hand (the whole coat was little more than a single, enormous revers), with the other she wanted to pry from her brow her tight-fitting green deerstalker cap, but she was having so much trouble doing that, and it hurt her so much, that she was hissing & scowling; meanwhile she knocked the parchment shade from one of the small lamps with her elbow, making a noise like a quietly tapped drum; for a couple of minutes the bare light bulb was seen, white, like a shamefully untimely bismuth star.

Everyone looked over that way: that was Halbert's direction. The little powder magnet was as though she had greeted him like an eager hunter or shepherd boy would a newcomer. As always on an occasion like this, a shudder ran though Lea and merged into Halbert's steps as he approached. The green-hatted girl gradually settled, or rather, squeezed with self-ironic crawling movements into the hole lined by the tablecloth and the fur coat, between the chair and her partner's legs: while down below, around her knees, those linings and casings were indiscriminately muddled up in trailing down, higher up her dress flapped and flickered tautly, cleansed free of disturbing husks, & even higher up was the pastel velvet of her powdered neck and shoulders — the burning little shepherd looked like the informative cross-section that is made of certain fruits in which all manner of rinds and shells can be seen at the foot of the page, above it fewer, & at the very top, the nakedly gleaming seed itself. The star burned glitteringly; the red hair fluttered gently in the slow breeze that was bathing it like a doused firebrand, above which was the green hunter heap that flitted now lower, now higher, thereby regulating the fires of expectation.

---

the ancient infertility character of beauty

When Halbert appeared in the doorway and drew closer to Leatrice, it was natural that the schema of an angelic annunciation should flit through her brain as through that of any woman at such a time: news of redemption was on its way and she accepted it with helpless humility, like water trembling in a flat dish does the shadows of its own waves on the bottom of the dish. The big annunciation always comes from within, and lay

& civilian angels bringing the public news are merely symbols of an unexpected, groundless blooming of a woman — at least that was how Leatrice felt in those minutes, and then again she did not resemble her species. But at the same time, when her spirit went through that gesture of infinite acceptance, which is most aptly symbolized in gymnastics by the reverse touching of the arms extended behind one's back (an embrace that is so wide open that the person who is being embraced has no sense of arms being around herself or himself, only the atmosphere of an enormous obtuse angle of 360° in which the two stems coincide, somewhere falling remotely far away from her), at that time, thinking of her own beauty specifically drew her soul more tightly together, practical vanity and a desire to be attractive crushed her body into a small withered point. Her face did not go together with desire; indeed, it often works in precisely the opposite direction: when the desire for love (that plan for self-denial naturally merges with the waves of affirmation experienced as self-contradictory since the time of Eve) grows broad and ample petals around itself, then it is as if the petals were shadows received from the horizon hovering Sun, extended to infinite length, yet the most fleeting thought that related to her eyelashes, to a piece of cotton wool placed under a garter (on the site of a not yet fully developed pimple), or to the inexplicably rapid evaporation of her perfume, stubbornly pushed her from the free world of love into a so to speak suicidal corner, into the barren lair of her own beauty.

Never before had she felt that duality between love and beauty, so it made her shiver and she would have liked to cry. Is happiness not, therefore, a personal matter; are one's own arms, eyes (metaphors of gambling with atropine), & skin unable to follow the irresponsible games of the soul? Does the annunciation straightway compel an abortion? Is that dualism perhaps too the dualism of Venice? But before that, in its own million-digit irrationality, beauty had been playing exactly the opposite role, & now, when the man was approaching, all at once it had shriveled like a big sheet of writing paper thrown amidst small flames — nothing more than a blind little bud of death? She would have liked to rip the mask of beauty off and along with the wanting of vanity, toss it rattling like a skeleton into the living water of love: Vendramin, Loredan, Cavalli & Foscari into the nihilist mirror of the Venetian canals.[164] Compared to the freedom of the annunciation scene, the unexpected rigidity of beauty so greatly resembled genuine infertility that she felt her womb was a residence which had been locked on the inside & so was impossible to enter, and nobody was going to come out since the resident had committed suicide — whereupon, though lacking every practical aspect of motherhood, she hankered with romantic stubbornness for a child, simply for an incitement into the love of individual beauty.

before that a Venetian novella

When she visited Venice as a child, she had heard an impossible story about the love of a Doge's boy and a famous courtesan, the main point of which was the young boy. The 15-year-old Doge's son had no idea about how children were born, and he had the most fantastic ideas about women; as for the aging courtesan, she fell pregnant against her will: some witty friends of the Doge's son put her to sleep and tricked the boy. During the pregnancy, the boy seldom met the woman, whose behavior toward him became impossible, besides which everyone around him took to whispering and making veiled allusions that he didn't understand, as a result of which he was driven to the verge of madness: all the 'highly civilized' bits had been invented by Leatrice, because she felt that, on her, beauty was an incomprehensible feature, much like the Doge's son must have felt about his aging lover's dimly conceived pregnancy, which was threatening from every hand. For the impending birth was more a symbol of infertility than of pregnancy: for the boy a suppressed secret, constant confusion; for the woman a tragic caricature, foolish toying with her life. The tale had it that she gave birth to the child on the night of Christmas Eve near a little bridge somewhere on a canal densely covered with tree branches — the throes of labor made the gondola dance awkwardly on the barely flexible water and with her shrieks (which were truly strong to the point of materiality) she tried to create for herself a third and fourth arm in order to be able to hang onto the branches. When the child was born she rolled over into the water. That was when the Doge's son arrived: the woman's body did not sink but swam speedily along the canal, the boy after it. The child was found by a spy for Turkish merchants who was hiding in the city disguised as a priest, nosing around for the families of wealthy Venetian mariners and suppliers. He was just about to be exposed that night, but in good time he had snatched hold of the child found in the gondola and started preaching about him to the people, who piously listened to him. Those who had wanted to expose him did not dare seize him after all, so well did he play the holy man.

She remembered that horror story only dimly, but it was good enough to appease her sense of barrenness and her ridiculously explicit desire to give birth: no doubt the good emblems are the ones that can mean anything — more backdrops calling one to action than specified characters. Does childbirth symbolize infertility? Beauty a swimming body or a suckling babe in a spy's hands? She had no idea about that sort of casting, she just felt that she was now confronting a real 'women's disease' of the kind she had heard whispers about in childhood — it was not a matter of the spirit but of the body; perhaps she ought to take some medicine. She was in the comical situation wherein she was afraid that Halbert would notice her beauty; instead of paying attention to her love, he was going to treat her as a woman squeezed into a conserving jar and would not wish to creep into the branchless clump of leaves of desire (only this word 'desire' could be freer of kitsch).

At the next table sat two elderly American women with negligible amounts of deeply cut clothing; they clattered loudly with their cutlery and their bracelets; jumping around them was a young, naïve, & continually blushing blonde-haired waiter, his shirt so limp on his chest from perspiration that it was like a handkerchief which has mopped up so many tears that it was hung out between draughty doors only to dry; the wee waiter performed nothing but diminutive movements, whereas the two elderly women took over and continued the waiter's tinkering of the torso with broad gestures; hardly had he pushed over some lettuce with humble waiter's chic than the more undressed of them had immediately snatched at the bunch of leaves & set about lifting it up, with everything a blur of white flesh, spring foliage, jewelry and dazzling spoon — as if with bored pathos she were making a sacrificial offering to an unknown person who was coming closer.

Ordinariness and liturgy, stereotyped movement and ritual gesture, triviality and myth, were always kindred notions in the arts, but nowadays triviality and a philologically resurrected, artificial mythology are *consciously* linked, whereas in the past the two were self-evidently one & the same, the self-standing, untimely nature of stylization was lacking. The faces of the elderly Americans were rugged and mauve, as if they had just been shaved; one of them had hair as white as snow with yellow, nicotine-like blotches dotted here & there; her eyes were huge, like those on Hindu pictures (there is always a cock-eyed realism in them, whereas with the Egyptians the eye has so much a hieroglyphic character that it would never occur to one to envy them their closed little globes), with an unnatural acuity.

---

then, a big allegory on aborting fetuses & against;
first of all, the conversation of a young theological director
with two American women

A theological scenarist went over to one of them & quietly, but in a persuasive tone of voice, which is such a concomitant characteristic of some priests (they whisper the truth as if it were a sensational secret; an incredible fixity of belief glows in the warmth of their breath, which seems a perverse greed rather than a virtue), saying to her no more than this:

— It is necessary that you, Americans, be there at the feast of love. The feast is not written in accordance to my taste, because the joy in it is a lie, the suffering merely a curio, whereas I love unpolished joviality in joy and cruel simplicity in suffering. Despite which, I permit this small Russian to carry on by its own lights right to the end since I like plays; indeed, it is not possible to accept them from any other point of view. And, above all, we sometimes need to see what people want to do. I admit, we don't want that to be of assistance to them, but in order to have our own dogmatic impatience, not to say Elysian-limitation, loved still better. Not all of my celestial colleagues acquiesced in what, in their view, is a cruel diversion, but instead deem to see a particular tragedy in humanity's perpetual labors and restorations of the soul, but those were mostly rural parsons or art-historian types of modest talent who would put on exhibitions of 'ecclesiastic art' in one place or another in which one could see how they would rub their little lyrical 'problems' off onto God's back & with enchanting unscrupulousness write down their stylistic invoices to God's expense. I noticed that God did not take them too seriously, & indeed up on high there is a society of earned scholastics who undertake research into what kind of irony is displayed by God — His irony unannounced to people, or to the blessed and the saints (within His boundless mercy and justice), which was gathered precisely from His rewards and style of mercy & justice, and I have come to you now on behalf of God's Irony Club of Paradise to dispatch you to Lea's love scene: not as extras, because in farces like that there is no difference between a heroine and a carpet — we simply have need of the two of you.

Not unnaturally the two pretty elderly American women immediately asked: — Why?

The theological scenarist replied with a smile:

— Without you the staffing of a love research laboratory would be incomplete these days. Of course, Lea will be actively in love, but somehow every woman in it will be compromised, because the important thing here is not the sentiment of love and whatever, but female existences as such, passive, condensed; Lea's individual role is there just to enliven the existence troupe. A naïve prayer leader who makes the spectacle somewhat melodramatic; up on high, in your cases, the intellect does not exclude a love of genres drenched in the current of time.

The two women naturally again leveled a "Why?" at the guest, though one of them had already put her feet on the low cabinet belonging to the mirror (with a sudden, lively movement, as if something inside were painful, so that its lightning-quick speed was not due to strength but to helplessness) in order to take off her street shoes and embezzle her feet across into the dancing pumps quivering like flowers of light in the corner (the theological director paid calls on the two women at home):

— Why? You should know full well, scholastic pater, that we were taught to give sharp definitions & precise golf strokes, so we acquired the purest technique of thought; but only the technique. Because we did not have behind us folk and blood for whom a thirst for syllogism and the water of doubt would have caused a confusion lasting decades. Pure thought was not a well-honed skill — we simply learned logic, like a crochet stitch, uncompromisingly, without having heard grandfathers tell tall tales about the various properties, specific gravity, durability & rigidity of thinking. Thus we ask for definition not because that is our rationalist instinct, and not because we want to feel out the plastic art of truth with our mental fingers, no, for us the truth is neither plastic nor attractive, and we were not looking for a reason for our anatomical photograph (it may be that it is there): define for us your goal because that is 'fair play,' because that is the right thing to do, because it's the best manufacturing trick & packaging patent for thought. Answer.

— You imagine me to be a dime-a-dozen scholastic-model puppet, and I will not deny that, for if I remember correctly, just a week ago a book was put on board that explores the memory of our earthly life and demonstrates that we were very passionate and whimsical; our syllogisms and definitions were full of romantic exaggeration, Gothic asymmetry, truth-masked hysteria & devil knows what else. I myself no longer remember exactly what I was like, it was quite a long time ago, and one soon forgets one's own biography up here — suffice it to say that only some post office mix-up can be the reason why you are not yet acquainted with the book and you speak to me like some wax statue of the ice order, not a Baroque comedian who wrote "*nec dicta de dispensatione dictis de essentia admiscenda esse*"[165] — only by way of various mechanical terrorist inhibitions — instead of 'a kiss-positive ferments logo-nothings' (as if thought were a fixed material, an area that, if you stock it with your neo-cherry-ish lips — and with what else would you stock it? — all sorts of plants would grow on it, plants which do not at all resemble the color and shape of the mouth & always yield a big, hypocritical flora of syllogism).

The woman who placed her foot on the mirror cabinet suddenly stood up and quietly inquired with a tickling overtone of screeching:

— Why?

— You start with conspicuously good omens of love; with a new body, a cold, muscular, and Edisonian manufacture-innocence, with past-free thinking. Your bodies do not possess any strange history of love; you are freshly exposed like rolls that have just been taken out of the oven onto the table.

— Father, you have as vulgar an opinion of us as we do of you.

The other American, who had been bored in listening to all that, nervously interjected while throwing her nailbrush at the scenarist like a prematurely aged child tossing a pebble at a ghost appearing before them, signaling that they are fed up with this whole specter business:

— There really is no sense in concealing your ignorance with loquaciousness. It's deeply offensive in respect to us that you have chosen us, because we are not types, we don't represent anything, and any normal person will realize that there is a ridiculously big distance between your obsolete picture of America & our individual specialty. Even an Eskimo better fits your type of 'new body'-vacuums than I do. Enough of it.

— It may be very vulgar, but it would be best if you get used to that very thing, my children. Because there are properties, symptoms, on the body of a nation, like ember-flowers that glow through fog, observation of which yields sharp diagnoses of woodcut crudity: I truly do not envy anyone that kind of diversity. It would greatly spoil the game if I were to pare you down to complex components — and in any case you yourselves would be tired by any obsessional conformity to that diagnosis.

---

seascape: as presented by the young director

The sea was blue and thin as paint on a fresh fresco under which a wall is still visible; behind it houses soared upwards, like white basalt-giraffes, or a clumped-together bed of reeds hungrily stretching their heads toward the foliage hay of the clouds; a Riviera-clarity sparkled in the water, and on the swaying blades of the houses and the cloud-collared stems of the roofs was also a Blakean-world that had nevertheless been created by civilization; picture of nature it may have been, but in such a way that this is suggested by technology and is a comfort to humanity, the most profound brutality, or Freud-stigmatized frankness coupled with perfect hygiene, comfort, and the apotheosis of pragmatism.

For it is natural that not even the Elysian father pursues self-serving visions into reality, where at the end of the image we only come across more images, but wanted to show the American women the simple nature of their own beauty, the essence of which consisted of truly and absurdly primitive instinctiveness and absurd technical perfection; or rather, the absurdly, merely technical perfection was already presaging a virtually new cultural formation, civilization's state of inebriation might be the embryonic phase of a culture. Old people were needed, haggard, slim, white-backed and half-naked old folk, because a new industry was already required to create that beauty: youth is an old invention, while glittering spring-hued old age was already a classic example of the new beauty. What is naivety and mental vacuity going to call for with this perfect industry? Venus can again be arisen from the waves according to the finger-pointing of crafty guards: on big whistling clam shells, only the final point of which brushes the water, otherwise the whole thing scuds in the air on stamen water-clouds: when the visionaries of old codified their notions, they always contained history, morality, and dregs of the past, but what do those record-Venuses see when the force of nature bursts out of them & there is no pressure of the past in it, only the mottled possibilities of mechanical comfort?

---

then the old director gets round to showing the young his own vision drama; the protagonist of this vision is a young woman who wants to have her child aborted by a physician

---

The celestial Arivarius muttered a threat to the scenarist:

— Watch out that it does not leak out straightaway at our first rehearsal that there is nothing naïvely elementary in their simplicity, at most they are a trifle stupid; but Lord, oh Lord, stupidity is not yet something primary; but take care that your other pole of protection, that mechanicalness, does not compromise itself: it will come to light that in the substitute mystery of love it is not a matter of the geological folding of the Freudocene and Mechanary periods, just of slightly loopy women using a bit better armpit hair remover than was used in our own time.

— No, it can't be about that: it's a matter of new forms of fantasy, a new nature of beauty in which utilitarianism has transformed into an as yet indefinable mass, and that is precisely its greatest value, it is the streaming material that has not yet solidified into a cultural base: it is in a transitional state; you will be able to see, indeed you have to see, that beauty is born willy-nilly from everything; delightfulness, comfort, elegance and petit bourgeoisie unite in order to blend into the new formula of beauty, and that beauty will become the new culture.

— Yes, sure, it's always about that — some barbarian demand is conventionalized — then he added, in the shoulder-shrugging tone of the elderly: — A new thievery is brewing. You are making a dogmatic-sensational New World portrait & you announce that this will take the place of our old culture: you seek to re-daub European culture with a glib definition like that — after all, your entire fervor is not addressed at Americans but at the European spirit, which appropriates America by means of an analysis and, by thus stealing them, fornicates with its decorative plunder & brings artificial pseudo-descendants into the world.

The old man went a bit closer and winked that the young man should follow her.

— Look, I, too, have a crafty breed of culture here, if it comes to that. It is not made of pathetic manufactured formulas like yours is, containing no autumnal electro-Venuses that sprout with supposed profiles from gleaming motors and white barber's napkins & among rainbow-colored flacons of lilac; it's an airy, naïve little culture that will come to nothing, yet its inhabitants will occasionally swim.

The scenarist paid attention. A pale, skinny woman stood in the doorway to a villa, the walls were white like sails, almost fluttering in the breeze — the whole house could have been an altar erected to the spirit of the Diaspora, it disintegrated into nothingness, into light, wind, and sea, although only a gaunt algebraic law was asserted in its walls & its glass skin.

— See, this rather fashionable villa on the Florida seacoast very much fits in with what is happening here. The whole style involves devotion to line, contour is the sole precept, and it's precisely a villa like that which disintegrates (metaphorically) in the world. For the time being all you see is that I wish to prove an awkward paradox, which in truth would ill suit my old noggin, but I want to guide you to a much simpler reality with these finger-pointings — the paradox is of no interest.

The woman was extremely slender, as slim as a green glass rod, her hair fluttered in the breeze; she had on a green suit, in one hand a pair of long white gloves reaching down almost to the knees.

— Are her lips covered in blood?

— No, not at all: it seems that I went a bit vulgarly overboard in marking the place for kisses like Neapolitan movie ads do the tracks of pistol shots. There are constantly lapses of taste like that in didactics, but I set greater store on robust pedagogy than on the big definition-thirst of the young, their desire to harness incipient semi-formations, which of course results in them merely penning down their own desire for definitions in lyrical poems.

The woman leaned a little back on the wall; she was almost transparent. On her white skin the green suit was like a lampshade behind which a kind of Plotinus-Ltd naked light surges from underneath upwards; the hair was none other than a freezing into material of what was beyond the shade. Around the hips the two ends of her belt hung above one another like two crossed hands with rigid fingers (brotherhood) in armorial bearings or mute wings placed in the shape of an x, and on that area the green was denser. On the place of the mouth there was just an amorphous red inkblot. The gloves lay limply in her hand like the adagio ears of a run-over Vizsla. Everything about the girl was funereal; her enormous eyes were closed but her beauty shone above all her weariness like an otherworldly coat of arms, or a watermarked stigma that exists faintly in the air but with a stubborn sense of being destined for precisely this spot.

— How melancholic everything that was dynamical is here. As if I could see the essence of the contour, notwithstanding that all I feel is dispersion. That is an ecstatic degree of the scintillating Gothic art of the bodies of Anglo-Saxon girls, but in all of her flights into the sky, all I see is a sick stretching, the perverse linearity of agony; it would be futile my explaining that perhaps I do not see the essence, only tricks of distortion, I have a feeling that although you work with demagogic means you somehow flip toward the essence.

In parallel to the girl's pose, solitary sunflowers stood beside each other, scrawny and gnarled, like soliloquizing backbones, the rocking and rising vertebræ ending in broadly grinning petal-roulettes. They were standing far from each other and bore a great resemblance to the girl leaning on the door; it was as if the clear-as-glass spinal column had sparkled the length of the girl's flesh: a rocking trailer, a snake on the verge of bending into a dream. With her fatigued hands she tightened her lips, & shining golden rings revolved around her hips like around Saturn — she bowed her head and placed her hands flatly over the hurtling golden belts, not caressing them, just resignedly & taking official cognizance of them. A seagull teetered above the door, as if it wished to break in.

— You know very well — the old-timer said — that all kinds of things could be said about me on earth, but no one could say that I had taste, that I could somehow have held the arts in more profound esteem. I therefore ask you repeatedly that if you see motifs of, in part, *trecento*-angelic greetings[166] & high school-level educational wall pictures mixed up here, don't let that take your interest away from grasping its in any case modest meaning.

The golden rings suddenly curled as if their racing geometrical lines had got caught in an invisible reel-filter, and after they broke up into miniature springs and slivers of light, they turned into bees unexpectedly and continued to buzz round and round her waist. The girl grew even scrawnier, her whole body asceticizing into a sleepwalking plant stem. This scene unified all the youthful splendor of turning into a flower, and all the rigidity of emaciation to bones; her body, on which bone and costume united, was like a far-off figure reflected from a third windowpane. The face suddenly broke up; only the little kiss blot remained in the form of a strident poppy.

— From now on this can continue as an animal tale or a flower fable, I don't mind if you understand the matter on the basis of an English children's book, or from the point of view of cynical Æsop, in any case it is just a prelude to my culture colony.

The poppy blazed (it is fairly conventional for them to do so) like a flame, it arranged the white house around it like a chalk vase before going on to circle the whole peninsula to its root like a shawl, and the sea as well wound funnel-like around its stem, so that in the end the fire-flower was like a fountain combined with mediocre taste in the middle of a garden; there was no conflict between a Cubist vase and a 13th-century garden.

— The battle of the poppy and the bees? Of the kiss & the hips?

— Well, maybe not — the old man coughed as if he were a bit shamefaced. The bees again turned curly-lined, then grew back into circles of geometric exactness, and finally they completely came to an end, leaving a big black shadow on the woman's waist. The poppy became a mouth; indeed, a very pale mouth. The girl went over to a little table on which a huge cactus was standing (three lopsided, unshaven erysipelas ovals), beside which was a crumpled *Herald* with enormous pictures and red seal, *Late*

Extra. The shadow followed on her hips. She produced her big handbag and reddened her lips: every muscle fiber was focused on that, and she even kept a tight hand on her ancestral spirits in forcing them into the act; she squatted at a little mirror propped up on the table as if it were not about cosmetics but a religious licking of a blood amulet — her thin knees were set a long way forward into the nothingness under the table, her legs strained at the ankles, she was raising her ankles in the air like two tension-balancing keys; she turned her head in wild twists, her hair flowed, echoing back & forth from itself; her hips meanwhile became ever blacker and she pressed her knees up ever closer to the table, & therefore the table to herself, so that its edge dug deeply into her belly. Thereupon, showing profound pain, she tried to rise.

the 'pedagogic Guignol' *commences;*
the woman calls the doctor by telephone

— Father, what a pedagogic Grand Guignol.

The woman went over to the telephone. Her legs were slender like those of the hyper-deer that are blown from glass nowadays; her breasts, too, were two hidden nonentities, a sand surface over which an infinitesimal breeze respired for 0.46 seconds — her waist, on the other hand, was as swollen as the crossed legs of seated Buddha statues: as if thick plaits were hanging from her as a bandage for a massive animal, or like a tube-shaped thermophore. As if she had been two persons (here, by accident, this is not the symbolics of an apparition, but an ordinary civilian observation). One was the hand that just before had still roved distractedly over the lines of a newspaper lying in front of her, then one of her fingers all at once started to nervously search more exactly for an advertisement in a smaller area, & when she found the name she jumped over it with the edge of the finger, part in impatience, part in laziness, like a ballerina dancing on points or a gramophone needle stuck in a groove — the other person assembled around the headphone & was poised like the dependent variable of a function, ready to react at a moment's notice, indeed, had made nebulous noises more than once in the belief that the party who had been called was answering: her eyes exploded over the paper at one time, at another internally, slipping into the Eustachian tubes, until the person called eventually answered. It was then that she noticed that the finger pointing to the address she was seeking had meanwhile slipped, and although its rigidity was hurting, it was now positioned in the wrong place (on a picture of a restored gas factory, on the belly of the Trade Minister); she hurriedly looked nearby for the address while uttering (by now quite loudly) meaningless syllables into the receiver in order to fill in time until she had found the address again.

— Yes... Yes, just a moment... Doctor, Doctor... Him? Of course... Yes... — (she suddenly hit on the name: her body had hitherto only just been in contact with the receiver, but now, all at once, she tucked it in like an umbrella hastily gripped in a gust of wind) — Doctor Morris. Yes, him. Is he not home?... Where? Yes? Yes??? That's marvelous. I'll give him a ring straightway. Yes, OooK, OooK... Thanky... Pardon? Yes, OK, OK. Thank you.

She was too tired to drag the telephone book over. She threw herself onto a chair and rang for the chambermaid.

— I can't be bothered to put in a call to Doctor Morris. He's not at home but somewhere in the neighborhood, at the house of the Lennings, or some such name, and he left a message that if anyone should ask for him, that was where he should be called. Would you be so kind as to find the number for me, then lay the table for afternoon tea on the small veranda.

The chambermaid pulled toward the crown of her head the cap that had slipped onto her forehead and began to scour through the massive telephone book (the small ads printed on the sides of the pages showed fresh deformations at every turn, as if one were looking at regular geometrical figures in a distorting mirror): a lay ministrant to a lay Bible. There is a disproportion between the incoherent voices of a call and the inhuman clamor of a ring that hits its goal — it may be that some kind of pulley system is at work by which a disproportionately large job can be completed for little effort. When Lenning answered the woman spoke:

— Bring the handset over to the table, please. Here! That's right, here.

She wearily pulled the telephone to herself, from which the mouthpiece hung like a galosh caught on a fishing hook *à la ballade des pendus.*[167] She began talking in a cheery tone:

— Good morning, my dear Doctor Morris. Excuse me for the interruption... That's very kind of you, thank you... Well, no, it's not an emergency exactly, though... to be honest, I don't know. Urgent... but, but... No, he went off early... That's possible, in fact it's all the same to me... Fine, fine... You'll get a cup of tea as well, freshly brewed. It's here in the sideboard — (for a moment she put a hand round the mouthpiece & called out to the maid: — Take out from the top drawer that pack in silver paper that came by post this morning. It wasn't you who was on duty? Then it must have been Lucy. No matter... There, there!... — she took her hand off the mouthpiece and the dry, tetchy, bureaucratic face again transformed into the conversational smile that is so characteristic of phone callers: in part they assume the rigidity of visionaries, a blend of an ability and a disability to fix on things, and besides that a naïve & homely absentmindedness). — Don't get me wrong, I was thinking of you. A cup of tea will be waiting: I'll show you my new assortment... Oh, no! No! No! Not a bit of it. No! No!... How? Perhaps that... But no I take that back. Not that either... In any case I don't believe it... Who's there? Hang on a second, let me guess. You say only yes and no. Wait a moment... Only Wilson, then. No point in being polite. Come over, do come. Thanks, ta. Bye-bye.

---

the troupe of monkeys files in

She contentedly put down the receiver and got to her feet from the chair. Her hips showed pronounced elephantiasis, and she was emanating a sharp, pungent odor. She lumbered across to the mirror (made of a ribbon of glass, it hung down from the ceiling, not reaching the floor; to the right and left were two gleaming metal cylinders, one bigger than the other, with a bare rod mounted from the larger one to the center of the mirror at the end of which was a lamp held between two parallel black lacquer plates) when the maid ran in fit to burst and yelled: "There's someone outside, he won't give his name, he's coming and I can't..." her white cap had slipped askew and her face had gone blue as Roquefort cheese, she was stumbling and slipping on the carpet (patches of carpet lay only here and there on the lurid yellow floor: the chambermaid slipped on one of them like on a raft or an iceboat) and then fell and stayed on the ground, weeping.

The young scenarist said to the craftily twinkling old man with a smile.

— A detective story according to the principles of the Schola?

— It's an old piece from the repertoire of allegories of the past — I tried — how to put it? — to give it a more youthful look for you but that wasn't much of a success; wherever I could I used the *'dernier cri,'* but where I couldn't I eked it out from some fine morality plays of my childhood with only the unity of meaning really present.

— It's an entirely fresh proposition, Father, fashionable-artificiality, and cumbersome symbols-miracle brewed together; indeed, the raw coarseness of symbol per se already counts as esthetic chic.

— Stuff & nonsense!

A commotion could be heard from over by the door to the hallway; somewhere in the distance a telephone was squawking with strange obstinacy. A black chef wearing an enormous white hat burst into the room, overturning the lamp by the door (it was a glass replica of a tombstone set in the floor of an old temple: a large crystalline plate with a red, engraved band of writing all around its border and in the middle a little scene: a troubadourish pseudo-bull is paying court to Europa, who in one hand is holding a burlesque medley of pan-European coats of arms). He bellowed at the top of his voice: "The police are coming!"

From the next-door house an infernal shrieking could be heard, shouts of applause and booing, barking, mewing, the incessant hammering of tiny bare soles. The very next moment a giant monkey leaped in; its nose was like a dog's muzzle & its skin fitted like badly pulled-on gloves, its eyes were horizontal like in Japanese pictures where they are designated by just a single line; its pelt was colossal like a peruke, the spokes of which densely fringed the red dent of its brow. It spoke as if barking and with a nervous scurrying, drumming the air from right to left, making use of the typical aimless gestures of monkeys, perpetually taking fright.

The monkeys were tumbling over each other like eggshells atop a fountain; they rocked on the spot, their heads shone like light bulbs; every one of them beamed, smirked, and gibbered.

The maid and the cook could only lie stupefied; a fist-sized little marmoset squatted on the girl's shoulder and with a mixed action of nervousness & comfort, fiddled in her dangling, freshly waved hair. Weeping, the 'heroine' crouched out of fear; her face was white like foam; her whole body was a ferment of glass at the center of which sizzled dense bubbles; the room was dark, and the sun appeared behind the sea as when it is wont to be scattered through fog into unarticulated bronze-breaths; the silver blinding strip of mirror was full of monkey heads; all red skin, festival wigs of blue fox, & above them sizzling pure light.

— We won't get anywhere with sentimentalism. You are impossible to understand; when you spoke about pure humanity you described the most tedious and most bestial of all beings. When you wanted to demolish the dams of passion, you restored the bedroom of a goofy grandpa, and even your philanthropy is the biggest conspiracy against humanity. Kiss, kiss, kiss instead of suffering; what is a kiss? — he thereupon jumped over to the woman, who shrieked as she covered her face with her hands.

When the 'head monkey' threw himself forward with his rude question, a company that had been quietly whimpering & gibbering in the last minutes suddenly pressed forward anew with cheering on with a squeal; indeed, certain groups completely transformed into greyish-green bubbling water & lapped in waves of hot foam to the middle of the room in such a way that the carpets moved from their positions and began to float toward the veranda. The telephone cord swam on top of the shallow lakelet like a dead snake.

— Don't torture me — the woman said plaintively, though with the particularly disciplined theatricality of someone who is only playacting the entire scene. — Don't torture me. What do you want from me? That I should start with untrue denials, that I should condemn my mouth, that I should curse about showing off how chic my swimsuit is, that I should recite

»Eros is not for eroticism,« for me to rush back to my lovers, who are serving on who knows what ship, or keeping the accounts at I don't know which corporation, and correct back your understanding into our embraces? I know why you are coming. I am not rebelling against you, but I cannot comply.

She uttered that last word crying, almost submissively, yet with the desperate obstinacy with which a half-successful Magdalena was able to declare about herself when she had dressed in rags, tousled her hair, and gripped a slothful book under one arm to read in her cave: "Dear God, I would gladly do it, but all the same it is absurd how badly all this suits me."

The head monkey threw off the fur coat from its head and bald-pated jumped on the woman, at which the others all rushed over there, whipping-up & splattering the water as it rose in the room. The woman and the monkey wrestled. The Sun peeped out of the fog for a moment, and at the place where it shone on the garden, cataracts of poppies spurted forth from the ground, the water, the walls and the sea's salty extreme billows; they did not look like flowers so much as seething packs of hummingbirds, their wild colorfulness unexpectedly deadening the monkeys' voices. With their silent seesawing resonance, the poppies at the silvery-dandy edge of the sea were standing in the melodious giddiness of sudden birth like in those new flower stands that are regularly made of colored, semitransparent glass and extremely flat, like a tray, but the flowers are held up in unnaturally vertical solitude in a separate perforated stem holder. The Sun again dimmed with shreds of fog growing above it like petals that by night fleece the flashily flaming capsule of seeds between their frugal fingers. Three figures wreathed forth from the waves like ghosts carried along by the rising tide. The first was a pinkish-colored boy all squashiness and spreading out: once upon a time it must have had a wholly human form but it has smeared apart like an amœba in the water.

The young spectator gently said to the old man:

— When I look at this picture what comes to mind are our long-past cogitations about the two sorts of visions — the one social, the other psychological; in one, whole classes of people are at work, big societies will be squeezed into puppetry-style symmetry: those are the algebraic visions, for divining which maybe a chess- or card-playing mentality is best-suited; the other, the psychological vision, is confined to getting embroiled in senseless distortion, chasing associations; in the geometrically social the Totality (does it exist?) is insisted on, in the other the Fragment (does it exist?) is deemed more mystic, and in any event our senses are invoked. I was somewhat scornful of them both, kind Father, even though there is a lot of fatiguing mental effort in those kinds of things; in truth, I am not sure that I was not guided by hidden laziness disguised by self-deception when I let myself get carried onto the dreamy paths of syllogisms instead of thinking out such a complex construct as Totality or Fragment.

— I don't believe that 'Totality' and 'Fragment' are what differentiates over-symmetrized visions & associative visions: what prevails in both of them is our appetite for monistic pabulum, only in one of them it is the external appearances which are intellectual (that is not a good choice of words since the other is also intellectual in regard to its form), which arouse an impression of unity, of '*monos*': the structure of a picture or poem suggests a structuredness of the world — whereas in the other the prime ideal is dynamic relationship, streaming-infinite totality, non-hierarchic continuation. Thus, it is not 'Totality' & 'Fragment' that are opposed in the two types of visions, but pseudototality & eternal continuation.

the three bad apocalyptic lackeys of pseudo-love; the first: effeminate lyricism

The pink-colored figure half hung down in the water in the way that dense bands of distant rain tend to plunge into the sea like the misty teeth of a comb, half swung his hands in the air the way children do a paper dragon weighed down by water; his head was lying somewhere in the clouds like a dropped fruit. Together around his mouth were roses, snails, birds and flags — with tiny purple feathers, leaves ringing from blood, and carmine-ribbons — a separate world which drifted among the clouds like a burning nest.

— I have abandoned everything — he said, half dreaming, half in a whining, entreating voice —, in order to search for just that red, I have erased divinities via libraries so that my finger is half worn down, then I calculated new gods of scarlet and with philological force I inserted a new history into the past so only that would be the soul of history, that the credentials of every god, that flag, shade, & scorch the politicians' faces; I have consumed my body in desire, spared it the trouble of working, given it a hatred of civilization, stripped it of the irrational springs of action — that was how I exposed it to the lights of the red constellation; the sea's monotony was my companion because the energetic aimlessness and majestically cloaked nil-prestige of the waves corresponded to my so-called shallowness — the unethical pomp of the trees, birds, & rainbows also suited me, because they exemplified the Narcissus-strength of existence, in contrast to the wastefulnesses of action — you always see drama in nature, or even at times when it is passivity, then a rationalized 'essence'-symbolism, which once again is a lie: all it has in it is redness, not the search for redness, nor its attainment and possession, but redness without any humane timetable, which makes anachronisms of the gods, renders history into a comedy, politics into hypocrisy. Oh, perspective…

The old man meekly noted:

— The devotee — that is the No. 1 kiss lackey.

The figure in the pink body truly had no strength — he lay as a pallid prey of trade and antitrade winds above the coasts of Florida, like the northern lights, like used-up daylight above the barricades of the clouds, celestial inspiration in the shape of uncertainty which, even though it flutters above the waters at martyr grade is nevertheless cowardly, servile, and gives only a confusing impression of femininity. On the shore men in swimming costumes ran about yelling & pointing in the air; some of them tugged black cloaks onto themselves, clapped flat, tasseled headgear on their heads without taking off their hairnets; a red-haired, gangly man bellowed for a telephone, others aimed cameras on high and, in view of the poor lighting conditions, set off flashbulbs; at such times the pink face could be seen more sharply between clouds for a moment: an oddly sanctimonious piety of uselessness slumbered in his eyes, his brow was as broken as the Moon, in the place of his lips birds twittered in a cardinal nest in the way the very first do after a storm, distractedly, selecting from their old repertoire with capricious uncertainty.

With a barking, the monkeys set off for the seaside, their tails held up high like the ends of tassels on a forest of lances, or the rampant beanstalk on which Münchhausen wanted to climb to the Moon — they jumped onto the roofs of the beach huts and like an enormous wave which for a while struggles with a resisting cliff, just roaring at its foot, but later on, when it has welled up like at a weir, all of a sudden, with a couple of hair's breadth thin crests, or rather merely with the flecks of surf detaching from the edge of a crest, it pushes its way over, so too did the monkey troupe at first bustle around on each other's backs, forming ladders & somersaulting at the foot of the row of cabins, only getting onto the roofs some while later. After that they plunged with a crash onto the other side of the roofs as if they had been spilled out of a high dangling bucket on a crane. They raised a huge cloud of dust on the shore as they rushed over to the water. They yelped at the sky and meanwhile, baring the whites of their teeth, they attacked the men gamboling in their swimming costumes and robes. The chief monkey sat solitarily on top of a swing frame, with two small yellow baboons swinging on two pairs of flying rings like two demented pendulums underneath him — when, after a while, they were running in parallel, they screamed long and hard like maids at a carnival.

The heroine lay on the ground in a ripped dress with water all around. She slowly lifted her eyes, and when she saw the sick ghost of a weakling among the clouds, she was suddenly overwhelmed by lilac docility, tears came to her eyes, & she was just like those stylized modern pictures that were produced for 18th-century books; again something from the aforesaid Magdalena salon: elegant paleness, hair theatrically fanned out, on her face only just enough pain as a court priest is capable of imagining at a ducal wedding when speaking about "the difficulties which may follow in life," in the piety of her eyes is a cynical fastidiousness, maybe they also manifest tragedy, only not in regard to the subject which is being sketched — but, for all his mawkishness, he rouses an expansive atmosphere of pomp, coerces darkly melodic colonnades behind him. Kings are in the habit of donning the military uniform of whatever nation they happen to be visiting: in the heroine as well some such assimilation of etiquette took place, only she was better looking than the ghost floating above her — all that was floating in the air was a program, with at most as many esthetic accessories as can be expected at all of a program, whereas in the woman there was at least God-given femininity.

On the shore, at the end of the colorful row of cabins, stood a pink and white building planned in accordance to Anglo-Saxon Gothic art — on its top floor was a big observatory & room for gymnastics. The girls were in the middle of doing gymnastics when the pink-colored romanticism puppet floated above them with the curtsy of an expiring Chatterton. Some of them, gushing with devotion, threw themselves to their knees before him, at which the ghost kept on dropping perfumed poppies toward them, though they had been pressed together by perspiration, so long had he been clasping them in the palm of his hand (while favorable winds carried them this far from Europe). A few girls frantically applauded a gentleman with a Girardi hat,[168] who, without spitting out his chewing gum, began to deliver a speech from a dais (it was reserved for a lifeguard to watch out for any accident on the beach).

— Behold! Beauty came among us in person and when young; we, who roam about with weary heads either among the tables of statistics of the real sciences or on the grey paths of daily life, or in the abstract halls of philosophy — Behold! she has came among us, who no longer see divinity and nature, science & the everyday, as opposites, or painful dilemmas, because she is beauty, or the latest newsreel which unexpectedly sprang from the festive depths of dawn — she is our goal through everything, because she consoles with her wonders, she keeps a belief in tomorrow alive in us, because she finds the meaning in all things, without philosophizing or explaining, and she is present, though that presence can only be surmised, we cannot fasten onto it with the bleak devices of our learning — there will always be universities, academies, and observatories, indeed they have to be in service, not so that her cloud-covered beauty be dissected with anatomically rigorous insensitivity, but in order for us to draw attention to her presence, to spread her veneration, the enjoyment of her, it being impermissible to mingle the disharmonious sawing sounds of thinking into that, only the embracing silence of the soul...

On a scruffy little island in the sea rose a huge tower of shining gold. The gate was reproduced in Byzantine style with philological accuracy, in accordance to Roman style on the second story, and to Gothic taste on the third, while on its peak huge revolving letters in neon lights proclaimed: Beauty Research Institute.

dispute about allegory & symbol

The young spectator, losing patience, slapped his knee and exclaimed:

— One would not find a more vulgar parody in even the vilest suburban cartoon column. This is what happens to a rationalist when he commits the faux pas of wanting to be a mystic. However stupid it might be, one needs to have mastery of it, like of sword swallowing or tightrope walking. Do you recollect that when he was in his fifties Father Sixtus had a vision, having spent thirty years pouring scorn on sniveling visionaries? He wept and was despondent because he had had a vision; while kneeling on the altar steps, he railed against God to be merciful and not make him a visionary; he did not wish to be a seer, and when he was visited again by apparitions, he fell sick, and only recorded them for himself as a curiosity. What visions they were! But he kept them secret. Those here? Any binding respect that I have for age ends.

— I find your agitation peculiar as I held the view that there was no need for me to repeatedly explain to you that allegory is by its very nature a vulgar genre; this is a question of spoon-feeding, spoon-feeding on a scale that can truly only be found in a few outdated cartoon columns where certain political parties are represented by various naïve chimeras, slogans by intrusively explicit heavenly bodies. I myself do not have an overly complex opinion about anything; for me analysis means no more than noticing two or three things and synthesis no more than my putting three things alongside each other, or I might as well say: leaving them alongside each other — analyzing is no more than noticing something, & 'editing' is simple listing. Do you, perhaps, take delight in pastels with their fine shadings? Do you, perhaps, look for pretentious allusions, a discrete salon-technique of hidden references? Come now! What can discretion have to do with symbols? Why were symbols needed in recent times to be psychologized into sentimental obscurity? You lot always seek some intellectual piquancy in a symbol, since with your pampered bellies you fancy metaphysics is a tingling nuance that only weak-nerved experts notice at the foot of things, as if it were a flirtatious old maid who every now and then lifts up her crinoline then vanishes — though what good that hide-and-seek serves, what is the point of including symbols among the deciphering games of conjecture and riddle? A symbol does not wish to arouse impressionist inspirations but to explain; clearly, crudely, finger-pointingly and unmistakably: it is not art, nor a feeling, nor a parlor game, but trashy didactics. By a symbol you explicitly understand something skeptical, something unfailingly evocative of a mood — you don't want me, do you, greybeard as I am, to let me show you a sniveling-nostalgic vision? I have no imagination so I compile — first and foremost from old cartoon columns. Caricatures were the last refuge for thinking in symbols (of course, you would prefer to hear from my lips, wouldn't you, the term symbolic-'vision' or, maybe, symbolic-'feeling'), but now they have also grown tired of symbolic thinking and in its place something has been left that you sometimes call stylization, which is truly 'fine,' and therefore impotent. A symbol is raw, because anything intangible in things (e.g., their system, internal symmetry, the naïve forms of causal relation, or a certain domestic simplicity of interconnection in general) is for it something very obvious that is easily expressible. In my view the world is not secretive, only at most it may sometimes speak quietly, in which case I move my ears a couple of centimeters closer & everything will be alright. What is worth more, it is a matter of taste; a naïve reduction that has been prepared with the incorrigible narrow-mindedness of old fogies or, on the other hand, an indefinite cultural inspiration that is still just loafing about at the stage of rocky premises or what the hell, because those are the two alternatives the two of us have — an attack with rusty weapons or celebration with wreaths of a quite uncertain color, whichever you choose. — So saying he shrugged his shoulder once, wiped the corners of his mouth with a wrist, and with a murmur and fidgeting, composed himself in his place. The youngster was red, and repressed questions broke out in the form of spots on his skin, even his clothes. Finally, looking aside in order to indicate what a lot he would like to say, he noted as he fiddled with a button:

— Symbols are anyway matters of technique; they are not metaphysics, only optical games, a mechanical synthesis with tricks — not an intellectual judgment. There are those as well. Anyway...

The old man paid attention, but only with his eyes, and when his young companion had finished his unsteady muttering, his eyes returned anew to the end of his own utterance.

the second bad apocalyptic lackey of pseudo-love: automatic fashionability; priestly opinion about the morals of the times

After the pink body had slowly swum on, fashionability stepped into the place of 'neuresthetic' love — while the first figure carried its outlines with itself like a woman a knot of hair without hairpins, at one moment undoing one and letting go another, the second clown was sharp as if incandescent light were flooding onto him, indeed looked among the clouds like a close up. He, so it seems, had nothing to say because maybe words do not belong among the appurtenances of agreeable masculinity; the same figure appeared first in a tuxedo, next in rugged golfing-tweeds, then in pajamas, yet again in hunting furs, smiling, lighting a cigarette — in this parody there were, indeed, a lot of anachronisms of a priestly elderliness.

At any time priests see Don Juans as in part much more dissolute, in part as much more innocent, than they are in reality. In their heads, for one thing, the great epitome of a fall from heavenly grace is constantly looming: in minute conventions, where erotic excitement is barely to be found under normal circumstances, they still see the hissing snake & the frightening whiteness of the bitten apple. They finger the big Miltonian-mask of love for its own sake in naïve deeds of vanity, which are a long way this side or the far side of eroticism — when a woman dabs powder on her nose simply because it is greasy, they are inclined to recognize a theatrical and apocalyptic gesture of temptation.

To that extent they imagine more sin than is actually there. On the other hand, less, because they are only superficially acquainted with the forms of 'modern' life (the 'dance of today,' the 'theater of today,' the 'clothing of today,' etc.) & therefore the million forms of wickedness remain hidden to them — hidden not in a naïve sense of the word, as if they did not have an encyclopedic knowledge of the artificial and forbidden forms of eroticism-action, but hidden in the sense that they never so much as suspect the capillarity of sin, the luxury of mood, the innumerable minute surprises of committing it, and the incalculable circumstance-contributions. They operate with two notions: one is the seashell-roaring, clumsy urn of 'big sin,' the other is the superficial conception of 'modern diversions' — for Don Juans, one is too ample, the other too constricted.

The heroine's reaction was a consenting smile — a brief contact of the kind which is so characteristic of a technically perfect degree of love; the sentiment was so evidently on her like a small ribbon on a big drum; sensuality is not dark and passionate but no more than consent in the impishly consistent ticking of a little clock at work — that is the way women habitually clasp hands, with Tacitean terseness and sportive sex-puritanism; the heroine regarded the floating man in that sort of style. Both were familiar with the game, albeit skeptically so, but for the sake of 'style' they had kept a memory of some of the old rules of the game in miniature ('modesty,' for instance, was long ago a Merovingian-enameled chain round the neck, whereas nowadays it is just a bit of golden thread poking out of a buttonhole), and that evokes a mixture of irony & emotion in the participants; mutual consent bestows a degree of unanguished facility & hygienic security to the tempo. Sport: a sole remnant of the medieval concept of social order — symbol, outward appearance, self-denial & inhumanity are united here, too, in the interest of the most human human — and that has been transmitted by both women and men into love as well; a symbolic rhythm & puppet-like piquant mechanicalism; the true 'sportiveness' of love always signifies that — the upholding of a certain theatrical etiquette, from which the moral spirit of etiquette is already lacking as it does from sport, but both, via certain external technical rules, are reminiscent of that.

the third lackey: pedantic vitalism

After the puppets of unhealthy lyricism & clerically updated fashionability, the last drastically simple pedantic bogeyman: bespectacled, naked; its nipples swung to and fro like whip ends, two clouds smoked up high from its heels like gigantic Mercury-wings — in one a jungle as resplendent, unifying in itself every naïve precision of a supplement to an encyclopedia and an accumulation resulting from a fever of fairytale illustrations, giving a bizarre and enticing mixture, which avoided the uncouth extremes of science and dreams and attested more to the imagination of a semi-educated 'nature lover' where the fluctuations of 'knowledge' substitute for the precision of science and childish decorative exaggerations for the silly whimsies of inspiration: one eye of the outwardly cockeyed Caliban with eyeglasses fixed that landscape on the sky — the other eye flickered on the other scene like a somnambulist bee grown into a flower: huge towers of books and the implements of civilized alchemists grew in it above one another, but scarlet stalk leaves bent over among the books until a given book or periodical with an alarmingly tedious cover flew over like a frivolous seagull into the forest canopy; a bird of paradise, swollen up by a convention, and a stagnant-blooded book gull cracked together in an off-key kiss.

The man was a sick compilation; his mosaic-like character proclaimed polytheism; there was a bit of Apollo in him, kneaded together from a poor schoolmaster's acquaintance with mythology and his aborted outbreaks of love; in his movements an unfailing 'Faun-Ism' competed with a tragicomic faunlessness: he was Pan who, not getting hold of the universe with a brutal knight move (though he had hoofs like secondhand gaiters) rather absorbs it in alphabetic order, organizing the weekend-chaos in encyclopedic scissor-&-paste jobs. His lap was covered by a small armorial-tablet on which a red flower stem and a black paragraph were laid crosswise in a golden field.

The heroine got up proudly although her waist was like waves on the sea; her dress, ripped as it was, was crumpled and white flesh was frothing out of it as if a person secreted in a huge lump of dough were trying to wriggle out; she spread her arms apart and in drunken happiness she greeted the three figures — the pallid fin-de-siècle figure hung around there like the half-torn-off leaf of a wall calendar with a huge black 13 — with the triumphant smile, the perfect golfer whizzed his slim club in the air, describing a propeller-halo around his head with much sweat whilst the balls sped in fizzing frequency toward the one & only target; finally pseudo-Silenus with the Zeiss-aspheric lens hammering with a long glass tube the heraldic wedges of his modesty bib like a paging or gong-beating waiter.

---

the spirit of the child that is to be aborted makes an appearance, masked as Donatello's David, in order to plead for his life from his mother; within this: two styles of biographical writing

---

While the ghost of vitalism blundered its way through a last curtsy to the heavens, two scuffling fellows burst through the door: one was a deer-legged young man, an exact double of Donatello's David but in the dress of Swiss playing cards, with legs in long and tight red pantaloons, in shoes with trembling points — a short black jacket, a pale face almost as green as a candle; the hair ash blonde & softly wavy as it tends to be after recent thorough washing; a broad-brimmed hat above the quivering shampooed mop of hair, worn-down in a somewhat clerical manner, the brim rolled-up with stylish limpness, like 18th-century women's hats; around it an unreal light-green wreathe, silvery like shivering tinfoil, and fresh, like some highly strung salad embellishing a beaf-steak for its own good.

Although the movements and garb were reminiscent of a girl doing gym exercises, the lethargic arrogance of the profile pointed to the relief of a broken-nosed Holy Roman Emperor, yet nonetheless he radiated the fervent force of a young man honest to a fault. At the same time, death, a great sadness of being haunted. He jumped through the doorway with a swish of a cane, white resignation standing out in his fleetness of step so that his strength and dexterity did not display a true spring but only the movements of a desire, for a spring that was dancing with stubborn energy. His dusty hat and irresolute wreathe spoke volumes about his journey: through forests and valleys, among flowers and scattered showers, very wearily, very much in vain. Of particular appeal is the melancholy of these weary *plein-air* travelers, because they establish a connection between the world's side scenery, which merrily passes us by, and our experience of perpetual agony (there is probably no need at all for such a connection, but that is beside the point).

— That does at least have about it a touch of the graceful — the young spectator commented. The old man suddenly & quietly plucked at his companion's arm.

— That is the sole person whom I love and about whom I would be unable to endure any criticism. Steer clear of him! I have grieved enough at being unable to express my love of youngsters & youth simply enough with a figure — because that somebody, whom you at least found a touch graceful, is a much clearer and more elementary person than muscles & clothes, but sadly the matter always breaks down with the object of one's love being an infinitely simple, unitary affair, but one's avowal of love, whether stupid or erudite, being always verbose. One is unable to bear that what is so strong and manifest in one's soul should come to so little in words, color, and form. I wanted to append to my child an ethereal role, a heavenly mask, yet I have amassed so many of those kinds of æro-components that I fear the end result has been a far too burdensome proposition. What comes to mind is an old difficulty I had with the lives of saints. How did Brother Leo manage to write twelve lives in just three months? He called on the assistance of the saints. The inspiration was a short & simple off-the-cuff prayer, then he made a pilgrimage to the saint's memorial church, viewed the relics, a statue or pictures of the saint, and that was all; they were genuine Roman life stories: the prayer was just a formal prayer, the 'life' itself a couple of stripped-down and strikingly groundless but all the more convincing actions; miracles of potato-eating simplicity and the convoluted & holy wilinesses of doctrines symbolized into a few ungainly theses, & in so doing everything was floating, sensitive, & poetically deconstructible. I myself made a start on a biography; I frequently called on the Holy Ghost, but that, too, was already in a faint-hearted manner — my love for my favorite saint was a muddled fire that covered & consumed the figure; I loitered around him like a sick bird above the burning bush, suffocated by fumes — I corresponded with fifty monasteries and they wrote back fifty different versions of where the saint's birthplace was, which could in no way be reconciled. How simply that was dealt with by Father Faustin: he constructed a *Vita Unica* and a *Vita in Mirroribus*[169] — in the latter he worked up how the one and only life was mirrored in the conception of the various towns and peoples; in *Unica* he communicated 'dry' facts (his psychological lack of rhythm exemplified the theatrical dictatorship of Providence, as a consequence of which God emerged as a curiosity-loving, somersault-centered, & radically-witty director who was able, with cunning magic, to conjure up as one a never-ending harmony and never-ending handstand, a mechanical tempo, and metaphysical babble) whereas in *Mirroribus* he indulged his own talent at variation: "*teutonici crederunt sic*"[170] was in the margin of the page, and there he related that, alongside scholasticism, St. Olympius was also familiar with falconry, although perhaps only "*analogiam videbant quasi cum oculis quomodo erat consuetudo illorum*"[171] (did "*illi teutonici*" naively translate a flight of thought as hunting?). For me those chapters in *Mirroribus* epitomized historiographic hygiene. Psychological possibilities and a flirting with symbolism in the history of ideas were blossoming here in a still naïve state — '*in mirroribus*' and '*unica*' were two sharply separated worlds for Faustin, and thus he traced doubt simply as poetry, as a parrot-colored catalogue of possibilities. The illustrator (whose name I have already forgotten) carried on by painting the picture of *Unica*, which he called '*Idemidem*'[172] and painted in a simplifying style, whereas he arranged the *Mirroribus* pictures around himself as if they were the sprouting branches of the trunk, and he called those *alteridem*.[173] Related to that was a fashionable poem of sorts: "...and he wove his false garland from many flowers, mixing the corolla of *idemidem* with the fragrance of the soul and the wicked taste of those spices of which the name is *idemidem*" or something like that; later that style of double life story was banned because it became rigid and dogmatic and my style became the official *nihil obstat*-manner,[174] though not one true life was written in that style. I ought to have got Father Faustin to have written the script about my favorite son, for then many unfitting shreds of the over-meticulous compilation would not have been left in it (incipient blotches of color made to pale back into darkness by incipient doubt). What can I do when at one end of my table the most glittering colors are lying in gigantic plates, whereas at the other end is just prickly analysis — the devil knows how elementary colors and overly outlined drawings could be dragged together into one. How could the target of desire and intensity of desire be brought into harmony for me? Perhaps a radical choice should be made and two unconnected dramatic mythologies created — one from pure-pure-pure colors (the nihilist language of intensity), the other from a formalized sketch of the object — thereby creating an absurd dual dominion. But the intensity of the desire cannot exist and be expressed without its object; *Deum deformans est amor realis Dei*[175] — I like something in it, but that something has to be destroyed in the blaze of affection; there was a lot of wrangling about this with heretic mystics, back then I was quite bored with all that... "*et in caecitate amoris Dei bonitatem quasi respirationem daemoniacum viderunt*"[176] — and the river was in love with the hill, whereupon it ceaselessly embraced and kissed it with its rapid green billows until finally all that was left of it was flat land; indeed, still later it became a valley, as a result of which the river, which had been impressed by the vertical udder of the hill, has ever since been dropping into a hollow on that spot, its eternal admiration of upwards aspiration leading to the birth of the waterfall, et cetera, etc. *Singularis causa inspirat amorem sed causa illa per amorem destructa est.*[177] See, I call for your forgiveness at such length when I am showing you the boy, just so that you steer clear of him.

The countryside was blue, like a globe of ink through which a moon has shone its light; the mountains were high and skinny, like basalt cylinders, & snow stood on their tops in a star shape like: a) a dollop of cream on a tart; b) a white Hebrew hexagram on the shoulders of alchemists in blue robes; c) the white zigzag spheres inset in the end of certain fountain pens. The night was transparent as a woman's blue stockings, & without its having broken up, trembling into dots, it fell with a quiet sound like snow — up on high it was dark and shaggy like a root pulled up from deep down in which side branches and soil do battle in a confused mass; downwards, however, where the sparkling darkness, falling in horizontal bands, reached the white of the hills like a foam curtain that is lapping the footlights with the swishing of the sea's skirts, it was entirely light like the glass of an optical semaphore line.

The heroine's body was coiled around one of the black hills, which had struggled upwards into the ringing & reposing night rather like those stumps that shoulder their way out of the azure in seaports *Unica* bathing resorts. The body wound and wove like the pink, thigh-tightening sandal ribbons did on the legs of Greek girls in archaizing operas; it was like a serpentine path twining in the lightness of spring on which the Donatello-copy leaped up in dance steps like the piper stripling following the forest of tails on posters for rat killers.

But it was not rats that were scurrying before him, forcing up a forest of lances from the earthworms of their tails, but his own miniature alter egos, like a buzzing and humming pilgrim army of red bees; in the blue night, between the black idol-ribs of the hills, they took around with themselves little shields of sunbeams, like a golden leaf which the wind had driven on them like a swinging baldachin; the whole army came to a halt from time to time &, throwing their hats, began to sing — the heroine lay with her head on the hilltop like someone carrying synods as a necklace, her bodice was embroidered with a map of Basle, leaving a hole on the site of the market square where a nipple poked out with marbled defiance on which swung hundreds & hundreds of little Donadavids like jittery beetles on a purple-pointed flytrap — on her waist Ephesus dangled like a yellow belt on which the Donadavids divided into parties, and the two parties bestowed a Parisian chic on the frame and pin of the buckle — her legs were twined around by Nicea, & the blue of the sea radiated almost white as snow above her knees, where the little synodist-scoundrels stamped their feet on veined sheets of marble while the same melody was hummed on the fourth floor besides a puritanical Gothic-crenellated castle wall.

---

something about synods (truth & landscape);
"syllogismus amoris *imago"* [178]

— This is the confusion in which I am well pleased — the old man said with a laugh and suddenly clapped a hand on his lips because his saliva was flowing from laughter. — What has all this got to do with synods? Synods were occasions on which big problems were raked up, life's basic questions, & those debates were accompanied by mass phenomena, like sports games or parliaments holding still in times of crisis; such hurrahing followed the establishment of each abstract principle like a goal in a football stadium, and it's precisely on that account that I love synods so greatly — they have in them the finest *'humanum'*: big abstractions and childish passions. I enjoy that they occur at a defined geographical place, and thus the very particular encounters the giddily divine — I see Byzantine ships on the waves of the Ægean Sea, I see Swiss lakes and Rome's poppy countryside as the idea of Christ's divine humanity, the meaning of sacraments or the immaculacy of the Virgin Mary rises out of them — I forget the active participants in the drama; all I see is the landscape of the synod and the supernatural doctrine and I take pains to forcibly bring those two discontinuities together; a naïve cooperation of trees, southern seas, & northern pines in the drawing up of dogma. I would like to express every great beauty with the dramatics of a synod; truth is attractive if dispersed in waves of mass passions, boundless ambitions are attractive if they carry their scent from finite milieus toward the heights — that is why I composed for you these small synodic-*klenodiums*[179] from my children for my heroine's body. The fact that these small figures do not demand groupings in these synod drawings by reason of their nature, that, too, maybe has its own significance; the nowadays fashionable technique of expanding thought that consists mainly of striving to amalgamate or unify stereotyped evidence, the most popular basic concepts acquired about a subject in the most arbitrary way possible (under extraordinarily high pressure, naturally), & thereby arrive at the truth, is not a bad technique — this is a principle that can be used in a technique of visions, inasmuch as the crankiest pictorial inconsistency will create such a subversive lack of balance that springing from this into a new balance will reveal entirely unknown areas. Love is the great intellectual force: "*syllogismus amoris imago*," and the other, currently more important principle of Crescentius: *relationes rerum amoris sunt opera*[180] — I am very fond of children and very fond of synods, and affection brings the two into connection.

— That is roughly identical to the latest production at the Folies Bergère, only a lot more immodest — the young spectator commented.

— There is nothing easier than being a pessimist vis-à-vis the 'efficiency'-techniques of visions. It was with infinitely chance groupings of still lifes that I felt the need for a new concept that was not a blending of chance and eternal form but a new kind of unsuspected *unio hypostatica*[181] of the two; an expression that does indeed relate, not the 'radiation of infinity into the finite' (that is deadly boring and a lie), but the '*accidens per se non-accidens*.' Here, for example, I cooked together all the associations of 'youth' into a Brueghel-miracle — perhaps it will not be 'a particular boy,' nor the notion of 'youth,' but a new third.

Aged pottering around? In the entertainments of old age you will always find certain childish forms of empiricism mixed with the most refined theoretical prejudices and logical superstitions — perhaps that soil will give rise to a good philosophy that we perhaps missed down there and pursue merely as a sort of patience-game up here.

With a laugh he patted his young companion on the shoulder & playfully, in a glib tone, threw out:

— Hey, don't knock it.

(That is already the third place that labors on the same obscure purpose: a decadent set of torsos as a logical St. Ivan's Eve. *Sachlichkeit* & codex *Bio-ornamenticus*; *Sachlichkeit* and system of heraldic symbols; Brueghel-hodgepodge or masqueraded Plato.)

— I wouldn't dream of doing so — the other responded —, I simply remarked that some of that error has also rubbed off on you Father, as if life were tantamount to certain disproportionate chance events, perpetual randomness, and, above all, associations, & therefore you set out from there in alchemizing a new concept of essentiality for yourself, though life is precisely the opposite of the aforesaid things; life, by which is meant the normal average way of looking at things and ordinary, dime-a-dozen perspectives, is full of proportions, hierarchies, balances and the most Baroque series of logical connections; the more vulgar a person, the more instinctively the world is seen to be in 'order' (naturally, I do not mean that everything is found to be legally, morally, or artistically good); an ordinary person lives their everydays in the most radical Platonism, and every time I hear life spoken about I feel that what is important, first & foremost, is the average point of view, and that is symbolic & pan-logistic. So, if you want to 'vitalize' something, then it is not possible to start from a cumulative vision, because that is already not a 'life' on its own animal scale but, on the contrary, the highest cultural luxury; an association is always already the result of activities of higher-order abstraction and counts as an artificiality divorced from life.

— I don't know, but there was a time when we thrashed out the pacifist idea, reassuring to adherents, that mystics and rationalists tread on a common path representing the two wings of the Holy Ghost connected into effective flight by the unique head of truth — my histrionics are even now somehow based on that; it's as if the Holy Ghost were not waddling up to the top of a stepladder scaled from branches for the syllo-coconut but was being whipped by a desire for the truth at such a furious pace as eroticism does to those left to their own devices — the picture is one of emergency exit-rationalism, of starved-to-death deductions or masturbatory inductions, for which reason they can be forgiven.

the physician arrives

The heroine's red hair streamed in the glittering azure of the night like the sails that sunken vessels leave on the surface of the sea; the little Donatello clones in crimson cloaks and scarlet cardinal's galeros advanced along the serpentine path to the woman's head, which was showing the greyness and materiality of melting ice, as if the donatellos were seeking to hustle the phalanx of dogmas drawn up from blood into an untimely coulisse; the crimson cloaks cracked in the wind like buds clanging like rifle bullets — after each clang on their heads blonde hair cascaded in all directions as if their whole body were only a capsule, from which this fibrous, snowy cream were flowing freely; of course, the flat, swamp rose-mallow hats slipped from the hair like helpless rafts onto the slippery mossy threshold of a waterfall — above them the heroine's frail head listlessly hovered like fog.

The monkeys were also there, jumping around them with their flashing eyes and unkempt, old-style perukes. (— They ingeniously masked their duality: their large perukes seem to signify the old-fashionedness of their thoughts, whereas their frolicking somersaults are imitating the expression of antiquated principles with modern refinement — the young spectator commented distractedly.) The little red cardinals assembled in big masses on enormous leaves: they swarmed there on three green plates like cherry stones — the heroine rose to her feet and turned toward her defenders. On one side stood the doctor in a black gown with a huge white Dutch collar, in a tower-high black stovepipe hat, twirling a flashing nickel lasso in the air. The monkeys kicked up a tremendous howling & flung themselves on the gleaming instrument, their backs full of blue shreds, as if the night and the sky had flowered into a single bough and the leaves got caught between their hairs. On the other side the army of cardinals knelt down, as if the wind had brought a patch of poppies to the ground with a single big gust, & prayed aloud.

The night grew increasingly white and fresher than the Mediterranean; dawn swung gently oscillating hills into space as if a dense mass of water had blown over, & now in its wake little islands the color of green peas would appear from the bottom, sending friendly smiles toward the cardinals, dropping asleep as they were from the loud tiredness of praying — the sea surrounded them, the hills wreathed a cool umbrella above them, and they were sprawled in a jumble as if heretic-adventurers who had only donned cardinal shells borrowed from a theater for the sake of an anticlerical masquerade: high-toed shoes, pink faces, crumpled hats and tousled hair (people tend to depict overflowing champagne that way for ads) — the whole thing was like a hill that had been cyclopsed together from dumplings of red rock with blond brooks burbling forth from several places. Above all that the huge cornflower of dawn bloomed like a huge and virginal apology.

The heroine's body came undone from the black basalt stakes like an unbuckled belt and stretched at length in the dawn sky like a sooty firebrand. The poet, the worldly one, and the vitalist, so it seems, somehow wanted to hide the girl with the physician's aid — one of them did his utmost to carve from her a curious villa, the second wanted to pour water from the blue sea of dawn over her, but she was visible from the crystal billows like the leaden skin of a dead walrus; the third started to paint frescos on her but they quickly became very ridiculous because the moment she moved, the pictures began to stretch as if they had been painted on a rubber ball that was now suddenly about to swell into a gigantic balloon.

The poet recited verses, the worldly one courted her, and the vitalist watched the whole thing from a stuffy attic room to which a small chunk of peeling-off sky was attached with a bit of string while a telescope curled over the woman's mouth; sometimes he stroked a chunk of the tamed captive piece of the sky like a circus animal that has to be cunningly coaxed — then he went on to orthochromatically photograph the redness of the lips and jumped above the pictures like a eunuch bullock above a female nominal suffix.

The whole thing was like a French puppet theater from the age that everyone thinks was empty-headed and mannered, though according to imagined revisionist scholars it ought to have been (o!) tragic crudity (Gothic Watteau, ascetic Boucher, et cetera). All of a sudden, a fountain unexpectedly sprang up toward the sky between the left bank (where the army of slumbering child cardinals was lying under the blue conch of dawn) and the right bank (where the heroine with her red hair was lying in the canopy bed of the night, receiving in parallel the poet's rhyming disease and the worldly one's unrhymed health) from the center of the troupe of monkeys, sending a howling monkey flying into the air, then the water split into two branches and in falling froze to right & left into a slim bridge. The chief Donatello jumped up like a startled hunter. Behind him was the dawn like a combed flag, in front of him the bridge like a burning glass arrow: facing him was the physician friend, invited by phone, in a turtleneck & with a caviar sandwich in one hand.

dispute of the boy & the physician

— Now we can at last pit our wits against each other.

— Look here, don't use old-fashioned phraseology, and in particular desist from naïve ambitions — whereupon a monkey leaped into the boy David's arms and like a solicitous mother looked up and down at the boy's face, which was wet from the morning grass.

— It may be that my phraseology is old-fashioned, but if I'm allowed across the bridge to hoist a blue flag on the black shore, then it will be in my power to utter current subjects and fashionable predicates — in regard to style only the past is available to me right now, but now it is not a matter of style. I am going to have to fight this battle with tattered furniture in order to be able to fight new ones with new weapons. What is my mother doing?

— Have you gone nuts? Anyway what's your idea of who is taken in by your company and side scenes? Didn't you read in the papers that the age when traveling circus performers were able to hire themselves out as prophets has come to an end?

One minute you're asking where your mother is like a little girl who is left alone for a second in the entrance hall because Mommy had to do something before the stroll — the next thing you come up with all kinds of heroic tricks & red uniforms to cheat us. In any case, I declare once and for all time that the zeros remain zeros, even if they do acrobatics on the trapeze.

The monkeys wanted to jump, but the young David restrained them; on one side his red partners lay above the sea like an overturned basket of cherries lying on the Riviera instead of Menton, on the other side, the humbly cantankerous monkeys cuddling tightly on top of each other like the slopingly gliding wing of a fur cloak that has been let go of halfway to the ground. The pale boy stood alone on the edge of the glass floor of the bridge between the two escorts.

— I am neither a prophet nor a young girl, you must know that full well. As to red being our color, that's only natural — red lips wanted us to exist, and from the moment we suspected that we can exist, we have burned & blossomed from the desire to exist. Redness is both our rawest instinct and our most traditional etiquette. It may be that this is brutal & naïve ceremony on grey everydays — but then neither did you consider the redness of kisses to be a medieval heraldic fuss, any more than you thought the red impatience of your desires to be unlawful obstinacy, and it never so much as occurred to you that, actually, it is kitsch-fanaticism to put your own lives, as well as our own unasked lives, to a single monotonous redness, the poster redness of the kiss. Our redness is no more than yours, a redness of kiss and a desire to live. Only in our puritanical & poorly equipped world we do not have as many comfortable devices as you do to mold, distil, and ridicule elementary redness into prose in so many ways. We are uniformly public romantics, even though I put on red tights and have adopted a Donatello-mask in order that my role should have some sort of form in this comedy, & I should not be stripped ethereally naked like an ordinary textbook draught of a ghost (I have no power over your dress) — I repeat, don't let the odor of second-hand shops deceive you in regard to my actuality, just as I was not deceived by your cynicism in regard to your red desires when your will operates so naïvely and monochrome redly like the corolla of a pedigree poppy. Where is my mother? Why do you always speak in her place, why do you force yourself on her? Push off! Eat your sandwich and don't wave that silver hook around in the air like a dilettante fisherman in water.

— I was hugely diverted by your discourse on your idiosyncratic *Farbenlehre*,[182] although if the same metaphor applies to you as well as to me, that in and of itself does not yet signify a sure common basis on which we might converse as equal-ranking parties, since nowadays people are not grouped by community of metaphor any more than by hat size or star chart. Spare me, please, your proof in terza rima that the zodiac is the most topical financial question and hat size is in fact the most realistic metaphysical kinship — we shall get nowhere with colored sophisms. I don't know whether I should address you with informal thees and thous, or more formal Misters or Monsieurs; in masquerade phantoms there is something of the buffoon and something of hieratic authority, which is not an advantage, of course; nothing, but nothing, is self-evident...

the boy's apology

— Mother, why do you listen to this windbag of a lawyer? If I am slandered, you are defined in ugly domains. Come over to my place on this glittering bridge, which is transparent like the soul of a god, hard, and sure as his will. There is no pseudo-modesty in me: look how beautiful I am. Look, I'm taking my hat off; just look at my hair — I'm a bit grubby & dusty, a little tired as well, because I had to walk such a lot to be able to reach you. We live far away, beyond every dawn & years and time of day, beyond the strange dualities of dreaming and wakefulness, but there was once a time when we nonetheless heard your voice — in our indescribably simple sky a red star flared like a drop of blood on a wall of unclouded quiet, and we were alarmed. We didn't know what to do, whereat a god happily dispatched us. We came & here we are, but you are hiding away from us, now among rococo eiderdowns like a naughty cat, now among white-washed Florida villa walls, listening to bad verse, dancing-master tricks, and adolescent biological-theses, as if you had completely forgotten about us. We hear the call even now; it sighs in us like the breathing in our lungs — so let us in.

The bespectacled, swim-suited man set some giant poppies before the heroine's bed, close to each other like a folding privacy screen.

— Mother, are you now turning against us the signs with which you called us? Do these glistening trophies from which we sketched out armorial bearings that express the essence of our pilgrimage now proclaim, now treacherously and with sudden conceit, that we are negligible quantities? If you have got tired of the Madonna pose as of a sugary sweet oleograph, then the fussy cultivation has taken hold late — we are wedded to your sentimental Madonnahood as greasy peasants are to a strip of land. Reply, Mother.

— Don't torture me to death, don't seek to force me between the blades of a maddening dilemma like Inquisitors. You are always spouting about life but you are not life: in the name of life do you want to ruin real life for the non-living? I never invited you; I will not permit you to torment me. You are not beautiful. Because a person who is not beautiful cannot become that, & what makes you beautiful is just a stolen mask.

— Tell the reverend Father — the physician stuttered back — that the sisters of the mission sewed a very fine garment for you for the celebration of charity, but it would be disgraceful to spoil the game by taking the roles so seriously. See you! — And with that he lifted back the steel visor that lit up in the night like a dead rainbow.

— You always make reference to the big advantage of actual existence, though it is based merely on a crude optical illusion: life is not constructed from pounds of flesh, but from forces. That is naïve material pharmacy, not life. Life is strength, a dynamic game of chance, a big tissue of concrete possibilities — for that reason it is not life here which confronts nothingness, not reality well provided with flesh which confronts the ghost, not reality exaggerated into mysticism which confronts a borrowed marionette — that is just the way your bad eyes and good styles imagine it: here there is no question of a conflict between us. Force confronts force — on one is flesh that has been borrowed from a butcher, on the other is an art-historical reproduction which the parish priest had sewn for him; which is the better-looking mask is a matter of taste; in other respects, we are alike. I also brought along my siblings, they all wanted to come; I brought them along in order to make something pathetic & vulgar with them: propaganda. Mother says we are not beautiful and covers her eyes. Mother says that we are not nobodies, but if she did not invite that insolent gentleman with the steel scissors, she could not sleep on account of us. Excuse us, Mother, for coming to you this way, like peasant rebels or soldiers demanding their pay, the only reason for it is because you thrust us into such uncertainty; otherwise we are as gentle as lambs, always, but always good and loyal.

The heroine stood at the far end of the bridge with her head hung low. She had shoes of green crocodile leather on her feet, grey, ash-colored stockings, a green tweed costume with enormous lapels, and a broad black buckled belt. Around her neck was a gigantic silk scarf, the swollen and soft knot of which hid & filled out her chest. Her hair was parted in the center. In her hands dangled two black gloves with green inserts. Her handbag was lying on the dressing table along the big black lid of which ran a slanting green band of bone. She looked wearily at the watch on her wrist. She sat down in front of the mirror & with a sigh shook her hair, the way women are accustomed to do; as if the technical tricks necessary to satisfy vanity formed a wearisome and melancholy set of problems that were no longer being undertaken for themselves out of a selfish and infantile desire to please, but as a universal moral obligation (their own femininity was not conceived practically but with mythical dizziness in which, inter alia, operated the notion of 'exhaustion' & an acquaintance with physical disgustingness. "That's life," they feel at times like this, and they feel rouge and powder in their hand as if it is 'Fate' that is fulfilled with sensual automatism). She pressed her long fingers next to one another, and pressed their tips to her brows, close to the corners of the eyes.

the boy wants to win over his Mother for himself

The ghost gently crept behind the woman and quietly put its hand on her shoulders from the back: "One has to get through some initial intrusion, I admit and accept, but after that I shall be gentle and eager to oblige."

The woman was at first startled but then began to speak, stonily directing her words at her mirror image as if she wanted to hang onto it against the boy's possible arguments or lyricizations; she felt that two figures were recovering: one of them was objectified beauty, which rose solitarily and with decisive strength above everything, and herself, full of the burdensome risks of thinking, the pale but disturbing outlines of honesty & truth, with all the dialectical obligations of an attorney-at-law who has to shape the cool records of the mirror image into principles; she felt bitter antagonism between the image and herself, it tired her that she had to interpret the alogical model for herself; as if for a moment she might have suspected that her beauty and beauty in their so-called legal essence were not apologizable, that they fall apart as soon as we seek to fill them with a human commentary, like a foam statue at the first touch of a fork. The boy saw this sort of a duel between the image's dumb cleanness and the confusion of the projected sacrifice he himself was ashamed of.

— I would like to invoke this duality of yours, Mother, your abstract beauty and your human struggles; you lie between the two like a naïve child, unversed in diplomacy, who has to entice two parties who yearn to be together but are nevertheless hostile by their very nature, into meeting; you struggle with your beauty like with some abstract & excitingly everlasting calling, you would like to carry on building it, you would like to enter fully into its service, & when you take a first step in that interest you feel that you have not been working on the mirror image but on your own fragile life — I am the sole person who is able to unify this nervous Platonic stubbornness of yours and your wise doubt, thereby giving new meaning to your beauty, not in the form of a lesson, as a suspect codicil to your lengthy meditations, but from your blood, your soul, if you dare to let me in. Otherwise, the bad fire of a miserly ideal will always burn before you in the mirror, and you will crouch and shuffle along like an outcast — I would ripen fruit from the flower of your beauty; then the ghostly flower and the stormy cult that you pursue in its interest would dissolve into each other. It could be that I am extemporizing a stilted mythology, but that is in some degree as a tactic in regard to you, whom I imagine as being more of a snob and a rationalist (albeit illogical) seeker of joy than a boring poppy crank.

The mirror went up very high and, along with itself, elongated the figure shivering in it — her red hair was piled up like a complex fountain that had started with, at that very moment, jets of water spurting out of the wall at ever higher levels at successive delays of a second, and while in the lower basins of the fountain the shooting water was already becoming blurred in glittering clouds of steam around the uppermost disks, the silver direction of the water jet was still sharply visible; by the time the topmost knots were boiling in reddish bubbles, the whole thing dropped back with the theatrical morality of geysers in which the shorn-misty rhythm of the proud line of radiation and the stepwise fall melted into a shallow symbol.

Under the laborious fountain of her hair her face shone white like a Canova-torso under a water sheath; with the semi-ascetic, semi-fashionable accuracy of the outline hit upon by girls of the last century with the cunning intuition of a sculptor (encountering the cosmetic predictions of French-neoclassical statues); they realized an essentially ideal-abstract & 'coolly' stylized form as 'flesh' as if they had sought to proclaim in the *civitas Dei* that 'cold form is more sensual' than the bumpy-dimpled flesh-bouquets of reality (N.B. There is no wish whatsoever for all the world to make use of girls for fashionable 'abstracto-philiac' propaganda purposes; for a second thing, due respects for the simple variant of the above draft wording: "Slim girls are gorgeous.")

There has to be a sensible reason why that Canovan *'platonisme mondain'*[183] (to use the language of the *Jardin des Modes*)[184] suits us in its harmonious entirety: à propos some kind of phenomenology of slimness, that mirror scene would be no bad thing. (Or if complete logicality cannot be accomplished right now, a pseudo-solution could at least be sought in an analogy.)

(Slim poplars shoot through silver hips toward the stars — their trunks are fatally linear, markedly 'positive,' and it is precisely on account of their linearity that they are able to so enticingly float, sway, and swing in the blue waves of the winds — let us reduce that, too, to the fairly boring game of opposites, that "its linearity makes its uncertainty possible, & the grace of swaying back and forth is inherent in the sure central line" and thus: does the rhythm of slim girls inhere in a fine compromise between frivolous decay and piquant firmness, & does our whole erotic interest in essence circle around a mathematical problem or the mechanics of proportions?)

---

the vision comes to a halt in order to yield place to the investigation of methods of pseudo-expression. The starting point is the dualism of the modern female body in the vision: the 'Hellenism' of glass gauntness, the 'Gothicism' of painting lips & eyes

---

Her eyes, or rather eyelids, took on the form of pitching dolphins: a big & a small hump ending in the opposite direction over toward the tail, as if her eyes had a form that was being renewed every moment, with its waves striking the white plateau of the face; her mouth was red from pigment, and the question of 'abstraction & sensuality' stood on the shape of that just as much as on the whole body: improbable hyper-mouth, exaggerated in the direction of linearity — it is not the redness that was coquettish, but its outline; indeed, the layer of make-up pigment itself was valuable more because it occupied a sure space, because it means 'a place' and not a colored material; what was needed was not a pigment & not lips, but a 'fixed space.'

The 'modern' woman is something grotesque in an elemental manner. Faces are set into a uniform composition: a few lines, a few blots, and that neo-primitive lucidity delights us ('logical delight' as some textbooks put it), and it does one's historical erudition equally good that the 'refined' modern face can undoubtedly be associated with 600-year-old colored wooden statues (that was touched on when we designated as Kermess-crudity[185] certain 'refinements' of Paris fashion).

Two paths for abstracting-symbolization: the Hellenistic and the Gothic directions, and they both meet in the face & body of the woman of today — over-refining lines, the parallel sharpness and ethereality of contour on the one hand, and the symbolization of certain (often distorted) body parts, in spite of itself, a symbolization stemming from naïve medieval naturalism (over-lighted mouth, ellipso-manic eyes). On the one hand, the body's refinement into glass; on the other, the overcorporealization of corporeality to the point of unreality. In the form of a trilogy: in the middle is the average body, to the left of that the exaggeration in glass (forms, rhythms) — to the right, the anatomic exaggeration of individual body colors and forms (the mouth, eyes, hands, nails, hair) — whereupon the average woman vanishes (is of no erotic interest) and the hyper-colors settle on the glass body: that is approximately the style-chemistry of today's woman as was now apparent in the mirror as well. But is there anything more superficial than style chemistry? The forcing of certain superficial analogies into three-dimensionality is, actually, no more than a theatrical alibi for the avoidance of psychology.

The most essential feature of the façade of a building, let us say, consists of the windows being surrounded by quite narrow red stone frames — the surrounding houses resembling it perfectly in every respect except for the quantitatively minimal difference of the small red bands of stone around the embrasures of the windows. That difference is nonetheless enormous; naturally, however, I did not manage to express the experiencing of that big difference by simply remarking that "the windows of this villa were festooned by reddish strips of stone."

I have a feeling that I was operating on a much more elementary plane when I spotted the difference; it implied a radically intellectual excitement as if my mind had a layer that reacted, intelligently and justifiably, to these 'rational' impressions, but that stratum was so far away that I did not hear the rational motivations clearly, despite my having the strongest sense of the fact that this logical explanation exists. Close attention and the patience of an ascetic would be needed to hear it out, much as with the reading of the worn rows of a Phœnician epigraph engraved in stone: only individual words and half-lines out of the uniform text of Reason, which lives at the bottom of every nervous reaction and automatism of the instincts, can penetrate the thick mental layers extending above it, the clear, purely-logical commentary glowing at the middle point as a mathematical point is dissolved and dulled by blotting-globes that one after the other surround it spherically — one rarely takes the trouble and instead takes refuge in hypocrisy and self-delusion. One does not describe the precise logic of one's ecstasy but makes a multiplier, quantitative mythology of the objects causing the ecstasy — as if that were able to substitute for the dramatic silence of the one and only cause.

three literary pseudo-expressions: infinite wordplay synthesis, mimicry of musical motifs, hyper-Balzacian dumping of types; pseudo-expression in the history of ideas ('morphology,' etc.)

All the houses were constructed from black bricks, but the special one had red garlands around the windows: I take the red as the material of a certain sculptor or pastry of an Xmas baker & make all kinds of figures out of it: I describe a synod of parrots in the style of medieval animal symbol books; I create a gigantic park where regiments of salvias emerge from the black earth; I have a monologue recited by a red-haired villain and afterwards devise an indicative martyrology in which the blood's bland redness becomes the sole actor and backdrop; I sketch a 14th-century map on which the Red Sea is actually painted red, and I guide the reader into one of the immense factories of the land of Liberté at the time of a sunset, which could be counted as a calamity from which two million Phrygian caps are exported every day to various countries of the world that have a need of that kind, etc.

This operation is completely identical to the situation as if in a huge basilica one were standing a great distance from the priest who was preaching so that his words were not audible or could only be heard very fragmentarily, so instead one would pay attention to his gestures & their elongated shadows (these outsized flickers of shadows are the megaphone of a mime), and when back home one is asked what was heard, one does not relate the content of the sermon but presents a ballet pieced together from the gestures, a dance instead of a train of thought. The protean multiplication of the surface is smuggled into the place where penetration-below-the-surface should be; that is how many empty Psyche-avoiding mythologies and allegories are born in art (by Psyche, we now happen to mean some ineradicable Reason-likeness).

Sometimes a Pindaric music-like handling of 'motif' is put in the place of a quick train of thought (thus a Pythia of the French embassy); another will try to express the enormous effect of simple things with the endless Gothicness of eternal wordplay: the simplicity of a splendid river with a nominalist 'heteroonania' — there is no other word — that mixes the names of the rivers with any conceivable fluidities (as the anathematized Irishman), or it can be that an attempt is made to render perceptible the secret of a single quiver of sentiment by deploying masses of people, society, & history at large, the entire external world (certain English vitalists). 'To render perceptible' instead of analysis: to lie instead of telling the truth.

Just as in art the structure of musical motifs, a synthesis of wordplay, and a hyper-Balzacian series of types substitutes for the logicality of experiences, so too in science (as previously mentioned) the mystery of superficiality and mythologizing of externality have developed in place of logic & are propagated under the banner of "morphology of the spirit": deadly humbug of the most barren Platonism. The situation there is the same as at the red window frame; there is a writer in whom the same southern-Italian courtly characteristics can be found, as in the other contemporaries in the area of Naples, with the small difference that he is also colored by the morality of Spanish stoics. The difference has to be expressed, and instead of analyzing the psychology of the connection (its most profound reason), he created two stage puppets: 'stoic-Inquisition morality' and 'Sicilian-Arabic etiquette,' personifying the most superficial & most striking characteristics ("noticing the writer & supplying him with an epithet happened at first sight"); instead of analysis a farcical battle of epithets. The red window frame turned into parrots, the Spanish tang was turned into Hegelian-cultural totems, the epithets into artificially enlarged 'horizons' — with shared technology, science and the arts go about their hypocritical business, working hard to hide their analytical incompetence.

Touqué's three studies: "Pseudo-Symbols," "The Physiology & Esthetics of Harmony," "Thèse et Scrupules"

Mention may later be made of an article to which Leville-Touqué gave the title "Pseudo-Symbols" and in which he investigates the question of morphologist-synthesis and symbol-types, contrasting abstract pseudo-marionettes with true or healthy symbols, of which virtually only the name is some generality, but otherwise their every feature was formed by the most restricted experience, or else they are purely formalities, printer's clichés, festive stereotypes, so-called soulless allegories lacking all laziness, which might be called *'geistiges Sein,'*[186] which is incapable of walking along the clutter of small streets and which is only able to enjoy bird's-eye pictorial maps. In that connection he subsequently posed general stylistic questions of hygiene and in place of the clumsy antithesis of truth and symbol strove to create some sort of identity between the two which, as a matter of fact, illustrated a therapy of raw perception; first and foremost, it meant a diet.

Harmonious means greatly impress one's sober mind or metaphysical sensitivity (it doesn't matter what name is given to one and the same thing), but there is another sympathy (one that cannot, with brutal perfunctoriness, be called an 'artistic sense'), which is simply bored with precisely these ideal results which, with respect to time as well, stand at the end of artistic development and greedily escape toward a parallel realization of one-sidedness or extremes.

Mention was made just before of the various forms of alibi-analysis, which are supported by our sore need to break our observations into 'many pieces' and the so-called feelings that arise in their wake, but instead of shredding the experience into its constituent parts, we stage a series of comparisons. All that stands on one side: mythologies, symbols, in short: quantum. On the other side stands psychological analysis, which is not seeking compromises, stylizing respites. From the point of view of an 'average style,' then, psychology is the other extreme. A 'harmonious mean' would be left with, for instance, the 19th-century novel technique in which psychology and the doubts and surrogates arrayed against it concurred on a compromise that might possibly be called harmony. All the same, one is separated from that style by a profound, possibly insurmountable aversion.

Leville-Touqué confronted that problem constantly in *Anti-psyche*. The Middle Ages were much more disharmonious and one-sided than the style of the 19th-century bourgeoisie — and yet… For that reason he introduced a differentiation between 'technical' harmony and 'human' harmony, applying the latter, naturally, to the Middle Ages. Every compromise-theory ought to logically arrive at the average 19th-century style, but when the whole theory was just a couple of millimeters from that crevasse suddenly, at the very last moment, he reversed the process in the opposite direction, not knowing himself whether that was with force or unexpected consistency.

All this restlessness first made itself felt in a critique of painting, which naturally proceeded parallel to an appropriate love experience, and the two (painting and woman) became closely 'co-logicized' (as he wittily put it). He wanted to demonstrate the superior quality of a codex illustration in contrast to a 19th-century picture, which was intermediate between impressionism and naturalism and where colors, forms, and composition gave a more perfect 'harmony' than the codex picture. The codex enthused him; the 19th-century picture was a bore.

As indicated, he wanted to wave off the matter by positing a dizzyingly vast distance between human (biological) harmony and theoretical (technical) harmony, and in *The Physiology and Esthetics of Harmony* he attempted to heat that contrast to the extreme and thus, of course, to a provocative denial of history. The harmony of a person's naïve functions does not imply graphical harmony or symmetry (e.g., even classicism has nothing to do with the true average person or 'human' harmony in general) — if it were possible to project 'human' harmony into certain formulas, then one would end up with the most bizarre picture, geometrical nonsenses & physical torsos (among them, of course, possibly symmetrical ones), which it would not be permissible to suddenly call romanticism in the habitual meaning of the word. The codex picture hit upon those 'human' lines of harmony, as opposed to the 19th-century one, which created an abstract, specialist technical balance.

His love of harmony had to be reconciled with his love of unnaturalness and artificiality, or rather, since he discovered both of them in himself, he had to clarify their common cause. Incidentally it was in connection to the frictions with Halbert that he realized that his 'person'-centeredness was replete with theoretical point-rigor and the sparkling restlessness of artificiality in contrast to the truly human simplicity of the 'person' that had evolved in Halbert's romantic attractions. So then he started to defend the average 19th-century novel and average painting, because the Middle Ages were much too interesting to serve as a basis for establishing an esthetic-free, practical beauty.

That was a period when a troubled colorless-phase commenced in *Antipsyché* (the July–September 1931 numbers), in which problems of human health and style were mixed; the trivial way of life and historical microscopies of the change in style went through fitful identifications, so that in the September 1931 issue Leville wrote a leading article under the title "Thèse et Scrupules" in which (in line with his tradition) he narrated a love story as an experiment. For the time being in three styles, with three watercolor illustrations — as if that naïvely resumed experimental method could lead back to the brutal virginity that had characterized the periodical's first number ("*... il y a des scrupules qui ne sont points maladifs — au contraire, ils sont le sport de notre âme, des tragédies hygiéniques en miniature, composées du scepticisme alerte et du sang superflu dont la thèse, qui conduit à la fatigue, a toujours besoin. Ce sont de véritables arabesques rationnelles: vérités-jeux, je les appellerais. La pensée, comme une matière vivante, après avoir fini son courant logique, continue l'art pour l'art son mouvement et crée un automatisme pseudo-logique avec des pseudo-problèmes et pseudo-relations — tout cela n'est point gothique au sens pathétique ou morbide du mot, mais la fonction la plus simple et plus thérapeutique des muscles mentaux ...*"[187] et cetera) ...

---

return to the vision: the boy asks for his life

The slim heroine radiated toward the sky, and the exciting prestige of her beauty provoked a dispute of 'form' & 'soul'   'form' failed and the 'soul's' alluring but almost unreachable distance shimmered goldenly in its self-evident victory — until a third person of emaciated exterior, as a schemer in the history of style, actually the 'average,' for a while obscured the radiance of the victor's face more with his shadow than by a brave taking to the stage.

Jumping between woman and mirror, the boy whispered as follows:

— When you, Mother, hear my name, you always feel a sour coolness as in poorly imitated outer-suburban Gothic-workers' temples; somehow 'virtue' comes to your mind, which for you is roughly as much as a crinoline or an aunt's funeral that you are obliged to attend. At present, I, too, feel no sympathy toward the tasteful spectra of sin, but mark you well, I myself am also no allegory of virtue; I am not necessarily identical to the sermons delivered in my interest, or to sanctimonious natural histories about me of possibly shaky grammaticalness. I am pure, that's not my fault, the shadowy Baroque art of mistakes has not yet made my essence 'tragically-human' (as you people are wont to say in your philanthropic, ludicrous jargon). I am life in the first place, not a moral provision, a humorless imperative. Life, opportunity, i.e., whatnot — propensity to evil, art, inconsistent love, hypocritical politics and tawdry business. Thus, even my clown's clothes are a bit symbolic, because as strictly monochrome as my honorable advocates in the world may be, I am in no way equally comparable to them. It may be that in my old age I shall drive you out, be your incestuous lover. What's the use of the many unpleasant possibilities, you will say, when a flawless, predictable machinery delivers the stock of voluptuous experiences to your door like a printing press that colors your life now red trances, now sepia spiritual clouds, at one time flashing petty revolts, at another the moraloid smudges of convention. The fact that I offer & introduce myself like a fairground barker should not lull you into thinking that your stance toward me is like that of a blasé customer toward a salesman having oriental volubility at his command, who, if he sends him away, is making a simple commercial decision. I have to be accepted; the only reason I have for praising myself with such naïve industry is because I know that so much disadvantageous tittle-tattle has reached your ears that it will do no harm if I correct with a spot of intelligence the portrait of a monster that is not at all illustrative of me. I have colleagues who go so far in pro domo zeal that they style their birth pains as being wonderful, and do so with an artistic sophistication that I don't find appealing: I don't go in very much for this exaggerated trickiness & lime-twig mother hunting, so I won't deny that I would be a brutal interpolation into your life and your flesh — grasses, walls, and flower beds will have to be dug up in order for a villa to be built there.

---

formation of the landscape, the monkeys

The next moment the physician in the pullover jumped on the boy's back — the short, little figure on the young blond man's slim body was a fairly grotesque sight. The man in the pullover meanwhile gave a whistle, whereupon men in snow-white coats jumped into the room from every corner; the mirror grew like a clamshell, swinging up to the ceiling & filling up with minute light bulbs. The boy suddenly grew dizzy from the wild light and covered his eyes with his arms. The monkeys ran into the figures in white but could not grab hold of them because they slipped through them as if they were air.

The sea was grey; enormous, flat step-waves that were almost marking time reached right up to the room; the monkeys drowned in the water, barking desperately at the seagulls, which etched unconcerned parabolas in the exultant air, surrounding the wearily idling boy like negative Holy Ghosts who had come not to enlighten but to obscure life; their wings beat around the boy's head like swords, their shadows bound the fugitive colors of his clothes into a restless jacket. The Sun speedily slipped up to the sky like the reverse shot of an evenly accelerating fall in the movies & fused with the disk of the operating lamp at the tip of the sky. The steam above the wet backs of the tumbling and wailing monkeys thickened, as Fig 1, Fig. 2, Fig 3... in text-books of watercolor painting show the richer forms developing from the first version of the blot, the fog becoming detailed ever more sharply and colorfully, at first following the annular, pollen-bearing samples of the billows, like a first draft of tree boughs; later the groups of boughs broke up into leaves, though at the edges fog not used in creating the foliage rocked in yellow clusters with the alluring frivolity of superfluity — the transition of sea and forest was barely distinguishable so that it was fairly miraculous that one had not seen before now (stronger than a formalism of semblances) the sea's branches, flowers, & vein-stretching chlorophylls as well as the billows of the forest, the high tide of branches.

The monkeys hung like dark nests among the branches as if a dark sponge had been pulled right through from the zenith to the rocky bottom of the sea basin, with the sponge leaving after it a dark streak but which finally got caught on the sclerotic knots of the branches. The more lemon-like the self-identity of the sun lamp as it illuminated the items of the land's precepts, the more mournful the dinginess with which the stricken cocoons turned black; there was a wise comedy in their darkness and muteness, a humorous blaséness with which they preserved their veto power much better than unorganized & programmed deadness with its senseless defiance.

The sea's waves smoothed into steps of semicircular shape; the horizontal slabs retained the greyness of the sea, whereas their low, vertical edges retained the whiteness of its spume; of course, the difference between architecture and waves was not definite — the boundary zone looked like the houses we see shivering & bowing through bluish-invisible smoke if a mobile bitumen-spreading machine emits smoky fumes when repairing the road. The leafy boughs, full of flowers and senseless fruits, broke through the clouds & returned in the direction of a rainbow after a semicircle storming from internal complications to the edge of the step; it was splendid to see the gentle tussle of the clear line of the semicircle & changeable sliding of the foliage in the valley, the dew-scaled compromises between the overreaching beauty of an occasional swaggering branch and an abstract arch of triumph sweeping with Romanesque-style consistency.

Slender women in swim suits came from the sea at every hand; a rubber cap dangled in the hands of some like a slick little basket that was going to be filled with silky locks of hair & submarine paleolithic moss the next minute (the Staalbreck clinic up in the north lived on associations of that kind): one could foresee their heads in the taut caps so much that they were considered young martyrs who, in the next second of their foam-Venusianness, would swing their own heads into the air like a catapult.

---

comparison to the swim-suited girl:
Hindu codex painting & Manet

Oriental painters were familiar with a certain technique of painting foliage that in essence consisted of sketching slightly zigzag-edged ellipses above and behind each other which covered each other for a while like playing cards held like a fan; these oval shapes, which assumed the pattern of stretched, propagating spores, were repeated within the big leading ovals, which, naturally, was a healthy falsification of a three-dimensional impression of real foliage. What on the real tree was soft shortening here became dizzy falling, what was shivering shadow there was here two sharp surfaces, an example of subtracting light of almost experimental perfection — every single property was separately placed and solved, but when all is said & done, setting them beside each other again seemed to be an 'Impressionist' style precisely on account of the naïve dissonance of the individually elaborated elements.

When the blot technique of 19th-century impressionism endeavored to accomplish a picture of the instant it created for itself a big synthesis-style, harmoniously coordinating relaxed forms and sliding hypotheses of color, so that this coordinating discipline of design completely excluded the impression of an accidental, psychologically asymmetrical, temporally sophisticated thing: rather, it preserves what lies within the capriciously fixed boundaries of the moment and it creates a classical interdependence among those things that are within it instead of giving an idea with the picture of how bizarrely arbitrary and out-of-balance the relation between 'moment' & 'time' is.

There is much more restlessness on these trees of 'naïve' technique, which are not the result of summary, momentary oglings, but of meditative observation & workmanship-lengthiness; as if space were filled with *ab essentia*[188] internal differences (with the aid of a stick dipped in water one is forced, all of a sudden, to face the most drastic shift in perspective) — just as geographical areas differ extraordinarily from the common denomination of a map, so behind the most abstract space there are motley variants of essence, and a painting or a tree bough shows us this philosophical 'variorum edition,' stuffed full of surprises, unexpected contradictions, dilemmas of lighting — equally, time loses the synthetic paleness stemming from 19th-century French pictures, the dogmatically uniformizing drill of the 'moment': in its place we get various expressions of prismatic time broken into the soul; big extents, and in the golden background of the big extents, capriciously cross-stitched minute blots, flashes of thickenings of color, as if the theatrical gold color of abstract & amorphous time were transformed into colors — divine heresies of green, red, blue and yellow — through thickening, compressing into human moments. That truly arouses an 'impressionist'-impression besides which Manet-boughs bore us with the timeless stiffness of a scholastic grisaille.

The girls sparkled above the sea in these colors of Hindu codices; each swimming costume, each body clashing with loud autonomy with its neighbor — perhaps one best feels the dramatic strength of that diversity if one finds various handwritings on one sheet of paper immediately alongside and after each other; not only does one sense the forms before one's eyes as different but one also knows for sure that every conceivable inference which can be drawn from these graphic signs will be different in its last permutation than the sum total of further possibilities of the neighboring writing; just as when every figure has a separate sky onto which shadows fall as they do on a folding screen standing a mere few centimeters away: at times like this one feels that if one could extend the figures in the direction of their lives behind the picture, then the further we would move away from the surface of the picture the more they would move away from each other, like the points of a compass dial; the picture relates to the elements it contains in the way that the 'classical' trunk of a tree does to its own impressionist branches.

This technique of 'otherness' has an effect that engages the nerves of our most impressionistic, most profound reactions; the effect is so deep and universal that in the final analysis it must nevertheless express an ancient harmony. And indeed so it does; one takes delight in the greatest contrasts not because they are full of divergent suggestions of space and time but because this technique best fosters our elemental sensuality of balance & harmony.

To use a trivial starting simile: when tightrope walkers keep themselves in balance with a pole to the ends of which two big iron balls are attached, they usually perform the most symmetrical movements with it, and if one were to map on millimeter-squared paper the deviation line of the centers of the two balls — all one would get is a picture of some sort of snaky neurasthenia: yet the certainty of balance would glow in it, invisibly & obviously. With the tree, every single twig & leaf, all greenery of which would embody a different style of twig, leaf, and greenery, indeed different worlds in the form of isolated premises & self-serving conclusions, thereby giving an impression of the 'absolute' relative — with that tree it is precisely the extreme chaos of directions that makes it clear that there is a basic relationship behind the breaking-up of veins, a 'monad' of force (Oh! what a tear-wrenchingly pedantic happy end!).

logos, time, life

In a popular historical novel taking place in the golden age of North African Arabs, one might fit around the love scenes the meditations of a walk-on figure who would bore readers with a theory of the 'three stages,' in accordance with which there is a clear logical root cause at the bottom of every life function, an intellectual- or primal-logical-'monad' or point (i.e., the basic stage); a vitalized form of that ancient truth principle is always some graph or other: the 'monad's' first movement toward life, or rather its first trace in life — the point-like monad hovers in one place, but time runs on in front of it, and the monad draws a line on it, and since time does not run precisely, it draws a snaking line (cf. the rocking rope walker) — that is the second stage; finally (after the point & the graph) the third, the visual stage, follows: life itself, which is a Baroque fugue, or a continuation and exaggeration of variation formed from the subject of the graph.

This popular walk-on figure would perform the three stages in the direction of 'monad — abstract-logical mechanism — sensual-logical mechanism,' but even if one starts from the picture one rapidly scales down 'disharmonies' to abstract lines of force, & the lines of force chopped apart in the mirror of time to an elemental point — that is the physiology (or mathematics, which comes to the same thing) of the enjoyment of impressionist pictures. Behind Manet's technical harmony is an elemental chaos; behind the technical confusion of Hindu 'impressionism' is elemental harmony — that the latter, the elemental harmony, is more important, is realized by anyone who ever gets round to examining the most ancient forms of their sensuality.

"I made clippings of these ornament assistants — said the celestial showman — from various swimsuit ads and brochures for bathing resorts, which explains their lack of esthetic justification; I myself also found it interesting that although the extent to which the two figures on the far right hand side count as relatives in respect of psychological content, & gestures expressing that, yet simply because they are made of different material they show the most grotesque possible contrast; one of them is pointing toward her cabin, the other is looking precisely in that direction (I was highly delighted to unearth that figure), but on the other hand the first one is drawn in poster style, in garish colors, in a technique that smuggles muscle, swimsuit, and shade into a single angular column, which was decreed more by the color-printing presses than by the artist's hand — whereas the second is all anxious scientificity, a specialist photograph that brings to the surface even the most hidden properties of the material of the swimming costume, with the two kinds of representation-technique making totally alien figures that are harmonized as to content."

disharmony of characters & life in the vision

These days photograph clippings are all the rage; these are not put into a frame together with the background, only the outlines of the profile are cut out and squeezed between unframed glass plates — however, a heavy price is paid for that game, because the cut-away background and discarded continuation are nevertheless there in ghostly form and fill the environs of the photograph over quite a large area with a photographic 'sense of space' that cannot be abolished simply by sticking other photographs directly next to it, as in the latest magazines, or slices of posters, as in this improvised mechanistic vision.

The swarm of women's faces jarred, utterly out of place, in the whole comedy — as if the scholarly pater had only just invented a theoretical helix & now, suddenly, wanted to popularize the whole thing and for that purpose was thinking of going to the most famous revue theater in order to seek out people to personate it: what was lacking in the invention was that obscure state that consists of the mixture of the thought *per se* and the as yet only half-sketched actors' faces: he did not regard the actors as one of the waves of the work of art itself, only as an article that could be bought in a shop that is just added to an already written drama in the way of a luxury binding to a much-loved old book. He slapped the manuscript under one arm, looked around the street, saw a sign: "Theater," opened the first door, met an host of women, giving them his piece so to speak over the counter, commenting: "Do it very well." However much the father spoke of the direct buds of thought in the picture and the rationalism of hallucination, precisely the opposite made itself felt: a creaking duality of spectacle & theory, a naïve diversity of the two crafts, as if there were exact borderlines or social distinctions between the 'picture guild' & the 'mind guild,' their shared creations being the result of at best a good-natured cooperation, far from an identity of cause. The pictures were now substituting for actors, but the process was the same — thought & actor did not break down into a molding.

There was a time when some people explained the verse form of the most ancient poems with the fact that rhyme had arisen to serve easier memorization — the same specific gravity of naivety is given by the other, which sees in a dramatic representation not the art work part of a work of art, only the practical performability. As a result, the well-known amusing situation (typically 'priestly,' as lay taste would put it) arises: the subject matter is chastely untimely and abstract, whereas the personators are wildly modern, because being an unversed author, having imagined the 'woman of today' in theory, he had gone out to inquire where the most modern roster of them was to be found, in what theater or what magazine, and he had turned straightway to the address he had been given since he wanted the most perfect. The most arbitrary map of utopia, and, on that wily soil, human samples that are very drastically stamped with tomorrow's date, are thus all there in the performance, or (as its own inventor called it) such an aperitif-vision.

The case is much the same with a poor person who, when he hears that the king is going to drop by on his way home from hunting, rushes over to his neighbor in order to borrow some money and then races off to ascertain which is the most distinguished restaurant and there places an order for the very best dinner, which will indeed be perfect, but for the poor person it does not, as it happens, constitute a 'perfect dinner,' but rather a foreign concoction that he believes (to use the words of others) "will evoke in the king the idea of perfection."

reality & representation, an actress on stage & in reality. Childish, idyllic in even the most naturalistic piece

It should be remarked that in social plays (or at least in the few that have endured) & comedies the 'modern woman' is likewise extraordinarily simple, her illustriousness (without the 'simplicity' being perceptible as the goal) being such, both in gesture & word, that even a simple viewer who is totally analphabetic in matters of elegance, fully understands. On spotting the actress who represented this readily intelligible modern lifestyle at the stage door, she will all at once be laden with secrets: it is now that the true 'modernity' begins, she will suddenly become mystic; a few minutes before, that person had still formed a kinship with the actress in homely-sentimental, democratic-community and, with naïve gullibility, noted himself down beside that day's date, but the white feather boa that she had worn in the last act has become, all at once, an outlandish allusion, an incomprehensible hieroglyph — how comprehensible, honestly social an institution that item of clothing had been just beforehand, and now, taken out of the dramatic work's regular, consolidated atmosphere, it has gained a wicked, brutal autonomy, standing in sharp inimicality to the spectator, who in a trice has become anachronous.

Any kind of modernity is unrepresentable, because in every representation there is sugary docility; in even the nerviest, shameless pictures there is an undeniably childish streak, modesty in regard to all-out stripping, motherliness in their critique. In every representation there is structure, rhythm, and expediency, for at the bottom of even the most heroic and demonic differences in rhythm ticks just a single rhythm — a "lulla, lulla, lullaby, sing with grace, Philomel";[189] in other words, the baby orderliness of the playroom.

There was a time when people used to talk about game theory in esthetics; an artist very rarely plays, to be sure, being much more likely to suffer, but out of the unhappy series of martyrdoms, something nevertheless always arises that produces the impression of a game. There is, perhaps, little to contemplate in regard to the dichotomy of reality and representation, but there is something perennially intriguing in the fact that even the hairiest pieces of the detectives of reality can seem to be mere naïve ballet dancing in relation to the couple of words and movements said and made by the parting actress on her way from dressing room to car.

There are pieces in which the entire argot of the so-called demimonde is utilized, so that the spectators, even a begoggled college kid in the gods, feels the language stands completely to reason (that is why quite young children dare to fall in love with the actresses in plays that are bristling with frivolous & 'hypermodern' allusions, because they sense a charm in their face that is congenial, a child's crying in their lamentations, a playroom joy in their sensual swaying: if they genuinely lacked that trait the children would, in all certainty, not be in love with them), and rushes happily to the stage door at the end of the performance, and when the heroine appears an oddly accented word leaves her lips, accompanied by a curt, flippant gesture — that, or even anything faintly like it, was not in the play. From that movement on the play ceased to be 'realist' & 'modern'; the observations stored up within it & the exaggerated and fastidious 'naturalism' of the actors were empty lies, or at best a deceptive fairy story, as if there had been some sort of conspiracy on the part of the actors that they would never perform the true reality.

Why? If a writer much wiser than them imagined cynicism in love as being the way it is in his play, then why does that style of cynicism not rub off on the actresses in everyday life as well: it is a cynicism that the staid spectator is familiar with, understands, is able to argue, work, and fence with, but when he is confronted with the actress outside her stage role he is all of a sudden faced with a cynicism of unknown psychology and mimicry. The spectator continues to compose the play letter by letter: that makes the actress laugh at him as if he was a stammering nursery-school child. How can it be that she sometimes studies a role for years on end, its psychology and its movements, studying it in such a way that she carries her "whole life" into it, yet when the spectator turns toward her with precisely that kind of lifestyle, then he finds the loudest mockery on the part of the actress? If the style is so ludicrous, how on earth did she find the strength to study it for years on end?

If it was a matter of her being aware that on the stage she is not seeking to represent life, but a puppet, a large-scale pictorial sophistry in which she supplants the old mask with a mask she has developed from her own self: but then she fills even stylized plays with realist misgivings, bringing 'life' onto the stage is her life's most Harpagonesque snobbery. When she portrays a psychological somersault on the boards the audience feels a great calm, an almost hummable comfort, as if the actress lay completely in its power, after all the audience is very well acquainted with hysterias, with 'unexpected' outbursts of that sort, and it has long been, as it were, reckoned into its judgment of human nature.

A 'realist' play always resembles memory: a few scintillating points of analogy, lasting just a couple of seconds, are enough for the audience's relevant subjective memories to extend to the whole stage scene; the knowledge that the audience does not have to interfere in actions beyond the footlights allows them to feel stage life as being, in large measure, the same as the life that is stored away in their own memory traces stylizing stage life *ab ovo*: the audience are unaware that they are now enjoying an extremely perfunctory simulacrum, and they believe that every detail of their lives harmonizes with the details of the play —

the piece awakens feelings, and those energetic waves of feeling smuggle long interpolations from their very own lives among the words of the play.

Every activity of a member of the audience is based on the past while the play is in progress, but their experiences (which even in the case of the most dry-as-dust, practical person, turn from day to day into more poetical and artificial forms) do not have to be forced into action, so that when 'regret,' 'jealousy,' or 'hope' runs through their body, they feel them in an abstract perfection such as never succeeds in real life; in reality, motifs of regret suffuse feelings of regret with undue force and weight, whereas in the theater, motifs of regret are just minute springs of action, fleeting off-beats, making the feeling itself all the clearer and more powerful — precisely that (a little motif, consisting of a subjective memory torso, almost a transcendental feeling) gives the illusion of naturalism. An extraordinary intensity of feeling is at work in the audience, and that lyrical tension lulls them into illusions of 'lifelikeness,' though what causes that intensified resonance of our feelings is precisely that it is in the most abstract situation: it utilizes memories without needing to apply them for even a fleeting moment to the following action; the entire scent-content of memories appears in the form of a brain-vapor, which at the time of being directed to action is, naturally, already engaged.

simile: dream & opium

Just as one is lifted into a state of visual laziness by sleep and some narcotics, so the theater draws one into a general laziness of life — there looking is for looking, and when a tree catches the eye, that is far from fitting into the series of what was seen before, and still less (and more importantly) does it come up with the claim (a constant in life) of serving as a stepping-stone for a subsequent picture: the tree fills the future with itself as well, transforms into the next image, indeed, with any one transformation it substitutes for the chronologically arranged series of the past — the whole is a passive optical-jogging on the spot, a denial of time and action: movement which nevertheless does not signify time and drama.

Many dreams always attempt to accomplish this pictorial paradox; as if they were, irrespective of time and action, precise projections of being, the strength of existence having hitherto been distributed into the long funnels of time, but now such a funnel was squashed, and thus these lines compressed into themselves would yield those peculiar spirals which one can find, for example, in the notebooks of opium smokers (if they are genuinely sincere). When they awaken from an opium rush they always see Hobbema's alley or Hooch's intercommunicating rooms; in life as a whole: perspective & succession; yet in perspective there is a hierarchy, & in hierarchy — a moral element, so that natural, naïve, lifelike-optic is already fraught with a lot of tedious morality.

Some such drama, free of time and action, surges in the minds of the audience under the influence of the stage action; in that respect the pseudo-life inside a playhouse resembles incense, where a small amount likewise arouses huge clouds of illusion, which then line the glittering golden apses with a fur of obscurity — as if the fire would not live its own 'natural' life on the line of a civil ordinate but would burst into a new flame in a violent manner on a perverse, perpendicular abscissa detached from life, a new flame that naturally preserved in its atmosphere all of its so to say bourgeois strengths but, being completely under other pressures and climatic influences, produces unknown fragrances, corollas, & light puzzles.

Like a dose of cocaine, one of the actress's movements launches this self-serving musing and action in the spectator, like a syllable which does not carry on into the next intelligible syllable of prose but suddenly dizzies into a melody and unrolls with heretical verticality — they unconsciously change time in one, and a film going at the normal speed of life is suddenly transformed into a slow-motion film, but that slowing is already another time outside the body of time that the spectator had arbitrarily selected from his memories, and that jealousy, joy, or sense of vengefulness does not gallop through the obstacle walls of life (like a bullet through the pages of a notebook) but in a vacuum of space: something like that was felt by a philosopher talking about the fact that a thought could be developed in two directions, one of which was a further development of its logic, the other an onward flight in a hypothetical plane, driven without any resistance by, as it were, the moment of the inertia of its own intellectual content.

It seems that this property is detectable in every aspect (action, optics, thinking), namely that practical movement differs infinitely from self-contained movement, and that duality falls sick into what is sometimes a very irritating question, such as when one inquires with hypochondriac apprehension which of the two is 'true' life: the one in which I work the motifs fully into feelings then immediately transmit the feelings into newer motifs, meanwhile continually assimilating the utterly unpredictable sea of external chances, relentlessly, with the uniform minute-length duration of minutes in the predestined life-directedness of deeds (as, for example, when I begin talking to the lady without camellias) — or else is 'true'-life when the balance between motifs and their effects is the most symmetrical because I use only the minimum of motifs (that memory thrust my way like the lazy final quiver of a tired wave) but in contrast enjoy the maximum emotional effect throughout, a totality for which practical life never gave opportunity (as, for example, when I watch the agony of the lady without camellias on stage). For the eye the true Garden of Eden is the one that is explicitly anti-Hobbema: dream makes possible a continuation of the picture without its progression, its motion without the constant discipline of action; only this logic-free space is a redeeming mental paradise for the brain.

While a duel is fought through to the end on stage, concluding in the scarlet death of one, all the audience sees of the parties is a vibrating coat-of-arms motif woven from two crossed swords, an action-free symbol-tower, charged only with lyricism, which rises (an action-rainbow beyond the action-shower) in a sky based on some basic rule of melody.

---

another simile: last edition of an Italian novella, illustrations & typography

---

All that is reflected in an old Italian romantic novella. With naïve superficiality, to be sure, but with a great deal of unintended precision (often a maudlin outburst of bombast is nothing more than the scientifically enlarged photograph of a neglected truth: there is a species of 'empty rhetoric' that is a veritable storehouse of nuances), it relates the love of a young poet for an actress whom he met when still essentially in his childhood, when she was a model, and when he had accompanied her mother to a dressmaker's; he had not seen her for a long time, and already when he had the opportunity to watch her in three or four different dresses, she had grown into those dresses and in recollection caused unsettling disturbances in his soul; green velvet, scarlet silk, and yellow lace started to bloom in his mind, with a different color predominating every night, the way it is customary for a card party to pass off under a different constellation of trumps;[190] the childish sensitivity to colors & snobbery about external appearance produced gardens and souls in dreams: yellow all at once vibrated apart into selfish botany but equally into definite shades of character (and he thereby realized something that nowadays is realized *ad nauseam* by others, to wit, that being bamboozled by surfaces may be a more philosophical attitude than tantalizing toward the murky x's of unknown 'depths'), and he did not know which he loved most truly: the face, dress, flower or character?

He finally saw her once again in the street. Like a drunken scholar who has suddenly hit upon a formula that redeems his lengthy deductions: he spied the girl, looked at her, and followed her in the street, compared her to his dreams, yet he didn't know "whether the dream had made the girl of life fairer, or the dream had the daytime to thank for every secret" (one of the lines of a children's poem in which systematizing anxieties deriving from stylistic game-melodies and observation-sharpness are the same: as if the center of gravity would jump from note to note between melody and truth; one of the keyboards opens toward the dance's wave-lines, the other toward hypochondriac self-philology, & the little ditty brushes against now one, now the other, with its hesitating fingers — that perpetual two-way flirtation is also one of the greatest charms of some of the better kinds of poems).

Seemingly, the poet is only rhyming around the dream's commonplace, contemporaneous prestige vis-à-vis reality — only the most recent criticism had noticed that the hero of the novella observed & nourished his dreams in the interest of reality. And when he glimpses reality after all that dream-theory, he goes off to acquire opium even before he could reach home: this is not a trivial denial of day but a gallop into the 'laboratory,' as if only scientific dream methods were able to pry the most ancient nature of reality, its final character, out of the body of reality, as if with an ultra thin yet ultra strong lever, because genuine reality had so coalesced with the apocryphal material of all kinds of conventions, 'reality' conventions. "My sage dreaming set off singing like a flying high tide on the taciturn water": it was good to comment a bit shrewdly on that adjective 'sage' as it had seemed to nearly shrivel up forever on the pages of the ant-faced concordance.

Thus, those little reflections in parentheses and seemingly merely ironic passages in which he remarks that the relationship of reality to dreams is like that of two seas looked different: in one of the seas (i.e., reality) the waves continually succeed each other as if they were the acrobat's body of time, one swallows up the other, ever newer ones come, and the result is a big monotony of identity; in the other sea, which is moved by the soul 'with an eternal trinity,' every wave that is born is preserved as a separate wave so that when the booming current of the second is rounded in the wake of the first, there are two of them, both isolated, each one different, each naturally embedded in a different time sphere.

It is quite interesting to see the final edition of this novella in which the still classicizing copperplates that illustrated the first edition are juxtaposed with the text in a font from those days, then the author's notes, and finally colored woodcuts by a modern illustrator: one gets a complete stereoscopy of the same thought, indeed, as is mathematically readily conceivable: 'corporeality' is raised to the power of 'corporeality.'

Strolling on the street of a small Italian town is a girl in a crinoline dress with breasts resembling a fruit dish suddenly thrown anarchically apart, her hair built up from tiny autonomous curls (little electromagnets): the whole picture is full of shade and assembled from minute points (those are not due to the artist but are a product of the printing), which, in the end, again serve outlines, the definiteness of the outline being achieved without sharpness. Loosening lines into a plane and making shadow undulations suddenly glow into lines has nowadays become a mechanical technique: how much finer the magic of the 18th-century outlining with dots.

At the time of the Italian Renaissance there were artists who tried to opticize a statuette and fog into a common material, in the north there were artists who knew how to chemicalize lightness out from darkness as if the identity of the two were the most banal physical fact; there were people in England who were able to make excessively-Brusselian-lace-of-lights out of the contrast of darkness and light — and even now there are those who want to make the mass of the whole material world unreal with the help of light and shade: with the aid of elucidations new syntheses arose, and those very arbitrary optical forms (e.g., so-called 'pure film') can truly step in before us with the claim that (as in a long-forgotten mythology) we grasp the whole world only as an experimental or mathematical game of light and shadow. (That was illustrated well by a French artistic humor magazine called *History of the Art of the Chessboard*: in that the B & W squares are pictures drawn à la Leonardo, à la Rembrandt, à la Beardsley and à la Picasso.)

Those 18th-century moments were magical in art history: scholars would habitually tack on the prefix 'pseudo-'; light, shadow, and form were not scientific questions, they were not mythological protagonists, nor were they entirely petit bourgeois concepts either, or the stock articles of dreams, they were not entirely artistic, more technical (printing press!). (The book's first illustrator was a so-called uninventive Prud'hon epigone.) The negative enumeration of the previous sentence may possibly suggest that the elements enumerated 'somehow' coincided — however, if one takes the matter seriously (and who could not take it seriously when it is possible to relive a moment of heavenly beauty), then one has to immediately concede that the elements of that beauty are just as possible to positively distinguish as individual yellow & individual blue dots are in a green layer of paint under a microscope (just as it is amusing if we regard 'pointillism' as a style, seeking thereby to construct a picture of the world into a unity, so it is exhilaratingly reassuring that the nowadays cursed craft of atomization stands at one's disposal against everything) — those illustrations, just as much as is generally the case with miniatures, ought to be magnified as much as possible, & then to such horrendous wrecks of sentences as "in the petit bourgeoisie roundness of her face lurks some Hellenic arch, as if the Biedermeier were only a loosely-waved mask adopted out of Romantic self-irony behind which the vulgar rhythm of Greek ornamentation were blooming, and not deeply either but in exciting proximity" — and similar over-complicated circumlocutions in the way of 'intuitions' one could give a clear content: one could see molecules & atoms of style, one could point to those millimicrons that are Hellenistic particles of line, which are by now not further decomposable, and point to others that are likewise unequivocally of Biedermeier character — 'mixing' light & shade would no longer be mixing in the empty decorative sense of the word, but the placement of blackness and whiteness could be seen from point to point & thus expressed numerically — after all, those poor down-at-the-heel essayists who sprinkle their reviews of pictures full of the suspect petals of gaudy epithets also struggle toward precision of that kind, even the cheapest epithet being a perverted form of the number, in the way that the most paradoxical sexual straying is also, in essence, a logical impatience of Platonism.

within the latter simile: old illustrations, the value of Prud'hon-style painting & copperplate engraving; relationship of morbid & absolute (or: ideal); two kinds of dream

The girl strolling in the street was surrounded by a foggy corona of clouds; those clouds themselves displayed the harmonious transitional state in which the roughness of the ribbons in the codex had, by and large, weakened, but it still stood far from true meteorological and psychological clouds; it contained a couple of traits of a devoutly imitative nature, a couple of traits which were a modest experiment at rendering the mystic perceptible, & it also bore a couple of traits which were there simply to serve as a frame or sheath for the dreams of the heroine of the novella. From those variations did indeed emerge goddesses created from various dresses, genuine women ripened from outward appearances: very long ago the difference of reality & dream used to be represented with a slight local shift, and the dreams were woven into a little frame, & one end of the frame (which would otherwise have hung freely like the plant-form spirals of initials) was twisted around the neck of the dreamer so as to signal the connection between the two; now they are drawn completely mixed up, like the different cards on the backs of two parcels.

Both were far from the 18th-century 'pseudo'-artist (printer). If one were to enjoy the picture first with Helmholtz-style resonators, then without them, one would see the golden mean in its own totality, which is truly full of gold, because it created a transition between naïve commoner art and art of the spheres, which is inexhaustible in gentlemanly excitements. The artist set out from the petit bourgeois, swung over into dream, then immediately backtracked to prose only the next moment to nevertheless trill over into the world of 'creation' — the mental mosaic comprised the tiny jumpings back and forth of glittering hypocrisies; reality was not a '*misera moles*,'[191] because unconscious prejudices refined its material, the 'ideal' was not agonizingly absolute strangeness, but only a flirtatious hint, dream was not a mechanical tragicomedy of associations, but the *dolce niente* reflections of slightly muted logic, and though reality and daytime were full of order, that happened without any asceticism & Baroque consciousness. The 'ideal' was in essence a convention, the artist did not find it in the stamped vision of the night but in the sentences of conversation, in the formulas of dances, despite which it was not so prosaic as not to be heated up by some passing fever of a metaphysical plus: as if the 'ideal' were sprinkled in a colloidal state among the bushes of reality.

A certain sick taste, which sometimes replaces the 'ideal,' was present in larger measure than in the polyhistoric nature of the compilation of illnesses of later decadence, hence they were nevertheless able to make probable the percept that nowadays seems to be just a withered aphorism — "there is a real relationship between the morbid and the esthetically or logically perfect." Primarily, the face of that girl in the picture had decidedly naturalist claims; it forces us to set the face before us in life size, in color, and with three-dimensional extension, but at the same time, in that imaginary metamorphosis, around the eyes and under the lips, it carries with it the shades and tender leaden mosses that signify only a minimal surplus in the drawing in comparison to reality but would give an extraordinarily mystical quality to the face if they were to become flesh.

When one imagines a face, two steps can be distinctly distinguished in the imagination; first of all, the evocation occurs either in a neutral space (e.g., while reading a novel one has the entire plot take place on such an isolated private stage — one can almost write down the average spatial relations of the fantasy, the average brightness of the dreams, the almost Protestant-cubism of the backdrops of the concept) or, even if the environs and time are indeterminately present in the picture, the whole thing takes place outside one, the picture usually not being life sized.

The second state of the dream print is when one pictures the figure (with decidedly palpable physical force) as life sized, setting it in the real surroundings that happened to be given, so that, for instance, it also covers the real objects in front of one and the voice is not the usual wordless reflex (as when, instead of the outlines of a bronze statue, all one sees gleaming in a ray of sunshine is a point of light on the metal which really has nothing to do with the body of the figure) but a genuine sentence of the neighbor's conversation that is drowned out.

It is interesting how relatively uncommon this second type of conception is in life, indeed in one's dreams: hence dreams featuring totally unknown figures, never seen landscapes, in an intercalated time that never occurred in the past, seem much more real (indeed, even before one recollects them, nostalgia for them at dawn is much more concrete, one might say full of more practical forces) simply because they were featured in life size, and the usual amateur stage appeared as unnoticed as a natural ebb tide under the soles of one's feet, the primitive confusion of the backdrops was simplified to a couple of monumental people, trees, and hours. These dimensions are much more important than the contents; as if here the tendency that often tempts one to the generalization that, at the root of everything in psychological life, one is looking for a spatial experience, and one classifies the horoscope-diagram either among the select theological truths or one of the masks that, purely out of morphological adolescence, the soul hangs on itself when it is only clear about the most superficial surfaces and is too lazy to put its own face in order.

Admittedly, this picture deriving from a Prud'hon epigone can only be evaluated when cast under the second procedure: in reality, these small shadows will make one shudder much more than, for example, those horrendous Ceylonese ritual dance-masks as conceived in the first instance. The neoclassical face will be completely human, but to the greatest degree foreign and secretive, because its lurking devilishness (poor word) will emanate from precisely those whisper-thin lines that ended up in the engraving in the interest of 'idealization': the lines of the eyes and lips on the drawing show the banal, unstrung bow of Amor's scroll — in the other conception this is tantamount to an anatomical revolution, the shadow is not a whisper-thin arching but will show a picture of a grotesque disease or degenerate race of humans, meanwhile one will constantly feel that this is the line that we have so many times found ethereally sweet, chastely sensual, and in general the freshest perennial and indispensible convention.

The easy line of gesture that was like a mythicized memory trace of summer breezes now looks to be, all at once, womanly weariness, blasé eroticism, & physiological semi-scandal, though one has never seen such a perfect embodiment of the female ideal of the period in a picture. If all at once it is the method according to which a group of poets, having specified in verse all the sensual qualities of the woman in question, indeed having stripped her before the astronomical public of the whole solar system — abruptly recasts her as a symbol of virtue and with such melodic conviction that it would not occur to one that the poet is hypocritical, but that by 'virtue' he meant something idiosyncratic, closely related to the previous scale of lips, eyes, & neck. A deep void separates celebration of the ethical quality of beauty and the fantasizing of sensuality into a moral law, and they can never have anything to do with each other.

The regular reciting of body parts rippled the poet into rhythm, whereas these melodious ripples (the music of the spheres is perhaps already too raucous for us to engage it anew for an analogous scene, despite its having been pensioned off) lull the poet into an illusion of 'world order' & he projects that symmetry of play and harmony of feeling in the tune back onto the woman — who is not 'Virtue' because she is faithful and chaste, but because she served as a pretext for an inspired flash of a staged meditation on harmony. Now here is the visual trial by fire of Platonism: it commenced with sensual details, carried on with a world-weariness of harmony, and now one suddenly stiffens into material this rainbow-hued figure rising to the sky in the vapor of 'spirituality': that is when one gets the picture of beauty which the Prud'hon epigone portrays. Healthy vulgar-naïve lips, Arcadian coral-mouth, & a kiss-cornice withering in the autumnal sultriness of fever: those three, in this sort of logical connection, without any looping of relationships of reason, in this kind of philosophically causal relationship, without the delving into deeper strata being attended by the childish surprises past ends of acts of old — few have resolved that game as successfully as has this illustrator.

There were painters, like the primitives, who conceived of floating as simply an arithmetical subtraction of the plinth — there were those, like certain Baroque snobs of force, who saw it as dynamic action — or there were those who could only comprehend it as an optical obsession, or, like a few fresco painters, entrepreneurs of the firmament, as an immoral sexual deviancy of perspective, but there were extremely few who, making use of the shades of physical vertigo that approach toward miracles, and along with that the latent humanoid features of the absurd, uniting the two, were able to make it credible as a basic stage of existence, an encounter between some physiological allusion & a gentle metaphysical piano.

Naturally, the floating did not pervade the whole body: the hips were a bit recumbent on the bed, the feet, on the other hand, were rivals of the clouds, the hair put one in mind of a pillow minus, but despite that the closed eyes flew in the air like two ash-colored petals, blown by the wind. As a result, picture and second notion again came into conflict: in the first, the floating of the conventional allegory, in the second, the struggle of body and soaring, showing the almost frightful rhythm of agony united with a girl's face so tired from dancing that she can only smile, as if the body wanted to break up, and while the hair streams crosswise in the air with discreet dishevelment on the other side, her waist breaks sharply like a column in the first moment of toppling down. The game is unending: at times this magical convention is suffused with the purest sweetness, at other times we are obliged to find 'harmonious perfection,' 'ideal' a slowly burning disease, or a torso causing physical nausea.

---

text of the Italian novella

A shade rougher expression of the subject was the poet's actual text in the published edition of the novella in verse. The fusion of analysis and rhythm was not a problem in the illustration; the duality was more acute in the poem; the nascent outlines of thought began to extend across the landscapes of poetic impulse. We said that there were few more attractive moments in the history of art than that of the *'ratio florealis.'*[192] The conjecture (that philosophical speculations made so improbable by eagerness being more perceptible from them than fact) that "feeling and thought are the same, only a chronological error muddles them together" — here that was truly convincing.

There was a good-natured suggestiveness in poetic similes: as if in landscapes and flowers some thought were really written that no intuition, botany, short-sighted pantheism or theological realism is able to understand so perfectly and make credible as this transitional state in the history of art, when the coldest symbol-argot and the most girlish mood-extensions were swimming on the boring billows of time.

Intuition would be an overheated hothouse for flowers, one in which they would wither in seconds, leaving behind a shriveled figure, as if anatomy were the same as essence; botany is worth a lot more, classification is more than that smuggling-into-the-soul called understanding, but so accurate that its scientific immaculacy makes it a eunuch from the start vis-à-vis the more erotic stimuli of truth; pantheism is death for a flower, the driest, most ascetic death that can be envisaged — the molting of flower love into flower theology, the transubstantiation of gardens into fog and words (impotent lovers insist on the amusing idea that the object of their love is a goddess); 'healthy'-realism, which sees the corollas of plants and some kind of meaning in the world simultaneously, may be the most sage state, but it lets slip the mood which consists of the way the two are connected.

Still in the margin of the last example (Italian novella),
modern illustrations: color prints.
Combinative possibilities of 'ratio & flos' [193]

That restless harmony has completely ceased in modern colored-wood engravings, the sole subject of which was the representation of that harmony. What with the Prud'honists had been the half-intended counterpoint to the shadows here became an exalted theosophy of shadows, a skeptic parody of shadows — but those kinds of contrasts, since moral *'sic-transit'*[194] lessons can also be drawn from them, are only of interest to old gentlemen. In those pictures *'superratio hyperflorealis'*[195] (too wordy a word?) stepped in to replace *'ratio florealis'*; it was undeniably lovely, & the brightness of the colors was truly intensified by the fact that it was not the poppies but a doctrinaire poppy-principledness that compelled them to paper; the intellectual elements luxuriated, every color burned with rationalism, the roses explained themselves into schemes with endlessly-fresh tautology: it was genuinely *'ratio* and *flos,'* but by no means a 'flower-thought.'

The easy mastery displayed by some people consists of their imagining the elements inherent in things (e.g., *ratio* and *flos*) as being 'buds' that have to be developed (an evanescent reflection into stable analyses, a passing scent into a state of atmosphere), 'logically constructed further': there is no way of knowing where on earth they got the obsession with 'buds' from (maybe from natural science?). (If one were not ashamed of the vilest hocus-pocuses of wordplay, the Prud'honian state might be called *'raflotirao'*:[196] this is the total unity of intellectual and sensory element; the textual variant the aforesaid *ratio florealis*; modern color prints *ratio et flora,* and finally the fourth, the dissertation of the philologist who edits the text *'Distinctio Critica et Analytica Rationalitatis ac Florealitatis.*)[197]

problems of expression again (cf. p. 671) 'melodizing' literature; a certain species of 'empiricism'; the essence & value of superstition; dozing as an automatic practicing of expression

Humans have a humorous instinct (as if they were motivated by a carping and unschooled goblin) that constantly stimulates them to use different types of methods, instead of a so to speak official and at the same time workaday technique of thinking; some people consider those techniques to be the essence of art as opposed to logic, some see in them the occasionally instructive but, at root, worthless games of a lazy soul — whilst there are some who deem to discern in them neither art nor game, but the biology of truth itself. I have a feeling or thought & I want to express it, which in any case entails my giving details: the thought or feeling is, as it were, at the center of my soul, just like a stone dropped in the center of a lake, whereas in reality a stone, through the usual concentric circles, comes into contact with the bank, in the soul it is up to me to develop such rings, moreover starting from the bank, starting with the biggest and thus (gradually narrowing the bands of the wave) reaching the equatorial minimum close to the body.

Expression therefore consists of proceeding inwards from the surface to the center, though that path inwards will show up in the expression as being in the opposite direction, namely a path from the surface to an outlying point that is just as far outside as it is from the surface to within the center. The question is always, actually, in what manner should I approach my center from my surface?

One of them is the aforesaid ringed-and-looped, typically irrational method, what might for short be called the musical method. A pseudo-expression like that often tends to finish in melodies, which is the death of expression. I have a feeling, I search for a near-parallel, then I unify the two parallels in a common wavy line, then I separate anew the constituent elements from the resinous sheath of the melodic common denominator, though by that time they bear on themselves the modifications that have arisen through the parallel, so that I shall copy a third around them, possibly interweave the two, and thicken the remaining third: I shall thereby end up with a rhythmic sporulation of lines and figures. One of the temptations of the aforesaid goblin, therefore, is expression with this 'melody,' which has no intellectual merit whatever: it stylizes a certain wave texture from the outlines of a stone dropped in water the way the blue lines of a sea on some maps further enlarge the outlines of islands.

(Everything here that relates to music's alleged 'irrationality' is, naturally, distortion and exaggeration, and only serves to signal the bigoted adoration of analysis that sometimes grips the Touqués et al. of this world. Intellectually analyzing individuals frequently feel that the development part of the sonata form, variation form, or expositions of the fugue, do not bring out any radically new details from the innermost 'secrets' of the subject. The whole, of course, to look soberly at the matter, is simply a question of hearing: in the course of a series of variations a person with a poor ear senses only that the composer is stating 'the same thing' over and over again, whereas for a person with a good ear the change of just one note in a musical subject of ten notes presents the subject as completely new, just retaining the link with the first form of the subject, so for that person those variations give the most rational, logically purest, and richest analysis of the subject: not parallels of 'the same,' similar to rings in a lake, but a series of revelations of differentness straining to the boundaries of identity. The above, therefore, can merely be in relation to a 'tin-eared over-analyzer,' and such gross simplifications as "melody is the death of expression" are something primarily against *literature* which plays melodies, fugue, and variations — the most exacting logic of music can be the most powerless tautology of writing.)

'Song' is the most abstract possible form of surface-repeating making lines, but there is a more naïve form of the same method that is a lot more worthwhile and in Podunk-lingo might be called 'an empiricist outline-tautology,' as opposed to the previous, for which the short name is 'music.' The word *'empeiria'*[198] must first be stripped of the grotesque peruke bestowed on it by the history of philosophy, which in truth had never suited it, for the notion of simplicity has been so driven into the holy-masked procession of other notions that in the end simplicity has etherealized into some transcendental meaning, instead of staying in Cincinnatian-like, clumsy chasteness.[199] For *'empeiria'* is not a philosophical opposite of 'speculation' in drama, but complete distancing from all drama — that is why the picture will be false when it becomes mysticized into sections belonging to drama in the history of philosophy.

This *empeiria*, Puritanical to baldness, can likewise go through the liturgy of lies like music, only with self-evidently more material tools — with words and pictorial analogues and thus as a naïve parallel to music, roughly this kind of procession will evolve: variant definitions one after the other, newer definitions around the words occurring in the definitions, the stylization of diptychs of broad antitheses arising from merely grammatical contradictions, with its constant rear-guard of organized similes until finally this flailing tautology automatically develops from itself a redeeming comparison, and at that point the process comes to a stop, one only has to sprinkle the whole thing retrospectively with a few trappings of true rationalism as if the preceding grammatical accidents had become the embryo fingers of logos. That is a much healthier situation because it shows the humorously human state when the theoretically absurd nature of miracles and the practical logicality of naïve truths unite: the natural history of dragons is written with just such a furnished brain, which contains a vast amount of scenery-like-ness but nevertheless seems to be utilitarianism, for there is so much semi-medical observation in it.

The word 'curiosity' most valuably expresses a type from which much could be expected, if it were to come into fashion again, even though it would come anew into the world with anti-rational burdens. It would be fairly entertaining if it were possible to definitively declare that no unique, single perfect 'attitude-to-truth' has ever led people to the truth, & the more truth one has uncovered, the further one gets from the pose and gesture that best resemble the ancient pattern of truth that lies at the bottom of all of life and existence; then one would have to decide in a healthy dilemma that was cut of old: to return to the era of the dragon's anatomy (or if not to dragons then to the attitudes of their biologists) and throw away every 'positive' and hygienic novelty in thinking, in the interest of a forgotten 'truth' lying in another direction — or carry on with the production of superbly working 'true precepts' and in that way possibly let slip the 'genuine' truth for the sake of a new, genuine variant of seaweed. *Un dragon? Comme c'est drôle*: & with that the matter was dropped.[200]

The healthiest grade of this empiricism is a superstition that will likewise have to be used as a treatment for the new thinking. (If one needed to define the path of the lie to a cure in a three-step analysis, then the sequence would be as follows: I. *de musica*: condemnatio fraudis; II. *de empirismo*: commentarii erroris; III. *de superstitione*: valores mytho-biologicæ.)[201]

Among the decorative methods of pseudo-expression I also ought to mention one that seems fairly valuable because it is lacking in consciousness *ad absurdum*, which cannot exactly be said of the first three, namely, the regularities of certain dreams and experiments serving to record them. Best are the dispositions of half-awakeness in the morning or the minutes immediately prior to falling asleep, or possibly the tiredness of a slight fever: I lie in bed and on the corridor the chambermaid is bringing breakfast. For her to be able to grasp the handle of the door to my room she is obliged to remove one of her hands from under the tray, hereupon it wobbles minimally, and for a moment a quiet, almost melodic noise arises from the plates, cups, spoons & jugs of water knocking together.

One is accustomed to controlling, as far as possible, every impression both logically & visually; that is one's first instinct here, too, but there are now two significant obstacles: one being the opaque door, the other & more important being my own laziness, the almost hundred-percent lack of nervous energy of my will, which inhibits me from turning toward the noise. However, a noise without a picture evokes an uncomfortable asymmetry. That, of course, calls out for me to restore the balance: that is indeed what I set out to do, and more particularly do so by the blindest and excessive application of the 'principle of the minimum expenditure of energy.' As if turning out abstract thoughts were easier for the mind, & associations relating to those abstractions slipped a lot more easily into the brain than those that were illustrated; at first I try to swing the noise into the balance of my mind not by visually supplementing the noise but by thinking along these lines: "life is full of disharmony, with a network of irritating responsibilities, the barbed wires of my relationships to people." For a moment that conditionally restores the balance: so exaggerated and large-scale is the moral commentary that it is able to approximately substitute for a naturalistic picture of a cup, along with the spoons and tray.

But, when it comes down to it, even at the bottom of that moral commentary is vision: the hypersensitivity of paying attention in a state of half-awakeness immediately registered the clinking in a slowed-down, analytical sound recording, so that certain elements of the rattling gave rise to a linear effect and were grasped in the form of dense stripes — that whole elementary line-like-ness, however, was not yet strong enough in the moment of its nascence to give rise to a single further pictorialization, and so it was as an assistant, as a springboard for the process of strengthening into picture form as it were, that it created a brief period of contemplation in which the lines turned into a moral net.

When I examine the true & hypocritical forms of 'expression' in general then it is possibly very useful indeed to pay attention to these dream resonances, these infinitesimally small pictorial echoes, because it is as if they were automatic strivings of the mind for expression: the most ancient amœba-movements of esthetic action and thus the main areas for 'bio-ornamental' experimentation. Here, for instance, we have hitherto seen as a reaction (the rhythm of unconscious reflex, however infinitely refined, is undoubtedly present in the artificial structure of the most arbitrary expression) a microscopically small and almost indeterminately short linearity, or rather linear impulses, immediately followed by a moral reflection, but the two came so quickly after each other that the possibility of exchanging simultaneity and succession naturally entailed with it a similar exchangeability of vision and reflection — and that is a fairly interesting '*milieu et moment*'[202] in examining the elements of expression. After reflex has replayed those two stages, it swings over into a third picture of by now painterly fullness, e.g., an agglomeration of golden needles, gradually growing and forming in quarter circles, fills the whole page from the lower right corner of the inside page of a book cover. I say 'golden needles,' but the whole point of those pictures is that, insofar as one perceives the constituent elements of our dreams as forms, instruments, & materials that are self-evident, positive, & in common use, so they are just as indefinable, similar to everything and nothing when one wakens: reflection, after the double impetus of abstract geometrical and abstract intellectual poles, has reached unreal hyper-plasticity; just as at the end of material one finds only a negative and positive charge, this trinity is to be found at the bottom of an artistic, or an 'adequate' expression, in general, in the prehistoric humus of unconsciousness — three charges in the atom of 'expression' (which is always a reflex).

This characteristic compilation picture as a final reaction to the clinking in front of the door resembles a pile of gramophone needles, hatpin ornaments bound together from tiny hummingbird feathers, matchsticks dipped too deeply in gold, and fans fronded together from brown ultra-lace, but all those indications of materials deem to be lamentable torsos when I recount to myself in the morning the naturalness of the picture.

From time immemorial it has been considered that one of the most miraculous things about the soul is that it assembles not by pasting fragments next to each other, but by transforming them chemically. As if it were mandatory for every impression to reach the collecting box of the mind in duplicate: one goes onto the shelves of the library (thinking is made up of the continual regrouping of those books), one is for absolute dissolving in some lake or other (dreaming consists of the automatic oscillation of these. Here 'dream' and 'thought' were taken in their banal senses — taken seriously, there is no difference between them). The chemical efficacy of an impression is very attractive to people on account of their natural torpidity, as it needs no energy, in contrast to the physical efficacy of an impression, which no longer plays out in the sweet choppy waters of the lake but among the strict rows of book shelves. These elemental chemical figures should be listed next to the three aforementioned forms of expression: IV. *de chemia psychologica …* [203]

return to the vision (cf. p. 641). A fleeting meditation about beauty; Eros ars veritas[204]

... there was a devout kinship, a natural transition of styles between the flowers of the cave of Venus and the mechanical elegance of girls thronging from the sea toward the shore: in those moments, the essence of the flowers was truly just the abstraction of color and line, whereas the fashioning and the color arrangement of swimsuits were only comprehensible insofar as they were continuations of flowers. It is as if it were a dramatized esthetic assumption in which one of the leading roles had been given to the mechanistic lily, the other to lilyfied female fashion, in order to arrive at a definition of beauty through love.

At first sight it seems to be a silly theatrical trick to link the academic evolution of the theory of beauty and the mystified technique of artificial infertility, but sometimes such non-stop reductions are necessary for truth-like symptoms to burst out onto the apron of the stage.

The young scholastic spectator suddenly poked his head forward like a hunting dog that is being driven insane by the smell of game but nonetheless has no idea where it is and, for that reason, whimpers at length in the imagined direction of the scent; as if, all at once, everything had become clear in the old complex of 'flower — female beauty — applied art — truth': the connections beamed like the white spines of sunny viaducts, causes and influences bloomed before him in such delirious proximity or half-mergence, like a fruit that had woken up from the flower on the branch at precisely that moment — he would have liked to rejoice because for him the Don Quixote question of "What is beauty?" was no longer so 'greyly' problematic.

When he bowed his head, however, suddenly his mind was again enveloped in darkness, and by the time he looked back at the picture, again all he saw was acting. Still lying in his hand like a charred scroll (which may still retain its exactly original form, but the first time thoughts are turned to it, it immediately powders away into insubstantial ashes) were old formula-stubs (...beauty is the intersection of amorphous vital energy and amorphous vital intelligence... graphic speculations about two pendulums, one of which is so big that it continuously completes a single sweep, departing & rising from the resting point, & another which describes only small oscillations before the other — combined drawings of the planes of oscillation of these two pendulums... et cetera), but before his eyes the connection between flowers & women, love & beauty, had already ceased to be sincere. He was in the humorous state that one will almost always attain if one makes an excursion into life with giraffized question marks — puritanical-looking conventional surmises which are as simple as the weapons of the Paleolithic Age as against sensually-complicated variety shows; an illegal show of corollaries around asthmatic matrons of 'basic concepts'; our truths are infinite Narcissuses, our themes are annoyingly merely decorative. At times like that the splenetic hours or minutes of fear of causality follow, in which truth formulas still continue, but the more public the disclosures of relations and layers the more it awakens in one the experience of mendacity — as if truth were suddenly being automated, & one rightly hates that.

The young scholastic also found it at first infinitely natural that the essence of flowers was in 'abstract' colors & abstract rhythms, that these were, so to say, the first microscopic froth of metaphysics that spilled over onto the lower plate of the earth (in tiered wells there are four, five, or ten such basins set under one another like a series of flat elderflowers); he found it just as natural that rhythm and color were the sense of girls (*vous croyez?*)[205] and thus for a second he enjoyed 'syllogized eroticism' instead of sexualized æsthetic (is a permanent summer of sense only to be found in dead words?); he, too, suddenly postulated a little theorilla (anew & not for the last time) that just as the eye is capable of receiving only part of incoming irradiations as colors, so the brain, too, is only capable of grasping a part of phenomena as thought truths, but it is possible to imagine a brain structure that is sensitive to infra-logical and ultra-logical truths as well, and for that brain, 'red' and 'yellow' will be rational percepts, et cetera, and therefore art, love, & truth are self-evidently the writhings of a single material under three kinds of sensory organs.

At the time, this triplet scale was no murky fog equation for him as in later centuries when the girlish-sleepiness of 'conjecture' threw a veil on the strict profile of the blazing sun — on the contrary, they were very raw timber columns in a village reason barn. When Father Alphonse first spoke about these connections he brought three matters to the attention of young minds. 'Conjecture' could not be of much satisfaction to the Father, one could see that from his exterior: a very old head, the face rugged, almost black, like a split beetroot, the brow and skull — above which fluttered sparse white cotton fluffs like wisps of morning clouds over a cold valley — a pale pink as if the peasant redness of life and the unbroken snow of thinking were mixing on him into a symbolic skullcap; a big, thick, soft nose, plaited in several directions like challah, with two tiny blue eyes inserted between the bends of his jug ears, in just the spot where they happened to fit in; when he prayed it sounded like the mutterings of someone conducting a defense case in court, spiked with all kinds of rude remarks, whereas each and every one of his amens was a singing lamentation.

It was hard to think of anything more grotesque than when he stood under a new statue of the Virgin Mary, slender as a reed,

& pointed at the picture with a palm of the hand (he never used fingers to point: the organ of analysis was the palm, the gesture that expressed accuracy was grabbing hold — though his hands rivaled ancient Assyrian pots with their clumsy lines), and with a quarrelsome, impatient accentuation, in the grumbling manner bachelors have (it is typical of this bachelor that the natural & artificial-scientific intelligence that had developed with the passing of years have become one — in him, truth became biologically identical to grumbling bachelorhood, which is a completely different link than the empty superficial mésalliance of 'science' & 'venerable age'), he explained that love was the starting point of everything, virtually prime matter that developed the animal duality of the mother & her son from its own intrusive solitude for it later to be realized in the Elysian dialogue of Jesus & his Mother; the investigation of beauty started with the philosophical, animal, and divine threefoldness of love (with an over-agitation of love with almost political extremity), he continued with praise of the beauty of the Virgin Mary, then, as a market auctioneer at a celestial auction, he considered the successive details of the exterior of the statue, hammering into the harshly washed heads of the young audience with his ball-shaped fist that only true superficiality will lead to the explanation of beauty, that essential matters are located in outward appearances (in its own time this was not a paradox-faced idea but a natural application of the commonplace that "*Deus est evidens*":[206] God constantly and ubiquitously strives to the surfaces with extraordinary tension, tearing through material and settling in millions of buds on the highest branches of material and reality; he imagined a practical dynamic in God's soul, which thus takes up position, in accordance to the laws of physics, like a fountain welling up in the communicating vessel of the world), & that art is based on work flowing from love, on the handiwork of overflowing love.

"Eros" here was the Virgin Mary, *"ars"* handiwork, *"veritas"* the human body: these similes and identity carnivals, of course, were soon withered by the warm winds of doubt — the caterpillar apportioned into the cocoon of hieratic masks assumed new forms, new experiments at a system floated before him around the old trinity: beauty's erotic (vital) and abstract (conceptual) elements lighted so sharply in the picture, with a glowing of the question that automatically melts it into a response, because it had two protagonists: woman & textile.

There were eras that constructed magnificent cathedrals or brought superb frescoes to maturity on the white foliage of walls, but the greatest artistic creation of the modern age is the architecture of women and textile arts. The design of the so-called new type of woman is an architectural task on which strict geometricians and small-town foreman-builders have worked. Today nothing is so perfect, nothing so commensurable to the great works of art of past ages, as the new, current woman and the textile arts that are in her service. It naturally intensifies the mixing of Eros & art to the utmost. It is obvious that the definition of beauty (*trattando l'ombre?*)[207] would not be brought into the world by the age in which the most beautiful pictures were painted or the best poems were written, but by times that are of the character of a specimen living on the energies of conjectures in which sounds the Circe-song of naïve extremes.

woman & beauty

As was said, a memory along the lines of the intersection of 'extreme abstraction' and 'primary life' went through his mind regarding the nature of beauty: yet all the same it was as if the female form now floating before him were showing that a too consistent vitality and brakeless abstraction are unable to offer an honest esthetic. The female body was a symbol of all life, her clothes and the surrounding objects of the applied art — a symbol of every abstraction: but as has been said, just as photographs of Platonic ideas seem to be clinical specialties, here as well, when the constituent elements of a definition were accomplished with overzealous plasticity (beauty is equivalent to 'life and abstraction,' but on the other hand, life is straightway equivalent to woman, abstraction equivalent to an elegant dress), he got something significantly different from what the definition was prepared for (for that reason any kind of imitation of style, if made by a person who can be made extremely hysterical in matters of logic, is something exciting & original, but then that sort of thing is rarely encountered in history; the relationship of Greek architecture & fantastic Baroque architectural fantasies, which exists only in Indian ink sketches, likewise consists of the re-realization of reality & the definition of reality, showing the extremes of cocaine usage to which an instinct of searching for the essence leads, eternally leaving the well-known moral at the end of the story: the pristine purity of the 'essence' and the unruliness of frivolous epigonism are psychologically identical).

This 'modern woman' was a type of hieroglyph in which one can still perceive the quivering of a bird's wings but which already includes the timeless anonymity of an algebraic sign; her main beauty lay in the dithyrambic negativity that it emanated, the darkening and fragrant tragedy of beauty, as if one always finds the superlative of beauty most completely where the grey homily that 'beauty is impossible' asserts itself most splendidly. At that moment the following definition of beauty shone with almost the softness of a tune: "beauty is that which reveals most elegantly the non-existence of the concept of beauty."

There is a self-consuming propensity about beautiful things; works of art of the highest rank are self-destructive; precisely by virtue of the vertiginous straining of perfection they radiate with smiling melancholy the modest but perpetual denial of "this is not *that*." From a sentimental point of view it is a very ordinary experience when harmony and tragedy, culmination of proportion and sterile blaséness, are identical, but invaluable are the moments when, tired of the games of our limited little neuroses, all of a sudden, as a landscape from an outside world that has nothing to do with us but has existed forever, all the things that we deemed to be mere asinine flirting of our emotions appear with positive outlines at the edge of a distance: what hitherto had been philistine drowsiness in us now all at once beckons toward us with startling outlines from the outside world in this kind of form: "in the big world order there also exist certain negatives, not as a nervousness of deficiency, but as facts."

Beauty is nothing more than rendering perceptible the role of the concrete negative in the world order — that is what came to mind when he looked at the woman. That negative naturally cannot contain any kinship with the known meaning of the word: it is not nothing, not a flirtatious counterpart of beings, nor some sort of underhand maneuver in logic, not a heresy against life, but something different, the material of beauty. It was also typical that the whole comedy was organized by the old pater out of a certain *vanitatum vanitas* inspiration,[208] and nevertheless in the end, where a sharp accent of criticism fell, he seemed to proclaim that beauty served its own end, as if the most malicious satire would automatically transform into a defense, signaling that "*difficile est apologiam non scribere.*"[209] As a result the makeshift criticism of sterility metamorphosed (or rather it did not metamorphose as that was simply what it was) into a nice experimental game: abortion was not a moral torso but the conclusion of the theory of beauty.

the physician sets about the surgical operation

— You might perhaps take your coat off — said the visional physician with a smile as he leapt behind the woman's weary back, waiting with arms eager to be of assistance for the costume jacket to be taken off and indicating with his eyes to a little helper who was a cross between a naïve executioner-extra and a blasé medical student. For a second the woman looked up at the Donatello-masquerader declaiming his rights; his figure, bent hollow-chested in a semicircle, was in stark contrast to the arrogant gesture with which the physician waited for her to take off her coat; as if for a minute the gently didactic antithesis of *'façon'*[210] & man could be seen — the physician's politeness-dance was not addressed at the person but at the technique of humanity, the ironic and symbolic routine of women, with which the real woman had nothing to do: the perfect woman's dress is always a vivid caricature — it was that woman fused into a dress-irony to whom the physician's waving movement was addressed: "You might perhaps take your coat off."

The woman suddenly straightened, and although she now completely filled the dogmatic borders of irony set by the cut of the dress, she coquettishly retained an appetizing surplus of the tragedy of her race.

— No, I won't take it off, I have to hurry, and anyway this room is very draughty — whereupon in the region of her hips she pulled together the two enormous clacking buttons of her green coat, which (they quietly clicked on her ring) were heavier than all the textile.

The helper jumped over to the window & pulled it down: the glass pane was so gigantic that one couldn't hear any movement or noise, only a thickening of the gloom, like in a glass of water into which a white powder is suddenly sprinkled. The red-suited boy managed to leave the spot with a Hamletian ancillary gesture: half weeping, half in adolescent unruliness, he cut his way through the girls flocking on the beach, squeezing their necks with his white hands with enough force for the blood to appear on his brow, though all his hands were to the girl's neck was windblown feather grass. The monkeys crouched darkly and with an endless monotone emitted a single grumbling sound: a sleepy yelping, a bestial sorrow. The sky darkened, the water swept the flowers away like the mud-steeped girders of a corroding ship, & in the middle the surgical light blazed blindingly white.

— Oh, you're ready as quickly as this? You're like confectioners or scrupulous cooks, you jump and dance around so much.

— Come this way by these small steps.

the heroine & her woman friend

A short little woman burst into the room through one of the doors: in one hand she was dangling a straw hat, under her armpit a huge handbag with its top askew, with two crumpled fashion magazines in it (like protruding slices of ham between two pieces of a roll); the rolled-up lapels of her opened coat were also rumpled, topping all that were the lace ornaments of the blouse squeezed out of the coat — the whole ensemble was like a cross-section of a savoy cabbage, in which, funnel-like, the inner leaves were cut shorter, the outer ones longer. She plumped herself down in an armchair, jammed the handbag and fashion magazines into her lap, and spread the coat wide open like two lazy wings of a diptych that has tired of being closed, whereat the squeezed wave of the lace insert suddenly smoothed down in her chest and with a peaceful shiver jumped back into shape — the insert somewhat resembled Rococo-era men's neckties; it was fresh, like an artificial aerial flower, & although it as good as covered the whole chest (it had been ironed in the way that flower sellers habitually twist paper to wrap a bowl and excessively bare branches), the Egyptianly-'correct' and cool line of the body under it could still be seen clearly.

— You still here, are you? — she asked in amazement. — I guessed as much, by the way... I guessed you are here. I heard something to that effect, but it never occurred to me that it would take so long...

— I think we'll be done soon.

— That's right — said the physician with a laugh and pushed the white table further. The heroine adjusted her dress and while she fastened, as if even with her voice, on her two-piece suit a button that was not easily seen and hard to reach, asked in a distracted tone:

— So, has the plan to tighten the girdle worked out?

— I have no interest in tightening the girdle or in doing the Lacedaemonian Leap. Guess what an appalling dilemma I was in: my tailor merged with Robert and today was their unveiling show. How could I go when it's not even been half a year since Robert dumped me? That is really tragic, I reckon: when you have to get your old sheik to make your clothes. Pay him for leaving me? Utterly grotesque, I must say.

— There's no need for you to go without fail to the launch. After all, your tailor can show you his stuff separately, you can easily arrange things so that Robert gets no wind of it.

— What a comedy that would be! Going in secret to my tailor, ordering things under a pseudonym, constantly trembling that my old sheik might turn up the next minute? Or am I to make appointments for him to come round at night? Dreadful.

— You could send Octavia, she's got good taste.

— I know, but she's a tricky devil, she's capable of singing the praises of the scruffiest rags so I won't look pretty and she won't be shown up for not having any money. It would be madness to put any trust in Octavia.

— I don't believe she's like that.

— You don't believe it? You should have seen how awfully she behaved last year in Paris. She got drunk in the buffet, and afterwards, half howling with laughter, half choking in jealousy, she hung around one countess after another, blurting out all manner of insults and flatteries. The sort of woman who has only one dress to their name is a pest — all she wants is to win allies among other one-dress women and slaughter those who have ordered two or three.

She got up and, hand on hip, asked: — Is it worth waiting? — Without taking a look at her wristwatch, she gave her wrist a slap.

---

death arrives with its ravens

A sound of crowing and a chaotic flapping of wings came from the ceiling and the next minute several big ruffled black birds dropped down as if some places in the sky had first become blackened with lead, then one of the ends of the dark area had snapped off like stage scenery that was on fire and tumbling down, and the shapeless fans of clumsy, dusty feathers were bursting forth from behind it. Pushing forward among the ungainly bodies of the birds, like a belated actor through a thronging crowd of overzealous extras, a gentleman in a black stovepipe hat and mourning wear approached, at times elbowing birds aside (one of the wings of some of them was still completely grown into the clouds, like a torso only one end of which has been modeled by the sculptor), sometimes snatching off his resonant top hat, hitting its brim with a big clacking against their beaks. Even before he could fully disentangle himself, he began to speak loudly:

— Actually, I needn't have come in person, still less with this gallery of ornithological heralds; it would've been enough to send a single elegant little black feather, or indeed not even that, and just infect the participants psychologically, tastefully, and modernly, but nevertheless I was overcome by some old-age or childish conservatism, & I thought that, even if I can no longer appear in my old picturesqueness or dramatic splendor, I can still arrange a spectacular little parade in a place where, when all is said and done, I am honored with a quite positive ceremony. I won't tell you my name because it sounds highly grotesque by way of an introduction, but even when nameless I am fairly explicit.

For a moment the physician was dumbfounded, but then he said with a laugh:

— Oh, it's you? But we are very old acquaintances, relatives even, somehow or other, on my mother's side of the family — only, of course, I long forgot that mythical role of yours. To be honest, I was not prepared for it. As best I know, if I were to offer you a seat, you would take that to be parody. But would you be so kind as to tidy up your birds. They are very dusty, & you aren't too elegant yourself.

The heroine suddenly rose up on the bed: the sun was not shining at all, only two beams of yellow light were scattered as if in the dense darkness it were a material that did not dissolve, only snaked back and forth in the foreign liquid, with growing cohesion, like rolling streaks of sealing wax in the seconds before setting — one of them fell on the woman, the other on her 'son,' who was lying palely, like a cadaver, among the branches of a bush with gigantic thorns; the lower branches of the bush were full of leaves, while even lower (as if it was a waxworks-performance of Ovidian verse) the body parts of the swim-suited girls swayed already half as branches, half as water, with slender white legs. The speckled blotches of the swimming costumes were capricious big flowers, like living coats of arms of mechanized beauty — their hair spread into yellow snake boughs, as a botanical esthetic of raw eroticism — above those, however, tangled bare branches like some sort of cage-like iron nest from which moon-colored spikes protruded: at the top, as between the claws of a crab, lay the disavowed child in golden light.

Choking, the doctor started yelling:

— There is a limit to everything, to bragging as well, so let's cut this vulgar comedy to the end. Why have you extinguished everything? Right now? Hey, where's my assistant gone to, heeey!

The next moment the assistant jumped out with a small dark lantern. The sun's two beams had also already ceased, all that shivered above the woman's body like a hypochondriac bee was the small electric light. The woman quietly moaned like a cat in the bone-dumb night:

— Done? done? dooone?

In the corner a rustling could be heard like the opening of a light paper parcel; on the wall of darkness, like an X-ray embellishment, the woman friend who had arrived not long before with a grey dimness staggered: she blossomed into her own symbolic anagram, from which the strangest algebraic formulas transpired — including propositions like "the morphology of fashionability is identical to the morphology of death." The night was like a primitive school blackboard, & the girl's grey outlines like a deduction that had been chalked on it. They were exact signs, though they had no resemblance to writing nor numbers — they were simply alternating abstract motifs of her life, neither analyses of figure, nor analyses of associations, but something much simpler, more logical, more self-evident. Two heads could be seen in the ring of light of the small dark lantern, one naked body, and a tired woman's hand with a green coat and dangling gloves drooping like the hanging lamb in the insignia of the Order of the Golden Fleece. Sometimes a glass clinked as if a metal tool had been dropped on or lifted off it. The next moment the two heads vanished from the ring of light.

---

death's speech. The heroine dies: end of the vision

— Ready! — a sharp cry could be heard in the dark, but it was not the physician's voice. The darkness suddenly lifted, and the figures of the woman friend became sharp & colored.

— Ready. But at least truly & consistently ready — said the man with the flock of dark birds. — I have discreetly and quietly attended so many of those sorts of ceremonies that it was time I warned you that the deity to whom sacrifices are made genuinely exists. I know that for a while my concreteness has been dependent on a pensioner's world of anachronisms, and I have played the part of all kinds of refined substitutes, aside from the banal ancient cases. I've started to have enough with the fact that wherever I was evoked, they would always talk about someone else, indeed, precisely about my greatest adversary. It was too much that, with the greatest naivety, my liturgical dance, which certain handbooks used to call agony — "*Mme dans sa candeur naïve*"[211] — was proclaimed to be vitalism. As a matter of fact, I was always keen on contrasts & brutal paradoxes, because it is my deep-seated opinion that they do not signify the dancing balance of truth, but the gallows humor of decay — yet, ladies and gentlemen, you have too much of a good thing, and I can't deny that with me consistency of craftsmanship (you may well have guessed it by yourselves) is stronger than my languid estheticizing moments. My strong side, when it comes down to it, has always been that of an empiricist in drawing conclusions and the rough-and-tumble of acting: it's true that I sometimes psychologize myself to bits as a Proteus, and I pay visits on my clientele in the incorporeal form of opalizing nervous complaints, but that is all just mosaic art, deliberate dilettantism, which can amuse one for a while, but is soon taken for granted and bamboozled into all manner of eccentric and untruthful list of names. Well now, I resume what, admittedly, is the nasty craft of consistency and play out the histrionics. If my personality and productions are a downright offense against the principles (that I, too, was fond of, though in a somewhat over-Platonic sense) of social and artistic taste, at least I satisfy certain just demands of the intellect. On this hygienic white table that I so favored the lady is dead. Death is a big energy, not just a hint, not just a treatable shadow for hypochondriacs. I will admit, there are times when I can be wayward in showing off that energy, but now I blessed my hand with logic as well. That is the practical side of matters. On the other side, you can see a deduction where I briefly signal (jumping over a lot of intermediate propositions) what a positive factor I am in the chemistry of the most elementary functions of life, and that those chemical equations can be transformed with a few simple arithmetical tricks in such a way that my decisive participation is made obvious. I know that this is boastfulness, but that is such an old appendage to my way of operating that it would be snobbery on my part to communicate these matters to you in an all at once humble tone. On that note I have ended: I am not in the habit of expressing myself in branching points but in a monotone lecture style. My birds will carry away that young man with the mien of an actor who tried to wring as much theatricality as possible from non-existence, but for vanquishing whom just as much strength was called for on my part as for the finales of much older colleagues — and my birds will carry away his mother, who was a bit too stupid to evade my peasant and jealously practical brain. I'll carry off that doctor gentleman as well, because, to be frank, I wish to hold a little demonstration apart from the usual harvest to steady my nerves. It is my belief that this bunch was too limited in proclaiming the universality of life and erotic beauty, so that I, too, am therefore obliged to present the universality of death in tableau fashion. Both you & I know that one need not take that universality literally, with such tragic pedantry, as is suggested by this awkward scene, but I too have party passions, I too have overreactions, and I have given them full vent. I won't say "Till we meet again," because sometimes I am better able to keep my humor under control than my deeds. It was you who provoked what I have done — & with his top hat he seized altogether the woman friend, the 'Mother,' the physician, the assistant, the 'child,' & a few other symbolic, shuddering figures.

Sachlichkeit & anti-materiality in modern fashion

One has a sense of a certain scale of identity from these three elements: fashionability — vision — death. For expressing sensitivity to identicalness the theatrical, Ovidian technique, is naturally always more appropriate than the logical and honest way. I set before my eyes an amazingly fair & square Parisian woman: her superb but short hair, red as copper, is stuck to one of her cheeks in eel-stripes like the patterns on some bookbinding papers that are ploughed into the paint with a broad-toothed comb — on the other side of her head is a little white cap crocheted from a thick, coarse string material with huge holes, not askew but vertical, like a drying net. The padded mass of soft but strictly modeled, golden-red hair is in sharp contrast to the splintery, clumsily curving lines of the Emmenthaler weave cap. Running right round the edge of the cap is a short little double wave of pale-pink veil material, like a colored shadow or hypothetical butterfly: a foreign and coquettish doubt, poised between the color tensions of hair & cap.

On the body a white coat, which is stretched to bursting point on the shoulder blades but in front suddenly loosens, is seized by a toga-like languor and at the same time starts to turn grey before turning into startling black lapels after three or four shell-ribbed wrinkles craving for each other. The whole coat is an asymmetrical triangular revers between the legs of which are prologue-wrinkles arousing an ironic impression. The skirt is white, like the blazing-hot funnel of a luxury yacht in the sun, and whilst the stifling pose of the blackness of stylized night emanates from the lapel, the skirt is as full of dry and clear mundaneness as an unused towel in an hotel room. On the side, with deliberately vulgar stitching, is sewn a rose-tinted tulle snake (just like on the cap), seeking malapropos discreet excitement in the spectator.

A woman dressed like that never gives the impression that she is a mere patchwork of practical ornaments, but a momentary constellation of faddish yet symbolically frivolous energies. The hair is a streaming cascade sweeping toward the spherically-slippery landscape of the shoulders with coppery opalization, above it (in the rustling haze of reddish reflexes), grotesquely solitarily, flies the snow-white string net that the big gestures of the wind had also tossed a bit into the air: a landscape, full of thirsty and luxuriating disproportionalities, the essence of which is a healthy cynicism toward the solidities of the material world.

The material of hair and string are very antithetical — one of them hypocritical and lazy as water, which embraces all forms with perverse exaggeration, its whole life consists of improvising pedantic negatives of every merely cursorily acquaintance from its own body — the string, on the other hand, is rough and stiff, like decrepit veins which spin a gnarled wire hedge against the body's original forms: how far from elegant would be a cap which tried to carry on the hair's suggestion of material (and the references inherent in it) like a sentence left as a torso — sometime and somewhere that, too, was elegance, but an evil and immoral elegance because it was flattery toward material (servile snuggling up to the bodiness of the body): that kind of thing always consists of grouping materials in accordance to, in the strict sense of the word, a '*materia-*'list point of view, as if in things (gems, cloths, etc.) there were some creditable system, a cunning, microscopic hierarchy, or a sensitively trembling connection to which the female body and person had to adapt.

It's all mannered materialism: 'discreetness,' 'fineness,' 'harmony' and 'tasteful' all belong to its lexicon. A tired pessimism runs through a woman dressed in such 'taste' and so 'finely' — her body is wiltedly stationed among selected materials. On the other hand, the string tatter that has been nominated as a cap: it laughs loudly at the bow before every material, doesn't give a damn about the subtleties of transitions and the cheap illusion of 'harmony' — harmony is also what the illustrious little bit of rag on her head represents, like a sparrow explosion that had freshly sprung there, but it has enough Christian astuteness to know that harmony is not a notion of chromatics, of tactile-consistency or comfort, but of chuckling defiance. It represents the kind of frivolity from which moral sense sprinkles, as from a fountain that is suddenly caught on one side by the wind.

When one looks at a woman like that, the first lesson can only be that material is senseless, textiles are a ludicrous clown-gear, animals' furs are a transient-masquerade, jewels are a jest accidentally turned into material. That, though, is moral enough for a streetcar-stop impression. These two good properties are lacking from 'finely' dressed women: the possibility of landscape vision and Christian nonchalance vis-à-vis sleeping objects. A part of humanity considers it perversity that leading tailors create women's garments, hats, and shoes from the most impossible materials, with a pathological forcing of incoherence: that is truly perversity from the standpoint of the material, but it is morally simple, indeed in a theoretical plane it is a downright ascetic matter from the viewpoint of the human soul, which is familiar with just one order: its own creative whim, the inconsistent surf-dance of its own will.

The string cap was not long-lasting & not much time was needed to make it: there was no time-masked deceptive prestige of 'work' behind it, before it not many months that it will endure — it was thrown together by a tousled Parisian milliner in under five minutes, and it will disintegrate after the first rain like the vineyard's label on a bottle of wine that is stood in water. But it is just as well that that is the way they are, because the dress has to be short-lived, beauty has to bloom full of anxiety every minute: the shadow of anachronism-intrigue has to roam in its proximity — otherwise it will become respectable & eventually we shall believe that there is something positive in material, that perchance some wise reality is slumbering in fine styles with a long life, like a tortoise.

It is also fitting that nowadays, when artists and fashion designers presume to respect material for the sake of material, rawness for the sake of God-given rawness: precisely now it is not a ponderous materialist-lesson that is epilogized at the end of the game but an impertinent clip on the ear against material that has lost all authority: the lattice of twine that is swinging above the woman's hair in keeping with unknown but in any case drunken gravitations is undoubtedly the most extreme honoring of material, indeed, if you will, its apotheosis, after all, there is nothing there but string, the whole thing is two and a half meters of string woven, in the simplest manner in the world, like the squares in an arithmetic exercise book, or in other words '*Sache für Sache*'[212] — and what is the result? The most unmistakable cynicism in the face of dignity, interpreted with bureaucratic obtuseness, both of man as of material — the whole thing is ethereal, floating, immaterial: maximal concreteness, material materializing for itself is full of irony, freshly tingling uncertainty and doubt of material.

If one compares this allusion of a cap, '*ur-sachlich,*'[213] to the point of immateriality (after all, it is not a cap, only this naked, but sharp proposition: "how ridiculous it is that a person has to wear a cap"), with an old hat creation one has the impression that when a lot of material is juxtaposed (velvet, stones, copper buckles, veil, silk, cardboard and plush), set in a nice 'composition': that is spiritual, whereas the one and only piece of material is material. The intentions, of course, played the game throughout in the reverse order, as perhaps always: when complicated hat structures were assembled, the idea was that the spirituality of the designers had won over material's massive irrationality; now the '*sachlich*'-designers have sought to free material from the intrusive style-superfluousness of the human mind in order thereby to marvel in the scarlet-matte of brick, in the autonomous-nudity of wooden sheets, or in the Calvinist-solitude of whitewashed backdrops.

Nowadays we can see well that it was precisely in the old hat that material suppressed spirituality, whereas materialistic material stripped of style pluses impels the soul forever toward the slippery world of uncertainties, silverly glittering assumptions, and transience. Dispatching this abstract tirade to the more honest stage of history, no doubt many kinds of variants of *Sachlichkeit* will stand before us, and there is a chance these will include some which have not reached (in the way Parisian fashion and applied art unquestionably did reach) the modest tenet of "absolute material = maximal hypothesis," but truly remained plaster Narcissized in plaster, or in other words, where material-simplicity did not become so extremely simple that the metaphysical openness of mono-elementariness became excitingly visible; there the *Sachlichkeit* is impure because it did not look for the truly uttermost borders of material but was satisfied with an external puritanism, with clumsily geometrical poverty.

In practice, for example, an impure (and thus falling far from every automatic morality) *Sachlichkeit* is the huge number of urban tenement blocks, which are more bleak cartridges of predestination than realizations of the cleanness of material: these houses are 'simple' only in a stylistic sense, but in the biological sense of material, not at all. The 'notion' of simplicity is a genuinely moral concept: but houses that are in accord only with that 'concept' will not become ethical.

On the other hand, take a luxury villa made of glass (the sole, monotonous, but active hero of this book), the furniture of which consists only of that couple of grey shadows cast by a few panes of frosted glass among the other layers of glass; the staircase connecting the two stories seems to be no more than a snaking copper spring from a distance (like in a transparent horror box, where the head of a jack-in-the-box is pressed under the lid of the box on the end of a spring); the only ornament for the façade is a flat waterfall which, all the same, is maybe the fulcrum of the whole building — that is the sole massive axis around which, actually, everything else is just chiaroscuro: its cement is mere mirroring, its concrete is periodic interference. This is not a house built according to an ethical concept of simplicity, but a perverse luxury villa, but it is created from the extreme limits of materials.

Anything that is 'anything' here is as if it would only drop from the pallid petals of a medieval lip as strict and cold anther. The girl with the string netting is therefore elegant because a need for a vision of moral value emanates peremptorily from inside her; at first, of course, it is only that naïve, literal vision in which the string caps become an otherworldly net, the thick red hair a cascade, the waves of which relate to each other in form and motion like the crazy wheels of a locomotive that are accompanied by a revealing movement of the pistons into the womb of speed.

Endnotes

1. The word "Greenwich" is in English in the original. All further instances of Szentkuthy's own English will be signified with the font Scala Sans.
2. Pure And-ness, absolute So-dom.
3. A Latin phrase coined by Szentkuthy, meaning roughly: An opening is forever additive.
4. Inversion of the inscription on ancient Roman constructions: "Made by the Pontifex Maximus" (i.e., President of the Pontifical College of senior citizens who ruled over the city), literally chief bridge-building priest or pontiff.
5. *The Studio* was an illustrated magazine on fine and decorative art published out of London (1893–1964).
6. Objective Person, presumably in the sense of *Neue Sachlichkeit* (New Objectivity), a term coined in 1923 by Gustav Hartlaub, director of the Kunsthalle in Mannheim, as the title of an exhibition he mounted to display a new post-WWI trend of representational rather than abstract art (e.g., Otto Dix, Georg Grosz, et cetera).
7. In 16th-century Late Latin, *ens* (pl. *entia*), meaning literally 'being' (from Latin *esse*, 'to be'), meant a real thing (an entity) as opposed to an attribute.
8. In quantum mechanics, the concept of matter waves or de Broglie waves reflects the wave-particle duality of matter, the theory being proposed by the French physicist Louis de Broglie (1892–1987) in 1924, giving rise to the de Broglie hypothesis that any moving particle or object has an associated wave. A de Broglie equation relates the wavelength *É*... to the momentum (p), and frequency (f) to the kinetic energy (E) of a particle. In 1934, de Broglie also advanced a neutrino theory of light, according to which a photon is equivalent to the fusion of two neutrinos.

9. "Truth is founded in the being of things." Thomas Aquinas, *Scriptum super libros Sententiarum* (Sentences of Peter Lombard), Book 1, Distinction 19, Question 5, a. 1).
10. My sinner (transgressor), Leatrice.
11. I don't believe because it is credible?
12. Ruled by Externals.
13. For My Body.
14. Max von Laue (1879–1960), a German winner of the Nobel Prize in Physics (1914), laid the groundwork for X-ray crystallography by surmising that the regular arrangement of points in a crystal would serve to produce diffraction effects on incident X-radiation.
15. Szentkuthy's own Latin: propriety is a gleaming afternoon refri-gerator.
16. A tax levied by regularly debasing the coinage of the realm with ignoble metal (such as copper) and requiring compulsory exchange of all money ("for the profit of the treasury") by the Hungarian Árpádian kings (e.g., a yearly tax on all coinage brought in by Andrew II in 1222).
17. By the book.
18. Re-embarkation for Cythera.
19. We will not [i.e., do not wish to] know.
20. This roughly translates as "Heideggerian 'Ahead-of-itself in already-being-in' & Neue Sachlichkeit [New Objectivity]: Nothingness as Thing." The reference is entirely spurious, intended to give an impression of familiarity (or as a satire) with German philosophy, as Antal Szerb noted in the second paragraph of his review of *Prae*: "References do occur, but strictly to non-existing books." See the journal *Erdélyi Helikon*, № 8–9 (1934) 547–49. Reprinted in *A mítosz mítosza. In memoriam Szentkuthy Miklós*, ed. Gyula Rugási (Budapest: Nap Kiadó, 2001) 20–23. An English translation can be found in *Hyperion: On the Future of Aesthetics*, Vol. 7, № 2 (July 2013) 93–96.
21. To the lesser glory of Heisenberg.
22. Being or existence in the most general abstract sense; entity.
23. Developed first in Florence in the early 15th century, principally by Filippo Brunelleschi, this emphasized symmetry, proportion, geom-

etry, and the regularity of parts (e.g., each of the eight segments of the dome of Florence Cathedral was constructed by a different sector of the city).

24. God: a Jumble of Boundaries.

25. A possible reference to Nietzsche's enigmatic phrase "circulus vitiosus deus." Cf. *Beyond Good and Evil* §56, and Pierre Klossowski's *Nietzsche & the Vicious Circle.*

26. Suetonius attributed the phrase *alea iacta est* ("The die has been cast") to Julius Cæsar, who supposedly pronounced it as he led his army across the Rubicon in Northern Italy to begin a long civil war against Pompey.

27. A pseudo-Heideggerian coinage meaning roughly: "The woman's making herself unauthentic to win being-there."

28. In Greek mythology, Atlantides was the name given to the Pleiades, the daughters of Atlas & Pleione. In order to save them from being pursued by Orion and his dog Sirius, Zeus first transformed Atlas & Pleione into doves, then stars, thereby creating the Pleiades. Cf. Hesiod's *Works and Days.*

29. A well-established saying in Hungarian is *úgy tükröződik (benne), mint vízcseppben a tenger* — "It reflects (in it) like the sea in a droplet of water" — all the typical properties of a whole are apparent in a small part (i.e., like breeds like, et cetera).

30. Behold the blossom of deceit.

31. Villefranche-sur-Mer, near Nice & Monaco, has one of the deepest natural harbors in the Mediterranean Sea.

32. The Gay Parrot.

33. Szentkuthy uses a Hungarianized version of the German *Spieß-bürgertum.*

34. I hate the unholy [rabble].

35. Preeminence, distinction, excellence.

36. I.E., at the age of 58. The personage is presumably an invention of Szentkuthy's.

37. Solveig is a Scandinavian female given name and probably hints at the plaited braids that the character Solveig in Henrik Ibsen's *Peer Gynt* typically used to don in Szentkuthy's time.

38. "Brehm's *Life of Virgins*" — a pun on the title of a 10-volume encyclopedia co-authored by Alfred Brehm (1829–84) and commonly known as *Brehms Tierleben* (Brehm's *Life of Animals*), first published in the 1860s.

39. François-Louis Cailler (1796–1852) was the first Swiss producer of chocolate. The company Cailler (now owned by Nestlé SA) still makes the Frigor brand of luxury chocolates.

40. Richard Dedekind (1831–1916) was a German mathematician who made important contributions to abstract algebra (particularly ring theory) and algebraic number theory. In 1888, he published a short monograph titled *Was sind und was sollen die Zahlen?* (What are numbers & what should they be?)

41. Sophie, Countess of Ségur (née Sofiya Feodorovna Rostopchina, 1799–1874) was a French writer of Russian birth, now best known for her novel *Les Malheurs de Sophie* (Sophie's Misfortunes).

42. Assicurazioni Generali S.p.A. is the largest insurance company in Italy and one of the largest in Europe, with headquarters in Trieste.

43. Cf. "I will not go to Canossa" (where Holy Roman emperor Henry IV sought pardon before Pope Gregory VII in 1077).

44. Literally: Be gone, Satan!

45. Summers as opposed to years of age.

46. Danzig (Polish: Gdansk) was a semi-autonomous city-state within the province of West Prussia, a so-called Free City, which existed between 1920 & 1939 when *Prae* was first published.

47. Latin for a morally lost woman, i.e., harlot.

48. Kontor is an archaic German word for 'office' while the Latin title translates as *Institutes of the Christian Religion* (Calvin's seminal work, published in 1536).

49. Tasteful Gomorrah: a German Hypothesis.

50. Angel's skin.

51. Hermann Minkowski (1864–1909) was a mathematician who used geometrical methods to solve problems in number theory, mathe-matical physics, & the theory of relativity. Szentkuthy also refers to him in §9 of *Towards the One and Only Metaphor* (Contra Mundum Press, 2013).

52. The primal substance — a concept dealt with by Hegel, especially vis-à-vis Schelling.

53. The historical origin of tone is called tono-genesis, with tono- meaning stretching, tension, or tone. Præsens = 'at hand, in sight, present, in person.'

54. Ψ is the wave function of the quantum system published by the Austrian physicist Erwin Schrödinger in 1926 (just eight years before *Prae* was first printed).

55. A Few Remarks Concerning the Legitimate Source of Narrative Poetry, or the Adventure Novel as Absolute Analysis.

56. Sketch of a Transcendental Topography of France.

57. Ernest Rutherford, 1st Baron Rutherford of Nelson (1871–1937), a New Zealand-born physicist, became known as the father of nuclear physics.

58. Presumably a reference to the secret revelation of the Apostle John, in which John sees the heavenly throne with a rainbow around it, having "the One" seated in it (Rev. 4:3).

59. In Greek mythology, Deucalion (said to have been aged 82 at the time), with the aid of his father Prometheus, was saved from a deluge Zeus had caused in his anger at the Pelasgians, surviving (somewhat like Noah or rather, Noah somewhat like him...) by building a chest in which to hide.

60. A porcelain factory has existed at Veilsdorf, Thuringia, in Germany, since 1762 (cf. the first in Europe was at Meissen, since 1710).

61. Literally: the end to which, i.e., the aim, the terminal point.

62. Szentkuthy's own cod Latin, meaning roughly: everywhere here inflammation is aroused.

63. Cross-blooming here is intentional arousal, or rather about the identity of Motion & Space: stability is a virtual space, and Motion is always the same space, but alive.

64. Plural of *Eigenbild*, meaning roughly: self-image.

65. I.E., French for shock, impact, knock.

66. The Calais-Mediterranée Express, *le train bleu*, was a luxury night express train, which operated from 1886 to 2003.

67. Landscape included.

68. Quantum numbers describe values of conserved quantities in the dynamics of a quantum system. A quantized system requires at least one quantum number.

69. Gaius Mucius Scævola was a Roman youth, famous for his bravery. In 508 BC, during the war between Rome and Clusium, the Clusian king Lars Porsena laid siege to Rome. Mucius attempted to murder Porsena but mistakenly killed Porsena's scribe. He was captured and thrust his right hand into a fire that was lit for sacrifice and held it there without giving any indication of pain, thereby earning for himself and his descendants the cognomen Scævola ('left-handed').

70. *On the Ontological Masking of Hysteria in Modern Myth-Interpretation* (Heidelberg, 1932). Probably a fictitious reference, though it indicates Szentkuthy's early familiarity with the thinking of Heidelberg *et al.* in Germany.

71. Hamiltonian Differential Calculation of Transerotic Love, or the Symmetrical Coefficients of Antivital Bio-sexuality. A spurious reference, possibly parodying the work of Wilhelm Reich, whose seminal book, *Die Funktion des Orgasmus: Zur Psychopathologie und zur Soziologie des Geschlechtslebens*, was published in 1927.

72. *Erotic Syllogistics of the Mirror.*

73. Female cardinal.

74. Aristotle distinguished a genus proximus ('nearest genus') from its differentia specifica ('specific difference'), with the differentia being the set of attributes that unambiguously distinguished members of the species from other members of the same genus.

75. *On Morbid Hyperontics and Polylinear Zeroscopy as Neurotic Binary Constants.*

77. *János Háry* is a Hungarian folk opera in four acts (premiered in 1927) by Zoltán Kodály, based on the story of a veteran in the 19th-century Austrian hussars who spends his days sitting in the village inn and entertaining listeners with tales of his derring-do.

77. The book title is given by Szentkuthy in English. The person in question is Ernest Rutherford, 1st Baron Rutherford of Nelson.

78. Attitude to Culture and So-called Pure Reason.

79. "In principle there was the flower" (cf. John 1:1: *In principio erat Verbum* ... (In the beginning was the Word ...)
80. The word seems to be of Szentkuthy's own coining (also written as "syn-opia" in the original), possibly relating to synopsis, though as far back as 1853 several marine amphipods (crustaceans) were given the generic name *Synopia* (*Synopia angustifrons* Dana, *S. gracilis* Dana, & *S. ultramarina* Dana).
81. Greek for form, shape.
82. Russian for brothers.
83. A shot of Venice.
84. Roughly: a fit of profanity / swearing.
85. Roughly: adore through slander.
86. Insight or outline.
87. A painting by Meindert Hobbema entitled *The Avenue at Middelharnis* (painted in 1689) is now held by the National Gallery, London, Great Britain.
88. French for conforming to accepted standards: correct, proper.
89. Meaning approximately Linea = line, Anadyomene = Greek for rising from the sea.
90. United Peoples, which was the motto of the house of Habsburg-Lorraine. SMS *Viribus Unitis* was the first Austro-Hungarian dreadnought battleship of the Tegetthoff class, launched in Trieste in June 1911, and sunk by a limpet mine on 1 November 1918.
91. Eternity.
92. Yiddish for little father: an affectionate diminutive of *tata* ('Dad') that might be used by a young boy.
93. The word here is "abcúg," which in Hungarian usage has come to mean "down with ...," but it is derived directly from the German word *Abzug*, as used in the Austro-Hungarian army, & meaning a "withdrawal."
94. In Hungarian this Yiddish term (*handlékat*) is used with particular reference to junk (antique) dealers.
95. Friedrich Gundolf, born Friedrich Leopold Gundelfinger (1880–1931), was a German-Jewish literary scholar and poet, one of the most famous academics of the Weimar Republic. Szentkuthy also

refers to him in §4 of *Towards the One and Only Metaphor* (Contra Mundum Press, 2013).

96. The reference is to the physical phenomenon of Brownian movement, named after the botanist Robert Brown (1773–1858). While looking through a microscope at particles found in pollen grains suspended in water, he observed minute particles executing a continuous jittery motion & went on to demonstrate that the effect was not life-related.
97. Sophisticated manners / breeding, fashionable society.
98. Established in 1929, the fashion house of Mainbocher operated in Paris (1929–39) and then in New York (1940–71). Bernard was a French fashion designer (1886–1940).
99. *The Twentieth Century: A Radical Counter-isolation of I and E.*
100. The references are possibly to István Csók's *Bathing Woman (Susanna)* (1920–28) & Francesco Hayez's *Bathing Bathsheba* (c. 1834).
101. It is not clear whether this is a genuine artist (possibly the émigré Russian-French Mariya Ivanovna Vassilieva, aka Marie Vassilieff, 1884–1928), and / or painting that is being referred to.
102. Hypothesis on Love.
103. Conjugation of *introeō* (to go in, enter) in the first-person singular future tense — a word particularly associated with a line in the Mass: *Introibo ad altare Dei* ("I will go in to the altar of God.").
104. Alluvial Impromptu or Heideggerian love — Neo-rational Impromptu or Carnapian love.
105. A German word for 'smart, stylish' which (as *fess*) has passed into Hungarian usage.
106. Short for German *spießbürgerlich* = roughly 'philistine' (as adjective), narrow-minded.
107. Childhood of…
108. The Preliminary Games.
109. A concocted (and highly sarcastic) term: culture-schematic deflo-wering.
110. Literally: world spatiality — a concept most closely associated with Martin Heidegger, who contends that while being (*Dasein*) dwells in the world spatially, it has no specific coordinate in actual space (as conceived of by Descartes). Cf. *Being and Time* §§ 22–23.

111. Around us.

112. *Umbra* = a shade, shadow; *mendax* = given to lying, false, men-dacious.

113. Another spurious reference parodying Heidegger: The Eroticism of Place-boundedness & the Asceticism of Space-boundedness.

114. Love-letters (NB plural).

115. Phenomenological illusion of spaciousness.

116. The opening line (*Kék a kökény recece*) of a Hungarian folk song (nóta).

117. Approximately: card index of apparent entities.

118. System of the world, i.e., the world order as represented in an astronomical model.

119. A method of proving a hypothesis by reducing it to a unique pro-position.

120. Oh, unhappy recital/catalogue of woes — a phrase that Szentkuthy himself seems to have made up.

121. Miracle of Finiteness. The phrase is close to one that Heidegger was using in 1920–21 when he drew up a lecture series called *The Phenomenology of Religious Life*.

122. A pictorial slogan — an image that conveys as much meaning as a block of text.

123. Between Sea & Shoreline.

124. Fall is summer inverted.

125. Body-time clothing eroticism.

126. The Grand Duchy of Mecklenburg-Schwerin was a territory in Northern Germany held by the House of Mecklenburg & residing at Schwerin. Among the figurines made of silver in honor of the wedding of Crown Prince Frederick William of Prussia and Cecilie of Mecklenburg-Schwerin in 1908, was one depicting the bride naked.

127. Swinemünde (Polish Świnoujście) is a city & seaport on the Baltic Sea & Szczecin Lagoon, located in extreme NW Poland. "Come to Swinemünde: strength, games, & principles! Strictest discretion!"

128. Turn down, dim, dip.

129. A step away from Parnassus (i.e., the mountain in central Greece that was sacred to Dionysus, Apollo, & the Muses) — an inversion of the more usual *Gradus ad Parnassum*.

130. "Shamed be he who thinks evil" is the motto of the Order of the Garter, the highest order of British knighthood (irreverently quoted by the humorists W.C. Sellar & R.J. Yeatman in *1066 and All That* (1930, ch. 24) as: "Honey, your silk stocking's hanging down.").

131. The water to the fish.

132. *Max and Moritz* (*A Story of Seven Boyish Pranks*) is a German-language story told entirely in rhymed couplets, written & illustrated by Wilhelm Busch (1832–1908) and published in 1865.

133. Little cosmoses (plural), and little sticks of bread (plural), deriving from the Italian *pane.*

134. In one of the oldest recorded uses of a contraceptive diaphragm (cap), Cleopatra is supposed to have used half a lemon. Casanova was also said to have made similar use of a lemon, though Szentkuthy makes no reference to this in his *Marginalia on Casanova.*

135. Sposalizio (marriage in Italian) comes from the name *Lo Sposalizio* (The Marriage of the Virgin) given to a painting by Raphæl (now housed at the Pinacoteca di Brera, the main public gallery for paintings in Milan, Italy).

136. Either a simple flute or a 4- or 8-foot organ stop that sounds like a flute.

137. Mourner.

138. To name is to know.

139. Most Customary Artemis.

140. Contributions on Neo-positivist Lachrymology.

141. Johannes Tauler (c. 1300–61) was a Strasbourg-born mystic, Dominican friar, & theologian. In 1338 or 1339, the Dominicans were exiled from Strasbourg as a result of tensions between Pope John XXII & Lewis of Bavaria, and Tauler spent his exile (c1339–43) in Basel. Here, he became acquainted with the circles of devout clergy and laity known as the Friends of God. He is now known only for his sermons, printed first in Leipzig in 1498, reprinted in 1508 at Augsburg, and then again at Basel (1521 & 1522), etc., which were considered among the noblest in the German language — not as emotional as Henry Suso's, nor as speculative as Eckhart's, but rather touching on all sides the deeper problems of moral & spiritual life.

142. Listening intently.

143. Plulogical present — a made-up tense based on the word 'pluperfect,' which is derived from the Latin *plus quam perfectum* (more than perfect).

144. *Pro* is Latin for 'for' and *domo* is the ablative case of the noun *domus* 'home,' so the whole phrase translates literally as: 'for home.'

145. Truth will liberate you?

146. There is no fear in love. The opening phrase of the Latin translation of 1 John 4:18, which continues: "but perfect love casteth out fear: because that hath torment. He that feareth is not made perfect in love."

147. Remembering is not human.

148. And form is always, by definition, jesting.

149. And fixed quiddity is always, by definition, tragic.

150. "I am artificial, therefore I am the way, the truth." The latter part recalls John 14:6: *"dicit ei Iesus ego sum via et veritas et vita..."* (Jesus saith unto him I am the way, the truth...).

151. Latin, standing for: part (taken) for the whole.

152. Total, whole.

153. Roughly: Five O'Clock Nicean Martyrology.

154. Perhaps a reference to Matt Cimber (born Thomas Vitale Ottaviano in 1936), an Italian-American film producer, director, & writer as well as the last husband of film actress Jayne Mansfield.

155. Introduction to the Parallelism between Realistic Cognitive Theories & Trends Toward Deliberate Deformation in Fine Art.

156. Trademark for a construction set, first patented in the UK in 1901, from which mechanical models can be assembled.

157. Author, book, and quotation are fictitious, although it is of interest that there exists a 1787 painting by Élisabeth-Louise Vigée Le Brun (now held by the National Gallery of Art, Washington, DC, USA) entitled *The Marquise de Pezay, and the Marquise de Rougé with Her Sons Alexis and Adrien*. The passage translates as: Pezay, *Artificial and Approximate Dogmatics of English Common Sense or Burghes' Empiricism*: "This one speaks to me of synthesis & the other of picturesque disorder: I give my assurance that I have never seen either a composed polyrhythm or vitalist chaos — I see some things that order themselves & then dissolve, or it is a not a matter of extremes,

but of simple daily *movement*. Movement: a vulgar guarantee of synthetic rhythm."

158. Literally: man to man, never man to woman.
159. The male of *duenna* (i.e., the old man).
160. Approximately: physical non-nature.
161. Surmounting Metaphysics by a Logical Analysis of Speech.
162. A quotation from St. Thomas Aquinas' *Summa Theologiæ*, question 104, which translates as: "man is *not* ordained to his neighbor as to his end."
163. Anteros, avenger of unrequited love, was one of a host of Greek winged love gods called Erotes. As a whole the phrase then simply means: Eros & Anteros.
164. The Palazzo Vendramin-Calergi, built around 1500, the Palazzo Loredan, designed in the 15th century, the Gothic building of the Foscari palace, & the Palazzo Cavalli-Francheti all lie on the waterfront of the Grand Canal in Venice.
165. Roughly: there was no talk about provision but about being an essential admixture.
166. I.E., the 14th century, especially in reference to Italian art & literature.
167. The *Ballade des pendus*, also known as the *Epitaphe Villon*, is the best-known poem by François Villon. It was published posthumously in 1489.
168. Alexander Girardi (1850–1918) was an Austrian actor & tenor singer in operettas who used to wear a straw hat with a flat crown and brim. The hat became popular and was known as the Giradi Hat.
169. Should there be any remaining doubt, Szentkuthy invented the name & titles: in addition, e.g., the Latin for 'mirror' is *speculum*, *analogia* is more Greek than Latin, etc.
170. Germans believed as follows.
171. My analogy they perceived as if with their eyes, as was their custom.
172. The same the same.
173. Second self.
174. Nothing hinders — the phrase used by Roman Catholic censors to declare that publication of an item is not offensive to faith or morals.

175. God deformed is the true love of God.
176. And in blindness they saw the benevolence of the love of God as devilish breathing.
177. A single cause inflames love, but a cause like that is torn down by love.
178. Syllogism is a representation of love.
179. Treasures.
180. Propositions of the things of love are work.
181. A term Szentkuthy Latinized, meaning roughly: a union of essential natures.
182. Theory of colors.
183. Fashionable Platonism.
184. Title of a monthly women's magazine, first published in 1923 until, after several more or less prolonged breaks and changes of ownership, 1997, and covering the more avant-garde designers of the day.
185. The reference here is to the crude faces in Dutch paintings (particularly those of Brueghel) representing kermesses.
186. Being spiritual.
187. "... there are scruples which are not unhealthy — on the contrary, they are soul sport, miniature hygienic tragedies, made up of alert skepticism and an excess of blood whose theory, which leads to fatigue, is always necessary. They are truly rational arabesques: I shall call them truth games. Thought, since it is a living matter, after completing its logical wave, continues its art for art's sake movement and creates a pseudo-logical automatic functioning with pseudo-problems and pseudo-relationships — all that is not Gothic in the pathetic or morbid sense of the word, but the simplest & most therapeutic functioning of the mental muscles ..."
188. In essence.
189. A paraphrase of a passage from *A Midsummer Night's Dream* (2.2), presented by Szentkuthy in Hungarian translation.
190. The Hungarian here says *á-tout*, but this is probably a mistaken spelling of the French *atout*, 'trump.' In card games the trump suit may be fixed as in Spades, depend on the outcome of the previous hand as in 99, be determined by drawing a card at random as in Bezique, etc.

191. A wretched large structure / dead weight.

192. Floral doctrine.

193. Reason and flower.

194. Clearly short for the Latin phrase *Sic transit gloria mundi* (thus passes the glory of the world / glory fades).

195. Roughly: hyperfloral super-doctrine.

196. A neologism from fusing *ratio* (reason) and *flora*.

197. As the author has already indicated, an obvious title that utilizes the expressions just mentioned to make up a title that roughly translates as: A Critical & Analytical Distinction of Rationality & Flo[wer] reality.

198. The Greek word *peira*, *πεῖρα* (a test, attempt; experience).

199. Although the city is named after him, this is not a reference to Cincinnati but to Lucius Quinctius Cincinnatus (519–430 BC), the Roman aristocrat & statesman revered for his civic virtue.

200. A dragon? How funny.

201. I. Proceeding from music: a condemnation of cheating; II. proceeding from empiricism: a note of error; III. proceeding from superstition: mytho-biological values.

202. The French critic & historian Hippolyte Adolphe Taine (1828–93) was notable, above all, for his three-pronged approach to the contextual study of a work of art, based on the aspects of what he called "race, milieu, & moment."

203. Proceeding from psychological chemistry.

204. Eroticism is an art of sincerity.

205. Do you think so?

206. God is manifest.

207. The line is from Dante's *Divine Comedy* (*Purgatorio*, Canto XXI, line 136), which T. S. Eliot translated as "treat the shadows like the solid thing."

208. In the Latin version of the Bible the whole verse (Ecclesiastes 1:2; 12:8) runs *Vanitas vanitatum dixit Ecclesiastes omnia vanitas*. In the King James Bible, this is translated as: "Vanity of vanities, saith the Preacher, all is vanity, vanity of vanities, all is vanity."

209. The quotation is from Juvenal's *Satires* (I. 29): "It is difficult not to write satire." But here it is turned upside down: it is difficult not to write an apology.

210. Manner.

211. Madam in her naïve candor.

212. Point for point.

213. Primitively objective / objective from the earliest times.

COLOPHON

PRAE
was typeset in InDesign.

The text & page numbers are set in *Adobe Jenson Pro.*
The book title is a CMP exclusive recut from the original types used in 1934.

Book design & typesetting: Alessandro Segalini
Cover design: Contra Mundum Press
Image credit: Front cover spread based on a drawing by László Nagy;
maze image by István Orosz.

PRAE
is published by Contra Mundum Press.
Its printer has received Chain of Custody certification from:
The Forest Stewardship Council,
The Programme for the Endorsement of Forest Certification,
& The Sustainable Forestry Initiative.

CONTRA MUNDUM PRESS

Contra Mundum Press is dedicated to the value & the indispensable importance of the individual voice.

Our principal interest is in Modernism and the principles developed by the Modernists, but challenging & visionary works from other eras may be considered for publication. We are also interested in texts that in their use of form & style are *a rebours*, though not in empty or gratuitous forms of experimentation (programmatic avant-gardism). Against the prevailing view that everything has been discovered, there are many texts of fundamental significance to *Weltliteratur* (& *Weltkultur*) that still remain in relative oblivion and warrant being encountered by the world at large.

For the complete list of forthcoming publications, please visit our website. To be added to our mailing list, send your name & email address to: info@contramundum.net

Contra Mundum Press
P.O. Box 1326
New York, NY 10276
USA
info@contramundum.net

OTHER CONTRA MUNDUM PRESS TITLES

Gilgamesh

Ghérasim Luca, *Self-Shadowing Prey*

Rainer J. Hanshe, *The Abdication*

Walter Jackson Bate, *Negative Capability*

Miklós Szentkuthy, *Marginalia on Casanova*

Fernando Pessoa, *Philosophical Essays*

Elio Petri, *Writings on Cinema & Life*

Friedrich Nietzsche, *The Greek Music Drama*

Richard Foreman, *Plays with Films*

Louis-Auguste Blanqui, *Eternity by the Stars*

Miklós Szentkuthy, *Towards the One & Only Metaphor*

Josef Winkler, *When the Time Comes*

William Wordsworth, *Fragments*

Josef Winkler, *Natura Morta*

Fernando Pessoa, *The Transformation Book*

Emilio Villa, *The Selected Poetry of Emilio Villa*

Robert Kelly, *A Voice Full of Cities*

SOME FORTHCOMING TITLES

Federico Fellini, *Making a Film*

Robert Musil, *Thought Flight*

Oğuz Atay, *While Waiting for Fear*

SZEN
TKU
TH
Y

CPSIA information can be obtained at www.ICGtesting.com
Printed in the USA
LVOW04s2103240615

443701LV00029B/1620/P

9 781940 625089